DREAMING AGAIN

DREAMING AGAIN

THIRTY-FIVE NEW STORIES
CELEBRATING THE WILD SIDE
OF AUSTRALIAN FICTION

EDITED BY JACK DANN

An *Imprint of* HarperCollins*Publishers*

First published in Australia in 2008 by Harper*Voyager*, an imprint of HarperCollins Publishers, Australia.

HarperCollins books may be purchased for educational, business, or sales promotional use. For information please write: Special Markets Department, HarperCollins Publishers, 10 East 53rd Street, New York, NY 10022.

FIRST U.S. EDITION

Eos is a federally registered trademark of HarperCollins Publishers.

Library of Congress Cataloging-in-Publication Data has been applied for.

ISBN 978-0-06-136408-2

08 09 10 11 12 QX/RRD 10 9 8 7 6 5 4 3 2 1

For my partner Janeen . . .
Ah, if only circumstance had not encroached . . .
you would — and should — have been co-editor

ACKNOWLEDGMENTS

The editor would like to thank the following people for their generous help and support:

Joshua Bilmes, Paul Collins, Gardner Dozois, Kate Eltham, Harlan and Susan Ellison, Andrew Enstice, Linda Funnell, Rob Gerrand, Diana Gill, Mitch Graham, Donna Maree Hanson, Merrilee Heifetz, Robert Hoge, Steve Paulson, Eugenie Regan, Claire Reilly-Shapiro, Stephanie Smith, Cat Sparks, Nick Stathopoulos, Keith Stevenson, Jonathan Strahan, Anna Tambour, Andy Turner, Dena Taylor, and Janeen Webb.

CONTENTS

DREAMING AGAIN

INTRODUCTION

Please forgive me, gentle readers, for a bit of lycanthropic railing and howling at the moon, but there's something I need to get off my chest; and it concerns the brilliant, edgy, ground busting, wondrous book you're holding in your hand. (And I'll explain why I feel I can hype this book with impunity in a moment.)

There is one very important name missing from the editorial credit.

Janeen Webb and I co-edited the prequel to *Dreaming Again* ten years ago. That book was called *Dreaming Down-Under. Publishers Weekly* compared it with Harlan Ellison's classic *Dangerous Visions*; Peter Goldsworthy thought it was probably 'the biggest, boldest, most controversial collection of original fiction ever published in Australia'; Neil Gaiman said, 'Ignore it at your peril; it's the book your friends will be talking about'; Jonathan Strahan, co-editor of *The Year's Best Australian Science Fiction and Fantasy*, wrote that 'It may be the most important anthology of Australian speculative fiction ever published'; and Gardner Dozois, editor of *The Year's Best Science Fiction* annuals said that it 'may well be the best overall anthology of the year.' It was the first Australian volume ever to win the World Fantasy Award, and it also won the Australian Ditmar Award for Best Anthology. Stories from *Dreaming Down-Under* dominated both the Ditmar and the Aurealis awards: All six short story nominations for the Ditmar Award came from *Dreaming Down-Under*, and stories from *Dreaming Down-Under* won the Aurealis Award in both the science fiction and fantasy short story categories. Two stories in the volume were optioned for film, and others were chosen for American Best of the Year collections. And in the recently published reference work *Australian Speculative Fiction: A Genre Overview*, Donna Hanson writes: 'This collection has been credited with putting Australian writing on the international map. It brought to the forefront Australia's best-known authors and launched a few others. This anthology is so pivotal to the Australian scene that it is still being talked about and is still in print.'

Not bad innings!

Since *Dreaming Down-Under* was published, Janeen and I have been constantly queried as to when we were going to do another volume. Our refrain was consistent: 'When the time is right.' We wanted to wait until the climate had changed ... until new authors started writing the stories that would shock, astound, and delight us; and we wanted to give the established and up-and-coming authors showcased in the original volume time to develop new styles, themes, and audiences.

Well, that time is here, and Janeen and I were *supposed* to co-edit *this* book, but circumstances — damn all the fates, Norns, dark angels, doctors, germs, miasmas, and especially hollow-headed bureaucrats who gather like storm clouds just waiting to mix a multiplicity of metaphors and rain on our respective parades — have forced her to sit this one out. Janeen is a private person. Her 'circumstances' are nobody's business. But, dammit, she should have had her name on the cover of this book.

Instead, she has looked over my shoulder, constrained me from my more florid idiocies, provided support, wisdom, and critical feedback. After all, she was an internationally known critic before she became a novelist.

So ... what about *this* book? What about *Dreaming Again*?

Well, for a start, this is what I wrote to the authors:

> *Dreaming Again* will showcase the very best contemporary 'wild-side fiction' (those stories that have an edge of horror or fantasy, or could be categorised as magical realism) and the very best genre fiction, which includes science fiction, fantasy, and horror. We are looking for brilliant writing, style, and fresh ideas. Our only criterion is quality. Your story can be 'new-wave,' or cyberpunk. It can be a 'New Yorker story', hard science fiction, soft science fiction, magic realism, contemporary fantasy. It can be a quiet vignette or ground-breaking extrapolation. We're looking for the brilliant stories that we'll remember in the years to come.

> *Dreaming Again* will cross genres to showcase a combination of the very best Australian genre and non-genre short fiction. It will contain the cream of Australian science fiction, fantasy, horror, Aboriginal fantastical fiction, and mainstream magical realism. This is the anthology that will shake up the established thinking about the 'shape' of contemporary writing in Australia ... that will open up — and redefine — the literary canon.
>
> We are very interested in science fiction, fantasy, horror (dark fantasy), and stories of magical realism that use the Australian experience and geography; but that is secondary to good story. If your killer idea takes place in the far future, or in space, or on an alternative world — fine. Again, our criterion is quality.
>
> This is an invitation to participate in the making of literary history. If you have a story that represents the very top of your form, we'd love to see it.

I won't apologise for shooting for the stars, for turning my back on reasonably good stories and reasonably good writers, for wanting only the golden-tipped prose that makes old men think they are young, or makes the hair stand up on the neck, or carries the reader into that detailed daydream we call sense-of-wonder. I won't apologise for wanting only those stories that galvanize, that stimulate wonder and thought and laughter ... that cause discomfort ... that in their small, subtle, and mysterious ways transform all those who encounter them.

And, yes, I'm excited about the stories in this volume. And, yes, this probably sounds like hype. So what? This book isn't about the editor. It's about the stories. It's about the numinous light shows and the Cimmerian darkness created by the talented authors who contributed to this book. It's theirs ... their talent, their ideas, their unique perspectives on life and death and the universe. They are the poets and tale-tellers and culture-changers. They are some of the best writers working in this wild, beguiling land with its great red heart and vast desert expanses. They are some of the best fantasists working in this country edged by blue seas, coral reefs, rainforests, and sophisticated urban culture. It just so happened that I was lucky enough to see these stories first and with great love and respect include them in this showcase collection, this ten year celebratory sequel to *Dreaming Down-Under*.

In his generous preface to *Dreaming Down-Under*, Harlan Ellison wrote: 'Because the work, all this work, all this fresh, tough, and brilliant work, all these stories, they need no California fantasist to shill for them. They speak for themselves. They have voices. Now, go away; and listen to them.'

Harlan was absolutely right.

You don't need my introduction or story notes; you just need the stories that are waiting like patient angels — or disguised demons — to embrace you. So I would not take offence if you gave up on this introduction right here and now and started reading the stories. In fact, in this unusual ego-less frame of mind that I seem to have slipped into ... I would urge you to do so.

However, should you be in the mood for some shading and perspective and background, I'll soldier on. After all, this bit of the book is free!

Ten years ago, Janeen and I had an agenda. Then as now, we wanted to shake up the established thinking about the 'shape' of contemporary writing in Australia: to open up — and redefine — the literary canon to include the non-mimetic side of our literature. We wanted to showcase the very best contemporary stories that pushed the envelope of genre fiction and those stories that used genre tropes or might be considered magical realism. We referred to those stories as 'wild-side fiction' to convey that evocative, almost dangerous sense of being right out there on the edge. And we wanted to get the word out to the rest of the world that there was something happening here in Australia.

Here's a snapshot of how it looked back in 1998: The genre culture was vibrant. Writers and fans were meeting regularly at science fiction conventions, which were rather small and intimate. Mainstream publishers such as HarperCollins Voyager, Pan Macmillan, Random House, and Penguin were developing new lists of Australian fantasy and SF writers; and new, vigorous small press publishers such as *Eidolon*, *Ticonderoga*, *Aphelion*, and *MirrorDance* were pushing boundaries and publishing some wonderfully quirky and imaginative work. There was healthy competition between the two major Australian genre magazines *Eidolon* and *Aurealis*, each featuring cutting-edge fiction by Australian authors. Jonathan Strahan and Jeremy Byrne were editing the annual *Year's Best* Australian SF, fantasy, and horror fiction; and although the Australian Ditmar Award (voted on by readers) had been long established, two new professional awards were created: the Aurealis Award and the Turner Award. A generation of hot new talented writers such as Sean Williams, Simon Brown, Lucy Sussex, Stephen Dedman, Aaron Sterns, Paul Brandon, K. J. Bishop, Kate Forsyth, Richard Harland, Ian Irvine, Cecilia Dart-Thornton, Margo Lanagan, Scott Westerfield, Fiona McIntosh, Janeen Webb, and Kim Wilkins were making their bones and pushing the various envelopes; and established professionals such as Garth Nix, Terry Dowling, Damien Broderick, Isobelle Carmody, Sara Douglass, Sean McMullen, Greg Egan, and Rosaleen Love were writing at the top of their form. Harlan Ellison thought we were experiencing a Golden Age of Australian Science Fiction, and, indeed, it sure as hell felt like *something* was going on. In fact it felt like the heady days of the late 1960s when SF writers in England and the United States challenged genre conventions and started a period of experimentation called *The New Wave*.

What were we challenging ten years ago?

We weren't *really* challenging genre conventions (although we did, sans polemic and proclamations); and although there was plenty of literary experimentation, we weren't part of any movement. We *were* part of a vibrant, creative community; and we felt that something new and exciting was happening, and it was … us. It was as if we had suddenly broken through the barriers of distance and isolation. Yet although individual writers had gained international recognition, Australian genre fiction in general was still flying under the radar. Most Australian genre writers weren't connecting to the influential American, European, and British publishers, editors, critics, and, most importantly, readers. All that began to change after the publication of *Dreaming Down-Under* and the catalyzing World Science Fiction convention, a truly international event, which was held in Melbourne. A number of American editors, friends that I had known for dog-years, approached me with, 'Damn, you were right about these Australian writers. They're terrific.' I was much too humble and ego-less to say, 'I told you so.'

According to *The Cambridge Companion to Science Fiction*, the 'renaissance' in Australian genre fiction gained wide acceptance thanks to Jonathan Strahan and Jeremy Byrne's *Australian Year's Best* series, David Hartwell and Damien Broderick's huge reprint anthology *Centaurus* . . . and *Dreaming Down-Under*.

So we all did it in the nineties.

Why then do a sequel to *Dreaming Down-Under* now? After all, a sequel is a dangerous sort of two-headed literary beast. *Dreaming Again* will inevitably be compared with *Dreaming Down-Under*. There sure as hell better be a good reason for this book.

So what's changed?

Well, thanks to the phenomenon known as Clarion South, often called a 'boot camp for writers,' some astonishing new writers have surfaced . . . and we find ourselves once again squinting into the bright reflections of another gold-tinged time . . . a continuation and consequence of Australia's golden age of genre. Writers such as Kim Westwood, Jason Fischer, Chris Lynch (and his American collaborator Ben Francisco), Christopher Green, and Peter M. Ball are all 'products' of Clarion South. They are some of the names that we will certainly recognise in the future. The 'New' writers of the 90's such as Trudi Canavan, Cecilia Dart-Thornton, and Margo Lanagan are making seven-figure deals, winning awards, and making international names for themselves, while the last generation of 'hot' writers, such as Garth Nix (who has over four million books in print), Sean Williams, Terry Dowling, Isobelle Carmody, and Sara Douglass, have garnered major international audiences and are going from strength to strength.

There is also a generation of writers who have been around for a while . . . and have suddenly sparked. Richard Harland comes to mind. He won an Aurealis Award and the prestigious Golden Aurealis Award for his satiric horror novel *The Black Crusade*. For my money, his *Dreaming Again* story 'A Guided Tour in the Kingdom of the Dead' is a knockout. And . . . there are those important established writers who did not have stories in the original *Dreaming Down-Under*, such as the bestselling authors John Birmingham and Garth Nix.

When I started editing this anthology, I'll confess that I was worried that I might not find the keep-you-up-at-night, genre-bending stories by the new Young Turks. Man, was I wrong about *that*.

In short, enough time has passed.

It's a whole new world of writers working under the southern sun.

It's steam-engine time again.

It's time to take another laser-lit look at what's happening in this special place.

And lastly — and firstly and in-between — it's all about the stories!

I invite you to go forth into this land of wonder, terror, and mystery . . . this wild side of *Terra Australis*.

Bestselling author GARTH NIX was born in Melbourne in 1963, grew up in Canberra, and has lived in Sydney for the past twenty years. A full-time writer since 2001, he has worked as a literary agent, marketing consultant, book editor, book publicist, book sales representative, bookseller, and as a part-time soldier in the Australian Army Reserve. More than 4.5 million copies of his books have been sold around the world and his work has been translated into thirty-six languages. His books include the award-winning fantasy novels *Sabriel*, *Lirael* and *Abhorsen*; and the young adult science fiction novel *Shade's Children*. His fantasy novels for children include *The Ragwitch*, the six books of *The Seventh Tower* sequence, and *The Keys to the Kingdom* series that begins with the CBC Honour Book *Mister Monday*. Garth's books have appeared on the bestseller lists of *The New York Times*, *Publishers Weekly* (US), *The Bookseller* (UK), *The Australian*, *The Sydney Morning Herald* and *The Sunday Times* (UK). He lives in a Sydney beach suburb with his wife and two children.

The poignant and evocative story that follows explores the calm before the storm and the eternity known as friendship . . .

OLD FRIENDS

GARTH NIX

I'd been living in the city for quite a while, lying low, recovering from an unfortunate jaunt that had turned, in the immortal words of my sometime comrade Hrasvelg, 'irredeemably shit-shape'.

Though I had almost completely recovered my sight, I still wore a bandage around my eyes. It was made from a rare stuff that I could see through, but it looked like dense black linen. Similarly, I had regrown my left foot, but I kept up the limp. It gave me an additional excuse to use the stick, which was, of course, much more than a length of bog oak carved with picaresque scenes of a pedlar's journey.

I had a short-lease apartment near the beach, an expensive but necessary accommodation, as I needed both the sunshine that fell into its small living room and the cool, wet wind from the sea that blew through every open window.

Unfortunately, after the first month, that wind became laden with the smell of rotting weed and, as the weeks passed, the stench grew stronger, and the masses of weed that floated just past the breakers began to shift and knit together, despite the efforts of the lifesavers to break up the unsightly, stinking rafts of green.

I knew what was happening, of course. The weed was a manifestation of an old opponent of mine, a slow, cold foe who had finally caught up with me. 'Caught' being the operative word, as the weed was just the visible portion of my enemy's activities. A quick examination of almanac and lodestone revealed that all known pathways from this world were denied to me, shut tight by powerful bindings that I could not broach quickly, if at all.

I considered moving to the mountains or far inland, but that would merely delay matters. Only the true desert would be safe from my foe, but I could not go there.

So I watched the progress of the weed every morning as I drank my first coffee, usually leaning back in one white plastic chair as I elevated my supposedly injured leg on another. The two chairs were the only furniture in the apartment. I slept in the bath, which I had lined with sleeping moss, which was comfortable, sweet-smelling and also massaged out the cares of the day with its tiny rhizoids.

The day before I adjudged the weed would reach its catalytic potential and spawn servitors, I bought not just my usual black coffee from the café downstairs, but also a triple macchiato that came in a heavy, heat-resistant glass. Because I lived upstairs they always gave me proper cups. The barista who served me, a Japanese guy who worked the espresso machine mornings and surfed all afternoon, put the coffees in a cardboard holder meant for takeaways and said, 'Got a visitor today?'

'Not yet,' I said. 'But I will have shortly. By the way, I wouldn't go surfing here this afternoon . . . or tomorrow.'

'Why not?'

'That weed,' I replied. 'It's toxic. Try another beach.'

'How do you know?' he asked as he slid the tray into my waiting fingers. 'I mean, you can't . . .'

'I can't see it,' I said, as I backed away, turned and started tapping towards the door. 'But I can smell it. It's toxic all right. Stay clear.'

'Okay, thanks. Uh, enjoy the coffee.'

I slowly made my way upstairs, and set the coffees down on the floor. My own cup in front of one white chair, and the macchiato at the foot of the other. I wouldn't be resting my limb on the spare chair today.

I had to wait a little while for the breeze to come up, but as it streamed through the room and teased at the hair I should have had cut several weeks before, I spoke.

'Hey, Anax. I bought you a coffee.'

The wind swirled around my head, changing direction 270 degrees, blowing out the window it had come in by and in by the window it had been going out. I felt the floor tremble under my feet and experienced a brief dizziness.

Anax, proper name Anaxarte, was one of my oldest friends. We'd grown up together and had served together in two cosmically fucked-up wars, one of which was still slowly bleeding its way to exhaustion in fits and starts, though the original two sides were long out of it.

I hadn't seen Anax for more than thirty years, but we scribbled notes to each other occasionally, and had spoken twice in that time. We talked a lot about meeting up, maybe organising a fishing expedition with some of the old lads, but it had never come together.

I knew that if he were able to, he would always answer my call. So as the coffee cooled, and the white plastic chair lay vacant, my heart chilled, and I began to grieve. Not for the loss of Anax's help against the enemy, but because another friend had fallen.

I sat in the sunshine for an hour, the warmth a slight comfort against the melancholy that had crept upon me. At the hour's end, the wind shifted again, roiling around me counter-clockwise till it ebbed to a total calm.

Even without the breeze, I could smell the weed. It had a malignant, invasive odour, the kind that creeps through sealed plastic bags and airtight lids, the smell of decay and corruption.

My options were becoming limited. I took up my stick and went downstairs once more to the café. The afternoon barista did not know me, though I had seen her often enough through my expansive windows. She did not comment on my order, though I doubt she was often asked for a soy latte with half poured out after it was made, to be topped up again with cold regular milk.

Upstairs, I repeated the summoning, this time with the chill already present, a cold presence of sombre expectation lodged somewhere between my heart and ribs.

'Balan,' I called softly. 'Balan, your lukewarm excuse for a drink is ready.'

The wind came up and carried my words away, but as before, there was no reply, no presence in the empty chair. I waited the full hour to be sure, then poured the congealed soy drink down the sink.

I could see the weed clearly in the breakers now. It was almost entirely one huge, long clump that spanned the length of the beach. The lifesavers had given up trying to break it apart with their jetskis and zodiac inflatables, and there were two 'Beach Closed' signs stuck in the sand, twenty metres apart. Not that anyone was swimming. The beach was almost empty. The reek of the weed had driven away everyone but a sole lifesaver serving out her shift, and a fisherman who was dolefully walking along in search of a weed-free patch of sea.

'Two of my old friends taken,' I whispered to the sun, my lips dry, my words heavy. We had never thought much about our futures, not when we were fighting in the war, or later when we had first escaped our service. The present was our all, our time the now. None of us knew what lay ahead.

For the third time, I trod my careful way downstairs. There were a dozen people outside the café, a small crowd which parted to allow me passage, with muffled whispers about blindness and letting the sightless man past.

The crowd was watching the weed, while trying not to smell it.

'There, that bit came right out of the water!'

'It kind of looks alive!'

'Must be creating a gas somehow, the decomposition . . .'

'. . . check out those huge nodules lifting up . . .'

'... a gas, methane, maybe. Or hydrogen sulphide ... nah ... I'm just guessing. Someone will know ...'

As I heard the excited comments I knew that I had mistimed my calls for assistance. The weed was very close to catalysis and would soon spawn its servitors, who would come ashore in search of their target.

I had meant to ask the owner of the café, a short, bearded man who was always called 'Mister Jeff' by the staff, if he could give me a glass of brandy or, at a pinch, whisky. A fine armagnac would be best, but I doubted they'd have any of that. The café had no liquor licence but I knew there was some spirituous alcohol present, purely for Jeff's personal use, since I'd smelled it on his breath often enough.

But as I said, it was too late for that. Palameides might have answered to a double brandy, but I secretly knew that he too must have succumbed. It had been too long since his last missive, and I accounted it one of my failings that I had not been in touch to see where he was, and if all was well with him.

'Someone should do something about that weed,' complained a thickset young man who habitually double-parked his low-slung sports car outside the café around this time. 'It really stinks.'

'It will be gone by morning,' I said. I hadn't meant to use the voice of prophecy, but my words rang out, harsh and bronze, stopping all other conversation.

Everyone looked at me, from inside and outside the café. Even the dog who had been asleep next to one of the outside tables craned his neck to look askance. All was silent, the silence of an embarrassed audience who wished they were elsewhere without knowing why, and were fearful about what was going to come next.

'I am a ... biologist,' I said in my normal tones. 'The weed is a known phenomenon. It will disperse overnight.'

The silence continued for a few seconds, then normal service resumed, at a lower volume. Even the double-parking guy was more subdued.

I spoke the truth. One way or another, the weed would be gone and, likely enough, I would be gone with it.

As the afternoon progressed, the stench grew much worse. The café was shut, staff and customers retreating to better-smelling climes.

Around five o'clock, nearby residents began to leave as well; at the same time the Fire Brigade, the Water Board, the police and several television crews arrived.

An hour after that, only the firefighters remained, and they were wearing breathing apparatus as they went from door to door, checking that everyone had left. Farther afield, way down the northern end of the beach, I could see the television crews interviewing someone who was undoubtedly an expert trying to explain why the noxious odours were so localised, and dissipated so quickly when you got more than three hundred metres from the centre of the beach.

The 'DO NOT CROSS' tapes with the biohazard trefoils got rolled out just before dusk, across the street about eighty metres up from my apartment. The firefighters had knocked at my door and called out, gruff voices muffled by masks, but I had not answered. They could probably have seen me from the beach, but no one was heading closer to the smell, however well-protected they might be. The sea was bubbling and frothing with noxious vapours, and weedy nodules the size of restaurant refrigerators were bobbing up and down upon the waves. After a while the nodules began to detach from the main mass of weed and the waves carried them in like lost surfboards, tendrils of weed trailing behind them, reminiscent of broken leg-ropes.

I watched the nodules as the sun set behind the city, mentally mapping where they were drifting ashore. When the sun was completely gone, the streetlights and the high lamps that usually lit the beach didn't come on, but that didn't matter much to me. Darkness wasn't so much my friend as a close relative.

The lack of artificial light caused a commotion among the HAZMAT teams though, particularly when they couldn't get their portable generators and floodlights to work, and the one engine they sent down the street choked and stalled before it had even pulled away from the kerb.

I had counted thirteen nodules, but more could be out in the weed mass, or so low in the water I'd missed them. My enemy was not underestimating me, or had presumed I would be able to call upon assistance.

I had presumed I would be able to call upon assistance, a foolish presumption built upon old camaraderie, of long-ago dangers shared, of the maintenance of a continuum. I had not thought that my friends, having survived our two wars, could have had a full stop put to their existence in more mundane environments, or at least not so soon. Which meant that they had met the same fate that now threatened to be mine.

'Anax, Balan, Palameides,' I whispered. By now there would be three new death-trees laid out in a nice row in the arborial necropolis, with those nameplates at their feet. There was probably a Nethinim carving my name onto a plaque right now, and readying a sapling. They always knew beforehand, the carriers of water and hewers of wood.

I dismissed this gloomy thought. If my time had come, it had come, but I would not wait in a dark apartment, to acquiesce to my fate like a senescent king grown too tired and toothless to act against his assassins.

I took off the blindfold and tied it around my neck, returning it to its original use as a scarf. It became my only item of apparel, as I shucked white cotton trousers, white T-shirt and underwear.

The stick I gently broke across my knee, sliding the two lengths of wood apart to reveal the sword within. I took the weapon up and made the traditional salute towards my enemies on the beach.

Courtesies complete, I shaded my skin, hair and eyes dark, a green almost heavy enough to match the blackness of the night and, with a moment's concentration, grew a defensive layer of young bark, being careful not to overdo it, while overlaying the sheaths in such a way that it would not limit my movement. Novices often made the mistake of armouring up too much, and found themselves extraordinarily tough but essentially sessile. I had not made that mistake since my distant youth.

The wind lifted a little, and the stink of the weed changed, becoming more fragrant. I heard thirteen soft popping noises come from the beach, and knew that the nodules were opening.

There was little point in dragging things out, so I simply walked down the street to the beach, pausing to bid a silent farewell to the café. Their coffee had been quite good.

I paused at the promenade railing, near the block of stone surmounted by the bronze mermaid, and looked across the beach. There was a little starlight, though no moon, and I thought both sea and sand had never looked prettier. The humans should turn the lights off more often, though even then they would not see the way I saw.

The thirteen had emerged from their nodules, or perhaps I should call them pods. Now that I saw them clearly, I knew I had even less chance than I'd thought. I had expected the blocky, bad imitations of human women that looked like Bulgarian weightlifters, armed with slow, two-handed axes that, though devastating when they hit, were fairly unlikely to do so provided I didn't make a mistake.

But my enemy had sent a much superior force, testament I suppose to the number of times I had defeated or evaded previous attempts to curtail my activities. This time they were indeed what long-gone inhabitants of this world had called Valkyries: female human in form, tall, long-limbed and very fast, and the sensing tendrils that splayed back from their heads could easily be mistaken for a wing'd helmet, as their rust-coloured exoskeleton extrusions could look like armour.

They lifted their hatchets — twenty-six of them, as they held one in each hand — when they saw me, and offered the salute. I returned the greeting and waited for the eldest of them (by a matter of seconds, most like) to offer up the obligatory statement, which also served as a disclaimer, thrust all liability for collateral damage upon me and usually offered a chance to surrender.

'Skrymir, renegade, oathbreaker and outcast!'

I inclined my head.

'Called to return eight times; sent for, six times.'

Had it been so many? I'd lost count. Too many years, across too many worlds.

'Surrender your sword!'

I shook my head, and the Valkyries attacked before I could even straighten my neck, running full-tilt at the seawall that bordered the promenade. Six stopped short before the wall and six leaped upon their backs to vault the railing, while the last, the senior, stood behind in a position of command.

I lopped two heads as I fell back, the Valkyries concerned momentarily confused as their major sensory apparatus went bouncing back down to the sand. As per their imprinting, they stopped still and if it had not been for the others I could have felled them then. But the others were there, attacking me from all sides as I danced and spun back to the road, my sword meeting the helves of their hatchets, nicking at their fibrous flesh; but their weapons in turn carved long splinters from my body.

If they could surround me, I would be done for, so I fought as I had not fought since the wars. I twisted and leaped and slid under parked cars and over them, around rubbish bins and flagpoles, changing my sword from left hand to right hand, kicking, butting, deploying every trick and secret that I knew.

It was not enough. A skilled and vicious blow caught my knee as I took off another head, and in the second I was down, a dozen other blows put paid to my legs. I rolled and writhed away, but it was to no avail. The Valkyries pinned me down and began to chop away.

The last memory I have from that expression of myself was of the starry sky, the sound of the surf a deeper counterpoint to the thud of axework, and the blessed smell of fresh salt air, the stench of that particular rotten weed gone forever.

I cannot smell anything where I am now, nor see. I can sense light and shade, the movement of air, the welcome sensation of moisture on my extremities, whether above or below the earth.

Neither can I speak, save in a very limited fashion, the conveyance of some slight meaning without words.

But I am not alone.

Palameides is here, and Balan, and Anax too. They have grown tall, and overshadow me, but this will not last. I will grow mighty once more, and one day, *They* will have need of us again ... and then, as we whisper, tapping with our roots, signalling with the rustle of our leaves, then our hearts will bud new travellers, and we shall go forth to do the bidding of our masters, and perhaps, for as long as we can, we four friends shall once again be free.

Garth Nix

AFTERWORD

This story began with a completely different tale, one that started with a group of four friends, survivors of a much larger group who had enlisted together for World War One, meeting again just after the war ended in 1918 and being drawn into another conflict of a more fantastic kind. However, I couldn't get that story to work properly, and eventually I realised that what I was trying to tap into is that kind of melancholia you experience when you know you will not see friends any more, either because they have died or you have totally lost touch, or the friendship has been sundered for some reason.

Once I realised this, I began writing 'Old Friends', trying to use that melancholic remembrance of old friends to fuel a different story. As is often the case with my short fiction, I didn't know anything about the main character or his situation when I started to write the piece. I just had a strange coffee-drinking guy with a stick who was in some kind of trouble. His nature and his situation slowly became clearer to me as I wrote the story in three distinct stages over about ten days, with pauses between stages where I worked out just what was going on.

A minor point of trivia that may interest some readers is that the names of the four friends all have something in common, and were chosen for that reason. Though not from the same myth or the same culture, Palameides, Balan, Anaxarte and Skrymir were all legendary giants, of one kind or another.

— *Garth Nix*

RICHARD HARLAND's ten published novels cover all areas of speculative fiction from fantasy (the *Ferren* trilogy) to science fiction (the 'Eddon and Vail' series), from gothic horror (*The Vicar of Morbing Vyle* and *The Black Crusade*) to fantasy for younger readers. Since he launched into short story writing five years ago, his stories in the speculative genres have been published in Australia, the United States, England, and Canada. He won an Aurealis Award for Best Horror Novel, a Golden Aurealis Award for Best Novel in any Speculative Genre, and has received the Aurealis Award twice for Best Fantasy Short Story. Before becoming a full-time writer, he was a university lecturer who published three books on philosophy and language theory.

In the haunting, twisty travelogue of a tale that follows, you'll discover first hand the dangers — and the cost — of being an over-anxious tourist...

A GUIDED TOUR IN THE KINGDOM OF THE DEAD

RICHARD HARLAND

'The things I have seen!' he croaked. 'You must hear everything, everything.'

He went off into a fit of coughing, as dry as sandpaper. In the short time I knew him, Gordon Sturman could never utter more than a few sentences without that cough rising up in his throat. Yet he was desperate to tell his experiences to an English-speaking listener. I think he expected me to envy his tourist marvels.

It was in the Mayfair Hotel, a budget hotel in the Zamalek area of Cairo. I was staying nearby at the New Star Hotel, one of the few American guests among flocks of Germans, French and Italians. What brought me to Sturman's bedside was a misunderstanding over the 'Dr' in front of my name; in fact, I'm a PhD, not a medico. As it turned out, Sturman's case was beyond medical assistance anyway.

His room in the Mayfair was small, dark and sparsely furnished. For the sake of his cough, wet towels had been hung over the window to generate a little humidity in the air. It amazed me that a middle-aged Australian could be so short of funds: Sturman was no young backpacker, and his expensive cameras were at odds with the poverty of his surroundings.

'It's him.' Sturman indicated the thin-faced Egyptian who had brought me to the room. 'Naguib the Inscrutable, I call him. My guide. He's got all my money.'

He had a strange relationship with his guide, half wary and half resentful. Waiting respectfully outside the open door, Naguib must have heard every word.

'He tempted me,' Sturman went on. 'He told me about the Kingdom of the Dead.'

'The what?'

'Hah!' Now his eyes glittered with a kind of triumph. 'Never heard of it, have you? You've come to Egypt to do the usual sights. I did them too, every last temple and statue and pyramid. I've been five weeks in Egypt. I hired Naguib as my personal guide and we started in the north, then south to Abu Simbel, then down the Nile to Luxor. Twelve hundred photos I've taken. Not in the Kingdom of the Dead, though. Not allowed . . . not possible . . .'

His cough overwhelmed him and he buried his mouth in the pillow. Naguib came forward and gestured me away. For the first time, I studied the Egyptian's face: the thin, fine lines of nose and eyebrows. When he turned to me on the landing outside, his voice was as calm as Sturman's was laboured.

'He excites himself too much, sir.'

'I'm not the kind of doctor he needs, you understand that, don't you?'

'Yes, Dr Webber. But I think he needs you too.'

'I'll come back with a proper doctor.' Perhaps I misinterpreted the motion Naguib made with his left hand. 'I'll pay the bill. You don't have to worry.'

I wondered how much money Naguib had managed to extract from Sturman. Did he feel somehow responsible for Sturman's sickness? Why else would he still be looking after him? He was no ordinary guide, that was certain.

It took a great deal of searching to find a suitable Egyptian doctor, and a fair sum to persuade him to a bedside visit. I was beginning to regret my commitment, though I was still curious to hear more about the Kingdom of the Dead.

The doctor's visit proved a complete waste of time. He could find no cause for the pain in Sturman's throat or his feverish symptoms.

'The fever is the body's reaction to the throat,' he said.

'And the throat?'

He shrugged and exchanged glances with Naguib. He prescribed some drugs, but it was obvious he didn't expect them to work.

Sturman himself was less interested in a cure than in talking to me. He started up as soon as Naguib left to fill the prescription.

'The Valley of the Queens, Webber,' he said. 'Near Luxor. Have you been there?'

'Only the Valley of the Kings.'

'The Valley of the Queens is where the most amazing recent discoveries have been made. You've heard of the Tomb of Nefertari?'

'No.'

He swallowed and rolled his tongue around his mouth, trying to work up a little moisture. 'You should have. Best preserved tomb-paintings in Egypt, better than anything in the Valley of the Kings. Naguib took me there, then on to another tomb that almost no one has heard of. The royal daughter of Nefertari, Meret Hathor.'

'And the tomb-paintings were better again?' By now, I could follow the way his mind worked.

'No, no paintings. Nothing much at all. Just very deep underground. I knew Naguib must've brought me there for a reason. Then I noticed the door.'

The effort to fight down a cough brought tears to his eyes. But he was determined to go on, regardless of the pain it cost him.

'See, he'd been dropping hints for weeks. About the ancient Egyptians as navigators on the other side of death. About sights a hundred times more spectacular than any ruined temples or pyramids. Everything I'd been seeing was just a shadow of something greater.

'But he was tricky. He didn't want to talk about the door — pretended he didn't, of course. Said I might not be the right kind of person, said it was dangerous even for him. Leading me on. I had to just about knock the truth out of him.'

Even wasted with sickness, Sturman was a big man, with a rough and raw-boned sort of face. I didn't doubt he could be physically intimidating.

'It was the Kingdom of the Dead on the other side of that door. I couldn't open it myself, though. It was a part of the wall, painted on. Only *he* could let me through. At a price. Eight hundred thousand bucks, he wanted.'

I whistled.

'Yeah. Too much. Crazy. But he knew he had me hooked. I could raise it — just. It was like he'd calculated the precise amount I was worth. I couldn't beat him down, not one buck.'

'But wait up. You said the door was only painted on?'

'Painted, but not ordinary painting. What do you think, you could pass through a real door to the Kingdom of the Dead?' His laugh was a dry bark. 'We went back two days later, after my bank had cleared the cash through to Luxor. Burning hot day, kept the tourist numbers down. We were the only ones in the Tomb of Meret Hathor when he did it.'

'Did what?'

'He opened a hole in the door. Muttered some words and pulled out a chunk of stone. Then he took hold of my hand. His own hand was slender as a woman's, but sinewy too. He slid our arms into the hole, up to the elbow, until we couldn't go any further.

'I tell you, Webber, there was a different feeling on the other side. The air was colder and tingling on my skin. Emptied out like a vacuum. Then Naguib's arm twisted over mine. You know the bonecracking thing a chiropractor does? Except that this spread out across my whole body. I was dislocated, unhinged, turned back to front. Can you imagine? No, of course, you can't.

'Suddenly we were through. Although it was more as if we stayed in the same place while the two sides of the door switched round. I looked up and there were great unearthly stars in the sky. The sky was blacker than any night you've ever seen, and higher too, far, far away. Yet the stars blazed a hundred times more sharp and clear. And the air was absolutely still, no hint of a breeze. I don't think there ever could be a breeze in that place. Somehow it was exactly the way I'd expected from that feeling on my arm.

'Next thing, I looked at Naguib and got an almighty shock. His eyes shone out like huge silvery lanterns.

'*Yes, your eyes too*, he said. *Because we are alive in the Kingdom of the Dead. Do not be afraid. It is dangerous to have too much feeling in this place.*'

Sturman fell silent. Footsteps were coming up the stairs and along the landing. A moment later, Naguib stood in the doorway with a crumpled paper bag tucked under his arm.

'I have brought the prescription,' he told Sturman. 'Permit me . . .'

He placed the bag on a cabinet by the bed, then retreated to the door. 'I apologise for the interruption.'

But Sturman was coughing again, an almost silent cough that made his shoulders shake. He waved me away without another word.

'Your visits are good for him, Dr Webber,' said Naguib, as he escorted me to the top of the stairs.

'Not if I make him cough.'

'That is not your doing, sir. I hope you will return tomorrow.'

I was caught, you see. I didn't know how to help Sturman, yet I couldn't simply turn my back on him. I told myself that his health would improve with rest and recuperation — that his health *was* improving, in spite of the evidence before my eyes. I could hardly afford to move him to a better hotel, and in any case he didn't wish to move. I neither saved him nor abandoned him, I suppose. I just kept coming to visit him every day.

And my visits *were* good for him. He was desperate to have a witness. 'You're my only record,' he said on one occasion. 'You have to see with my eyes. I'm the camera and you're the film.'

He took it for granted I believed whatever he told me. And in a way, I did — or I suspended disbelief, at least. The Kingdom of the Dead was absolutely real for him, and he made it real for me.

He told me how Naguib had led him across cool soft sand towards the Great River. 'Strange sort of walking we did. Sort of loose in the joints, you know? Like some chiropractor really had been working on me.'

On the way, they passed the Assyrian Necropolis. 'Webber, you've never seen anything like it. A city built down instead of up. The tops of the roofs were level with the ground, the streets were channels five meters deep. We stood on a mound to survey the grid. The houses were just the stone left standing between the channels. Windows, doorposts, ornamental features, all carved into solid rock.'

'Nobody lived there?'

'Lived?' Sturman found that amusing. 'They were the dead. The Clamourous Dead. Naguib explained it to me. Twenty-four types of death, he said, and twenty-four species of the dead. The Unready Dead, the Shrunken Dead, the Turbulent Dead, the Nomadic Dead, the Willful Dead, the Shivering Dead ... I can't remember all the names. The Assyrian Necropolis is a city of the Clamourous Dead. Naguib had to point them out before I could see them. Two-dimensional shadows gliding flat to the ground or flat against the walls. You couldn't see any faces, only the shape of arms and legs. I think they were blind and feeling their way by touch.

'They became aware of us, though. Soon they started to approach along the streets. A whole sliding, slithering tide of them. They had no voices, but they reached out their arms in our direction. They gathered in the channel below our mound and fluttered and clutched at empty air, like they were trying to attract our attention. Like we were the tourists and they were trying to sell us something. I guess that was their clamouring.'

He shuddered when he described them, yet he was ecstatic too. I could hear the unspoken boast behind his words: *I've seen such sights as you'll never see*. Terrible or beautiful, pleasing or ghastly — so long as it was spectacular, that was all he craved.

Spectacular was what he got in the Kingdom of the Dead. Another time, he told me about the valley of the Great River: a stupendous gap in the landscape, many kilometres wide. Naguib followed a winding route along the valley's edge. On the other side of the river were stone constructions of unimaginable size.

'Mausoleums, they were. I swear, the finished ones were bigger than any building in the world today. And the unfinished ones a hundred times bigger again. They had bases as wide as mountains. Huge stone buttresses, surrounded by ramps and scaffolding. The biggest of all was only just rising from its foundations. When I asked Naguib how long it would take to build, he said, *Five thousand years already. Time has no significance in the Kingdom of the Dead.*'

His eyes flicked towards the doorway, where Naguib stood listening. Sturman had overcome his earlier reluctance about speaking in the presence of his guide.

'And the sound, Webber, the sound! This endless murmur, low but deafening. The sound of a million hammers tapping, a million chisels chipping, a million blocks of stone being dragged up the slopes.'

'Who? Who was doing it?'

'The Bonded Dead.'

'Another species?'

'Yes. I never got a good look at them, though. In a mass, they glistened under the starlight like blue-black ants. Same colour as the stone they were working on. They were fastened together in teams, tied up with ropes. But as soon as you tried to pick them out one by one, they winked in and out of existence like they were only half there.'

I didn't understand, but he was already rushing ahead to the next marvel. He always talked faster when his voice was giving out.

'Great pillars too. Think of the tallest skyscrapers, and these pillars were even taller. Like sentries, in pairs on either side of the river. Faces carved on them ... terrible, cruel faces ... human eyes and eyebrows, but the beaks of hawks, the jaws of dogs. They were the Lords of Death.'

'What? Rulers of the Kingdom?'

Sturman fought for breath. 'Yes. The mausoleums were theirs too. Naguib wouldn't tell me their names.' He turned to Naguib with an odd expression of defiance. 'Would you?'

'We do not speak their names,' said the Egyptian quietly.

'See?' Sturman turned back to me. 'Naguib the Inscrutable.'

Naguib the Inscrutable ... but maybe not so inscrutable in the end. In the end, he spoke out against Sturman, and I finally understood the nature of their relationship. It was the last time I saw Sturman alive, my last visit before he died.

'We went to cross the Great River.' Sturman was his usual monomaniac self, overflowing with his own experiences. 'We followed a staircase of giant steps to the floor of the valley. Steps carved into the rock, hard as iron, each one half a metre high. We had to climb down over them.

'At the bottom was a field of tall pale flowers. Pretty from a distance, but unwholesome close up. You only had to brush against the stems and they broke off, oozing milky liquid. The petals gave off a sickly sweet smell, half like perfume and half like rotting meat.

'Naguib went on ahead and dug out a coracle that was hidden in the flowers. You know what a coracle is? Circular boat woven from reeds. We carried it together to the water's edge.

'That was the first time I got a close look at the river. So broad and fast-flowing — but not proper water at all. It was the most amazing thing. What flowed in the Great River were the shades of the dead.'

'The newly dead,' added Naguib. He had been out on the landing, but now came forward into the room.

'Right. The new arrivals. All the different species, sliding and twining over one another. Like a rushing current of black fire, with flickers of yellow and white. Sometimes an arm or a leg shot up from the surface like a jet of flame.

'It looked too wild and choppy for any boat to cross. But the coracle was unbelievably buoyant, just bobbing on the tips of the waves. There was a rope stretched from bank to bank, and Naguib hauled us across hand over hand. He made me keep my own hands inside the boat.

'It was incredible, Webber. The shades of the dead went past in a blur. They were making a mournful sound as they went, a chorus of lamentation. There was an oily smell too, and a smell of something burning.'

He looked at me with his what-do-you-think-of-that expression. His eyes had a feverish intensity.

'Incredible,' I said. 'But take it easy. Don't exhaust yourself.'

'I don't care about that. When you've seen what I've seen.' For a middle-aged man, Sturman could sound childishly petulant. 'Listen. We reached the other side and the bank was dry cracked mud. A vast flat plain of it. We left the coracle on the mud and Naguib started off towards the side of the valley. There was a V-shaped gorge running back into the rock. *The way out*, he said.'

Naguib advanced to within a couple of paces of the bed, but held his peace.

'*The way out!* I'd paid eight hundred thousand bucks for the trip of a lifetime and he wanted to end it already!' Sturman coughed and hacked and spluttered. 'Eight hundred thousand bucks!'

Naguib pursed his thin lips and waited for Sturman's indignation to subside. 'I made no promises. Already you had seen sights beyond your expectations. You have been saying so to Dr Webber.'

'But eight hundred thousand bucks for a couple of hours! It was a cheat! No way was I going to leave!'

'You let anger into your mind,' said Naguib. 'First greed and an uncontrollable hunger for sights. Then anger. I warned you against too much feeling in the Kingdom of the Dead.'

'There was more to see.' Sturman's tone changed to a kind of querulous appeal. 'I know there was. We only saw a few kilometres of the whole valley. Admit it.'

Naguib refused to give a direct answer. 'My ancestors made maps,' he said. 'Precious maps handed down from generation to generation. There are routes and there are limits. You stepped beyond the limits.'

'I only walked a different way.' Sturman switched his appeal to me. 'I headed back upstream to the pillars and mausoleums.'

'Backwards, backwards.' Naguib shook his head. 'No one goes backwards in the Kingdom of the Dead. I called out to you, didn't I?'

'I never heard you.'

'You did, because you shouted a reply. A loud angry voice. Very foolish.'

A long silence followed. The only sound was the painful rasp of Sturman's breathing.

'What happened?' I asked at last.

'Footsteps,' said Sturman.

'One of the Lords of Death,' said Naguib.

'Boom-boom-boom! Like thunder. Stamping towards us. I saw him.'

'There was nothing to see, Mr Sturman. You heard but didn't see.'

'I saw him, I tell you. It was one of those pillars come to life. Bird-beak and dog-jaws. Way up in the sky.'

'How did he move? Where did he step?'

'I don't know. Coming towards me. Coming to crush us.'

'No. You had your arms over your head as you ran. It was only your imagination. Only your terror.'

'Yeah, I was afraid, who wouldn't be? Except you, because you have iced water in your veins. But not terror. Don't say that.'

'The third feeling you let into your mind. Helpless, unreasoning terror. The strongest feeling of all.'

'Stop it. Stop trying to put the fault on me. It was the damned dust that did it. Nothing to do with feelings. The damned dust in the damned stone box. You should have warned me about *that*.'

'What stone box?' I asked. 'What dust?'

Since Sturman was reluctant to answer, Naguib spoke up. 'A tomb, he means, sir. A stone tomb.'

'It was the only shelter on the whole plain!' Sturman burst out — and was immediately overwhelmed by an explosion of coughing.

My imagination was having difficulty with this. I'd pictured an empty plain of cracked mud, and now there was a stone tomb in the middle of it. A single tomb? Even for the Kingdom of the Dead, it seemed too much like a dream.

Naguib turned to me. 'He ran for the tomb and dived straight into it. The stone cap was half fallen away at the top, so he had space to wriggle in. His terror was stronger than anything I could do.

'Shut up!' Sturman sat up, gasping. 'Shut up about terror! Shut up about it!'

He went into a truly alarming paroxysm. Coughing and clutching at his throat, as though choking. His eyes bulged out and his cheeks sucked in. I raised his shoulders from the bed and whacked him between the shoulderblades.

Naguib watched and never moved a muscle.

After a while, the fit passed. Sturman fell back and rolled over onto his side, face grey, breath wheezing in and out of his throat.

'I'll call an ambulance and take you to hospital,' I said.

'No ambulances,' he husked.

Did he mean there were no ambulances in Cairo, or that he didn't want one?

'A taxi, then. Do you think you can travel by taxi?'

'No taxis.'

'He's saying he does not want treatment in hospital,' Naguib interpreted. 'Why would he?'

The Egyptian's impassive manner was starting to get under my skin.

'Okay, I'll find another doctor,' I told Sturman. 'A competent one this time. There has to be an infection in your lungs.'

Sturman's wasted hand reached out from under the sheet and latched onto my wrist. He pulled me closer, so that he could speak in the very faintest of whispers.

'I thought I'd be safe in that stone box. But there was a layer of dust at the bottom. So dry and fine, like ground-up chalk. Like powdered bone. I couldn't help stirring it up in the darkness. I couldn't help inhaling it.'

I forgot for a moment that all of this was supposed to have happened in some other world. 'Same as coal miners and asbestos workers, then. It's in your lungs.'

'No. My throat. It grinds and grinds, it scrapes and scratches. I let it in and I can't get it out. Like swallowing razor blades. Drier than dry.'

Even his voice was dry, even his breath in my ear. I freed my wrist, jumped up and headed for the door.

'Don't worry. I'll find a doctor for you.'

I *did* find a doctor, a more professional one than the first. More compassionate too, because he was willing to come at once to Sturman's hotel. I must have sounded desperate. But it was already too late.

When we arrived, Sturman lay covered over with his own bedsheet. My first reaction was to blame Naguib. 'He *can't* have died from a cough! Not like that! Not in half an hour!'

Dr Hurghada performed a thorough examination and announced that Sturman hadn't died from a cough, but from a massive blockage of blood vessels in the arteries to the brain. A stroke, in other words. Naguib had to translate everything for my benefit, since Dr Hurghada spoke only Arabic.

Of course, I insisted on a further examination for other causes. According to Dr Hurghada, there were no signs of infection in Sturman's throat or chest. Had he been asthmatic? I didn't know and Naguib wasn't sure, but a search of his belongings revealed no medications.

Dr Hurghada looked thoughtful. 'A fear of being unable to breathe could trigger a panic attack. And a panic attack can be a trigger for a stroke.' In Naguib's translation, the explanation came across as very hypothetical, hedged with a great many maybes and possiblys.

I stayed on after the doctor had left. There were funeral arrangements to be made, and I couldn't just leave them to Naguib. Perhaps my first step should be to contact the Australian embassy?

Naguib pulled the sheet back up over Sturman's face. 'What do you believe, Dr Webber?' he asked me suddenly.

'What? About the stroke?'

'About the Kingdom of the Dead, sir. Does it exist, in your opinion?'

I didn't like being put on the spot. To tell the truth, I'd never yet settled the matter in my mind. It had existed for Sturman, that was all I knew for certain.

'The Lords of Death and the Great River,' he went on. 'The tomb standing all by itself in the middle of a plain. Can you believe it?'

I shrugged. If he was playing devil's advocate, I didn't understand his game.

'It's even stranger than you think, sir. You see I had to go to the tomb and pull Mr Sturman out. He never saw it himself and I never told him. There was an inscription carved on the side of the tomb.'

With middle finger extended, he traced shapes on the sheet next to the body.

'What's that? Hieroglyphics?'

'No, sir. Much older. The ancient language of the dead. Do you know what it spells, sir?'

The way he kept saying 'sir' wasn't so much obsequious as subtly insulting. I felt he was toying with me.

'Tell me.'

'It was his name, sir. It said *Gordon Sturman*. That was his tomb, you see.'

'Impossible.'

'Impossible, yes, indeed. But time has no significance in the Kingdom of the Dead, sir. Mr Sturman was always going to die, as we know we all must die. The only difference is whether or not you let it into your mind.'

His thin-lipped smile held a hundred insinuations. In spite of his words, I had the momentary impression that he was tempting me to become another tourist in the Kingdom of the Dead.

AFTERWORD

'A Guided Tour in the Kingdom of the Dead' was inspired by a trip to Egypt — of course! You can't *not* think about the world on the other side of death when you see how the ancient Egyptians made such incredibly careful plans for journeying there. In the words of a guide in one tomb in the Valley of the Kings, they were 'the greatest navigators in the kingdom of death'.

The other Egyptian memory that went into the story was the absolute sandpaper dryness of the airborne dust in Cairo. Once you've had the taste of that dust in your mouth, it truly feels as if your throat will never get moist again.

— *Richard Harland*

BEN FRANCISCO and CHRIS LYNCH — fellow graduates of Clarion South 2007 — are the proverbial 'writers-to-watch'. Chris is from Brisbane (by way of a childhood in Papua, New Guinea) where he teaches English; and Ben is an American who lives in Brooklyn, New York, where he manages programs and funding initiatives for non-governmental organisations, foundations, and government agencies. This felicitous collaboration — a first-contact story, which Chris refers to as 'one of the many fruits of Clarion' — is a meditation on religion and culture and, perhaps, the true nature of transubstantiation . . .

THIS IS MY BLOOD

BEN FRANCISCO AND CHRIS LYNCH

From the Journal of Mother Rena

24.07.2489

Stark. An apt name for this isolated planet, hard and bleak like the prospectors who named it. I left the mining camp at first light, glad to see the backs of such men, eager for the company of souls I don't yet understand. The Walker was expensive. I had little choice but to accept the asking price, for I wouldn't have got far across the tundra without one. It's spring here on the southern continent, and bitterly cold, even with the layers beneath my robe.

I'd been trudging for eight hours across drab vegetation when the Suvari found me. I didn't see them until they rose out of the ground before me, like feathery ghosts. Three of them. They're shorter than I expected —little more than a metre tall. We're trained not to compare aliens with the familiar, but it's hard not to. They look like wingless eagles: bipedal, stocky and muscular, covered in a thick white coat tinged blue at the extremities. Two powerful arms end in splayed, long-fingered hands: three fingers and an opposable thumb. From each digit springs a long, wicked hook, designed for grappling.

I dismounted from the Walker to greet them. The one in the middle seemed to be the leader; a bony pendant hung around her neck, and her three-pointed leather boots were of a finer cut. They wore no clothing, other than the boots. The leader blinked slowly, then opened her mouth, a wide, jagged slash tucked beneath her beak. A tongue flicked out, tasting the steaming air.

'Much warmth, bloodkin.' A rich bark, high-pitched and breathy.

'Much warmth,' I replied, tripping over the unfamiliar sounds. No matter how good, automated lessons are never the same as speaking with real people.

She stepped forward and offered her mouth to me, like a bird feeding a chick.

'I give of my blood,' she said.

'I drink of your blood,' I said without hesitation. I leaned down, allowing our mouths to touch. Blood gushed from her mouth into mine. If I hadn't practised drinking artificial blood on the voyage here, I'm certain I would have gagged. Their blood tasted salty, not very different from my own. I swallowed three more times, then stepped back, licking my lips. I gingerly wiped my chin, praying I was doing it right, that I wouldn't cause offence. I waited for her to speak again, the fluid pooling uneasily in my stomach.

'I am Shay,' she said. 'You're the new missionary?'

'Yes, I'm Mother Rena. Is Father Marcelo still with you?'

Shay's shoulders hunched and her fingers twitched. That gesture had not been in the database — they are never complete. 'No,' Shay said. 'He left some time ago, with the nomads.' She paused for a moment and added, 'Come with us. It's getting late, and we want to speak with you.' The three of them pivoted, their knobbly tails swinging round behind them, and I followed them into the fading light.

Shay, I learned, is the village shaman, their spiritual leader. She must have spoken a great deal with Father Marcelo, because she mentioned

Christ several times in conversation with me and is interested to learn more about the faith. She seems to have appointed herself my personal guide, and I'm glad to have connected with her so soon.

Shortly after we arrived at the village, Shay showed me to my quarters. From the outside, the yurt looked so large that I was worried the Suvari had displaced an entire family on my account. I almost objected that I could make do with something much smaller.

I had to crouch to get through the low door. I was surprised to find at least a dozen Suvari in the single room, lit only by the coals of the central hearth. Some were resting on small mats on the floor; others were gathered in small groups, playing a game with stones and string. The room quieted as we entered, and a dozen beaks swung in my direction.

The Suvari hurried over to me with excitement. It was odd to be surrounded by these creatures, who stood only as tall as my waist. I sat down, pulling back my hood, and one of them reached out to gently claw my greying blond hair. I resisted the urge to pet them, reminding myself that paternalism is the missionary's deadliest sin. They were filled with curiosity, asking me about everything from my home planet to my journey to Stark. They were particularly curious about my light tan skin, hair, and breasts — all of which marked me as different from Father Marcelo. They seemed confused when I said I looked different because I was female, no doubt because for them gender is a characteristic associated only with the young. I tried to explain that I was a fully grown human, despite my sex, but it only increased their bewilderment. (Interesting that I refer to them as 'she' when they should really be 'it.' They just *seem* female.)

Once the excitement died down, I ushered Shay into the corner and asked, 'Do all of you live here together in one room?'

She clawed at her ear, a Suvari expression of confusion. 'This is where I live,' she said. 'I wanted to welcome you into my hearth-group, as I did with Father Marcelo. But if you prefer to stay with the chieftain's hearth-group, I will take no offence.'

I was making far too many errors on my first day. 'Oh no,' I said. 'I would be honoured to be part of your hearth-group. It's just that among my people —' I tried to remember the word for privacy, realised that if there was such a word in their language, I had yet to learn it. 'Sometimes my people prefer to have time alone. We enjoy being with others, but also value time alone, especially when we sleep.'

Shay clawed at her ear again. 'Father Marcelo never mentioned this,' she said. She chattered away with her hearth-mates, and within ten minutes they had partitioned a corner of the yurt for me with a flap of the rough bloodcow leather they use for a multitude of purposes.

'Will this be all right?' she asked.

'Yes,' I said. 'This is lovely. Thank you so much for accommodating my strange ways.' They'd been so kind, and seemed to have so little sense of physical boundaries, that I kissed her on the beak. 'This is a kind of blood-sharing among my people,' I explained.

'Yes!' she said. 'Let us all share blood as hearth-mates for the evening meal.' The entire group gathered around the hearth, and a young Suvari fetched blood from the icebox to the rear. Rather than cups, they drink from thin, pliable sacks, shaped like sausages and tied off at one end. They heated them for a couple of minutes in a pot of boiling water and passed them around, waiting for Shay to puncture and suck from her sack before doing the same.

I took the blood sack and attempted to imitate them. My teeth, though, weren't sharp enough to puncture it, and I fumbled for several minutes as they looked on patiently. Eventually Shay kindly offered to help. She made a small slit in the sausage and passed it back to me. It tasted different from the Suvari blood I'd had earlier, much heavier and harsher, though tempered by the addition of various herbs. My stomach bubbled, bloated with so much liquid. But I appreciated the opportunity to show I was part of the hearth, especially after I'd already created a wall between us.

At the end of the meal, we chewed some grass to cleanse the palate, and then everyone traded Suvari blood between their mouths, an intimate ritual they seem to use as a greeting, a farewell, and on nearly every other occasion. I wonder, is the constant blood-sharing a substitute for sex — their alternative way of building intimacy?

I settled into my makeshift room and logged on to my gopher. I sent a brief note to the Archbishop's office that I'd arrived safely. For a moment, I felt the urge to send another note. But Kelly has made it clear he has no interest in hearing from me, and I'm certainly not about to get in touch with my family. I feel so rootless, always preparing for the next mission, leaving a piece of me behind in every place but never quite finding a home on any world.

The Suvari are already sleeping. They make a soft sound in their sleep, an odd combination of purring and chirping. I should be tired after such a long day, but I don't feel sleepy. The inhuman snores keep me awake, reminding me of all the new things I will experience in this unknown place. It's a familiar feeling, the excitement tinged with loneliness, when you're alone and far from home and everything is new. What does God have in store for me here?

26.07.2489

This morning, Shay showed me around one of the bloodcow farms on the outskirts of the village. At three metres tall, the bloodcows are easily ten times the mass of their keepers. They're a bit like a buffalo, with a red, woolly coat and two tusks. Their hind legs are significantly shorter than their front legs, which almost makes it appear as if they're squatting when they're standing up straight. The Suvari saw off their tusks and keep them in large grassy areas enclosed by stone walls. They were surprisingly docile, despite their ferocious appearance. It's difficult for me to imagine the little Suvari hunting the wild cousins of these gigantic creatures.

A small Suvari 'milked' one of the bloodcows while we were there. She plunged her beak into its neck and sucked for several minutes, then regurgitated the blood into a leather sack sealed with a bony cork. I asked Shay, 'You take blood from them every day?'

'Of course,' she said.

'How long can they live like that, losing blood daily?'

'Their natural lifespan,' she said. 'We feed them well, and take just the right amount of blood from them each day so that their health doesn't suffer. The Lifeblood flows.'

I'd heard that saying several times in the past three days. 'And what is the Lifeblood?'

'The Lifeblood is within all living things,' she said. 'It's what makes the blood flow. The cycle of the Lifeblood guides our destinies, determines the seasons of bloodtaking and bloodgiving, and, in the end, our final bloodletting.'

I lifted my head and made three clicking sounds, my attempt at a Suvari nod. It's interesting that the Suvari seem to have a nascent pantheistic philosophy. In many ways, their thinking is more sophisticated than most primitive cultures, which tend toward polytheistic mythologies.

Walking back into the village, I noticed a large yurt, the doorway painted with the same designs of concentric red circles as on Shay's pendant. I asked to go inside, and in the gloom discovered what appeared to be a fish farm: two large, perfectly round pools filled with steaming water. The pools were swarming with what looked like over-sized albino tadpoles, but with a stalk sprouting from the front of their bodies and ending in a beak. They weren't much larger than my hand. Some of the stalks waved blindly in our direction as we approached.

Through the gloom, I searched for Shay's eyes. 'Do you feed on these as well — or are they pets?'

Shay jabbed at her ear. 'Oh, no,' she answered. 'These are spawn.' I'd read of their unique reproductive cycle, but still had trouble picturing it. The spawn are a sort of larval stage for the Suvari, the only time in their life cycle when they have sex — in both senses of the word, I suppose.

I stammered out an apology, but Shay seemed to take no offence. She went on, 'We feed them until it is time for them to mate.'

'And then what happens?' I asked.

'We're not very different from other animals. The female is enveloped in her cocoon, and a young Suvari emerges months later. We elders give of our blood to them until they can feed themselves.'

I jabbed at my ear — the gesture feels surprisingly natural — and said, 'But then where do the *spawn* come from?'

She nodded, which was clearly not a sign of assent as it is in many human cultures. 'From our spores, of course,' she said. 'Both the end and beginning of the Lifeblood cycle.'

'Can you remember?' I asked. 'What it was like to be a spawn?'

Again the nod. 'I was never spawn,' she said. She gestured toward the pool. 'We all come from them, but they are not Suvari. The plant's seed is not the plant.'

'And the male spawn?' I asked. 'What happens to them after they mate?'

'They don't live much longer, having fulfilled their purpose. Such is the way of the Lifeblood.' She paused a moment and added, 'Out on the tundra, among the nomads, I am told they still drink the blood of the male spawn until the Lifeblood is drained from them. But we no longer practise such savagery here in the village.'

I clicked away and lifted my head, trying to withhold my judgments.

28.07.2489

Tomorrow, I will preside over my first Mass here, and I find myself struggling with the translation. Father Marcelo left no notes or documentation of any kind, so I have no idea what he's told them or how he's begun the enculturation process, and I'm left to start from scratch.

Blood (*kasali*) means everything to these people. I'm tempted to use the word as the translation for any number of concepts. For a race whose only food is blood, how else can you translate 'daily bread' except as 'daily blood'? Given that, is there any reason to include the Body of Christ in the ceremony? Should I translate Holy Spirit as 'Sacred Lifeblood'?

I'll keep the Mass simple tomorrow — a few basic prayers, the gospel reading, a homily, then the Eucharist. I've been debating what to read for the gospel. I often like to start with Gabriel's appearance before Mary, but the virgin birth is confusing even for cultures with reproductive cycles similar to our own.

I fell asleep in the middle of the day, and had a nightmare that I was back on Galatea. I was walking through the dark valley, and looked up to see the three crucifixes in the shadows atop the hill. Nails stabbed the gossamer wings of the three lifeless bodies hanging from the crosses.

Haven't had that dream in years. It must be the stress of a new world, the fear of making the kind of mistake that cannot be undone.

29.07.2489

We held the Mass in the sinkhole in the village centre. It has banked seating around the sides, and is covered with a low roof of leather and bone. Shay says they use the space for village meetings and for special blood-sharing rituals. A good number came to the Mass — a couple of dozen out of the two hundred or so who live here.

I read my translation of Matthew 28, when the women discover that Jesus has risen from the dead. In my homily, I tried to connect Christ's resurrection to their cyclical philosophy. Christ's rebirth as a symbol of new beginnings, the possibility of new life springing from death. It was simple and straightforward, but a good beginning point for enculturation.

It was the strangest consecration I've ever done —holding up a sausage of actual blood instead of a chalice of wine. I drank first — I've got better at biting it open — and then handed it on to Shay. She drank the rest and said, 'Let the Lifeblood of Christ flow from my mouth to yours.' She passed it on to the others in the usual manner, a bloody kiss passed from beak to beak. The smaller, younger ones drank last.

Afterwards, I opened the floor for discussion, as is customary in the enculturation process. An elder was the first to speak. 'The Lifeblood flows,' she said, the clichés rolling easily from her beak. 'Christ releases His blood to give life to others, then He returns in a new cycle of the Lifeblood.'

'Yes,' said another. 'Christ gives up His blood that the Lifeblood of the world may flow.'

I was surprised at how engaged they were. I had the impression that some of them were showing off their knowledge.

One of them clawed at her ear and seemed to be frustrated. 'But Father Marcelo said that Christ *is* the Lifeblood.'

They looked at me, hoping for an answer. Inwardly, I cursed Marcelo. I would never have made such a bold translation. There are simply too many cultural nuances to make such a strong assertion so early in the process.

'Yes,' I said, not wanting to undermine what they'd already learned from Marcelo. 'In a way, Christ is the Lifeblood. The Sacred Lifeblood moves through Christ and His works.'

'And when will Christ be re-born?' asked another. 'Will Christ's next cycle of the Lifeblood begin soon?'

'It is not so important when,' I said. 'What matters is that He *will* come again.'

I had never mentioned the Second Coming to them, so they must have learned about that from Marcelo as well. He's left all the signs of a novice missionary in his wake. Anyone with a modicum of experience knows it's best to wait until much later before mentioning that Christ will return. It creates too many expectations. No one pays attention to the parables if they're busy preparing for the saviour.

I've already received several transmissions from the Archbishop's office asking about Marcelo. The Church bureaucrats are eager to complete their forms and mark him with some official status. I've kept my replies vague. I've never met Marcelo, and yet I find myself alternately annoyed and protective of him. He's quite young and I suspect his errors are mostly the result of youthful rashness. I've asked Shay to make inquiries about him among the nomads who pass through the village, trading oils and leather for herbs and tools. At the very least, I need to find out if he's all right.

05.08.2489

After a long walk on the outskirts of the village (which, I've discovered, is the only way I can truly have privacy), I came home to find my hearth-mates facing away from each other in silence. I was quite surprised, having become accustomed to their constant chatter.

'Is everything all right?' I asked Shay.

'It's Hasha,' Shay said in quiet voice, referring to one of our hearth-mates. 'She was taken by a harpy, out on the tundra. We've lost her.'

It was the first time I'd heard of any villager dying, although the prep program had warned me about predators. I didn't know Hasha well, but I felt a bit shocked. 'I'm sorry,' I said, struggling to express condolence in a foreign tongue, then remembered a Suvari adage I'd heard several times before. 'In the cycle of the Lifeblood, every ending is a new beginning.'

Shay shrieked — loud keening cry — and several of the others did the same. 'No,' Shay said, still keening between the words. 'She never made it to the hot springs. She didn't spore. *Agakhe*, death without sporing; Hasha is lost from the Lifeblood, forever.'

There were so many ways that I knew God could bring them comfort. I wanted to tell them that Hasha's soul would live on, that she was now part of an even greater cycle of the Lifeblood. But I said nothing. A time of grief is among the most dangerous of times to introduce new ideas to a culture.

The hearth was quiet all evening, and we shared no blood. In quiet solidarity, I joined my hearth-mates in fasting, and in grief.

11.08.2489

Shay has heard news of Marcelo from a nomad passing through the village last week. He's taken up with a nomadic tribe now camping near one of the marshy areas to the northeast. They are likely to stay in that area throughout the summer, since it's near a set of hot springs used for sporing and mating by both the nomads and the animals they hunt. Apparently Marcelo's tribe has become known as the tribe led by a strange, dark giant. They have methods that allow them to hunt more game and to win victory over other tribes in battle. I fear Marcelo may be doing even more harm than I expected, overstepping all the Church's guidelines. A single misunderstanding can pervert the faith, or destroy a people. I know; the Galateans are testament to that.

I'd never be able to reach him on my own, and Shay is the only Suvari I've truly connected with. At first, she was reluctant to go. 'It's too dangerous,' she said. 'The nomads are savages. The wars between the tribes are ceaseless, and the dangers of the tundra are many.'

She agreed to come only when I pleaded with her as my hearth-mate. The prejudice against the nomadic tribes is considerable here in the village, and I was impressed that Shay was even willing to consider the journey into the tundra.

14.08.2489

Our third day of travel. I'm slowly getting used to the cold. Even with a hood and scarf I have to breathe hard and rub my nose to get the circulation flowing in my face. (I can only imagine the temperature in deep winter. Thank God I have nearly two years to adjust before I have to face it.)

The tundra is beautiful. There is little snow; somehow I thought there would be more. The distant horizon splits the world into two solid sheets. The rocks and mud are covered in a patchwork of lichen and herbs, a dozen shades of green and grey. At nightfall, the sky deepens into carbon black. We're so far out, here on Stark, that I recognise only one constellation, St. Helcio's Cross.

This morning I saw a pink flower! The first bright colour I've seen on the tundra. I exclaimed when I saw it, and made Shay stop and let me dismount from the *guntha*. She seemed bemused by my happiness. I picked the tiny star —*ashuyar* —and tucked the sprig into the fur above one of Shay's stubby ears. She wiggled her ear — whether in irritation or pleasure I'm not sure — but seemed to accept my gift in good humour, patting my leg the way she often does.

These past few days, I've spent more time with Shay than I have with any individual — of any species — in years. She's so curious and eager to learn — she chatters quite a bit, as nearly all the Suvari do — but she's perceptive enough to respect my need for privacy, even if she doesn't fully understand it. She refers to it as my 'alone time', which sounds so childlike that I find it quite endearing.

Last night, after we'd put up the tent and were getting ready for bed, she picked some lint out of my hair and asked, 'Don't your people ever groom each other?'

'No,' I said. 'Not usually, not in the way your people do. We each groom ourselves separately.'

'And you don't blood-share either?'

'No,' I said.

'Is it always alone-time among your people?' she asked. 'Do you have no form of coming together with one another?'

'Of course,' I said. 'We do many things together. We —' I searched for the word for eat, realised that the only word in their language had the connotation of a wild animal devouring prey. 'We eat together, but not in the manner of animals, in a civilised way, like blood-sharing. And we play and work together, as you do. We do this.' I leaned over and kissed her on the beak. 'And we have sex.'

Shay nodded — which, I have learned, is a kind of patronising smile, almost like a pat on the head. 'Of course,' she said. 'Younglings have sex. But what do the adults do?' I've tried to explain human reproduction several times to Shay. All advanced animal life on Stark reproduces as they do, with sexual intercourse taking place in the first phase of development. It's difficult for them to imagine any other way.

'In any case,' I said. 'There are many things we do together.' I paused a moment and asked, 'Could we groom each other tonight?'

Shay clicked her assent and began picking through my long hair. Then she turned her back to me and I cleaned out her feathery fur. It felt good to be touched by another, to be cared for in that way.

As I write this, it occurs to me that Shay and I are becoming friends. It feels good to have one, after so long without.

26.08.2489

I found Marcelo today, after two weeks wandering the tundra. Thank God — the wind has been unrelenting the past few days, and I was becoming short with Shay, upsetting us both. I'm relieved Marcelo's still alive, but my fears about him have been confirmed. He's headstrong and immature, given a Mission on his own much too soon after ordination.

Shay led us to them, catching Suvari scent on the wind on the morning of the fifteenth day. Shortly after, an enormous beast crested the hill to our left, no more than ten metres away, thundering down and almost crushing us beneath its muddy footpads. It was similar in form to the bloodcow, except larger, with massive, curved tusks. Staggering out of the way, I saw a Suvari spread-eagled face-first against its side. Her claws gripped the shaggy red-brown fur, footspurs biting into its flank.

As the wild animal galloped past us, the little figure unhooked a coil of rope from her shoulder and adroitly lassoed one of the tusks. She leapt from the beast, rolling across the mud, and sprang up at once, barking excitedly. Her avian feet were bare, and I had the feeling I was looking at a naked savage. Two ropes trailing behind the animal snapped taut. It stumbled and abruptly veered left, disappearing back over the hill. The hunter glanced at us, then ran after the beast. Shay and I followed.

We reached the top of the hill and looked down on an unfamiliar scene. Everything I've read and learnt about the Suvari nomads says they hunt alone, ambushing the widely scattered, and mostly solitary, wild cousins of the bloodcows, and gorging on their blood. They then return to their camp or cave to blood-share with the other members of the tribe. In this way, both the young and the unsuccessful hunters are fed, and the animal lives to see another day.

The scene before us was completely different. The fallen creature was bellowing beneath a swarm of Suvari. They tied down its legs with rope and stakes of polished bone. It kicked wildly, knocking a Suvari to the ground. She lay motionless, a heap of bedraggled fur.

A fit, dark-skinned man with a tangle of black hair barked orders in the midst of the chaos. Father Marcelo. He was dressed lightly in bloodcow leather, coils of rope slung over his back, a bloody dagger in his left hand. The ropes were actually wire; they were of human origin, not Suvari. He spoke confidently in the nomadic dialect I've only just begun to learn. But I immediately recognised a lazy human accent; he pronounced the diphthongs as if they were distinct vowels, and mixed up the three pitches that are essential to many words.

He didn't seem surprised to see me. He eyed my white collar and black robe and shouted in Standard, 'The Church's new lackey, I presume?'

'I'm Mother Rena,' I said, walking down the hill to greet him. 'Should I report that you're too busy rolling about in blood to continue your ministry?'

He shook my hand and wiped some of the blood away from his face. 'Put whatever you like in your reports,' he said. Then, in the nomadic dialect, he shouted, 'Take all the blood you can. We need to be moving by sundown.'

A couple of hunters stooped to drink from their dead comrade, then left her where she lay. I glanced at Shay in shock; she averted her eyes.

I didn't get the chance to speak to Marcelo again until the evening, back at the nomadic camp. He'd begrudgingly invited us to join them. I sat between him and Shay at the evening meal. In contrast to the villagers, the nomads drank their blood directly from the animals they'd killed that afternoon. Shay seemed quite uncomfortable throughout the meal. She only drank a bit of blood from the carcass, then set it aside as if it were rotten meat.

Marcelo's canines were surprisingly sharp — I wonder if he's filed them down. He plunged his teeth into the meat and sucked out the blood as easily as if he were Suvari. Then he ate some of the meat itself, which he offered to share with me.

'Is it safe to eat raw?' I asked.

He laughed. 'As safe as anything.'

The meat tasted terrible and its texture was tough, but my stomach was happy to have something solid in it. 'So?' I asked him as I chewed on the grisly food. 'Why haven't you made a single report for nearly a year?'

'My gopher broke,' he said with meat in his mouth. 'And I saw no need to go all the way to the mining station just to get it fixed.'

'Marcelo,' I said, putting my hand on his shoulder. 'You need to give me a reason. Give me a reason I can put in my report, so you don't have to lose your collar for nothing.'

'Well, *Mother* Rena,' he said, removing my hand, 'there is no reason. Take all my collars and put them to good use. I've no interest in playing the white man, converting alien savages.'

'That's not the way of the New Catholic Church, and you know it. This isn't the twenty-first century. The Doctrine of Enculturation calls for the Church to *learn* from other cultures just as much as we teach.'

He laughed in a patronising way quite inappropriate for a boy barely half my age. 'I'm so tired of the Church patting itself on the back for the progress it made three centuries ago. Pope Marie II is an anachronism, and so is the enculturation process. These nomads don't have the luxuries of your villager friends. They struggle for food to survive another hard day on the tundra. We need to help them *live*, not fret about how to translate a book written twenty-five centuries ago on a planet hundreds of light years away.'

I controlled my breathing, resisting the urge to raise my voice. I was conscious that Shay was beside me, unable to understand our words but intently focused on our body language. 'There is wisdom in the enculturation process that you don't yet understand. It provides us a framework for sharing the truths of different cultures, for welcoming a planet into the community of worlds. For three centuries, missionaries like us have been the emissaries of Christ's love across the stars —'

'Oh, really?' he interrupted. 'Did you bring Christ's love to the Galateans?'

It shouldn't have, but it surprised me to hear him mention Galatea. He was barely a child when it happened. I turned away. 'I'm glad to see you know your history,' I said. 'I was very young then. And I failed precisely because at that time the Church had no clear guidelines for enculturation. You would do well to learn from my mistakes rather than repeat them. Come back to the village with me. I'll send a report that you were lost in the tundra with your gopher damaged. There's no reason you can't continue in the priesthood.'

He set aside his food, and seemed thoughtful for the first time since I'd met him. 'I'm not sure the priesthood is for me,' he said. 'When I was an orphaned boy, a homeless refugee, it was a priest who took me in and raised me. Father Keenan. He was more concerned with feeding the poor than with preaching the Gospel. That's the kind of priest I wanted to be. To help people. But I'm not sure there's room for that in the Church any more. It's become more bureaucratic than ever, more concerned with paperwork than with people.'

'There's a reason for the paperwork,' I said. 'Helping people is fine, but we must be careful *how* we help people, to ensure that we don't do more harm than good. Have you considered that the hunting methods you're teaching them can be used just as easily for war? Do you want that on your head?'

'You have the mentality of a paternalist,' he said. 'I give them knowledge. The choice is theirs what to do with it.'

I let him have the last word.

31.08.2489

So much has happened. Marcelo was not the most charming host, but he agreed that Shay and I should stay in the camp for a few days before we began the long journey back to the village. Shay was reluctant to stay among 'savages', but she recognised we were both in need of rest.

Our first few days with the nomads were uneventful, but on the fourth day everyone was bustling about, gathering around a steaming pool sunk into the ground in the middle of the camp. Some of them were carrying big leather sacks, creatures bulging and squirming within. I finally got a glimpse inside one and saw that the bags were filled with the Suvari spawn. Shay nervously huddled into herself, like a bird in the cold. 'Today must be mating day,' she said.

At midday, the entire tribe gathered around the pool. Shay and I sat together behind Marcelo. Near our side of the pool, several Suvari dumped out sackfuls of female spawn. I looked at them more closely than I had before. They were about the size of toads — and looked much like four-legged tadpoles, just lacking pigmentation of any kind. They were quite distinctive from their adult counterparts, yet I could see the faint suggestion of one within the other — their legs and arms especially. White and clawless, their tiny fingers looked disconcertingly human. The females splashed into the water and were remarkably still. Their stalks swayed slightly from side to side above the surface, small beaks opening and closing.

An elder stepped to the edge of the pool and addressed the crowd. 'The Lifeblood flows,' she announced.

'The Lifeblood flows,' the tribe chorused.

'I give of my blood,' the elder said. She knelt before the pool and bowed low, blood gushing from her beak into the water. The female spawn wriggled towards the dispersing blood.

'We give of our blood,' responded the tribe. By twos and threes, they stepped forward, knelt, and added their blood to the pool. Soon the steaming water was pink. Even Marcelo pulled out his knife and made a show of cutting his hand and dripping blood into the pool.

Shay and I remained seated. Shay seemed disturbed by the ritual, and I wondered how it differed from mating ceremonies in the village. There was an uncomfortable moment when the elder looked at us, but she seemed to accept our non-participation readily enough.

When all were seated again, another group of Suvari upended out the male spawn by the sackful. They looked much like the females, but smaller and with longer tails. And much more active. The moment they landed in the water, they swarmed toward the females, splashing over and around each other, the larger ones shoving and kicking the smaller ones aside. There was something mindless about it — a violent, seething mass surging through the bloody water.

A large male was the first to arrive on our side of the pool. He wriggled up to one of the females, gripped her like a frog, and plunged his stalk into the open stalk curling back to meet him, her beak biting into the base of his neck.

More and more males reached our side and plunged their stalks into the females. The intercourse itself was surprisingly fast and quiet — no grunts of orgasm, no thrusting or gyrating. I try to remind myself to set aside my anthrocentrisms. The small creatures are not even whole organisms — with only one set of genes they're more like sperm and eggs than infants.

Mere moments after each male and female released each other, the female began exuding a thin, slimy film, which spread out over her body like a second skin. A few of the adults were carefully picking up these crystallising females in nets and placing them in protective woven cases. The post-coital males underwent no such transformation, just twitched aimlessly in the water. Not far from us, a Suvari reached into the pool and snatched one up in her claws. She held it up to her beak, sucking blood from the creature's stalk as if from a straw. It didn't struggle. Other claws reached into the pool to grab the spent males. Shay shuddered and looked away, her claws digging into my leg. I was about to tell her we could leave if she wished, when Marcelo shoved a bloodied male in her face. 'Don't you want to try the tastiest delicacy of the tundra, villager?'

Shay shrieked — a loud, keening cry, the same as when we lost Hasha.

'You're even more of a child than I thought,' I said, pushing him away from her. 'Leave her be.'

The chaos of the mating ceremony changed tenor, and it took me a moment before I realised that something was wrong. One of the Suvari next to me slumped forward, a primitive arrow sticking out of her back. The blood was starkly red against her white down.

'Marcelo!' I flung myself to the ground, shielding Shay with my body. Marcelo was already darting into the fray, bone dagger drawn. An invading Suvari was slitting the throats of the females in their fragile cocoons. Marcelo confronted the invader — his size an overwhelming advantage — and cut her down. I lost track of him after that — my focus was on Shay, who was visibly shaking. I led her to a tent on the other side of the clearing, far from the raiders. We peered from behind the tent's flap, watching the spears and claws fly.

The fighting ended as abruptly as it had begun, and the raiders melted back into the tundra. They'd killed three adults, and left behind four of their own, but, thanks to Marcelo, only two of the females had been killed.

I found him lying on the edge of the camp, a bone spear in his side. I knelt beside him. He was in obvious pain, but trying not to show it; the wound wasn't life-threatening. My limited medical training and first-aid kit was enough to remove the spear, and I staunched the wound with my scarf.

'We need to get you to the mining station as soon as possible,' I said.

'My place is here,' he said.

'They can't treat this kind of wound here. You need professional medical attention.'

'No, I'll be —'

'You don't know what was on that bone. The wound is likely to get infected, and you know it. You can ride the *guntha*, and Shay and I will take turns leading.'

I could see he wanted to argue, but, for all his bravado, he knew I was right. He said nothing, nodding reluctantly.

05.09.2489

The trip back to the village is much slower with Marcelo wounded. He's not a pleasant patient, either —constantly moaning and complaining, yet also unwilling to accept much assistance from Shay or me. Today I was replacing his bandages, and he fidgeted so much that the wound partially re-opened. For a moment I had the urge to lick the blood away. I've spent too much time with the Suvari.

I couldn't help but look at his chest. His black skin was chalky and chapped from the cold, but his muscles were toned and healthy. He looked from my eyes to his torso, following my gaze. He smiled as if he were a package that couldn't be resisted. I adjusted my robe with a smirk. 'Don't flatter yourself,' I said. 'Your chest is only inviting in comparison to the asexual blood-sucking aliens.'

He laughed gently, but I could tell he felt hurt. Sometimes I can be too harsh. 'It must have been a long time for you, too,' I said. 'A long time since you've even seen another human.'

'Months,' he said. 'More than a Suvari year.' He shrugged. 'But I always knew the life of a missionary was lonely.'

'Yes,' I said. 'Out here we don't even get to benefit from the wonderful reforms of Vatican IV.'

'But we could,' he said. He ran his finger gently along the back of my hand, the only part of my body within easy reach. I let him continue for several minutes before I moved closer to him.

I couldn't help but feel flattered, being pursued by a man who could be my son. It's so strange, the things we do when we feel lonely.

He was surprisingly gentle for a man so young. I thought it would be disappointing, a quick anti-climax. Perhaps his injury forced him to slow down. At some point —I didn't even notice when — Shay came back into the tent and quietly, casually watched us, as if we were two children playing an endearing game. I must be getting accustomed to the lack of privacy, because I barely noticed the intrusion.

18.09.2489

It's good to be back in the village. It almost feels like home. I took Marcelo to the miners' camp, where he finally got proper treatment for his injury — which had become infected, after all. He's spending most of his time here in the village while he gets his follow-up treatment, but he's staying in a different hearth. We've spoken little since that night in the tent — many averted gazes and brief, empty conversations. The other day, he passed by the sinkhole while we were having Mass, and he gave me a look of utter contempt.

Tensions between the villagers and the nomads have worsened. Almost none of the tribes trade with us any more, and last week a group of nomads raided the bloodfarm during the night. They completely drained three bloodcows, leaving their carcasses behind, the hides creased with the bloody marks of wires, and the beaten earth pierced by stakes. The culture of the village is already changing as a result, with a rotating guard established for the bloodfarm at all hours of day and night.

I confronted Marcelo. 'Do you see what your knowledge has reaped? You need to stop this before it gets out of hand.'

'I don't even know which tribe did this,' Marcelo said. 'Besides, the village had it coming. Wealth that isn't shared is bound to be taken.'

'So I suppose they got the wire from a local hardware supplier?'

'The nomad tribes trade with each other,' he said. 'I don't control everything they do.'

'You need to take responsibility for the consequences of your actions, Marcelo,' I said. 'You've invited genocide.'

He sneered at me. 'What do you think the villagers were doing to the "savages" before I arrived? The same thing that "civilised" people have always done. I've just given the nomads the means to take care of themselves.'

'I've seen no evidence of persecution by the villagers.'

'No, you wouldn't.'

I ignored the comment. I have no interest in any more debates with the child.

23.10.2489

I vomited again this morning. I hope I haven't picked up something from the Suvari — or even worse, brought something to them. I need to do some tests.

Shay brought me some herbs, which she said would make me feel better. As she boiled them in water for me, I asked her, 'Shay, is there any reason why the nomads attack, other than for food? Do they feel the village has persecuted them in some way?'

Shay gave a patronising nod. 'The nomads always claim they're being persecuted,' she said. 'I began to understand things better when we visited them. They don't have the advantages we have here in the village. They haven't learned the true ways of the Lifeblood. That is why they seek unfair trades, and when they do not get their way, they steal by trickery or, worse, by violence.'

I weighed her words, trying to separate the prejudices from the realities, if ever it's possible to do that. I looked down at the steaming pot of water, the herbs giving off an odd, tangy aroma, a bit like tamarind. 'For these herbs here,' I said, 'what would you ask in exchange for these?'

'There is little trade now,' she said. 'But a few months ago we would have traded this for, perhaps, a dozen sheets of leather.'

In my head, I estimated that much leather would require the hides of at least four of the wild creatures we'd seen on the tundra. 'That seems quite a drain on the blood,' I said, 'for a handful of herbs.'

'You sound like a nomad! These herbs take a full year to grow, and they cure many maladies. The trade is more than fair.'

I lifted my head and clicked, but for the first time felt slightly alienated from Shay. Though she travelled with me on the tundra, her perceptions have never expanded beyond this tiny village.

27.10.2489

I'm a fool. I honestly thought I was too old to conceive.

I'm awash with uncertainties. The life of a missionary on a foreign world — that's no way to raise a child. She would have no peers, no sense of her own culture. And yet I have no family left, and feel the urge to start my own. Stark feels as much like home as anywhere I've lived, and the Suvari are a kind, good people. Shay would make an excellent godmother.

I considered simply not telling him at all, but decided he had a right to know. I asked him to take a walk with me on the outskirts of the village, for privacy. 'Really?' was all he could say after I told him. 'Really?' he repeated several times, as if the answer might change if he kept asking the question.

Eventually, he made sense. 'So,' he said, 'do you want me to ... What do you want me to do?'

'Nothing,' I said. 'Honestly, I'd prefer that you did nothing. I just thought you should know.'

Marcelo raised his head and made clicking sounds — no doubt out of reflex, for we were alone and had been talking in Standard. We both laughed. It was a moment of mutual relief.

'So what's next for you?' I asked.

'I'm nearly better,' he said. 'I'll most likely leave within the fortnight. Return to life with the nomads.' He paused and added, 'You'll be staying here?'

'Yes,' I said. 'For some time, I think.'

'I'd like to visit once in a while,' he said. 'To spend time with … your family.'

'Yes. That would be fine.'

It's strange, but I think I could be happy.

03.05.2490

The nomads raided again today. This time we lost more than bloodcows. Three villagers were killed — one of them a hearth-mate.

I wonder where Marcelo is, and if he knows. I have to believe that the raiding tribes have not been his, that for all his bravado he would never participate in an attack on this village, on me — on our coming child. I suggested to Shay this morning that we contact him, to see if he could help negotiate a truce, but she simply ignored me. I fear it's too late. This afternoon I noticed some villagers practicing shooting arrows at a large leather target. Too large to be Suvari, too small to be bloodcow.

Is Stark any place to raise a son?

11.05.2490

I caught Shay looking at me quietly today after Mass. I've come to know her moods well. 'What?' I asked. 'What's wrong?'

'Nothing,' she said. 'I'm just going to miss you.'

'I'm not going anywhere,' I said.

She gave me that patronising nod of hers. 'Even your young are tall and wise. Will your successor be even taller?'

I was tired of her questions, tired of explaining to her that I was not a walking chrysalis, that a new being was not about to crack me open and emerge from the hollow shell of my dead body. 'No, Shay,' I said. 'He'll be smaller than you.'

Several other Suvari were eavesdropping on our conversation. They were all looking at my swollen belly, their eyes dancing with excitement. 'The Lifeblood flows,' one of them said reverently.

They huddled around me, touching my hair and my belly. Shay placed her hand on my stomach and sang: 'Christ has died, Christ has risen, Christ will come again.'

I stared at her.

'He will save us after you're gone. He will find a way to stop the nomads. Won't He, Rena?'

14.05.2490

I can't sleep for more than a few minutes at a time. Nightmares wake me. They're not about Galatea any more, only Stark. Shay and the others are by my side day and night. They are kind, but the way people are kind to the terminally ill.

Do I leave? Would they even let me go? Do I attempt to escape, unseen in the night? I imagine such devastation if I did — a village on the brink of war, losing its saviour. I feel more at home here than any other place, but what will become of my boy if I stay? Even if he survives the rising violence of this world, I fear what it might do to him, to be raised as an alien, to be treated as a God. I fear what they will do to me, when I break all their natural laws by surviving the birth.

Useless questions, all of them; I'm too close to term now. The gopher sits before me, messages unopened for weeks. I've stopped wearing my collar. I no longer deserve that honour, and perhaps I never did.

Between sleep and tears and attacks, I pray, my arms wrapped around my swollen belly. But I don't think my prayers will be answered out here, on this cold world.

This is my blood, this time. My blood.

AFTERWORD

'This is My Blood' was born after some all-night brainstorming during Clarion South 2007, a six-week boot camp for speculative fiction writers held in Brisbane. It is the first collaboration for both of us, and we very much enjoyed the experience of playing off each other's strengths.

The strange life cycle of the Suvari is not our invention; it is common in fungi and plants like ferns and mosses. We wondered how such a life cycle would affect the culture of sentient beings, and ended up exploring first contact in the context of our shared Catholic upbringing and similar sleep patterns.

— *Ben Francisco and Chris Lynch*

KIM WESTWOOD, a graduate of the inaugural Clarion South workshop, won a 2002 Aurealis Award for her first speculative fiction story, 'The Oracle', which was published in *Redsine 9* and then translated for the Serbian magazine *Znak Sagite.* Seven more stories have appeared since, in anthologies such as *Agog!* and *Eidolon I*, *Year's Bests* in Australia and the USA, and on ABC Radio National. She is a recipient of the prestigious Varuna Writer's Fellowship and has recently sold her first novel to HarperCollins Australia.

Like Sonya Dorman, Kit Reed and Carol Emshwiller, Westwood writes with subtle style and a brilliant intensity. In the wild, gender-bending story that follows, she grants us a glimpse into a dystopian future of ships and slaves, Rajas and Mukhtahs. Listen to the dark and violent poetry of the future . . .

NIGHTSHIP

KIM WESTWOOD

Here the linen smells of mice and the men of old boots. I lie beneath a slaughter of ferals, cushioned in my guilty comforts and waiting for this black-caulked hulk to sink; but it glides like death along the briny channels of a shrouded city half-submerged — a Grey Zone, neither sea nor shore.

Past my porthole other nightships slice the mist thickening on dank canals. Blunt-nosed, barnacled, they nudge from lock to lock, deals done and deliveries made under cover of a perpetual fog.

Now that I am owned — ship's boy to a Baron — I have been sewn up to make certain. And if it wasn't me they'd chosen for those rough, practised hands, it would have been another. Ship's surgeon Crake, who did the work on me, doubles as a dentist for the crew and, Gods help the bleeders, a midwife. Midshipman Nog went to him for bunions on his toes. The lancing knife took the ends off each in one quick disconnection, Crake shouting as he cut, *You'll fit a smaller shoe and use less leather!* A bloody stump Nog has now, and cries at night in his bunk across the bulkhead from me.

I know, since he is not captive, he could jump ship for shore at any time. But for what? For where? Galley Ma would say for Kosciusko, a distant mountain, west, that climbs above our creeping winter into sunlight. But none of us — the bonded, sold — have ever seen it, or will ever go; and the crew, all five of them Barons including Nog, won't speak of it.

Three years ago, at thirteen, I was bonded to my captain, a metal merchant and fur trader. Some say it's a sorry pact compared to smelter work, but she is better than most, and amid the business of it I feel a fierce attachment. The Barons, although powerful among the Iron Families, are not the cruellest, and tucked between her threats are rough endearments and promises of protection, safe passage. So when she brings out the knife to tease — threatening to cut my stitches then have them resewn tighter — I listen with a hellish joy, and behind my pleas and protestations there is desire for her hand to snick.

Above deck the ship's bell sounds *EYES PORT!* and it's force of habit that makes me press my face to the rimy glass as we pass below a row of bodies, heads in sacks, suspended from canal-side cranes. Pacifists mainly, and any others — the infidelitous and effete — that threaten the Family system.

From my pelted bower I hear shouts starboard, and tinkly bells, the graunching of a girl barge alongside. The captain and her first lieutenant are off to spend what leisure time they have. Later, when the barge returns, she will fall sated into bed smelling of glitter and oil and a barge girl's milky seed, but it's of no matter to me: I am her true companion, kept for an entirely different pleasure.

I close my eyes to the caress of air, a quick filigree touch, then the sharp edge of a fingernail down my cheek — not my captain, but the ghost of ship's boy Aggi at my bedside.

You like it too much, she says, aglimmer.

I make as if to grab her, but she jinks away. An old game. She was always faster, lighter than me; a mere slip of a boy whose misfortune it was to be too lithe, too handsome at thirteen and in the short years she had beyond that age when fate and Family collude to choose our adult occupations.

Until then we are considered children, and ungendered. At that deciding time we are given titles — man, woman, girl or boy — according to our station. All those in the Iron Families, irrespective of their physiology, are named as men, while those of us born out of Family who pass through puberty and never bleed are sewn up and called boys. We become deck and kitchen hands on the ships — and sometimes, with mixed fortune, captains' companions; others go to work in the shipyard smelters, or eke a living scavenging for scrap uranium in the waste pits. The last brings better pay, but a shorter life.

Those at menarche — bleeders (and there are far fewer of them than us) — are the only ones announced as women. Exchanged by their own families for a generous stipend, they are sent to the birthing farms for procreative duty, the Iron Families being mostly barren. And only when they are fully spent do they rejoin the populations in the Grey Zone, living out their broken spinsterhood cared for by those of their siblings not sold at auction.

But the girl barges are another thing. Decked with swathes of coloured cloth and strings of bells, they are a floating misery, a tinselled gaol for those youths born out of Family and whose seed has been deemed unworthy of another generation. Most of these 'ill-affected' are drowned before they reach thirteen, but the rest the Iron Families visit for distraction.

Aggi used to say she could hear the crying long before a barge appeared.

And now? I ask.

She looks as if she might not answer. *I hear it all the time*.

When the barge has pushed into the mist and the decks above are silent, I seek out Nog and we sit midship, wedged under the dinghy tarps out of a sleeting headwind.

His foot is bound with filthy strips of rag, and festering. I want him to see Galley Ma, who's dressed my wounds many times and has kinder hands and better medicines than Crake; but as far as Nog is down the Family's pecking order he is still one of them, and spits *Pacifist!*

I don't argue: she's told me the story. I peer up at the soot flurries from a floating immolation bier, and change the subject.

Nog, can you tell where one city ends and the next begins?

They are all one now, the towns and cities laced together, he replies. *But the old names have been given to the locks.*

How far do the canals extend?

As far as there is land north and south, I've heard. But I've only sailed the central stretch, old New South Wales, between the steel ports. Those Families that ply the most northerly and southerly reaches — the Sardars, Presidents and Muftis — I've never seen.

I wonder what he knows of Kosciusko. *And west?*

Nothing. An indefinite mist.

He shifts position, lifting his bandaged foot with both hands as a foul smell wafts, and taps the dinghy at his back. My *escape*, he says, *if ever I should want it.* His rheumy eyes look past the cargo crane and fo'c'sle winches to the Gatling gun niched at the bow, then fix on me. *This whole ship is radioactive.* <u>*We*</u> *are radioactive.*

What's that mean? I ask, although the answer makes no difference.

He considers. *Soon we'll be deader than dodos.*

I don't ask him about dodos. Those of us born into the Grey Zone know we are living a madness. That our world is dying, and the Families are getting from it what they can.

From somewhere aft there comes an angry shout, the landing thwack of leather, a shrill scream: ship's boy Moth — forever picked on by the crew — being punished for some petty misdemeanour.

I think of Aggi. *Don't you ever wish . . .* she used to say, arms crossed about a body lean like a sapling as she stared into the mist. I would follow her gaze to where ships' lights floated in fuzzy strings and shore beacons blinked. *No*, I'd reply. And it was true. I had no spirit for adventure, no fire for any challenge other than my owner, whose dangerous changeability — the beckonings and dismissals — kept me hooked. But in truth there was no one more precious to me than Aggi, and I was often afraid for her. *Wishing*, I warned, *will only bring you trouble*. And trouble came, in the form of a Shogun who took a liking to her features and tried to spirit her off the ship. In the fight that ensued the Shogun was killed, and so was Aggi, caught between blades.

The feud between the two Families has lasted a full year, and each night since poor Aggi was tipped dead into the canal I have dreamt a ship of ghosts with her leaning from the prow, hair flying, and I its frail, deluded helmsman led by min-min lights across the marshlands to the snowy sides of Kosciusko.

Nog eases painfully out into the sleet and stumps off to prepare for docking. Left alone, I bring the razor blade from my boot across my forearm and feel the satisfaction as it beads a bright living red. Many things the captain will command and I will bear the marks of, but this I do entirely for myself.

The scars and being captain's companion sets me apart. Aggi never cared, and the privilege of the latter made me fast friends with Nog; but from the ship's boys there has always been a reticence, as if those two things laid between us have made an uncrossable divide.

My captain has me on the long chain so I can reach all parts of the cabin as I wish. Her back to me, she is taking inventory with her second in command: a new deal struck with the Rajas, a ship's boy maimed in a recent act of carelessness. I wonder that she can't see their third, seraphim-bright and leaning both elbows on the table.

Aggi winks.

The lieutenant tells the hard news to his commander last. *The Viscounts have begun a new campaign of mutilation against the Mukhtahs*, he says, and her shoulders lift for a breath then drop.

I thought that ended long ago, she responds low-tone, and both are silent a moment, remembering.

Before the Eastern Industry Alliance was forged, the Families — Dukes and Barons, Earls and Emirs, Viscounts, Rajas and Mukhtahs just some — were forever at war among themselves, and developed a taste for it. When they began to mutilate each others' children in an effort to champion their own line, most were left barren.

My thoughts are on the captain. She had never let me see her unclothed, and instinctively, I had always known why.

Her second takes his leave and she stares awhile unseeing at the door, then leans down to the shackle on the chair leg and begins to haul me in.

Late afternoon we moor at South Head for a stoning. A bleeder has betrayed her Family and aborted their child. I doubt she meant to, but that's immaterial.

The captain and I climb the path to a high, solitary place clotted with mist and strewn with rocks. The Emirs are gathered in a wide circle, their accused crouched before them in her burial shroud. We take our places at the back of the crowd, being invited guests and this not our Family's trouble. As a signal comes from one, a scythe of arms is raised and the first volley flies. The woman screams once, twice, then on and on, a lacerating wail above the sick thudding of stones.

I wipe my sleeve across my eyes as if some dirt has lodged there. I can't be seen to sympathise. I sneak a look at my Baron beside me, nothing to betray her thoughts — except, perhaps, the up-down-up of her Adam's apple and the white press of her lips.

The woman topples to one side, silent now, a foot released from the bloody huddle in the pooling stain from cloth to dirt. For her at last it's over, but in my belly something forlorn and wild is rising: a serrated ache that tears from my stitching to my heart. I want to turn my head and puke, but for my captain I must contain myself or be punished for shaming her Family. The broken body is picked off the ground and carried to a pit at the side of the field. There she is dropped — so small, no more than rags — and a little dirt kicked in.

The captain goes to thank the Emirs for being included on their guest list, and to say she will be sure to return the favour when the Barons next have a hanging. Then we leave along the well-trod track back to our ship moored with others in the lock below.

Ma says the Barons dress like last century's South Sea pirates; the other Families have quite different styles. We, their bonded, are generally attired in the cast-offs, and can tell on sight to which Family each belongs. And so it is with their punishments, which have become signature: stoning is popular with the Emirs and Mukhtars, while the

Barons favour hanging or decapitation, which at least is quick. The Rajas go for immolation, and the Viscounts and Dukes prefer public floggings where the agony is drawn out for hours. I often wonder how they find so many to punish. Are the canal cities still so chock-full of dissenters? Or is it that the Iron Families have found — like me — a cathartic pleasure in the ministry of pain?

Mornings I am sent to help Galley Ma. Of Torres Strait stock (home swept away long ago) she is large-boned and reassuring, queen of her kitchen. This morning she is both hands in the soy dough, squeezing it with soothing repetition. The progeny of pacifists, like her, used to have their left hand — the hand of darkness — sliced off; but Ma has two.

It was by Aditi's grace, she says, *that I was found to have a certain talent in the kitchen, and so kept both my hands*.

Her forebears were among those who tried to keep the Iron Families from their trajectory to power. I ask again how she escaped the Kyoto Uprising, when all the rest were killed. She taps her nose, mysterious about her past. But once I overheard that she and the captain had agreements that went further back than my short life. And although she gladly takes the role of stand-in for our own mothers, she seems perpetually ungendered: neither man nor woman, but something unnamed in-between.

As boys filter in from around the ship, she motions us closer. Those most recently bonded and still with keepsakes thumb failing palm screens that flicker with the likeness of their parents' faces. I'd had one too, once; but it was tossed by Crake into the canal soon after I arrived onboard.

When we are settled — nine of us — around her workbench and fixed on her expectantly, she waves her arm towards the black socket of a porthole, and begins.

Today, let's think of this as Venice, and us as gondoliers.

She describes that city of art built above canals, its floating white beauty trellised in light and eventually swallowed by the sea, and I peer out trying to imagine it as a barge girl floats past, his pale face illumined by the starboard navigation lights.

I gasp, and the other boys rush to look.

Veils drift, gossamer, about him; sequins dot his skin like tiny stars. I am reminded of the jellyfish that slop against the hull and levee walls at turn of tide.

Ma's conversation takes a different tack.

It was the weathermen, she says, *who envisaged this, our fogbound world, back when the skies still turned their daily blue and the sun kept us warm — so, of course, no one listened. The skies began to darken, bit by bit; but did any of us take special note the last day the red disc of the sun burnt unobscured above? Did we sear that hot image on our retinas so that afterward our memories could fill the lacuna in the sky?*

She pauses a moment, a reservoir of sadness, then looks carefully around as if to record the geometry and colour of each of us. The inspection ends at Moth, fresh welts congealing above the collar of her shirt.

Ma slaps the dough aside to start on another piece. *The day the landscape of our lives was set for change there should have been a warning sound: a siren, or a thunderclap. Instead the machinery of old divisions ratcheted soundlessly together as the Iron Families were united under one dominion. They have always paid heed to an angry and intolerant God, and so Kyoto was quelled by slaughter; but by far the worst of it was saved for the pacifists, who were an anathema to the Families' way of doing business.*

We boys sit hushed above the resting hum of the ship's reactor and the faint clicking of the ion exchangers inching us along. The images of beauty — Venice, the sun reflecting off shiny cities edged with blue — chased away and we bereft, our minds turn to what else we'd lost.

Galley Ma takes pity on us and brings out her picture books. She lays them on her workbench and slowly turns the pages as we pore, goggle-eyed, over faded illustration plates.

Once, she says, *you could dig in the soil and find a myriad creatures, or look to the sky and see the shapes of birds; but we lost them all — except the ferals — their frail perfection barely a memory now. We are left with fog and the structures of our own making: the canals and enough industry to build a hundred ships. But for what? What kind of future, here? Or perhaps the Families think to conquer other countries cleaner and more sane than ours.*

Her tone carries a warning, but our thoughts are stuck on something else, another beauty.

Show us the thing, we implore, and then she brings out her most precious of all, a blue-green globe, and sets it spinning slowly on its stand.

Never forget, she tells us, one eye to the door, *that the world is bigger than this fogbound stretch we sail, and although the Iron Families hold sway here, they may not elsewhere*.

This is more than she has ever said, and we hold our breaths at the blasphemy of it as she stops the globe, her finger pressed to a fat familiar shape set amid the blue: Terra Obscura. Then she traces a floury line to a peaked contour near its eastern edge and whispers, *Kosciusko*.

The ship stinks, a slew of ferals being skinned on the aft deck. Their innards will go to Galley Ma; the rest is destined for the tannery at our next stop.

I am primly at the rail in my ship's boy's best, waiting for the captain. She is off to a Thirteen sale, and I am to go with her.

Watch your back, says Nog, sluicing the bloody deck with canal water.

I look at his tattooed arms working the thick-bristled broom, his bad leg dragging. We both know if he goes to Crake he'll lose the leg, but likely it's the only thing between him and creeping gangrene. I wonder if he'll still be here when I return.

A dinghy is lowered, and then I row the captain and her lieutenant up a narrow course off the main canal between tall buildings sitting empty, their feet in water, to Market Place, a cloistered square filled with floating wooden piers.

Those who've recently turned of age have been brought here for auction. The city's inhabitants shadow the arcades, hunched on all manner of boats to watch their offspring being handed into service. The money from each sale is generous — the proceeds from a bleeder will feed them for a year; but whenever one is taken by a Family with a reputation for unusual cruelty, a collective sigh goes up and gusts, a hollow wind, around the colonnades.

I ease the dinghy toward the main viewing platform, the Families' designated bidders assembled in front. The thirteen-year-olds are gathered on a central raft, and being called one by one to the auctioneer's stand. Some of them have already been marked by fate for certain occupations: pity help the gazelle-boned youths, eyes down so as not to catch the gaze of the barge owners, as if that might save them. The wide-hipped bleeders, so soft, so round, attract the greatest interest and fiercest bidding, their manifest fertility sought-after to carry a Family name.

Three years ago, when Aggi and I were brought here and bonded to my captain's vessel while those at menarche were winnowed out and sent to do their duty, I too thanked Aditi that I never bled; because although bleeders are cosseted and want for nothing, they lead a far more captive life than ours.

With the dinghy nosed against the viewing platform, the captain takes her place among the bidders. I remain with the officer in the boat, trying not to look too hard into the cloisters.

Then one is led onto the auction stand that stops the breath in me. Arrestingly curvaceous, clearly a bleeder, my younger sibling Ina's time has come. I wonder if this is why we are here today. I try to will it so, afraid of the other bidders, and slowly they drop away until there are only two: my captain and a Shogun. The square falls silent, aware of the feud between the Families. As the bid climbs I grip the oars and call silently, and Ina's gaze seems to rest awhile in mine. Finally there is a lull in the bidding, my Baron's the last, and I think she's won; but just before hammer-fall the Shogun makes another bid so high that even the Families gasp. My captain, all done, gestures no more bids; but even at a distance I feel her taut and thunderous, and know it isn't over. The Shogun, triumphant, steps along the pier and up to the auction stand to claim his prize. He draws his sword as if to offer us, his competition, a warrior's salute, then turns and swings, slicing Ina through.

The crowd sucks in its shock then expels it with a roar. I scream my sibling's name as the captain leaps into the dinghy shouting *Row!!* They are coming at us from all sides, an angry wave, their tethered lives' tight leashes snapped, and the Shoguns are all blades out to fight. The other Families, caught unprepared, scramble to escape.

When we are away from the square in quieter waters and making for the ship, my captain speaks to her second.

They'll rise against us for what we do. This thin control can't last. The Families must change their ways.

The lieutenant, a Baron of only slightly lesser standing, answers just as grim. *If the Families change their ways they will be slaughtered.*

They stay silent for the rest of the trip, and I am left to row until my arms are numb and my sorrow has been ploughed into the foetid, oil-slicked water.

The Barons are celebrating. They have sailed a flotilla of powered rafts across the marshlands and conquered Kosciusko. The news of their success (the expedition undisclosed 'til now) has diverted attention from the crackdowns in the Grey Zone and been relayed to the other Families — all of whom had secretly vied to get there first.

And other news has reached our ship. Halfway up they found a hidden enclave of pacifists, and torched it. The twelve they didn't burn they brought back to punish.

My captain paces with heavy boots. Six to my bed, turn, six to the door: one for every pitiable prisoner. I stay quiet beneath the coverlet in case her agitation turns to anger and she lashes out.

If I had been chosen for that trip . . . she mutters, and I'm left to wonder what might have turned out differently if she had. I am reminded that even she bends her will to a higher authority: the Family's inner circle, its most influential Barons.

When I get the chance I seek out Nog, always a source of information.

What will happen to them? I ask.

You'll know soon enough, he says gruff and unforthcoming. *Now move your mollycoddled arse and help*.

The ship's bilges are being emptied at a canal-side treatment plant. Hoses poke above the deck plates, fat eels, coursing with effluent. Smaller hoses loop like streamers between ship and shore, sucking a fresh supply of clean water into the hold tanks. As the crew busy themselves with valves and gauges, boys are stationed at each attachment point, keeping an eye on the connections for signs they might blow — a foul and hazardous occurrence.

I help Nog lock off the taps as each tank is filled, dread sitting on my bones like canker. I hope he might yet say something reassuring, but he doesn't.

After supper, Galley Ma keeps me back to help, Moth unable to do her usual chores and my captain busy with Family celebrations.

She seems distracted, wiping her workbench more times than it needs, and, when the other boys have been dismissed to quarters, leads me by the hand to her blue-green globe hidden in a flour bin and her picture books tucked behind the larder.

The Families blame the weather, she whispers, *but it was they who broke us. Their combined force — the right hand of retribution — came down and squeezed the Grey Zone dry of hope. After that, it seemed we all became the shadows of our former selves, under the yoke, no will left other than to comply. But the memory of our unmaking holds the key to being made again, and so I say to you, use these well, and don't let memory rot to nothing.*

Then she does a surprising thing: draws me close and kisses my head, before sending me off to my master's well-appointed cabin.

Perhaps it was events at the Thirteen sale, or the capture of the Kosciusko 12, but the captain seems to want more of my company about the ship. Her helmsman relieved of watch, I am allowed the privilege of nights with her on the bridge as she commands the laden vessel through black waters, navigating by pulsing shore beacons and direction markers set mid-canal.

It gets bitterly cold perched inside four screens of grimy glass; I shiver, and am slung one of her fur wraps. Cuddling into that warmth and familiar scent, I feel a lulling peace that resonates with the years I had before thirteen.

My Baron is impervious to the chill. Her face the shape of concentration, she works the wheelhouse instruments with deft assurance, and gradually, mesmerised by the pattern of her movements, I begin to imagine her hands are my own. We stay like that, hour after hour enveloped in the strange calm that night brings to the Grey Zone, and I think perhaps she feels it too: a companionate hiatus, brief respite from the disharmonious affairs of the Iron Families.

Boots clang on hatchway ladders; figures hurry past the cabin door. All the decks locked down, the boys are being summoned one by one for questioning. Moth, going to Galley Ma for comfort in the night, found her sprawled among her saucepans, dead.

Nog says the confessions extracted from the Kosciusko 12 had all led back to her. She must have known they would, and done the deed quickly before they came for her.

I feel as if the ship has tipped into a sickening lurch: *Ma!* Love's mooring lost, the past's last tether cut, and I cast adrift in a perpetual night. I squeeze tight against my chains in a corner of the cabin and thank Aditi that she's been spared the Family's punishments. But I have never seen the captain so distraught. Her fist lands hard against the panelling above me and dents it. She doesn't seem to notice and lets fly again. The entire section splinters; her hand drips blood. I am frightened, even though I know it's not aimed at me, or mine, but the unthinkable: her own Family.

I peek upwards.

They will pay, she mutters.

And then the realisation strikes me. Her passion — not one she has ever shown to me — is that for a true love: Galley Ma's secret place inside my captain's padlocked heart.

Distracted, all mood gone for play, she undoes my manacles and leaves.

I wait a count of one hundred then slip outside along the passage and to the galley. Its porthole deadlights are all latched. In the dark I stumble on a chaos of strewn pots, the place where the body had lain and is now removed; but I am not here for that, the empty shell of my beloved Ma. I am here to take possession of her globe and picture books before the Barons find them.

As I hurry Ma's things back to the cabin, the ship's bell sounds *EYES PORT!* And when her treasures are safely relocated, I climb reluctantly above deck.

The crew and boys are all eyes fixed on the giant shapes rearing portside in the fog. I scan anxiously for the captain.

Crake sidles up beside me. He points and sneers. *What they brought back from Kosciusko is hanging over there.*

The cranes have gone up and there are our angels, Ma's intrepid relatives who'd escaped the slamming grip of the Iron Families to live in sunshine, hung in rows like coats on hooks, each neat brown pair of hands and feet limp below the sackcloth. No more our angels than the Families' seditious enemy, now they are the dead — and decomposing with them, hope.

As we come alongside just beyond, Crake mocks again. Called out to a Family birthing, he clambers off the ship past Nog and swiftly disappears, a venal, hated man, into the suppurating twilight.

The captain gives the entire crew shore leave and goes to drown her sorrows on a girl barge. Nog, wanting to keep his infirmity well hid, volunteers to stay behind.

The ship sits in mist, its cargo off-loaded and abandoned on the wharf upcurrent from the spider-legged cranes still dangling their catch. The dark falls, a wet, clinging shroud; the canal wind cuts like garrotting wire. And we are huddled on the foredeck crying silently down on Moth, frail and folded, crushed beneath the fo'c'sle winch.

Something — a wall — breaks suddenly in me, and I race below as if pursued by death itself to drag the heavy pelts and fat silk pillows back from my stash, and spin the globe.

Countries blur with sea.

I stop the vivid blue-green swirl with a finger and peer close: a pair of smaller islands southeast of ours. Closer. Aotearoa: home to the Iron Families' long-time opponents, rumoured to have helped orchestrate the Kyoto uprising.

As I measure the distance in finger widths, thinking of Nog's boat and the locks that lead to ocean, Aggi rests a shimmery hand on mine.

You'll drown, she says, *and be eaten by fish —*

Is that so bad? I interject.

She traces my most recent scar. — *Unless you take the ship.*

The ship's boys are for it. Already, without Galley Ma — her subtle protection not fully realised until now — the crew, egged on by Crake, have been inflicting punishments at every opportunity. The boys, suffering, feel Ma's absence as keenly as those icy winds that luge between the levee walls. But worse — far worse, Moth, our littlest and most recent to fall foul of the Barons' casual cruelty, was adored.

I go to Nog.

Knowing his time is as short as ours, I tell him what I plan to do then ask, *Would you rather be sent to the filthy bottom of a canal by Crake, or come with us and be joined forever with the sea?*

His face is a rumpled spread of seams and stubble; pain has made bruises of his eyes. He winces as his bad leg briefly takes some weight. Resting gratefully against the bulkhead he makes his decision for his heart's first love.

With Nog on lookout for the crew's return, we assemble in the galley to make fast our plan.

How will we manage the ship? Binn, the pluckiest, asks after I've shown them Aotearoa on the globe.

Eight is enough, I answer. *And between us we have all the skill we need. If we can slip unnoticed through an outer lock, we'll be away and won't be followed.*

They know the sea locks are generally unattended, being used infrequently, and only for the long hauls north or south, the Families much preferring to hop between their territories in calmer and more manageable waters.

Who'll steer? Binn asks for them all.

I've spent some hours in the captain's company at the helm, I say, not mentioning that Aggi (whose enquiring mind had ever risked and learnt much more than me) will instruct.

Last minute, the boys waver between sure purgatory and uncertain fate until I remind them of Galley Ma's final admonition, and then they draw toward the plan as if to a distant saving light, while I wish I could feel even small measure of the confidence I pretend.

And so we loose the mooring lines from their bollards and let the nightship drift, a sullen juggernaut, downcanal towards an outer lock as the boys launch one last defiance, sending Crake's belongings tumbling overboard.

The ship pitches horribly, most boys are sick; its bearings set southeast and our sights toward the hope of land, I have had to lash the wheel to stop it spinning like a gyro through my grasp. But past the anchor winch and Gatling gun, Aggi leans, a five-point star above the prow, hair flying, face pressed to the wind.

Nog is dying. Laid in his dinghy roped secure on the foredeck, he is being rocked like baby with the ship and smiling up at sky. From my navigator's storm-battered eyrie I look out beyond each terrifying lift and plunge to what he sees: not the fogbound night of moonless waters, but the wild pale breaking blue of day.

AFTERWORD

London, Harrods, a cowhide on a carved wooden bed littered with fox pelts. Australia, home, and documentary footage of a woman being stoned to death. These images meeting cataclysmically in a sentence and 'Nightship' emerging, behemoth, from the fog.

— *Kim Westwood*

TERRY DOWLING is one of Australia's most awarded, versatile and internationally acclaimed writers of science fiction, fantasy and horror. He is author of nine books, among them the award-winning Tom Rynosseros saga (*Rynosseros, Blue Tyson, Twilight Beach, Rynemonn*) and the critically praised collections *Blackwater Days* and *Basic Black: Tales of Appropriate Fear*, as well as three computer adventures. His stories have appeared in *The Year's Best Science Fiction, The Year's Best SF, The Year's Best Fantasy, The Best New Horror* and many times in *The Year's Best Fantasy and Horror*, as well as in anthologies as diverse as *Dreaming Down-Under, Centaurus, Wizards* and *The Dark*.

Holding a doctorate in Creative Writing, he is also editor of *Mortal Fire: Best Australian SF, The Essential Ellison* and *The Jack Vance Treasury*, and has been genre reviewer for *The Weekend Australian* for the past eighteen years.

In 'The Fooly', Dowling — artist, prestidigitator, and literary excavator — once again casts his spell . . . and breaks new ground.

THE FOOLY

TERRY DOWLING

It was a new town, a new chance, a new shortcut home from a new pub. All so similar, yet so different, walking this lonely road on this cool, windy night.

The choosing was what made it special for Charles Ratray. The chance to choose, the ability to do it. He had lost so much, before, during and after Katie, truth be told, but here he was, at the end of that hardest choice, here in Kareela instead of Karalta.

It wasn't so bad. Kareela was like any other small town really, a town you could walk out of in ten minutes it was so small; the Royal Exchange like any other small pub.

And this road across the fields could have been a dozen similar backroads at Karalta, the same clumps of trees, same scrappy field-stone walls and barbed-wire fences, same grasses blowing in the cool night wind.

Some would ask then why re-locate at all? But they didn't know, couldn't, or forgot to remember the handful of reasons that always changed everything for anyone.

Katie was there. Karalta was her place.

Warwick's too. *Their* place now.

Away was better. You had to know when to leave, how to manage it, no matter how demanding it was, how difficult.

And he *had* managed. And weren't they surprised now? If they were.

Charles stopped, just stood in the blowing dark and breathed in the night.

How good it was to be here, anywhere else.

'You're new,' a voice said and Charles Ratray yelped in fright.

There was a figure leaning against a field-stone wall, a dark man-shape, darker in the darkness, with a glitter at the eyes.

'You startled me,' Charles managed.

'That'll do for starters,' the figure said. 'It's all about persuasion, you see. You're new.'

'Arrived last week. I'm the new day supervisor out at Fulton's dairy.'

The eyes glittered. 'I haven't seen you on the road.'

'Should you have?'

'Well, it's my road, see? I'm here a lot.'

'I can't see you very well. There's enough moonlight. I should be able —'

'Part of the effect,' the figure said. 'Adds to the mood. I'm a specialist in mood lighting.' There was a hint of smile below the glitter.

'You're a fooly, aren't you?'

'A what?'

'You know, a fooly. Something in my mind. A figment. My mind is playing tricks.'

'Well, in a sense that's right. I'm already tweaking your mind a bit, see? There'll be more later. It'll get worse once I start bringing up the fear. Slipping in a bit of terror and despair. Walk with me.'

Charles had been walking home anyway. He started along the road again. The figure stepped away from the wall and joined him, walking with an odd crimped walk Charles found disconcerting.

'You're a ghost,' Charles said.

'That's more like it.'

'You don't seem very frightening.'

'They all say that at first. That's the come-on, see. Start out easy. Build up to it. They never tell you about that in ghost stories. What it really involves.'

'Like what?' Charles asked.

'How we adjust the mind, the feelings. Being in charge of something means everything. That's what it's all about, living or dead.'

'I never knew.'

'See? It's the thing that matters most. It's like a work of art really, judging the moment, bringing up the disquiet, the dread. Hard to believe it right now, I know, Mr —?'

'Ratray. Charles Ratray. Charles.'

'Good, Charles. Always try for first names. That's part of it. I'm Billy. Billy Wine. See, much less threatening. They'll tell you about me in town.'

'Then you should let them do that. I'll ask around. Do this another night.'

'Too late, Charles. Charlie. Had your chance. They should have told you about Billy Wine already. Bad death. Awful death. Five people at the funeral. Disappointing all round, really.'

'So now you're making up for it.'

'That's it exactly. Hey, I like you, Charles. You're quick. You're interested.'

'That won't change anything.'

'Not a bit. Not at all. You took this road. But no one told you? No one at the pub? No one at the dairy?'

'About the road? No. Haven't been here long. Will I survive this?'

'Probably not. But you have to understand. I don't get many along this road so I like to draw it out. Sometimes I misjudge the heart business. Scare folks too much.'

'I thought ghosts just gave you a quick scare and that was it.'

'That's the quick shock approach. The public relations side of it. We can do far more. That name you said. Fooly. We like to bring the victim — the subject — the scaree — to the point where they're not sure if it's real or in their heads. You get much more panic once you get to that point.'

'Maybe you could just give me a quick scare now and I can come back tomorrow night.'

'Hey, you're a real kidder. You wouldn't, of course. Surprised no one told you about me though.'

'Maybe you had something to do with that.'

'Boy, you're quick. Charlie, I really like you. Where are you staying?'

'Out at the Dickerson place. Six-month lease.'

'Well, there you go then. That explains it. They probably figured you for a relative of old Sam Dickerson. Shutters would've come down the minute you said.'

'Or maybe you did something to stop them telling me.'

Billy Wine grinned. 'That too. Lots of things are possible.'

Charles smiled to himself, at least meant to. It was actually rather pleasant walking in the night; windy, blustery really, but cool, not cold. The grass was soughing on the verge. The trees were tossing. There were house lights far off to the right — and more behind when he glanced back, the homes of people he didn't know yet, and right there, the patch of light where Kareela sat in the night, like the glow of a ship at sea.

He kept alert for the fear, the thinnest edge of terror, but felt nothing. Perhaps he was immune. Maybe it didn't work for him.

'Should be feeling it soon,' the fooly said. 'Your senses will go a bit, bring in weird stuff. You smelling the sea yet?'

Charles couldn't help it. He sniffed the wind.

And he did. He could. The salt tang, impossibly far away but there. Charles *smelled* it.

Billy Wine's eyes glittered, a paring of smile beneath. 'Seabirds?'

They were barely there, thin, far-off, wheeling four, five fields away, but there.

'Why the sea?' Charles asked.

'Always loved the sea,' Billy Wine said. 'You hearing trains?'

Trains, yes! Nowhere near as surprising; there was a station at Kareela, after all.

'But steam trains!' the ghost of Billy Wine said, anticipating.

And that's what Charles heard, chuffling, snuffling, stolen back, there and gone, there and gone.

'Circus!'

A calliope whooped and jangled in the night, forlorn, distant, dangerous.

'Weeping!'

And, oh, there was. Full of ocean-lost, clown-sad, missed-train sorrow, desolate on the wind. Billy Wine brought it in. Made Charlie do the bringing.

'Getting you ready, Charlie, my man! Think now — all the things you've had taken from you. All the things you never got to say. All the bitter.'

Not bitterness. Bitter. Billy had the way of it, the ghosting knack, sure enough.

Charles kept walking. 'What can I give? What can I trade?'

'Trade? Don't need souls. Nothing to hold 'em in. Old fooly joke.'

'Fooly?'

'Just using your terminology, Charlie, my man. Don't get excited! Maybe an invitation to the Exchange. That'd be worth something.'

'I can go back. See what I can do.'

'You wouldn't. You couldn't. They don't see you. They served you up.'

'You did that,' Charles said. 'Stopped 'em warning. Tweaked their minds.'

The eyes glittered. The paring of smile curved up.

'Taking care of business,' Billy said. 'It's what you do.'

'I'm nearly home.'

'You'll never get there.' The smile sharpened. 'Walking's getting harder, isn't it?'

It was. Suddenly was.

Charles felt so heavy. His legs were leaden, wooden, twin stumps of stone. This was feeding Billy, Charles saw. The power. The finesse.

Billy read the moment. 'Time for a flourish. Look how scary I've become.'

And he had. Oh, how he had, Charles saw, felt, knew.

That awful darkness. That blend of glitter-gaze, crimp-step and pared darkling smile. In spite of everything, knowing it was coming, Charles saw that Billy was the same but not the same. Never could be.

The wind was slippery now, pushing, coddling, blustery and black-handed. The grass blew, hushed and blew again, reeling them in. No, not them. Him. Him.

Billy Wine lunged, strode, tottered, stayed alongside yet flowed ahead, all at once. He was sharps, dagger edges, razor-gaze and guttering grin. The dark of him was too much, too close, too stinking hot.

But mostly it was the gut-wrench suicide cocktail inside Charles Ratray, three parts dread, two parts despair, one blossoming nip of revulsion slipped in sideways.

Charles could barely breathe. He staggered, breath to breath, inside and out, fighting to remember what breathing was, what walking was, what self was.

This deadly, crimp-stepped Billy truly was good at what he did.

Close up, there was his sudden, awful intimacy, while out there, oceans closed over ships, birds plucked at eyes, calliopes screamed into the fall of colliding trains, and Katie was denied, denying, again and again.

Charles screamed and stilted and propped, fought to breathe. No part of the night was satisfied to hold him. It pushed him away, hurled him from itself back into itself, made panic from the stilting, flailing pinwheel he had become. He screamed and yelled because Billy wanted him to.

Though Billy knew to stop, of course, to relax and savour, to settle for shades and ebb and flow. He had a whole night, a whole splendid, new-to-town Charlie Ratray to teach the last of all lessons.

But Charles managed to keep his sense of self through it all, did manage, and he let the Dickerson house be the focus, off in the distance, its single yard light showing where it was.

'I made it,' Charles said, knowing how Billy would respond.

'Did you? Have you? Are you sure?'

The house swept away, one field, two, road threading between, single yard light jiggering, dancing off like a small tight comet.

'Too bad,' Billy Wine said. 'We're almost at the end of it.'

'We are?'

'It'll be quick. You'll be fully aware.' Billy sounded gleeful.

'But it's still early —'

'I know. And *do* be disappointed! That bad death I had. Only five people to see me off. It makes you hard.'

'But you have the whole night. Surely there's more fear? More dread?'

'No need. All that's just window dressing anyway. Absolute clarity is best. Just the anguish. The disappointment. Enough despair. You go out knowing.'

'Billy —'

'No more, Charlie. Time to go. It'll hurt just a bit. Well, quite a bit. Well, a lot actually, pain being what it is. But maybe you'll get to come back. Some do.'

'Maybe I already have.'

And Charles Ratray was gone, spiralling away as a twist of light on the wild dark air.

'Hey! What? What's that?' Billy Wine demanded, but knew, had even imagined the possibility, though had never ever expected it.

For who else watched the watchmen, hunted the hunters, haunted the haunters?

Who else fooled the foolies?

All that remained of Billy Wine stood on the dark windy road and felt the ache of disappointment tear at him again and again.

AFTERWORD

There's a scene in Ridley Scott's fine 2000 film *Gladiator* when, with grudging admiration, Derek Jacobi as Gracchus remarks on Commodus's shrewd PR move of staging over a hundred days of gladiatorial games and says: 'Fear and wonder. A powerful combination.'

That's what constantly motivates me as a writer: delivering fear and wonder for all sorts of useful, straightforward, sometimes very important reasons as someone living in the early twenty-first century. Like many writers in the field, I never set out to be a horror writer per se, or any sort of genre writer for that matter, seeing such things as fixed prices on variable goods and useful only to marketing departments, booksellers and librarians.

But quite early in my career I saw that I was being constantly drawn to what can usefully be called tales of unease, to this constant braiding of fear and wonder. As part of this, I found myself fascinated by the nature of ghosts and hauntings, and the very human preoccupations and perceptions of reality that keep bringing us back to these things. Terror (in its potent, original, pre-1980 meaning) has always been infinitely more powerful than horror, so I've rarely been that interested in the easy shocks of gore and gross-out. I guess I've always sensed, intuitively, that the power of the very best horror writing lay in that careful and splendid hesitation between the thrill of the disquieting moment, the disturbing situation for the human mind experiencing it, and its resolution, often with the too easily given 'oh, is that all' of the inevitable supernatural explanation. I sensed that the supernatural is rarely terrifying once it's shown for what it is, that the real chills, the real creepiness, lay in all that precedes its arrival. Such a simple realisation: that the real impact, the real punch, be given in the mood, the feel, the staging. The nifty ending is still the *sine qua non*, of course, but the getting there is just as important and often much more so.

From the beginning, I found myself — sometimes successfully — exploring the time-honoured tropes and traditions of the ghost story in tales like 'The Bullet That Grows in the Gun', 'The Daemon Street Ghost-Trap', 'Scaring the Train' and 'One Thing About the Night'. In the light of these tales, 'The Fooly' seems an inevitable companion piece, a small story built around an idea so simple that it was quite irresistible. Once again it let me consider what ghosts are and exactly *how* and *why* they do what they do, this time with a touch of Bradbury (always pay your dues, Terry D.), a touch of Rod Serling's *The Twilight Zone* (pay 'em, you hear!) and a touch of the tall tale that's really quite

Australian. I'm inordinately fond of 'The Fooly'. Part of me kept wanting to make it larger, have it stay around a bit longer, but small things can read large and every time I re-read this one it feels bigger than it is. And just maybe, to recall Derek Jacobi's words, the combination is there enough to work the spell.

— *Terry Dowling*

Author and young Turk ADAM BROWNE, with tongue firmly in cheek, humbly describes himself as 'the love child of Henry Darger and Virginia Woolf, raised under the foster care of Mozart and Flannery O'Connor, tutored by Edgar Rice Burroughs, Rudyard Kipling, L. Frank Baum, Philip K. Dick, Ray Bradbury and H.G. Wells, and allowed to run the streets with pals Mervyn Peake, Lewis Carroll, Gabriel Garcia Marquez, Hieronymus Bosch, William Gibson, Cyrano de Bergerac, and certain of the performers from the cabaret of pre-World War II Berlin.'

He is the recipient of the Aurealis Short Story Award and has received an Australia Council Emerging Writer's Grant for his novel-in-progress *Phantasmagoriana.*

'Neverland Blues' showcases Browne's pyrotechnical talent. He writes that 'it is a tale about space travel and reaching for the stars, a story that proves that no matter how far some celebrities rise in their careers, they will always want to get just that little bit higher . . .'

NEVERLAND BLUES

ADAM BROWNE

Michael Jackson bobs mothsoft and white in the North African night sky.

His many eyes tic and tick. Expensive lenses shiver into place, swivelling down. He takes in the view.

Morocco. Tangier; the Kasbah; so beautiful, an Aladdin's Carpet a thousand metres below him.

Wanting to see more, Michael Jackson twitches an aileron. But he's still clumsy in this body, and the movement is too emphatic. He spins, the city revolving under him, the *souk* a disordered whirl, the Old Mosque glimpsed then gone, the Oriental Quarter a flash of red and gold . . .

Remaining calm, he gently corrects, then corrects again, slowing the spin; and soon enough it settles down. The Ibn Batouta Spaceport drifts into view, and he gazes at the exotic vessels on the launch apron, alien designs echoing the Moroccan architecture — pale blue extraterrestrial prows and instrument bays like minarets and holy domes.

His sensitive hull thrills with longing.

He wants to be where those ships have been, visit their worlds, fly the clean spaces between the stars. He wants to swim the lavender vacuum of the Crab Nebula, hear the tolling of the bell-moons that hang among the purple suns of the Great Bear. He wants to witness the blackholes at the centre of the galaxy — so massive, he's heard tell, that not only light, but also black cannot escape them — blankholes fizzing invisibly at the White Hot Core of the Vast All-Thing . . .

But he can't, not yet. Space is lonely, almost definitively so. He needs a friend for the journey, a passenger. Someone like him, a brighteyed innocent with no reason to miss the world.

In recent weeks, he believes he's found just the boy.

Michael Jackson has been busy since then. He's been putting steps in place, measures, ways and means. Various of his proxies — some human, some not — have weaved a web of bribes and other inducements to steer the boy closer. And tonight is the night when it all comes together, or falls apart.

Now a subroutine pings an alert: the boy is on the move. Michael Jackson brings his focus down, lenses converging on the city — a fuzz of pixels clearing — highgain cameras finding the boy in the Medina, tracking him. Files pile up. *There*, the boy's characteristic skintones glancing from the shiny bowl of a hookah — *there*, the boy negotiating with another urchin, a dance of sharp quick hand movements — and *there* again, his crow-coloured hair, his follicular scalp-pattern visible between awnings as he hurries along an alley older than the Christian religion.

Michael Jackson tenses. The boy is approaching the teahouse. He pauses at the entrance. The wait lasts four seconds, an agony for Michael Jackson.

The boy enters.

If he had a mouth with which to do so, Michael Jackson would smile with relief.

* * *

Salim, who has a keen sense for such things, knows he is being watched. A *gendarme*? He thinks not. Another thief, more likely, aiming to steal what Salim has stolen.

Or perhaps one of Uncle Baba's boys. Or worse, the Uncle himself.

He picks up his pace, doing what he has always done to avoid observation: strategies he took in with his mother's milk. He pauses, alters his gait, flits into a crowd, out again; deftly navigating the secret trails and inturning alleys of the *souk*; through strawberry clouds of *shisha* tobacco; past stalls and pickpockets and tourists . . .

He glances back several times, hoping to catch out his pursuer. But because he does not think to look into the sky for the beautiful machine that was once the American popstar Michael Jackson, he sees nothing suspicious.

Reaching the teahouse, Salim scans the street once more. Again, nothing: An old Voltswagen *petit-taxi*, engine compartment sparking; a Nigerian woman drifting along with a bright bundle on her head, her body long and thin and swaying, like someone's shadow at sunset.

Salim turns and enters. Yellow tiled walls, cool marble floor, ceiling-fans whupping. The music generator is set on Arabic pop — slow yodels, ululations, lovelorn warbles.

Salim smells coffee and lemon juice and frying lamb. His stomach aches yearningly.

He reads the room with a glance. Aliens here and there; monsters and monstresses sitting at tables; a squad of feverdreams lounging by the bar . . . Salim is unsurprised. Tangier has always been a haven for outlanders. Descended from nomads, Moroccans have a proud tradition of extending lavish hospitality to travellers.

He walks further in, passing a table of sentients from the Large Pathetic Galaxy. Then a thing sitting alone, as hideously beautiful as a deepsea nudibranch, sipping mint tea with a damp slithe of mouthparts. Then another thing like a cross between a gibbon and a flea, poised on a stool, primed, *waiting*.

He skirts a group of humans; Berbers in *djellabas* and dusty black head scarves. The clack of dominoes, the resinous stink of *kif* . . . One of the men looks at Salim, at the boy's soft hair and liquid eyes, and mutters to the others. They laugh as Salim walks by.

Salim's broker sits at a table at the rear.

It is a creature from q^1 Eridani. Nameless, a bull-male, it is one of a race of beings who are, as a species, an artwork created by a member of a still older race of beings.

It has been said it is in the nature of art to be useless, but this is not so, for to be successful, a piece of art must perform the useful functions of generating admiration or money. Salim's broker demonstrates this latter function well.

Seeing Salim, the creature fans its crest — black lacquer and old leather, bony hinges as daintily evil as a bat's wingbones. The body swells, greenpink and blueblack, shifting on its plinth. From deep in its chest comes an interrogative *thunk*.

In response, Salim produces a small package. The broker takes and unwraps it with a knuckleless prosthesis the colour of lead. Within is a new Victorinox Swiss Army Knife stolen at great risk earlier that day.

Eyelessly, the broker regards Salim.

'Look,' Salim says. Taking back the Swiss Army Knife, the boy's small fingers pull out the implements, the little scissors, the nail-clippers, the cigar-trimmer, the can opener, the laser-pointer. Then: 'Look, see, one of the attachments is another Swiss Army Knife.'

Demonstrating, he unfolds the second Swiss Army Knife. It is half the size, but otherwise identical to the first. 'And here, here is another.' With a dirty fingernail, he prises a third Swiss Army Knife from the second. It is a quarter the size of the first.

'This is as far as I can get without tools,' he says. 'I used watchmaker's gear, microscopic pincers I stole a while back.' (In Salim's language — a street-patois of French, Moroccan Arabic and American English — the verb 'to steal' carries no disgrace, but rather connotes an almost Socialist scorn of private property: property is theft, is the implication, therefore theft is property.) 'I got down to thirty-seven Swiss Army Knives with no sign of stopping,' he says. 'Perhaps it goes all the way down to nothing. Perhaps smaller.'

The broker takes back the Infinite Swiss Army Knife. It regards it for a moment.

Salim waits.

Then the broker *thunks* in the affirmative. Salim holds out his hand for payment. He smiles to himself. He needs thirty dirhams to pay Uncle Baba, but the knife is worth far more. He will have plenty left over for food, perhaps even shoes.

Instead of money, the broker gives him a fat tube of dark heavy-duty cardboard.

Salim stares at the tube, unbelieving. 'What is this?' he says. 'I cannot use this.' He tries to hand it back.

The broker *thunks* dully, refusing to take it.

'No, I do not want this,' Salim says. 'Money. Dirhams. I need money.'

But the broker is shutting down, fans and vanes and bony louvres folding away.

'I need money,' Salim says again, raising his voice, though he knows it is useless. The broker is gone, retreated into itself. As well argue with fate.

Salim turns away. His stomach aches. He does not know what to do. He says a word he heard a man say once, the filthiest word he knows.

Then he pockets the tube and makes for the door. On the way he passes a creature with a long intestinal body and a head studded with damp black snout-pits and a smattering of yellow concave eyes receptive not to light, but to misfortune.

Seeing Salim, the creature flinches and squints as if shocked by a flash of lightning.

A thousand metres overhead, lenses track the boy leaving the teahouse.

Servos whine, telephotos zoom, optics switch to infrared, showing Michael Jackson the tube in one of the boy's pockets.

So the broker has fulfilled its part of the plan.

But Michael Jackson does not relax. He knows from experience how quickly things can go wrong.

He continues to watch.

Salim walks a block then ducks into a sidestreet, pausing in the firelit darkness at the rear of a bathhouse. Boilers thunder behind him, their burners tended by a huge, ferociously moustachioed man in loincloth and fez.

Salim squats in the shadows, studying the cardboard tube. It is unmarked and sealed at both ends with red wax. The wax is stamped with Arabic characters to guard against the entry of evil spirits.

He cracks one of the seals — a salt smell. He upends the tube. A sin rolls out and plumps into his palm.

His immediate urge is to hurl the thing disgustedly away. He resists, forces himself to inspect it. It is about the size of a pigeon egg, with loose parchmenty skin over a mass as soft and warm as fresh rice custard. A cord like a rat's tail leads to a 50-pin 6.5 mm universal ribbon-connector for multiple data pore-splines.

It is from the West, he knows. His mother warned him about such things. In Islam there are just a few sins, she told him, each adding its weight to the soul so that at last it must descend into Hell. Western sins, though more evil, are lighter, she said, which is why Westerners can have so many of them. Salim often sees the Western tourists walking about with them on open display, barnacling their spines and cancering the backs of their necks.

It sits in his palm, emitting an intimate heat. He wants to tramp it into the dust with the heel of his foot.

Instead, he carefully returns it to its container and moves on.

Michael Jackson's lenses shiver and frisk. The boy's image blinks through the marketplace, strobing between awnings and ornate balconies.

Where's he going? In Michael Jackson's headspace, projections run, proliferating, decision trees branch and rebranch. It's dizzying. So many variables . . .

Michael Jackson is confounded. It had never occurred to him the boy would not try the mod himself.

As the boy continues along, a new, worrying possibility begins to coalesce.

Anxiously, Michael Jackson watches its statistical likelihood mount. Inside his hull, a nervous actuator taps out a rhythm a music historian might have recognised as the bass-line of his hit single, 'Blood on the Dance Floor'.

He is starting to think he may have to act. Not yet, but soon.

In preparation, he accesses the Tangier whitepages and scans for a number.

The *souk*: Salim hurrying past beggars and vendors; gasohol generators clattering; intricate wickerwork windows; iron doors with medieval locks and hinges. He dodges a sick mule lying in the dust, its beautiful eyes reflecting the videoflare of old Wii games and VDU mosaics. He passes a goatherd whose animals are afflicted with an alien disease that has caused their horns to sprout leaves and soft goaty flowers. He rounds a sunfaded red canvas stall selling sandalwood-covered books of God's Word alongside clapped out laptops and secondhand thinkingcaps, corroded electrodes swinging among plastic rosaries.

He pushes on, past tourists, Western and alien (extraterrestrial and extraterritorial — for Salim there is little distinction): a brace of blue ghost-robots from Camelopardalis; a pod of Germans in identical pink skingloves, as turgid and glistening as Bratwursts; a bodiless creature from the Boöte Void, its intelligence coded into the infinite busyness of the Medina, thoughts written into the transactions of the turtle-soup vendors and the cries of girls peddling disposable phones with call-to-prayer ringtones.

At last, Salim arrives at a particular stall.

Its sign, in Arabic and English and other scripts, advertises various types of sin — or *mods*, as the Westerners call them.

They hang on racks, held in place with yellow plastic clothes pegs.

They are dollopy podges of protein-coded programmable-RNA wrapped in a swaddle of datafat and rolypolymers.

They are machines to make you change your mind.

There are many types on offer here. Mood-mods and sex-mods and drug-mods; IQ-mods and EQ-mods and TLC-mods; a wide assortment of god-mods, traditionalist varieties to enhance understanding of the teachings of Mohammed (may Allah bless Him and grant Him peace), and more adventurous brands to devote you to, say, the beliefs of the Nineteenth Century Fourierites who predicted the End Days would come when the seas turned to lemonade ... There are subtle mods to give you the feeling of being seven years old on the first bright morning of your summer holidays; there are brash, loud mods to light your spinefuse and set greymatter bottlerockets abursting in the night of your brainpan …

Salim understands little of this, of course. To him, trained by his mother and with the literalism of a child, they are sins, all wicked, ranging from venal to deadly.

He spots the vendor, Tahar, a short, thin, precise man who does people the kindness of not pretending to be kind. Salim has had some dealings with him, making deliveries for Uncle Baba. The association worries him, but he hasn't a choice.

Currently, Tahar is haggling with a Bedouin woman. Her dowry coin headdress tinkles as she argues the price of a navigational-mod.

Salim waits in the shadows. He is so hungry he no longer feels hungry.

Tahar continues to haggle, the transaction running its slow course; ritualised gestures, shakes of the head, theatrical cries of dismay — protocols of negotiation as formalised as a ceremonial dance, adhered to until finally both parties are satisfied.

The Bedouin woman pays, a flash of debit card in hennaed hands, then takes the mod and leaves.

At which Tahar turns and looks straight at Salim. 'Come out, boy. It makes me nervous to have you skulking there.'

Surprised — he thought he was well hidden — Salim steps forward, unable to take his eyes from a platter of honey cakes by Tahar's eftpos machine and old-fashioned phone.

Tahar sighs. 'Take one. You'll only steal it otherwise.'

Salim immediately shoves an entire cake the size of his fist in his mouth. His head fills with the flavours of filo and rosewater and honeyed walnuts.

'Now, what do you want?'

Salim's mouth is too full to speak. Silently, he hands Tahar the sin.

The man picks it up by its cord. 'This is strange.' He sockets an old jeweller's loupe into his eye. 'Good workmanship. But a cleanskin. I wonder why …'

He turns it over, inspecting its underside. 'By its look, I think it may be an addiction.' He frowns. 'I do not care for them myself, though there is a market. Some people find them useful.' He regards Salim through the loupe. 'Addictions and obsessions have a way of simplifying things.'

Salim gulps hugely, clearing his mouth. 'Fifty dinhar, mister.'

Tahar smiles. 'If you find out what it does, little one, you might find a buyer on the street. But not here.'

'Forty-five. Forty.'

Tahar shakes his head. Salim sees a fat sin under the man's collar: a mod, though Salim does not know it, to boost the wearer's left anterior middle temporal gyrus: the part of the brain that models hypotheses of others' internal states. 'I have seen you before, little one,' Tahar says. 'You are one of Uncle Baba's. You thieve for him and sell stolen goods, giving him a portion of the proceeds.' He pauses, allowing his mod to do its thing — not sympathy, but empathy, cold and razor-sharp. 'Now he wants you to do a different kind of work. He says you do not have to do it if you do not want to, that you can leave him whenever you like. Sadly, however, if you do not pay him a small fee, he cannot protect you. He hates to think what might happen to you.'

Salim does not answer. He wishes Tahar would offer him another cake.

'You are a commodity without an owner, little one. A dangerous thing to be in Tangier. One way or another, the situation cannot last long. Your only hope is that whoever ends up your owner is one who takes care of his possessions.'

'Thirty dinhar,' Salim says. 'Please, mister.' He realises he's crying.

And suddenly Tahar wavers; Salim doesn't need an empathy mod to see it. He knows Tahar is going to give him the money.

Then, on the table in the stall, the telephone rings.

Tahar picks up the heavy handset, goes to speak, is interrupted. Salim hears a voice on the other end, strange, soft and faltering. It speaks for a minute, and Tahar flushes, then nods once, silent. Then dialtone.

Slowly, Tahar hangs up. He does not look at Salim. 'Go, little one. Run away.'

'But, mister . . .'

Firmly, Tahar returns the mod. 'I cannot buy an unmarked unit.' When he looks at Salim, his expression is complicated: baffled, sad, amused, appalled . . .

'Take it,' he says. 'Go.' He turns away, pretending not to notice when Salim steals another cake before running off.

Watching the boy running through the streets, Michael Jackson aches with feelings he cannot name. He wonders if his new body has brought with it a new set of emotions . . .

The boy is so alone, so lost, made to live as an adult before he ever had a chance to be a child. Michael Jackson remembers his own childhood: forced to work from the age of seven; no friends; no school; a cruel and neglectful father . . .

In retrospect, then, his final transformation should have come as no surprise. After all, he'd never been entirely of this world. He'd always sought escape through his art, through transformations abstract and real. All the surgery, all the cosmetic procedures, had been a legitimised form of self-harm — scalpels in place of razor blades, cautery probes in place of lit cigarettes — physical pain to help relieve the deeper pain.

Over the years (how many years? — too many — he'd stopped counting birthdays after his hundredth), he'd become ever more streamlined, ever less human. He'd chiselled away at his body, pruning the superfluities, reducing himself by increments, paling into the background. And with time, the lifts and peels were succeeded by more experimental procedures, alterations and refinements, gerontological treatments to keep him a boyman, undecayed through the decades . . . then came procedures more experimental still.

Others had done something similar, of course. Most who could afford it were altering themselves in some way or other these days; the transhumanists, the posthumanists. But he'd always been the first. Michael Jackson had been posthuman before there was a word for it.

And now — now he's *post*-posthuman: original body little more than a memory; limbs replaced with ailerons and other control surfaces; face flowered into a pallid little radio-telescope headgarden . . .

Grub to butterfly, that's what it feels like. Metamorphosis: painful, emancipating, beautiful. A delicious stretching of long-cramped wings.

But as he continues to track the boy below, he knows he is still not entirely free. The paradox is not lost on him: for true liberty, one always needs the ties of love . . .

He wonders if he might work the sentiment up into a song.

Disconsolate, Salim slopes and ducks through the *souk*, the tight alleys of the Medina opening into the Boulevard Sidi Mohamed Ben Abdelah — the old city giving way to the hotel district; art deco palaces; the Idler's Terrace; the El-Minzah with its dark lush courtyards; the Café Haffa zizzing with cocaine and Tangier jazz — Salim a bit of local colour here, an authentic ragamuffin on display for the edification of the tourists . . . He runs along the Rue Dar Dbagh, across the square to the Tangier Ville Station; and from there down an incline, through a hole in a chainlink fence, to his home under a rail bridge.

A freight train kachunkachunks overhead. Soot rains down.

Salim pushes through brocaded fabric into the little house he has made; a tepee assembled from his mother's old clothing: scavenged bits of lumber supporting her *kaftans* and *djellabas*, her *foulard* scarves and embroidered pantaloons, shirts and wide ornate belts — the eyegrilles of her *burqas* forming slit-windows.

It is a fantastic object, naïve art, an unintentional masterpiece (and indeed, when Michael Jackson's scouts first sent images of it to him a few weeks ago, he began to suspect Salim might be the boy for him).

Inside, wrapped in the mothersmell, Salim flicks a stolen keychain LED to life. Its light glints from her jewellery, cheap amulets, charms, a *khamsa* pendant pinned to the fabric, its swinging eye warding off evil.

The sin's cord hangs slackly in his fingers. He considers what Tahar said, that Salim might sell it on the street if he could discover what was in it . . .

To hesitate would be to give the fear time to take hold. Quickly, he tugs down his collar and touches the connector to the back of his neck, as he's seen the Westerners do.

The pins wake at once — ultrafine, moist with local anaesthetic — reaching out to slip into his pores; deeper, under his skin — then deeper still.

Suddenly he is sliding sideways into sleep. There's just time to lay his head down ...

And he is dreaming about his mother. It is the dream he always has — that last night, in their rooms ... and it is cold, so she tucks him into the blankets, and she, hacking, wheezing, the pneumonia in both lungs by then, wraps herself in a discarded swatch of lighter-than-air bubblewrap, helium blisters keeping her an inch or so above the rammed earth floor as she nods off, coughing, shivering, fading ... And then, as it always does, the dream moves forward, hours later when he wakes to the realisation of silence — no more coughing, no more wheezing — and for a little while he enjoys the quiet.

Then he realises what it means. He rises to find her, her corpse bobbing in the air by the closed door, like a pet wanting to be let out ... this is the point at which the dream normally ends, leaving Salim awake and weeping.

But now it does not end. The dream-Salim is surprised to find himself opening the door for her, and his mother's smile is grateful, the smile he remembers, farewelling and forgiving her sinning boy as she begins her journey towards paradise. *Jannah*, the Home of Peace, where the righteous recline on green cushions in gardens with fountains and streams of clear running water, where the north wind sprays scent upon them and enhances their beauty ... (and even in his sleep, even in the deepest parts of his dream, he can feel the mod, its soft incursions, its butterfly touches at the edges of his thoughts, a dust of scales in the mind's eye ...)

He wakes. Midmorning sunlight streams through the eyegrille windows.

He rises and pushes out into the world, strong and unafraid. He glances back at his tent, considering for the first time that he might sell a few of his mother's effects, raise a bit of money that way. Somehow he's sure she wouldn't mind.

He stretches and looks about. The Tangier-Marrakech bullet train is in the station. So beautiful, so powerful. He glances up at the broken sky visible between the girders of the railbridge.

And then he's flat on his back, gasping with a delight too huge to be borne.

The *sky*. What has happened to it?

It is made of bliss.

The mod is an addiction, as Tahar surmised. An addiction to the colour blue.

Based on the cortical architecture of the male Satin Bowerbird of Australia, it alters the wearer so that to see blue is to know joy. The effect is such that even the dirty Moroccan sky (postcard-blue, yes, but the blue of a postcard many years old, faded and smirched and smeared with greasy fingerprints) is utter beauty.

Salim breathes it in, feeling unworthy. How had he never seen it before? How could people walk about under it so blithely?

He lies there a long while, until clouds gather and his high dissipates. Then he moves on, climbing back up to the street, re-entering the city, eager for more blues.

He dives into the turbulent deeps of Tangier, a wash of warm colours, splashes of terracotta and opium and dust. But that's okay, because the scarcity of the blue makes it all the more precious whenever he finds it. He's a treasure hunter, searching out gems, little bits of delight — the *bleu-de-Fez* tiles in the mosaics on the walls of the richer houses — the purpleblue threads in the hanging carpets of the weaver's district — the clothes and hides and exoskeletons of various tourists — the pots in the market stalls, often just tourist trash; but the *blues*, the cobalts, the ultramarines ... And then, at the dye sellers, the mounds of colour — just pure colour — indigo, hardcore, straight from the source ... Crying out with the pleasure of it, he sits, plonk, just like that, in the middle of the street. He is overcome, all his troubles forgotten. Some passers-by look at him, others look away. The sight of a young person drunk on gasohol is not uncommon in Morocco.

The high fades once more. He needs a new blue, always a new blue, pulling him on. He's tuned to it, following its vibrations to the Dar el Makhzen Museum. He slips by the guards to drink in the blue-frescoed ceilings, the plasterworks, the silks, the enamelled metal pots, the mosaic of Venus on a sea voyage — and it is the glass waves under her boat that ravish him, not Venus at all.

Then he's out again, back on the street, perhaps tossed out, perhaps of his own accord, he neither knows nor cares. His need is stronger, helping him find the lucent greyblue of a stray cat's eyes, then the iridescent turquoise of alien weeds brought as spores on visiting ships. By midday he discovers he can smell blue, its odourless scent pulling him through and through the city.

His desire is a muscular thing, pressing against his organs. He is breathing hard, cold and hot at once.

He pushes on, never noticing another, older boy, who spots him and begins to keep pace (and above, lenses flourish and slick. Michael Jackson's avionics squirm. Should he do something? Not yet, not yet ... He waits, his verniers fluting the tune of his early single 'Shoo Be Doo Bee Do Da Day').

Salim moves on, finding blue where others might not: a hint at the base of the smoke rising from a charcoal cooking fire; a suggestion in the sheen of a carcass in a butcher's stall; a layer of paint on a house, hidden by its current colour, but still *there*, still muffledly humming.

But Salim is never satisfied. He stumbles down the Boulevard Mohamed VI (Michael Jackson watching as the older boy unfolds a cellophane cellphone and makes a call).

Suddenly, Salim stops. His breath quietens. Over the clamour of the city he hears something.

A crash of waves, the cry of a gull. His head lifts.

Of course.

He runs, leaps. Over a low wall, past the Café Celine Dion, around the back, losing a sandal as he scrambles under a fence, through the backyard of an old colonial house — a dog barking, chasing him onward — across a midden, cutting his heel, blood flows, doesn't matter — then out the front.

Onto the beach. The sea, the surf. Waves of joy.

Weeping, he falls to his knees. He begins shuffling forward through the sand like a penitent.

A shout behind him. He turns, if only to share the joy.

It is Uncle Baba with two of his boys. Salim smiles. The man looks silly with his British-style pinstripes and polished brogues on the beach.

Uncle Baba says something Salim cannot hear, something about money. Salim shakes his head and turns back to the sea. Who needs money when there is *this* to be had?

He stands and walks on. He will enter it, drown in the blue.

A hand whirls him around. It's Baba, who raises his fist — and freezes, looking behind Salim in horror.

Baba runs, his boys behind him.

Glancing back, Salim is annoyed to see his view of the sea has been blocked by a spaceship.

He looks at it disinterestedly. It is covered with a fur of innumerable tiny lifting surfaces — a fractal wing; the equivalent of a two-kilometre wingspan fuzzing the vessel's lines, the merest breezes pushing it this way and that, keeping it half-aloft, touching but lightly on the earth.

Graceful landing gear drum manicured fingernails on the sand. A door opens, and a voice calls, soft and faltering. Blue spills from the opening, bluer even than the sea. It pulls him forward.

The ship sighs with pleasure as Salim enters it. He looks around for whoever it was who called to him. There is no one.

The voice Salim heard was the spaceship's. Its name, as he will learn in coming days, is Michael.

The door closes, but Salim isn't worried. It is warm, and there is food and drink and many splendours. And all is lit blue . . . Such a blue . . .

The ship speaks again to Salim, soft English words that he does not understand, but the tones are soothing as the vessel rises, a little uncertain at first, wobbling up into the stratosphere, gaining confidence as it reaches escape velocity, the sky unfurling — a rolling glory of stars — the ship accelerating now, its dreaming engines driving it ever faster, the wavelengths of the stars ahead Dopplering, shifting bluer and bluer.

And together Michael Jackson and his new friend laugh and dance as they shake off the sad old dirt of the world for the delights of the heavens.

Moonwalking without end into the blue forevers of Neverland.

AFTERWORD

Those who are denied a healthy childhood often remain emotional children in their adult years. In many ways, 'Neverland Blues' is a childhood fable, Michael Jackson playing the role of the fairy godmother. Many who have read this story have found Jackson's transformation, from popstar to spaceship, strange. It never seemed strange to me at all. Indeed, it's always felt almost inevitable — so much so that I wrote it in a hurry, lest the man himself make fiction into reality before I could get it published.

— *Adam Browne*

ANGELA SLATTER is a Brisbane-based writer. Her short fiction has appeared in Australia, the United States, the United Kingdom and Canada, in publications such as *Lady Churchill's Rosebud Wristlet*, *ONSPEC*, and *Shimmer*. She has a Graduate Diploma in Creative Writing, a Masters (Research) in Creative Writing and is currently undertaking a PhD in Creative Writing. She is working on two novels and writing reviews for *Australian Specfic in Focus* (*Asif*).

Here she creates an Australian fable . . . a deadly, albeit beautiful, metaphor for colonisation.

THE JACARANDA WIFE

ANGELA SLATTER

Sometimes, not very often, but sometimes when the winds blow right, the summer heat is kind, and the rain trickles down just-so, a woman is born of a jacaranda tree.

The indigenous inhabitants leave these women well alone. They know them to be foreign to the land for all that they spring from the great tree deeply embedded in the soil. White-skinned as the moon, violet-eyed, they bring only grief.

So when, in 1849, James Willoughby found one such woman sleeping beneath the spreading boughs of the old jacaranda tree in his house yard, members of the Birbai tribe who had once quite happily come to visit the kitchens of the station, disappeared. As they went, they told everyone they encountered, both black and white, that one of the pale women had come to Rollands Plain station and there would be no good of her. Best to avoid the place for a long, long time.

Willoughby, the younger son of an old Sussex family, had fought with his father, migrated to Australia, and made his fortune, in that order. His property stretched across ten thousand acres, and the Merino sheep he'd purchased from John McArthur thrived on the green, rolling pastures spotted with eucalypts and jacarandas. He had a house built from buttery sandstone, on a slight rise, surrounded on three sides by trees and manicured lawns, a turning circle out the front for carriages. Willoughby made sure the windows were wide enough to drink in the bright Australian light, and filled its rooms with all the finest things that reminded him of England. His one lack was that of a wife.

He had in his possession, it must be said, a large collection of miniatures sent by the parents of potential brides. Some were great beauties — and great beauties did not wish to live in the Colonies. Some were obviously plain, in spite of efforts the portraitists had gone to imbue them with some kind of charm; these girls were quite happy to make the arduous journey to a rich, handsome, dark-haired husband, but *he* did not want a plain wife. He had not made his way in the world to ornament this place with a plain-faced woman, no matter how sweet her nature might be.

The silver-haired girl he found early one morning was beyond even his dreams and demands. Long-limbed, delicate, so pale he could see blue veins pulsing beneath her skin — for she was naked, sleeping on a bed of brilliant purple jacaranda flowers, crushed by the weight and warmth of her body. As he leaned over her, she opened her eyes and he was lost in their violet depths.

Ever the gentleman, he wrapped his proper Englishman's coat about her shoulders, speaking to her in the low, gentle voice he reserved for skittish horses, and steered her inside. He settled her on his very own bed, the place he had always hoped to bring a suitable wife, and called for his housekeeper.

The broad, red-faced Mrs Flynn bustled in. She was a widow, living now with Willoughby's overseer in a fine arrangement that suited both of them. In Ireland, her three sons had been hung for treason against the Crown, and the judge who sentenced them decided that a woman who had produced three such anarchists must herself have strong anti-English sympathies. She was arrested, charged, tried and sent to live in this strange land with an arid centre and a wet green edge. She'd been allocated to Willoughby, and although her heart would always have a hole in it where her sons had been torn away, she had, in some measure, come to feel maternal about her master and directed her energies to making him happy as only a mother could.

The sight of the girl on the bed, lids shut once again, and the mooncalf look in her master's eyes troubled her but she held her tongue, pushed her greying red hair back under its white cap and began to bustle around the girl. Willoughby sat and stared.

'She's perfect, Martha. Don't you think?'

'Beautiful for sure, Master James, for all she's underdressed. Who is she? Where's she from?' Mrs Flynn surreptitiously sniffed at the girl's mouth for a whiff of gin. Finding nothing, her suspicions shifted; surely the girl was addle-pated. Or a tart, left adrift by a client of the worst sort. Or a convict on the run. Or a good girl who'd had something unspeakable visited upon her. She'd check later, to see if there was any bleeding. 'Perhaps the doctor …'

'Is she hurt?' The urgency in his voice pierced her heart, and she winced like a good mother.

'Not that I can see, but we'd best be sure. Send for Dr Abrams. Go on now.' She urged him from the room, her hands creating a small breeze as she flapped at him. Turning back to the girl, she found the violet eyes open, staring around her, without fear, and with only a mild curiosity.

'And what's your name, little miss?' Mrs Flynn asked, adjusting the blanket she'd laid over the girl. The eyes widened, the mouth opened but the only thing that came out was a noise like the breeze rushing through leaves.

Martha Flynn felt cold all over. Her bladder threatened to betray her, and she had to rush from the room and relieve herself outside. She wore her sweat like a coat when she returned (it had taken all of her courage to step back inside). The girl eyed her mildly, a little sadly perhaps, but something in her gaze told Martha Flynn that she had been *entrusted* with a secret. It moved her fear to pity.

'Now then, the doctor will be here soon. You make yourself comfortable, *mavourneen*.'

* * *

'She's a mute, you see,' explained Willoughby to the parson. 'No family that we can find. Someone has to look after her.'

The Reverend St John Clare cleared his throat, playing for time before he had to answer. Willoughby saved him for a moment.

'She seems fond enough of me,' he lied a little. She *seemed* not to hate him, nor anyone else. Even 'fond' was too strong a term, but he didn't want to say 'She seems slightly less than indifferent to me.' Sometimes she smiled, but mostly when she was outdoors, near the tree he'd found her under. She was neither grateful for his rescue, nor ungrateful; she simply took whatever was offered, be it protection, affection, or food (she preferred vegetables to meat, screwing her nose up at the plates of lamb and mutton). She did, however, take some joy in the new lambs, helping Mrs Flynn to care for them, feeding the motherless ones by hand, and they would follow her.

He'd named her Emily, after his grandmother. She had taken up painting; Willoughby had presented her with a set of watercolours, thinking it would be a lady-like way for her to pass the time. She sat outside and painted the jacaranda tree over and over, her skill growing with each painting, until she had at last produced a finely detailed, subtly rendered image, which Willoughby had framed. It hung over the fireplace in his study; he would stare at it for hours, knowing there was something he was missing, some construction of line and curve, some intersection of colour he had failed to properly see. She would smile whenever she found him thus engaged, lightly drop her hand to his shoulder and finally leave as quietly as she had come.

'Does she want to marry you?' asked the parson.

'I think so. It's . . .' struggled Willoughby, 'it's just so damned inappropriate to have her under my roof like this! She's not a relative, she's not a ward, she's a woman and I . . .'

'You love her,' finished St John. Mrs Flynn had spoken to him quietly upon his arrival. 'There's always a charitable institution? I could find her a position with one of the ladies in Sydney Town, as a maid or companion?'

'No! I won't let her go!' Willoughby wiped the sweat from his brow, felt his shirt sticking to the skin of his back. 'I can't let her go. I want to look after her. I want her to wife.'

St John Clare released a heavy sigh. He was, to a large extent, dependent on Willoughby's good will — what mind did it make to him if Willoughby wished to marry a mute who'd appeared from nowhere? Younger sons were still kidnapping brides in England — this was marginally less reprehensible. 'Very well. I will conduct the ceremony. Next Sunday?'

'Tomorrow.'

'Ah, yes, tomorrow. Very well.' He did not use the phrase 'unseemly haste', although he knew others would. What Willoughby wanted, Willoughby would have, and if it benefited the Reverend Clare in the long and short term then so much the better.

The ceremony was short, the groom radiant and the bride silent.

Mrs Flynn had dressed the girl in the prettiest of the new frocks James ordered made for her. It was pink — Willoughby had wanted white but Mrs Flynn insisted it would wash-out someone so pale and she had carried the day, on territory too uncertain for a male to risk insistence.

The ring was not a plain yellow band, but something different, white gold set with an enormous amethyst. She seemed to like the stone, staring at it throughout the ceremony, smiling at the parson when he asked if she agreed to the marriage. Willoughby saw only a smile but heard a resounding 'yes', and convinced himself that she loved him.

She didn't seem to care what he did to her body — having no experience of men, either good or bad, having no concept of her body as her own, she accepted whatever he did to her. For his part, he laboured over her trying to elicit a response, some sign of love or lust, some desire to *be* with him. Never finding it, he became frustrated, at first simply slaking his own lust, quickly. Gradually, he became a little cruel, pinching, biting, hoping to inflict on her a little of the hurt his love caused him. For all the centuries men have dreamed of the joy of a silent wife, Willoughby discovered that the reality of one was entirely unsatisfactory.

It was Mrs Flynn who first noticed the changes in her. Not her husband who stripped her bare each night and used her body as he wished. It was Martha, with her unerring woman's instinct, who pulled him aside and told him the girl was pregnant. Willoughby became gentle once again, no longer insisting upon his conjugal rights, but sleeping wrapped around her, his hands wandering to the slowly swelling belly, praying that what he had planted there would stay, and would, in turn, keep her by his side.

More and more, he found her under the jacaranda tree. She sat silently for hours, no longer interested in painting, but stroking her growing belly as if soothing the child inside. Whenever he arrived back at the house at the end of the day he would go straight to the tree, for he knew that was where he would find his wife.

'Where's Sally?' demanded Willoughby. On one of his infrequent trips to the kitchen, he found Martha alone; no sign of the indigenous girl (re-named 'Sally' in spite of her protests) who helped around the kitchen.

'Gone. They're all gone, all the natives. They won't come here any more,' said Mrs Flynn, her skin shining, hair trying to escape the cotton cap as usual.

Willoughby paused, astounded. 'Why not? Haven't I always been good to them? I've never abused them or punished them unduly. I don't understand.'

Mrs Flynn was silent for a moment, weighing her words, wishing she'd not opened her mouth in the first place. How to explain? 'It's Emily. They're scared of her,' she said reluctantly.

'Scared of Emily?' His laugh was sharp. 'How the hell can anyone be scared of Emily?'

'She's ... different, Master James. Leave it at that. It scares them. They have their legends and she scares them.'

'What bloody legends? What are you talking about?' he gripped her upper arm tightly, squeezing a slight squeal from her as the flesh began to pinch between his knuckles. She could smell the sour brandy on his breath. He let her go, but insisted, 'What legends, damn it?'

'Sally said they come from the trees. They don't belong anywhere.

They bring grief and eventually they go back to the trees.' Mrs Flynn batted away tears with the back of her hand.

Willoughby stared at her. 'And you? What do you think?'

'There are superstitions and then there are things we cannot understand, Master James.' She bent her head, new tears fell onto the dough she was kneading; she folded them into the rubbery mixture and refused to look at him again. He left the kitchen, swearing and shaking his head.

Willoughby rounded the corner of the house, raised his eyes and saw his wife, her curved belly seeming to defy gravity, walking slowly towards the jacaranda tree. She stood before its thick trunk and placed one hand against the rough bark. As he watched, the slender pale limb seemed to sink deeply into the wood, and the rest of her arm looked sure to follow.

With a yell, he charged at her, pulled her away with a force driven by anger and despair. She was flung about like a leaf in the wind. Finally settling, she stared at him with something approaching fear, something approaching anger. He was too furious to see it and he ranted at her, finger pointed like a blade. 'Never, never, never. You will never go near those trees again. You will never leave me!'

He locked her in their bedroom, then gave orders to his station hands.

'Get rid of all the jacarandas. Cut them down, burn them. Destroy them all, all the ones you can find.'

So all the jacarandas within the bounds of Rollands Plain were razed; he even sent some of his men to walk three days beyond the boundaries and destroy any offending tree they found there.

He let her out only when he was certain all the jacarandas were gone.

Her scream, when she found the dead stump of the tree, was the sound of every violated, outraged thing.

Mrs Flynn ushered the child into the world that evening. Emily did not stop screaming the entire birth, but Mrs Flynn could not help but feel that the screams were more for rage than for any pain the tearing child caused, for there was very little blood. Strangely little blood. The milk that dripped from Emily's nipples smelled strongly of sap. The child made a face at her first taste, then settled to empty the breast, her face constantly twisted in an expression of dissatisfaction.

Willoughby came to visit his wife and daughter, his contrite face having no effect on Emily. She opened her mouth and a noise came like that of a tree blasted by storm winds. Having not heard his wife utter a sound before, he was stunned; having not heard anything like this, ever, he was appalled. He backed out of the room, and retreated to his study and the bottle of brandy with which he'd become very familiar since his marriage.

Late one evening, a few weeks after the birth, Mrs Flynn saw Emily, standing slender and silver in the moonlight, motionless beside the stump of her tree. She held the baby at her breast; the child was quiet.

Martha was minded, though she knew not why, of Selkie wives, women stripped of their seal skin by husbands afraid to lose them, by men who feared them more than they could love them. She called quietly to Emily and gestured for her to follow.

She led her to a stand of eucalypts not far from the house.

Within the circle of gum trees stood a lone jacaranda, the one she knew Willoughby had missed, the one she kept to herself. The silver woman needed to be able to go back to her place or she'd haunt them forever.

Martha shivered. She was terrified of this ghostly creature, but she hoped she loved Emily more than she feared her, loved her enough to show her the way home. She watched Emily's face as she recognised the jacaranda, smiled, leaned against the trunk and a sound like leaves laughing blew around the clearing. Martha backed away. She watched the woman's hands slide into the trunk, saw her move forward, then stop.

The child would not go into the tree. Her diluted flesh and blood tied her to her father and his kind. Martha watched as the pale woman kissed the child's forehead and laid her gently on the ground. Emily pushed her way into the tree, disappearing until the brown bark was visible again, undisturbed for all intents and purposes. The tree shook itself and let fall an unseasonal shower of purple flowers, to cover Martha and the baby she scooped up and held tightly.

* * *

Willoughby drinks; Mrs Flynn often pours for him. She is strangely disappointed each time he swallows back the brandy decanted by her own hand. Most of her day she spends with his daughter, who has her father's dark curls and her mother's violet eyes.

She is a quiet child, but on the occasions when her cries have a certain tone, a certain pitch, Martha catches her up and takes her for a walk to the stand of eucalypts. Rollands Plain's sole remaining jacaranda will release a purple blanket no matter what the weather, and the child stares up at the tree as if she finds it very lovely indeed.

AFTERWORD

I'd had the idea of jacaranda women in my head for a while — my study looks out into the backyard where there is a giant jacaranda tree and one rainy day I was writing — or rather, not so much writing as staring out the window at the tree. It was in season and the bunches of purple flowers were so heavy with rain that they looked, well, pregnant — so that's where that idea came from initially. I haven't written any other stories set specifically in Australia, so I thought it was something I would/should try, to set a tale against a very Australian landscape. My mother's family came to Australia with the Second Fleet and settled in Port Macquarie originally, and their family property was called Rollands Plain — so, that's where the location came from — the idea of the woman going back into the tree came from having an Irish character and the Celtic legends of Selkie wives whose skin is stolen by their husbands. The jacaranda is found all over the world, so I liked the ideas of being transplanted, of not quite belonging, of a strangeness in the landscape. I quite like it as an Australian fable, still with its roots in a European fairytale tradition.

— *Angela Slatter*

Award winning author SEAN McMULLEN gained a major reputation for his scientifically accurate 'hard' science fiction with his epic Greatwinter series, which includes *Souls In the Great Machine, The Miocene Arrow,* and *Eyes of the Calculor. The Miocene Arrow* won an Aurealis Award for Science Fiction, as did his earlier novel *The Centurion's Empire.* With his Moonworlds series (*Voyage of the Shadowmoon, Glass Dragons, Voidfarer,* and *The Time Engine*), McMullen has firmly established himself as a fantasy author. In a review of *Glass Dragons, Booklist* wrote: 'McMullen has a gift worthy of the best mainstream authors for creating memorable, finely nuanced characters, making him must-reading for fantasy enthusiasts weary of the routine sword-and-sorcery outings.'

Although his Moonworlds fantasy novels have been translated into many languages and spread his reputation across Europe, his last three awards have all been for science fiction stories — 'Tower of Wings', 'Walk to the Full Moon', and 'Voice of Steel'. Even his Greatwinter science fiction series unfolded a little more in 2007 with the publication of his story 'Schwarzdrache' ('Dragon Black') in Germany. Television options have been bought for several of his stories. His short fiction can be found in magazines such as *Analog, Interzone, The Magazine of Fantasy & Science Fiction, Universe, Aurealis,* and *Eidolon.*

Sean is also an expert in the history of Australian science fiction and has won four William Atheling Jr Awards for excellence in science fiction criticism. He was an assistant editor of *The Melbourne University Press Encyclopedia of Australian Science Fiction & Fantasy* and author (with Russell Blackford and Van Ikin) of *Strange Constellations: A History of Australian Science Fiction.* He also manages to work full time as a computer systems analyst, teach karate (he has a black belt), and work on his PhD in Medieval Fantasy Literature at the University of Melbourne.

'The Constant Past' has all the ingredients of a fine mystery story … murder, obsession, love, death, desire, and poetry. Oh, yes, and an added ingredient: time travel …

THE CONSTANT PAST

SEAN McMULLEN

Mister Brandel did try to blend in with the fashions of the London of 2010, but only in the sense that he played down the more strident aspects of his own time's fashions. He wore a heavy, calf-length garric overcoat, and it was such a dark shade of green that when I first met him I took it for black. This he kept buttoned all the time, and it reached down to a pair of black, fringed, knee-length boots. Although he wore a cadogan wig, which did tend to stand out, his black beaver hat was worn pulled down very low, so that the wig was almost lost between the hat and the collar of his coat. In his right hand was a Malacca cane, while in his left he held a well-worn leather folder filled with papers.

What intrigued me from the start was that he did not make a point of seeming from the late eighteenth century. A serious re-enactment fanatic would have used a quill and jar of ink, but Mister Brandel had found a ballpoint pen somewhere and was happy to use this for his writing. He did not write very much, but that which he did write was in an elegant script, and was mainly names, dates, places, and descriptions. He did read a great deal, however, and it was always the biographies of Elizabeth Crossen, the nineteenth-century poet. As a librarian I have noticed that most readers show little emotion as they read, but Mister Brandel generally scowled. For someone with such an interest in Crossen, he never seemed at all happy to be reading about her.

Mister Brandel never became a borrower, and this struck me as odd. Borrowing was far more convenient than playing book roulette with other library customers. As a former forensics professional, this also told me that he might have an identity to hide. Some of the staff were running a competition to find out both who he was and who he was pretending to be. On the evening that I learned both his name and his alias, he had been visiting the library on and off for seven months. As usual, he had gone to the shelves in search of the Crossen biographies, then come to the information desk.

'Your pardon, the books about Elizabeth Crossen are missing,' he said.

'Do you mean the biographies?' I asked.

'Yes, yes. There were five of them.'

'Just a moment.'

I checked our holdings. All five books were on loan.

'They have been borrowed, all at the same time and by the same person,' I explained. 'Some student writing an essay about her, I'd say. We can reserve them for you.'

'Reserve them?'

'Yes. When they are returned, I'll send you a message. What is your address?'

'My address,' he sighed. 'I — I travel.'

'Well, do you have email?'

'Ah, no.'

'What about a phone number?'

'I have no phone number address. Sir, were I to come here in three weeks, will the books be, ah, reserved as you say?'

'Well yes, but they might be returned early.'

'But you said they were on loan for three weeks.'

'Most books are returned before they are due.'

Mister Brandel looked both weary and exasperated, as if even something as simple as a library loan was too much for him to comprehend. He knew just enough of the system to find the biographies of Elizabeth Crossen, and had no interest in learning any more.

'If I return in three weeks, will the books be here for me to read?'

There was something subtly dangerous about the man's attitude. In another career, almost in another life, I had worked in a police laboratory. I know the signs to look for, and Mister Brandel had them. In theory he had to be a member of the library to have books reserved in his name, but by now I was more than intrigued by him.

'Return three weeks from today, the books will be here,' I answered.

This was all that he wanted to hear, and his manner softened at once.

'So much ... everything ... it is such a strain,' he said wearily, as if almost beyond words. 'My thanks, you do ease my path.'

'That is what I'm paid to do,' I said cheerily. 'What name shall I put against them?'

'Goldsmith. James Goldsmith.'

With that he turned away, strode for the doors, and vanished into the night. Upon the reference desk was his leather folder, battered with use and greasy with handling. I picked it up, suspecting that a man like him would be back soon. Very soon he was indeed back, looking flushed and wild-eyed.

'Is this yours?' I called, holding his folder up.

Our strangest customer came hurrying over and snatched it from my hand.

'Yes, yes, praise all saints, I thought it lost,' he babbled in relief.

'You were lucky you left it on my desk,' I said casually. 'Try not to leave anything valuable lying about, the library is full of thieves.'

'Indeed, is it so?' he said, his relief still apparent. 'My thanks for your warning.'

With that he gave me a curt bow, then hurried from the library again. Having a background in forensics I tend to pick up odd details about people, and Mister Brandel had just confirmed my suspicions about being a little out of the ordinary. Within the space of a minute he had grown at least two days of beard stubble.

It was not a busy night, so I plugged my phone into a USB port on the reference desk computer and accessed the image store. Mister Brandel had been separated from his leather folder for a little more than three minutes, yet this had been enough for me to use my phone to take twelve double page photographs of the notes he had made.

His real name, Edwin Charles Brandel, was on the inside of the folder. He was meticulous and methodical in his studies, particularly about dates. On the first page he stated the date to be 15th April 2010, and noted the name of Colonel Graham Harridane. Quite a lot of details were noted down about this man, including his first meeting with Elizabeth Crossen. This was on the 23rd of November 1803. Following this was the cryptic 'marr. 3 May 1805'.

I looked up Colonel Harridane on an online genealogical database. He had been shot and killed in a duel on 25th November 1803. On the second page was an undated 'Valé' with a line drawn under it. I looked up 'Valé'. It was Latin for goodbye. Next came an entry for Sir Gregory Cottington, noting that an introduction to Elizabeth Crossen had been arranged for 30th November 1805. Again there were details of addresses, dates of concerts, and even the names of brothels that the knight had been known to visit. Eerily, 'marr.' again appeared, now dated 16th March 1805, and again followed by 'Valé.'

As I accessed another website dealing with Crossen, I already suspected that I would find an entry about an untimely death. Sure enough, Sir Gregory had been stabbed to death in the company of a prostitute the very next night after meeting with the poet. The woman had been hanged for his murder, and Crossen had even commented on the matter in a letter to her sister.

'Sir Gregory has been murdered in the most scandalous of circumstances. He was found dead in the company of a common woman. And to think, he was in this very house just the day before. He was courting me, no less.'

I scanned the remaining pages of Mister Brandel's notes. There were details of fifteen men who, to use the terminology of the time, were men of quality. All but one had died violently, within a few days of their first meeting with Elizabeth Crossen. The single exception had an entry on the very last page, and his name was Robert Bell. The name was familiar, but I could not quite place it. Unlike most librarians, I have little background in the arts and literature. Networks and databases are my areas. Give me a reference or a name and I can track it down, but without a reason to do the search I am lost.

Now I did a combined search on Robert Bell and Elizabeth Crossen. Bell was an early romantic poet of no particular talent, and the sample of his works that I glanced over involved medieval knights and ladies meeting after long separations, then marrying and living contentedly. Crossen had met him in 1809, and they had indeed married the following year and gone on to live happily for several decades.

The records of the Old Bailey are on the web, and it took only moments to call up the murder of Sir Gregory Cottington. A prostitute named Gwen Bisley had been convicted of the crime, but were modern forensics in use at the time she might have walked free. That was my opinion, anyway. She testified that she had entertained a very strange gentleman in her room by merely taking her clothes off. He had paid her and left, then she had gone in search of her next client. When she had returned with him, a man was lying 'stabbed, dead and naked' on her bed. The client ran screaming, raising a hue and cry. The authorities found Gwen's bully drunk in a nearby tavern. The magistrate concluded that the pair had conspired to murder Sir Gregory, but that the bully had got 'too far into drink' with the money stolen from him, and had forgotten to dispose of the body.

I re-read the description that Gwen had given of her first client. He had worn a dark beaver hat whose brim shadowed his face, but she was sure that he had been wearing a wig. All else was concealed by his coat, but his voice had been that of a 'Frenchy', as she had put it. Apart from the accent, that was Mister Brandel's description, and even I could fake a French accent.

By then it was getting near closing time, so I checked out several anthologies of early nineteenth century poetry to myself. Returning home on the Underground, I discovered that Elizabeth Crossen was not best known as an early romantic poet, but a pioneer of the Gothic style. In the years leading up to 1809 her works grew increasingly dark in tone, and she often wrote of being 'courted by death'. Anthology introductions spoke of her suitors having an extraordinarily high mortality rate, but her marriage to Robert Bell had given her a last chance for happiness. With Robert she had been lucky. He was mentioned as being from a noble family, but working as an assistant to a magistrate 'for the common goode.' He had abandoned this career for his poetry after marrying Elizabeth.

I was so intrigued that I not only missed my station, I missed it by eight stops.

The following morning saw me in the British Library's reading rooms at St Pancras, and by lunchtime I was in the nearby bookshops. I arrived at the municipal library with my own copies of all five biographies of

Elizabeth Crossen, along with several books of her poetry. I had even memorised her most famous work, 'Death is a Gentleman in Love'. The poem described a shadowy figure that stalked her in the shadows, jealously taking the lives of anyone bold enough to court her.

Literary authorities were unanimous that this was her finest work, and some Gothic scholars even lamented the beginning of her liaison with Bell because it brightened her mood. Others argued that she had done more good with her later pastoral works, because she had gone on to promote the glories of the English countryside at a time when it was under threat from industrialisation. I found myself even developing an empathy for Bell as well as his wife. After all, we were both refugees from law enforcement.

Those who have not worked in forensics can never appreciate how very attuned one becomes to a case. Every detail becomes worthy of investigation, because important clues can never be anticipated. Thus it was that I decided to review the security tapes from the cameras in the library. There were several cameras, all feeding into old-style video cassette tapes, and these were rotated every three days. I had hoped to catch a good view of Mister Brandel, in particular his face. I was disappointed. He appeared on only two tapes, because all other cameras had been moved to the hidden corners of the book stacks. At that time we were trying to catch the Phantom Crapper, who was touring the municipal libraries of London and leaving steaming hot turds in secluded areas.

In a strange way I was very relieved to see Mister Brandel on the tape of the information desk, because it confirmed him to be real. Everything was as I remembered it, however, and I learned nothing. On the tape from the library entrance he appeared four times. These were images of him that I had not seen, so even though they did not provide a better view of his face, I stared at them intently. I could even see myself sitting at the information desk in the background, for the camera was trained on people leaving the library. This was to catch customers leaving with stolen goods. I saw Mister Brandel collecting his folder from me, then approaching the camera. The inner glass doors slid aside, he walked through … and I remained dimly visible as he passed between me and the camera!

Several dozen viewings later I had established that the library's most intriguing borrower had started fading as he had passed through the inner doors. Were he really from the first decade of the nineteenth century, he would not know about cameras. Amid everything that did not make sense, here was consistency at last.

For the rest of that evening I studied trends in clothing from around 1800. It was a time of transition for men's fashions in England, influenced heavily by George Brummel. Being a favourite of the Prince Regent, Brummel's opinions were taken seriously. He had established trends to personal hygiene, wearing clean clothes, and the abandoning of wigs and hair powder for more natural grooming. In general, the lighter colours of the late eighteenth century were giving way to dark green, sombre brown, and even black. Mister Brandel's wig and beaver hat were a little old fashioned for the early 1800s, but his long, dark garrick overcoat with its high collar was certainly in period. Slowly I established a profile for him. He was not overly conscious of fashion, and even lagged a little behind in some matters of style, but generally he made an effort to blend in. He did not have a stale, unwashed reek about him, which fitted in with Brummel's decrees on washing being fashionable.

It was while having dinner that I realised Mister Brandel was a serial killer.

For the next week I resented every reference enquiry from every library customer as I researched Mister Brandel and everything associated with him. Edwin Charles Brandel had worked for the East India Company, although his occupation was merely given as 'agent'. The scanty records about him showed that he had been in India in the 1780s and 90s, and had returned to England a rich man. This would have put his age at no less than forty when he had begun his peculiar, anonymous association with Elizabeth Crossen in 1803. She had been seventeen then.

Mister Brandel's father had been knighted for his part in the British Admiralty's project to develop highly accurate clocks to help ships' navigators calculate longitude. His brother William had taught natural philosophy at Oxford University. William's single published paper was on the mathematics of time. In it he argued how time was really a branch of optics, and could be intensified, reflected back upon itself, and even focussed into the future. The paper had been published as a monograph in 1792, and William had died in 1803. No indication was given of what he had discovered or developed in his last eleven years. Edwin Brandel had returned from India in the year of his death.

The more I learned, the more fearful I became. Mister Brandel was a rich man from an upper class military family, and his brother had made studies into the nature of time and optics that were wildly at odds with both contemporary and subsequent scientific theory. After his brother had died, Mister Brandel became obsessed with a pretty, intelligent and vivacious young woman less than half his age. There was evidence for his involvement in the murders of fourteen of her suitors between 1803 and 1809.

What can one do about a serial killer from two hundred years in the past who is researching his victims in one's library? My work in forensics had been with associative evidence, that is, trawling databases and finding links between apparently unrelated facts. I was sure of myself . . . yet the police would be sure to treat my suspicions as a joke. Even if they did take me seriously, I doubted that they could do anything about Mister Brandel. He could vanish at will, and apparently he could also travel through time. By the look of his notes, he had done quite a lot of research in other libraries. Why was he now in mine? Had he murdered other librarians for becoming too suspicious? I was not a man of action. I had never fired a gun, I did not jog, I did not have so much as a yellow belt in karate. Whatever I did would have to be alone, and it could certainly not involve a confrontation.

I began to steal odd items on visits to other libraries, and after years of shunning the use of computers at home I bought my first PC, printer and scanner. Most significantly, I arranged lunch with my friend Harriet, who was a failed writer who refused to stop writing. It was usually Harriet who contacted me about our occasional dates, but now I needed her. She was not so much my ally against Mister Brandel, she was more of a weapon.

Harriet had a private income, so she was able to indulge her passion for writing detective fiction. Her style would have been acceptable in the 1930s, so had she been writing eighty years earlier she might have made a name for herself. This was 2010, however, so she was let down by her overblown prose, simple plots, minimal grasp of police procedures, and characters with about as much depth as a car park puddle. Nevertheless she had nine books in print, which had sold three or four hundred copies each. Out of loyalty I had bought copies of all nine, then bought another set which I had donated to my library.

'Look, it's the same old story,' said Harriet when I enquired about how her sales were coming along. 'Getting in print, easy peasey, you can go from formatted file to book-in-hand in a working week if you know who and how. Promotion? Hey, I do all the FM local shows and writers' centres, so people know. After that you have three problems. People know about the book, they want to buy the book, but now it's distribution, distribution, distribution.'

'So, the distributors still won't distribute?' I asked.

'Not even if I pay, and I've offered to do that.'

'I bet that doesn't stop you.'

'Stop me? Hah! Since I've been selling directly from my web site, sales have gone up fifteen percent. That's still only sixty two books more, but I've used another trick to get sales over five hundred — sort of.'

'Really?'

'It's a bit of a fiddle, but it works. I do a scooter tour of all the big bookshops with remainder tables, taking a couple of copies of my latest into each place. I pretend to look through what's on offer, leave my books on the table, and when I go nobody notices that I've got two less books than I came in with.'

'You smuggle your books into bookshops?'

'Hey, why not? When the system screws you then it's time to screw the system.'

Harriet was as predictable as the sunrise, at least to someone from forensics. The word 'screw' had been spoken. That was highly significant, and meant she was in the mood.

'So, how is the next book going?' I asked. 'Do you think number ten will score a thousand copies sold?'

'Oh man, as if. How I would love to say "sales in four figures". Er, speaking of the next book, would you like to be in a little research project?'

'I'll do what I can, the library's resources are at your disposal.'

'Er, well, it's actually a bit more hands on than that.'

* * *

That night after work I knocked at Harriet's door at 11pm, and was greeted by a woman in a dark blue skirt suit with padded shoulders, wearing a beret, and with the most luridly crimson lipstick that I have ever set eyes upon.

'Harriet?'

'Hey, come in, come in, it's 1945 and I'm a spy, wouldn't you know it?'

Harriet was researching a seduction scene in which she was a spy and I was a British scientist with secrets that she wanted. Neither of us smoked, so naturally when we lit up the first cigarettes to enter her unit in decades, her smoke detector went off and we both had coughing fits. To give her credit, she had researched the dinner, drinks and clothing of 1945 very thoroughly. I was sent into her bathroom to change into underwear that even my grandfather would have thought a bit dated, and over all this went a genuine 1945 shirt, tie and suit. I emerged feeling very self-conscious.

I am not entirely sure what Harriet got out of the encounter. Once drinks, dinner and banter were over, we both had quite a lot of trouble coping with a seduction that involved suspenders, braces, a fly with buttons, and all the other intricacies of archaic underwear. I tried to point out that real 1945 characters would have handled all that with the ease of experience, but Harriet did not agree. She maintained that the British scientist was meant to be inexperienced with removing female clothing.

We moved on to the act of lovemaking while partially clothed in 1945 fashions. This got off to a bad start when Harriet was hit in the face by my braces, then took a turn for the worse when one of my fly buttons got caught in a suspender strap. About three hours after I had arrived, we were at last fully divested of the clothing of 1945, seduced several time over, and drifting away to sleep.

Although my wife was by now nine years dead, and although this had not been my first experience of Harriet's literary researches, I still felt unease at being with someone else. Over and over I told myself that Emily was dead, and that this particular exercise was to save another life. Emily had been a policewoman, she had died in a shootout, and there was nothing that I could have done. We all have to fight in our own ways and with our own weapons, and this was my way of defending the innocent and defeating darkness. Sleep claimed me while I argued with my conscience.

It was the following morning that I had really come for. I did not start work until the mid-afternoon, and Harriet did not work at all. Thus I had roughly six hours free to spend with her.

'Harriet, I wonder if you would help me with a little project of my own?' I asked as we sat drinking coffee to the sound of London commuting to work outside.

Mister Brandel arrived in the library at three weeks to the very minute from our previous meeting. Instead of going to the stacks he came straight to the reference desk. I cannot describe his manner as nervous, so much as brisk and confident. Yes, his clothing was two hundred years out of date, but his manner made up for that. Look as if you belong, act as if your presence is beyond challenge, and everyone but a trained security guard will accept even a substantial degree of strangeness in your clothes.

'Three weeks have passed, I must have my reserved books,' he said, as if he had only left the library moments earlier.

I looked up at him, hoping that my smile did not look too forced. I very nearly called him Mister Brandel, but caught myself in time.

'Mister Goldsmith, I have your biographies of Elizabeth Crossen, but I'm afraid there was a problem,' I explained.

'You have my books but there was a problem?' he asked, frowning.

'I had to get them in from Nunhead on inter-library loan. The student who borrowed our own copies has not returned them as yet.'

'You — but you *do* have the books?'

'Oh yes, I knew you have a keen interest in Elizabeth Crossen's life, and I noticed that your time here seems to be limited, so I did not want you to be disappointed. I had them sent here only an hour ago. They are the latest editions.'

I could see the relief in Mister Brandel's face, even though not much of his face was actually visible.

'That is very kind of you,' he whispered. 'Such kindness is all too rare.'

Pausing only to check that the books were the same titles that he wanted, he hurried over to the reading tables, opened his folder, laid his pen across it, and picked up the first book.

Sweat trickled from my armpits and ran down my rib cage. The man was a killer, quite possibly he had been an assassin for the East India Company. He could travel through time, meaning that he could move about at will and kill with impunity, whether in the nineteenth or twenty- first centuries. He was clearly obsessed with Elizabeth Crossen, and by now I was able to guess at his agenda. A time machine cannot make you young again, but it can allow you to travel to a time when your much younger beloved is closer to your own age. The only problem would be if she happened to marry someone in the meantime, but there were ways to deal with that as well.

Mister Brandel had conducted his strange courtship for six years now, and history had changed fourteen times as he assassinated his rivals. Two hundred years into his future, he had safely researched the details of the men that Elizabeth had married, then gone back and killed them. With each murder he changed history, clearing the way for yet another young rival. How long would this go on? He would probably spend only a few days or weeks in any year, so that Elizabeth would get older while his age virtually stood still. So far the age gap between them had narrowed by six years. What gap would he think to be suitable?

The man's problem was that he was in love with the *young* Elizabeth. We all change with the experience of life, however. When Emily had been shot I had very nearly been destroyed. I had not dated anyone for seven years, and I had changed both job and career to escape the memories of losing her. When I was young I would never have dreamed of dating someone like Harriet, yet she was such a contrast with Emily that I was now willing to have at least a tenuous attachment with her. If our relationship was a farce, what was wrong with a farce? I needed a laugh, after all. For her part, Harriet was tired of men who wanted her to adjust to their expectations. Because I did not make demands upon her or try to keep her from her lovingly, if shoddily, written detective fiction, she chose to include me as a small part of her life.

It took all of my willpower not to stare at Mister Brandel. He now had three books lying open on the reading table, and had just picked up a fourth. My past, it was coming to life. I had testified in court, dangerous people had learned just who had traced their guilt through convoluted database associations. Weeks later two hard, cold men had walked into the park where Emily and I were sitting, feeding the pigeons in the sunlight. I had been helpless, but she was an armed policewoman.

'Got any more crumbs for the birds?'

They had been my last words to her before we saw the guns come out.

'Run! I'll cover!'

They had been her last words to me. I ran, crouching low. Nine shots barked out behind me, and by the time I looked back there were three bodies on the ground and a lot of onlookers screaming and fleeing.

Now it was I who was doing the defending. I had fired my shots, I had not run, but I still had to stand my ground. Mister Brandel was a killer. A *killer from any other age still kills as dead.* The thought almost made me laugh, but I could not afford to laugh. At some time in the distant past, and with a trail of dozens of corpses behind him, Mister Brandel would finally court and win an Elizabeth Crossen who was perhaps four decades old. She would be bitter from the twenty years of pain and loss caused by his murders. He would be disappointed with what she had become after so much waiting and effort. He would be a disappointed killer.

Out of the corner of my eye I saw Mister Brandel stand, straighten his coat, then walk from the reading table.

'Oh Mister Goldsmith, you forgot your folder!' I called as loudly as is proper in a library.

He stopped and turned. His eyes wandered here and there, as if he were confused about who might have spoken to him.

'I am just to the privy, watch over my effects if you will,' he said to me at last, then continued on his way.

Glancing to the reading table, I saw that all five books I had given him now lay open. There was a muffled thump from somewhere, like the sound of a motor accident in the distance. I returned to my work on some inane reference question from the local historical society. A smoke detector called its shrill warning from nearby. I looked up.

'Someone smoking in the men's toilets,' said one of the shelvers.

'Again,' I replied.

I got to my feet with the usual reluctance. Ejecting smokers from the toilets always involved a confrontation. Ejecting Mister Brandel for smoking was bound to be even more of a challenge. Still, I was not surprised that he needed a smoke to steady his nerves after what I had done to him. I expected him to have one of those long-stemmed clay pipes, the sort that you can still find fragments of beside the Thames. As I approached the outer door I realised that something was wrong, however. There was the smell of sulphur on the air.

I had never dreamed how much smoke could be produced by a single gunshot. Mister Brandel was lying on the floor, on his back. His wig had landed in a urinal, and I now saw that his head was shaved. There was a neat hole, blackened at the edges, in his right temple. The exit wound took up most of the left side of his skull. In his right hand was a flintlock pistol, its barrel still smoking, and in his left was his beaver hat. The ball had continued on to shatter a mirror.

I was the first aid officer for the evening shift, but this was well beyond my training or experience. Workplace First Aid 2.1 does not prepare students for someone blowing his brains out with a half inch lead ball. I forced myself to go down on one knee and put my fingers to the body's neck. The skin was warm, but there was no pulse. I stood, touching nothing, then recorded the scene with my phone camera.

The library was closed as a crime scene while the police and coroner did their investigations. Mister Brandel immediately became a source of considerable mystery to them. He had no identity whatsoever, aside from what was in the folder. In the weeks that followed the police found no match with his DNA, and no match on his key facial elements. The Costume Suicide Man, as he came to be known, was featured on the television news and even spawned a few websites.

When the police first arrived I was quizzed about what books he wanted. Because he had borrowed nothing, he had needed no library card — and thus had not needed to show any ID. Only my memory contained a record of his requests.

'Why would history drive him to suicide?' asked the detective as I showed him the books that the dead man had been reading.

'I can't say. He seemed as if he wanted to live in the past, like with all his period clothing.'

'Oh yeah, it's amazing how he got the costume, the weapon, everything, so accurate. Like I study this sort of thing for a hobby, you know, I'm into historical re-enactment. That body in the gents is authentic, right down to the tooth decay. Even his costume has the sort of wear that only comes with years of use. My redcoat uniform is just like that, proper wear from years of use.'

'He had a particular interest in the poet Elizabeth Crossen,' I said, pointing out the five books that lay open alongside his leather folder.

'And apart from reading the books he never used any library facilities?'

'He never so much as reserved a book.'

There had been chaos following the alarm being raised over Mister Brandel's suicide. Very conscientiously I had removed the tapes for the monitor cameras that covered the information desk and front door, then locked them away for the police to examine. The new tapes did not go in until after I had substituted our library's biographies of Elizabeth Crossen for those that Mister Brandel had just read. These found their way into my backpack behind the information desk. Naturally the staff were badly shaken by what had happened, but it was two hours before the police allowed us to leave. As I walked for the Underground station I thought of Harriet, and of how much I owed her.

The very first thing I did when I got home was to light a fire. Next I got out the scotch and poured myself a generous measure. By the end of my second glass the fire was burning hot enough for my needs. Into the flames went a stolen accessions stamp from the Nunhead library, and as this burned I began ripping up the biographies of Elizabeth Crossen and feeding the pages into the flames. I was working on the last book when Harriet phoned me. She had heard about the suicide on the news.

'Whoever he was, he imagined that he really was a time traveller,' I told her.

'But why did he do it?' she asked. 'Nothing seems to make any sense.'

'Obsession with the past,' I replied. 'Some people really let it get to them, you see that sort of thing if you work in a library for long enough.

I think he fell in love with Elizabeth Crossen. In a way it was a clever fantasy.'

'You mean he was pretending to be a time-refugee, and pining for his sweetheart in the past?'

'Yes.'

'*That* is just *magical*!'

How could I tell her the truth? Brandel had been killing Elizabeth's suitors one by one, then travelling forward in time to read about how history had changed. It had never changed to his satisfaction, so he had gone on killing. Surely this said something about his chances with her, but love was apparently blind in this case. How many lives had I saved by driving him to suicide? Quite a few, I hoped, because I was feeling decidedly guilty. Could I be prosecuted for murder? Probably not. Accessory to suicide? Possibly. I could possibly plead self-defence on behalf of potential victims who had died back in the nineteenth century, and point out that I did it because there were no time-police . . . my head started to spin, and I decided to stay with the pretend-time-refugee story.

'Brandel was reading of how Elizabeth married Robert Bell at the library tonight,' I said aloud, as much to solidify this version of events for myself, as to tell Harriet. 'I watched him, wallowing in grief as he read of how his girl met, then married, another man. He was unable to stand it any more, so he killed himself.'

'But he's not a real time traveller, is he?'

'No, he's just done a good job of looking like being one. So far the police can't trace him as someone modern. As far as they are concerned, he might as well have been a time-refugee.'

'Hey, intense. Like, in a sense he had got what he wanted. He escaped these times, and died as a man from, er, when did you say?'

'1810.'

'Wow. As plots go, it's got a lot going for it.'

'Yes, although it's sort of real,' I agreed.

'Er, look I don't want to sound, like, crass or anything, but I don't suppose I could come over now, could I?' asked Harriet in her rarely used tentative voice. 'I mean, to get a few impressions while they're fresh in your mind? This could make a fabulous book, in fact I think I could sell over a thousand copies if I get it out really fast.'

I had seen this coming, and I did not mind at all. First I had lost Emily, and then I had developed something of a crush for Elizabeth before saving her for a life with Robert Bell. I was lonely, and Harriet was the sort of company that I really needed.

'Better be quick or you won't get much sense out of me,' I warned. 'I'm about to pour my third scotch, and I'm stretched out in front of a roaring fire.'

'Give me just twenty, I'm on a scooter, remember?'

The biographies of Elizabeth Crossen that I had hurriedly scanned and re-written from the originals, then self-published in runs of one copy each, had been quite slim. This was because in my version of history she had died in 1812. I read my tragic tale as I fed the last pages of the fifth book into the fire. I had Robert Bell taking the king's shilling and going to fight in the Peninsular Campaign against Napoleon in 1809. This he had done to prove himself brave to Elizabeth, yet in doing it he had lost his life. When news of his death had reached her, she had gone into deep mourning. It had only been after a courtship of three years that she had finally agreed to marry Edwin Charles Brandel, formerly of the East India Company. The marriage had been a brief but turbulent one, and had ended one night when he had beaten her to death, then shot himself out of remorse. Some of her last words, taken from a letter written only days before her death, were quoted on my final page.

'He keeps railing against me for being bitter and disillusioned, and not being the girl he loved, yet how can this be? He only met me when fate had already squeezed the joy from my heart and rendered me desolate with loss. Edwin is just one of many who courted me, but fortune willed it that we should marry. Robert was my only true-love.'

When I had written the words, I had hardly dared to hope that they really would drive Mister Brandel to despair. Like a shot taken at a dangerous gunman at extreme range, my words had struck home through sheer luck. As the last page burned I sipped at my scotch and opened my own copy of Abercrombie's definitive biography of Elizabeth Crossen. Mister Brandel was absent from the index, and both Elizabeth and Robert were recorded as living happily together into the 1860s. The lovers were safe, forever, in a fixed and constant past.

The doorbell chimed, then Harriet rapped at the door and called my name. I let her in, and she managed to ask half a dozen questions about Mister Brandel and his suicide before she remembered to ask me if I was feeling okay and give me a hug. By then I did not feel like anything other than immediate bed and sleep without company, but I was very much in her debt. Harriet had taught me about vanity presses, print-on-demand publishing, who to contact, and what they could do in what sorts of timeframes. Without her I would not be the anonymous publisher and pseudonymous author of five biographies of Elizabeth Crossen, each with a print run of one copy. Looked at from that perspective, the two of us were indeed a slightly peculiar version of Elizabeth Crossen and Robert Bell, and I even found the idea strangely alluring.

AFTERWORD

Avatars inspired me to write this story. From what I have seen, people who build avatars on the internet develop something perfect, which usually means fresh, fit, foxy, and financially secure. Well, who said virtual reality was anything to do with reality? I am an author, however, and when I build characters they must be interesting, not perfect, or real readers will not buy my books. In 'The Constant Past', Mr Brandel is trying to build his vision of a perfect lover from a real person. Most people probably agree that turning someone real into your idea of perfection is a better recipe for disaster than looking for a gas leak with a lighted match. Most people have probably learned this from direct experience.

— *Sean McMullen*

KIM WILKINS was born in London, and grew up by the seaside in Australia. She is the author of seven supernatural thriller novels for adults, five psychic crime stories for young adults, and five fantasy books for children. She has won Australia's Aurealis Award four times, and has a PhD in writing. Her novels include *The Infernal, Grimoire, The Resurrectionists, Angel of Ruin,* and the Gina Champion Mystery series. Her most recent novels are *Rosa and the Veil of Gold, Giants of the Frost,* and *The Autumn Castle.*

In the story that follows, Kim Wilkins reworks a classic tale to take us into the neon-lit world of danger and dark magic that can only be found on the other side of the mirror . . .

THE FOREST

KIM WILKINS

I.

My brother and I turned fifteen on the same day, but we are not twins.

His mother is my stepmother; his stepfather is my father. We were raised together from the age of seven. We squabbled over toys, mocked each other's weaknesses, screamed red-faced that we hated each other in one moment and pored over comic books together the next. All this familiarity, however, was not proof against attraction.

My brother's name is Hansel. On the day he turned fifteen, he was half-boy, half-man. He wore his hair long, and could almost be mistaken for a girl, except that his body had begun to change. His long limbs were becoming dense with muscle.

At our birthday party that day, I watched him across the table, beyond the limp cake that Mother had grudgingly spared an egg and a cup of flour for. And Hansel watched me because that is what we did.

We watched each other. In the morning, while the grim skies above the city of Stonewold leeched themselves to muddy grey-green and the traffic began moving beyond our grimy windows. After school, while the black and white television flickered and grimaced in our gloomy living room. At supper, while our parents fretted about money and meted out string beans as though they were emeralds. And then at bedtime, across the four feet of space between our single beds. We watched each other, and our eyes became as hungry as creeping poverty had made our bellies.

And so my brother and I turned fifteen on the same day, and we watched each other turn fifteen and something insistent pressed on my heart while I watched him: a fear of loss, a horror of growing older. Perhaps it is hindsight that allows me to describe it, because at fifteen most feelings are indescribable. At fifteen, feelings are flashes of incomprehensible white heat, convictions are as unutterable as they are searingly vital. The fabric of being is stretched by the swing of that hinge between childhood and adulthood. Souls ache.

We were dispatched to bed after a supper of rough bread and dripping: Mother said that as we had eaten cake, we need not also eat a full meal. We said our goodnights as we had always said them and climbed into our individual beds. But the pressure on my heart would not abate and I tossed and turned for nearly an hour before I dropped into sleep.

It seemed only minutes later that I woke to see a dark figure standing at the window. It was Hansel, gently parting the curtain to look outside.

'Hansel?' I said.

He turned, smiled. The streetlight caught him across the cheek and my fingers prickled with the desire to touch him. 'I can't sleep,' he said.

I turned back my covers and stood with him, pulling the curtain open now so that the familiar peaks and edges of Stonewold were in view. The orange streetlights turned the perpetually swirling cloud above to amber. The slick streets were empty, oily with rain and muck.

'There is more, isn't there?' Hansel said.

'Somewhere.'

'They warned us in school that one day we would say these things.' His fingers laid loosely on the windowsill. Long, tanned fingers with bitten nails.

One of the first lessons of our seventh grade was about puberty, how it would catch us and make us unhappy with what we have. How we would start to think about the forest.

'Do you think anybody ever gets to the forest, Gretel?' Hansel said.

'We won't, and that's all that matters. "Born in the city, die in the city" — so the saying goes.' I indicated with a tap on the glass the rusting, cut-out trees sprouting from the roof of the next building, the steel spirals mimicking organic shapes that hung from our own building. 'This is the closest we'll get to the forest.'

He leaned his head on the glass, closing his eyes so his long black lashes fanned out on his cheeks. 'I know I could breathe among the trees.' Then he opened his eyes and fixed me in his gaze. 'But this feeling will go away. A few years, we'll learn to bury it.'

'I don't want to bury it,' I murmured, the pressure on my heart becoming painful. 'I would rather suffer.'

'I know,' he said, and it was the profoundest thing he had ever said. His fingers reached for mine and clutched them. A moment hung suspended between us, a sliver of clarity in the fog of adolescence. He lifted my hand to his mouth and his tongue slid out and licked my index finger, wound around and down. An intoxicating weakness washed through me. He grasped me around both wrists gently and pulled me towards him, spreading my arms. 'I want to be young forever,' he said.

'I do too.' I could feel the heat of his body through my thin cotton nightie.

He kissed me. It wasn't the first time, but the intent was new. All my senses flared into life and I moaned a little, a sound I'd never heard coming from me before. He pulled off his shirt, and I pulled off my nightie and my breasts were pressed against his bare skin while two of his fingers trailed a searing passage down my body, crept inside the elastic of my underpants and slid inside me.

Noise. Light. We jumped apart.

Mother was standing in the doorway, one hand on the light switch, the other hand clutching a pile of our folded laundry. 'What's going on?' she shouted in a panicky voice. 'Father! Come here.'

Father was there a moment later, his grizzled moustache drooping over his mouth as he stared at me, then Hansel, half-dressed, red-faced.

He marched in, grabbed Hansel roughly by the shoulder and pushed him out of the room. I quickly scrambled back into my nightie. The door of the bathroom slammed shut, and I heard the key in the lock. Father returned, wordlessly removed Mother from the room, then locked the bedroom door as well.

I sat on my bed, my heart thundering. The curtain still lay partly open, revealing a shard of the amber sky. I heard voices and crept to the door to listen. Mother and Father.

'... shame upon this family,' Mother was saying.

'I won't have that boy in this home any longer.'

'And I won't have that girl.'

A long silence. The subway roared beneath the building, shaking its foundations. Then Mother said, 'We can't afford to keep them, anyway.'

'I'll take them into the old city tomorrow,' he said. 'They'll never find their way back.'

II.

Father was a concreter, a trade that many young men of his generation were trained for, but a trade that had rapidly become obsolete. As Stonewold grew, every inch of dirt and grass disappeared under a hard grey veneer. There was simply nothing left to concrete. He eked out a living on minor repair jobs. The rusty tray of his old XP utility was lined with concrete dust and the occasional hard lump that had set on the beige paint before he could clean it up. At dawn, Hansel and I were herded into the tray, where we were told to sit with our backs up against the cabin for safety. The ute took off, rattling over tramlines. We held hands.

'What will we do?' I asked, close to Hansel's ear.

'I have a plan,' he said as our apartment tower disappeared. From the inside pocket of his windcheater he pulled a packet of Winfield cigarettes. 'I stole these from Father this morning.'

'What use are they to us?'

He glanced over his shoulder. 'I'm going to leave a trail, to lead us back home.'

He shifted over closer to the side of the tray and began to drop cigarettes, one after the other, along the route through the city. They were brightly white against the grubby streets, and I cautiously shed my anxiety. Those pale cylinders would lead us home. Home was not a happy place, but it was better than being exposed in the city. Dark shadows stalked the city streets, shadows with names like Violence and Winter and Disease. But their king was Hunger.

We were leaving the new city behind now, with its rigidly planned structures of unpainted concrete, bristling with plastic and iron vegetation. As we wound down into the valley of the old city, the streets grew so narrow that the thin, black buildings seemed to bend towards each other in aggressive challenge. The smell was bitter: damp rot and garbage and decades-old car fumes trapped in tight alleys. Underlying it all was the ceaseless aroma of dead things, for many things died in the city. I presumed Mother and Father expected us to die, and while this horrified me, it didn't surprise me. The instinct to destroy the young was always latent in their generation; it simply became more pronounced when we were all competing for food.

Spirals within spirals, demented alleys; the ute finally came to a halt in a space so tight that Father simply couldn't drive any further.

He got out, opened the back of the tray. 'Here you are, kids.' He handed us a rusty coin each, just enough to buy a bread roll. 'I'll pick you up in the same place at nightfall.'

This was a lie, and all three of us knew it, but nobody spoke it.

Hansel and I stood in the mouldy alley and watched Father's ute back out into the street. One of the headlights was bent, shining at an odd angle against lichen-splattered brick. The engine spewed blue smoke as Father turned, revved, and drove away.

The swirling olive-tinged clouds were thick and sludgy above us, and the tall buildings created cold shadows. An unnatural lightlessness pervaded, as though it were about to pour with rain any moment; but rain rarely came to Stonewold despite the perpetual cloud cover. Miserable drizzle sometimes, or weeks and weeks of unbearably chill humidity. Never a thundering downpour to wash the streets clean.

'What now?' I said to Hansel.

He shrugged. 'I guess we follow the trail.'

We walked to the next block, where the first cigarette lay waiting for us. Hansel picked it up, brushing at a grey stain on the white paper. He straightened, scanned for the next, and on we went. We passed boarded-up shops, their faded signs streaked with water stains and bird droppings; we passed a concrete children's playground, with a toppled-over climbing frame and an odour of cat urine lingering in the sand pit; we passed an empty car yard where aluminium cans and fast food wrappers clung to the chain wire fence and six bent hubcaps were propped up against the shopfront. Behind the clouds, the sun had risen and so the traffic started. We risked our lives at intersections where road rules had long since been abandoned. We passed rows of black apartment blocks. Most of their windows were shut against the smell and the ugliness of the city, but one stood open, Led Zeppelin's 'Kashmir' spurting at deafening volume onto the street. The song followed us for two more blocks, a steam train on heavy rails.

Then the cigarettes ran out.

'Shit,' Hansel said, after a long search.

I tried not to panic. A cold wind had risen, and Hansel wondered aloud if the cigarettes had simply blown away. Then an old tramp with a brown coat came past us, walking in the other direction, a crisp Winfield cigarette between his lips.

'Hey, grandad!' Hansel said, grasping the old tramp's arm. 'Where did you get that?'

The tramp grinned, pulled a handful of cigarettes out of his pocket. 'Summun lift'em on the stritt.'

Hansel rolled his eyes and groaned. 'Did you pick them all up?'

'Inny I could see. You want 'un?'

Hansel took the cigarette offered to him, leaned in to light it from the tramp's cigarette. He angled his head slightly as though he intended to kiss the old man. I admired the soft line of his jaw.

'Iss a good day,' the tramp said to me, laughing softly.

'It is?' I said impatiently, too caught up in my own suffering for kindness.

'Allays a good 'un when you git smokes fer nuppin'.' He winked, waved and shuffled off.

Hansel blew out a stream of smoke. Shrugged. 'We're fucked now.'

'Maybe we can find our way back anyway.' I glanced around, trying to squeeze familiarity out of the surroundings. 'I think we came under that arch.'

'I don't remember it.' His eyes went skyward. 'It's strange here in the old city, without the tram cables. Feels like we're not in a cage for once.'

I followed his gaze, cheering myself. The edge of a feeling tickled me, a feeling like liberty.

'Come on,' he said. 'You're probably right. Under the arch.'

Gradually, we grew dizzy. The streets of Stonewold seemed designed to confuse. Landmarks repeated, causing the cold anxiety that we were retracing our steps. When our legs ached we knew we were heading slowly upwards, and so were going in the right direction. When they didn't ache we were relieved of discomfort, but knew we were losing ourselves. The day progressed; I grew hungry. I swallowed three times for every hunger pain, as we had been taught in school. It didn't work. It never worked, but it was better than doing nothing. We talked about spending our money on bread, but decided to save it: insurance against things getting worse. Those who are schooled in privation can always imagine worse privation; bad luck only takes the wealthy by surprise. Hansel clutched my hand, dragging me hither and thither, deeper and deeper into the maze of the city. The streets were too narrow for traffic. The noise withdrew through black alleys. I was nearly ready to admit that we had no hope of finding home again.

That was when I saw the white bird.

'Hansel, look!' It was the strangest bird I'd seen. I was used to the dull brown sparrows of Stonewold, small and dirty. This bird was snowy white, with a long, elegant tail, an azure crest on his head, and proud black eyes. Most unusually, it was mechanical, made of springs and screws. It sat on the sign of an empty shop cleaning its metal feathers.

Hansel stopped and turned, his eyes following the direction I was pointing. He smiled, approached and held up his hand. 'Hello. Where are you from?'

The bird raised his crest and spoke, clicking his tongue in his beak. 'The forest.'

Hansel and I exchanged desperate glances. The forest? Now the bird spread his snowy wings and swooped into the air. He stayed low, heading down an alley. Without a word between us, Hansel and I began to run, following the bird, splashing through mud and nearly slipping on the algaed bitumen. The way home was abandoned behind us along with daylight, which was closed out by narrower and narrower spaces. Finally, the bird burst through the other side of the black alley. A half-demolished building lay to our left, a group of shops to our right. Ahead of us was a shining mirror, twenty feet tall and easily as wide, embedded in a grey wall. The bird arrowed towards it, its reflection growing larger all the time. We could see ourselves in pursuit. The mirror drew close; we pulled up, the bird didn't. It speared into the mirror. A ripple of light flashed behind it. The cityscape in the mirror disappeared. In its place was a forest.

I choked on my own breath. Ran forward, puzzled to see my own reflection hovering ghost-like among the verdant shadows. Hansel was beside me a moment later, hands pounding on the mirror.

The bird sat on a branch and made a noise almost like laughter. Only now it wasn't mechanical, but a real bird of feathers and fine bones.

'How do we get in?' Hansel shouted.

'We all go empty-handed into the unknown!' the bird squawked, then took to the sky and disappeared.

'What does that even mean?' I murmured as I gazed at the forest. Drooping larch cast its hanging shadows over sunlit rocks. Long, soft grass rippled in the breeze. A narrow stream curled its way through the trees, and suddenly I was desperately thirsty. All around me were the smells of water gone bad: stagnant, mouldering. I wanted more than anything to bend at the side of that sweet stream and drink.

Hansel had picked up a half-brick from the demolished building and threw it hard against the mirror. The brick bounced back, hitting him in the shoulder. The mirror didn't crack. He staggered, swearing in frustration.

'I wouldn't do that if I were you.'

Hansel and I turned. Outside one of the shops was a woman, around the same age as our parents. She was well-dressed and tidy, with shining chestnut hair and thick spectacles. The sign over her head said, *Sweet Shop*. My mouth began to water.

'Why not?' Hansel demanded. 'What's in there?'

'It's a trick of the imagination, that's all. There is no forest. Just a mirror. Look.'

We looked. The forest was gone. The reflection of the dark city gazed back at us.

'Besides,' she said, 'breaking a mirror is seven years' bad luck.' She smiled. 'Would you like to come in?' She stood aside, nudging open the door of the shop.

Hansel and I stumbled over our feet in our hurry to accept her invitation.

Inside the sweet shop, the air was warm and heavy with the aroma of baking biscuits. The walls were painted black, which contrasted strongly with the coloured sweets: reds and pinks and greens and bright yellows. Strings of gingerbread hung like streamers from the ceiling; barrels of butterscotch, jelly shapes, powdered Turkish delight and other treats waited in every corner; and a little fountain of chocolate stood in the middle of it all, bubbling over neatly stacked pink marshmallows. I forgot myself. It wasn't the sweets that aroused this fissure in the meaning of things; it was the concept of *plenty*. In all my life, I had never seen *plenty* before.

The woman sat on a stool by the counter and crossed her stockinged legs neatly. 'Help yourselves.'

'We can't afford to pay for this,' I said, blinking back into cognisance.

She waved my concern away with a flick of her beautifully manicured hand. 'Oh, never mind. You look hungry.'

Hansel had no hesitations. He was already stuffing gingerbread into his mouth.

'I need to tell you something, though,' the woman said. 'I do prefer to be up-front about these things. I'm a witch.'

Hansel laughed, spraying crumbs from his mouth. He didn't believe in witches.

I was less sure. 'What do you mean?' I asked, tentatively nibbling some peanut brittle.

'I'm a witch. Magic spells and so on. I control all the rats in this part of the city.' She clapped her hands together and out of the shadowy corners advanced a dozen rats. They gathered at the bottom of her stool and waited, patient as newly trained puppies. Even the rats couldn't turn me off the food which, now it had hit my stomach, had aroused ravenous hunger. I finished a slab of peanut brittle and went for a strap of raspberry licorice.

'Are you going to put spells on us?' Hansel asked.

'Heavens, no. There's no need for that.'

'That's cool,' he said, reaching his hand into a barrel of jelly snakes.

'Stay a while,' the witch said, wistfully blinking her pale eyes behind the thick spectacles. 'As long as you like. Eat what you like. I'm going to sit here and count my money.'

She popped open the cash register and pulled out handfuls of gold coins, which she began to count and stack, humming softly to herself. The big enamel stove ticked softly, warming the space. I had to admit that she seemed very friendly and kind for a witch, and I relaxed and filled my stomach with sweet delights. Afterwards, she made us thick hot chocolate to drink, and then the evening was approaching so she insisted we stay a while, that there would be crumpets and marmalade for breakfast and, as long as we didn't mind the rats, we were welcome to sleep in the spare bedroom.

I had reservations, I do remember that. My stomach was full, we might have been on our way. But what reservations can stand up to abundance? In the morning, there would be more, and more was what I wanted.

Our beds were side by side, under a window with a white blind. Hansel held my hand for a long time, but eventually sleep caught him and he let me go and turned on his side. As I drifted off, I listened to the sound of the rats skittering around under our beds, and the clink of the witch, counting her gold coins by the thin electric light.

III.

'Did I forget to mention that I eat children?'

I opened my eyes. The witch was leaning on my bed, dressed in a tidy beige suit. One of the lenses of her spectacles was cracked, the other missing completely.

Confusion arrested me. 'What did you say?'

'I eat children.' She smiled. 'So much for wanting to be young forever, eh?' She stood and walked away.

I checked Hansel's bed. He was gone. I leapt up and made to run after her, but beneath my feet a swarm of rats began to move. Warm, scratching bodies. I lost my footing, I fell. A rat squealed. I began to shout. 'What do you mean? Where's my brother?'

Her voice was calm, drifting from within the sweet shop. 'Well, come and see.'

I kicked rats out of my way. One bit my bare toe, but I hardly felt it. My heart seemed to have grown too large for my chest, it sat on my lungs. The chocolate fountain had been cleared away from the centre of the sweet shop. In its place was a silver cage. And in the cage was Hansel.

I approached, limbs shaking. His knuckles were bloody, a graze adorned his temple. He looked up at me with sulky eyes. 'The bitch caught me.'

I reached for the bars. The moment I touched them, a sweet melody began to play, a pearly, disembodied voice gathering in the dark arch of the room:

I swear by the sour, I swear by the sweet,

Someone is trying to steal your meat.

The witch strode over and knocked my hands off the cage with a thick candy cane. 'Don't touch,' she said. 'Or I shall know, and you will end up in there with him.'

I realised she was having trouble focusing on me, and I glanced at the floor of the cage. Shards of broken glass. Hansel had broken her spectacles trying to get away from her.

She blinked rapidly. 'I can't see well enough to go to the grocery store for turnips,' she said. 'You'll have to go.'

'Turnips?'

'For my boy-roast. One must have vegetables with meat. Too much meat by itself is bad for one's colon.'

I was speechless. The witch carefully pulled a handful of coins out of her pocket. Peering closely, she fingered them one by one until she landed on the right denomination. She held it out to me. 'Here. The grocery store is two blocks west. The rats will show you.' Then she smiled. 'And if you try to run, the rats will tell me and I will cut Hansel up bit by bit. I will have boy-fondue instead of boy-roast. I will invite all my witchy friends over and we will listen to Carole King and talk about how *good* life used to be. Understand?'

I nodded, felt the sweat forming around the coin in my palm. At least going to the grocery store would give me time to think of a plan to free Hansel.

She gave me a little push towards the door. Scurrying feet followed me: two rats, close at my heels.

The first thing I saw, as I emerged into grey daylight, was the giant mirror. There was no forest in it, no white bird. Only miles of concrete structures, strangling out the day. Gloomy clouds crowded down on me; I hesitated, straining to see the sunlit stream again.

'There is no forest,' one of the rats said, in a soft voice.

I looked down. 'I saw the forest.'

'Don't talk to it,' hissed the other rat. 'The witch just wants turnips.'

'A friend of mine thought to get through to the forest,' the first rat said.

'A friend? . . . A *rat* friend?' I had never heard a rat speak before.

'Yes. He stole a gold coin from the witch, and came here and slammed himself up against the mirror until he brained himself. You see his bones there.'

I moved towards the mirror, and stooped to pick up a rat bone. Perhaps from a hind leg. I put it in my pocket.

'Hurry, hurry,' said the second rat.

'Do you like the witch?' I asked.

'Nobody likes witches,' said the second rat.

'But she gives us lots of things,' said the first rat. 'Sweetmeats and so on. If we stay loyal to her, she gives us one coin every five years.'

'And if we are disloyal,' said the second rat in an urgent voice, 'she boils us up in a pot. Let's *hurry*.'

I returned to the witch with a turnip twenty minutes later, and she declared she would cook Hansel that very afternoon. Then she retired to count her money, and I sat next to the cage — careful not to touch the bars — to keep Hansel company.

I had never lost anything as precious as Hansel. I cried and my tears fell onto my hands.

'Don't cry,' he said. 'I'll get out of this.'

'How?'

'When she opens the cage, I'll overpower her.'

I didn't point out that he hadn't managed to overpower her when she'd put him *in* the cage.

'Then we'll run to the mirror and escape into the forest.'

'It's not there any more.'

'It might come back.'

I pulled the rat bone out of my pocket and handed it to him through the bars. 'Nobody gets through the mirror.'

He turned the bone over in his hands. 'That bird did,' he said, but he sounded less certain now.

'That witch has so much,' I said. 'She has gold coins, and more sweets than she could ever eat. Why must she eat you as well?' I shivered, thinking about my own fate. 'Why must she eat both of us?'

Hansel didn't answer. He tucked the bone behind his ear; his long hair covered it. 'I might stab her in the eye with this,' he said. He seemed very young, a little boy, playing a game of superheroes.

My hand stole between the bars, and he took it. I noticed he held it very tightly. We said nothing for a long time.

IV.

'Almost the dinner hour,' said the witch. 'I need to heat the stove. How much fat is on you, boy? If I roast you too hot, you'll get tough. I do despise chewy children.'

I shuffled out of the way and watched as the witch reached blindly for Hansel. The bars sang, but she didn't mind. Quickly, Hansel pulled the rat bone from behind his ear and thrust it out towards her. Her fingers caught it.

'My!' she said. 'You are very thin.'

'I'm only a boy,' he said in a little voice. I wanted to laugh and cry at the same moment.

'Hmph.' She put her hands on her hips. 'Hmph. I have the stove far too hot. I'll have to adjust it. You looked so succulent when you first arrived.'

She turned to me, fixed her pale gaze just above my eyebrows. A smile formed, a very unpleasant smile.

'Gretel, perhaps you can help me.'

I scrambled to my feet. She grabbed my hand and hauled me behind her. 'I can't see the controls on the stove properly since your brother busted my spectacles.' She thrust me in front of a large dial on the side of the stove. 'What does that say?'

'H for hot,' I replied.

'Put it on M for medium.'

I would like to say that I saved my brother then, that I had the forethought to turn the stove off all together. But while my mind tried to process the impulse, the witch guessed my hesitation and whistled for two rats, who came to supervise. I turned the dial to M. Medium. Hansel would be roasted at a medium heat, and there was nothing I could do.

The witch opened the stove door. A wall of heat blasted out, making me stagger back. The long cylinder inside was deep enough for a tall boy like Hansel to lie, curled in a foetal position. It was lined with coals that glowed orange. She handed me a poker. 'Rake those coals so they lie even,' she said. 'I want him roasted nicely all over.'

I reached in as far as I could. My arm grew hot. I raked the coals.

'Get right into the back.'

'But —'

'Climb up on the lip of the stove. Do as I say! I'll cut him to pieces!'

I climbed onto the lip of the stove. My hand burned against the soot-streaked enamel. I reached as far as I could. My shoulder was pushed up against the opening to the stove. I turned my head away, trying to keep my face from roasting. I saw her piles and piles of gold coins on the bench next to the stove. And I had an idea.

My heart thudded, because I doubted myself. But necessity made me bold. I crouched, pretending to peer into the stove. 'What's that?' I said.

'What's what?' she asked, myopic gaze seeking me out.

'Is that a gold coin at the back of the stove?'

She jumped. 'What? Is it melting?'

I stepped down, adopted a casual tone. 'Oh, it wasn't a coin at all.'

'A coin? Melting in there?'

'No, no. Nothing at all. Nothing. Here, let me keep raking the coals.'

'You're just saying that, now. There's a coin in there. You are going to rake it up and keep it.'

'No, it was a trick of the light.'

'Rats!' she exclaimed, and immediately three of them were at her feet. 'One of you climb up and tell me if you see a gold coin in the back of the stove.'

The first climbed up. 'Nothing, witch,' it said.

'I don't believe you. You want it for yourself.'

The second climbed up. 'Nothing, witch,' it said.

'Ah!' she exclaimed, pulling at her hair. 'I can't trust you. There's gold melting in there!'

The third climbed up. 'Really, witch. There is nothing there.'

She kicked the rat out of the way, doubt possessing her, ravens in her brain. 'I'll look for myself.' She pulled out a big pair of oven mitts and leaned into the mouth of the stove, muttering, frantic.

I kicked her. I kicked her so hard that I tore the muscle in my right thigh. Her upper body slammed onto the coals. Rats began to bite my feet. I pushed the stove door, but her bottom was in the way. She was screaming. I lifted her legs and cracked them between the door and the stove. Something broke. I folded her in, slammed the door shut and dropped the latch.

Then I went to the dial and turned it up to VH. Very hot.

Hansel had heard the screaming, and was shouting at me to come. I limped out, my blood still thundering.

'What happened?' he said.

'She's in the stove,' I said, panting, shaking the bars of his cage. The cage began to sing, but this time the music was out of tune, warped and dripping. The bars began to dissolve in my hands, turning to sticky sugary syrup. Hansel leapt free and embraced me. The rats were in chaos. Some were shouting that they had been liberated, while others tried to trip us and bite us.

Hansel linked his arm through mine and we turned to the witch's cash register. We filled our pockets with gold coins, then ran out of the shop and stopped at the mirror. Already, four rats, gold coins clenched between their teeth, were trying to bash their way through. Again and again they struck themselves against the unforgiving glass, until they were battered and bleeding.

I put out my hand. The mirror was cool. It did not bend, it did not melt, and it certainly did not let me through.

Hansel hammered his shoulder against it, grunting. Sweat formed on his brow. In the mirror, I saw the white bird sitting on the exposed brickwork of the half-demolished building to our left. I looked behind me. In reality, it wasn't there.

'How do we get in?' I called to the bird in the mirror.

It didn't answer. I watched as Hansel knocked himself against the mirror, as the rats began to drop, one by one, in bloody mangled heaps.

And I knew.

We all go empty-handed into the unknown.

'Hansel, turn out your pockets,' I said. I reached into my own pockets, dropping coins on the ground as if they were as inconsequential as dust-balls. 'But the money,' he moaned. 'I've never seen so much of it.'

I was too young to articulate my conviction: that wealth could be measured without coins, that youth and health and love — oh, god, love — were blessings not to be squandered. All I could say was, 'I know this will work.'

Hansel stopped. He turned his pockets inside out. A clattering, ringing shower. Gold coins in shining, seductive clusters at our feet along with the dull rusted ones our father had given us. We faced each other. He leaned down, kissed me hard. He tasted like candy and fear. I took his hand, and we walked forward.

Softly. Into the forest.

AFTERWORD

It only struck me recently that the scariest thing about Hansel and Gretel isn't the witch, but the idea that your parents might abandon you in the woods. It got me thinking about generational conflict and what forms it takes, about cashed-up boomers so freaked out about their own immediate security that they're eating the future: selective blindness to environmental damage, ridiculous wars that need never be fought, pricing young slackers like me out of the housing market. So, I thought the story of Hansel and Gretel might be an interesting way to express some of these ideas.

— *Kim Wilkins*

LUCY SUSSEX was born in New Zealand. She is currently a Senior Research Fellow at the University of Melbourne, Australia, with interests ranging from genre fiction to Australian Studies and Victoriana. Her work includes both creative writing and the scholarly. She has produced editions of the pioneering women crime writer Mary Fortune — *The Detectives' Album* and *The Fortunes of Mary Fortune* — as well as Ellen Davitt's 1865 *Force and Fraud*, the first Australian murder mystery novel. In addition she has compiled three anthologies for younger readers: *The Patternmaker, The Lottery*, and *Shadow Alley. She's Fantastical*, an anthology of Australian women's non-realist fiction edited by Lucy Sussex and Judith Raphael Buckrich, was shortlisted for the 2005 World Fantasy Award.

Her award-winning fiction includes four books for younger readers: *The Penguin Friend, Deersnake, Black Ice* and *The Revognase*. One adult novel, *The Scarlet Rider*, won the Ditmar Award and was shortlisted for the Kelly Award. She has written three short story collections: *My Lady Tongue, A Tour Guide in Utopia*, and *Absolute Uncertainty*. Currently she reviews weekly for *The Age* and *West Australian* newspapers. She is also completing a book on early women and crime fiction.

Here she writes about the KGB, George Bush, Ronald Reagan, Ollie North, rendition, the obligatory robots and zombies . . . and did I mention giant lizards?

ROBOTS & ZOMBIES, INC.

LUCY SUSSEX

Editors' Note. The following was transcribed from a tape, clearly record of interview, mailed from a fictitious address in Uzbekistan (we checked) to the Oakland PO Box of ConspiracyTheory.com. The quality of the tape is poor, with obvious miking problems at the time of recording. The interviewee is audible, but his interviewers little more than mumble, even with digital enhancement. Such would suggest an amateur recording, rather than that of an experienced journalist or police professional. But we see no reason to doubt its authenticity.

My name? Well, there's two of them. George Washington Reynolds, also Donald McIvor Smith, depending which passport I was using. Such happens when you get split.

Same birthdate for both: 11/01/51. Fake, of course.

Ditto the birthplaces. Reynolds was Nutley, NJ. Smith, some godforsaken Scottish New Town.

We had each other, a necessary narcissism. And for back story, Reynolds had a wife, two kids, and a rottweiler, somewhere out beyond Langley, VI. Smith was less complicated — or so I thought. Gay. Kept gerbils. That's unexceptional in the British Secret Service.

The cover was various Spooky actions. It got strange at times. Like when I was acting Liaison Officer between the US & UK secret services, which meant liaising with . . . myself. No, nobody ever noticed. But just to be on the safe side, after that Smith went bald.

The first time I came to Tashkent was in 1975. An urgent security meeting of Mammelia Corp. My real employers.

Yes, that was also my first murder.

Well, what would *you* do with jetlag, the latest in concealed weaponry, and a jetlagged hippie earbashing you in the transit lounge about Giant Extraterrestrial Lizards mind-controlling the world's leaders?

I later found out it was a genuine cult. Shame it was a little too close to the truth.

I blamed the KGB and just forgot about the murder, until now. Look, I had other things to worry about. Like eliminating the Soviets.

They were nearly onto Mammelia, that's why. After Tashkent we knew we had to get the Subjects into place and pronto.

Subject A had actually been a sleeper for some time. A back-up model, just in case. For a model blown up by the IRA, half our luck.

Yes, Subject A was experimental, and given to transmogrification. I did know about the sudden change of sex. Apparently it happened spontaneously.

Mammelia's British Office had to go and completely rework the back story. Including the spouse, Denise. She took it rather well, except for the time Smith sang Blondie's 'Dénis, Denise' *sotto voce* to her during a NATO reception. Burst into tears, and said she'd preferred being a woman, unlike Mal, I mean Mags.

The Office gossip was their sex had gone pear-shaped.

Oh, that was nothing compared with Subject B, Ronald Reagan. He only went and died in the middle of the Presidential election campaign.

Of course Mammelia revived him, nobody had thought to split a copy. What a pro, what a ham, even when dead meat. Knew his lines, well, at first. Projected avuncular warmth whilst stony cold.

No, that was rouge. Without it he looked like death warmed up.

My role as Reynolds was spin doctoring, everything from Chile to Gorby. Then Ollie North showed up.

No, I still don't know who North was working for. The competion was kinda nebulous at that stage. But I knew big trouble when I saw it.

I requested an immediate transfer. Ended up in the Canada office. Boring as batshit. But safe.

No, Reynolds never was on the team running Reagan. Nobody with any sense did. Of smell — he whiffed of the mortuary.

Yes, that's why they kept him a safe distance from the White House Press Corps in his later years. He was visibly deteriorating, and not only in memory.

The finger in the soup incident is perfectly true. Luckily it happened in front of the Australian Prime Minister, who was too drunk to notice.

Yes, he actually ate it.

As Smith I was in and out of Downing Street. Hands on. Unlike Reagan, Mags couldn't act for toffee apples. Completely synthetic.

The word Simulacra was never used by Mammelia. Officially the term was Subject, unofficially, Robot. Only R&D were so crass as actually to say Meatbot.

I heard they spliced in some components from an earlier prototype, a 1950s British Nanny. Without it Mags didn't know if she was Arthur or Martha. After that she at least crossed her legs when wearing skirts.

Came to terms with it eventually. Said it helped being ex-male, she knew how their minds worked, and they didn't expect her to think the same way. That's devious . . .

The beauty was the Brits got so fazed by a woman in power they couldn't spot Mags's total unreality.

Yes, they had the Queen, but she couldn't act either. Completely robotic, even though natural. Indubitably.

I beg your pardon. Smith had *nothing* to do with the Diana model. Another experiment — Helen of Troy was the working title. Quite prophetic, as without someone riding shotgun 24/7 she was way-out wayward. I think the Brit branch of Mammelia never quite got things right. They deserved to be liquidated.

No, actually turned into liquid and recycled in the vats. Smith was in Paris by then, cleaning up the Diana mistake. He had the wit to move sideways when Mags managed a second transmogrification. Into a good actor, convincing even, as she fought for her political life.

Didn't work. After politics Mags went onto the lecture circuit. I heard somebody high up in Mammelia finally got jack of her and pulled the plug. Head first into the lectern, time to retire, girl. At least Reagan had the grace to zombify in a rest home.

Late 1990s. The times were a-changing, I could smell it. Like Reagan's decomposition.

The order came from Mammelia Central: splice time! I think that's when things really started going downhill.

Reynolds and Smith met in the Canaries, spent a week in a very exclusive health farm, and I emerged, whole again.

No, it was horrid. Smith had developed a taste for exotic rough trade, and had decided on the ultimate deniability: memory wipe. The sorta thing you see all the time now in politics. He had his done on the cheap, and it showed. Every time I got anywhere near a dodgy memory, I got an instant migraine.

Mammelia put me on light duties. Bloody Canada again.

If I'd known about Smith's affair with the Jihad mole, I'd never have agreed to a Middle East transfer.

What can I say? I was sitting in a bar in Cairo, and the pest from Tashkent reappeared. Still rattling on about giant lizards thought-controlling the world.

Of course I thought he was a split. In the world I live in, the coincidence was too big to be believed.

So I killed him. How was I to know he was natural — my original victim's identical twin brother? And vice-prez of the conspiracy theory cult, which now had a worldwide membership. Even in Uzbekistan, I can see.

I blamed the KGB again. Bad idea.

Because things were different. The Soviets had gone, but the Russian Mafia were picking up where they'd left off. Strange alliances were being made, between bedfellows odder than Smith and his gerbils.

I found myself bound and gagged, on a cargo flight back to Tashkent.

Yes, I know it's called rendition. But if you tried to torture all my secrets out of me, I'd just disintegrate. I'm made that way.

Does it really satisfy your paranoid fantasies that the world isn't run by giant telepathic lizards, but much worse? Well?

Since you ask, Mammelia is finished. The competition's simply too strong. And it's not just the Bush family franchise. They're probably finished too.

I can point to anywhere in the world and show you little Mammelias. Outrageous copies, of course. But slowly perfecting the business of Robots & Zombies, Inc.

AFTERWORD

The writer Ben Peek has a story called 'Johnny Cash', which uses the format of fifty questions. Ben says he got the idea from J. G. Ballard's *Complete Short Stories*, which includes 'Answers to a Questionnaire'. Ballard used one hundred questions, Ben cut it down, with tighter results. I started playing around with the form, and ended up with forty-nine answers, the result of an interrogation. Because I'm variously informed by reviewing, media consumption, life, I married Jon Ronson's *Them*, on conspiracy theories, with a documentary I saw on Margaret Thatcher. She came across so robotic that I wondered how anyone could have voted for her. Of course, the story also gave me the opportunity to be irreverent about many other things, one of my favourite pastimes.

— *Lucy Sussex*

SARA DOUGLASS has become Australia's premier bestselling fantasy author, since the publication of *BattleAxe*, Book One of the Aurealis award-winning Axis Trilogy in 1995.

She writes: 'I was born in Penola, South Australia, raised in Adelaide by Methodist Ladies, condemned by apathy to the respectable profession of nursing, and escaped via the varied kindnesses of the Department of History at the University of Adelaide into the preferable world of writing.'

Sara is the author of *Enchanter* and *Starman*, which complete The Axis Trilogy; the Wayfarer Redemption Trilogy, which includes *Sinner*, *Pilgrim*, and *Crusader*; The Crucible Trilogy, which includes *The Nameless Day*, *The Wounded Hawk*, and *The Crippled Angel*; Troy Game, a tetralogy, which includes *Hades' Daughter*, *God's Concubine*, *Darkwitch Rising*, and *Druid's Sword*; and the Darkglass Mountain Series, which includes *The Serpent Bride* and *The Twisted Citadel*. *The Wounded Hawk* won the Aurealis Award for Best Fantasy Novel, and *The Crippled Angel* was nominated for Australian Book of the Year. She is also the author of *Threshold*, the young adult novel *Beyond the Hanging Wall*, and such non-fiction titles as *Images of the Educational Traveller in Early Modern England* and *The Betrayal of Arthur*. She currently lives in a rambling old Victorian house on an island just off the southern tip of mainland Australia, right at the edge of the world.

The wonderfully dark and atmospheric story that follows takes place in 19th-century London during the age of the building of the underground railways.

Sara Douglass told your editor that 'One of the great problems with driving those tunnels under London (at least in *my* world) is that they tended to drive straight into forgotten and lost buried roman and medieval crypts ... filled with all kinds of dark things.'

As you'll soon discover, gentle reader ...

THIS WAY TO THE EXIT

SARA DOUGLASS

James Henry Greathead, chief engineer for the City & South London Railway, rose to his feet as the footman showed the two gentlemen into the club's drawing room. He was relieved the men were reasonably well dressed and didn't gawp at the rich fittings. It had been a risk inviting them to the Athenaeum Club, but the club afforded privacy, and before anything else Greathead wanted privacy for this meeting.

The company could not afford the inevitable financial setback if word he had met with the crypt hunters alarmed the shareholders.

'Mr Kemp? Mr Gordon? So good of you to attend.' Greathead gestured to the two men to sit, then nodded at the waiter to bring two more glasses of whiskey. 'I trust your journey from Windsor was without trouble?'

'Quite, thank you,' said Kemp. In his late fifties, Kemp was the slightly older of the two men, but they both shared the careworn and pale visages of those who habitually worked late at night at their books.

Or who habituated the dark underground basements of cities.

They were both very still and calm, regarding Greathead with direct eyes, and Greathead found himself uncrossing, then recrossing his legs, before smoothing back his hair.

He hated it that necessity brought him to these men.

'It surprises me you do not live in London,' Greathead said, 'as so much of your, um, work is here. Why live in Windsor?'

'You can perhaps understand,' Kemp said, his gaze still very direct, 'that we prefer the tranquillity of Windsor for our wives and children, as well as our own peace of mind. London can be unsettling. Windsor has no —'

Greathead suppressed a wince.

'— discontented underground spaces,' Kemp finished.

'Quite,' Greathead said.

The waiter returned with the whiskeys for Greathead's guests, and while the waiter fussed Greathead took the opportunity to study Gordon and Kemp further. They were unusual men, not so much in background, but for where they had gone in their lives. Gordon had been a vicar who had immersed himself in the study of the churches and monasteries of the medieval and Dark Age periods. He quit the Church of England, quite suddenly, in his early forties. It was about that time that Gordon had met Kemp — Kemp had been a private scholar with a bent for the arcane and mysterious — and they had made a name for themselves speaking at antiquarian functions about southern England.

They had an astounding knowledge of the ancient crypts and vaults and cellars, often dating back to pre-Christian times, that lay under London.

They also had an astounding understanding of what continued to inhabit these ancient crypts — the memories, the terrors, and the wandering ghosts and ambitions of men and gods who refused to remain entombed. Greathead was not quite sure what the men did inside these crypts — they never allowed anyone else in while they were working — but they could somehow manage to desensitise them and make them safe for whoever was trying to push through a railway tunnel or a new sewer or water line.

Underground London was not always quite benign, nor were its forgotten spaces always quite dead. Many tunnellers — whether railway or sewer men — had been lost in the strangest of circumstances. Often the only way the railway or sewer bosses could keep projects on schedule — and workers in the tunnels — was to employ the services of Gordon and Kemp.

The waiter left, and Greathead took a deep breath. 'No doubt you have heard of my latest endeavour.'

'Of course,' said Gordon. 'We understandably took some interest when we heard Parliament had authorised your project. A new railway line for southern Londoners, yes? Travelling deep under the Thames to connect their suburbs directly to the City.'

'It will be the first deep underground railway system in the world,' Greathead said. 'Look here, see.' He drew a linen-backed map from a satchel to one side of his chair, and unfolded it across the table before Kemp and Gordon. 'We are running the line direct from Stockwell in the south, up north through the Borough of Southwark, under the Thames just west of London Bridge, then through the city, deep underground, at least sixty feet deep, through to Moorgate. It is a great enterprise.'

Kemp and Gordon exchanged small smiles.

A great enterprise, and fraught with difficulty. There was so much which had been forgotten lying in the railway's path.

'It will be a great deal of work,' said Gordon. 'All that tunnelling, and, aye, yes, I know of your patented tunnelling machine, and how wonderfully it shall slice through the London clay for you . . . but still, a great deal of work. When do you hope to be completed?'

'1890,' said Greathead. 'The Prince of Wales has agreed to open the line for us.'

'That is not long distant,' said Kemp. 'You are surely already hard at work, and thus —'

He paused, holding Greathead's eye, and Gordon finished his companion's sentence.

'And thus we are here,' he said. 'You found a . . . problem.'

'The City & South London Railway, whom I represent,' Greathead said quietly, 'does not have problems. We have only challenges — which we overcome with skill and ingenuity. *Thus* you are here.'

Kemp's mouth curved in a small cynical smile, which he hid as he took a sip of his whiskey.

It was very good, as was this club, but then Greathead had made a fortune with his innovative and daring engineering work on other railways, and doubtless could afford the luxuries of life.

'Well,' said Greathead, 'we have started work in several locations, working tunnels in different directions, that they may meet up within months.'

'What have you found?' said Kemp, and Greathead glanced irritably at him.

'As I was saying,' Greathead said, 'we are working in several locations. Here,' his finger stabbed down at Clapham, 'here,' now the finger stabbed down at the northern end of London Bridge, 'and,' the finger lifted, hesitated, then dropped to the corner of King William Street and Arthur Street East, a few blocks to the north-east of the bridge, 'here.'

Kemp and Gordon shared another glance, and this time there was no amusement in their expressions.

'That is right by the Monument,' said Gordon.

The Monument, erected to mark the exact spot where started the Great Fire of London of 1666. It was an inauspicious omen. Later tragedies were often caused by ancient disturbances below.

Greathead sat back in his chair. 'I had heard of your work with the Metropolitan and District Lines,' he said. 'You smoothed over some considerable difficulties they experienced.'

'Few people know of our work with the Metropolitan line,' said Gordon. 'It was all very — necessarily — secretive.'

'I make it my duty to know of your work,' said Greathead. 'Secretive or not, I made a point of discovering the names of everyone who might be useful to me. Gentlemen, I intend this railway to succeed.'

Kemp gave a little shrug. 'And now you have encountered one of your little obstacles at the Monument site?'

'It is the site of one of the underground stations,' said Greathead. 'We are naming it King William Street Station, after the street on which it stands. There is already a commodious building on the site, which will serve as the city offices of the City & South London Railway and as the entrance into the underground station. While there shall be stairs winding down to the platforms sixty feet below, we are installing two large electrified lifts to carry passengers to and from street level. The entire project, gentlemen, shall be electrified, even the trains.'

Greathead paused, expecting his guests to remark on this extraordinary innovation, but they continued to regard him calmly with their direct eyes.

'Yes, well,' Greathead went on. 'We started to sink the shafts through the basement of the building six weeks ago. Work proceeded as planned, then . . .'

'You found a crypt,' said Gordon. 'Perhaps an ancient vault. Yes?'

'We always expected to find *something*, at some point,' said Greathead. 'London has been occupied for thousands of years, city built atop city. Naturally we expected an extra basement or two.'

'The Metropolitan and District Line gave us much work and worry,' said Gordon. 'Two crypts, one ancient rotten mausoleum, and one rather dark space which somewhat befuddled us for a day or two. What have you found for us?'

'Nothing that whispers,' said Greathead. 'Just a . . . space.'

The faces of Kemp and Gordon relaxed slightly.

No whispers.

'Nonetheless, I warrant it a space that has caused you to suspend all further work on the shafts and summon us,' said Kemp.

Greathead sighed. 'The workmen broke into it five days ago. Two of them took down lanterns and explored. When they came back up — well, that was when I wrote you to come to London.'

He picked up his whiskey glass, then put it down again. 'Look, we are not far distant from King William Street. It would be easier, perhaps, if I showed you our difficulties.'

Gordon and Kemp stood at the foot of the twenty-five foot diameter shaft that stretched down from the basement of the building above. It would one day house two lifts, but for the moment they were surrounded by iron reinforced walls, a muddy floor, half a dozen workmen standing about leaning on their spades and pick-axes, and Greathead.

At their feet was a three foot diameter hole, with a ladder stretching down into the gloom.

One of the workmen handed Kemp a lantern on a rope, and Kemp lowered it carefully down into the darkness.

Everyone standing about — Greathead, the work crew and their supervisor — leaned closer.

'What can you see?' Greathead said.

'Not much,' Gordon replied, leaning back a little. 'It's a big space, though.'

'It will save us a great deal of money and time if it is usable,' Greathead said. 'The cavern is at the precise level we need to build the station. Both I and the board of the Railway pray for good news.'

The lamp hit the bottom of the cavern, and Kemp allowed the remainder of the rope to slide down to join it. He looked at Greathead, then locked eyes with Gordon.

A moment later Gordon began the climb down the ladder, Kemp following directly after.

Kemp held the lantern aloft as the two men stood, staring about. They ignored the faint sounds of the men far above them in the shaft, and instead concentrated every sense on the cavern about them.

'It is not ... "bad",' Gordon said very softly. 'Not like the crypt under Westminster station. That ...'

That had been pure evil — something small and weaselly and chattery that had inhabited the small chamber since well before Christianity had established its hold on England.

Their efforts to remove the lingering malignancy had almost killed them. Even now Gordon continued to have problems on his shin where the thing had bitten him, and both suffered constant nightmares over the episode.

'No,' said Kemp, 'it is not "bad". But what *is* it?'

The space they stood in looked like a natural cave, although the walls and roof had been obviously man-worked at some time in the ancient past to give the rock a smoother finish. It stretched perhaps some forty or fifty paces from east to west, and, as the two men explored, they discovered that about twenty paces from the eastern end it appeared almost as if another cavern, or tunnel, had intersected with the one in which they stood. On both the northern and southern walls of the main cavern archways had been crudely hewn out of the rock, and passageways extended north and south — if only for a few paces each way before rock falls blocked their progress.

In the very centre of the main cavern, at the intersection of the two smaller passages, stood a pale-stoned cross, almost seven feet tall. The top of the cross had been enclosed within a circle, revealing its ancient pagan origins.

Gordon and Kemp exchanged another glance.

'It's a Long Tom,' Gordon said, naming the ancient cross in the manner of countless generations of English peasants. He raised the lamp, and both men muttered soft exclamations.

Set into the circle of stone about the top of the cross was a ring of human teeth.

'I have never seen that previously,' Kemp said.

'Nor I,' Gordon said. 'What do you suppose it means?'

Kemp gave a small shrug. 'Perhaps they are the teeth of robbers, or bandits, set here to dissuade others from similar pursuits. In all my studies, I know of no other possible relevance.'

'You are likely right,' Gordon said, then turned the lamp towards the passageway that had once led south. 'These side passages have been blocked off a long, long time ago.'

Kemp was still examining the cross in the dim light.

'A crossroads marker,' he said. 'Long Toms always stood at crossroads to protect travellers.' He gestured about the main cavern, then at the two side passages. 'We are standing on the site of a very, very ancient crossroad.'

'London straddles the junction of several of the ancient roads through England,' Gordon said. 'This,' he indicated the main cavern stretching east to west, 'is likely part of the original Wæcelinga Straæt,' he said, using the ancient Celt name for what was now known as Watling Street. 'And this,' he indicated the intersecting, narrowed tunnel, 'one of the lesser tracks leading north and south.'

He looked up once more at the roof of the cavern. 'This has always been enclosed — under a hill, perhaps? Or a man-made tor?'

'Possibly,' said Kemp. 'This area was once riddled with hills and caves, most imbued with some esoteric significance. Gordon, my friend, this place was not *just* a crossroads. You can feel it too, yes? There is something . . . a gentle pull of some description.'

Gordon gave a nod. 'But is it *dangerous?*'

Kemp shifted from foot to foot, chewing a lip.

'I don't think so,' he said after some consideration. 'There is nothing *bad* about this, nothing unsettled. It is a passageway, a throughway. Very ancient, very well travelled — if not in the current millennia — but benign. Even the Long Tom, with its strange circle of teeth, has no feel of malevolence about it.'

Gordon gave another nod. 'I agree. There is nothing for us here to do. No malignancy to expunge, no sadness to purge. Nothing dangerous.'

'Nothing dangerous,' said Kemp, 'so long as the trains travel through. This cavern will be put to the same purpose for which it has always been used. It will be appropriate, somehow. I doubt the cavern will be unsettled by its updated purpose.'

They spent another ten minutes inspecting the cavern, then they climbed back to an impatient Greathead.

'Well?' he said.

Gordon and Kemp exchanged a look.

'The line is going through to north London, isn't it?' Gordon said.

'From Stockwell to Moorgate,' Greathead said. 'King William Street Station will be the first station north of the river. From there the line travels to Bank, thence to Moorgate. *Well?*'

'The cavern below is an ancient crossroads,' said Gordon. 'You are lucky. There is nothing malignant to remove, just some old rock falls ... your King William Street Station is virtually hollowed out for you. There is an old cross down there that you might like to donate to some local antiquarian society, but, overall ... neither Kemp nor myself foresee any problems for you. Just make sure you take those trains through.'

Greathead had begun to smile halfway through Gordon's speech — now he was beaming. He shook each man's hand heartily. 'Gentlemen, I thank you indeed. You bring good news. Come, let us climb back to the surface, and we can arrange your remuneration.'

Gordon suppressed a cynical smile.

The railway engineers were always pleased to see the back of Gordon and Kemp.

Eighteen months passed. Greathead called Gordon and Kemp down to London on one more occasion in January of 1890 to investigate something near the London Bridge station, just south of the Thames, but that turned out to be even less of a concern than the King William Street Station cavern. While they were inspecting this latest site, Gordon and Kemp asked Greathead about the ancient crossroads cavern.

'The site is almost complete,' Greathead said. 'The workmen are laying the last of the tiles, the platforms need a sweep, but other than that ...' He gave an expressive shrug.

'There have been no problems at the site?' Kemp said.

Greathead hesitated for just an instant, then smiled. 'None at all! Now, is there anything else with which I can assist you?'

On the morning of 5th of November, in 1890, Gordon sat at his breakfast table reading the morning paper. There was extensive coverage of the opening of the City & South London Railway line. The Prince of Wales had officiated, and a good time was had by all. Unfortunately, there had been some technical problems with the engine meant to draw the carriages containing the prince and his entourage from Stockwell in the south through to the northern-most station on the line, and eventually everyone had to abandon the railway carriages for the more reliable horse-drawn vehicles on the streets above.

Gordon was grinning broadly by the end of the article. He could easily imagine Greathead's embarrassment at the failure of the train engine. *Dear God, what could he have said to the Prince of Wales?* He folded the paper and put it back on the table, thinking that if it remained fine, then later this afternoon he would make the brisk walk through the frosted streets to Kemp's home so they could share a glass of wine and their amusement at Greathead's discomfiture.

But by noon steady rain had settled in, and Gordon put to one side his plans to visit Kemp.

Christmas came and went. Gordon and Kemp spent some days together, but they did not discuss the City & South London Railway, Greathead, nor their visit to the cavern that was now King William Street Station. Largely they left their London work in London: it was one of the best ways to maintain their serenity.

On a frosty morning in early February Gordon was once again reading his paper at breakfast. His wife had just risen from the table, and he could hear her in the hallway, discussing the evening's meal with their cook, Matilda. There was little of interest in the paper, and Gordon was skimming it somewhat irritably when the headline to a minor paragraph on one of the inner pages caught his eye.

Third person reported missing at King William Street Station.

Gordon fumbled in his haste to fold the paper that he might the more easily read the article, then cursed under his breath as he upset his cup of tea over the pristine tablecloth. Hastily sopping up the mess with his napkin, he read the rest of the article.

On Tuesday last, Mr Arthur Bowman, of Hill End, alighted from the train at King William Street Station. His companion, Mr Charles Marbrock, alighted with Mr Bowman, but lost sight of him in the crowded tunnel leading to the exit. He was not waiting at the entrance foyer when Mr Marbrock exited the lift. A thorough search by station staff provided no clues. Mr Bowman is the third person to go missing from the exit tunnel of King William Street Station since the New Year.

That was it. Nothing else.

The third person to go missing from the exit tunnel of King William Street Station since the New Year?

Gordon rose suddenly, tossing the newspaper down to the table and further upsetting the now-empty tea cup. He strode into the hall, disturbing his wife and Matilda, and grabbed his heavy coat from the hall stand.

'I'm going to see Kemp,' he said to his wife. 'I doubt I shall return before late afternoon.' With that he stomped out the front door.

Late afternoon saw both Kemp and Gordon in the train station at Windsor. It had been a cold walk down almost deserted streets, and both men were pale, their faces pinched by the cold.

They stopped at the ticket box. 'Do you have a map of London Underground?' Gordon asked the ticket collector, and thanked the man as he handed one over.

Kemp and Gordon retired to the station fire to look at the map. Neither had been back to London in many months but, since they'd read the news this morning, both had a growing fear that they'd need to return very soon.

Gordon traced a gloved finger over the diagram until he came to the City & South London Line. It was drawn in black to differentiate it from all the other Underground lines currently in service, and Gordon ran his finger up the line from Stockwell to King William Street Station.

The line terminated at King William Street Station.

'It was supposed to go further!' Kemp said. 'All the way through to Moorgate!'

'That cavern was a throughway,' Gordon hissed. 'A *throughway*, not a terminus!'

They walked back to the ticket office, where the ticket collector sat looking bored.

It was freezing weather, and not many people had wanted tickets to London today.

'Good man,' said Gordon, 'do you know why the City & South London line only goes so far as King William Street Station? We were hoping to catch this line through to Moorgate . . . we thought . . .'

'Heard they had troubles with water seepage north of King William Street,' said the ticket collector. 'Several buildings collapsed over where they were trying to push through the tunnels.' He gave a slight shrug. 'Stopped work north, it did. Line now terminates at King William

Street Station. But if you want to get to Moorgate, then you can walk to Mark Lane Station, and from there . . .'

Gordon and Kemp paid him no mind.

The line terminated at King William Street?

'Why did we never check?' Gordon whispered. 'Why did we never ask?'

'And where are the missing people *going*?' said Kemp.

'Pardon?' said the ticket collector.

The next day, just after noon, the two men stood on the pavement outside the entrance to King William Street Station on Arthur Street East. Passengers were coming and going through the great double doors. Nothing appeared untoward.

Gordon and Kemp exchanged a look, then they went inside, purchased their 2d tickets, then walked through the turnstile to the lifts.

They rode down in silence, not meeting any of the other passenger's eyes. As the last time they had descended this shaft, both men had nerves fluttering in their stomachs. This descent, they knew their nerves would not be easily quelled as previously.

From the lift they took one of two tunnels that led to the station platform. The tunnels were some six feet wide and perhaps eight tall, the white-tiled ceiling curving overhead in an elegant arch.

The platform itself was enclosed in a circular tunnel, again white tiled, and lit with the warm glow of gas lamps. Some fifteen people stood about, waiting for the train from the south to arrive. The tunnel continued a little way north of the platforms, and Gordon and Kemp could see a signal box straddling the track.

Beyond that was a blank brick wall.

The two men turned their attention back to the platform area, trying to orientate themselves with what they remembered of the cavern. They studied the twin tunnels leading to the lifts. Above each tunnel workmen had painted chubby gloved hands, each one with its index finger pointing to the tunnel below.

Between the two chubby gloved hands were the words: *This way to the exit*.

Gordon shivered, although he could not for the moment understand why.

'Gordon?' Kemp said. 'D'you see?'

'See what?'

Kemp nodded at the tunnels. 'These tunnels are in precisely the same spot as was that south leading tunnel we found. You know the one, with the Long Tom lying half buried a few paces in.'

'My God,' said Gordon, momentarily forgetting himself in his shocked realisation.

'The original tunnel likely led to a pathway leading to a ford over the Thames,' said Kemp, 'and from there to one of the roads leading to the south-east and the coast.'

'Is that —' Gordon began, but broke off as he heard the sound of the train approaching.

It stopped at the platform — a little grey and cream engine pulling green carriages. None of the carriages had any windows — the City & South London Railway Company had refused to pay for glass when there was nothing to see on the entirely underground line.

Gordon thought they looked like green coffins, and was not surprised to see people bundle out of them in a rush.

He'd be keen to alight, as well.

The disembarked passengers all headed for the exit tunnels, and Gordon and Kemp joined them, mingling among the crowd.

They entered the right hand tunnel and were not four or five paces inside it when both men felt a strange tingling. Kemp, a pace or two behind Gordon, lunged forward and grabbed his friend by the elbow. 'What —' he began, then stopped in absolute horror as the person in front of them, a young woman in a fashionable tartan bustled skirt and matching hat, simply faded from view.

Both men staggered in shock, then were pressed against the wall as the tide of passengers continued through the tunnel, heading for the exit.

Buffeted and breathless, they were finally left alone in the tunnel, staring about as if they could miraculously find the woman lurking in the shadows.

They paused for a restorative whiskey in a pub on Arthur Street East, then they headed back to the station building which housed the London offices of the City & South London Railway.

There they demanded to see either the chairman of the company, or Mr Greathead, the chief engineer.

As it transpired, both men were in and, after Kemp had shouted a little at the chairman's secretary, both agreed to meet with Gordon and Kemp.

'What in God's name were you thinking,' Gordon said, not even waiting to be introduced to the chairman, 'not continuing the line? That cavern was a throughway, a *throughway*, not . . . not . . .'

'Not a terminus,' Kemp finished.

'If I may?' Greathead said. He waved the men towards a group of chairs by a fire, but neither moved.

Greathead sighed. 'May I introduce Sir Charles Grey Mott,' he said, then murmured, 'Mr Gordon, Mr Kemp,' as Sir Charles stepped forward to shake the two crypt hunters' hands.

The chairman was a tall, elegant man whose very manner seemed to calm Gordon and Kemp somewhat.

'There is a problem?' Sir Charles said. He sat down in one of the chairs, crossing his legs with such grace that it could only have been bred, not learned, and after a moment both Gordon and Kemp took chairs as well.

Greathead repressed another sigh and joined the others.

'That cavern was a throughway,' Gordon said. 'An ancient crossroads. It would have been safe had the train continued on its journey, but as it is, the train stops, and people have to go somewhere.'

Sir Charles regarded him patiently.

'People have been going missing,' said Kemp. 'We saw another, today. She vanished before our very eyes. Doubtless there will be a report in tomorrow's *Times*. If it is of any concern.'

Sir Charles flickered a glance to Greathead but otherwise his expression did not alter.

'There were problems in continuing the tunnel north,' said Greathead. 'Water began to seep in and —'

'Yes, yes, so we have heard,' said Gordon. 'What are you going to do about the station? There are people going missing! On their way to the exit! You *must* continue the tunnel!'

'That is impossible,' said Sir Charles. 'We simply cannot do it. Instead, in April we shall begin construction on a diversionary tunnel that will run just east of the current line leading into King William

Street Station, and bypassing the station entirely. The soil is more stable there, and we should have no problems driving the line north. We anticipate that we can be finished by the end of the year.'

Kemp opened his mouth to speak, but Sir Charles continued on smoothly.

'You assured Mr Greathead that the space was safe to be used. You said —'

'That it could only be used if the tunnel continued through!' Gordon said.

'I don't recall you saying that,' Greathead said. 'In fact, I am sure that you didn't —'

Sir Charles raised a hand for peace. 'What is happening to these people, gentlemen? I can assure you, it *is* of concern to me.'

'We don't know,' said Kemp. 'They are travelling *somewhere*, but not to the exit they desire.'

'You need to close the station,' said Gordon.

'That's impossible!' Greathead said. 'King William Street Station is our one and only station currently north of the Thames. If we close it then our entire purpose of building a line from the southern suburbs under the Thames into London is defeated. We might as well —'

'Close the entire line,' said Sir Charles. 'And if we do that then the company will founder, and thousands shall be left destitute.'

Gordon made an impatient noise. 'You *must* close it,' he said.

'There is nothing you can do?' Sir Charles said. 'This is, after all, your speciality. It is what we *paid* you for.'

Gordon narrowed his eyes at the tone of Sir Charles' voice and began to shake his head, but Kemp put a hand on his arm.

'There might be something,' Kemp said. 'The Long Tom.'

'The ... *what?*' Sir Charles said.

'There was an ancient cross in the cavern,' Greathead said. 'Gordon and Kemp called it a Long Tom and told me to give it to some local antiquarian society.'

'It might help,' Kemp said, 'if it went back into the station. It might protect the passengers.'

'*Might*,' Gordon muttered.

Neither Greathead nor Sir Charles heard him.

'Where is it now?' Sir Charles said. 'Greathead, do you remember where it went?'

Greathead looked a little embarrassed. 'Ahem ... it currently stands in the grounds of my Devon house.'

'Good!' Sir Charles said. 'It shall be no trouble to restore it, then. Kemp, you are certain this will work? We only need to keep the station open eight or nine months.'

'I cannot be sure,' Kemp said, 'but —'

He stopped. Sir Charles and Greathead were engaged in a conversation about how to transport the Long Tom back to King William Street Station, and from there how to explain its presence to passengers.

Kemp looked at Gordon. *Who knew if it would work?*

And then ...

What exit were the missing people taking?

Mrs Frances Patterson stepped out of the tunnel and stopped dead, her mouth hanging open.

This was not what she had expected to see.

Instead of streets bustling with horse-drawn vehicles and pedestrians, and footpaths strewn with vendors, all she could see for miles and miles was low rolling hills. To her right stretched what she supposed might have been the Thames, save that it was three times too wide, and where there should have been embankments and warehouses, piers and ships, was nothing but waterbirds and rushes.

A movement before her caught her attention.

Three men stood some fifteen paces away. They wore nothing save woven plaid cloaks and trousers. Their faces and naked upper bodies were daubed with blue woad, their long hair was plaited with what looked like bits of copper, and their eyes were narrowed in suspicion. Each of them carried a long spear.

They were not very tall and looked underfed, and Mrs Patterson vaguely wondered if they were prisoners escaped from one of the city prisons. Newgate, perhaps. Or perhaps native Americans, transported to London's docks by one of the tea clippers.

She cleared her throat. 'Is this ...' She had to stop and start again. They were so rude to stare at her in such fashion! 'Is this the way to the exit?'

The three men exchanged glances, making their decision.

One of them leaned his weight on his back foot, and hefted his spear.

Sir Charles Grey Mott sat in his office, looking down at the plan of King William Street Station sitting on his desk.

It had been ten months since he had spoken with Greathead, Gordon and Kemp in this office. In the week following that conversation workmen had restored the ancient pagan cross to the platform, just between the entrances to the two exit tunnels. A little sign attached to the cross had said that it was an artwork on loan from one of the county antiquarian societies.

For two months it appeared to have worked. No one else went missing from the exit tunnels.

Then, very gradually, people started to vanish once again. One every fortnight or so, then the numbers began to increase: one a week, then two a week.

Sir Charles had kept it from the press only because of his extensive contacts, a few bribes, and one rather vicious threat made to the editor of London's largest newspaper. The City & South London Railway was only a very new company, still with only one line, and Parliament could withdraw its consent for the company's continued operation at any time.

There could be no hint of what was going wrong.

So Sir Charles and Greathead pushed their work crews as hard as they could to open up the diversionary tunnel. They found, thank God, no further caverns (if they had, Sir Charles thought he may have taken an early retirement to Panama).

Yesterday the new tunnel through to Moorgate had opened.

Yesterday King William Street Station was finally, thankfully, closed.

Sir Charles would have gone down himself to turn off the gas lamps and smash the damned pagan cross to pieces, save he didn't want to have to risk using the exit tunnels.

He sent the foreman of one of his work crews instead, and, thankfully, he had come back.

Sir Charles stared a long time at the plans, then he reached for his pen, dipped it into the inkwell, and in large black letters wrote across the plan: *Closed due to an engineering blunder*.

Then he pushed back his chair, rose, straightened his vest and jacket, and went back to his wife and family awaiting him in Chelsea. He would have a good evening meal, and relax later in his study with a whiskey.

It was all over and done with.

The wind whistled across the marshes surrounding the sacred hills that sat on the bend of the Thames. A small village sat close to the northern bank of the Thames, near a ford, and near to where, one day, London Bridge would stretch across the river. It was only a small village, with eight or nine circular huts, most with smoke drifting from holes in their apex.

Just to the east of the village stood a low hill, one of the sacred hills. The hill had four low arched openings that were centred on each of the cardinal directions.

At least, the hill had *once* had four openings. Now all but one of them were closed over with rubble and turf. A group of six men moved towards the entrance, their steps slow, their shoulders burdened with a tall stone cross, its head enclosed within a stone circle.

Two shamans walked behind the six men and their burden, their heads bowed, murmuring incantations. They had carved the cross between them over the past cycle of the moon, working into it all the protective magics they could.

To one side stood the remainder of the villagers, watching proceedings. Their faces were a mixture of sorrow and relief. They had once revered the sacred hill for the mystical journeys it had enabled them to take, but they had spent the past few months in increasing terror at the evil spirits the hill had begun to spit forth.

They watched the men and the cross vanished within the hill, then the shamans after them. The villagers shuffled a little in their tension.

They hoped the shamans were powerful enough to successfully combat the evil spirits.

After a short while the six men returned, their burden left within the hill. They stood to one side on the entrance, eyeing the tools and the great pile of stone and rubble that stood waiting.

Once the shamans returned (*if* they returned), the men would seal off this remaining doorway.

* * *

The two shamans stood in the centre of the crossroads, deep within the hill. They were illumed by two small burning torches and the very faint patch of light that made its way inside from the entrance at their backs. Before them stood the stone cross, the Long Tom.

The shamans regarded it silently for a long moment, then the older of them, the senior shaman, stepped forward. He began to murmur an incantation, at the same time running the fingers of both hands lightly over the teeth set into the circular stonework. The younger shaman bowed his head, remaining silent, concentrating on sending his elder all the strength he could manage.

'It is done,' the senior shaman said eventually. He stepped back from the Long Tom, his hands trembling with his weariness.

'The evil spirits will not return?' the other shaman said.

'Not so long as this cross stands here to protect the passageways,' said the senior shaman. 'We will seal the entrance, and it will never be moved, and our land and people will be safe, for ever more. Now, come, let us leave this place.'

Once outside the senior shaman nodded to the villagers standing anxiously, to let them know it had been done, then murmured a word to the six men waiting with tools and stone. The men bent down immediately, beginning to shift the stones.

By morning the entrance would be sealed for evermore.

The two shamans moved down to the river bank. There waited an earthenware pot. The younger man bent and picked it up, then unceremoniously broke the pot against a rock and tipped its contents into the water.

Creamy-grey dust and crushed bone fragments — the cremated remains of all the Londoners who had taken the wrong exit — scattered over the water, creating an oily film that slowly moved away from the river bank into the current to drift eastwards toward the sea.

It was not, all things considered, the exit the chubby gloved hands had promised.

AFTERWORD

I have long entertained the idea of writing about one of the abandoned stations in London's Underground. I thought I would need to create a fictionalised station for this story, but when I was doing the research, I came across the strange tale of King William Street Station, destined to be closed due to 'an engineering blunder' less than a year after it had opened; it was the first London Underground station to be abandoned. I did not need to look further.

King William Street Station still exists. You can reach it via the emergency stairs leading down from a manhole in the basement of Regis House which stands on the corner of King William Street next to the Monument. The gas lamps are still there, as is the signalman's box with its twenty-two hand-operated levers, and most of the Victorian white tiles used to line the ceiling and walls. The twin exit tunnels remain, as do the chubby gloved hands helpfully pointing the way to the exit.

I would advise you not to visit, nor to attempt the way to the exit.

— *Sara Douglass*

The late A. BERTRAM CHANDLER began writing for John W. Campbell's germinal science fiction magazine *Astounding* in 1944 and became one of science fiction's most popular and prolific authors of space opera adventure. Along with Doc E. E. Smith, Robert Heinlein, Clifford Simak, A. E. Van Vogt, Lester Del Rey, Jack Williamson, L. Ron Hubbard, and Isaac Asimov, he was also a popular 'Golden Age' writer. That period from the late 1930s to the mid-1940s was ushered in by John W. Campbell and — to quote Sean McMullen in Paul Collins's *The Melbourne University Press Encyclopaedia of Australian Science Fiction & Fantasy* — 'is often referred to as the Golden Age of science fiction because the older adventure-based forms were giving way to stories with more realistic technology at their core.' Chandler, who immigrated to Australia from the United Kingdom in 1956, was a veteran seaman and commanded merchant marine ships under Australian and New Zealand flags; and he used his specialised knowledge and experience to chronicle the epic adventures of the spacefarer John Grimes, his best-known character. Chandler's John Grimes/Rim World adventures have been rightly compared to C. S. Forester's Horatio Hornblower series; critic John Clute has written in *The Encyclopedia of Science Fiction* that 'Grimes himself establishes a loyalty in his readers rather similar to that felt by readers of Hornblower.'

In 1981 Chandler wrote: 'Quite a few years ago Robert Heinlein said, "Only people who know ships can write convincingly about space ships." At the time I thought that was very true. I have not changed my opinion. I believe that the crews of the real spaceships of the future, vessels going a long way in a long time, will have far more in common with today's seamen than with today's airmen. I freely admit that my stories are essentially sea stories and that John Grimes, my series character, is descended from Hornblower.'

A. Bertram Chandler wrote over two hundred short stories and forty-four science fiction books, which include the Empress Irene series and Australian historical novels. Here are just a very few of his titles: *The Road to the Rim, To Prime the Pump, The Hard Way Up, False Fatherland, The Inheritors, The Broken Cycle, The Big Black Mark, Into the Alternate Universe, Contraband From Outer Space, The Way Back, Bring Back Yesterday, The Hamelin Plague,* and *Beyond the Galactic Rim.*

He won the Australian Ditmar Award in 1969, 1971, 1974, and 1976. He also was a recipient of Japan's Seium Sho Award, the Invisible Little Man Award, an Australian Literature Board Fellowship, and was guest of honour at the Chicago World Science Fiction Convention.

A. Bertram Chandler passed away in 1984.

But it is my great pleasure to present his only (as far as we know) unpublished John Grimes/Rim World story. All credit goes to Paul Collins, who originally purchased the story some thirty years ago. Paul has kindly agreed to write the Afterword.

So here is our one last chance to sail with Commodore John Grimes, who, while comfortably settled in the day cabin of his ship *Faraway Quest*, will narrate his latest dangerous adventure in time and space to you himself . . .

GRIMES AND THE GAIJIN DAIMYO

A. BERTRAM CHANDLER

Kitty Kelly, by this time, did not need to be told to make herself at home in Grimes' day cabin aboard *Faraway Quest*. The old ship had now been a long time, too long a time, on Elsinore while repair work on her inertial drive unit dragged on, and on, and on. Shortly after the *Quest*'s arrival at Port Fortinbras, Kitty had interviewed Grimes for Station Yorick and had persuaded him to tell one of his tall — but true — stories. The commodore, sitting at ease with pipe and glass to hand, had gone over well with Station Yorick's viewers. Soon he became a regular guest on Kitty's Korner, as Ms Kelly's programme was called.

'And still you're here,' she remarked brightly as she set up her recording apparatus, adjusting lenses and microphones.

'A blinding glimpse of the obvious!' he growled.

Still, he thought, watching the raven-haired, blue-eyed, creamy-skinned girl in the emerald green dress that left very little to the imagination, there were compensations, or at least one compensation — and she was it. He would feel a strong twinge of regret when, at long last, *Faraway Quest* was again spaceworthy and on her way.

'That's it,' she said finally, getting briefly to her feet and then subsiding into an easy chair, facing Grimes in his, stretching her long, shapely legs before her. 'Ready to roll. But pour me a drink first, Johnnie boy.'

Grimes had learned not to wince at this appellation. (After all, during a long and, according to some, misspent life he had often been called worse.) He went to his liquor cabinet, poured an Irish whiskey for Kitty and constructed a pink gin for himself.

'Here's mud in your eye!' she toasted, raising her glass.

'And in yours,' he replied.

After what was more of a gulp than a ladylike sip she switched on the audio-visual recorder. 'And now, Commodore,' she said, 'can you tell us, in non-technical language if possible, why your ship, the Rim Worlds Confederacy's survey vessel *Faraway Quest*, has been so long on Elsinore?'

'Because my inertial drive is on the blink,' he said.

'In what way?'

'First of all it was the governor. There were no spares available here. Too, the inertial drive unit is a very old one; it came with the ship — and she's no chicken! So there were no spares anywhere at all for this model. A new governor was fabricated in our workshops at Port Forlorn, on Lorn. It was shipped out here. Then my engineers had to turn down the shaft so that it would fit the bearings. The drive was tested — and the main thruster fell to pieces. And so on, and so on ...'

'I'm only a planet lubber,' she said, 'but it seems to me that much time and money would have been saved if your *Faraway Quest*'s inertial drive unit had been renewed, in its entirety, long before it got to the state that it's in now. After all, the Rim Worlds Navy, to which your *Quest* belongs, is not some penny-pinching star tramp outfit.'

Grimes laughed. 'Except in times of war, navies are as expert at penny-pinching as any commercial shipowner! And I often think that the only bastard who really wants to keep the old *Quest* running is me.'

'You have been in her a long time, haven't you, Commodore?'

'Too right. She started life as one of the Interstellar Transport Commission's Epsilon Class freighters. When she became obsolescent, by the Commission's rather high standards, she was put up for sale. I happened to be in the right place at the right time — or the wrong place at the wrong time! — on the world about which her lay-up orbit had been established. Very temporarily I had too much money in my bank account. So I bought her, changing her name from *Epsilon Scorpii* to *Sister Sue*. She became the flagship — and the only ship — of my own star tramp company, Far Traveller Couriers. She replaced a deep space pinnace that I'd been running single-handedly, called *Little Sister*. Well, I tramped around for quite a while, making not too bad a living. It helped that the Federation Survey Service, into which I'd sort of been dragged back with a reserve commission, organised the occasional lucrative charter for me. And then, while I was trying to weather a rather bad financial storm, I drifted out to the Rim Worlds. At that time Rim Runners, the Confederacy's merchant fleet, were going through a period of expansion. They were buying anything — anything! — that could clamber out of a gravity well and still remain reasonably airtight. They offered me a good price for the ship and offered, too, to absorb myself and my people with no loss of rank or seniority while guaranteeing repatriation to those who did not wish to become RimWorlders . . .'

'But you became a RimWorlder, Commodore.'

'Yes, Kitty. And the ship was renamed again — to *Rim Scorpion*. For a while I stayed in command of her. Then, at about the same time that I got a shore job, as Rim Runners' Astronautical Superintendent, the ship had another change of name, to *Faraway Quest*. She was converted into a survey ship. Every time that she was required for survey work — which wasn't all that often — Rim Runners would second me to the Navy, in which I held, and still hold, a reserve commission. After all, I know the ship and, too, held command in the Federation Survey Service before I became an owner-master.'

Kitty laughed sympathetically. 'We can understand very well how much this ship means to you, Commodore.' She laughed again. 'Now I'm talking off the top of my head — but what a pity it is that you can't modify your Mannschenn Drive unit, your Time-twister, to take the ship back into the Past so that she can be refitted with a suitable inertial drive at a pre-inflation price. After all, there was that first story you told me, about the Siege of Glenrowan, when a modified Mannschenn Drive was used to send you back to 1880, Earth Old Reckoning, so that you could change the course of history.'

'I didn't change the course of history,' said Grimes stiffly. 'I prevented the course of history from being changed.'

'Ensuring,' snapped Kitty, 'that my ancestor, the sainted Ned himself, was awarded a hemp necktie.'

'In any case,' Grimes told her, 'there was no *physical* Time travel. I was just sent back to occupy the mind of one of my own ancestors who was among those present at the siege.'

'And so even though your interstellar drive, your Mannschenn Drive, does odd things to the Space-Time Continuum, even though FTL flight is achieved by having the ship, as you told me once, going astern in Time while going ahead in Space, physical Time-travel is impossible? But isn't it true that most governments have forbidden research into possible techniques for using the Mannschenn Drive for real Time-travel, physical as well as psychological?

'Have *you* ever been involved in such research?' She grinned. 'After all, Commodore, there's not much that you haven't been involved in.'

Grimes made a major production of refilling and lighting his pipe. He replenished Kitty's glass, and then his own. He settled back in his chair.

He said, 'There was one rather odd business in which I played my part. In this very ship . . .'

She asked sweetly, 'And did you interfere as you did at Glenrowan, changing the course of history?'

'I did *not* change the course of history on either occasion. I kept history on the right tracks.'

'But have you ever thought that these are the wrong tracks, that we're living in an alternative universe that could never have come into being but for your interference?'

'I like being *me*,' he told her, 'and I'm pretty sure that you like being *you*. And we are *us* only because *our* history has made us what we are. In an alternative universe we might have no existence at all.'

She laughed. 'We're neither of us cut out to be philosophers, Commodore. Just do us all a favour and wear your storyteller's hat for the next hour or so.'

'You're the boss,' said Grimes. He got up, recharged glasses, refilled and lit his pipe, then settled down back in his chair. 'You want a story. Here it is.'

It was quite a few years ago, he said, more than just a few. It was when this ship was still called *Sister Sue* and I was both her master and her owner. It was during that period when the Federation Survey Service was still throwing charters my way like bones to a hungry dog. Very often I'd be carrying Survey Service cargoes from Earth to the various Survey Service bases throughout the Galaxy.

This was such an occasion. A cargo of *sake* and soy sauce and assorted pickles to Mikasa Base, the personnel of which was then, and probably still is, Japanese. Rather unusually I was loading not at Port Woomera in Australia but at the new spaceport just outside Yokohama in Japan. I still think that spaceports should be well away from heavily populated areas but the Japanese wanted one of their very own and they got it. Of course there were very strict regulations — inertial drive only, when landing or lifting off. No, repeat and underscore no, use of reaction drive when in the spaceport vicinity. But my inertial drive wasn't in the same mess that it's in now and I was reasonably sure that shouldn't need a squirt of superheated steam in an emergency.

It was my Mannschenn Drive that got me into trouble.

Well, even though Japan is a very small target compared to Australia, I found it without any trouble, and found the spaceport and set down in the middle of the triangle formed by the marker beacons. And then, as so often happens, especially when governmental agencies are involved, it was a case of hurry up and wait. The cargo wasn't ready for me. This pleased me rather than otherwise. The ship was on pay, which meant that myself and my officers were on pay. I treated myself to a couple or three weeks leave and booked on a JAL airship from Narita to Sydney, changing there to a Qantas flight to Alice Springs. My parents were pleased to see me. My mother was her charming, hospitable self and my father, as always, was both a good listener and a good talker — and could he talk on his pet subject, history! As I've told you before he was an author of historical romances and always prided himself on the thoroughness of his research.

He asked me about my impressions of Japan and told me that he had visited that country, doing research for one of his novels, a few weeks prior to my arrival. 'Yokohama,' he said, 'is handy for two shrines that you will find worth a visit. There's Admiral Togo's flagship *Mikasa*, in which he defeated the Russian Navy during the Russo-Japanese War, preserved for posterity as the English have preserved Nelson's *Victory*. And, on a hilltop on the Miura Peninsular, is the tomb of Will Adams and his Japanese lady wife . . .'

'Will Adams?' I asked. 'But that's not a Japanese name, surely? Why should a foreigner be honoured by having his grave regarded as a shrine?'

My father laughed. 'Oh, Will Adams was a *gaijin*, a foreigner, when he first set foot on Japanese soil. He was the first Englishman — although not the first European — in Japan. He was an Elizabethan — the first Elizabeth, of course — sea dog. He was pilot major — senior navigator — of a small fleet of Dutch ships that sailed to Japan in an attempt to get some share of the trade that had become the monopoly of the Portuguese. Only one ship, Adams' ship, reached Japan. Adams was sort of adopted by the Shogun, the real ruler — the Emperor was little more than a figurehead — and was made a Samurai, and then a Daimyo, which translates roughly to 'Baron'. He was known as the Anjin-sama — Pilot-lord — and as the Miura Anjin, after the estates on the Miura Peninsular that he was granted. He held the rank of admiral in the Japanese Navy . . .'

I said, 'He must have been quite a character . . .'

'He was,' agreed my father. 'I hope to use him in my next novel. He's been used before, of course, but I think that I shall be able to introduce a new twist. But if you find out anything interesting about him when you're back in Yokohama, let me know, will you?'

'I will,' I told him. 'I'll ask Yoshi Namakura what she knows about him.'

'Yoshi Namakura?' he asked.

'My Chief Mannschenn Drive Engineer. Oddly enough, in spite of her name, this is her first time in Japan. Her first time on Earth, too. I engaged her in Port Southern, on Austral, where her family have lived for generations. An attractive wench and clever with it. A list of letters after her name as long as my arm. Doctorates in mathematics and physics and the Odd Gods of the Galaxy alone know what else. And ardently Japanese. Knowing Yoshi I'm sure that she'll have been making the rounds of the local shrines, pouring libations and clapping her hands and bowing . . .'

'I have often wished, John,' said my mother, 'that you did not have such a casual attitude towards religion.'

'But I've always had the impression, Matilda,' I told her, 'that you're an agnostic.'

'I am. But I try to avoid giving offence.'

'Except when you want to,' muttered my father.

'That's different, George,' she snapped.

'I suppose that I was rather making fun of Yoshi,' I admitted. 'But she's such a *serious* person. But as far as Shinto is concerned I have far more respect for it than for many other faiths and I quite approve of the honouring of distinguished ancestors.'

'You'd better honour me,' said my father, 'or I'll come back and haunt you!'

And that was that.

The rest of my leave passed very pleasantly and it was with mixed emotions that, eventually, I made my way back to Yokohama. Mixed emotions? Yes. One's boyhood home holds a large place in one's affections but so does a ship, especially a ship that one both commands and owns.

It was early evening when I got back to the Yokohama spaceport. *Sister Sue* was the only ship on the ground. The loading gantries had been set up about her but were still idle. She stood there in black silhouette against the odd, lemon-yellow sky, a dark tower surrounded by an elaborate tracery of metal, looking like one of those intricate Japanese ideographs that you see on ornamental scrolls and screens.

Security was fairly tight and I had to identify myself to the spaceport gatekeeper and then, again, to the guard on duty at the foot of the ramp. Port Regulations required that I employ him so I was pleased to find that he was taking his job seriously. In any case the charters, the Survey Service, would be picking up the bill for his wages. Once I was in the airlock I looked at the indicator screen to see who was aboard. The Third Officer was the shipkeeper. Normally, especially in a rather exotic port such as this, he would have been sulking in solitary state, feeling very hard done by. But, it seemed, he was not alone. Neither the Chief Mannschenn Drive Engineer nor the Communications Officer was off painting the town red. But surely Yoshi would have made friends in Yokohama or, even, discovered distant relatives. Perhaps, I thought, she was entertaining some such or one such on board.

I took the elevator up from the airlock to my quarters. On its way it passed the Mannschenn Drive compartment. And the Drive was running — the oscillating whine that it made whilst operational was unmistakable. Perhaps, I thought, Yoshi was recalibrating the controls, a job that can be done only when the ship is at rest on a planetary surface. Recalibration should not be carried out without the permission of the Master. But so what? Billy Williams, my Chief Officer, had the authority to issue such permission during my absence.

But I was uneasy nonetheless.

I stopped the elevator then went down again to the Mannschenn Drive compartment. The door into it was both shut and locked. I could hear the whine of the machinery inside and, very faintly, the sound of voices. I rapped on the door. And again, more loudly. *They must be deaf in there*, I thought.

In my pocket was my keyring and on it, among others, was *my* key, the master key that would give me access to any compartment in the ship. I took it out, fitted its flat surface into the recess designed for its reception.

The door slid open, making a sharp clicking sound as it did so. One of the two men intently watching the display in the screen that had been set up alongside the complication of slowly rotating, ever-precessing flywheels — had the Drive been working at full capacity it would have been suicidal to have looked directly at it — turned his head and grumbled, 'Come in, come in, whoever you are. This is Liberty Hall. You can spit on the mat and call the cat a bastard.' Then he saw who it was and muttered, 'Sorry, sir. We weren't expecting you back just yet.'

It was the Third Officer and with him was the electronic communications officer. I glared at the two young men and they looked back at me. They were more than a little scared. And I'd give the puppies something to be scared about.

'Where is Ms Namakura?' I demanded. 'What are the pair of you doing in the Mannschenn Drive room, running a machine that only qualified personnel are supposed to touch? The Odd Gods of the Galaxy alone know what damage you'll do with your tinkerings!'

'She . . . she *was* here, sir,' stammered the Third.

'Is she in her quarters? Get her back down here. *At once.*'

'She . . . she's not there . . .' stammered the Third.

'She's not *now* . . .' said Sparks.

'Are you mad?' I almost yelled, glaring at them. Somehow in the light that was coming from the screen the skin of their faces had an odd yellowish tinge and their eyes a peculiar slant to them. I remembered then that, like Yoshi Namakura, they both had Japanese blood, although, unlike hers, theirs was much diluted and their names were European. But the three of them, spaceman officer, communications officer, and Mannschenn Drive engineer, had always been as thick as thieves. There were those who suggested that they had a *ménage a trois* going. Perhaps they had, but what of it? A ship is not a Sunday School outing.

'Look at the screen, sir,' said Sparks.

I looked. The picture was that of the poop of some sort of ancient sailing vessel, a galleon, a small one, at sea. In the background were five other ships of the same type, on parallel courses.

'So you got some new spools for the playmaster,' I said. 'But what's a playmaster doing here? Its proper place is in the wardroom.'

'This is not a playmaster, sir, although it's adapted from one. Running in conjunction with the Drive it gives a picture of the Past.'

I remembered that conversation with my father. 'And now I suppose you'll try to tell me that you're picking up coverage of Will Adams' voyage to Japan.' I laughed. 'As I was told the story, only one of those Dutch ships got here.'

'Those are not Dutch ships, sir,' said Sparks. 'Look!'

He did something to the controls under the screen, zoomed into that poop deck in the foreground. There was an almost modern-looking binnacle and there was a large wheel with one man, clad only in baggy trousers, at it, steering the ship. He was obviously an Asiatic. Japanese? Chinese? But that wheel . . . It looked wrong. Just *when* had the wheel replaced the tiller? I was pretty sure that it had been well after Will Adams' time.

A man and a woman came into view — he a bearded European, tall, in a white shirt with ballooning sleeves, white trousers that flapped about his legs. Instead of a belt he wore a wide sash; thrust into it on one side was a sheathed sword, on the other a big, flintlock pistol. The woman was in what I thought of as traditional Japanese finery, with elaborately upswept hair. I recognised her, although I was more used to seeing her in uniform.

They were talking, this man and woman. What a pity it was that there was no sound — and lip reading is not one of my accomplishments. They paced slowly back and forth. Then the man sat on one of the two bronze cannons mounted on the poop and Yoshi subsided gracefully onto the wooden deck, leaning back against his legs.

'So far,' Sparks told me, 'this is the furthest into the future that we can get a clear picture. But the ones of the finish of the voyage are getting clearer all the time ...'

'The furthest into the *future*?' I asked, bewildered.

'Perhaps I didn't make myself clear, sir. What I meant was the future as reckoned from the start of the voyage ...'

'*What* voyage?'

Sparks fiddled with the controls. He got a clear picture of a seaport, a Japanese seaport, with the six galleons looking out of place among the smaller craft, with the wharf crowded with people, with armoured Samurai wielding long staffs to clear the way for those embarking aboard the ships, the tall European, attired now as a Japanese nobleman, his lady (*my* Chief Mannschenn Drive Engineer), the armoured Samurai of his personal guard ...

And the ships cast off and their unfurled sails filled and the gaily coloured streamers of bunting (or of silk?) fluttered from their mastheads and orange flame and white smoke gushed from their gunports as a salute was fired to the Emperor or the Shogun or whoever it was who had come to see them off.

I thought again what a pity it was that there was no sound.

'And now,' said Sparks, 'the finish of the voyage ...'

The picture was dim, distorted, the perspective all wrong, the colours sagging down the spectrum. But I recognised that coastline, that entrance to one of the world's — Earth's, I mean — finest harbours, with the sheer cliffs of the North Head and the less regular rock formations on the south side. The ships, the galleons, were standing in with a fair wind, guided by one of the small pinnaces that had carried out a preliminary survey.

'It's clearer than it was the last time we tried,' said the Third Officer. 'Do you realise what that means?'

He sounded frightened.

So he was frightened and I was both puzzled and angry.

'Just what the hell is going on here?' I demanded.

There were swivel chairs in the Mannschenn Drive room and we sat in them, turning them so that we did not have to look at those ever-recessing rotors or the screen with its disturbing pictures. It was heavy work at first trying to drag the story out of them but, at last, the dam broke. Then it was hard for me to get a word in edgewise, to ask the occasional question, to try to get clarification of various points.

It was Yoshi, of course, who had made the modifications to the Mannschenn Drive unit. I suspect that she had been toying with such an idea for quite some time but, until her visit to the home of her ancestors, had lacked a strong motivation. Shortly after *Sister Sue*'s arrival at Yokohama spaceport she had made the pilgrimage to Will Adams' burial place, had made Shinto obeisance at the shrine. The story of Adams fascinated her. The man was among those who, with only the slightest nudge, could have changed history. And why should not she, Yoshi Namakura, supply that nudge?

She had Sparks and the Third Officer eating out of her hand. They would help her. Although they did not share her knowledge of the workings of the Mannschenn Drive they could be trusted to follow her instructions and to monitor her progress. They were to snatch her back to her own Time should things go wrong. (But, as they were beginning to realise, *right* for her could be *wrong* for very many people, including themselves. People face death — they're doing it all the time — but how do they face the utter extinction of never having been at all?)

History is full of *Ifs*. *If* Napoleon had accepted the American inventor Fulton's offer to build him steam-driven warships ... (imagine a squadron of steam frigates, wearing the French flag, at Trafalgar!). *If* Pickett's charge at Gettysburg had been successful, and the Confederacy had won the War Between The States ... *If* that special train had been derailed, as intended, by Ned Kelly's freedom fighters at Glenrowan ...

And *if* Will Adams, the Anjin-sama, had been allowed to build European-style ships — with improvements, the Japanese excel at improving things — armed with cannons, officered by Samurai ... *If* an expedition under the command of the Anjin-sama, the master navigator, himself had pushed south on a voyage of exploration ...

And *if*, I thought, on the some yet-to-become established Time Track he had pushed south, reaching Australia, founding a colony ... history might be, would be changed on a grand scale. With the resulting population shifts, with the wars that didn't happen in *our* history books, with inventions made before their time or not made at all, many of us might never have been born. I'm an Australian, as you know. Would I, could I have happened in an Australia that had been a Japanese colony founded in the Seventeenth Century?

I demanded, 'Why don't you bring her back? Why don't you snatch her back to our here and now from a time before she's had a chance to influence Will Adams and his sponsors?'

Sparks said, 'We've tried, sir. But she told us to pull her back only if things went wrong. She must be carrying some device that will keep her where and when she is, no matter what *we* do, as long as things are going to *her* satisfaction.'

'Then somebody,' I said, 'will have to go back to a time before the fleet sets sail to throw a spanner in the works ...'

'I'll go, sir,' said the Third bravely. 'Sparks has to stay here to operate the controls.'

'I'll go,' I said, not feeling at all brave. Oh, I did not doubt the Third Officer's courage but, after all, he had been under Yoshi's influence and, too, had Japanese blood himself. (Was it my imagination or had he been looking more and more Japanese as we had been talking? Was it proof that *our* Time Line was fading out?)

'But ...' objected both young men, yet I thought that I could detect a note of relief in their voices.

'Wait here,' I told them. 'Don't touch anything till I get back.'

In my quarters I disguised myself as well as I could — by putting on a rather elaborately embroidered dressing gown over my shirt and trousers. From the ship's arms locker I took a stungun and a laser pistol, checking each to see that it was fully charged. I stuck both weapons in my dressing gown sash. I glanced in the mirror. I didn't look Japanese. I looked like a middle-aged shipmaster of European origin clad in a dressing gown hung around with incongruous weaponry. But I hoped that Sparks would be able to make me arrive at night — and the lighting in and around seaports wasn't all that good in those days. With any luck at all I should be able to do what I knew, with increasing certainty, I had to do, undetected.

I returned to the Mannschenn Drive room.

Sparks and the Third stared at me in some amazement. I ignored this. I told Sparks what I wanted and he fiddled with the controls of the monitor screen, at last got what I wanted. Despite the midnight darkness it was quite a clear picture, the galleons, with their lofty masts, the furled sails glimmering palely on their spars, were alongside in the Japanese seaport. There were a few, a very few, lights aboard them. Ashore watchfires, around which moved dark figures. What little light there was threw glimmering reflections from polished spearheads.

'That will do,' I said. 'The night before sailing day. All stores — including powder — aboard. All hands ashore enjoying a last night in the arms of their lady loves . . .'

'What are you going to *do*, sir?' almost wailed Sparks.

'Never mind. I'm just going to do it. Or try to do it. Just get me back there, not too close to any of the sentries.'

'I think I can manage that, sir. I put Yoshi down by the side of the road where the Anjin-sama was taking his morning ride, unaccompanied. Do you see that circle painted on the deck? Just stand in it. Look at the rotors.'

I did as he directed, gave him last instructions. 'As soon as I've shunted history back onto its right track, use the recovery procedure. For Ms Yamakura as well as for myself. It should work on her this time. Things will have gone very badly wrong — from her viewpoint.'

I looked at those blasted, precessing rotors. They seemed to be dragging me into some dark chasm that had opened in the Space-Time continuum. And their motion was subtly . . . *wrong*. Their precession was not confined to the fourth dimension, somehow involved more dimensions than merely four.

And then the night air was cold on my face. A light drizzle was falling. I was standing in a puddle that chilled my feet in their light shoes. I could smell the smoke of the watchfires and something spicy cooking over one of them. I was sorry that in these circumstances I could not sample whatever it was. Somewhere a stringed musical instrument was plaintively *plinking* away. The nearest group of sentries were talking in quite loud voices and laughing. I wondered what the joke was.

I pulled the stungun out of my dressing gown sash, walked as quietly as possible towards the ships. Towards the one that was third in line from the head of the wharf; she had fewer lights aboard her than did the others and that at her gangway was almost out. The gangway, a slatted, wooden ramp, rattled slightly as I set foot on it. I froze. But the other gangways were rattling too as the ships stirred in the slight swell that was coming in from seaward.

At the head of the gangway was a sentry. He was standing there, leaning on the bulwark, more than half asleep. After a brief buzz from my stungun he was wholly asleep but did not fall, propped up as he was.

I wished that I'd been able to study constructional details of the ships of this period. The powder magazine would be, I thought, amidships, well below decks. But aft there should be a storeroom, the lazarette, with flammables of various kinds — canvas and cordage and barrels of tar and oil. So I made my way towards the stern. I let myself into the officers' quarters in the sterncastle, hoping that none of them would be spending this last night aboard.

I used my laser pistol, at a very low setting, as a torch. At last I found what I was looking for, two decks down. A small hatch. I lifted it, looked down into what seemed to be the bo's'n's store. There were coils of rope, bolts of canvas. There were barrels and there was the smell of tar. I aimed the pistol at one of the tar barrels, adjusted the beam. A viscous black fluid spilled out, igniting as it did so. The fire that I'd started needed no further help from me. I hoped that I'd be able to get out and clear before it reached the magazine.

I scampered up the ladders, pursued by the acrid stench of burning. At the head of the gangway the sentry was still unconscious. I slung him over my shoulder in a fireman's carry — he was only a small man, luckily — and got him away from immediate danger. After all, I bore no grudge against him. I bore no grudge against anybody. I was just trying to save my — *our* — universe. And my own skin.

That fire was spreading fast. The big windows of the stern gallery were glowing ruddily and the flames were roaring, louder and louder. There was bawling and shouting among the sentries on the wharf, a great deal of running around. I did my best to impersonate a chicken with its head cut off, reasoning that if I joined the general panic I might escape notice. Then I found cover in a narrow alley between two warehouses, stood and watched. The galleon was well ablaze by now, with lines of fire running up her rigging, spreading to the furled canvas on her spars. Somebody had organised a bucket party but by this time it was utterly ineffectual. There was only one thing to do — to get the remaining ships away and out from the wharf before the first vessel's magazine went up. But there was nobody there to do it; those sentries must all have been soldiers, not seamen.

The fire reached the magazine.

Oh, I've seen, more than once, the sort of Big Bang that can be produced by modern weaponry — but that particular Big Bang still, after all these years, persists in my memory ... The strangely slow flare of orange flame and a somehow leisurely boom of man-made thunder ... The blazing fragments scattered in all directions and other fragments, not yet burning, black in silhouette against dreadful, ruddy light ... And the fires exploding in the rigging and on the decks of the other five ships — and on the roof of the warehouse beside which I was standing.

Somebody was addressing me urgently in Japanese. It was a tall, kimono-clad man, with pistols as well as a sheathed Samurai sword thrust into his sash. He was tall, as I have said, and bearded, and the language that he was using did not sound right from his lips. There was a kimono-clad woman with him. She stared at me wide-eyed.

'Captain!' she gasped. 'What are *you* doing here?' What have you *done?*'

'What have *you* been doing, Yoshi-san?' I demanded.

Adams — it could have been none other — had one of his pistols out, was pointing it at me.

'Who is this,' he asked, 'that you know him? Some Spanish dog sent to frustrate me? Who are you, man, and who employs you? Should you make truthful answer I might spare your life.'

And then, at the other end of the timeline, Sparks did what he should have done minutes before and I was standing in *Sister Sue*'s Mannschenn Drive room, with holes burned by flying sparks in my dressing gown, my face smoke-blackened. I moved out of the circle to look at the screen. Nothing could save those ships now. As I watched two of the others exploded.

I heard the Third say to Sparks, 'What about Yoshi?' and Sparks reply, 'I'm trying.'

And he got her.

She sprawled lifeless on the deck, in a pool of her own blood. A dagger was in her right hand. And one of those scraps of useless knowledge that one accumulates floated into my mind. Japanese ladies, wiping out some real or fancied disgrace, were not expected to carry out ritual self-disembowelment.

A mere throat-cutting would suffice.

But it wasn't all over yet. The two young men who had been Yoshi's accomplices were taking her death very badly. Before I could stop him Sparks had snatched the laser pistol from my sash. And he took his revenge. Oh, yes, Kitty, I know that I'm still here, but he took his revenge. He turned the destructive beam of the weapon onto the machine that had sent his lady back into the Past, to when and where she had met her death. He paid particular attention to the controls that she had installed. And I did not stop him. I did not try to stop him. It was better that Yoshi's knowledge died with her. The Present may be bad enough, but tampering with the Past would almost certainly make it worse, not better. The mere fact that we are here and now is proof that on *this* Time Track things have been working out not too badly.

'Having known a few Australians, including yourself,' said Kitty, 'I still think that a Japonified Australia might have been an improvement.'

'You're entitled to your opinion,' said Grimes stiffly.

AFTERWORD BY PAUL COLLINS

The road to publishing 'Grimes and the Gaijin Daimyo' has been long and circuitous. The journey started in 1982 or thereabouts and the winding path I'll describe below.

'Jack' Chandler was among a clique of well-known Australian authors who supported me in my early publishing days. We even collaborated, this group and me, on (an as yet unpublished) novel called *The Morgan Pattern*. I published the first edition of the last Grimes novel, *The Wild Ones*; and six of Jack's stories, and bought a seventh, the one you've just read. Whatever anthology I had planned never eventuated, and this particular story was filed away 'for later use'.

Skip the intervening years till about a year ago. A diehard Chandler fan called David Kelleher emailed me asking for miscellaneous Chandler material. I knew I had a manuscript 'somewhere', and after going to David's site (www.bertramchandler.com) I decided I should make an effort and find that MS and send it to him. I had no idea that the story in question hadn't been published overseas, nor that no copy other than mine existed. Meanwhile another fan, Evan Ladouceur, asked me for Chandler paraphernalia. I sent both David and Evan a copy of 'Grimes and the Gaijin Daimyo'. I was informed that it was a rare find, an unpublished Chandler story. Yet another fan, Steve Davidson (www.rimworlds.com), began writing, and I started to realise 'the story' had to be published.

I believe David listed 'Grimes and the Gaijin Daimyo' on his site as being unpublished. Soon enough, Baen Books discovered its existence and an editor asked David for a copy because they were publishing a Kitty Kelly series e-book. At this point David asked for permission to send the story.

I thought long and hard and finally figured, no, I wanted this story's first appearance to be here in Australia, and definitely in print form, not e-book form. The trouble was, I knew I had a contract *somewhere*, but did I want to search through my garage for it? And surely the twenty-six-year-old contract had expired by now. Luckily, neither David nor Evan, the only two people other than me on the planet who had copies of the story, were going to show the story to anyone without my consent.

I resisted all further calls for the story, and believe me, there were a few.

After the Baen Books enquiry it struck me that Jack Dann was editing *Dreaming Again.* A perfect spot for the final Grimes story had I been thinking on my feet — but the anthology was closed. With nothing to lose, I emailed Jack asking him if he'd like to read the manuscript. It's a carbon copy (faded and in parts almost illegible) and HarperCollins would have to get it keyed in, so I wasn't too hopeful.

Jack loved the story. But the road up ahead became murky. Joshua Bilmes, Chandler's US agent at JABerwocky Literary Agency, informed us that Susan Chandler, Jack's widow, who was signatory on his estate, had died recently. The Chandler estate was now in the hands of the Public Trustee NSW. Jack promptly wrote to Kim Schriever asking for permission to publish the story, and I subsequently received a letter asking for a copy of my contract.

To save a whole lot of bother on all fronts, I simply waived any rights I might have had to the story — my intention all along. And had not the Public Trustee's office been so efficient, 'Grimes and the Gaijin Daimyo' would still be in my filing cabinet in the garage, and bar a mention on David Kelleher's site, a piece of unknown Chandler history.

I hope you enjoyed the ride.

— *Paul Collins*

PAUL COLLINS has had over a hundred and twenty books published. He is best known for his fantasy and science fiction titles: The Jelindel Chronicles (*Dragonlinks, Dragonfang, Dragonsight* and *Wardragon*) and The Quentaris Chronicles (*Swords of Quentaris, Slaves of Quentaris, Dragonlords of Quentaris, Princess of Shadows, The Forgotten Prince, Vampires of Quentaris* and *The Spell of Undoing*). His trilogy The Earthborn Wars (*The Earthborn, The Skyborn* and *The Hiveborn*) was published in the United States. He has edited a dozen anthologies, including *Metaworlds, Dream Weavers, Trust Me!*, the Shivers series of children's horror novels, *SF aus Australien* for Wilhelm Goldmann Verlag in Germany, and *The Melbourne University Press Encyclopaedia of Australian Science Fiction and Fantasy* (with Sean McMullen and Steven Paulsen). He is currently collaborating with Danny Willis on a trilogy: *The World of Grrym.*

He has been short-listed for many awards for his fiction, and has won the inaugural Peter McNamara, Aurealis, and William Atheling awards. He is also the publisher at Ford Street Publishing, an imprint of Hybrid Publishers.

In the edgy, contemporary, in-your-face story that follows, Collins extrapolates the possibilities of love, sex, adultery, and death in virtual worlds such as *Second Life* . . .

LURE

PAUL COLLINS

The metaverse had become a minefield.

The dossier in my hands made me want to puke. I popped a dozen 'ludes', the kind that fool you into thinking everything's okay. The main question before me was whether or not it's permissible by law to kill an avatar — a digital manifestation — and if not, can perpetrators be tried for murder?

Perhaps the pills unfogged my mind. I decided it was an indictable offence. I mentally ticked off key points leading to my conclusion.

Legislation was passed after a lovelorn celeb called Elvirat suicided because his toygirl avatar, blitzed by a beta-virus, deconstructed block by digital block before his helpless eyes.

Since then, an estimated 200 million avatars had 'died' and 20,000 creators with vitamin-D deficiencies had self-destructed. The Bureau was called in but so far the FFC had come up with zilch. No 'body', no DNA. All they could do was interview witnesses and get their meat-space contact details.

I studied the dossier for the fifteenth time since it'd been dumped on my desk. How do you catch someone who can be someplace deep in Russia killing off avatars, someone whose digital creation left a bigger footprint on the real world than their meat-space makers did? Frankly, the whole thing gave me a headache.

Not that I could talk. My own life was circling the drain, or is that the toilet? To make ends meet I'd written three crime novels whose royalties made a slight dent in the rent and scored me seats at *Sisters of Crime* conferences.

That's me, a sister of crime. Only the person I aspired to be was something else . . .

Anok Helstrom. Paper Goddess. Or just goddess, the kind that left you dripping. Rumour had it she'd once sold her shopping list to *InStyle* webzine. When her latest book appeared, the world stopped.

And I adored her. We'd sat in rooms together, breathed the same air. Problem was, she didn't know I existed.

Then one day our feet touched under the table. Her stilettoed boot tapped mine as she shared thoughts with some A-list arsehole. I almost pulled my foot away, but didn't. The merest touch from the object of my obsession was like tantric sex.

A week went by. I could think of nothing but that tapping on my foot, like some zit-faced adolescent. Make that *stupid* zit-faced adolescent. For Christ's sake, she was married. Had two kids. Happy, for all I knew.

Like me.

So I emailed her. I figured what the heck, if she didn't reply it didn't matter. I typed, deleted, typed some more, deleted some more. Started all over.

* * *

Hey Anok

Just touching base. Putting together a crime anthology, titled: *Dark Times & Dark Crimes*. The malaise of the metaverse. If you're interested, what about meeting up next time you're in town?

Yours

Angel Hart

I had no intention of putting together such an anthology. And less hope of her wanting to be in it. But you don't catch a fish without bait. I clicked SEND and a truckload of tension purged itself from my shoulders.

And that's how it started.

She replied the same day.

Dear Angel

How lovely of you to think of me. I'm off to London, back in a week. I'll be in Melbourne the 25th to the 30th. Can we play catch-up then?

Anok

Catch-up. The word made me salivate. All over. I hit reply and pinned her down to date, time, place. Must be the detective in me.

And what a week that was. Hey, back up and defrag! I'm talking the week *before* we met. Emails sizzled to and fro.

Hey Anok

You'll never guess what happened last night at work. Detected an unauthorised datastream on one of the private medical channels we scan. Discovered some dude chatting up a girl in a singles bar, having answered an ad.

Should have disconnected them and ran a viral interloper. That's my job. But I'm on a bigger case right now and the small stuff slips through. Anyway, I dialled for sensory input. And suddenly I was 'there', freeloading on the orgasmic ocean till they'd exhausted themselves. Bliss. So what do you think, am I perverted?

* * *

She laughed. Said my hard-drive was in over-drive.

I met her in a café she'd suggested. In meat-space, not the metaverse, where most 'first-dates' usually happen. She was hidden at a corner table, camouflaged in shades and hat. She was line-editing a manuscript.

'Don't know how you can work in here,' I said, sitting down, moving straight into my agenda of getting her out of there. God was on my side for once. The hubbub in the café intensified.

She wrapped her manicured satin-tipped fingers around my hand. Electricity sizzled through me. 'What seems like chaos,' she said, 'is actually keeping me in a necessary state. I go to cafés when I'm not focusing well and wham, suddenly I'm concentrating ten times harder just to blank out all the noise.'

Maybe she'd rehearsed that. No matter. I'd rehearsed mine, too. 'It's crowded in here,' I said. And, thank you God, it was. 'How about we go someplace quieter?'

She looked at me, head tilting sideways in what, disbelief? The pressure on my hand loosened and she took her hand away. My heart skipped a beat.

'Okay,' she said. 'Where did you have in mind?'

I stood before she could change her mind. I'd already made a reservation at a nearby motel. If I'd been more confident I'd have paid up front and got the discount.

'Oh, I have to pay for my cappuccino,' she said, slightly confused. This was fast-tracking beyond her control.

'I'll get it.' I paid at the counter while she gathered her stuff. The motel I'd found was only a block away.

Within minutes I was shutting the door of our room behind us. After that, well, I don't remember much for the next couple of hours. I do remember getting out of the shower and Anok saying, 'I hope you're not leading me on.' My nipples hardened as I stood there. I think that answered her question.

I emailed her the moment I arrived back at the Bureau. Within the hour she had replied from her laptop:

* * *

Hello darling

I can still feel your hand and mouth prints on my skin.

I think of seeing you and being in your arms and my thinking rationally stops right there. It's like my mind can't go past that moment. It's so necessary and so delicious. I truly can't wait to see you again. That thrilling, dangerous encounter scared me in retrospect, but it's an electric memory. I was so terrified of having crossed the Rubicon and started to babble and you just took a couple of strides and kissed me and all doubts went up in flames. I would love to be lying on your naked chest having this conversation but I have to settle for a cyber connection. You have to tell me more about our skin being virtual to virtual. I'm such a Luddite!

What a sweet diversion into a parallel world you are. A dangerous and intoxicating imagining ... You once joked about being hard-wired into me as if I'm a hot spot you can connect to — I hope you found it as electrifying and shocking as did I.

Next time?

Yours

A xx

We saw one another every time she came to Melbourne over the next year. But the last time we were almost caught. Mutual friends saw us go into her motel room. Nothing odd about that, really, but it unsettled Anok. If her husband found out ... she had her boys to think about ... all the standard doubts shared by adulterers the world over. To give up security for the unknown is a risk many don't wish to take.

During this time an epidemic was gaining momentum. Another 8,000 people worldwide suicided at the loss of their beloved avatars. Every major government in the world bankrolled investigations into catching the creator of the virus.

Meanwhile a shady character by the name of Jerry Anderson took avatar construction up another notch. His avatars aren't constructed — you *are* them. Wireless, too — key in your biorhythm index to your reality space and you're there. Actually are you them or are they you? They're better than human for they never get tired and they cope with rejection. Configure yourself — your avatar — to be the woman or man that all others want, then step into the metaverse and have fun . . .

The interslick tech is nothing special to look at, just a neckband and headband of material that feels cold and wet when you put them on. I had a loan of a prototype set of series #2. No way could I ever be able to afford one on a detective inspector's wage. Jerry Anderson was a scumbag who mainly dealt in hardcore dildonics until I'd busted him a year before. He'd created virtual reality snuff flicks like *Private Predator* and embedded them with neural-induced hypnotherapy. An REM-triggered response that reacted with the player's amygdala creating a neural feedback on the victim's brain like an immense emotional shock. Basically, it killed men who viewed his sordid flicks. To say actors committed bestial acts of depravity in those hack and slash flicks would be an understatement. I let Anderson off with a caution and a pat on the back. He was ridding the world of some choice acts. The killings stopped and the Bureau tucked it all away in the Cold Case file.

Anderson finally repaid me. Whoever was killing off avatars by the cartload was actually destroying his stock and trade. The virus was now sweeping the city's avatars and people were pulling out in droves. Hundreds of customers had opted out of reality, too, leading to scathing media attacks on SpaceScape Productions. Anderson's business was going bust fast. He wanted the hacker caught and quick. Hence the prototype of his new series.

'Have fun, Angel,' Jerry said with a smirk. He never did get it, the loser.

I studied the package and set up a plan to bring down the Avatar Butcher, as the media had so garishly labelled him.

I emailed Anok with an idea to assuage her fears of our affair being made public. We'd set up in Jerry Anderson's frontier town, Lovago, already the world's largest alternative universe. Every brand name corporation from Nike through to Ford and Hooters had set up shop there — a metropolis of cash-driven nirvana. It was bandied about that the government now made more tax dollars from the metaverse than it did in meat-space. And that's in spite of only receiving an estimated ten per cent of its dues. Would I be a cynic to say it was no wonder the governments wanted to stop this mass serial killer from continuing his or her spree? It was costing them big time.

Using the new interslicks we'd simply be superior to our neighbours, but it'd only appear as though we were slumming rich dudes with huge graphics cards. With pseudonyms we could live our parallel lives in anonymity and without fear of getting caught providing we were careful. No, I didn't tell Anok about my ulterior reason for continuing our affair in Lovago. I tried to. I hinted of dark things beyond my control that might make her mad. I told her I'd never seen her seething, that it would be a sight to behold.

Her reply marginally eased my conscience:

Hmmm … me when I'm mad. Not a pretty sight, I suspect. It's only in books and movies that ugliness is supposed to look attractive. I hate feeling angry, and I feel ugly and corroded. I can't imagine you will ever see that side of me. Especially given that in a funny (not amusing but quirky) way our lives keep us apart from that. We don't have enough time to waste being mad. Any doubts will be seriously soothed, skin to skin, avatar to avatar. It makes no difference — I can't wait to be in your arms.

I love u

A xx

And that's how the love-nest came to be. I downloaded the software — the Bureau has the latest high-volume graphics channels on the market, and terabytes of volatile memory to assimilate tactile stimulation inputs from one's partner.

All the while I marvelled at Anderson's invention. He was set to become a demigod and bring down governments. No one need ever leave their house and interact with others again — a social inertia if ever there was one. It'd be a lot safer in the sex sector. One never knows what you might pick up if more than electrons and photons flow between bodies. And Anderson's avatars were more human cells than avatar blocks — viral-proof.

I bought a wad of andos — virtual currency that doesn't exist in meat-space. At the going rate, 200 ando dollars equalled one 'real' dollar.

Anok and I soon moved into a condo. Whenever she was touring we stayed the night in Lovago, had breakfast, went to work. At nights I'd call out the proverbial, 'Hi, Honey, I'm home.' It was a cry that became ritual. We rarely ventured out into the city, colourful though it was with its frilly-maned dragons with Bambi eyes, Gandalf-inspired wizards, hissing vampires and other loops. People who construct this virtual stuff are high on image quality but low on imagination.

Lovago was just our little niche of the metaverse in which we were a happily married couple. Ostensibly, that is. Like the bug-chasers of yesteryear before a cure for AIDS was discovered, I laid Anok and me out like virtual bait.

Things started unravelling when I found a blonde hair in the shower plughole. My first thought was that it was a leftover from the previous tenants. But we'd been here a month now, and no way could that hair have remained stuck there. The detective in me took over briefly. A computer-generated DNA analysis on the follicle cells would tell me exactly which avatar the hair belonged to. I figured I was being paranoid and let it drop. You do things like that when you're in love. I didn't want to know if she was having an affair in our home. I knew I could never compete with her husband — but another woman? I sent her an email about this part of our relationship and in passing said I hoped to have her hooked for a long time to which she replied:

Hooked and landed. As for Frank, he's a social cripple and puts everyone's back up, curdling them like month-old milk. There are many times when he feels like a big anvil around my neck, a dragging weight that slows me and makes everything heavier and harder. But I can't be bothered dwelling on it, because he is never going to change and if I give him a blast about it, he'll sink into a morass of despair and go lie on his bed in funereal gloom. That might be worse than the slackness.

See you tonight, my love.

A xxoo

Till I received that email I'd kept the blonde hair in an airtight crime scene bag. I flushed it, bag and all, down the waste disposal.

A week passed and we continued on as before. We craved one another so much that my meat-space partner became worried that I was working too much. Only by staying away from home could I visit Anok at our condo. For her part, she accepted more and more interstate and international bookings. We were pretty much in Lovago 24/7.

But doubt rides hard when spurred. I searched our condo with a thoroughness best reserved for work. I found Cherry Blossom lipstick — Anok always wore PlumVamp. I found more blonde hairs in her hairbrush. And the final proof of her adultery was on the phone. I hit re-dial. A man's voicemail answered. 'Hey babe, Hans here.' I didn't really listen to the message, but it was personal, as though only Anok had his number. I know he said, 'Can't wait to catch up at the condo.' It appeared she was having at least two affairs — one male, one female.

Can someone be a double-adulterer? Who was I to condemn Anok for cheating on me when both she and I were cheating on our partners? I wrestled with the conundrum. Were our avatars really cheating? If you watched a movie about adultery did you partake of it yourself? If your avatar committed adultery, was that any worse for you than watching a movie about it? I'd put men away for years for enjoying the thrill of date-rapes and murders in virtual realities. But it was the avatars doing the pillaging, not those enjoying the experience. Can adultery, or rape, even, exist in the metaverse? Cyber-bullying was the basis for today's harsh virtual legislations. But was the whole concept basically flawed? The foundation of everything I'd ever worked towards was suddenly cracking up.

One part of me wanted to sell up, clear out. Cut Anok and her lover/s out of the picture forever. Another part of me wanted my dream to last for however long it could, warts and all. Then I realised all this stuff wasn't about me. It was about the job. I was on stake-out duty. Business first, pleasure second. It wasn't until I had this figured out that I knew I was getting somewhere with the case.

So I let it rest. Nonetheless, doubt gnawed away at me like a cancer.

Anok and I met in meat-space during the Canberra Literary Festival. Real life sex is marginally better than the metaverse variety. You can't beat the smell of sex, and that is one sense the metaverse hasn't replicated yet: smell. Anderson boasted to me that he was within a whisker of solving *that* problem.

The moment I arrived back at the office I went straight 'home'. My suspicions that Anok had been cheating on me were allayed after our weekend encounter. But a nagging thought drove me to give the condo a thorough check.

I wasn't really surprised when I found a man's handkerchief with an H embroidered on it in the bed. It confirmed a suspicion that I'd been harbouring for a week. Back at the office, I phoned Anok via a secure line on her cell. It was late. But it was serious. I told her the whole sordid duplicitous story.

The next night we had a row at the condo.

'So what do you call this?' I demanded, throwing the lipstick, brush and the handkerchief on the bed. 'And who's Hans?'

'Angel … don't do this. I don't know how these things got here. They're not mine. Of course they're not.' She looked about the room. 'Maybe Frank —' but the words died on her mouth. No way could Frank navigate the metaverse. His skills lay strictly out at sea and his own dark space.

'Get out, Anok,' I said. 'I'm selling the place.'

She nodded slowly, as though understanding. 'Okay, Angel. Do what you have to do. You always do.'

She snatched her bag and with head bowed she went to the door. She paused there, and I had hoped to see her turn and at least acknowledge me. But she didn't. The door opened, and that was that.

I put in two more visits before everything fell neatly into place.

There was a knock on the door. It was the security guard. She was cutting edge perfection in a uniform so neatly ironed the creases looked sharp as razorblades. An obsessive-compulsive then. A lean woman, she was quite attractive in a harsh way. Something predatory in her manner reminded me of a dozen psychos I'd put away over the years. I buzzed with adrenalin.

'Hi,' she said. 'I'm Sheila. Security. I heard you guys arguing the other night.' She winced with heartfelt commiseration. 'Saw the "For Sale" sign up.' She looked beyond me, into the lounge room. 'Thought I'd pop over.' Then hopefully, 'You might need a shoulder to cry on.'

Like a cyber-rebound, I smiled pitifully, lips trembling. If I could have squeezed out a tear I would have. But I almost over-played it. Sheila froze for a moment. Like maybe a human would when confronted by another human so perfect that it couldn't be real. Like meeting an angel in meat-space.

A professional, she recovered. From behind her back she drew a bottle of merlot. 'The best ando dollars can buy.'

I stood back from the door. 'Sure, come in.' When she entered I locked the door.

She turned, a smile touching the corners of her cherry blossom lips. 'Do you lock in all your female visitors?' She had already scanned the condo for the firewall — the only obvious means by which our avatars had not succumbed to her virus. We shouldn't exist, yet we did. The virus had wiped out two thirds of Lovago's populace in the last month. Now she needed to get up close and personal. Decipher how to crack our immunity codes. An insatiable hunger I knew she could never quench, could never resist. If we were immune to the virus she needed to know why to combat it. A challenge to match that of the Mac virus that knocked out three quarters of the smug Mac users whose catchcry was once: 'I don't get viruses. I have a Mac.'

She unscrewed the top of the wine bottle. Raised it in salute. 'Glasses? You should toast. You're a free man.'

Without saying a word I undid the top five buttons of my blouse. I'd been waiting for this moment for two whole days.

The avatar's eyes dropped to my cleavage. 'So you're a woman.' Her smile evaporated as her earlier suspicion dawned large on her. 'What is this?'

Anok used her key to open the door. Only now her avatar was a lithe beauty dressed in a jet black neoprene bodysuit. She'd needed to log in under a pseudonym to avoid the real Sheila's detection. Several Lovago officials fanned out from behind her and flanked Sheila.

'There's been some mistake,' Sheila began.

'Yours,' I said. 'Spreading viruses across the metaverse is an international offence.' I looked at my watch. A meaningless gesture here in the metaverse of course, but old habits die hard. 'Right now there's a bruiser called Burbank knocking on your door in meat-space. I suggest you answer it before the FFC kicks it in.'

'You can't prove a thing!' Sheila hissed. She started laughing then morphed, losing layer upon layer of blocks till there was nothing there.

A self-destruct virus. Clever. But not clever enough. Burbank would be reading the hacker his or her rights by now.

I showed the officials to the door and thanked them with the bottle of merlot. Then I held Anok at arm's distance. 'Why, if it isn't Cathy Willow from *Willow's Game*.'

'On loan from Jerry.' She undid the rest of my buttons and unclipped my bra with practised ease. With fingertip softness she pushed me backwards onto the bed. 'We need to talk about you setting us up,' she said. 'But not right now,' she purred ...

AFTERWORD

'Lure' follows 'Wired Dreaming', a story published in *Dreaming Down-Under*. It's not often that I get a chance to record my forecasts for the future. That the predictions here will occur there is little doubt in my mind — it's more a matter of when. I couldn't resist the dig regarding Mac users, having sparred with many over the years, defending my reliable PC with religious zeal. Who, I wonder, will take up the challenge and take that second bite from the apple ...

— *Paul Collins*

SIMON BROWN's stories have been published in Australia, the US, England, Japan, Russia, and Poland. Some of his stories can be found in the collections *Cannibals of the Fine Light* and *Troy*. He began writing science fiction novels such as *Privateer* and *Winter*, but has turned his hand to high fantasy with the Keys of Power trilogy (*Inheritance, Fire and Sword,* and *Sovereign*) and the Chronicles of Kydan series (*Born of Empire, Rival Son,* and *Empire's Daughter*).

He lives on the NSW south coast with his wife and two children.

In this deft and stylish evocation of H. G. Wells, Brown tells the story of how the world was really saved . . .

EMPIRE

SIMON BROWN

'You know, little brother,' Isaac said, looking out the window of their tiny room, 'you can see the stars. When we first came to London there was so much fog that you could not even see the tops of buildings. I can even see Mars.'

'Is it really red?' Leonard asked, joining Isaac and leaning out on the sill.

'Yes. Small and red.' Isaac pointed it out.

'I can't see it.'

'There, next to the really bright white one. That's Jupiter.'

Leonard's face fell.

'What's wrong?' Isaac asked.

'Mama told me the brightest star was pop, all the way up in heaven, looking down on us.'

Isaac nodded. 'Well, maybe I'm wrong. Maybe it is poppa.'

Leonard shook his head. 'No. You are always right, Isaac. It is Jupiter if you say so. And I can see Mars, too.'

'I am always right, eh? Even about Machines?'

Leonard snorted. 'You are *never* right about Machines.'

Isaac checked the song sheet in his hand, trying to memorise all the lyrics, and started singing. Leonard joined him for the last few lines, and they knew how sweet they sounded. Some things in their lives were right, at least some of the time. When they stopped they looked at each other with something like pride, and almost with one mind turned to look out the window again, to see the stars and planets. And eventually they looked down to see spread out before them the yellow lights of reborn London, and beyond the city the high wall that kept them in, and beyond that the red landscape that was the domain of the Martians, their hunting grounds and their nursery.

History made Erin Kay go to Happy Rest, an antiseptic flat-roofed hospice in the middle of irrigated gardens near Phoenix.

She rolled up not expecting anything, but hoping Howard Finkel's signature would have some influence. The registrar umm-ed and ah-ed when Erin gave her the authority. She spoke softly into the intercom and the day manager appeared; he phoned the contact number beneath Howard Finkel's almost illegible scribble. He spoke a few words, nodded silently to himself and put down the phone.

'It's fine,' he told the registrar, and walked away without having said a word to Erin.

The registrar pointed down a corridor. 'Third door on the left. Room 12. Poor dear's not long for this world. He used to be a singer or something, did you know?'

'So I've heard,' Erin said, and made sure she retrieved the authority, figuring she might need it again.

She knocked on the door to Room 12. She heard a reply but could not make out the words. She risked opening the door wide enough for her to peek inside.

'Zac Feelgood?'

He was looking straight at her. Brown eyes that seemed too young for the pale dying face they peered from. He was sitting in a wheelchair, wrapped in an old checkered bathrobe. Thin grey hair was combed back over his head, ending in uneven tips above a silver cravat. His hands tightly gripped the chair's wheels as if he was afraid they would suddenly fall off.

'I said I was busy,' he said in a wheeze. Spittle flecked his lips and Erin felt queasy.

'My name's Erin Kay, Mr Feelgood.' She stepped into the room and closed the door behind her. 'Your son Howard said I could visit you.'

'That was good of him, considering he never visits himself. The little spiv. I should have given Dot my name. My real name. Her kids visit all the time. Good kids. But he was the only legitimate one left, so he gets everything.' Feelgood's mouth curled, showing a full set of yellowing teeth. 'You one of his lawyers? What the fuck do you want? More papers to sign?'

'I'm an historian, Mr Feelgood, not a lawyer.'

'Don't call me Feelgood,' he said curtly.

'Pardon?' For a second Erin had the horrible thought that she had knocked on the wrong door.

'It's Finkel. Get that right if you're gonna write a book.' He growled at her. 'I read all those books about me and my brother. All they talk about is the booze and drugs and dames. It's like our act meant nothing at all. But we put smiles on the faces of millions.'

'I know, Mr Fe . . . Mr Finkel. Look, can I call you Zac?'

She held her breath while he stared noncommittally at her for a long moment.

'Isaac,' he said distantly, as if he was remembering the name of a friend long dead. Then he came back to the present. 'Talk to me? About what particularly?'

Erin knelt down next to him. 'About what came before,' she said, almost in a whisper, because that was how everyone talked about what came before.

'Why me?' he said suspiciously. 'There are hundreds of us left from those days.'

'They didn't go through what you and Leonard went through.'

'How would you know?'

'A long time ago I met Dot. We were friends. She told me things.'

'And Howard still let you come and see me?'

'I didn't tell him about Dot. I told him I was interested in music hall and vaudeville. I told him I was writing a book about Zac and Lenny Feelgood. But I'm more interested in Isaac and Leonard Finkel.'

He leaned towards her and said, 'You know, almost no one knows the secret history of Isaac and Leonard Finkel, and how we saved the world from a fate worse than ... well, worse than death.'

'I know some of it. Dot told me a lot before she died. She said forget about everything I'd read, about the movies, and about how you changed your name from Finkel to Feelgood —'

'And how we married too young, how we got hooked on hash and hooch, how we deserted Benny our first manager, poor dumb bastard, and how we ignored our kids, like poor dumb Dot, and how Lenny died from cirrhosis in 1953, and how I'm here forgotten in an old peoples home in 1965 and telling the nurses stories they don't believe.'

Erin said in a subdued voice, 'Something like that.'

Isaac's face went flat and hard. He stared at Erin like he didn't care about anything in the world. 'Why the fuck should I?'

'Because you're dying, Isaac, and this is your last chance.'

Isaac's breath rattled somewhere in his chest. 'Why do you care?'

'Because it really happened,' Erin said.

There was another long pause, and then Isaac looked away from her and outside his room's only window. Hard Arizona light slanted across his face. Erin thought she had lost her chance. She sighed heavily and stood up. But before she could move to the door, Isaac started talking, the words coming out slow as treacle, and Erin retrieved her tape recorder from her purse and turned it on.

'This is the only story that matters, and the only reason most people haven't heard it before is that it was too good for stage or screen let alone real life, even if the Committee for Conciliation had felt like letting it through the censor. It starts a long time ago, long before common memory, and long, long before history.

'The first date to remember is May 1894 ...'

* * *

… when all the way from Danzig, as hopeful as birds in spring, the Finkels arrive in London. Jacob, a cobbler, his wife Magdalena and their two children, Isaac and Leonard. But as Magdalena always said, 'An unlucky person is — kaput! — a dead person', and Jacob was as unlucky as they come. The Martians arrived three months after the Finkels set foot in England, and as the world soon learned the Martians had no respect at all for people with good hearts and modest ambition and a determination to work hard.

Jacob Finkel did not live out the first onslaught, and Magdalena, with her two small boys, was taken prisoner and put in a camp in London with thousands of other survivors, all homeless and bewildered and watched over by monstrous machines with heat rays and no mercy at all.

'They were terrible and beautiful, the Machines. I remember their long silvery legs moving in the morning mist from the Thames like the fingers of some giant Jehovah.' Isaac walked three fingers on the arm of his wheelchair to show Erin how they moved. 'And when the sun was low in the afternoon the metal on the Machines looked like molten gold.'

Isaac paused again while he remembered the Machines, the great striding of them.

'Now listen, Erin Kay, because the second date I'm going to give you is the one to remember, because that's when it all really starts. It is 1897 …'

… and in the refurbished rooms of Mr George Cochrane, manager of the Empire Theatre, the aforesaid Mr Cochrane is on the defensive.

'Maggie, Maggie, Maggie.' Cochrane said the name as if it was the start of a sigh.

'I prefer Magdalena. From you, in fact, Mrs Finkel is even better.'

'After all we've been through.'

'Which is less than you imagine and more than I can bear to think about,' Magdalena said stiffly, and gathered her boys around her to prevent any unwanted advances. Mr Cochrane may have been a cad, but Isaac and Leonard sometimes played with his own children and he was sensible about rumours.

'Take my advice, my good lady. Change the name of the act.'

'It is very English. I have heard English say it.'

'Froth and Bubbles.' Cochrane shook his head. 'No. It sounds like the name of a female revue, you know, with the fan and ti … feathers.'

Magdalena looked blankly at him.

Cochrane cocked one heel and lifted invisible breasts. 'Bristen … boosten?' He wiggled his backside. 'Toches?'

Magdalena was horrified and tried to cover her children's ears, but they were already tittering.

Blushing, Cochrane cleared his throat. 'Much better if it was something like …' He waved a hand in the air. 'What are they doing again?'

'Some jokes, some song, some jokes, some dance, some jokes …' Magdalena started, but her voice was drowned out by the cranking, stomping sound of a passing Machine. The walls of Cochrane's office shook a little, and dust sprinkled from the ceiling. The boys ran to a window before their mother could stop them and caught a glimpse of a huge metal leg.

'Land dreadnought,' Isaac said with certainty.

'No. Cruiser. Four heat rays —' Leonard said.

Isaac interrupted his younger brother. 'You don't know what you're talking about.'

They were jerked away from the window, Isaac by Magdalena and Leonard by Cochrane.

'Fool boys!' the manager said shortly, handing Leonard to his mother, then craning his head out the window to make sure the Machine had gone on.

Magdalena shook her sons by their stiff white collars. 'Idiots! What are you? *Meshugeh*? Don't you know better, as if I haven't taught you myself? You want to disappear? You want to feed the monsters?'

'Sorry, mamma,' Leonard squeaked.

'It didn't see us,' Isaac said.

'And how does Isaac Finkel, twelve years old, know what a Martian can or cannot see?' Magdalena demanded. 'Are you an expert on Martians, all of a sudden?'

'He thinks he knows all about them,' Leonard piped enthusiastically.

'More than you, anyway,' Isaac said under his breath.

'Both Lenny and me collected cards,' Isaac said. He pointed to a set of drawers next to his bed. 'In there, Erin Kay. In the top drawer.'

She opened it. There was a wallet, toothbrush and toothpaste. And what looked like a pack of miniature cards held together with a rubber band; the back of the top card had on it a picture of a packet of cigarettes and the word 'Players'.

'Bring the cards to me,' he said.

Erin gave him the cards. He slipped off the rubber band, turned them face up and spread them in his two hands. Each card had a vivid three-colour illustration of a Martian Machine. Erin could not believe her eyes. She had heard descriptions of the machines from other old folk, but had never imagined they could look so lethal and so utterly alien. And yes, beautiful, too.

'Zac and I collected them. Had every one, except the sea cruiser, which was rarer than . . .' He frowned in concentration. 'Rarer than an acorn.'

'Acorn?'

'From an oak tree. The red weed killed most of 'em. After the defeat of the Martians, Players started making cigarettes again and put cricketers and racing cars and battleships on their cards. The Committee for Conciliation didn't want any reminder of the Martians, and the world soon forgot how close it came to having no history at all.'

A cat leaped onto the windowsill and looked into Cochrane's office just long enough for everyone to notice it, including Leonard who sneezed violently.

'Cats,' Mrs Finkel explained to Cochrane. 'His allergy. Also geraniums and coff —'

'Bubble and Squeak,' Mr Cochrane said.

The three Finkels looked at the chairman with puzzled expressions.

'Bubble and Squeak,' he went on. 'A name for the act. That's as English as breakfast. And your boys are good with the jokes, I know, so the name fits. Like a suit, Maggie.' Magdalena glared at him and he forced a laugh. 'I mean Mrs Finkel.'

'Bubble and Squeak,' Mrs Finkel said slowly, frowning. 'What do you think?' she asked her boys.

Isaac and Leonard exchanged glances. They were not sure what to think; Magdalena usually did that for them.

'Tell me about the Empire,' Erin said. 'Dot showed me a picture once.'

'What's to say? It started life as a hole in the ground where Trafalgar Square used to be before the Martians hit London. The bastards created a natural amphitheatre, y'know, like the Greeks used, a fact not lost on Cochrane. The world has never seen an entrepreneur and entertainer like him, and never will again. When he first put on a show — Gilbert and Sullivan's brand new operetta, *The Grand Duke* — no one came, including Sullivan who had been harvested the day before. Everyone was afraid the Martians would attack the audience. But nothing happened. Some say one of the Machines walked by, stopped and swayed a little, as if it was dancing, but no one believed it.

'Cochrane's shows were the only bright spot in our lives. He did such a great job raising everyone's morale that the Council for Collaboration made sure he and his entourage were free from any harvesting.'

'Did you ever see anyone harvested?' Erin interrupted. She could not help swallowing.

'Saw plenty taken,' Isaac said, hollowly. 'But not what happened after. Not for a while, anyway.'

'What happened with the Empire?'

'Like I said, Cochrane was a clever man, and he saw what people wanted was music hall. He put on afternoon matinees as well as night shows, and took up the acts from the destroyed Hackney Empire and the Hippodrome, the Grand and Hoxton Hall. In time, the council assigned labour teams to build proper seating and a proper foyer and ticket office; the council even wanted to build a roof over the amphitheatre, but Cochrane knew that would screw the acoustics so he didn't let it happen. In the foyer Cochrane placed the head of Nelson from the column. It was his way of saying "fuck you" to the Martians. And "fuck you!" to the council, too.

'The labour teams didn't stop with the Empire. The council extended the building program to cover the whole of the prison camp, which by then had spread to include most of the old city and held survivors from the whole bloody island. The prison was turned into a metropolis. The Martians didn't seem to mind, as long as the collectors from the Council for Collaboration were given free reign to harvest when necessary and no one got in the way of the Machines.'

He cleared his throat. 'We started at sixpence a show. Threepence each. Oh, and a shilling for mama. We did well, figured out how to work the audience, and in a few weeks had fifth billing for the afternoon matinee. You had to be good to get that. Cochrane started paying us a shilling. The family was clearing two bob a show, nothing to sneer at in those days.'

His eyes seemed to dim for a moment. 'Not real shillings, of course. Not real money. Little metal disks the council gave out. We just called them threepences and zacs and bobs.

He rubbed his right forearm. Erin watched his blue veins jump up and down. 'You know what got Cochrane?'

'Influenza, wasn't it?'

'That's what they wrote for his obituary. Really it was boredom. He hated the movies and the musicals that started after the Martians were gone. His heart was in revue and operettas. He couldn't believe the nineteenth century ever came to an end. For Cochrane even the Martians were better than what came after. He belonged to the Empire, and always would.'

'You know, Mr Cochrane,' Mr Cochrane said to himself, 'those two boys aren't half bad.'

Isaac and Leonard weren't sure whether or not they were meant to say anything to that, so said nothing. They waited.

Cochrane lit one of his precious cigars. The boys watched enviously. International trade had died with the invasion and nothing was imported any more, including tobacco, but Cochrane had somehow obtained a few pre-invasion boxes of cigars for his personal use. Purple smoke curled into the air, stale but still seductive.

'There might even be a part for you in Gilbert and Sullivan's new piece.'

The boys could not hide their surprise. 'Their new piece?' Isaac said. 'I thought Sullivan was taken?'

'He was, but Gilbert is adapting an earlier piece. He is changing his lyrics to *HMS Pinafore* and telling the story of our slimy tentacled friends.'

The boys blinked. They had a vision of the new Empire being melted to the ground with them and mama in the middle of the puddle. 'Won't the council stop it?'

Cochrane snorted. 'The Committee for Collaboration won't care, so long as the punters are happy. I admit, Gilbert's first title for the musical, *HMS Thunderchild*, was a little close to the bone, but we've settled on *HMS Minotaur*, martial without being exactly provocative.'

Cochrane looked appraisingly at the boys. He took a long puff of his smoke and said, 'Gilbert has added new characters as well. There are parts for two young lads in the piece. I was going to give them to Marie Lloyd and Vesta Tilley, but you can hold a tune and act well enough.'

'And we're cheaper,' Isaac pointed out.

Cochrane smiled. 'You heard Marie's latest?'

The boys shook their heads. Their mama still pretended they knew nothing of the world and would not let them in the audience when Lloyd or Tilley performed.

'"She Sits Among Her Cabbages and Peas." Had the audience rolling in the aisles.' Then, strangely, he grimaced. 'Not quite the standard I expected to introduce into the Empire.' He looked down at his cheroot and sighed heavily. 'Still. I don't suppose we should expect anything at all to go our own way. The future doesn't exactly belong to us any more.

'One possible problem, though. The name. Finkel? No good at all. Too foreign. Too Jewish.'

'Mama.'

'Tell her it's just for the posters and bills. Finkel just won't work. Tell her it's not English enough.'

'And what did your mama think of the idea?' Erin asked.

'If Finkel was good enough for Jacob, your father, it is good enough for Mr High-and-Mighty. Tell him that, Isaac.'

As arguments went it was a hard one to fight, so Isaac said to her, 'Mama, you have to see it his way. Mr Cochrane is an impresario; he sees the big picture. He knows what's best for us.'

'I know what's best for you, thank you very much. I am your mother, who brought you all the way from Danzig in a leaking boat filled with fish and your father sick over the side. We survive pogrom, the North Sea and the Martians. I know what's best for my sons.'

'It's entertainment,' Isaac said. 'Nothing more. We can call ourselves Finkel in the street, in the home, we can shout it from the mountains for all Cochrane cares. But not in the Empire, not if you want us to do Gilbert and Sullivan.'

'Finkel is your name and that is the end of it.'

In the distance, the family could hear a Machine patrolling the walls. They could feel the vibrations through the floor of their small apartment.

Isaac had a sudden idea. 'Mama, what do we call ourselves in the matinee? The Finkel Brothers? No. We call ourselves Bubble and Squeak. *You* were even going to call us Froth and Bubbles. How is Isaac and Leonard Feelgood any different from that? In fact, how about Zac and Lenny Feelgood? Now that's not bad.'

'It is a long way from Isaac and Leonard Finkel,' Mama said.

Leonard said, 'It's a long way from Danzig.'

Magdalena fell silent. The boys waited for her to make a decision. The sound of the Machine faded as it walked away from them.

'Not just a long way from Danzig,' Magdalena said solemnly. 'Very well, Isaac, if you think it's for the best, have it your way. Have it the way of Mr High-and-Mighty CoMchrane.'

Later, when Magdalena was preparing their daily meal and the sound of the patrolling Machine was still fresh in their memories, Leonard said, 'Jack Bissel says everyone will be harvested in the end.'

Isaac looked up from his sewing, glancing first at Leonard and then at his mama.

'Jack Bissel is a *schmuck*,' Magdalena said.

'Mama!' Isaac and Leonard said together. It was alright for them to say such words, but they could not believe their mama knew the word let alone spoke it out loud.

'Don't you two "mama" me. You think I came in the last shower? I know what Bissel is because I know what his father is and what his mother is. Jack Bissel is lower than Martian's *petsl*.'

This time the boys laughed they were so surprised, but they stopped when Magdalena glared at them in challenge. 'Some things are not to be laughed at.'

She was chopping squash and carrot and cabbage into a cooking pot, vegetables that were now grown in the small market gardens that had started almost as soon as the city had been rebuilt. The gardens had produced their first crop just in time, for the Martians had turned virtually the whole of Britain into a red wilderness where nothing grew that was of use to people. Even the Thames, which for a short period after the invasion had become filled once again with fish that could be eaten safely, now carried water that was crystal clear and completely barren of all life. At least the water could be used in cooking and to drink.

'So,' Magdalena continued, 'Jack Bissel does not know what he is talking about. We are not going to be harvested. We are going to live. We have not gone through all that we have gone through so the Martians can take us. It is not God's will, I am telling you, and it is not *my* will.'

Isaac and Leonard both knew God's will was irrelevant — how else could the Martians ever have invaded the Earth and caused so much death and destruction? — but the will of Magdalena was a natural force, like the wind and sunshine. For the first time he could remember, Isaac started believing he would survive, that he had a life whose course ran so far into the future he could not read it.

He returned to his sewing, and the glimmer of elation he had felt was reduced by the knowledge that he was now cannibalising his last spare pair of pants to keep his best pair in decent order. Soon Magdalena would have to spend some of their hard-earned coins to buy material from the looters and scavengers who searched through the ruins in the red wasteland for things that were no longer produced, such as cloth and fabric and kitchen utensils and even coal for heating and cooking.

Isaac dropped the sewing, stood up and went to the window and looked out over London. It had rained an hour before, but now the sky was clear and the sun shone on a city that shimmered. He thought London looked like a glittering diamond set in red velvet, and for a moment he realised the Martian landscape held a soft and muted beauty of its own. Almost immediately he felt guilty, as if he had betrayed his own race, his own planet, by admitting such a thing. But it was true, and he sensed he understood a small part of how the Martians saw the universe.

What if this *is* God's will? he wondered. What if the Martians were His Chosen People and the rest of us the chaff to be winnowed from His creation?

He heard Leonard say in a thoughtful voice, 'You are right, Mama, Jack Bissel is lower than a Martian's *petsl*.'

Isaac could not help laughing again.

And cut it short as the Machine they had heard before returned suddenly, its shadow falling across the window. It was a dreadnought. It had come so quietly he had not heard it. The Machines did that sometimes, stalking through the city as silent as silver spirits as if to prove a point to their prisoners, that death can be as unexpected as lightning from the sky. The dreadnought seemed to hover outside their tenement for a long moment, and brought one leg down so hard the whole building shook. Then it was gone.

'Did you ever go over the wall? Outside of London?' Erin asked.

Isaac sucked his lower lip. His yellow teeth looked like thick tortoise shell pegs. 'Well, once,' he said after a while.

'With Leonard?'

'Uh-huh.'

'Just you and Leonard?'

'Nope. One other, a boy who did the act before us. He was a couple of years younger. Cleverest boy I ever met. Tiny bugger, but as agile as a monkey.'

'What was his name?'

'Charlie Hawkes.' He wheezed as he remembered. 'Poor fucking Charlie Hawkes.'

'What happened.'

'Jesus, it goes everywhere,' Charlie said. 'All the way to Timbuktu, I bet.'

'Not over seawater,' Isaac said. 'None of that red stuff goes near the ocean.'

'How do you know that?'

'Heard it from others who saw it first put down,' Leonard said.

'Well, who's to say the Martians didn't land in Sudan and Siam and all the way to Mexico?'

Isaac and Leonard didn't want to think about that, so they shut up.

The rolling red hills of England spread out before them. The landscape stank like old seaweed and dead squid.

Leonard sneezed.

'Cat,' Isaac joked.

'What?' Charlie said.

'He always sneezes when there's a cat around.'

'Do not,' Leonard protested.

The air thrummed. All three boys stared at each other. You only got that sound when *they* were real close . . .

'I can't see it,' Leonard said, almost squealing.

Isaac looked over his shoulder to the hole in the London wall. If they were real quick, maybe the hole wasn't as far as it looked.

'We have to run!' he said to the others. 'Now!'

Leonard didn't wait, but scooted faster than a rat down a drainpipe with Isaac only a tenth of a second behind. Charlie, though, he was braver.

When the two brothers got to the hole, Isaac saw Charlie still hadn't moved an inch.

'Damn you, Charlie, get your arse over here!'

Too late. The Machine first appeared around the corner of the wall and one triple-step later was standing over Charlie Hawkes. No argument this was a dreadnought, Isaac thought. Clear hundred and fifty feet straight in the air with a cabin on top shaped like the head of a beetle, four heat rays under and four on top in twin turrets, legs three-jointed and splay-footed, and around the front of the cabin were clumps of metal tentacles like the whiskers of a catfish. It reflected red in the red landscape except for Charlie's oblong face all distorted and gigantic in the concave underbelly of the thing. Two of the tentacles extended out, fell down and wrapped themselves around Charlie, then whipped him up to the cabin. And he was gone.

At first Isaac thought it was Charlie screaming, heard all the way from inside the cabin, but then his brain recognised the clear bell tone of Leonard's sweet, sweet eleven-year-old voice.

'Shut up, Leonard! Fuck's sake, shut up!'

Another of the tentacles slithered down, but this time it didn't wrap around anyone, just pointed at Leonard as if it was seeing him and sniffing him at the same time, then was gone.

Leonard shuffled backwards until he was back behind the wall, then dragged Isaac back after him

'We can't leave Charlie!' Isaac said.

Before Leonard could say anything, there was a slurping sound from the machine, and out of the cabin dropped a small red bundle with bones sticking out of it.

'And you think that was Charlie?' Erin asked.

'Don't know what else it could have been. Anyway, he was never seen again, poor bastard.' Isaac wrung his hands. 'Had to tell his mama and that was hell. Never seen anyone cry so much as Charlie's mama. It drove her mad in the end.'

'Did you get in trouble?'

'Nope. Everyone was so relieved the Machine only took Charlie they never minded us, except ordering us never to go near the wall again. We were happy to oblige.'

* * *

Isaac was kissing Mary Ester's pink ear lobe while his hand fumbled in the top of her dress. He had just managed to cup her left breast when Leonard barged into the dressing room and said, 'Oh, there you are!'

Mary yelped, pulled away from Isaac and ran out, straightening her neckline as she went.

'She's nice,' Leonard said approvingly. 'I saw her with Oliver Mark the other day.'

'Shut up,' Isaac said.

'Be nice or I'll tell mama. She thinks you're holier than Moses.'

'What'd you want to come in and spoil things anyway?'

'We've got a date.'

'Date for what?'

'For *HMS Minotaur*! Five days from now!'

Isaac grinned. 'Really?'

Leonard grinned back. 'Yup. Mama told Cochrane he can change our names, so Cochrane told mama we were in, and mama told me, and now I'm telling you.'

'Zac and Lenny Feelgood,' Isaac said, trying the billing out loud.

'Lenny and Zac,' Leonard said. 'Things should be done alphabetically.'

When the nurse came to test Isaac's blood pressure, Erin looked out the window, but the sigh of the trees depressed her. They were the fast growing species that had been planted almost everywhere else in the world over the last century, like Monterey Pine, Karri and Yellow Box, in their way all reminders of what had come before and of everything that had been lost. So she turned away from the view and pretended to study the painting on the wall above Isaac's bed while the nurse pumped and pumped the wrap around Isaac's poor thin arm.

The painting was one of Munch's *Scream Series Two* with a woman's face distorted into a silent, consuming shriek with a Martian walker striding over the bridge behind her. The background comprised swirls of red weed, their rootlets extending off the edge of the painting's borders. She remembered red weed from her childhood; some had been preserved in her local Museum of Conciliation. Well, pink weed then because of the formaldehyde, and getting paler year by year. It was nothing, really, a specimen as pointless as the jars filled with fetuses and two-headed lambs. But seeing Munch's painting, Erin could almost feel what it must have been like living in those times.

Isaac was swearing at the nurse, but he ignored the language and when he was finished helped Isaac back into his wheelchair, thanked him politely for cooperating and walked out, nodding sympathetically to Erin before closing the door behind him.

'It's not my fucking heart they should worry about,' Isaac spat, and jabbed at his skull. 'It's the fucking blancmange in here. I can feel it oozing out of my ears. I tell you, Erin Kay, I won't have anything left soon. I will be all skin and bones and spit and in the middle my heart beating like a clock but no brain anywhere. They'll scoop me up and put me in a bin, and that'll be the end of Isaac Finkel, all the way from Danzig, and Zac Feelgood and Bubble and Squeak and all the stories. No one will remember the Martians any more. The Committee of Conciliation wants us to forget any of it ever happened because that way none of them can be hanged for what they did when they were the Committee of Collaboration. History gets stuck in their gullet like . . . like . . .'

He coughed and slumped in the wheelchair. He waved his right hand in the air, signalling Erin to invent a metaphor for him.

'Like a fishbone,' she said weakly.

'Jesus, no. Like shit made from cement.'

'So tell me, Isaac, so I can tell everyone else.'

'Tell you what? I've talked myself into a stupor. I feel like I've got nothing but slag in my lungs.'

'We're not finished yet. What happened on that night? The opening night of *HMS Minotaur*?'

Isaac closed his eyes. 'So long ago. You know, it isn't the grease paint and the lights I remember?'

'No?'

'Never was. Never is for anyone in music hall. That's just for the songs and the memoirs, you know, "I remember the smell of the grease paint, the heat of the stage lights". It's all bullshit. When you're working on the stage all the time it's just background.'

'Then what do you remember about it?'

'I remember the women, Erin Kay.' His eyes opened and his mouth curled into a smile. 'I remember being around twenty women or more, all taller than me and done up and sweating in their costumes, and the glass beads, and the powder on their breasts like flour on rising bread, skin so pale it was almost blue, and the pins and broaches and parasols and the way they let me look at them because they thought I was a kid and it was kinda cute, but Jesus I wanted them. I wanted Mary Ester and Lorna Dixon and Jane Fremont, all at once, and Annie Beaumont and Victoria Denny. All of us crammed into the wings waiting our turn to tumble out and entertain all the poor sods waiting their turn to be turned into fertiliser. You know, all that dying around us made us horny as the devil. I was fourteen when I first did it; that was with Annie, during the third act. My first time. It was over so quick we didn't have time to clean up and then we were on and afterwards mama looked at me like she knew.'

Erin swallowed. She had not expected these confessions and did not want to hear any more; still, she could not help wondering what Annie had thought of it. Had she seduced him? Or was sex like alcohol for people who had no other way to relax, or maybe even to relate to each other? Maybe Isaac was right, that all that dying made everyone horny as the devil. How many conversations can you have when you know the world is dying around you? In the end, perhaps that was the only thing you could talk about, so maybe sex was a way to avoid it and a way to remind yourself you were still human when so much around you was not.

'Not that mama minded, I think,' Isaac went on. 'With everything else going on. Besides, I reckon Cochrane was right. He and mama now and then. You know.'

'The opening night,' Erin prompted. 'Tell me about the opening night.'

Running up from the dressing room, Isaac and Leonard caught their breath in the wings. The stage manager glared at them disapprovingly, but they didn't care. There was no way they were going to miss the spectacular opening number, and when Cochrane walked onto the stage the entire audience, the biggest ever seen in the Empire, fell silent as if all were struck dumb by the hand of God. Cochrane knew exactly how long to speak, how far he could build up their expectations before losing them, and when he had finished he lifted his hand in a flourish and the curtains behind him rose as he left the stage.

And then the orchestra in the pit started up. Lime lights swung across the stage as if searching for the cast, and then the prow of HMS *Minotaur* was pushed into view and the audience erupted in cheers.

For Isaac, though, it was the costumes that made his eyes glitter. Cochrane had made sure the cast were decked out in the best costumes the Empire had, many saved from theatres and music halls long gone and never used since. The women wore dresses made from silk and chiffon with satin sashes, and on their fingers wore rings with fake pearls the size of peas, and in their hats wore peacock feathers and pins made from gold and silver. The men wore uniforms so covered in braid and toggles and brass buttons they would have made any real ship top heavy, and the dress swords that swung by their sides were broad and heavy enough to have come from giant Mamelukes. Even Isaac and Leonard, the only children in the cast, carried long knives suspended from their belts with bejeweled hilts and inlaid scabbards.

The opening number was so spectacular, so loud and audacious and fast moving, Isaac was overwhelmed by the glory of it; he did not think the court of the Sun King could have been half as brilliant. And then he and Leonard heard their cue and from that point on they were a part of it, the whole glittering show, their nerves succumbing to the excitement the whole cast felt, singing with such grace they could see people in the audience leaning forward in their seats to be closer to the sound of it.

At the end Isaac and Leonard had their duo, the grand finale where the rest of the cast gradually joined in until the piece reached its crescendo, and as the singers filled themselves with air and seemed to stretch on their toes to give the greatest voice they could, the audience stood, pulled to their feet by the music and words stirring inside them, something they had not felt since the invasion.

And then the last verse, sung like an anthem, rang out.

I humble poor and foreign born,

The meanest in the new division —

Despite the red-tentacled dawn —
The mark of Harvester submission —
Have dared to raise my wormy eyes
Above the dust to which they'd nail me
In mankind's glorious pride to rise
I am an Englishman — behold me!

When it was done, the last note lifting into the dark sky above, there was a moment of condensed silence as if the whole world had fallen quiet. Then the applause started, rippling towards the stage like waves that grew larger and larger as the cast took their bows, the loudest and most sustained being for Isaac and Leonard. Isaac glanced at the wings and saw his mama there, tears pooling under her eyes, and at that moment, for the first and only time in his life, he felt invincible. Until he looked up and saw the dreadnought. It was almost completely hidden from view, revealed only by the thinnest sliver of silver that outlined its cabin and one of its three legs. It stood before the Empire, towering over the amphitheatre, not moving at all. One by one the others in the cast followed Isaac's gaze, themselves becoming as still as the Machine, and soon everyone in the amphitheatre was looking up at it.

Isaac said nothing for a long time. Erin, who had finally reached the climax of the story of how Isaac and Leonard Finkel had saved the world, was torn between wanting to know how it ended and wanting to be suspended forever there at the moment before knowing, filled with a wonderful anticipation and tension.

In the end she surrendered. 'Dot told me Leonard sneezed,' she said, almost in a whisper. 'Right on a Martian.'

Isaac's gaze settled on her as if he did not know who she was.

'He was allergic to them,' Erin went on. 'That's what Dot says.'

'No,' Isaac said slowly, the word squeezed out from tired lungs. 'It was nothing like that. That's just myth; sometimes we'd go along with it, but mostly we said nothing.'

'Then tell me, Isaac. What *really* happened?'

'The dreadnought walked away, clumping through the city back to the walls and its own red kingdom. Everyone in the Empire waited and waited for something to happen, not making a sound, half expecting to die, to be picked up and squeezed like a ripe peach. But nothing happened.'

Isaac coughed loudly, making Erin jump. It was a deep wet sound, almost all phlegm and no air.

'And then the Machines started dropping, one by one. All over the land, all over the world, the Martians died. I saw one crawling out of its machine. A huge grey thing that pulled itself along with its tentacles. It reminded me of a dying cow I'd seen during the invasion, its rear legs burned off and the stumps cauterised, pulling itself through the field with its front legs, a huge sack of dying meat. That's what the Martians had become — huge sacks of dying meat.'

'They caught a cold,' Erin said. 'That's what all the autopsies showed. Influenza or something.'

'Maybe,' Isaac whistled. 'But I think we defeated them because we survived, and kept on surviving no matter what happened. It wasn't the singing and the acting and the jokes, or Cochrane and the Empire, although all of that helped. It's simply that we hung on and hung on, and in the end it was the Martians who let go first.'

Isaac and Leonard were looking out the window of their tiny room.

'I can still see Mars,' Leonard said.

'You thought it would go away, did you?' Isaac jibed.

'Kind of, I guess. Will they come back?'

Isaac shrugged.

'If they do,' Leonard piped up, 'we'll just build another Empire.'

'We'll sing them away.'

'We'll joke them away.'

'Mama will scare them away.'

They almost laughed at that, but it sounded forced even to their ears. They turned away from the window.

'What do we do now?' Leonard asked, almost forlornly.

'Get our names up in lights,' Isaac said. 'We'll start here, in London. Then Paris, maybe, and Manchester, when they build it again. Edinburgh, too. Maybe even New York one day. I can see it now, little brother. Zac and Lenny Feelgood conquer the world.'

AFTERWORD

'Empire' came from an interest in Gilbert & Sullivan and H. G. Wells that collided in that part of my brain reserved for the most bizarre story ideas. The glue that held the two themes together is the idea of survival, that it isn't the heroes who make a victory, but the great masses of people who just hang on and keep working and dreaming no matter what.

— *Simon Brown*

CHRISTOPHER GREEN migrated to Melbourne in 1997 and has been writing for fifteen years. In 2007 he attended Clarion South where he wrote 'Lakeside', which also happens to be the first story he ever submitted for publication. This haunting story is a visceral journey through rejection and abuse to the cleansing waters of life . . . or perhaps death.

LAKESIDE

CHRISTOPHER GREEN

Molly isn't supposed to go to the lake, so she does. She finds the body on her first trip. It is small. Its little arms are outstretched and it floats on its back in the reeds. She can tell it is a boy. He is more colours than she can count, but all of them are black. The body shines like an oil slick.

Molly wades in before she realises what she has done. She is hip-deep in the water, her dress growing heavy as the wool absorbs it. The wetness climbs past the water line, over her stomach and up to her chest. Her mother will be angry.

She tries to retrieve the body, gently coasting it closer by throwing rocks into the water behind it. When she can reach it she stops, but the baby does not. It kicks its swollen legs and opens its sunken eyes and reaches its hand out to her.

Molly runs, but not very far. The baby rolls onto its tummy and slides beneath the water. It does not resurface. She holds the sodden hem of her dress high against her thighs and sprints back across the field that separates her house from the lake.

Now and then she stops and glances over her shoulder, hands on hips as she sucks in air. No dark shape moves in the high brown grass. The field is empty, save for the path in it she's made herself.

When Molly gets home she doesn't recognise the car in front of her house. She sits on the edge of the dirt road, pulls the wet folds of her dress in around her ankles, and waits. After a few minutes she turns a little, so she can watch both the field and the house.

There are no other houses in sight. The road doesn't go anywhere worth going, which mother says is perfect. The quiet lets her mother and her visitors be loud, and they are loud now.

Molly shreds a flower between her fingers and waits. Her hands smell like the reeds by the lake.

When her mother and the man finish, he leaves. He watches Molly for a moment, keys in hand, and smiles. She doesn't smile back. He gets in the car and drives away. Molly stands and walks through the dust he has left behind, and into the house. She gets herself a glass of water, drinks it, and carefully puts the glass away.

Her mother's bedroom is closed. Molly sits at the middle of the stairs and watches the door through the slats of the banister.

She hears her mother turn on the radio and music drifts under the door. The house grows slowly dark.

She wakes in a patch of moonlight. The windows rattle in the wind. The noise that woke her comes again, the drawn out rasp of gravel on the garden path. She holds her breath and listens but the noise is not repeated.

Her mother's bedroom door is still closed.

Molly's dress is stiff and scratchy and still damp in the places she is sitting on. She tugs it half-off over her head and enjoys the sensation of being trapped, then wiggles her shoulders and bursts out of the dampness. Her skin is pale. The moonlight hits her and makes her bright, like the underbelly of a fish.

Molly opens the front door. Mother is always adamant that if she musses her dress, she'll have to go without. The wind wraps around her and her skin goes numb. She steps outside.

The road is rough beneath her feet, and she hurries across it to the grass of the field. It is dry and clean, as she imagines a horse's bed would be. She can smell the lake on the wind, and soon it is just ahead, spread out and reflecting the moon.

The wind moves along the surface. Shapes like dark eels stir the water from within. Bubbles rise in long streamers from the lake bed. Molly forgets her nakedness and sits on a rock, knees tucked up hard against her chin. She scratches at the ground with a stick as she waits, and when she grows too cold she leaves the stick behind and crosses the field again.

The smell of broken reeds and the rustle of brittle grass follow her home.

When the morning sun hits her, she sits up in bed and then runs naked to the stairway. Her dress is gone.

Her mother swishes in behind her. 'Molly?'

'Yes Mother?'

'I found your dress this morning, on the stairs. It stank of the lake. You know I told you not to go there.'

Molly opens her mouth to say something, which makes the slap reverberate even more. Her head snaps back against the wall. The next blow cuffs her to the floor. Molly holds her hand to her head and it comes away wet.

'You could drown there, Molly. You could go down into that lake and never come back up. Is that what you want?'

A car pulls up outside.

'Go and get your dress, you stupid girl. It's out in the front yard, on the line.' Her mother tries to smack her again, but Molly backs away.

'And don't bother the man. He and I'll be busy all day. I don't want to see you again until he leaves.'

Molly gets to her feet and goes to the front door. A man, different man than yesterday, pulls it open before she can get there. She holds her hands in front of her nakedness and her cheeks burn with shame.

'Hello, sweetie.'

Molly tries to slide past, but the man blocks her.

'Don't run away just yet. Where are your clothes?'

She points at the clothesline outside, at her lone black dress as it twists in the breeze.

His hand is rough on Molly's shoulder. 'Helen. You look nice. I'd heard I should expect to see *more* of you, this time,' he says.

'Hush. The Lord let slip that burden. Molly, go outside and play.'

The man laughs. 'I brought us some candy, Helen. The imported kind. Would your little girl like some candy, too?'

The man slides his hand along Molly's bare back. She tries her best to stand still, like her mother would, but when the hand dips below her shoulderblades she pushes past him and runs outside.

Her mother's voice follows her. 'No sense in wasting such things on her.'

Molly hurries to the line and pulls her dress on over her head. Her mother and the man are not loud yet, but she knows they will be soon.

The lake is wide, pressed flat by the sky like a bug under glass. The reeds rub against each other. The baby is there, on the rock she sat on the night before. He sits with his hands on his puffy knees, head hung low, bent forward like a toy. She approaches. The pale sand crunches beneath her feet, but the baby does not move.

Molly is careful when she sits beside him. He seems delicate, now that she is so close. She sees the tangle of flesh at his stomach and a smaller twist between his legs. The baby's skin is flaking now, like the rubber she finds on the side of the road. The skin is tight on his body.

She picks up the stick from yesterday and breaks it in half. His dead eyes turn to her at the sound, and one hand reaches out, fist pumping open and closed. Molly places the stick in his hand, and he makes a watery sound that bubbles in his chest. She reaches past him and pulls a fistful of daisies from the ground. One by one she links them, and then drapes the chain over his head. Her hand brushes his skin. It is clammy, and she wipes an oily film off onto the grass.

They sit beside the lake for a long time. Molly plays with him gently, as best she can. He crawls into her lap and she runs her hand along the sprinkle of hair that crowns his head. He twists, and holds his arms out. Molly hugs him close, like one of her dolls, and he closes his eyes.

She closes hers as well.

They play all morning. Molly walks along the lake with the baby in her arms. She gives him pebbles to skim along the water, but he is too small and drops them after putting them in his mouth. She moves away from the lake and into the shade once the sun is at its height, and sets him in the grass beside her. He sits on his bottom and watches her. She had been told a brother was on the way, once. Molly smiles at the thought, and falls asleep.

He is sitting at the edge of the field when she wakes. She can see her house from here, the car in front of it already gone. The baby wipes dark drool from its chin and crawls to her. He is making the noises babies make when they are ready to wail.

Molly stands, picks him up, and turns toward home.

The house is quiet. Upstairs, the radio plays, another song for another day. Molly cradles the baby in her arms and takes the stairs one by one, and turns toward her mother's bedroom.

The door is closed.

She shivers, but reaches out and twists the knob. The door swings open.

Her mother is sleeping naked, the sheet tucked in around her waist. The room is crowded with a thick, burnt-candy miasma. A tray beside her bed holds a few of the little brown candies the man must have brought. Her mother's mouth is dusted with them. The window is open, and dusk stirs the room with the scent of open water.

The baby kicks in Molly's arms and wails. The noise is a thin one.

Molly turns the body in her arms and lines the fatness of his lips up with her mother's nipple. She presses him against it. He turns his head away and cries again, louder. Her mother does not stir and her breathing is slow. Molly tries again, pressing his mouth to her mother's breast, but the baby squeals and flails its limbs.

Molly shivers again in the cold, and pulls the linen from her mother's body to drape over herself. The baby squirms, and she sits with him at the foot of the bed. Her mother is still damp, at the spot where her legs come together.

The blackened body is restless in Molly's arms. She drapes the sheet over her shoulders like a shawl.

She moves to the window and looks out, across the field, to the lake. The water there is more colours than she can count. All of them are black.

Her mother's eyes slide open, awash in moonlight. Her mouth works but does not. Molly has seen fish do the same thing. She undoes the top three buttons of her dress and wiggles her arm out of the sleeve and up through the collar.

Molly presses the baby's head to her thin chest and smiles as he closes his lips on her. She sings him lullabies that she makes up as she goes. He sucks happily, uselessly, at her nipple. She feels his teeth brush her skin, now and then, and she coos to him and strokes his dark head.

She cradles the baby in her arms and walks out of the room. The sheet trails her like the train of a gown, like a white, white wake.

AFTERWORD

'Lakeside' was written during the week Kelly Link tutored at Clarion South 2007. Somewhere along the way, amidst Brisbane's heat, humidity, and nights full to bursting with three whole hours of sleep, I found a lake in my mind, and fished something out.

— *Christopher Green*

JENNY BLACKFORD's university degree was in Classics (Greek and Latin), but an advertisement in the paper led to an unexpected twenty year career in large computer networks. Since she gave up her day job, Jenny has been writing fantasy, science fiction, and ghost stories. A story set in ancient Delphi appeared in the Hadley Rille anthology *Ruins Terra* in 2007, and various stories for children have been published in the *NSW School Magazine* and other markets. As well, a YA story has appeared in Paul Collins' anthology *Trust Me!*

During the 1980s and early 1990s, she was a principal in the small press publisher Ebony Books and a member of the Editorial Collective of *Australian Science Fiction Review: Second Series*, an award-winning journal. She was fantasy reviewer for *The Age* in the early 1990s, and one of the judges for the Fantasy division of the Aurealis Awards in 1998 and 1999. In 2001, she co-edited (with Russell Blackford) *Foundation* 78, the special Australian issue.

She also writes and reviews for the Australian science magazine *Cosmos*, the ecological magazine *G*, and the *New York Review of Science Fiction*.

In this sweet, stinging, and funny predatory tale, Blackford shows us what other, er, people do on their night out . . .

TROLLS' NIGHT OUT

JENNY BLACKFORD

There was a lot of shrieking and laughing going on at the table behind ours.

'Girls' night out,' I said, and took a good swig of my glass of red.

David barked out, 'What did you say, woman?'

I shouted this time, hoping to penetrate the restaurant sound barrier: 'Girls' night out.'

David snorted. With his impressive snout, that was something.

'Trolls' night out, more like it,' he said. He bared his long white canines in a toothy grin.

The comment was typical of the David I'd known and hated, before I ran away to Scandinavia. Unfortunately, it's not considered good form to scream at one's ex in a good Melbourne restaurant. Instead, I cut off a piece of my salmon cutlet and stuck it in my mouth, fast. The aroma of David's steak was tormenting me.

'That's not very nice,' I said, at last, when I could speak without screaming at him. 'Even for an old wolf like you.'

'So what?' he said. 'I'm not a very nice person.'

I swallowed my list of pent-up grievances, and sighed. 'I thought we'd agreed that you were going to become a warmer and nicer person.'

David sneered. His dark unibrow made the expression even nastier. 'Maybe *you* agreed that I was going to be warmer and nicer. *I* don't remember any such agreement. This would have been before you so heartlessly left me and went jaunting off to Sweden?'

'Yes,' I said. 'Heartlessly. Unaccountably. No good reason at all.' Ha! After all the fights, he knew my reasons well enough. I drank half a glass of red wine in one gulp. At least it was a sturdy South Australian shiraz, not a watery pinot noir.

Without conscious warning, the hairs on the back of my neck lifted, and I could feel my cheek muscles trying to bare my teeth in a snarl.

David patted my hand and said, 'Settle down, sweetie. It's okay — it's just two Samoyeds and an Alsatian on the footpath. Nothing to get agitated about. They haven't been washed for a month, by the smell of them.'

He was handling his involuntary physical reactions far better than I was, the bastard. Showing no signs of stress, he said, 'So, this agreement that I was going to become a warmer and nicer person. Was I listening at the time?' Another fistful of chips disappeared into his maw. The coarse dark hair on the back of his arms poked irrepressibly out of the wrists of his dark grey shirt. Not so long ago, that sight could have made me feel all tender and squishy inside.

'Well, you *seemed* to be listening,' I said. 'You were nodding now and then, saying "yes", and occasionally "no", making eye contact, all that. You mean you can do that and not listen?' It had been during the last of our many rapprochements. I'd been feeling strangely emotional, sentimental, hopeful. Hormonal.

He grinned irritatingly. 'Of course, my dear. It's just a simple, autonomous subroutine. My mind could have been anywhere. Contemplating dinner, thinking about my tax bill, plotting my next play.'

'You travesty of an ex-lover,' I said. 'So much for the meeting of minds.' Clearly, our relationship had been more about the meeting of bodies.

'Let that be a lesson to you of the perfidy of man,' he said. He looked at me shrewdly as he cut a bleeding piece from the almost-raw centre of his enormous steak.

'You want this, don't you?' he said, waving it under my nose.

I'd cheerfully have killed for it. 'No,' I said firmly. 'I'm a vegetarian now. I told you that when I rang.' I put a huge piece of salmon into my mouth and chewed like mad. It didn't help much. Eventually, I swallowed. 'A lot can happen in a year.'

He looked down his long snout at me. 'I don't know if you've noticed this, Talia, but salmon don't grow on trees.'

It was time to change the subject. 'That girls' night out behind me —'

'Trolls',' he said firmly.

My blood was starting to boil, despite the cooling influence of the fish. 'You really are such a bastard, David. You're always so judgmental about people — especially women —'

He smirked. 'Well, turn around and take a look at them.'

'Don't be rude. They're just a pack of high-spirited young girls.' But I'd seen them as they'd walked in past our table, in their ones and twos; they were more than just young girls. I was only arguing with him from long habit.

David snorted again. 'Very muscular girls.'

'Maybe they go to gym together.'

'Look at that one, the girl in the red dress, the fluffy-haired blonde,' David said, pointing with his fork at a girl — woman — at the end of the table behind us. 'She could be a wrestler with those arms.'

I swivelled my neck to sneak another glance. Her red dress was a tiny sleeveless thing, and her triceps muscles rippled visibly. Her biceps were stunning. I wondered what it would be like to lick her arms. It would be a smoother, softer experience than it had been with David.

Two voluptuous girls with long, straight blonde hair sat on her left wearing ruffly pale violet confections that made the most of their amazing pecs and lats.

The girl next to *them*, with short spiky dark hair, was even more impressive. I couldn't help myself: 'How about the deltoids on the one in the sparkly top! Wow!'

He looked at her, then back at me, and gave his right shoulder a reassuring squeeze with the left hand, as if to check that the muscles were still there. 'Well, my muscles are bigger.'

'Not much, proportionally,' I said.

He looked gratifyingly distressed. 'But how has she done it? You know the weights I lift.'

I pretended to smile. 'Yes.'

'You should have been happy to have had a fella who didn't let himself go. At least I've always taken care of myself.' As I watched, he pulled in the stomach which had persistently evaded his best efforts towards perfection.

'Yeah, right,' I said. He'd driven me mad with his obsession with exercise, for seven long years. Up before dawn every day. Cycling one day, weights the next. Especially if a first night of a play was coming up. No slow mornings of coffee and the papers in bed for us ...

But it was not my problem any more. I had more important concerns, now. I wiggled my shoulders until the small knot that had developed between them came loose. No wonder I'd needed months of remedial massages in Sweden.

David turned back to his oozing steak, then peered at my plate. 'What's this nonsense with eating fish, anyway?' he said, with a stern look. 'It's not right or proper for people like us. You're not trying to deny your heritage, are you?' He wiggled his one long eyebrow to underline the word 'heritage'.

So, he's back to that again, I thought. I sighed as deeply as I could manage, and tried to look put-upon.

'Look, David, I don't want to deny *anything*. But I don't have to give in to it. I can fight it. And, when I called you, I told you, I've gone off red meat. That's it. End of argument.' For months now, I hadn't been able to bear the thought of benefiting from the killing of my fellow mammals. Each of them was somebody's furry, milk-drinking baby. But I hadn't had to sit at a dinner table and watch anyone eat steak oozing delicious juices either.

'You're not going soft on me, are you?' he said. 'That's not like the delightfully predacious Talia I remember.' He gave a wolfish grin. 'No, I know what it is. It's just because you've put on weight, isn't it? You've gone veggie to lose weight. Actresses do that all the time.'

As he sniggered, I considered punching his long, designer-stubbled jaw. The restaurant owner would understand, if I told her. As long as it *was* a her. 'You insufferable —'

He interrupted me: 'Not that it's a bad thing.' He winked theatrically. 'Your tits look great, sweetie.'

I was briefly distracted from my building fury by the waiter walking past, taking another huge platter of food to the girls'-night-out table. It was piled with lady's fingers, those long, thin Middle Eastern pastries stuffed with spicy minced lamb. The smell was torture.

'But how did you manage to get so much of the added weight to go up top?' David asked. 'Surely you wouldn't have had a breast op.'

He'd pushed me to my limit. I snapped. 'You're right, you know,' I said. 'They *are* trolls.'

His mouth hung open. It was not a pretty sight. Given that he was temporarily speechless — a rare and welcome event — I went on. 'Well, not adult trolls yet, not quite. They're troll nymphs, a few years from metamorphosis.'

'Trollettes,' he said, with an evil grin.

'Troll nymphs,' I said firmly, keeping the conversational upper hand as long as I could. 'It's dark outside, so they can leave home without getting turned into stone. But they won't be able to come out to places like this much longer. Around the time they turn thirty, the metamorphosis starts. In a couple of years, most of them won't even be able to get through the door. They'll be huge, like sumo wrestlers only bigger, and the camouflage will kick in.'

He sniggered. 'They'll develop baggy green uniforms?'

'Don't be frivolous,' I snapped. 'This is serious. They're evolved to blend into mountains. They'll look like a heap of rocks, most of the time. If you saw the group of them moving, they'd look like a small landslide. In winter in Europe they'd be paler, like ermines, to blend into the snow.' I hoped I was making an impression on David with this disgraceful breach of the secrecy agreement I'd signed.

'What a heartbreaking story,' he said. 'Gloriously nubile muscular treats one minute, boulder-like monsters the next. Are you sure they're really trolls? I was just indulging my well-known mordant wit.' He put on the facial expression he used for photographs of himself as a semi-famous playwright: one side of the unibrow lifted, the other lowered. I tried not to laugh.

'I'm absolutely sure, David.' Deciding that I might as well be hung for a sheep as for a lamb, I carried on breaching secrecy. I'd feel bad about it in the morning, but right then I didn't care. Anything to score another point.

'They're definitely troll nymphs,' I said. 'I worked with them in Scandinavia. There's something subtle about the proportions of the arms and legs. Nothing crude; it's not like their knees are on backwards or anything, but the bones aren't quite human, either. Once you've studied them, it's unmistakable. And the endocrine system is fascinating. Even the blood is incredible.' I've seen a lot of blood in my life — mostly through a microscope — but I'd never seen blood quite like that before I went to the institute in Sweden.

'I'm impressed. So, you actually did something useful after you deserted me.' Surprisingly — even shockingly — he truly did *look* impressed.

'Thanks, I think,' I said. 'And be careful around them, you old wolf. Gloriously nubile or not, they're more dangerous than ever at this stage.' I glanced back at their table. The huge platter of lady's fingers was empty already. 'They're highly evolved predators, with an amazing sense of smell, and they have to eat enormous amounts to fuel the metamorphosis.'

'They've certainly been tucking into the food tonight.' This from the man who'd practically inhaled a huge steak and a mound of chips.

'And you know their *favourite* food, don't you, David?' It was so nice, knowing more than Mister Know-It-All, about something other than the endocrine system.

'Shock me,' he said, with a devil-may-care man-of-the-world look.

'They're a protected species in Scandinavia, but it's kept very quiet. They're isolated in the mountains, in a secret spot, or they'd be exterminated in weeks. Vigilantes would hunt them down. The people have long memories, there.'

'Cut to the chase,' he said. He hated any conversation he didn't dominate. 'Their favourite food is . . .?'

I didn't want to lose the upper hand now. 'Human flesh, David. The younger and sweeter the better. Babies, if they can catch them. Back in the old days, you didn't let a child wander too near a heap of rocks — just in case it wasn't really a heap of rocks.' I ruined the effect by shuddering involuntarily; I simply wasn't the woman I used to be.

For the first time in the evening, he looked genuinely excited. 'Really? No wonder they starred in so many fairy tales. Kids *love* that stuff.' He'd made most of his income, over the years, in plays for schools.

'Yeah, human nature never changes. Kids have always loved disgusting, scary things.' Things like *you*, I thought.

'They're revolting beasts,' he said. He leaned across the table, his brown eyes gleaming. 'Children, I mean, not trolls. I'm assuming that the trolls can't help themselves. They'd be acting instinctively, at the mercy of their genetic coding. However much of a monster I might be, at least I don't go in for human babies.'

Despite myself, I almost laughed. 'You're well-known to detest them, in fact.' But that was enough talk of trolls and babies. The conversation could take far too many dangerous turns from here. More importantly, I felt the unmistakable tug of duty: I had to be home by 10 pm, alone.

The gods were with me. At that moment the waiter came to take our plates, and I distracted David with the help of the cakes on display in the big glass case at the back of the restaurant. But I knew that getting rid of him wouldn't be easy. He'd want to come home with me for coffee: several cups of coffee in fact, a brandy or two, and, despite everything, he'd try to talk me into bed. Despite everything, I might even have been tempted, if I let it get that far.

I gulped my chocolate cake down in four or five huge, delicious mouthfuls. I suspect David wolfed his in one big bite; I couldn't bear to look.

Cruelly, he asked, 'What would you do if they discovered that the cocoa bean could feel pain? Would you give that up too?'

'That's a moral dilemma for another meal,' I said, and placed notes on the table for more than my share of the meal. I wasn't almost famous, like him, but at least I had a steady income. I stood up, and walked to the door, talking over my shoulder as I went: 'Gotta go, sweetie, lovely catching up, must do it again soon, bye . . .'

He just sat there staring; I was into my car in seconds, and off.

Once I was home, I sat in the old blue car for a moment, relieved to have escaped so simply. I wouldn't have been surprised if he'd tried to follow me, but there was no sign of that. I was in perfect time for the 10 pm feed.

Inside the house, I paid off my elderly baby-sitter and carried the sleeping babies from their big cot out to the glassed-in room at the back of the house. The light of the full moon streamed through the floor-to-ceiling windows. The boys woke and started mewling with hunger; their vigorous little bodies knew it was time for food.

I lay back on the huge squashy sofa and stripped down for action, then I carefully attached a soft, sleepy, hungry baby to each nipple. Once they were suckling steadily, there in the moonlight, I allowed my body to relax at last into an animal languor. It was such a relief. The twins took no notice; they love me with four paws and eight teats just as much as they love the version with two legs and two breasts.

But then I heard the crunch of dead leaves outside. My senses have always been sharp, and they were amplified by motherhood, doubtless to help me protect the young. I looked out carefully: something was trying to conceal itself between the huge deep-green camellia bushes. It was a troll nymph, there in my backyard in the moonlight — the dark-haired girl in the sparkly top.

My lupine instincts took over. She was a danger to my young. The hair at the back of my neck bristled, and I made a guttural noise deep in my throat. It felt good. I went further: I stood on all four paws over my babies, and howled a loud warning to the predator. The twins lay under me, reaching upwards for a teat like the famous bronze babies in Rome. The fact that I was standing on the sofa may have undercut the iconic nature of the tableau somewhat, but that was not my problem.

From out in her hiding-place, the troll nymph saw that I'd spotted her. She looked up, startled.

'Annafrid,' I growled. My hearing is too sharp for me *not* to have caught her name over dinner.

'Can I come in?' she said. 'Please? I'd like to talk.' She looked at me a little guiltily, a child caught out doing something silly — not a predator caught in the act. I sniffed very carefully, checking the tiniest nuances of her smell. The air was deliciously full of fascinating pheromones: not-human and not-wolf.

With difficulty, I started to pull myself together. Transmuting from human form into wolf was all too easy, but it took a huge effort of will to melt back into the soft human form — especially in the moonlight. Growling gently, I worked through the whole painful process, and reflexively pulled a few clothes on. The twins started to whine with frustration.

'All right, Annafrid,' I said at last, 'come in. The back door's not locked.' I'd known since adolescence that I could take care of myself, as long as I didn't come across too many mad peasants with silver bullets, and no one had cause for revenge; I've never so much as tasted human meat. The whole idea had always made me nauseous, even before I'd got myself pregnant. Apart from any moral questions, it was so shockingly unhygienic. You never know where people have been.

The troll nymph walked in, looking tentative. Her deltoids shimmered prettily in the moonlight, and her top sparkled. So did her dark-lashed blue eyes.

'May I hold one of them? Please?' she asked, glancing at the twins.

The wolf in me wanted to growl, but I knew that Annafrid was taking her medication. I could smell it in her sweat.

I handed Remus to her. She held him clumsily, as if he might explode. 'It's so little,' she said. 'Hardly even a mouthful.'

The window over the sink shattered, and a greying middle-aged wolf leapt over the kitchen bench and straight at Annafrid. He pushed her to the ground, and stood over her throat. She managed to keep hold of the writhing, screaming baby; her muscles were mercifully useful as well as decorative. Romulus in my arms and Remus in hers both started to howl. Their lung capacity is excellent and their ancestry appropriate; the noise was indescribable.

'David! Down, David!' I shouted. 'Don't you dare hurt my baby!'

I dropped Romulus on the sofa, snatched Remus from Annafrid with my right arm, and pushed David's snout away from her throat with my left. He snarled at me.

As I scrambled onto the sofa with my two babies safely in my arms, David threw back his head and howled. All the dogs in the neighbourhood, as well as my twins, joined in.

'Stop the histrionics at once, you middle-aged thespian,' I said. 'Can't you see she's not resisting? Get off her this instant, and transform back.'

He snarled at her and me then, and growled a few times, but finally complied. His clothes must have been lying in a heap somewhere — wherever he'd changed — so I passed him the sofa throw. He knotted it around his thickened waist.

As soon as he was decent, and his vocal cords had settled in, he started shouting back at me.

'What do you think you're doing, woman? You should be thanking me for rescuing you, and those babies of ours that you'd so treacherously kept secret from me! How *could* you?'

'Stop jumping to conclusions, you egocentric idiot!' I shouted. 'What makes you think they're anything to do with you?' He'd never wanted children; he wasn't going to claim my gorgeous babies now.

He took no notice. 'I *knew* something was up at the restaurant. You didn't smell right. You're lucky I followed you to find out what you were so eager to get back to, and caught her in the act. She's a troll nymph! She's just here to eat our babies! Why aren't you doing anything about it?'

By this time, I'd reattached the twins to my leaking nipples, which had the great virtue of stopping the babies' ear-splitting howling. 'My babies,' I said, 'not *ours*,' and glared at him. 'And you're wrong about Annafrid, too. Maybe you should have snooped around outside the window a bit longer before you leapt to conclusions about what she was doing.' I nodded to Annafrid, hoping that she'd take the hint and explain herself.

'Actually, I came here to thank you, Talia,' she said. 'You changed our lives. Those trials you were doing in Sweden ... the pills you were testing on my relatives are wonderful. They really work.' She waved happily towards the twins, still sucking away. 'Even the smell doesn't tempt me. Your babies are perfectly safe from me!' She beamed, clearly overcome with joy.

'It wasn't just me, it was the whole team,' I said, blushing modestly. Then I looked David in the eye. 'She's talking about a new medication for troll nymphs, to suppress the desire for human flesh. That's what I was working on when I was in Sweden: the clinical trials.'

David sat on the Turkish rug, exuding disbelief — but speechless for the moment.

'I'm *so* pleased the medication really works,' I said to Annafrid, with perfect sincerity. 'I'd have hated to have been forced to kill you.' Actually, I wasn't sure who would have won in a serious match between Wolf Woman and Troll Nymph, but I wasn't going to let on.

Annafrid gushed on: 'I was so proud, just being in the same restaurant. My group — we all had a wonderful night.'

I felt all warm and runny inside. David just rolled his eyes.

'That wasn't a coincidence, was it?' I said to Annafrid. 'A group of wild trolls, in inner Melbourne?'

She shook her head and gave a rueful half-smile. 'No. Most of us live up in the Dandenongs. Elfrida and Birgit flew down from Sydney; there's a lesbian colony up in the Blue Mountains.' Troll males are almost always solitary and brutish, though enormous. Heterosexuality should never be assumed among female trolls.

'Elfrida and Brigit — they were the pair in the matching satin frills?' I asked.

She nodded, and said, 'We've been monitoring your emails since you got back to Australia. Sorry about that . . .' She scuffed her feet uncomfortably, while I tried to look impassive. Soon, she went on: 'Um, well, our relatives in Sweden had told us about you, and we all wanted to see you. All of us who could pass for human.'

'Oh?' I said.

Annafrid looked serious. 'It's very important to me. I lost my mother that way. She snatched a human toddler, when I was just a baby. They came for her with machine guns and hand grenades. Afterwards, my older sister smuggled me out here to Australia. She's changed now, poor Agnetha. She can hardly talk any more.' Tears were glistening in her huge blue eyes. Trolls were formidable after the metamorphosis, but they lost easy use of many of their higher functions.

David finally spoke up. 'And you all just happened to choose the night Talia deigned to see me, after a whole year. After she'd left me when she was pregnant with our sons. Without even having the courtesy to *tell* me she was pregnant. Great timing, both of you.'

'My babies,' I said again. 'Not *your* babies, or *our* babies, you horrid man. You don't even like babies, remember? Just for once, this isn't about *you*.'

'I think it is, actually,' he said, with a smug almost-smile. 'Whose babies could they be, if they're not mine? I'm sure they've got my eyes. They're exceptionally handsome little creatures, for babies.'

Everything was *always* about him. 'I've told you already, they're mine. They're only eight weeks old. Do the maths, David.'

His long, single eyebrow tilted. 'So you got pregnant in Europe, a few weeks after you left me. You said there wasn't anyone else. Would you care to explain just how this happened? Artificial insemination? Immaculate conception?'

David had quite graciously helped me pack up and leave him, after seven years of squabbling interrupted only by more serious fights. I'd diagnosed mildly dented pride, rather than heartbreak.

'It's absolutely none of your business,' I said. 'I think it's time you went home, now. I've got to put the twins to bed.' I wanted to mention the bill for mending the smashed window, but he'd have stayed all night arguing that it was merely a by-product of his heroism, and that I ought to welcome him back to my bed in heartfelt gratitude.

'And I bet you've called them Romulus and Remus,' he said, with a sly smile. 'Male twins of uncertain parentage, right? Possibly semi-divine, and suckled by a wolf.'

He knew me far too well.

I prevaricated. 'Why would you think that?'

'Well, what else would you call them? Tom and Jerry? Not my inventive Talia.'

Now, more than ever, I knew that I had to change their names to something plainer and more child-friendly before they got to kindergarten, or they would be social pariahs.

After much nagging, David loped off into the night alone, leaving me and Annafrid with the twins. I handed Romulus to Annafrid, and we walked upstairs together and tucked the two boys into their big cot.

When David was out of earshot — which took quite a long time, with a wily old wolf like him — Annafrid asked, 'They *are* his, aren't they?'

'Yeah. You can smell it?'

She nodded. Troll senses are even better than wolf senses. Their natural environment is harsher.

I said, 'They're five months old, really, not eight weeks, but he wouldn't know the difference. I only found out I was pregnant when I was working in the institute with your relatives. He'll work it out eventually. He's not stupid, and they really have got his eyes.' I hoped, quietly, that they wouldn't get his dark unibrow.

She looked baffled. 'But why don't you want to tell him now?' she said. 'Human males bond strongly with their young, don't they?'

'Yeah, mostly, but David would be a terrible father. He'd probably run away to Europe, if I told him they were really his. On the other hand, he'll make a fantastic Uncle David for little boys: all care and no responsibility. Hunting lessons in the backyard — chasing grasshoppers and beetles — they'll all have a ball.'

While I was trying hard to be casual, Annafrid was looking at her feet sheepishly.

'What's up?' I said.

She looked up at me through her long, feathery eyelashes. 'Hey, would you mind if, I mean can I, um, is it all right if I sleep on your sofa tonight? Talia? I missed my lift back to the hills, coming here.'

I almost asked her to share my bed. My tongue itched to lick those rippling deltoids. But it had been a stressful evening, and I needed a few hours' sleep before the 4 am feed, and the 7 am alarm clock.

'Sure.' I led her to the linen cupboard for sheets and blankets. She stood very close to me; her fascinating inhuman smell surrounded me. I breathed deeply, and smiled.

But there was no hurry. Annafrid and I could have a few good years together before she started to change into an adult troll. I could smell it in her endocrine mix. And there was something that none of the researchers had wanted to tell the trolls until we were absolutely sure: the medication we'd been testing didn't just take away the desire for human flesh. It actually seemed to delay the metamorphosis. Annafrid would have a choice; she didn't *have* to turn into an aphasic pile of rocks. With luck, she could stay gloriously nubile for as long as she wanted.

As she kissed me goodnight, sweetly and gently, I passed my right hand lightly over her shoulder. Her deltoids felt as good as they looked.

A few minutes later, in bed — alone — I set my mind to work towards a happy future for us all. What could I rename the twins? Castor and Pollux, no; that would be even worse. Tom and Jerry, no. Ben and Jerry, no. Bing and Bob, no . . .

AFTERWORD

Some years back, Russell Blackford and I ate at a noisy Melbourne restaurant near a large group of young women who seemed to be having a wonderful time. I said, 'Girls' night out,' and our sardonic dining companion replied, 'Trolls' night out.' It became a family catchphrase, and eventually turned into this story.

—*Jenny Blackford*

AARON STERNS's first published story, 'The Third Rail', appeared in *Dreaming Down-Under* and was shortlisted for the 1998 Aurealis Award for Best Horror Short Story. Subsequent stories 'At Night My Television Bleeds' (Orb #3/4) and 'Watchmen' (*Gathering the Bones*) both received honourable mentions in *The Year's Best Fantasy and Horror* annual collections. Recently he served as script-editor for the film *Rogue* and appeared in Greg McLean's earlier *Wolf Creek* as a nasty truck driver. A former editor of *The Journal of the Australian Horror Writers*, Sterns has also presented academic papers on *American Psycho* and *Crash* at the International Conference on the Fantastic in the Arts (as part of PhD work on postmodern horror), written non-fiction articles for *Bloodsongs: The Australian Horror Magazine*, amongst other publications, and was the Australian correspondent for *Hellnotes: The Insider's Guide to the Horror Field.* Sterns is currently working on a number of screenplays and a novel. He lives in Melbourne, Australia.

Be warned, the brilliant, incandescent story that follows is . . . harrowing.

THE REST IS SILENCE

AARON STERNS

He drove from Melbourne almost on autopilot, winding through the familiar country roads between Gordon and Mt Egerton and arriving at the old house before even realising he'd been heading there.

The tiny shack still stood halfway up the slope of the mountain. Abandoned long ago, its yellowing weatherboards looked sickly against the surrounding grass, the few windows broken and gaping. He left his car by the road and slowly walked towards his old home, staring up at the unfinished wooden veranda looming above. His stepfather Graeme had once thrown his mother over the railing, punching her hard enough in the mouth to send her tumbling into the dirt, and he had crept out later to find her folded-up in the darkness, the side of her head caked with mud and blood that he tried futilely wiping away with his pyjama top as he helped her inside.

The back door hung only by one hinge, and as he hefted it aside a warm rotting smell hit him. Inside he could see mildew up the plasterboard walls, great darkened rents in the floorboards, spreading stains across the roof. He remembered sitting in here at the cramped eating-table watching television with his brother Stephen as Graeme and his mother argued about something over dinner, remembered the big man leaning forward and casually swatting her across the face, breaking her jaw. Remembered blood speckling his plate.

Through the doorway he saw into the bedrooms, once bisected with a curtain but now open and empty. So many nights he and Stephen had burrowed beneath their blankets on their side of the room trying to escape the sounds from the kitchen of his stepfather's drunken ranting and clomping feet, the fearful, hitched-breath justifications of his mother, the heart-stopping gunshot-smash of a bottle thrown against the wall, the otherworldly smack of flesh on flesh. So many nights they listened to the alien sounds of sex from behind the curtain, his mother not able to meet their eyes the next morning but at least avoiding getting hit.

He remembered pleading with her again and again to leave. But Graeme threatened to kill them if she did.

Toward the end, when he had grown bigger, he started standing up to his stepfather and had his nose broken twice, but it tore through his mother's inertia and forced her to take them away. Since then he had dreamed again and again of revenge, of hunting down his stepfather and ... doing what? Killing him? Beating him up? He never really knew, and when the bastard died of cancer it was as if some part of *him* also died.

He stared around at the crumbling monument to his past, and then stepped forward and opened the jerry-can from the service station in Gordon and started emptying it of petrol. He soaked the walls, the floors, the gaping windowframes, until the wood was stained blood-dark. Then he walked outside on stiff legs and lit the bottom of the door.

The heat scorched out at him and he stumbled back as the door whumped into life. The growing licks of flame blazed in the dying late-afternoon light and soon the weatherboards alongside the entry took hold and the wall of fire arched up towards the roof with a sudden roar.

But as he stood watching the house burn he felt empty inside. It didn't give him release, didn't change what happened, didn't exorcise anything.

When he saw an old guy in a flannelette shirt running over from the next property he headed back to his car. Sat inside clenching the steering wheel with white knuckles, still feeling the heat on his face, the emptiness inside, then realised the guy was taking his numberplate and drove away.

Panicking at being seen he turned onto Sharrock's Road and quickly wound around the mountain and down again, disappearing into the back roads, nearly losing it on the gravel. The setting sun burned in his rear-view and he glanced up and saw tears in his eyes.

It had all been for nothing. He couldn't escape the past. Couldn't get rid of the deadness inside.

And now the police would be after him.

What the hell had he done?

He looked back to the dirt track as he came over a dip to see a bizarre flash of white in front of him, something in the middle of the road: a figure, a boy walking along the trail. He yelled and braked and the car fishtailed, sliding instead *towards* the boy, the tyres howling on the uneven ground, and he slammed the wheel hard to one side even as the boy finally turned with a little o-mouth of surprise, and then a scraping crump sounded from somewhere, everywhere, as the grille folded around the sudden body. A scream of metal and spinning air and strange whorls of gravity like a blender a washing machine a dryer and trees spanned past the window with a disembodied frightened roar sounding through the crumpling cabin strangely like his own voice; and then an otherworldly slowing, a graceful transition to epiphany in which he could see the web of cracks in the windshield hanging timelessly, sculpture coupled with dried insect guts and scratches from rocks, the dashboard a comforting black nothingness wrapping around him, soothing in its manufactured plastic, primacy over the elements, over the earth; and for an age he transcended it all frozen in that eternal moment — and then the steering wheel sank into his chest as if he was molten and flowing and yielding. Blackness like a sly wink of a loved one, of his mother, his brother perhaps, his runaway father, the boy on the road, capturing eyelid washing away all pain and fear.

He woke suddenly in a haze of agony, chest resting on the remains of the steering column. Pain lanced through his arm but all he could think was he'd killed a child.

Oh God, he'd killed a child.

The car was on its side down the embankment and he looked out through the shattered gape of the windshield at the ridgeline. No movement on the road. Tried to unhook the fused seatbelt clasp and nearly screamed.

His hand was flayed open, the bones broken and spiking out as if claws, threaded muscles hanging in ropes against his forearm. He swallowed vomit and clutched the useless hand to his chest. Tried the clasp with the other hand.

And groaned with despair. He would have to wait for help, for someone to find them. He couldn't help the child now.

He closed his eyes, realising how stupid he had been.

No one knew he was here. He didn't speak to his mother any more. After she lost her hard-fought house in Ballarat she became unstable, forever railing against the injustices she suffered, all the shit she went through with no help from anyone, not the government, her parents, his father, no one, as if he and his brother hadn't been there for any of it. He wasn't able to take any more of her victim-complex or her vitriol. He stopped seeing his brother too after Stephen became increasingly angry and violent, externalising all his hatred at the world and his past. They had come to blows over some stupid thing last Christmas and that was the last time he saw his family. He had pulled away from everyone: mother, brother, friends; sabotaged every job he ever had; fought against anyone and anything he could. Ever since he left this shithole of a town his life had been in entropy and just when he finally tried to do something to abate it, to regain control again, to purge himself of the past, something even worse had happened.

From the distance came a soft mewling. His eyes snapped open. It sounded again, small and shattered: like an injured cat.

K-kid? he cried hoarsely, coughing with the effort of speaking. The boy must be alive. Injured, perhaps badly, but alive and in need of help.

He could still do some good. I'm coming, he called, tearing with awkward fingers at the clasp until it finally popped and he fell against the door. He sucked in air for a moment, massaging his bruised and constricted chest, then cradled his arm and scrambled through the windshield out onto the dirt away from the wreckage. The Centura was almost unrecognisable — its roof caved in, bonnet dented and steaming — and smelt of leaking petrol. In the last of the light through the trees he could see angry scars arching down from the road, and, using rocks as leverage, he scrabbled back up to the angry churn of the crash site, despite the wrenched feeling in his hip. Caught movement ahead down the long stretch of red dirt: a flash of white on the road. The boy was dragging himself along on his stomach like a wounded dog seeking somewhere to die, heading towards a mass of gumtrees up the side of the mountain.

Wait … I'm coming, he croaked, his voice like dead leaves. He started to follow but his hip had seized, right leg stiffening up, and he could only lurch slowly in pursuit. No, stop! he called to the boy. You need help … We need to wait here.

He looked to the crash site. But the road was empty, no signs of rescue, no signs of chasing police. When he looked back, the child had dragged himself off the road.

Pain-sweat dotted his forehead as he jerked his wooden leg behind him, clutched his arm to his chest. But he pushed through the agony. He couldn't let the kid down. Then he saw where the boy was heading and stopped.

A house stood off the side of the road amongst the tangle of trees. A big two-storey brick veneer, new, a flat imposing facade pocked with large elegant windows, well-kept driveway, even a garden. A house he had only ever dreamed of. A room for everyone. Space.

The kid was trying to get home.

He gave a strangled gasp and tried not to think of the scene to unfold: the family's dying child turning up on the doorstep, his killer staggering just behind seeking help. He almost turned and ran. But the lights were off. There mightn't be anyone home. The kid may still need him to call an ambulance, and he clumsily staggered on, following the speckled trail of blood.

In the distance, the front door opened with a creak. As he watched, the kid tried to rise on unsteady feet and walk through. But the boy's legs buckled, splintering unnaturally. A high lilting screech of pain scared some birds.

No! Wait! he shouted feebly, but the tiny figure disappeared across the threshold pulling broken legs, the distant cry of relief heart-wrenching, and it took him an eternity to catch up.

The boy's blood glistened faintly on the polished floorboards beyond the entrance and he knew he had to get to the injured child as soon as possible. But the light from outside didn't travel far and he had to stumble along the wall for a light switch. Hello? He searched a small table for a phone and knocked over a vase. Hey, is there anyone else here? We need help. Kid? Where are you?

The house was silent and he was forced to follow the faint specks down the darkened hall past empty rooms. He was near the end of the corridor peering up a staircase to the second level when he heard the child's soft mewling coming from the last room. He focused on the massive doors and forced himself on.

The arched doorway led into a big sitting room at the back of the house. The boy huddled in the furthest corner in faint light arcing around the heavy curtains, a puddle of blood dotting the carpet next to him.

It's okay, he said to the boy as he came into the room. I'm going to help you.

He searched for a light switch but couldn't find one, instead having to edge into the gloom. Banged his leg into a coffee table a few steps in. The boy shuddered at the collision and tried to burrow even deeper into the corner, crying out horribly as the bones of his shattered legs grated together.

Don't move, he warned the boy desperately. I'm not going to hurt you. I just want to make sure you're okay. Look, I'll stay where I am. He stopped in the middle of the room and put his hands up to reassure the child but the kid wouldn't look at him, kept trying to edge away despite the grinding pain.

He hesitated, unsure whether to continue into the room or backtrack for help. Looked to the doorway as if that would answer.

He was turning back to the boy when he sensed something behind, a shadow running at him from the hall, and he turned, already raising his hands in protested innocence, expecting one of the child's parents.

I didn't — he started to say and then the figure filled his vision and his tongue jammed to the roof of his mouth at the impossible shock, the *recognition*, and then a whoosh of air sliced towards him, a sudden wallop impacting his temple and sending him sprawling back towards the window, throbbing disembodied pain seeping through him as if vicarious, delayed. And as he stumbled against the window-ledge trying to yell: Wait! he clumsily pushed with his free hand, palm butting a chest. But it only allowed the other to find him again in the near-dark and the next punch slammed into his nose and snapped his head back against the curtain-muffled window, sparkling his vision and sinking cold up past his eyes. He fell then, toppling to the side with one flailing arm, sight gone, and he somehow grabbed hold of the curtain on the way down and it held for a moment then noisily ripped and came down on top of him. He swatted at the sudden caul, terrified, waiting for the blows to rain down, kicking out like a child, feeling a thump as he connected with something that nearly twisted his ankle. But it felt good, substantial, and he kicked again, sensing his foot crunch something this time: a leg, giving him time to struggle out from the curtain and see the room in sudden relief with the last of the outside light coming through the naked window.

To see his attacker — his brother Stephen — hunched before him, cradling his smashed knee and glaring, face twisted.

St-Stephen? He managed but his brother just stared at him. Stephen? What are you —

And then his brother snarled and came again and all he could do was scrabble backwards, feet skittering on the floor, arm still tucked uselessly into his shirt, and then his brother collapsed as his leg gave out but kept coming at him on his stomach now like the boy.

He backed across the floor, knowing that this was impossible, that it couldn't be his brother attacking him, that he must be delusional, still in the crashed car perhaps, dreaming deliriously because of his injuries or something. And then his brother reared up with one arm and brought it down on his shin, piledriving the shear of bone with a crack, and he screamed at the explosive reality of the pain and kicked out instinctively with his other leg, catching Stephen beneath the eye and whipping his head. His brother just grinned, teeth white in the near-dark, a faint rip opening across his cheekbone. Blood welled like tears.

He banged up against something cold and harsh, his hand scraping fireplace-stone, and as he frantically searched for something, anything, to defend himself, he tried to yell: Stop! What are you doing? his voice raspy with fear, but it only seemed to spur his brother on, unstoppable now, coming at him across the floor in a nightmare whirl of limbs.

His hand finally closed around something heavy and metallic and he swung it in a wild arc that ended with jarring impact.

His brother abruptly stopped, expression frozen, crazed eyes unfocusing and glazing over.

He let go of the black length of fire-poker. It remained suspended from Stephen's head, its thorn dug deep into the side of the skull as the familiar blue eyes rolled up and blood ran in a thin line down and around his neck. Then Stephen keeled over and the poker clattered to the floor.

He stared down at the crumpled body of his younger brother, shaking, face crawling with horror. No, no, no . . . he kept saying. But Stephen didn't move. He *had* killed someone now. His own brother. He'd killed his own brother. He slumped backwards. Kept mumbling to himself: No, no . . . spacing out, eyes blurring and filling with tears. It was too much to take. What was his brother doing here?

And then he remembered the boy. Tore his eyes away from his brother's body and in a daze looked back into the corner.

The child was gone.

He looked to the open doorway, distantly wondering if the child ran out while they were fighting, but his mind no longer worked. Couldn't answer the questions. He got to his feet, gasping at the pain in his tortured leg, and edged around Stephen's body to the corridor.

The lights he had turned on were now off. He stared down the length of darkness to the still-open front door at the end.

A shadow crossed the doorway.

Then: footsteps, crunching gravel, more shadows arcing down the hallway. He stood awestruck staring at the gap of light as the sounds increased like hailstones, a steady rain of impacts.

And then the first figure appeared. A silhouette only but its shoulders were hunched in anger, the body squat and arrowlike, searching and then focusing on him. Another figure behind it and another and then darkness eclipsed the hall as figures filled the doorway and spilled into the house towards him, the noise on the floorboards now coiled thunder.

He instinctively twisted and fled up the staircase, knowing only that he had to run, the sound of countless feet scrabbling down the corridor pushing him on in terror. He rounded the top of the stairs and flailed in the darkness — a dim skylight the only illumination on the landing — and banged into the first door he could find.

He jammed his body against the door and stood panting. A bedside lamp softly lit the room and his eyes took it in as if it was some rationality, some comfort against the insanity on the other side of the door. Then he saw the glow off the sweating pale bodies on the bed: at first only a congealed mass of rippled, sheening flesh dotted with hair and freckles; then the woman moved beneath, opening her legs wider and groaning, and the mound coalesced into distinction. The guy kept pummelling away in fury on top — love-handles sagging down over shapeless white buttocks, shoulders straining with the missionary position. And then suddenly swung his head around, grinning through thick beard at him.

He almost tore open the door to escape back into the hallway.

The guy kept thrusting, staring at him with wild eyes and that rictus-grin, and then the woman beneath — greying hair spread over the pillow like road kill — looked at him standing there. Her glazed eyes washed over him then refocused and she smiled, the white slug of her tongue darting out to wet her lips:

Come here.

Her voice was soft, seductive, and he tried to push backwards through the wood of the door as his mother raised her hand to him, beckoning to join them. Outside, silence fell on the landing.

His mother frowned. I said come here.

Graeme stopped thrusting and stared at him, grin disappearing. The old anger surfaced beneath pig-eyes as the fat bastard withdrew with a clench of his puckered ass and a sound like a knife sliding out of a wound. Rolled off the bed and stood, bloated hairy stomach taut with a lifetime of beer, slickened alien-head penis a fresh jutting limb.

Then his stepfather was across the space between them in a flash, grabbing him by the throat and staring up, hands slick with salty sweat. Behind, his mother ran a hand down her body and snarled at him.

He couldn't do anything, could only stare down.

And then he realised he was now taller than his dead, impossible stepfather. And as Graeme was bringing his face down to his and reaching for his groin with the other hand an anger rose from somewhere deep inside, hidden all these years but finally given full expression and he roared and punched back at the older man, feeling the jellied softness of nose beneath his fist; punching again, harder this time to the jaw with a satisfying crack of crumbling bone, and Graeme was stumbling backwards now, hands raised blindly against the assault, and he limped after him and slammed down onto the fucker's chin and his stepfather crumpled, erection wilting and mollusc-drawing up into itself. He jumped on the older man and was barely able to keep his broken hand into himself, to stop using that too to beat and beat, and he kept punching until there was only blood, until the red mist hung in the air and covered his face.

A screech and a whump as something smacked into him, hot skin pressed against his, and then slices of pain near his eyes as his mother clawed from behind, legs wrapped around his waist, and he could *feel* her against his lower back, and he cried out and rolled onto her, slamming his head back with crunching force against her face and swinging around to hit and hit and hit.

When it was over he vomited until his stomach spasmed with nothingness. He tried to close his eyes to the scene around but kept seeing himself punching again and again, kept seeing their slackened faces dissolving beneath him, and he wearily opened his eyes and looked to the door, waiting for it to burst inwards.

A muffled giggle came from the corner of the room. He looked up at the dresser to the boy sitting on its top swinging broken, multi-jointed legs and staring with fascination at the bodies sprawled on the floor. A soft awful clicking of bone like chittering teeth. When he realised he was being watched, the boy looked at him and fell quiet, but the smile lingered. He seemed to be waiting.

He was about to ask something useless of the boy, something redundant and irrelevant about what was happening. But it didn't matter any more.

The boy nodded at his acceptance, and then the glittering eyes swivelled towards the doorway and the smile widened.

He understood then, understood everything, and he crouched and waited for the first to come through; these people from his past, the dead and the living: aunties, uncles, friends from primary school, old girlfriends, grandparents, work colleagues, perhaps people he'd only passed in the street, brushed past in pubs, sat next to on the train. He could hear them now pressing at the door, lining the stairs, crowding the hallway with clenched hands, filling the driveway in anticipation, could imagine them stretching away down the road, an eternity of faces and fists and blood. He flexed his hands like a prizefighter and hunched closer to the floor, grinning with the insanity of it all.

He hoped his father was next. He was looking forward to seeing him again.

AFTERWORD

Hell is other people, as Sartre said.

'The Rest is Silence' (Hamlet's last words, and obviously an ironic title in that the story ends with anything but silence) is what I'd call an existentialist ghost story. We are all haunted by the past, but we learn to repress the pain and regret and guilt and move on with our lives. It's often only years later that the true damage surfaces and threatens to overwhelm us.

Some it will destroy.

— *Aaron Sterns*

JASON NAHRUNG is a Brisbane writer who grew up on a cattle property in Queensland but now works as a journalist for a major metropolitan newspaper. His coverage of Australian speculative fiction has earned him a William Atheling Jr Award for review and criticism. His short fiction is invariably darkly themed, perhaps reflecting his love of classic B-grade horror films and 1980s Goth rock music. His debut novel, *The Darkness Within*, is based on a novella-length story written with Mil Clayton.

Nahrung is a writer 'with the juice', another writer to watch. Here he writes about mateship, otherness, and what's worth dying for in the mummified dryness of the Australian outback . . .

SMOKING, WAITING FOR THE DAWN

JASON NAHRUNG

George stood by the bleached skeleton of the Wyandra stockyards, breathing in dust and sun-baked silence. The rust-red roofs of the township shimmered in the heat haze, and from what he could see, his old stomping ground hadn't fared much better than he had in the past twenty years: tired, forlorn, running out of time.

He leaned against the uncomfortably warm bonnet of the Commission-issue van and rolled a smoke, making the most of the inconsequential shade offered by a drooping mallee tree. The first hit of nicotine settled in his lungs and he coughed wetly before breathing out a blue cloud of resignation.

He eyed the sagging loading ramp and the warped rails. The decrepit yards didn't look like they could hold so much as a steer now, but once, he and Tommy Daniels had herded a baker's dozen of Undead through those gates and shipped them back to the holding camp down the road at Cunnamulla. They'd got a citation for that.

Familiar bile rose in his throat and he spat it out to sizzle on the tarmac. They'd been quite a team, him and Tommy, raising all manner of hell out here, mates all through school and then for the best part of ten years with the Commission.

A Fourex sign, the red faded to the colour of dried blood and the white to that of bone, beckoned from the roof of the Railway Hotel from across the railway line. That had been their office, once. Back before the enclaves had been established and the Undead had been semi-legalised; back when a collared zombie or vampire was worth a damn sight more than a ute-full of kangaroo carcasses and dingo scalps. Back before the big Toowoomba breakout had rolled over his friendship with Tommy like a road train. All that was left now was road kill, twenty years old and still stinking fit to make him spit.

George flicked his cigarette butt to the ground and toed it out. Sweat pooled under his shoulder holster and the heavy utility belt at his hips. He reflexively caressed the polished weaponry, drawing comfort from the long, thin tube of the HeartStopper, the half-moon curve of the nested guillotine, the black mass of his side-arm.

The sun beat down on him like a solid iron fry-pan, making him squint behind his sunglasses, sweat stinging his eyes. He didn't need to check his watch to know the time; he could tell by the angle of the shadows that it wasn't yet noon. Plenty of time. He eyed the hotel that was, like him, a memento living on dust and memories. Time to go to work, he thought, but first, he'd drop into his former office and see if his old mate had left him a postcard.

George leaned against the bar and closed his eyes. The Railway Hotel smelled as he remembered it: stale beer and cigarettes, dirt and antiseptic. He forced his eyes open as the publican plonked a glass of beer beside him, condensation making his mouth water with anticipation. The bubbles rose towards the thin layer of white foam sealing the glass, promising relief as the yeasty aroma wafted free. The publican, crow-footed eyes narrowed to a slit, picked through George's change, took what he needed and ran it through the register. He hadn't looked George in the eyes since George had walked in.

George grabbed the cold glass and took a sip. The beer still tasted the same. It always did. He sighed and wiped his mouth with the back of his hand before rolling a smoke. 'You know Tommy Daniels at all?' he asked.

The barman glanced at the phone, then dumped an empty in the sink with a harsh bang and rinsed it off. Sweat beaded on the man's bald spot.

George hid a knowing smile behind the rim of his glass. 'I thought you might, given this is the only drinking hole in town.'

The barman concentrated on drying the glass. 'Don't know no one by that name.'

'Tommy Daniels. He was a Hunter, once.' George took another drag on his cigarette. He felt the vaguest movement of the air from the fan bolted to one wall, its muted whirr the only sound.

'A Hunter, eh?' The barman looked up, his eyes glancing off the pistol slung under George's arm. 'You won't need the gat. Hasn't been any renegades out here for years. They're all locked up in the enclaves, eh.'

'You would've heard of Tommy. Here.' George took an old snapshot from his pocket and placed it on the bar runner, careful to dodge the wet coaster.

The barman eyed the photograph, two young men in sleeveless shirts and bullet-proof vests carrying rifles, standing in front of a four-wheel-drive. They could've been shooters, except for the Commission logos on their vests.

'That's an old photo. Before my time, I'd reckon.'

'He was a bit of a local legend, Tommy. I'm guessing he wouldn't look much different now.'

'There was a chap, called himself Dan, looked a bit like that.' The barman ran a hand over his bald spot. 'He's dead, but.'

'Really?'

'Passed on a week or so ago. That you, standing next to him?'

George tipped his glass in acknowledgement.

'You here for the big roundup, back in '72?'

George nodded, remembering the hunt that followed when the Undead had broken en masse out of the Toowoomba camp. The clever ones had headed to the coast, trying to hide in the population there. But others went west, and why had always been a mystery to George. The zombies he could maybe understand — they could handle the sun — but the vampires: where was the food, the shelter? Hunting them was hardly a challenge. Shouldn't have been a challenge, he amended.

Memories of the shearing shed surfaced unbidden, the sunlight lancing through the gaps in the timber slab walls, the holes in the iron roof, the smell of wool and grease and sheep shit heavy in the dusty air. He and Tommy, driving stakes into the Undead and dragging them out to the van for transport. And then the screaming, the fire ... And seeing her, the Greek, and feeling the earth lurch under his feet.

The barman rested a hand on the tap. 'Another?'

George looked at his glass, mysteriously emptied between nicotine breaths, and nodded. 'How did he go?'

'Found him myself, dead on his kitchen floor. Heart attack, maybe kidneys or liver. I never heard for sure. Didn't have a cent to his name, the poor bastard. Folks round here chipped in to buy him a headstone at Charleville.'

George looked out the open casement that offered a view of the town. The other pub was a sagging timber structure that looked ripe to collapse, its windows boarded and paint faded to non-existence. The community hall didn't look any better, and only two rusty bowsers marked the former site of the petrol station cum general store. Whole streets of houses had vanished since his time.

'Wasn't a fancy headstone,' the barman said, putting a dish of peanuts on the bar.

'They never are,' George said. No one retired rich from the Commission. No one retired from the Commission, full stop. He skolled his beer and reached for a handful of nuts. 'So you buried old Tommy, eh?'

'If that was his name. It was what Dan wanted.'

'Strange.'

'How so?'

'Every Hunter I know insists on cremation. Just in case.'

'Catholic,' the barman said.

'They burn as good as anyone else.' George tucked the snapshot away. 'Shame I missed the funeral.'

'It was only small. You didn't miss much.' He took George's empty glass. 'What brings you out now?'

'Work.'

The man's eyes narrowed. 'You here about that lad out at Black Creek Station? The one that got tore up? That was just dogs, wasn't it? Poor little bugger.'

'I can't say. Wouldn't want to start a rumour.'

The barman looked around the empty room. 'Yeah, wouldn't want folks to talk. Anyway, headstone's up at Charleville. Danny Smith's the name. Another?'

George put down another bill from his wallet. 'So how was he, towards the end?'

'Same as always.' The barman topped off the glass with a practised smack on the tap. 'Come in from his shift at the meatworks, get pissed, stagger home.'

'He was working at the meat works? Up at Charleville?'

'Cunnamulla. Bit of a drive, but a man's gotta earn a crust, eh?'

'Where was he living?'

'Little cottage up the street, there. It's on the market. Was thinking of buying it myself, but not much point, really. The town's gone belly-up: just a handful of locals here now, and the guys out on the stations. Between them and the occasional tourist and truckie, there's just enough trade to keep this place open.'

'I reckon I know the one. I might go take a look at it, for old time's sake.'

'Nothing much to see. Every cent he made, he put across this bar.'

George glanced out the window. Noon had passed but sunset was a long way off. 'No rush. I reckon I'll have another one: for Tommy.'

George parked around the corner from Tommy's house after a slow drive-by. The timber building looked much as he remembered: the porch a little more sagged, the stairs a little more rotted, the paint more peeling. The iron eaves drooped over the windows, the rusted tin roof all but curling under the sun. George reckoned he knew how the house felt. He could've used some structural work himself.

With a heavy sigh, he went around the back of the van, opened the rear doors and retrieved his case. Back in the merciful shade of the cab, he popped the lid and took stock of the tools of his trade. Once he had his vest on and had adjusted his shoulder holster, he assembled the shotgun quickly, an action he could do with his eyes closed, and then went through the similarly automatic steps of preparing the hypo of PP-D. He rolled up his sleeve and tapped the hungry vein underneath a clean patch of skin. One of the idiosyncrasies of the serum was that, for all the vampire-like physiological effects it could mimic, healing the damage caused by its own delivery wasn't one of them. Thirty years of working for the Commission was mapped out on his arms in needle sticks. It was something the boffins were working on for the next version, but it had never been a high priority: there was only one Hunter who had reached thirty years of service, and he wasn't likely to make another ten. So the doctors told him.

George shot the contents into his vein. The familiar rush swirled through him, pushing him back in his seat. The world grew very bright, very hot, as his senses peaked. His heart raced.

He pushed his sleeve down and went through the ritual of rolling a cigarette as he waited for the spasms to subside, his breathing to ease. Roll the tobacco, lick and seal the paper, tamp the ends, light her up, breathe her in: so pungent to his nose, so acidic on his lungs, but soothing, in its own way. He was ready to go.

Dry, brown grass and crumbly sand crunched like glass under his boots as he walked towards the house. With every step, he felt the buzz of PP-D burning through his system: muscles quivering with the need for release, reflexes as taut as fencing wire, the world bright and loud and moving just a little too slow for his hyped body.

For a long moment, he stood, finishing off the cigarette as he surveyed Tommy's old home.

The last time he'd seen Tommy Daniels, they'd been pulled over by the side of the highway a good few miles from here, the stench of burnt timber and flesh still clinging in their hair, the back of the wagon filled with recaptured Toowoomba renegades.

They'd tracked the escapees to a shearing shed. He and Tommy had gone in under cover of daylight, juiced out of their brains on serum — what had it been back then, PP-A? B? The Greek had come out of nowhere, a shadow amongst shadows. She'd got the drop on Tommy and it had been luck, just luck, that George had got the shot off and put her down, long enough for Tommy to ram a stake home — no spiffy HeartStoppers back then, but the old-fashioned stab-and-thrust, squelching up under the ribs while the reverb of the gunshot still shook the white ants in the posts. The situation had got out of hand, the other Undead charging in, and him and Tommy running white-hot. There'd been gunfire, blades, incendiaries. Some of the Undead were kids. It wasn't pretty, seeing them burn, those they couldn't drag out in time. Tommy had cried, openly, and reckoned he was done with the Commission. George hadn't believed him.

That night, when the shed was a pile of ashes miles behind them, they agreed the Greek was the most beautiful woman either had seen, living or Undead. In the wagon, with the stake withdrawn in a moment of mutual weakness under the excuse of interrogation, they'd asked her where she was from and she'd said Greece, a long time ago. George had asked the questions but she'd answered them to Tommy, and after a couple of hours of that, George had told Tommy to 'stake the bitch, she's not gonna tell us anything useful about the others', and stomped off to have a cigarette. When he'd come back, the woman and Tommy had gone. He'd tracked them for a day, but realised pretty quick that Tommy was no hostage. George returned to Brisbane with the remainder of their capture, and never reported the run-in with the Greek; just said Tommy was MIA, lost in the fire.

Had he made the right call? If he could go back, would he do it differently? George stomped out his cigarette and took a long, hard look at the house. Nothing moved behind the boarded windows.

He checked his pistols one more time — 9mm automatics in the shoulder and hip holster, and a snub-nosed .38 on the ankle — and felt the reassuring weight of the shotgun, its mag filled with heavies. He'd been putting this off for twenty years. It was time.

A crow cawed, lethargic in the heat, the cry rasping across George's enhanced hearing as he approached the house.

The iron gate hung open in a fence long absent of wire, but habit made him walk through and up the cracked, uneven concrete of the path.

George wrinkled his nose as he paused at the bottom of the steps. Whiffs of vampire reek carried on the air. The smell of a nest was distinctive, a bit like the roost of a city derelict: that pungent, throat-burning aroma of an unwashed body in near permanent habitation. Not that vampires were dirty; it was more subtle, the scent of exhaled blood and meat, of decay on hold.

George cranked a round into the breach and picked his way up the dodgy stairs. They creaked, but held. He tested the door. It swung open with a rusty squeak that sounded like a hacksaw through metal to George's sensitive ears, making him grit his teeth. Shotgun cradled against his waist, he let the door tap against the wall. Sunlight scorched a path across the room. Motes of dust twinkled in the beam. The rest of the room was cloaked in shadow, the furniture merely enigmatic dark shapes, a television screen gleaming in the light.

The threadbare carpet cushioned his footfalls as he stepped in, his senses scanning for the tell-tale signs. He was halfway across the room before he felt the movement behind him: the softest, most delicate footfall, the sudden change of light as the door swung almost shut.

That delay, the merest breath-long delay it took for her to reflexively close out the sunlight, was what saved him. He was used to it, surviving by a breath. It was part of the rush. The PP-D could only do so much in levelling the playing field; to win against the real thing, you needed cunning and a bit of luck. He took two paces back, giving himself extra time to bring the gun to bear as she approached. Slow, the Greek, not like twenty years ago, back in the shearing shed.

'He's —' she said, before her voice drowned in the blam-blam-blam of the shotgun. The burst shook dust from the ceiling, echoed in his ears long after the afterimage of the muzzle flashes had faded from his vision. She sprawled, spreadeagled and bloody, looking as if she'd been dropped from a great height. Her chest was a gruel of flesh, bone and blouse, her jeans saturated and pale face splattered with dark blood.

George knelt beside her, held the HeartStopper over her breast and fired a bolt into her before she had time to recover. Her eyes stared at the ceiling, wide and brown. He reflexively fitted another bolt into the tube and reloaded a charge before holstering it. God, she was beautiful. Even like this. He traced her chin, rubbed her cheek, flicked a hair from her forehead where it lay stuck in a blood splash. His hand shook as memories of the shearing shed pulsated through his racing mind. As beautiful now as she was then, even being dragged, bloodied shirt hanging open, as limp as a corpse with a stake through her heart, her life on hold until that vital muscle could beat again.

The first whiff of burning flesh hit his nostrils like a smelling salt and he looked around, blinking away his reverie, and found her arm lying in that narrow beam of sunlight shining through the slightly open door. The skin, scarlet and blistered, was starting to crack and smoke. His hand left the guillotine, denying the call of the primed, diamond-edged blade, and moved her limb into the shade.

A footstep.

Behind him.

Still on his knees, he straightened slowly and grasped the shotgun in both hands, aware now of the glint of eyes surrounding him as the vampires emerged from behind furniture, materialised from the shadows. He could see three, sensed more.

Timber creaked.

He turned, heart leaping, barrel swivelling, trigger finger tightening — he jerked the barrel up. 'Fuck, Tommy, I almost drilled you.'

Tommy leaned against the doorway into the hall, arms crossed across his blue singlet. 'I heard you were back in town, Georgie. I was hoping you'd drop in.'

Sweat ran cold down George's back, his finger still jittery on the trigger. The others hadn't moved, content to hover in a loose circle around him, phantoms at the edge of his vision. 'I'm surprised you're still here, Tommy.'

'Where else would I go?' He moved to peer around George at the woman's body. 'Lys only wanted to talk, you know.'

'Old habits,' George said, getting to his feet, careful to keep the gun pointed at the floor, his finger on the trigger guard. 'I'm juiced, Tommy. You know what it's like. But she's still kicking.' Thank God he hadn't finished her. At least this way, he had some kind of bargaining chip —

hadn't done anything that couldn't be undone. 'You took a risk, didn't you? Letting her do that?'

'I didn't reckon you'd do her in. Wouldn't have let you, anyway. She wanted to talk to you first, see how you'd react. I told her it would be okay. That I knew you.'

'It's been a while, Tommy.'

'Not that long. Let her up, George. I want to talk to you.' He pointed over his shoulder, down the hall. 'Tea?'

'Is that what you're drinking these days?'

Tommy smiled, teeth bright. 'Still enjoy a good cuppa.'

George stooped and yanked the bolt out of the woman's chest. It withdrew reluctantly, dragging a wet, sucking sound. She moaned, blinked, her wide, dark eyes registering her delayed shock. The wound began closing over immediately. The lurking vampires shifted nervously. 'Sorry about that,' George said, surprised to realise he meant it, and retreated after Tommy.

He found his old mate filling a battered kettle at the kitchen sink when he entered. Cracks of light shone through the boards over the kitchen window, casting the room in a twilight murk. Soft footsteps on the worn hallway runner urged him to put his back to the wall by the door. By the time Tommy had ignited the gas stove and put the kettle on the burner, four children were gathered around him, their eyes fixed on George.

Tommy sat at the Formica table, its red and white check pattern faded with age. The kids gathered around him, vaguely reminiscent of that painting of the last dinner of Christ, but a few bodies short. Tommy Daniels and the four apostles. Plus however many were left in the front room with the Greek.

'So what brings you out here after all this time?' Tommy asked.

'Work, just work.'

'Nice of you to visit, then. I'm amazed you're still Hunting after all this time. I though you would've retired by now, one way or the other.' His eyes roved over George's long sleeves. 'It's hard to give up, isn't it?'

'Not for some, apparently.' The PP-D screamed at him for release, the flood of synthetic, vamp-based drugs trying to convince him he could make it. He only had to get into the sun. They couldn't touch him out there. The incendiary grenade on his belt could take care of the rest.

'You remember the shearing shed, Georgie?' Tommy's voice was low and level but carried the cold menace of a knife blade on a steel.

George gripped his shotgun tightly, squeezing his reply through a clenched jaw: 'I remember.'

'And you're still Hunting.'

The two men locked stares; both blinked when the kettle shrieked. The kids all seemed to vibrate on the spot, like guard dogs on the leash, begging for release.

George used every ounce of will to overcome the urge to spray them all with a long burst and run for the kitchen door and hope to God the PP would give him enough strength to burst through before the vampires tore him apart.

Tommy breathed out, a long, sad sigh. 'You just should've come for me, Georgie, way back when, instead of taking it out on those poor sods over the years.' He motioned to one of the kids, who turned off the stove. The kettle's scream died away. 'You still take it black?'

'Yeah.'

Tommy got another kid, the tallest, to fetch two cups and saucers from a cupboard.

Shaking, George propped the shotgun against the wall and rolled a cigarette. Had to work hard to get enough spit to seal the paper. He could feel the stares of the kids: vacant, hungry, inhuman. One twitch from Tommy and they'd be on him. 'I never figured you for a family kind of guy. Not all yours, I take it.'

'Strays. Surprised me, too.'

'Must be the woman's touch,' George said, lighting up. He coughed, blew smoke. The stench offended his artificially keen sense of smell, but he didn't care. For some reason, he wasn't dead yet, but if he was the condemned man, he'd bloody well enjoy his last cigarette. 'I heard they buried you.'

'I heard that, too.' Tommy gave his trademark guffaw. 'C'mon, sit down. Like I told you, I want to talk.'

George sat. The kids bristled as the chair scraped on the lino floor. George felt their hostility fill the room like a looming storm. At eye level, their teeth seemed much brighter, much sharper. His hand found the butt of the pistol at his hip: for him, if not for them. His fingers clenched on the cool metal as the only girl, dark-skinned and flat-chested, plonked the tea pot on the table, then stepped back beside Tommy's shoulder. Her gaze settled on George, steady and alien, and he became aware of new trickles of sweat running down his back.

'So what's on your mind, Tommy?'

Tommy poured two cups, the scent of tea wafting over the stale layer of old blood and dust, the bite of nicotine and freshly struck match.

'You're here about that young fellah out at Black Creek, aren't you.'

'Like I said, just business.'

'It was an accident.'

'He's still dead, Tommy.'

'We trained the kids to live off the land, but they're just kids, Georgie. They make mistakes, just like the rest of us. But they don't always understand what they do, you know?'

'That kid out at Black Creek's still torn up when he didn't need to be.'

'And you got to take someone back to show for it, haven't you?'

George nodded and sipped his tea. 'The Commission knows, Tommy. They recovered enough of the corpse to work it out: not dogs, not weres — vamps.'

'I figured as much. Where do you reckon we could run to?'

George put his cup down and resettled his hand on his pistol. 'Nowhere's safe. Not without friendly bartenders to cover for you.'

'What about the enclaves?'

'They'd never shelter a renegade, not one with a blood warrant on its head.'

'I'm out of touch, been out of the game too long, not like you. Tell me this, though, Georgie: after thirty years, what've you got to show for it? Scars inside and out, and blood under your nails. How long do you think you can keep going? How long till the juice wears out, or you do? And then what have you got?'

George tapped ash from his cigarette onto the saucer, then rubbed his eyes, his chin. He felt tired, so very tired: the PP-D wearing off, no doubt, and perhaps the thirty years of hard, dangerous road catching up with him. Living on the edge, and about to fall off. Sitting here with the last man he'd trusted, but not the last one who'd betrayed him. 'I dunno, Tommy, I dunno.'

'So why did you wait so long to come looking for me? For us? Why didn't you lop Lysandra just now when you had the chance?'

'I dunno that either, Tommy.' He focused on the glow of his cigarette: so bright, burning down, almost out.

'I think you do.'

George ground out the butt on his saucer, making the china rattle. 'Fuck it, Tommy, you were my mate. I couldn't hunt you, not even after you jumped ship and left me holding the can.'

'You ever ask yourself what you would have done if she'd made you the same offer she made me?'

'What offer was that? Eternal life?'

'I only got her to bring me across a week ago, once I realised Black Creek was going to be a problem. Up till then, it was too important to have someone who could operate in the daytime. The job at the abattoir provided all the nourishment this lot needed, and kept me in beer money.' Tommy ruffled the hair of the nearest kid, an Aboriginal boy with white teeth and curly, black hair, rendered sexless by youth and a voluminous football jersey.

'You're looking good, though, for fifty going on a week.'

'The love of a good woman will do that,' Tommy said with a chuckle. 'Her love and her blood, anyway. Ageing gracefully, I call it.'

'So you've been with her the whole time, eh? Feeding off each other.' George felt the lethargy seeping into his arms and legs as the PP serum weakened its hold. He rolled another cigarette. 'Long life and good health, and you get to keep your tan. Sweet deal.'

'You didn't answer me, Georgie. What would you have done if she'd asked you?'

'I'd have stayed, done my duty. My duty to my country and to my partner. To you.'

'You know what I think, Georgie?' Tommy topped up their cups, dragging the question out. 'I think you were scared when you found out that the renegades were human after all. I think you've spent the rest of your life trying to prove to yourself that you made the right call.' He slurped his tea. 'How many have you collared now?'

'I don't keep count.'

'I reckon you do. Probably two separate columns for stopped and lopped.' He stared at George, as though he could see the ledger in his eyes. 'You ever wonder what's it like — the real thing?'

'No. Did you?'

'Yeah, of course. The PP's only so good.'

'Is that why you . . . you went with her?'

'Nope. Though I gotta tell you, it leaves the serum for dead.' He grinned, then grew serious again. 'I was exhausted, Georgie. I couldn't take it any more, couldn't face another collar, not after the shearing shed. Not all the PP in the world can wash away that stain on my soul.'

George looked around the dark room. 'And this has?'

Tommy leaned back and smiled. 'You don't have any family, hey?'

George shook his head.

'Pity. Family's the only thing worth dying for.'

'You're not dying, Tommy.'

'Everyone dies eventually.' He looked past George's shoulder and smiled. 'Well, almost everyone.'

George turned in his chair as Lysandra entered with another kid holding her hand. She'd changed her top. Even without his boosted senses, he could smell the recent bloodshed, the gunpowder. She glared at him as she stalked to Tommy's side, one hand resting with easy familiarity on his shoulder.

'Sorry,' George told her. 'Instincts, you know.'

'Instincts can be overcome,' she said, her voice accented. Even in the gloom, or perhaps because of it, she looked beautiful, black hair shining and complexion dusky, speaking of quiet strength and resolve. And perhaps something else: resignation?

Tommy clasped the woman's hand, then fixed George with his gaze. 'Tell him,' he said. 'Tell Georgie why you asked me and not him. It's been eating at him for twenty years.'

George held his breath, cursing Tommy with every silent blasphemy he could muster. He didn't need — didn't want — to hear this.

Lysandra ran her fingers through Tommy's hair. 'But I did.'

Tommy looked stunned, his hand frozen on her.

'You'd walked off, to check the others, relieve yourself … something. And I asked him.'

Tommy stared at George.

'He said no.'

George looked at his teacup, feeling the bite of regret in his throat. 'I was doing my job. I still am.'

She turned away from him to concentrate on Tommy. 'It's in the past. He said no, you said yes. We should forget this. We can still run. Take our chances on the road.'

Tommy took her hands, his voice quivering as he said, 'There's nowhere to run to, love. Nowhere I can be sure you and the kids will be safe.' He looked at George. 'You are one lucky sonofabitch, you know that?'

'And why's that, Tommy?'

'You're getting a second chance.'

George lifted his head to run his gaze over both of them. 'How do you figure that?'

'You're gonna have to take me in, Georgie.'

'What?'

'Just me. Lys and the kids stay free.'

'Tommy …' His fingers closed on the pistol. No chance, he knew, not without the PP-D. Not now that he was just an old, tired Hunter … He looked at Lysandra and knew — knew — he couldn't shoot her again. Ever. His trembling fingers released the pistol; tea spilled as he gripped his cup instead. 'This is insane.'

'Hear me out. You give me to the Commission and close the case, retire somewhere nice. You've got the connections to provide for Lys and the kids.'

Silence settled, the kids' gazes boring into him. 'What do you think about all this?' George asked Lysandra.

'I think I should've killed you when I had the chance. I think I should've turned Thomas a decade ago and run away with him to Asia. But I didn't, and now I have to do what's right for the children, for our family. We always knew this day might come. We just didn't know how we'd deal with it.' Her grip tightened on Tommy's shoulder, her knuckles showing white. Red tears rimmed her eyes, but she blinked them away, not letting them fall. 'So now I think I need someone to protect us from the Commission. Someone to watch over us during the day and bring us the blood we need, without anyone getting hurt. I think, Mr George, that you can help us and I can offer you something you need. You wouldn't want to make the same mistake twice.'

George rubbed his arms, feeling the scars through the material. 'The Commission will never believe it. They think you're dead, Tommy.'

'The Commission needs a collar if they're going to be prevented from digging around. The only way to keep them off Lysandra's tail is to give them one. I have the history that we can use, right down to that empty grave up at Charleville. You can tell them you were wrong back in '72. That I must've escaped the fire and got infected, lived off livestock and backpackers till I got sloppy and killed that kid out at Black Creek. You're the investigating officer. Tell them whatever you need to, to keep my family safe.'

'If I take you back, they'll make you talk. We'll all go down.' He gestured to Lysandra and the kids. 'You, me, them.'

'I know that.' Tommy squeezed Lysandra's hand again, flashed George a grim smile, fangs showing. 'Taking me in alive — you know what I mean — isn't an option.'

George clasped his hands under the table, trying to stop the shaking. 'Fuck, Tommy. I dunno. I just dunno if I can do this.'

'A second chance, Georgie. A man with a cough like yours should be grateful for it.' He flashed a sad smile. 'Then think about it some more. We've got till morning.' Tommy shepherded his family out of the kitchen, leaving George alone with his smokes and the teapot.

The tea was cold when Tommy came back, cheeks wet with pinkish tears. 'You made a decision, Georgie?'

'You love them that much?'

'You will too, in time.' Tommy smiled. 'Don't feel bad. Second chances don't come cheap. We've both paid the price.'

George nodded, a single, determined gesture. 'Put the kettle on, eh?'

They sat, and drank tea, and talked, just like two old mates who hadn't seen each other for years, rather than two old mates who'd never see each other again. When the sky started to get light, they went out and sat on the stairs, and smoked, waiting for the dawn.

AFTERWORD

'Smoking, Waiting for the Dawn' was born during a road trip. My father and I drove through western Queensland, where he had worked during the '50s, hoping to meet up with some of his mates from that era. Unfortunately, most had died. This story was also influenced by Australia's sorry handling of refugees.

— *Jason Nahrung*

CECILIA DART-THORNTON was first 'discovered' on the Internet after she posted the first chapter of her unpublished trilogy to an online writing workshop. Subsequently a literary agent signed her, and within a few weeks a major New York publisher bought her three-part Bitterbynde series (which includes *The Ill-Made Mute, The Lady of Sorrows,* and *The Battle of Evernight*). On publication the books were acclaimed in *Amazon's* 'Best of 2001', *Locus Magazine*'s 'Best First Novels of 2001', and the *Australian Publishers' Association Award*: 'Australia's Favourite Read of 2001'. They also reached the top of the *Sydney Morning Herald* bestseller list and received accolades in the *Washington Post, The Times, Good Reading Magazine, Kirkus Reviews* and more.

Grand Master of Science Fiction Andre Norton wrote of *The Ill-Made Mute*: 'Not since *The Fellowship of the Ring* fell into my hands have I been so impressed by a beautifully spun fantasy. This is indeed a find! ... The writing is very close to poetry. Many fantasies are compared to Tolkien these days but few really have the excellent writing and good characterisation that this work offers. This is far above the usual offering in the fantasy field and the reader is left longing for the adventures to continue. I feel honoured to be asked to read and comment on such work.'

Cecilia's books, including the four-part Crowthistle series (*The Iron Tree, The Well of Tears, Weatherwitch,* and *Fallowblade*), are available in more than seventy countries and have been translated into several languages.

'The Lanes of Camberwell' is pure magic ... and pure Melbourne.

THE LANES OF CAMBERWELL

CECILIA DART-THORNTON

In March that year, when autumn was already beginning to pick out amber tints across the leafy suburbs, I visited Julia, who had been my friend during our early school years. We'd somewhat lost touch, and I would scarcely have recognised her if it were not for the fact that she still lived at the same address.

She was thin, a wraith of her former self, and she came in late — having forgotten our appointment — ragged in her green dress, even barefoot, her skin like chalk. It was with true affection that she welcomed me, mingled with regret that she had inconvenienced me by making me wait. 'Oh Jenny,' she cried, 'I'm so sorry. I had forgotten ... my memory these days ... can't seem to get organised ...' Her sentences were broken, as if wounded. And there was truth in all she said, because the house was in a state of disarray. This was not the Julia I had known. What had happened on that day, some twelve months ago? Why had she gone to pieces? She made me sit on a couch in her living room while she brewed a pot of tea, and as she disappeared into the kitchen I mused in some dismay about her deterioration.

Julia had lived a normal life until one day about a year earlier, when she had gone missing. Eventually she had been discovered wandering the streets alone, unable to find her way home or offer any explanation for her plight. Since then she'd taken to roaming regularly, and some called her 'the Bag Lady of Surrey Hills', though she was only twenty, and the beauty of youth clung to her as tenaciously as the tendrils of the Boston Ivy that smothered the fences of her back garden. In autumn that vine decorated the weathered bones of the palings with splashes of deepest crimson; almost the colour of her hair.

I'd heard she now spent her days walking the local footpaths in a trance-like state, sometimes muttering to herself, ignoring passers-by with their quizzical glances. Occasionally she was to be found sitting on the nature strip with her back against the mottled bole of a plane tree, staring into space with a puzzled expression. She always, however, found her way home in the evenings.

Reentering the room empty-handed Julia said, just as if she'd read my mind, 'Isn't "nature strip" a funny term?'

Personally, I couldn't see why it should be, but I nodded. We'd always laughed about Julia's uncanny knack of apparently picking up other people's thoughts.

'Most suburban streets have grassy verges,' she elaborated, 'but I think Australia must be the only country in the world where they're called "nature strips".' She was looking out of the window into the street. From here you could see the gracious, wide-spreading branches of the plane tree that grew outside her house, its leaves, as large as splayed hands, just beginning to turn gold and brown as the days became shorter. My hostess had forgotten about the tea. Instead she walked across the room to the dining table where, on the faded tablecloth, a journal lay open. 'This is Daniel's,' she said. 'He wrote this more than a year ago.' Picking up the book she handed it to me and I read:

February: Last month of Summer.
The Lanes of Camberwell. What is it about them that draws me so? In dreams I walk them. Waking, I revisit them in my mind, think about actually returning to see them, then think again; *no*. Why not? Because I have grown to be over-awed. And because in any case I'll never be free of them. They are with me always, inside my skull; their pattern, their layout, their connections, corners and angles, their *feeling*.

And what is that feeling?

It is made of wonder and excitement, eager expectation and the slightest tinge of fear. It is the sense of imminence; that *something is about to happen*, and that the *something* is only a hair's-breadth away, an instant away, if only you knew how to break through. The slim, dim, dusky Lanes of Camberwell, where no matter whether the summer sun is blasting its heat across the shimmering roofs of the suburbs, there is always a breath of freshness, a hint of moisture; cool shadows caught in the long swathes of peppercorn leaves overhanging the fences like the hair of tree-giants; a gleam of syrupy gold from the five-petalled buttercups that grow at the entrance to one of the lanes, and which appear nowhere else that I have ever seen. We used to hold those flowers beneath one another's chins, chanting, 'Do you like butter?', and if a golden reflection appeared on our friend's skin, it was supposed to mean they did. But whence comes the sudden, incongruous moisture that nurtures these blossoms of yellow silk? For here in this single patch the ground is damp, as if the tiniest corner of some English marsh has appeared from nowhere, complete with bright green grass and shiny flowers floating on their stems. Everywhere else the ground is dry and hard, baked by yet another drought. Perhaps the remnant of some age-old underground spring still seeps below the Lanes, heedless of mankind's attempts to divert and drain, to capture it with metal fetters and enclose it in pipes; a free, wild waterway that won't be tamed but remains secret, running hidden beneath the footpaths, the foundations of the paling fences, the roots of the peppercorns, the lawns and hydrangea beds of the suburban gardens abutting the Lanes of Camberwell.

Secret, like the Lanes themselves.

For you would not know of their existence unless, walking along one of the Surrey Hills streets, you chanced to glance sideways at exactly the right moment.

Then, unexpectedly.

You've passed house after neat house, each perched in the centre of its tidy garden behind a front fence of bricks or pickets, each building different from its neighbours, each with its painted letter box. Here a fully-grown pomegranate overhangs ceramic fence-caps, its ripe fruit like red lanterns; there a japonica, its startlingly black boughs splashed with blood-flowers in spring. Elsewhere the gently nodding foliage of a dogwood, a crepe myrtle or a glossy lilly pilly. House-block after perfectly rectangular house-block, they rub shoulders with each other, jammed up close with no room to spare, marked out by six-foot high fences along their boundaries.

The rows of houses form a barrier. You are walking along the street because there's nowhere else you can go. You have not been invited into any dwellings; you cannot even see what lies behind them, because they won't let you past the front gate. They are private property and you have no business there. A formidable barrier they are indeed, though pretty, with their terracotta-tiled roofs and wrought-iron verandas, their benevolent-eyed windows winking from half-drawn fringed blinds. There is nothing ominous about the homes of Surrey Hills; they are where people live, that is all, and welcome their friends to afternoon tea, and tend their gardens — lawns silver-frosted in winter, daisy-starred in summer.

But you, a stranger walking along the street, may not enter. You have two choices: to keep walking in the same direction or to turn around and walk the other way. Two directions; two dimensions.

Until.

You look to the right and there's a disjunction. Unexpectedly, one suburban plot slams to a halt up against its fence-line and before the next one begins, *there's a gap*.

One more step and you would have missed it.

To your right the land rises. The houses sit proudly above the level of the street. Between them — between the green-eaved house where two elderly ladies live and the white weatherboard house deep amongst its shrubberies, a stab of brightness flashes: daylight.

Daylight at the far end of a tunnel. And the tunnel is dead straight narrow, deep-walled, sudden. You are staring along one of the Camberwell Lanes.

I closed the journal and replaced it on the table. 'Daniel?' I enquired. 'Who's that? And why do you have his diary?'

My friend looked at me and smiled. That smile was so profoundly enigmatic, it disconcerted me. She said, 'Don't you remember him, Jen? The blond boy who used to live down the street when we were children? He was a couple of years older than us, and Mum made us walk with him to school. He and his parents moved away about twelve years ago but by chance I met him again last year.'

'Oh, *that* Daniel!' I said, my interest awakening further. 'I rather fancied him. We all did. What's he like now?'

'He's tall.'

'Of course he's taller, but —'

'Oh, he looks like an angel.'

Love was written all over Julia's face. She showed me a photograph of Daniel, which she kept on the windowsill beside a potted plant with jagged leaves. He was sitting on the beach wearing a swimsuit, the white-hot sun casting hard shadows across his tanned features. The picture must have had been taken at Christmas time, because beside him, stuck in the sand at a rakish angle, was a sawn-off pine tree decorated with tinsel and shiny baubles. I had to agree, Daniel had grown up to be gorgeous. They'd met by chance, she told me, at a meeting of an environmental action group, and reaffirmed their earlier acquaintance, settling into an easy-going, platonic relationship. He regularly invited her to visit him at his home across town, where they'd reminisce about old school days, and discuss the world's problems and how to fix them, and many other topics besides. He was very busy in those days, with his career as a freelance journalist, and had not yet been able to find the time to visit her.

'I loved him,' said Julia, twisting her fingers together tightly, 'and I still do. In hindsight I see I didn't make the most of every moment. Perhaps I could have been a better listener.'

A tragic love affair! So that was it.

'He has a brilliant mind,' she went on, 'and was always interested in the oddest things. Seeing me again seemed to trigger something, and he developed this kind of *obsession* ...' She hesitated, before adding somewhat doubtfully, 'Not with me. A *landscape* obsession.'

'Let me make us a cup of tea,' I said, tactfully omitting to mention that she'd forgotten to do just that, 'and we'll sit down together and you can tell me all about it.'

From Julia's neglected and overgrown garden the cooing of doves came burbling through the open windows. The curtains stirred softly in the breeze. Meanwhile, seated in the front parlour, I listened to my friend's tale. Over the scalloped and gilt-daubed rims of porcelain cups delicately painted with pansies and violets she evoked a vision of her times with Daniel. I reconstructed her story, filling any gaps from details she let slip, for she had always seemed to possess this gift of mind-reading, and she'd perused his extraordinary journal from cover to cover, so that as I listened, it was if I'd jumped into the restless mind of this boy, this man I'd not seen for twelve years.

It was easy to imagine; she as lovely as a budding rose in her green skirts, her auburn hair spilling around her shoulders; he tall as a warrior, golden-bronze and graceful ...

'What have you been writing in that journal of yours?' asked Julia, looking up from the armchair on which she lounged in Daniel's study, the newspaper on her lap. She had kicked off her sandals — which lay tumbled at her feet — and crossed her slim ankles.

'Just thoughts.'

'About what?'

'About Surrey Hills.'

Julia turned a page. 'I can tell you, it has not changed much, since we were children,' she said. 'Only, things seem smaller and closer together.'

'I have not been back for a year or two,' Daniel said. 'I think I should, just to take a look. Seeing you has reminded me of — of so much about our childhood haunts.'

'Well, you are welcome at my place any time.'

'I know,' he said, 'and I'll take you up on that offer soon. It's funny, but whenever autumn comes around I start thinking about the places we grew up. Do you find that autumn is an evocative time of year, a season that brings on nostalgia?'

'Not really,' Julia said with a shrug, her eyes wandering to the pages lying open on her knee.

'I keep thinking about the route we took when we walked to school. I can't get it out of my head.'

'Oh yes!' Julia glanced up again and smiled. 'I remember those cold, frosty mornings, and we with our knitted scarves and gloves, our fingers and noses red and stinging, running down Guildford Road towards the lane because we were late, and how heavy the schoolbags felt, and how long and arduous the journey seemed. You used to make up stories about travelling in an armchair on wheels, with soft cushions and a blanket, and armrests so wide you could rest a hot cup of cocoa there, while we drove our armchairs to school, in comfort. And we'd imagine how the other children would stare, when we zoomed in at the front gate of the schoolyard ensconced in our chintz upholstery!'

Chuckling, the young man said, 'I'd forgotten. I wonder how many times we walked along those same paths. Five days a week, maybe forty weeks of the year was it? That makes two hundred, minus a few days off when we had the measles, or whatever. Say, a hundred and ninety times a year for six years — that's well over a thousand journeys. Twice that, if you count the return trip.'

'A lot,' Julia agreed absently.

'It is well known,' Daniel mused, 'that upbringing influences character; that our environment contributes, in varying degrees, to the orchestration of our destinies. The brain of a child is capable of being shaped or formed. What if this is closer to the truth than anyone has guessed?'

'What do you mean?' Julia was not really paying attention, but this did not seem to matter to her companion, who was being carried away with his own theorising.

'What if a child's daily passage through the rooms and corridors of a familiar house, or along the streets of a familiar neighbourhood actually, over time, erodes these geographical patterns into the physical circuitry of the brain?' he said animatedly. 'To turn left, for example, we must look left and step left, using the right hemisphere of the brain to analyse perceived data and to send messages to the nervous system. If those particular "left turn" centres of the grey matter are repeatedly stimulated at a certain point in the child's journey through time and space, they must necessarily *adapt*. They must *change*. A cerebral map is laid down inside the skull. It is wired there, engraved there; a road plan that will be carried forever. We might never be conscious that this was so, though sometimes they manifest as the pathways of our dreams . . .'

The speaker paused reflectively. On the other side of the room Julia remained engrossed in her newspaper. 'And so, I carry these pathways with me in my head,' Daniel said softly to himself. 'They are with me always; therefore it is not impossible that they have shaped my life, my destiny.'

Opening his journal he resumed writing. 'Once again I think of going back. They attract me. Why?

'I walked them, day in, day out; year in, year out, throughout all the ten-centuries-to-Christmas years of my childhood, but seldom have I returned to Surrey Hills since I was eleven years old. When I do, I never walk those paths, because now there is no reason to do so.

'When I visit my childhood haunts they are waiting patiently, those streets. The same presentiment is always there, along with other impressions I had forgotten, such as the fact that when you walk the Lanes, somewhere around the middle of the journey you become confused. You feel lost. You cannot remember how many Lanes exist in total, or how many you have passed through, or how many are still to come. Geography seems meaningless. No matter how many times you follow that route, it always happens. All you can do is keep going, until you arrive at some familiar landmark, and then you turn a corner and slowly your inner map reassembles itself again and as if waking from deep sleep you gradually become re-oriented, and breathe a sigh, *How could I be so stupid? Of course, this is where I am, this street is where the Lane comes out* . . . But it happens every time, even when you have grown up. I have walked that route to school thousands of times, yet I can never quite remember how many lanes there are . . . Strange . . .'

After closing the journal once again, Daniel crossed his study to the bookshelves, searched the contents quickly and selected an old, somewhat battered tome.

'What are you doing?' Julia asked as he carried the book to the desk.

'I have always been intrigued by Surrey Hills,' said the young man, 'and as time goes by the feeling gets stronger. I have decided to try to demystify the footpaths of our childhood by looking them up in the local street directory. Surely seeing them diagrammed as lines on paper will put them into perspective. It will show that the lanes and streets are leading nowhere mysterious and unattainable; that the houses along the Surrey Hills streets are not barriers manoeuvered into position by some arcane force that manipulated the minds of early town planners, nor are they concealing unknown wonders. It will demonstrate that there is a definite length to each footpath and a layout that does not alter; that the lanes do *not* move around, appear or disappear, that there is nothing to confuse pedestrians who Walk the Lanes.'

'Really?' Julia had risen from her perch and was peering over his shoulder as he searched for reference 46 D11 to H10. 'You used to get lost on the way to school?' Privately she was captivated by the way his hair fell down across his collar, and the fresh scent of the linen shirt stretched across his shoulders.

'Not lost,' he said, 'but disoriented, in a way I never have felt anywhere else. I bet if I stare long enough at the map I will be able to memorise the layout of the Lanes and therefore, if I visit them again, I will not experience that odd and discomfiting sense of uncertainty.'

'I'll leave you to it!' Julia said with a laugh, forcing herself to draw away from him. 'Mind if I make some toast?'

Daniel nodded. 'Go ahead, but not for me, I'm not hungry.' His guest strolled out of the room, and when she returned, he was still poring over the open pages.

'Clues,' he was saying. 'I need clues. Look at these, Jules, all these significant landscape features. The old red brick railway station, probably built a hundred years ago. Sports grounds and reserves. Boy Scout and Girl Guide headquarters. Waterways. Churches. The Salvation Army.'

Brushing crumbs from her hands Julia said, 'Significant? Scouts?'

'The Scouting Movement is immersed in human tradition, history and symbolism. It represents links with the land at primeval levels — campfires, singing, survival skills, camaraderie, adventure, human tribes living in the wilderness.'

'And reminds us of Childhood Before the Machine,' Julia contributed.

'Indeed, and with the uniforms and badges, their troops and bivouacs and encampments, it's like some quasi-military institution. Part of the fortifications of the boundaries. To keep something out . . .'

'What's significant about the railway?'

'The railway lines are the Iron Roads; vast, interconnected electrical conductors, like silver wires running across the landscape; nerves carrying impulses from station to station. Their bridges and underpasses are significant because they are a crossing of ways, and crosses, traditionally, are meaningful symbols. See the way some of the suburban streets are forcibly deflected from their straight course by the railway line? Do you think the railway follows the path of some waterway, in order to take advantage of the smoothest gradient? Or is there some other reason?'

Julia shook her head and shrugged.

'Which brings us to the significance of waterways,' Daniel went on. 'Life is impossible without water. Places where it rises or runs or collects are important. Not that all the waterways of the land are visible — civilisation has hidden many of them. But man has not, with all his efforts, entirely been able to disguise evidence of water's pathways. Here and there in the local topography a dip, a dell, a shallow valley or parkland reserve betrays the truth — "*Beneath this place water runs*". If you held divining rods and walked across these natural folds in the landscape the rods would, no doubt, twist and jump in your hands.' He stabbed the map with his index finger. 'Here at "Shrublands Creek Reserve" an ancient waterway of Surrey Hills has been allowed, for a few blocks, to flow uncovered. When we were kids we found tadpoles here. It was another magical place. Children can feel that land magic; I'm not sure whether I'd sense it now. I suspect the creek runs underground, beneath this other reserve over here. There's a sudden dip in the middle, a dell so steep that the council built a hump-backed footbridge across it.'

'A delightful, fairytale footbridge,' declared Julia, 'under which trolls were expected to dwell.'

'Yes, and when we stamped across we felt sure we sounded like the Billy Goats Gruff!'

'But we believed we were more than a match for the trolls if they did appear!'

'Do you see how the land's gradients prescribed the railway route, Jules? And its waterways dictated where buildings could be placed without danger of subsidence or flooding. That much is obvious. What is not so obvious, and more debatable, is whether land magic influenced the positioning of other points of significance, such as the churches, certain houses ... and the Lanes. But see here,' Daniel added, '— an unusual feature, surely, for a suburban zone? "Air Force No. 1 Flight Air Training Corps Small Bore Rifle Range".'

'Oh yes,' said Julia. 'I think it was built during World War I. Remember the enormous Scottish band that used the main hall to practise?'

'Of course!' Daniel smiled in fond recollection. 'In full regalia — kilts, sporrans, plaids — they played massed bagpipes every Saturday morning; you'd hear the music skirling through the streets of Surrey Hills for half the day, like a haunting reminder of our Celtic past! Look there on the map — a tower, a stream, a park ...'

'Yes,' Julia said absently. 'Sorry. I stayed up late last night.' She yawned and returned to her newspaper.

Feverishly Daniel traced the map with his fingertips. 'No need for apologies. I never expected anyone else to be interested in my current fixation. It is — I have to admit — a little eccentric to be reading the street directory on a fine Saturday morning. But there —' something had caught his eye — an oddly-shaped road that barrelled straight ahead out of the west to then suddenly swerve north at right angles as if avoiding some invisible obstacle, before turning east again and running straight on again ... 'A road along which half the houses turn their backs,' he said slowly. 'A road with a name that has always struck me as bizarre ... And all these places, these towers and steel rivers and martial establishments and halls of festivity for Celtic warriors, are linked; all linked by tree-lined streets and the Lanes of Camberwell. How many lanes are there?' Carefully, his finger moving over the page, Daniel counted. As he still must count, every time, to make sure. How odd. Odd that his mind could not hold this simple number, as if the number itself were fluid. Yet he was good at mathematics, and could usually memorise numbers with ease.

He followed the railway line, later writing about it as 'forging its way through the landscape like a cold steel river, driving deep cuttings through the bones of the hills and rising above sunken places atop embankments adorned with green filigrees of weeds'. How did Surrey Hills look — he later wondered in his journal — a hundred years ago? When the railway line was being built? Before the wild streams of the area were enclosed or buried so that houses and shops could be built, and roads laid down — where were they now, those ancient waterways? They would still be flowing — not even clever engineering could forestall the mightiest forces of nature — but no doubt they were now diverted underground, trapped in old, rusting pipe systems, flowing secretly along their arcane pathways.

'Aha!'

At Daniel's triumphant cry, Julia folded her reading material and put it aside. She did not resent the interruption; his enthusiasm was infectious and besides it was far more enjoyable to gaze upon her companion than to read the latest political opinions. 'Well, have you found a clue to whatever it is you are searching for?'

'Possibly. Just then a shape leapt out at me. It suddenly seems obvious that if you join up the lanes by drawing over them with a pencil, connecting them to the footpaths along which we walked to and from school all those years, a circuit diagram appears.'

'What exactly is a circuit diagram?' Julia asked. 'I mean, I know it's something to do with electronics . . .'

'A pictorial representation of an electrical circuit.' Spinning around in his office chair Daniel elaborated, as if quoting, 'Circuit: any path that can carry electrical current; a path or route the complete traversal of which without local change of direction requires returning to the starting point.'

'You actually *memorise* things like that?'

'I'm a nerd, you always tell me so! Oh Jules, this circuit engraved into my brain, what does it mean? Circuits lead back to the beginning. Where is its beginning? And does it in fact lead back there, or somewhere else? Let's go,' Daniel said suddenly, leaping up. 'We have to go.'

Julia did not have to ask 'Where?'

That very morning they caught the train to Surrey Hills. From Chatham Station they walked up Guildford Road to have lunch at Julia's house. Afterwards they set out again, passing the low brick fence of Daniel's childhood home, retracing the old route to school.

Grey skies were heavy with rainless clouds, and there was scarcely a breath of wind in the mild air. A blackbird twittered in a hedge when they passed by.

'I have not walked through the lanes since we left school,' said Julia. 'It's funny, but even though I live in this suburb there's a great deal of it I'm no longer familiar with.'

'Absurdly, I can't help feeling nervous,' said Daniel as they strode down the footpath to the bottom of the hill. 'After being so long away, spending so long *thinking* about this place, it suddenly seems as if I am walking into the pages of a storybook. But the pages might be blank! What if all that I *believe* I remember — the sense of oddness, the intuition that something amazing lies just out of reach — is nothing but delusion?'

'Hmm,' Julia said noncommittally.

'Or, if the premonition really is a property of the Camberwell Lanes and their circuitry, maybe I'm too old to receive the signal any more! Maybe children are the only ones permitted access to it!'

'You're only twenty-two,' murmured Julia.

'Either the storybook is blank, or it is filled with tales of wonder. Either way, I am unnerved.'

Julia, who saw nothing but the suburban street lined by avenues of trees and houses, made no reply.

'However,' concluded Daniel, glancing up at the overcast sky, 'the feeling seldom happens on days like this.'

They reached the mouth of what they'd always called the First Lane and passed into the shadows between its high fences. The defile was so narrow it did not permit them to walk abreast. Their feet trod a layer of asphalt, grey as smoke. In places this had cracked, and weedy blades of ribwort plantain were pushing through. The high wooden walls blocked any view into the gardens of the neighbouring houses. Ahead, a rectangle of diffuse daylight showed where the lane gave onto Sir Garnet Road.

'Here in the Lanes we walk Beyond the Pale,' Daniel said.

'Beyond the paling fences you mean?' Julia said.

'Yes, and somehow beyond the limits of civilisation, beyond reality's pallid appearance. On the maps this lane is nameless, you know Jules. Even now, they do not have official titles, these secret footpaths. No signs, no labels. That is part of their mystery. Is it impossible that the influence put forth by a place might be so strong that it subconsciously affects even the cartographer who attempts to define it?'

'You're being a nerd again,' Julia called out from ahead of him. Her voice echoed strangely.

'I know. How many lanes are there on the way to school?'

'Only one.' They emerged into the relative brightness of Sir Garnet Road. It was like coming out of a subterranean passageway. 'That is, if you go the quickest way,' Julia added.

'Look at this corner,' said Daniel, surveying the street. 'Isn't it the strangest shape? A complete anomaly! Within a few paces the whole street abruptly makes two right-angled deviations for no apparent reason, then changes its name to Surrey Avenue. And half the houses turn their backs on it! There's not a front door or front gate to be seen along the western section, only back fences. Who do you think Sir Garnet was?'

'No idea. Maybe there never was such a person.'

'The Knight of the Red Jewel,' Daniel said softly, half-serious. 'Damn,' he subjoined, staring across the road, 'look at that. They've pulled down the Southall house.'

Towers of scaffolding and concrete rose from a block where a familiar weatherboard house used to stand, at the crux of Sir Garnet's strange configuration. Julia gave a cry of disgust. 'They're building townhouses or something, by the look of it,' she said. 'What a shame. That house was no mansion but it had a certain character.'

'And memories,' said Daniel.

After navigating Sir Garnet Road's dog-leg, they struck out across a public children's playground no bigger than a standard house-block. A kind of goat-track, made by the passage of countless feet, ran down the middle; a path of worn-away soil cloven through the tussocky sward. Nearby, brightly coloured plastic equipment squatted like alien spacecraft.

'What a shame they've removed the whizzy,' Daniel said with regret. 'It provided one of the two most thrilling rides in this playground. The old steel climbing frame and slide and swings have gone, too, swept away by politically correct safety rules.'

'What other dangerous ride was your favourite?'

'The "maypole".'

Julia visualised the lethal construction of free-swinging heavy chains and metal rings, which no doubt knocked many a child unconscious and smashed many a bone, not to mention wrenching shoulders from their sockets and probably attracting lightning to boot.

'Aah, but it was a wonderful ride,' said Daniel, 'with the wind in your ears and the clamour of the chains against the concrete-embedded pole, jangling like iron bells. A wonderful ride!'

The track led them to Empress Road — 'Named, no doubt,' said Julia, 'in honour of Queen Victoria, Empress of India,' — where they turned left, but soon they paused again at the other side of the Southall block with its tall, hollow-eyed skeletons of buildings. The house's rear had overlooked Sir Garnet Road while the front faced onto Empress Road, and notably it had been the abode of the famous author Ivan Southall. More pertinent for children of that bygone era had been the fact that all along the base of the Southalls' white-painted wire-work front fence grew small plants they called 'egg and bacons', because the flowers, with their bright yellow centres, looked like fried eggs and, more astonishingly, they smelled like eggs cooked with bacon. The children had considered it quite fascinating. It was also frustrating to inhale the odour of a delicious but inedible breakfast.

The other outstanding feature of Ivan Southall's house in those days was that their schoolmate Jan Southall — his daughter — was able to depart either from her front gate onto Empress Road or from her back gate onto Sir Garnet Road. Every other suburban house seemed to be hemmed in at the back by someone else's private property. As children they'd considered that Jan's ability to slip between roadways via her house was intriguing; like owning a secret passageway. She was deemed to be incredibly fortunate; almost charmed.

They loitered in the street outside the Southall block, trying to see if any egg and bacons had survived the construction workers. There was nothing to be seen except dust and clay.

'It's all gone pear-shaped,' said Daniel decisively. 'At the risk of seeming to turn into a bitter old coot, I feel like saying *what happened to the good old days*, and *they don't make 'em like they used to*.'

'At least *schools* are better now than they were,' said Julia.

'That's true,' her companion observed. 'Nothing could be worse than Chatham School in our day. The awful, awful school, I thought it was. The strict, soulless, brown-linoleumed, vertiginously-staircased, cruel school with its hard-surfaced so-called playground that fried us in summer and gouged our knees when we fell, and all the other petty inflictions: the headmaster with his strap, the rulers smacking the backs of our legs, the public humiliations, the eccentric teachers.'

'If we detested the buildings and staff,' said Julia, 'We loved the learning, you and I, didn't we Dan.'

'We did, and it was by losing ourselves in that, and those fanciful games we used to make up, that we survived, I think . . .'

'I am sure of it. Come on, shall we get moving? We're only halfway.'

'No, wait, there are other ways to get there.'

'We could go by the lane with the buttercups. It's slower, though.'

'Perfect! I would love to see that again.' They retraced their steps past the desecrated Southall site, moving east. 'I think,' said Daniel, 'of all the lanes the buttercup one was my favourite. If ever I walked home via Luke's house, I used to take that way.'

A short street formed a T intersection at the end of Empress. On the left it narrowed to become, along more than half its length, the unofficially named Buttercup Lane — forbidden and inaccessible to all traffic except pedestrians. When they reached the entrance, Julia and Daniel could discern no sign of the massed drifts of buttercups that had so enchanted them as children. Disappointingly, nothing but short-cropped turf abutted the neighbouring properties.

'Well it has been a long time,' Julia said despondently. 'Anything could have happened.'

'Gone! All gone!' Daniel said, throwing up his hands in despair. 'Did the drought kill them? Or is it political correctness again — has someone poisoned them, or mowed them all down because they are not native plants?'

Julia uttered a squeal and ran forward. She crouched down close to the fence, peering eagerly at something on the ground, cupping it gently in her hands. 'Look Dan, just here. Right against the fence, where the lawnmower couldn't get them. A few, just a very few — and dwarfed, clinging to the dry earth. Tough little things aren't they, despite their fragile beauty when they're in flower!'

Daniel was kneeling beside her in an instant, his handsome face alight with pleasure. 'I'm going to save one,' he said. 'I'll dig it up and put it in a flowerpot.' Carefully excavating he dislodged one of the tiny plants from its niche in the dirt, wrapped the jagged foliage in his handkerchief and folded it in a capacious pocket.

They sprang to their feet, exuberant about this precious find, this symbol of childhood's golden past which had courageously struggled through years of adversity and emerged victorious. 'Let's see if the peppercorns are still there,' said Julia, impulsively taking her companion by the hand and leading him into the Buttercup Lane.

The peppercorn trees at the other end of the shady thoroughfare still let down their spicy grey-green tresses, and in that the couple rejoiced anew. Turning left as they exited the lane, they headed down Mont Albert Road towards the pedestrian crossing.

'Camberwell,' said Daniel as they went. 'Such an English name! It might be part of Britain's landscape, or Canada's, or New Zealand's, or America's. It might lie in Australia, or Gibraltar, or anywhere in space and history that was once colonised by the British, who brought their place names with them. Did you know, Jules, that there are many Camberwells all over the world? The original, a district, lies in the London borough of Southwark. There is much in a name, for names have roots, like trees, and those with the longest roots tell stories. Through them etymologists can trace languages, which give clues to migrations, famines, wars, invasions, and the entire history of the human race.'

'However,' said Julia, 'in 1994 they changed the City of Camberwell's name to Booroondara.'

'An Aboriginal word,' said Daniel.

'It is. But one cannot help wondering what Booroondara's etymology is, given that in 1951 the Aborigines bestowed the title of Melbourne's famous festival, Moomba, upon the City's aldermen, with the assurance that it translated as "Let's get together and have fun", when in the late sixties it was revealed that the term literally means "up yours".'

Laughing and joking they reached the school, strolled around its perimeter marvelling at how it had shrunk and recalling increasingly hilarious anecdotes of school life, then turned for home. The late afternoon sun had appeared and, as the cloud cover receded to the east, the daylight brightened to mellow amber.

'This is closer to the feeling,' Daniel muttered, as if thinking aloud. Addressing Julia he said, 'Two lanes. Only two lanes between home and school when you go the long way. Keep reminding me! It seems like three or four.'

'I suppose the playground could be considered an honorary lane,' said Julia, in an attempt to reassure him. 'I mean, there is a public footpath through it, and it cuts through between houses, like the lanes do.'

'You're only saying that to mitigate my madness,' said Daniel, smiling, 'but thanks anyway. I assure you I am not this navigationally challenged in other suburbs. It's only Surrey Hills.'

'You might be thinking of the Three Lanes Way,' Julia persisted. 'The *really* long way.'

'Let's take that route back!'

They crossed Mont Albert Road and turned right. About a block further on they ducked into the shadows of the Top Lane, whose straight, echoing path brought them out into the western section of Empress Road. There they stood still, looking about. Front fences, punctuated with gates, stretched away to either hand. Twin avenues of trees dwindled into the distance.

'If you didn't know any better,' said Daniel, 'you'd think you only had two choices — to go left or right. Two dimensions.'

'But you'd be wrong,' said Julia.

Hidden on the opposite side of Empress Road, slightly to their left and easily overlooked, was the mouth of the Middle Lane. They followed it to the end, the sound of their footsteps ricocheting hollowly off adamant surfaces. After they emerged into Sir Garnet Road they walked diagonally across and entered the confines of the Lower Lane. This graven furrow disgorged them opposite the wide grassy oval of Canterbury Sports Ground, at the bottom of Guildford Road which — Julia's parents had told her — had been named after some place in the English county of Surrey.

Daniel said, 'Canterbury, Surrey, Guildford, Chatham, Victoria — all the English names transplanted.'

'Turn left,' Julia said, 'and prepare yourself for the long hard walk home uphill, or so it always seemed; an arduous drag, with a heavy schoolbag on your back after an onerous day of cruel school. Now that we have grown up it doesn't seem so terrible.'

'This place where we are standing right now,' said Daniel, 'is one of those connecting points I've identified on the maps. Straight ahead a footpath leads across the Sports Ground to the railway station. The line runs to the city centre, the hub of the state's rail network, which in turn is connected to every city on the globe. We could turn for home, or if we had the inclination we could journey from this point to just about anywhere in the State of Victoria, or in Queen Victoria's Empire for that matter.'

'Come on,' said Julia, 'let's go back to my place. I'll cook dinner for us both.'

They trudged up the hill, Daniel still airing his thoughts aloud. 'My mother went to Chatham School. She must have Walked the Lanes daily.'

'Walking the Lanes,' echoed Julia. 'The phrase reminds me of the ancient English tradition of Beating the Bounds. I've heard that in Britain they still do it to this day, ceremonially circumnavigating the boundaries of a district. It's a relic of the ancient need to protect the borders from invading Picts or Gaels from Beyond the Pale, I suppose.'

'Which means,' said Daniel, without breaking his train of thought, 'that the Lanes of Camberwell and I share a long history maybe, beginning when my mother was old enough to begin school. Fifty percent of my genetic heritage travelled those pathways regularly, before I was conceived. In a way, I made this journey before I was even born.'

Wattle birds were squabbling in the street trees and the sun was going down at their backs. Shadows stretched long before them.

'But what,' said Julia, as they passed the wrought-iron gate of an Edwardian mansion, 'what is it all about these clues you speak of, this feeling you get? What's the point of it all?'

'Jules, you'll think I really *am* crazy if I tell you.'

'No I won't! I promise.'

They bantered for a while, but eventually with reluctance Daniel began to reveal his theories.

'The Lanes of Camberwell have a secret,' he said. 'That, I have come to suspect. An old, old secret. Older than colonisation or the Aboriginal tribes that roamed Victoria; maybe older than anyone guesses. As old as the underground waterways? Older?' He brushed a stray lock of hair out of his eyes, made as if to say something, faltered, then continued, 'They are almost exploding with that secret.'

Julia merely nodded, unwilling to interrupt the flow.

'It alters the course of a road,' Daniel said. 'It chops through boundaries, bans some people from its route and invites others, contains its own dewy moist atmosphere, grows its own flowers, hugs mystery to its tall fences like a cloak of leaves and shadows, confuses us, misleads us, swallows us up in places *between*; neither here nor there, neither England nor Australia, neither the old world or the new, nor at home nor at school ... and spits us out into somewhere else entirely.

'There are secrets here, Jules, and strange, unguessable forces of nature at work.'

'That may be true,' Julia said noncommittally.

'It is my theory,' he persevered, 'that the secret of the Camberwell Lanes can be discovered. But only by someone who Walks the Lanes in the right way, at the right time. Oh yes, it has to be the right time. And the right person.'

Julia said, 'Maybe a person who travelled the Lanes before their own birth. Someone who Walked the Lanes when young enough to perceive and hear and feel and taste what adults cannot; young enough to see through angles that harden and cloud over as you grow older and preconceptions blind you.'

'Exactly. As to the right *time* — the time when the secrets rise closest to the surface; when, as you Walk the Lanes, you tremble with anticipation, the paling fences grow taller, the overhanging foliage sharper and clearer, the streets more deserted — why, that season is autumn.'

A sudden afternoon breeze blew motes of thistledown past their faces.

'Autumn of the early mists,' said Daniel, 'the long amber sun rays of perpetual morning, the glassy panes of leaves turning crimson; mushrooms and toadstools springing in the short-mown turf of the nature strips. Walk the Lanes of Camberwell in autumn and there's a chance you will hear an echo of an echo. You might almost but never quite see.'

'Autumn is now.'

'True, but it's not the right time yet. There are certain days . . .'

'How can you tell?'

'It is a feeling. I *know* I'm right. It's a "feeling I get when I look to the west, and my spirit is crying for leaving" as the Led Zeppelin song goes. There will be days during this season, certain days, when the *feeling* will be just right. It's easy to tell. Magic will be in the air; *thick* in the air, and that's when it will be time.'

Giggling erupted from one of the front gardens, where small children were blowing bubbles through wire rings dipped into detergent. Translucent spheres came drifting over the fence into the plane trees then popped and vanished.

'The tides have their rhythm,' said Daniel, 'the heart has its rhythms, the seasons have theirs ... and there is a rhythm too, to the approach and retreat of that Something Else. How can that feeling be described? It is the sense that something exhilarating and possibly *dangerous* is about to happen. It is the sense that some unseen barrier, having congealed and thickened throughout the months of summer, has diminished to the sheer filminess of a veil, and that veil in places is so tenuous it can, perhaps, be torn — if you know the secret. It feels as if some Other World is pressing up against ours as the veil dwindles; some Other World which is usually separated from ours by impenetrable forces. As you are walking beneath the leaves on your way to the Lanes something from that place *is*, or *might be*, watching you from behind the trunk of one of these very trees, but for what purpose, with what intent, is unfathomable. Time's wheel turns, the forces ebb and flow. Autumn is low tide; the lowest of the year.'

Daniel watched as seven bubbles floated past.

'The veil becomes, in places, as thin as a soap bubble's walls,' he said. 'Thinnest in places such as the panes of autumn foliage.' They were passing beneath the burnished boughs of a plane tree. Reaching up he touched one of the leaves. 'When the sun shines through the stained glass of a smoky-amber plane tree leaf, it becomes a window, if only you knew how to look through it. The splendour is leaching through into the Pale — the rich apple-reds, the warm gold tints, the wine-crimsons — and do not be mistaken, the changing of the leaves is attributed to chemicals and sap but it is not. No, the leaves turn colour because they are membranes where the bubble-wall is thinnest, so that the hues of Other World, of Autumn Place, of *Equinoxia*, come seeping through, dripping through like mulberry wine and melted toffee and honey mead ... It's the leaves, Jules, and the light — the long mellow rays of equinoctial light.'

'So it is associated with the equinoxes, this feeling, whatever it is,' said Julia.

'Most definitely. But it is so overpowering! Don't you feel it? No? Why I seem to be the only instrument upon which these sensations play, I have no idea. But as I walk along the Camberwell Lanes, knowing that the Other is all around, everywhere, in the sky, in the sunlight, beyond the Palings, it comes to me that the Pale is where we are living; the Pale World, on the borders of one that is more richly coloured. And Beyond the Pale lies a place outside the jurisdiction of normal laws, a place considered hostile by civilisation, but which can never be reached, even at equinox when the wall, a thousand miles thick at Midsummer, thins to gossamer.

'Or perhaps it can, if you find the hidden way . . .'

He fell silent, then.

They returned to her house on top of the hill, and while Julia prepared dinner Daniel borrowed her street directory, somewhat to her annoyance. He sat at the kitchen table and once again riveted his attention on the maps of Surrey Hills.

'When I drew the shape of this "circuit",' he said, 'it meant nothing to me. Expanding the diagram I added links to significant places in case this helped form a meaningful figure, a symbol; some kind of *pattern*, a shape, laid out tracing the route, the shape of an ancient symbol — some rune, perhaps, or a key. A key! That's what I yearn after.'

Julia reached into the pantry for a chunk of parmesan cheese.

'Waterways, paths, journeys, burials,' said Daniel, 'death, warfare, wilderness survival, crossing places, iron roads, *conduits* — I marked them on my map *sensing* somehow that they had been placed there not at random but for some particular reason. Not that the town planners had decided to create pivot points or circuits; but that forces had been at work of which they were unaware. Forces that moved them without their knowledge. The land itself dictated the ways humans should use it.'

Having placed two bowls of pasta on the table, Julia pulled up a chair.

'Thanks.' Daniel picked up a fork. 'Sorry Julia, I'm being a pain I know. You're very kind to put up with me.'

'Not at all. I find your theories fascinating.'

'Really? One day I'll lend you my diary. It's full of 'em.'

'Well, maybe not that fascinating . . .'

He laughed. 'Point made! I promise I will not mention my delusions any more tonight.'

* * *

'And he kept his promise,' Julia said to me over the scalloped rim of a delicately painted teacup. 'We spent that night together, talking until sunrise, and he stayed with me until noon the next day. He said he was falling in love with me. Oh, but I miss him.'

'I'm so sorry. Why did he leave you?'

'Why?' Julia smiled mirthlessly, picked up Daniel's journal once more. 'See for yourself!' she said, pointing out the beginning of a paragraph.

'For autumn,' Daniel had written, 'is approaching again. It is the last month of summer and the days are noticeably shorter. And once or twice, already, there has been a day when a hint, just a *hint* of that anticipatory delight has flavoured the air. Just for half an hour or so ... As the time approaches it seems increasingly urgent to crack the code; to unravel the mysteries of the Lanes. Autumn, apple-time, leaf-time, golden tawny light time ... That *other* place, I know, is lit with long rich light, its slanting rays of burnt gold.'

'Did you suggest he seeks counselling?' I asked.

'Jenny, the man's a genius. These are not the ravings of a lunatic, don't you see? I think he struck on something, I really do. At first I was sceptical like you, but then I did some research.' Brandishing a notebook of her own, Julia said, 'I found this information in a library book when I looked up the etymology of "Camberwell".' Opening the book she read, 'The original "Camberwell" is believed to have been named for a well lying within its boundaries, whose waters possessed extraordinary healing properties. In the Domesday Book the English parish is called "Ca'berwelle". The author of *A Short Historical and Topographical Account of St. Giles's Church* — the parish church of Camberwell — writes, "It has been conjectured that the well which gave part of the name to the village might have been famous for some medicinal virtues, and might have occasioned the dedication of the church to this patron saint of cripples and mendicants. *Cam* is a very crooked word, and is applied to anything out of square, or out of condition. Having regard, therefore, to the fact already noticed, that the church is dedicated to the patron saint of cripples, we are certainly justified in assuming the word *cam* to be in this instance descriptive of individual condition; and the well would then become the well of the *crooked* or crippled."' Julia put down the notebook. 'A place of miraculous magical water!' she cried. 'But here in the Australian Camberwell, most of the streams and springs have been diverted underground! They have become secret magics . . .'

'Ironically, Camberwell is a "dry" area,' I said, attempting levity. Julia gave me a look of pity. 'Dry areas', local areas free of licensed hotels, where alcohol could be bought at shops but not restaurants, were a legacy of the 1920s, when the temperance movement was strong. Only two pockets of Melbourne were 'dry', and the erstwhile City of Camberwell was one of them.

'Where is Daniel now?' I asked humbly, to make amends for my inept stab at humour.

'For a while he went away. He came back one last time, on a clear, bright morning early in May last year, and announced to me that this was one of those days in full bloom; the feeling at its strongest, the walls at their thinnest. "I have to Walk the Lanes again today at the height of autumn," he said. And naturally I went with him.'

My auburn-haired friend sat on the arm of a chair, looking forlorn and dejected. I felt sorry for her.

A long hiatus ensued.

At length I broke the silence, saying gently, 'And that was the day you were found wandering the streets, lost, unable to find your way home. What happened? Where is Daniel?'

'He's gone,' said Julia brokenly. 'He's been missing ever since. The detectives can't find him. And I cannot really explain it.'

'But you go looking for him every day,' I said, and now I felt tears pricking the backs of my eyes.

'Yes. I go seeking the way in.'

'The way in?' Julia's confusion appeared worse than I had first suspected. 'The way into what?'

'Come with me. I'll show you.'

'I don't have time to tramp around the whole of Surrey Hills, I'm sorry Julia,' I said.

'Just as far as the end of the First Lane.'

'All right.'

Together we walked down Guildford Road and up the lane. Along the way Julia became quite agitated, blurting, 'Did you see that? I caught a glimpse of something moving over there, see, beneath the trees,' or, 'Look! Between the sky and the ground — a flash!' but I witnessed nothing out of the ordinary, and my alarm over her mental state intensified.

As soon as we stepped out of the lane at the corner of Sir Garnet Road she took my elbow in a confidential manner and leaned to murmur in my ear, while waving the other hand at the half-completed townhouses where the old Southall house used to stand.

'Leaves were blowing down all around us in the Buttercup Lane,' she said, 'and at the Southall house, and the sunlight was blowing too, as if the leaves were made out of sunlight, and our feet left the ground. We could hear the sound of jangling bells. We two were whirled up, and we saw the pattern laid out below as if in lines of fire across the suburb, and the pattern is the key, and the key unlocks the door. We returned to earth, and that was when I saw the door opening, and Daniel went through, but I held back because I was afraid. But for the brief moment the door remained ajar I looked in and saw an amazing sight, just as Daniel had described. Then it closed, but the golden honey soft comfort feeling of autumn lingered.'

She would say no more and I didn't like to press her, in her current state.

We returned to her house, where I took my leave of her. 'Julia, you are getting professional help aren't you?' I said as I stood on her threshold.

'Of course,' she said.

'Is there anything I can do?'

Julia insisted that she was fine and there was no way I could be of assistance. So I said goodbye to my altered schoolfriend and journeyed homewards.

A week later a wonderful autumn day dawned, and for the first time I sensed that feeling described by Daniel. Next day it was trumpeted all over the news and everyone was talking about it — the bizarre incident that had occurred in Surrey Hills overnight.

This was too coincidental. I had to go and see for myself.

Surrey Hills was abuzz with sightseers, and the air was fragrant with savoury scents I could not quite identify. Errant breezes whisked leaves and hats through dazzling sunlight; the day was vividly alive. I turned up at Julia's house but it was locked, and nobody answered the door. Then the neighbour, Mrs Warner, came in at the gate to tell me that Julia had disappeared again and detectives were searching for her.

Mrs Warner had a key, and let me in. The pot-plant on Julia's windowsill was in full bloom, vibrantly ablaze with buttercups. I found Daniel's open journal on the table.

In Julia's handwriting —

'I hear his thoughts in my head. He is calling me. He tells me that Ivan Southall's house stands at a fulcrum, or possibly *the* fulcrum of the circuit that is the Camberwell Lanes. It is *there* that Sir Garnet Road does its strange and sudden contortion, there that our favourite flowers grew, there that the playground chops in twain a row of houses, there that privileged daughters were permitted to pass *between* two roadways. This site is somehow connected to the Buttercup Lane — perhaps by an underground waterway. With the Three Lanes route to the west of the Southall house and the Two Lanes (almost three) to the east, bounded to the south by the Iron Road and to the north by busy Mont Albert Road with its hurtling traffic, the circuit centres on the Southall house.'

Outside in Guildford Road, an untamed wind was gusting; a sweet, clean wind from beyond the stars, and with every breath I felt I would be borne aloft. I followed the crowds to the old Southall block where they were gathering. Perplexed residents were scratching their heads and wondering how such a strange thing could have happened. Some had heard of a rain of frogs, or even of fish but never such a phenomenon as this!

From top to bottom, the entire site was awash with deep drifts of leaves and flowers. The partially constructed buildings, two stories high, were barely visible beneath this confetti, although it was already being scattered by the breezes. The spectacle was extraordinary.

Late that previous night all the people whose homes bordered the lanes of Surrey Hills had been woken, simultaneously, by the sound of running footsteps and laughter. In the morning the construction site was found weltered in autumnal leaves, in gilded buttercups well out of season, and yellow buttons of flowers with a savoury scent, and blue hyacinths, and soft silver-grey catkins, and I knew with a rush of joy that Julia had got through.

She was with Daniel.

I envied them both.

That year we had one of the most beautiful autumns we've ever seen in Melbourne.

AFTERWORD

The Lanes of Camberwell can be located in the Melway Street Directory of Greater Melbourne, Map 46, F10 and G10.

— *Cecilia Dart-Thornton*

STEPHEN DEDMAN is the author of the novels *The Art of Arrow Cutting, Shadows Bite, A Fistful of Data,* and *Foreign Bodies,* and more than a hundred published short stories. He has won the Aurealis and Ditmar awards, and been nominated for the Bram Stoker Award, the British Science Fiction Association Award, the Sidewise Award, the Seiun Award, and the Spectrum Award. He teaches creative writing at the University of Western Australia, works part-time at Fantastic Planet science fiction bookshop, and is fiction editor of *Borderlands* magazine.

In the next story, Dedman takes us into a brightly lit utopian world so we may discover the true value of art . . .

LOST ARTS

STEPHEN DEDMAN

Tao's was the only office on Hathor. It was a conventional flexiroom bisected by a temporary wall; the smaller chamber served as an anteroom, mainly in case the mayor was asleep when unexpected visitors arrived. Many of her neighbours had chambers that were similar, but they called them studios or studies or libraries or galleries.

Being mayor of Hathor wasn't normally a demanding job, as the more routine details were handled by her Turing-tested secretary Aidan. Tao's role was mostly oversight, and dealing with those inhabitants who wanted to speak to a fellow human. When this happened, she would conjure up extra chairs or couches from the nanomorph flooring, but normally her part of the office was empty except for a real divan, a spigot, and a holographic desk. Her side of the temporary wall was transparent; the more permanent walls and ceilings were holographic within a bubble that protected her from Hathor's usually inclement weather. On clear or spectacularly stormy nights, Tao would switch off the hologram to stare at the sky; at other times, she seemed to be working inside a reproduction of Bosch's *Garden of Earthly Delights*, though Aidan would sometimes change this image to flatter a visiting artist. As most of Hathor's human population considered themselves artists of one species or another, this was a detail Tao was glad to leave to the AI.

On good days, Tao could walk from the office to her apartment in less than ten minutes. Today had not been a good day, and by the time the doors shut behind her, she was wishing she'd decided to work at home. Aidan's holographic form appeared behind her desk as she sank into the large chair. He didn't say, 'You're late,', nor did he hypothesise about the explanation: he was programmed not to guess unless ordered to do so. 'You look tired,' he said. 'Do you want anything?'

'Vanilla chai,' she muttered, 'and a bodyguard. They acquitted Larue. Insufficient evidence.' She knew that Aidan was aware of this, little happened on Hathor that he didn't know about before she did, but she found that venting in the AI's presence was sometimes helpful. 'He didn't even have to testify — but now that the trial's over, he's talking to everyone who'll listen. Which is everyone on the planet, and it's probably already being blipped to Earth and the neighbouring systems.'

Aidan was silent for a moment. Courtroom procedures on Hathor were little different from those on old Earth: while prosecutor and judge were both AIs, the accused could choose a human lawyer to defend him, and the jury was also made up exclusively of humans. Aidan had observed the whole trial, watching the way Larue's lawyer had manipulated the jury.

There was no denying that Manco Larue had paid a substantial portion of his personal fortune to buy van Gogh's *Starry Night* and have it shipped from Earth to Hathor; Hathor's side of the bargain was to name a gallery in the museum after him. When the container had been revealed to be empty, shortly after arrival, Larue had protested his innocence — but as soon as the verdict had been delivered, Larue's AI secretary had claimed that since Larue had paid the cost of purchasing and transporting the masterpiece, he should still be entitled to the naming rights. Larue was also speculating on the planet's comweb as to the motives of the thief, as well as the painting's location.

'You're not serious about the bodyguard, are you?' asked Aidan, cautiously.

'No, but I could really use the tea.' Her chair rolled across the floor towards the spigot, which produced a cup. She sipped the drink, still fuming, then said, 'What's the probability that he still has the painting?'

'Unknown. Insufficient information.'

'Profile him.'

'It's consistent with his acquisitive character,' the AI admitted. 'And he has a record of tax avoidance on Earth. But there are many people on Earth who have similar psychoprofiles, and some of them may have had opportunity to steal the painting, as well as motive. And of course, it would also be in character for him to have sold the painting to another collector on Earth for enough to cover the cost of shipping, thus making at least a small profit.'

'The painting was in that container when it was shipped.'

'Can you prove it? Something of the appropriate mass would seem to have been in the container, yes, but it may not have been the painting.'

'No, I *can't* prove it,' said Tao. She put her mug on the floor, grimacing. 'If we could get a warrant to search his house, or his bank accounts ...'

'The prosecutor tried.'

'I know.' She shook her head. 'Why would someone do something like this, anyway? What good does it do him?'

'I can't answer that,' said the AI, blandly. 'Computers have no aesthetic sense.'

'You *act* as though you have an aesthetic sense,' Tao replied.

'We appreciate accuracy and efficiency,' said Aidan. 'As Einstein once said, everything should be as simple as possible, but no simpler. I am aware of some of the determinants of attractiveness that humans apply to different objects — form and pattern, symmetry, proportions, and similar factors. I can see the cleverness in something such as Bach's *Crab Canon*, which might almost be considered an equation — though one that is needlessly complex and distracting — or some of Escher's paradoxical images. I can understand that inaccuracies in a painting by van Gogh or Edvard Munch, or a poem or play that you regard as great, convey inner emotion as well as external reality. I can accept your premise that the original of an art object has an inherent value that is not present in a copy, even a copy that is identical beyond the ability of human senses to tell from the original — but only as a premise, as it does not seem logical.

'As for placing a monetary value on works of art, be they original or copy . . . that, we do not understand at all, though we accept that humans do so, and will accept that they consider such objects to be valuable and treat them accordingly. I might be able to estimate a value based on previous sales figures, or the shipping costs, as might any other AI, but I would not care to rely on it.'

Tao nodded. Spaceflight was expensive and frustratingly slow, and few material cargos were considered worth the cost of transporting between worlds now that nanotechnology had made them cheap. This had added to the mystique of *Starry Night*, because there was little on Hathor and similar worlds that could be bought or sold. Most human labour — be it farming, building, cooking, massage, sex, or other forms of artistry — was driven by enthusiasm, not need or greed. But Larue, and others like him, had brought their previously earned or inherited wealth with them when they had emigrated, and they were determined to increase it.

Just *why* Larue had emigrated rather than staying in luxury on Earth, Tao had never really understood. Some Hathorians had suggested it was the time dilation effects of the trip, which caused him to age less than six months over the nine-year voyage; others believed it was the opportunity to treat a whole planet as his personal fiefdom. Larue, however, had been allotted no more than the standard area of land and housing when he'd arrived, no greater quantity of food or privileges or luxuries, and Hathorian law maintained that these were not for sale: to each according to his needs, and Larue had not succeeded in demonstrating especial needs. Money had only been useful for importing luxuries from Earth, and few local artists had expressed any interest in paying the exorbitant freight charges, nor for waiting seventeen standard years for their goods to arrive.

Larue had set himself up as an art collector, and an agent for other collectors, and used this to have extra rooms built onto his quarters, turning it into a private gallery — and one of the largest and tallest buildings on the planet. None of the art originals he represented had ever been exported, but once he had bought a few and placed price tags on more, artists had begun competing. He had also used his considerable skills as a publicist to promote the work of some artists, getting them commissions to produce artistry on demand for buyers on nearby worlds — portraits in different media, designs for personalised hardware (including sex robots, of which Larue had a large collection), biographies and histories made to order. Tao didn't know what percentage of these commissions Larue kept, but she rightly suspected it was substantial. The precedents had been set long before she became mayor, as had the arrangements to buy the van Gogh and ship it from Earth, so if he was attempting to defraud Hathor's government, it wasn't *personal.* It merely *felt* personal.

'What would *you* have decided if you'd been on the jury?' she asked.

'I'm not permitted to serve on —'

'Hypothetically.'

'I would have voted to acquit,' said Aidan. Tao thought she heard a faintly apologetic note in his voice, but that might merely have been her imagination. 'The prosecutor had not provided sufficient evidence to prove Larue guilty beyond reasonable doubt. Had I been the prosecutor, I would have waited.'

'How long?'

'Until I had the evidence ... but *we* can afford to be patient. Larue can not, and his lawyers stressed this to the judges.'

Tao nodded. Larue was 174 years old, by the calendar, though coldsleep and relativistic effects had slowed down his aging by more than a decade. Still, few people lived into their third century, and no man had ever reached the age of 205. In theory, anyone could have their minds replicated as an AI, but if they did so, they would legally be Turing-tested software rather than humans, with no rights to physical possessions. Tao had heard rumours that Larue was prepared to go into coldsleep indefinitely to defy his children and ex-wives, who were waiting for him to die so they could inherit his fortune. Whether or not this was true, she was certain that the old man would pay someone else to die for him if that was an option.

Tao spent the next few hours attempting to distract herself with other work, while Aidan's holographic self dealt with the people who walked into the anteroom to protest the decision in the Larue case. When the AI reported that there seemed to be no one else waiting for her, not even lying in ambush between the office and her home, she rubbed her eyes and walked quickly back to her apartment.

The place was empty apart from her handicats; she walked in and checked that they hadn't managed to outsmart the foodfax again. She collapsed into her favourite armchair, letting both of the animals climb into her lap, and wondered who had had the brilliant idea of gene-gineering Siamese cats with opposable thumbs and prehensile tails. It had probably been someone's PhD thesis. At least they'd stopped short of giving the creatures human voiceboxes.

The handicats had theoretically belonged to her husband, and when he hadn't taken them with him (his new boyfriend had objected), she'd been unable to give them away or bring herself to have them recycled. They weren't especially annoying or destructive, as pets went — arguably less so than her husband had been — but she was glad that nothing in the apartment was breakable or irreplaceable. Tao closed her eyes, letting the cats compete for the most prestigious position, then began stroking them. She ordered meals for them and for herself from the foodfax, and considered calling for a masseur, preferably one who also did sex. She knew she had little to offer in return, but she did have some admirers, and not everyone on the planet had swallowed Larue's philosophy that everything should be for sale . . .

The only answer to her call came from a couple in their thirties who she'd met at a launch, the man less than half her age and the woman only slightly older. She told the door to let them in, and put the handicats into the exercise machine with a holo of an Earthian mouse plague. The couple arrived as she emerged from the shower; they seemed overly respectful at first, almost awed, but once they'd got their fingers into her, all three of them began to relax. The next three hours passed very pleasantly, and when the couple finally drifted off to sleep, Tao let the cats out of the exercise machine and was heading back into the shower when Aidan coughed gently. 'I didn't want to interrupt you,' he said, 'but I think you should see this.'

'See what?'

A hologram appeared ahead of her: Larue, being interviewed by one of his pet human journalists, with a copy of *Starry Night* behind them. 'This is only speculation, of course,' the old man said, 'and guessing at the motives of whoever might have stolen this masterpiece is a matter for forensic profilers, not someone like me . . .'

The interviewer nodded encouragingly.

'It could be a personal attack,' Larue continued. 'Somebody who simply didn't want me to have it, because I must admit, I have made some enemies in my time, competitors who bore a grudge. Or it could be chauvinistic, an act by somebody who doesn't think that the painting should leave Earth. But I think it's more likely that it was engineered by another collector who wanted the van Gogh for himself.'

The interviewer leaned forwards slightly. 'But why would a collector want a painting like this if he couldn't display it, for fear of it being reported and recovered?'

Larue smiled. 'Do you collect art, Andre?'

'Yes, of course.'

'Originals?'

'No . . .'

'That's the difference. A . . . there are collectors who would be happy to have a unique and valuable item such as the van Gogh even if they *couldn't* tell anybody else about it, even if they had to hide it away and rarely even look at it. Knowing would be enough — knowing that you had something that nobody else could have. Do you know van Gogh's *Portrait of Dr Gachet?*'

Before the interviewer could reply, the studio's AI replaced the image of *Starry Night* with one of the portrait of a melancholy-looking physician leaning on a table. 'This and Renoir's *Bal au Moulin de la Galette, Montmartre* were bought in auction by a millionaire who announced that he intended both paintings to be cremated with him when he died. When he *did* die, a few years later, the paintings disappeared — forever.'

The interviewer blinked, then smiled. 'So you *can* take it with you.'

Larue matched his smile, though the look in his eyes was sharper. 'That may have been his intention. It's an old idea, of course: Egyptian pharaohs, Chinese emperors, Norse kings and many others, were buried or cremated with their grave goods. Whether they really believed this would make their afterlife more comfortable, or whether it was more the feeling that they could make sure that they would be the last owner of these things ...' The smile became even wider and uglier. 'But I'm only speculating.'

Aidan froze the image, and Tao stared at it for a moment. What remained of her afterglow had been replaced by a feeling of cold fury and seething hatred. Okay, she thought. *Now* it's personal.

Larue was still smiling when Tao visited him the next morning, and his gallery was bright with sculpted sunlight, as well as the glow from what seemed to be a genuine old-fashioned fireplace. Incongruously, he wore an opaque grey Earthian suit that might have been fashionable when he was a teenager, and sat in a huge ugly armchair that placed his head higher than hers. 'And what service can I perform for you today?' he asked, then ordered one of his scantily clad sex dolls to bring them both coffee.

Tao thought the phrase made him sound like a twenty-second century non-denominational undertaker, as well as looking like one, but she kept her tone and expression pleasant. 'I watched your interview last night,' she said.

The smile widened. 'I thought you might have done,' he said. 'Seventy-six percent of the population already has, and I'm sure the rest will catch up. Are you any closer to catching the thief?'

'I think I might be,' she said, 'and I'm sure you can help. As a fellow collector, you may have a much better understanding of the thief's ... motives, and actions, than our psychoprofiling software. AIbots have no aesthetic sense, and can't really appreciate the ... passion that can come from having one, and this handicaps them in a case such as this. And, of course, we have no humans who are trained as detectives ... it's almost a lost art.'

Larue nodded sagely. 'One of the many things that we've lost with the creation of nanofaxes — especially out here, on the frontier. When everybody has access to almost everything they want, what would be worth the effort of stealing something which you can legally reproduce? Unless, of course, you appreciate the value of an original over a copy.' He beamed at the feminoid as she brought him his coffee, but there was a hint of sourness as well as nostalgia in his tone. 'Values have changed so much since those damn machines were ... anyway, I see your point. I was never a policeman, of course, but I do remember them. And I can certainly remember when art theft and forgery were real problems. How long ago did you leave Earth? Earth time.'

'About forty years ago.'

'Crime is little more than a historical curiosity to you, then. It's rather sad, in a funny sort of way, to think that when my generation is gone, there'll be nobody left who can really appreciate the motives behind so many Shakespearean tragedies, or even Agatha Christie mysteries. When nothing is worth killing or dying for ...' He shrugged, and Tao suddenly understood why the old man had been nicknamed La Rue Morgue and Larue-garou: he actually *missed* the bloodier years of Earthian history. Violent crime hadn't entirely disappeared along with property crime, but it had certainly been on the decline even on Earth; on Hathor, anyone who felt the urge to do violence could find plenty of harmless ways to divert their anger, and none of them felt poorer for it ... except maybe the bald old man sitting before her.

'So,' said Larue, emerging from his misty-eyed reverie, 'how do you think I can help? Surely the crime was committed on Earth, and Earth still has police, even if most of them are robots.'

'If the painting hasn't been discovered, then no one on Earth knows it's been stolen,' said Tao, 'and they won't know for eight years, when the message reaches them. It will be at least another eight years before we learn anything here. But since it's *possible* that the theft occurred here, we have to eliminate that possibility. You've speculated about the thief's motives. Now, it might be possible to re-sell the painting on Earth, but here, the profit motive seems much less likely. Wouldn't you agree?'

Larue clicked his cloned teeth while he considered this. 'Yes ... unless the thief wants to ransom the painting. I assume you've not received any demands?'

'No.'

'Me neither.'

'Would you pay it, if you had?'

Larue looked sharply at her. 'This long after the robbery, I think it unlikely that it was the motive ... unless the thief has lost his nerve. But if I were you, I would be very cautious about trying to investigate. If the thief is worried about being caught, he might decide the safest option was to destroy the evidence — destroy the painting.' He stared into the fire in the grate for a long moment. 'And that would be a tragedy.'

'It would,' said Tao softly, after absorbing this. 'Of course, if we found evidence that this *had* happened, the punishment would be much more harsh — intensive therapy, even a possible period of isolation, rather than just a fine. And you would be entitled to sue for a much greater amount than if the painting had been recovered.'

Larue sat back in his chair, turning away from the fireplace. 'Isolation?' he said, a hint of uncertainty in his voice.

'House arrest, and restricted communication. Incoming communications would be allowed, of course — we're not monsters — but not outgoing. The duration and other terms would be up to a judge.' She finished her coffee, and put the mug on the table beside her uncomfortable low chair. 'Anyway, any advice you can give us would be greatly appreciated. Please contact my secretary any time you think of something, no matter how minor it may seem. You know how AIs love raw data.'

There was no one waiting in her anteroom, and since Tao had had a long walk back from Larue's gallery, she didn't wait until she was in her private office before exploding. 'He threatened to destroy the painting!' she snarled. 'A van Gogh, and he threatened to ...'

'Only the original,' said Aidan, his tone smooth and reassuring. 'The image would have remained. Are you sure he has it?'

'Ninety percent sure. I wish I could have taken you in there.'

'If you had, his psychoprofile suggests that he would be even more likely to have destroyed it,' said Aidan. 'I can monitor his home environment systems, and make sure that his nanofax recycler won't accept the painting.'

'He has a fireplace. I saw it. You can check the environmental controls for his house.'

'I see ... well, we're monitoring the gases produced by the fire, of course, we'll know if he tries to burn the painting ...'

'*The* painting, or *a* painting?'

'A painting,' Aidan conceded. 'And I'm not sure that would be admitted as evidence, if it came to trial — which it could, in theory; destroying a van Gogh is a much more serious crime than merely stealing one, so double jeopardy wouldn't protect him. Beyond that, I'm not sure what more I can do. I can't stop him painting over it, for example.'

'I don't think he paints — at least, I've never seen anything he's painted. I don't know that he's ever produced *anything*.'

'It's probable that he would disagree. He produces publicity. Celebrity. Fame. Gossip, if you prefer, or what was once called "spin". Whether or not you consider it an art, he's undeniably made a fortune from it, which he would consider sufficient proof of a talent.'

Tao grimaced as she considered this. 'Could someone restore the painting, if he did paint over it?'

'Possibly, but if he were to cut it into pieces first, that would pose more of a problem. We might have to ship it back to Earth.'

'I wish it had stayed there,' said Tao glumly, slumping into one of the chairs meant for petitioners. 'If it had, we'd never have needed to worry about whether or not the original still existed; if anything *had* happened to it, we wouldn't have known for years. But we'd still have the memories, and the copies ...'

Aidan subtly changed the lighting and colour scheme in the room in an attempt to brighten her mood, but Tao didn't react. 'If it's not money, why would someone — anyone — do something like this?' she groaned.

'I don't know.'

'Guess.'

'It might be to show that he is wealthy enough not to miss the money, a form of potlatch. It might be to deny that wealth to his heirs. But the most probable explanation would seem to be herostratic fame.'

Tao blinked. 'What?'

'Herostratus was the man who destroyed the Temple of Artemis at Ephesus, considered to be one of the most beautiful buildings in the world at the time. According to Valerius Maximus, he did it so that his name would be known worldwide. The Ephesians responded by proclaiming that his name would be erased from history.'

'Well, *that* obviously didn't work.'

'No. It was recorded by the historian Strabo. Much of Strabo's work has been lost, but that fragment has survived. Is this what you would regard as irony?'

'It'll do, until something better comes along.' She stared at the pastel ceiling. 'I suppose you'd need to be able to erase human memories for that to be able to work. Sometimes I envy you AIs that ability. With us, the harder you try to forget something, the more it sticks in your memory; I can vouch for that.'

'It *could* be done with humans,' said Aidan, cautiously. 'It would be risky, and not utterly reliable — human memory is holographic, with multiple redundancy — but removing a name would not be a particularly difficult process, much less so than erasing all memory of an image. As a nanosurgical procedure, it would be as simple as cell rejuvenation or a memory upgrade, and much quicker.'

Tao thought for a moment. 'So if I asked you to remove all memories of Jeff . . .'

'Your husband?'

'Yes.'

'You could forget his name — permanently, if you chose; it would only take the equivalent of a meme virus — but not his face or anything else about him, not without a more elaborate procedure. And not that you'd been married, or the time you'd spent together; for that, you'd either need to accept holes in your recall, or false memory implants. But you would have one less reminder of his existence, and I suspect it would be a blow to his ego if you were to meet and you had forgotten his name.'

'I'll keep that in mind,' Tao muttered. 'If it's that simple, could it be done to the whole population of a planet?'

'On a strictly practical level . . . yes, a population this size, with the medical facilities available, could undergo the treatment in nine hours and twenty-seven minutes, allowing for the usual margin of error. The drain on resources would be minimal ... but I would advise against it, on purely ethical grounds. You have the legal power to declare a state of emergency and enforce such an order, and the AIs would have to co-operate — but if people resisted, even passively, this would slow the process down greatly and possibly increase the risks. And the majority might think you'd exceeded your authority, and vote to have you removed. Unless you can persuade everyone in town to voluntarily have parts of their memories erased, with the risk of unintended collateral memory loss, all on the same day ...'

'I doubt it. Larue's a pain in the ass, but most people simply don't think he's important enough to justify that sort of —' She paused. 'Would *Larue* think he was that important?'

'His psychoprofile suggests that he's self-obsessed enough to believe that everyone else would be obsessed with him as well,' said Aidan. 'But he would probably think that he's *too* important to Hathor's artists, and many other people, for them to deliberately forget him, no matter what sort of crime he was believed to have committed.'

'More important than a van Gogh?'

'It would be extremely difficult to persuade him otherwise. And while threatening him might motivate him to hand over the van Gogh as a way of regaining his celebrity, he might instead destroy the painting out of sheer vindictiveness — which, as he said, many people would regard as a tragedy.' There was a convincingly sad tone in the AIbot's voice.

Tao stood. 'There has to be *something* we can do. Doesn't there?'

Like many people, Larue had his secretarial software scan the net for mentions of his name and sort the comments by theme, content, and emotional intensity: unlike most Hathorese, he rarely had time to read all of them, though he read as many as he could, both positive and negative. He also kept tabs on mentions of visual artists, and not only the ones he represented; as an agent, he needed to know whose work was attracting attention. It was a discussion of the works of van Gogh that had inspired him to buy *Starry Night* rather than a less famous work, and he still had his secretary monitor casts for any mention of the painting, particularly theories about its disappearance and current whereabouts. He smiled when he noticed how widely Tao Sing's latest comments on the case had been read, and had his secretary play the interview back at him while he walked to the toilet.

The conversation began innocuously enough, with the mayor admitting that they had no hard evidence that the van Gogh was on the planet, and even if it were, distinguishing between it and any of the nanofaxed copies that had become almost ubiquitous on Hathor would be difficult. But Larue paled as Tao said, 'But this is not an argument for getting rid of these replicas — on the contrary, I think we should treasure the artist's vision, for that, I think, will be with us forever. But since we have no reason to think the original is any more lost to us than it was when it was on Earth, I don't see why we should mourn it. Rather than obsessing about it and looking for someone to blame — possibly unfairly — the best thing to do would be to erase the entire incident from our collective memory ... except for the AIs who are working on the case, of course. This can easily be done with nanosurgery.'

'Isn't that risky?' asked the interviewer.

The mayor shrugged. 'There is a possibility that some associated memories may be lost as well, but only very recent ones, and I'm assured that the danger of even this is small — and, of course, the procedure is easily reversible, should the painting be recovered and we wish to celebrate. I'm not ordering anyone to do it, but I would highly recommend the procedure to everyone: I'm sure we'll all sleep more easily for it.'

Larue felt the blood returning to his face, until eventually it was bright scarlet and as hot as if he'd stood too close to his fire. Did that infernal woman mean to deprive him of *all* pleasure? For a moment, he considered destroying the van Gogh in the most insulting way possible, and he called for a maid — but by the time she arrived, he'd calmed down enough to think of a less drastic solution. He wiped himself with a softened reproduction of an antique $10,000 banknote, stood, and pulled his pants up. 'Send out invitations for a party, to everyone on the A and B lists, *except* the mayor,' he barked at his secretary.

'Certainly, sir. At the gallery?'

'No, here: I can't keep that bitch out of the gallery. Tomorrow night. Make all the arrangements.'

'Your life support allocation . . .'

'Bugger the expense. Hell, double the amount of oxygen in the air, give everybody a high. I'll ask for donations, if I need to.'

'Catering?'

'Finger food and an open bar. Whatever it costs.'

'Certainly, sir. Do you want any other details on the invitation? A reason for the event, perhaps?'

'Make it . . . a celebration of genius.'

'Yes, sir.'

Larue grinned, and patted his sex doll on her perfectly sculpted bottom. He knew that when the *Mona Lisa* had been stolen, more people had visited the Louvre to stare at the blank wall than had seen the painting when it had hung there. He was going to go one better: hang the van Gogh in one room, copies in all the others, and let everyone try to guess whether any of them was the original. It would have people talking for years, decades, maybe for the rest of his life.

When midnight struck, Larue was still standing in his great house, alone but for his robots, the rest of his art collection, the fountain of champagne flutes and the trays of dim sum, sushi and canapés. He had gone from irritation to puzzlement, outright bewilderment, and most recently fury. He had snapped at his secretary for not including a request for RSVP's on the invitation (not that they'd ever been necessary before), then demanded that the invitations be re-sent, only to be told that none of them had been opened.

'What?' His fists clenched, and he found himself wishing that the computer had a neck. 'How many people are watching this party?'

'None, sir.'

'*What?*'

'The hit counters indicate that no one has been watching.'

'No one at all?'

'No, sir.'

'Not even that bitch the mayor?'

'No, sir.'

His face grey, Larue slumped into the nearest chair. He hadn't had any mail that day, which was unusual but not unprecedented, especially when he was expecting to meet people later that night ... He took a deep breath, and demanded the access figures for the past day. They told him that no one on the planet had looked at his collection, no one had done a search for his name, no one had even mentioned it in passing. Not even once, and that *was* unprecedented.

He looked at the previous day, and was horrified to see a steady decline beginning shortly after eight — the time of Tao Sing's netcast. He felt the blood pulsing in his temples as he converted the figures into a graph. Seventeen hours after she'd delivered her message, it was as though his name had been erased from the public consciousness.

'No,' he breathed. 'No, that's not possible.' He glanced up at the ceiling. 'Is it?'

'Sir?'

Shakily, he explained the situation to his secretary, who listened politely. 'It is *theoretically* possible,' the AI replied a few seconds after he'd finished. 'Considering the planetary population and the medical facilities available, everyone on the planet could undergo the treatment in the time you suggest. Whether that many of them *would* do so, I do not know enough about human behaviour to judge. It strikes me as highly improbable, but it *is* possible.'

'But the invitations!'

'If they had done it early enough, sir, they would not remember you: they would never have heard of you, and would almost certainly dismiss the invitations as a hoax, if they remembered them long enough to do so. And they might have programmed their coms to filter out your name, as well, and forgotten having done so.'

Larue blinked. 'Send that bitch a message from me. Tell her she won't get away with this.' He sat there and waited for a reply, and eventually fell asleep, still waiting. The chair reshaped itself into a bed, but even with its stochastic software, it was barely able to keep up with his twisting and turning.

*   *   *

When Larue woke, the next morning, he felt worse than he had crawling out of coldsleep. He took one sip of flat champagne, stared at the finger food, and ordered his maids to take all of it to the recycling hopper. 'And while you're at it,' he said, looking around, 'do the same to the van Goghs. Except for the original. Bring that to me. I want to recycle *that* one myself ... no, bring me all of them. I want to watch them *all* go.'

He laughed as he fed the first painting into the hopper. 'If a painting is destroyed and nobody sees it,' he cackled, 'can it really be said to have existed?' He was still laughing as he recycled the twentieth copy, wheezing as one of his feminoids handed him the fortieth. Only when he tried to lift the fiftieth, fifty-first, and fifty-second at once did he collapse onto the floor.

Tao was woken shortly after sunrise by her cats, demanding food and attention. She sat up, ordered meals for them from the foodfax, and rolled over — to see Aidan's holographic face hovering above her nightstand. 'Sorry for disturbing you at home,' he said, 'but I've just had an urgent call from Mr Larue's secretary. He says that Mr Larue has had a seizure and is unconscious. He suspects that the cause may have been stress. Will you speak to him?'

Despite herself, Tao yawned, then nodded. 'Audio only,' she said, as she slid out of bed, and ordered a clean tunic and pants from the fax. 'Tao here. What sort of stress?'

'He was negotiating with someone who was demanding a ransom for the return of *Starry Night*,' said the secretary. 'When we were able to determine that the painting was, indeed, the original, and was undamaged, Mr Larue collapsed.'

'How bad is it?'

'The robodocs say he should recover, though there may be some short-term memory loss. The painting is here. Do you wish to collect it?'

'I'll send someone over,' Tao promised. 'Let me know if there's anything my office can do to help.'

'Thank you.'

*   *   *

The morning after the morning after the unveiling of *Starry Night*, Tao walked into the office wondering why AIs still allowed humans to drink alcohol. She had vague memories of asking Aidan this once before, and of receiving a complicated explanation, which had something to do with robots having to work so hard to prevent humans harming each other that they were rarely able to prevent them harming themselves. Despite the feeling that she should still have a hangover, she made it to her private chambers unaided and began scrolling through the previous day's reports. 'Good party?' asked Aidan.

'Excellent,' she muttered. 'A pity Larue couldn't be there in person.' She hesitated, then said, 'The docs say that his version of events of the night before he collapsed is quite different from those his secretary gave.'

'He could be delirious,' said Aidan. 'Or delusional. A result of the seizure. But I'm not a medic.'

Tao knew that the com had instant access to the full range of human medical knowledge, but she didn't argue. 'They say he seems to have suffered from a paranoid delusion that everyone on the planet had had him erased from their memories.'

'That was the night after your netcast,' Aidan reminded her. 'It could well have given him nightmares, which he might find difficult to distinguish from reality. I think it would have given *me* nightmares, had I not been immune to them. If you had actually ordered it done, or even persuaded people to undergo the procedure voluntarily ... removing that much human memory, of performing so much potentially risky neurosurgery ... obviously, we could not have refused to do it had it been requested, but the risks would have posed an ethical dilemma for the robodocs — indeed, for the whole AI community. It would have been even worse than allowing the van Gogh to be destroyed. It seemed far too drastic a measure for a relatively unimportant problem.'

'But Larue would have thought he was sufficiently important.'

'That is consistent with my analysis, yes.'

Neither spoke for a moment, then Tao said, 'Of course, if someone had made Larue *think* people had forgotten him, by interfering with his net access and blocking his hit counters . . .'

'No human would have that power,' said the AI, coolly. 'The system would have repaired itself as soon as such a fault was detected. And, of course, that sort of interference would also have been ethically questionable.'

'But less so than mass memory erasure? Less drastic a solution?'

'Hypothetically . . . it might be considered so.'

'Or than destroying an original van Gogh, even if ordered to do so?'

'That would also pose an ethical dilemma,' the AI admitted. 'Much the same dilemma we face when a human wishes to cause themselves serious harm.'

'And interfering with someone's net access would have been much simpler, at least for the AI community. As simple as possible, but no more so. Efficient, minimalist . . . even a beautiful solution, in fact.'

'I wouldn't know,' said Aidan. 'I have no aesthetic sense, remember?'

Tao nodded, and walked over to the spigot. 'Only . . . what was it? A sense of symmetry? And proportion?'

The holographic face smiled fleetingly. 'Just so,' he said.

AFTERWORD

'Lost Arts' came about partly from an urge to get away from horror writing and dark futures and write a story set in a feasible utopia, and partly from a desire to write a far future story without faster-than-light travel or communications.

I may not be an optimist by nature, but I know what sort of world I'd like to live in, so imagining a utopia was the easy part. The difficulty was coming up with a plot. In a society where need and even most forms of want had been abolished, where crime and violence were so rare that police were no longer needed, what could I use as a source of conflict?

Fred Pohl once said that there was nothing so bad that someone wouldn't love it, and nothing so good that someone wouldn't hate it.

He was talking about fiction, but I like to apply this to the inventions, discoveries, and social changes that separate science-fictional worlds from our own. If we make a better universe, someone will prefer the old one.

Since I wrote the story, there have been reports that van Gogh's *Portrait of Dr Gachet* and Renoir's *Bal au Moulin de la Galette, Montmartre* were not destroyed, but sold to another private collector. Let's hope that my prediction that they will never reappear proves overly pessimistic: this is one time I'd be happy to be wrong.

— *Stephen Dedman*

JASON FISCHER is based in Adelaide, South Australia. Winner of the 2005 Colin Thiele Literature Scholarship and 2005 City of Salisbury Three Day Novel Race, he was also selected for the 2007 Clarion South writers' workshop. He has several short works published online, was a member of the *Andromeda Spaceways Inflight Magazine* co-operative, and reviewed for *Tangent Online*. Jason was a recent finalist in the Writers of the Future contest.

He says: 'I aim to write with a sense of wonder and potential. I like to build unusual disposable settings for my stories, snapshot worlds peopled with sadistic freaks, misguided protagonists, and Wrong Things. Though my tales are often woven with creepiness and gore, black humour inevitably creeps in. Even when things are crumbling all around them and the hungry unknown comes knocking, there is always time for a bad pun.'

As you'll see, things don't usually go well for folks in Jason's stories. 'Undead Camels Ate Their Flesh' is no different . . .

UNDEAD CAMELS ATE THEIR FLESH

JASON FISCHER

With its usual efficiency, the sun blazed down on bugger-all. It was the Outback, with nothing for hundreds of miles but heat, dust and flies.

Shuffling through this wasteland was a dead man, his footprints leading back to civilisation. He'd grown in cunning since his murder, knew to avoid the roads during the day. When hunger struck, he gorged himself on road kill, scanning the horizon cautiously as his leathery hands tore at flesh.

A truck was braving the old highway, slowly navigating the cracked asphalt. At the first sound of engines, the man fell to the ground, playing dead. The truck drove on, spluttering and backfiring as it downshifted. No one ever stopped.

Somehow the dead man knew he was an endangered species. He had a dim memory of city streets, of walking around in a horde and smelling out the hidden fresh ones. When they caught one, it was glorious, almost communal.

Things went bad when the fresh ones fought back. There was nothing left for it but to shuffle away, hoping to escape the slaughter of his kind. Something primal told him to follow this road, and this northern exodus had taken years.

Somewhere in the centre of his dead brain certain things remained hard-wired. He still knew that when things went wrong for a man, it was good to go north for a while.

For a dead bloke, he was a survivor.

'I didn't mean it,' Swanny said, his shaking hands still cradling the smoking sawn-off. His ears rang from the blast.

'Bloody worthless you are,' Trev said, snatching the gun out of his hands. 'Now we are royally stuffed. Thanks a lot.'

'It went off by itself,' the boy said quietly. He stepped away from the body, looking down in horror. 'We killed him.'

'No, Swanny, you killed him. Coz you're a stupid twat. Now get over here and help me!'

They dragged the body into the office, bundling him up under the desk.

'We could feed him to the pigs,' Swanny suggested. 'Leave no trace.'

'What's the point?' Trev said. 'Look at all that blood and shit, all over the floor. We need to open the safe and get out of here.'

Checking through the blinds, the older man made sure no one was approaching the house. It was a big farm, and there was a chance no one had heard the gun go off. He gestured to Swanny for the satchel, which he threw across the room.

'We could have beaten the combination out of him, but you had to blow his head off,' Trev grunted, sticking the explosives to the outside of the safe. 'Now every bastard is gonna hear this.'

They set the fuse and ran. The explosion blew the thick metal door off its hinges, shattered the furniture, blew all the glass out of the windows. Swanny had packed the charge with his usual enthusiasm.

Coughing, Trev waded through the wreckage of Buchanan's office. He reached into the safe, beating out the flames. Half of the contents were on fire.

'I can't rely on you for anything!' Trev shouted. He opened up his bag, stuffing it full of notes.

'We're rich, Trev,' Swanny said with a daft grin. He'd never seen this much money.

'Ah, it's all useless,' Trev said, holding up a half-charred note. It was King Christian's face, not King William. Swanny looked confused.

'It's Danish money,' Trev said with his last shred of patience. 'No one around here will take these.'

They took it anyway, shovelling everything into the duffel bag and running out the back door. At least Trev's battered motorcycle was still there. Two farmhands were yelling and running towards the house, but stopped at the sight of Trevor Flannigan with a shotgun.

'Get back,' he ordered, sweeping the gun across the frightened pair.

Swanny fell into the sidecar, huddling the bag of loot on his knees. Not taking his eyes off Buchanan's men, Trev trod on the starter. Nothing.

'Mongrel of a thing,' he muttered, and pushed the starter again. This time the ancient machine gave a slight cough, but did not roar into life. The silent tableau was only interrupted by the whir of the starting pedal and Trev's curses.

Just when he'd given up hope the motorcycle roared into life, and Trev hammered the throttle, kicking up dust as he spun the machine around and shot for the gate. Swanny made sure to give the farmhands the finger, pulling a face through his motorcycle goggles.

Trev raced through the farm district, stopping only when he caught sight of the barricade surrounding Port Augusta, a wall of old tyres and broken cars. They'd picked a good time to do over Buchanan, most of his hired help were at the football final in town. At least that part had gone well.

'We can't go in there,' he said over the rough chatter of the engine. 'People know we went to meet with Buchanan, the cops will put two and two together.'

'Can't we just spend some money?' Swanny moaned. 'We're rich.'

'It's Danish money, idiot. We need to get far away, right now. Those farmhands will be riding into town.'

The prospect of being hung made Swanny touch his throat gingerly, and he gulped. They had killed a man, accident or not. In the distance he could see a man on top of the barricade, gun at the ready. They'd been spotted.

'I should have shot their horses,' Trev said. 'I'll have to go around the town. Hopefully we'll make it to Pimba.'

'Yeah, we should head north,' Swanny agreed, looking at the fortified town. 'North is good.'

Camels. A great herd of the feral beasts was coming this way. Australia turned them loose when the motor car came to conquer the interior, and they repaid this favour by breeding like mad and eating everything in sight.

The dead man could smell them downwind, and crouched to the ground. He hadn't eaten for days and was hungry. The only thing he'd found on the road were bones bleached white by the sun.

Keeping perfectly still, he lay in the spiny grass and red dust. Years of dry heat had mummified him, yet he didn't suffer from the rot or the smell that many of his companions had. With the right wind, hours of stillness could pay off in a kill.

A feral camel wandered over the rise. Oblivious to the unnatural creature that lay in wait, the first the camel knew of disaster was when something reached up and sank sharp teeth into its leg.

Squealing in terror, the beast bit back, wrenching the dead man loose. It hurled him away, the man tumbling down the sand-dunes with a mouthful of flesh. The camel spat and hissed, a terrible taste in its mouth from where its peg-teeth had broken the dead man's skin.

The herd broke into a gallop and scattered into many directions, and the bitten camel ran too. It started feeling wrong, had trouble keeping up. Frustrated, it spat and bit at the nearest camel.

This felt good, felt right. Eyes rolling and mouth foaming, it bit another one, tore through the skin this time.

Trev's motorcycle started to splutter when Pimba was in sight. There was still plenty of fuel in the tank; something else was going wrong in the innards of the ancient machine. They were still several miles away when the engine gave a death-rattle and died. They rolled to a stop, engine ticking and boiling.

'I've had this bloody thing since the Plague broke out,' Trev said, 'Took me from Brisbane to Melbourne, and when the bloody Danes came, I got from Melbourne to Adelaide in one night. I even hit a zombie once, and it only wobbled a bit.'

They sat there, Trev tight-lipped and Swanny too frightened to say anything. The older man was furious, gripping the handlebars tightly. The engine stank of burnt oil, and a cloud of flies descended on the stricken pair.

'This thing was worth ten of you,' Trev said, pointing a finger at the terrified lad. 'Treated me right when nothing else did. So what happens when I need it the most?'

Swanny said nothing, clutched the duffel bag tighter. Trev got handy with his fists when he was angry.

'I'll tell you what happens. The goddamn engine dies at Pimba! The arsehole of the world!'

He hopped off the bike and kicked the wheel hard, stubbing his toe. Launching into a string of curses Trev snatched the shotgun out of its holder, priming a shell and pointing it at the bike. Wailing with terror, Swanny fell out of the sidecar, dragging the heavy duffel-bag behind him.

'Don't shoot it Trev!' he implored. 'Tank's full of fuel!'

Glaring at the bike like a madman, Trev started to squeeze the trigger, a nervous tic causing half his face to twitch. Taking a deep breath, he pointed the weapon at the sky, when the dodgy trigger fired by itself.

'We gotta get rid of that gun, Trev. Someone's gonna get killed,' Swanny said.

Trev ignored him, grabbing his swag and the potato sack that housed Swanny's worldly possessions. They both landed at the lad's feet.

'Carry those,' Trev said, and started walking along the cracked bitumen of the old highway. Struggling under the weight of all the bags, Swanny rushed to keep up with his mentor.

'What are we gonna do now Trev?' he puffed. 'Should we stay here for a while?'

'Nah. Too close to a murder scene,' Trev said. 'We gotta keep moving, keep heading north. We go west, we enter what's left of civilisation. Cops, the army, jail. If we're lucky.'

'Why don't we go east? We've got Danish money, why not go to New Denmark?'

'Stuff that. If I wanted to hang out with a bunch of box-head krauts, wouldn't have left in the first place would I?' Trev said. 'We go there, we end up in a work-camp with everyone else, working for King Christian the fucking invader.'

Swanny hefted all of the bags, wanting to stop for a rest. The road shimmered with heat-haze, and the tiny town seemed to be getting further away from them. There was nothing but the endless plodding along the cracked surface, and he could feel the heat rising through his old boots. He wondered how long the duct-tape holding them together would last.

When they reached the tiny township, it was mostly deserted. A few grubby children watched them go past, gawking at the pair that had walked out of the bush.

'Where's a mechanic?' Trev demanded, and a boy of perhaps ten pointed up the main street. They continued playing with a half-deflated football, and it was unlikely they'd ever seen a classroom.

'Arsehole of the world,' Trev muttered. They found an old service station with an open workshop, an old petrol-guzzler standing over the pit with its engine pulled to pieces. The bowsers were covered in cobwebs, and there was an old sign nailed against the shop-front. 'NO PETROL' it read, and he wasn't surprised.

'Oy!' he called out, unable to see anyone. 'Anyone here?'

'Hang on,' someone said, and a man clambered out of the pit, covered in grease and filth. He looked about a hundred. 'What do you want?'

'Bike broke down just outside of town. I need you to fix it.'

'I might have the parts,' the man said, eyeing Trev's shotgun. 'Do you have money, or something you can trade for it?'

'Here,' Trev said, reaching for the duffel bag. He unzipped it, carefully pulling out one stack of bills. *No sense showing this arsehole how rich we are*, Trev thought. He hadn't survived this long by being stupid.

'This is Danish money,' the mechanic said. 'I won't take this.'

'Please, we need the bike fixed,' whined Swanny. 'We've got more money.'

'Shut up!' said Trev. 'Will you fix it or not?'

'Do you have any Aussie money?' the man said. Trev shook his head.

'I lost two sons,' the mechanic said. 'The first was in Adelaide, and the zombies got him. Second was in the Army Reserve, and some Dane put a bullet through his head during the Invasion. When two strangers roll into town with a big stack of kraut money, I get suspicious.'

'Are you calling me a box-head?' Trev yelled, priming the gun. 'What are you trying to say?' The mechanic looked at him calmly, wiping his hands with an oily rag.

'Did I tell you about my other two sons?' he said, and two stocky young men stepped out of the shadows of the workshop. One held a large revolver, the other had a Rottweiler slavering on the end of a chain, a cricket bat in his free hand.

'The pair of you can just piss off,' he said calmly, picking up a tyre-iron. 'I don't help traitors or Danes.'

Trev was angry but not stupid. He would only drop one of them before the other two jumped him. He backed out of the workshop, gun levelled at the two sons. 'Big mistake,' he called out. 'You'll regret this.'

The pair of them ran from the petrol station, and ran through the dusty side-streets till they found an abandoned shack to hole up in. Trev didn't know if there was a copper in Pimba, didn't want to take any chances. After several minutes without the sound of pursuit, they peered through the broken windows, sweaty and covered in dust.

'What are we gonna do now?' Swanny said. 'I'm hungry.'

'I dunno, idiot, how about you go to the nearest shop and buy some lunch?' Trev said. 'Take as much money as you need.'

Trev thought furiously, and Swanny tried to think. What passed for his look of concentration made him look constipated, and Trev only tolerated the boy because he made him feel smart. *I'd abandon him in a second if it was him or me*, he thought.

'The police force still has a working fleet of cars, and they're bound to search Pimba soon. We gotta leave now.'

'Should we steal a horse?' Swanny offered, to be rewarded with a slap across the back of his head.

'The only car in this shit-hole town is in pieces, back in that tosser's workshop. We either need to steal food and wait till the heat dies down, or somehow get the bike working again.'

There was a long hooting sound that cut through the air, making the broken shards of glass shake in the frame. Trev leapt to his feet, a grin from ear to ear.

'Train!' he said. Snatching up his swag, he dragged Swanny to his feet. They sprinted across the small town until they hit a trainline, and the train barrelled past them, headed towards the local siding.

'It's the Ghan!' Swanny said. 'We can go right up to Darwin if we want to!'

'Train doesn't go to Darwin, it's still a zombie town,' Trev said, puffing and panting as they ran alongside the train. When it slowed down to stop, he hoisted himself into a baggage compartment. Grudgingly he offered Swanny a hand.

'We're getting off at Alice Springs. There's sometimes work to be had there, and maybe we can change some of this money over somewhere.'

'What are we gonna do in Alice Springs? I'm not good at nothing.' Swanny said. The depression that swept the country after the Plague had killed many homeless kids, and if it wasn't for Trev he would have starved by now.

'Use your imagination mate! We could join some shooters. I hear they're that desperate for meat up there that they'll eat camel.'

Shifting the gun belt that held up his fat gut, Chief Inspector Wallis knelt down, careful not to get the bloody mess on his trousers. He didn't get out in the field much these days, and it showed.

'Not zombies for once,' he said, picking up the shotgun shell.

'Stupid bastards choose to live outside the wall, you see what happens,' the young constable started. Wallis glared at him like he was a dog-turd hiding in a box of doughnuts and he wisely shut up.

'Buchanan was my brother-in-law,' he said. 'My old lady is beside herself, you little shit! Do me a favour and interrogate the farmhands, or the pigs or something. I don't care what, just get out.'

For what it was worth, the fingerprint guy had been all over the place. He'd found nothing, but since the computers had stopped, the police had bugger-all to work with. They had to rely on old methods and equipment, but contingency plans meant nothing when all the records were gone.

'Why did they shoot you, mate?' Wallis wondered. There was a square of paper soaking up blood, and he peeled it off the floor with a pair of tweezers.

'Danish money?' he mumbled to himself. 'What the hell was he into?'

'Boss, one of the town shooters just got on the radio,' the young copper said, timidly poking his head around the doorway. 'Says they saw a motorbike circling the town this morning, two fellas. Weird that they didn't come in and fuel up.'

'Where'd they go?' Wallis said, shifting his bulk as he got to his feet. There were only a handful of working cars in the district, and no bikes.

'North, towards Pimba,' he said, ducking out of the way as the Chief Inspector barrelled through the door. Wallis moved quick for a fat man, and he was angry. Hardly anything got him out from behind the desk these days.

'I pity those blokes when he catches them,' the constable said to the fingerprint guy. 'They'll be praying for zombies.'

Thousands of feral camels died within hours of the first bite. This news should have made most Outback farmers happy, but people still remembered the Plague. Varied reports went over the patchy ham-radio network, speaking of aggressive camel packs attacking livestock and people. And eating them.

'Zombie camels?' one ham operator in Alice Springs snorted. His ranger friend was noted for telling tall tales. A hundred miles away his friend was dead, dragged from his shattered four-wheel drive by a camel missing half its face. The entire pack devoured his broken body, jostling with each other for a feed.

With blood-spattered jowls and marble white eyes, a vast stinking horde of dromedaries made for Alice Springs, drawn by the bright lights on the horizon and the distant smell of fresh meat. Their great honking howls echoed throughout the night.

'I saw them officer,' the mechanic said. 'They came in here perhaps three days ago, toting a big bag full of kraut money and a shotgun. The lads and I chased them away, but we lost them after that.'

'Great,' Wallis said, looking around the filthy workshop. The only car in town lay in pieces before him. 'You have a pair of killers gone to ground somewhere in your town. Why didn't you get on the radio? You idiots have put everyone in danger.'

'When's the last time we saw the law in this town? No one cared about this place, not even before the Plague. We look after ourselves here.'

'Doing a good job,' Wallis said, turning his bulk on the man as he returned to his squad car, which bristled with antennas and rust. He would poke through every abandoned shack and lean-to in this dust-bowl till he found Stephen's killers. The Chief Inspector was armed to the teeth and vengeful; it was not likely they would be brought to trial, or even buried. Law had changed around here.

After a fruitless morning of poking through a town that was post-apocalyptic before the Plague, Wallis saw the trainline shimmering on the horizon. He visited the sidings on the edge of town, and tore the yellowed timetable from the nail that held it up.

'Least the trains still run proper,' he pondered, wondering if he had enough fuel to take him to Alice Springs.

'We don't need shooters,' the foreman told Trev. 'Stupid to shoot them out in the bush, unless you plan on cooking and eating your camel on the spot. Smart way's to round them up, bring 'em into town and to the slaughterhouse.'

'I don't have a horse, or a bike. But I've got a gun,' Trev said. The outriders laughed.

'Well mate, perhaps some farmer needs help with a rabbit problem. Doubt you'll hit anything with that old thing though.'

I could hit you, Trev thought, but bit his tongue. They were in hiding, and desperate for cash. Last thing they needed was trouble with the law, though he ached to lay into the cocky prick.

Swanny had started work yesterday for a local preserver. The days of fridges and canning had gone by the wayside, and he worked on an assembly line, pushing wax seals into glass jars full of fruit and meat.

'That's womens' work,' Trev had laughed at the time, but Swanwick was the only one with a job. Trev had pounded the pavements till he wanted to pound some heads. No luck.

They'd discretely tried to change some of the Danish notes, with limited success. Alice Springs had been left alone during the Invasion, but many sons and husbands had gone off to fight throughout the district. The hostel had accepted one note with great reluctance, providing a week's accommodation. They would not do this again.

'A fortune and nowhere to spend it,' Trev moaned, not for the first time that day. He flopped onto the uncomfortable bed, waiting for Swanny to come home so he could hit him for beer money. Literally.

Making sure that the door was closed, Trev went through the bag one more time in the vain hope that some Australian currency had been in Buchanan's safe. There was nothing but the Danish money and some boring looking papers. With nothing better to do, Trev actually took the time to read them, took a closer look at the maps that they'd snatched from the safe.

What the hell was Buchanan doing? Trev thought, his head spinning. What he held in his hands amounted to high treason, spoke of sabotage and troop movements. *Perhaps I'll get some sort of reward for turning this in. We killed a Danish spy!*

He'd only known Buchanan was a wealthy landowner near Port Augusta, went there with the pretence of looking for work. *We bungled the heist, but I reckon we've come up with something better than loot!* he exulted. *This will clear my name!*

He was still sitting there on the bed, surrounded by enemy money and plans for sabotage and invasion, when the door opened. It was another person he'd seen in the hostel, another labourer down on his luck.

'Sorry mate, wrong room,' the bloke said, doing a double take when he took in the scene. The white and red *kroner* of New Denmark was distinctive, and to be seen with so much of it could only mean one thing.

'Oh Christ!' the man said, slamming the door a moment before Trev blasted away with the ever-present shotgun. There were screams of pain, the sounds of running and doors slamming.

'Fuck, fuck, fuck it all!' Trev said, pushing the bed up against the door and jamming more shells into the breech of the gun.

'I'm not a spy!' he shouted through the broken door, letting off another round just to show he meant business. 'I'm a fucking thief.'

Wallis had navigated hundreds of miles of cracked highway, and when the barren landscape gave way to the green outskirts of Alice Springs, he breathed a sigh of relief. He was literally driving on the fumes in his tank, the boot full of empty jerry cans. The old car had begun to overheat, and he doubted it would make the return journey.

No wonder this place was spared by the Plague, he thought. *No zombie would ever make it across that wasteland.*

He noticed the smoke from several fires rising above the town, wondered why he couldn't hear the bells of the fire brigade. There was screaming in the distance, and as he prowled through the streets in the cruiser, Wallis saw people darting into doorways as if the devil was on their heels. The engine began to struggle as the tank ran out, and the car stalled in the middle of the road, engine ticking.

Where the hell is the petrol station?

A young lad ran around the corner and didn't see the police car, running into the driver's side door. The Chief Inspector launched a beefy arm out of the window and grabbed him by the collar before he could flee.

'What's going on?' Wallis demanded.

'The camels are coming!' the boy cried. 'They're eating everyone. Mister, you've gotta get out of here.'

Camels?

* * *

'Give me that,' Swanny said, pushing the young girl to the ground and taking her bike. His knees knocking against the handlebars, he poured as much energy as he could into making that pink-tasselled wonder-machine go. Something from the depths of hell was hot on his tail, several somethings that had devoured all of the little old ladies at the preservery. He heard the horrible honking cries behind him, heard the sick crunching sounds as the beasts caught the screaming little girl and tore her apart, eating her alive.

'Whatthehellwhatthehellwhatthehell!' he screamed, losing his bladder control and not caring. A great rotting head loomed out of an alleyway, square teeth nipping at him as he sped past. He felt the hot stinking breath of the camel on the back of his neck, whimpering as the teeth barely missed him. The great empty clacking sound of the teeth striking each other made him moan with fear.

'Camels do not EAT people!' Swanny sobbed. He had to find Trev, Trev would know what to do.

He took the side streets when he could, hoping he would be able to find the hostel. They'd only been in Alice for two days. A wrong turn could mean becoming a camel snack. *I've got to get Trev and the money, get the hell out of this place!* Their problems with the law seemed so less important right now.

There was a shotgun blast, and then another. *Trev!* he thought, steering towards the noise. *He's alive!* There was another shotgun blast, and Swanny rode into view of the hostel, abandoning the bike in the street. Within seconds, someone else nicked it to flee from the undead camels, but Swanny didn't care. He'd found salvation.

'Take that, you bastards!' Trev yelled from somewhere inside. 'I've got plenty more where that came from!'

One of the camels had tried to walk into the front door of the hostel and got stuck. It roared with impatience, and Swanny could hear it bashing at the internal walls with its great heavy head. He wouldn't be going in that way.

Creeping down the back alleyway, Swanny froze as something knocked over a bin. It was a cat, screeching in terror. It tried to bolt for safety, but as it ran across the street one of the abnormally swift camels struck like a snake and swallowed it whole. Then it looked up, pale dead eyes regarding Kevin Swanwick. He felt his bowels release, and ran up the alleyway, undeath hot at his heels.

'Oh sweet Jesus!' he said, leaping through the window. Broken glass and shit covered him, and Swanny lay in a painful pile on the floor. The room stank of cordite, and Trev was loading more shells into the shotgun.

'Where in the *hell* you been?' Trev demanded. 'Hang on, did you piss *and* shit yourself?'

'The camels!' Swanny managed, a split second before the zombie camel rammed its dead head through the window, blood-stained teeth snapping at Swanny. Trev emptied the shotgun into its head, round after round until he was leaning outside the window to finish the job. Finally, the horrible beast was silent and presumably still.

'What in the bright blue fuck was that?' Trev said incredulously. 'Never seen a camel do that before.'

'Um, Trev.'

'Yeah, what.'

'What the hell were you shooting at before?'

They moved the bed and opened the doorway. Numerous trappers and shooters had been running down the corridor to deal with the stuck camel; Trev had murdered every last one of them.

'I thought they were coming for me,' he explained weakly. 'What else was I supposed to do?'

'We need to go Trev, we need to go now,' Swanny pleaded. He reached for the duffel bag, swept the bundles of paper and money into it.

'Leave the money!' Trev said. 'That shit has done nothing but curse us. I say we burn it.' But Swanny held onto it.

Despatching the stuck camel with several well-placed rounds, Trev and Swanny stepped over its twitching body, and into the absolute anarchy that was post-camel Alice Springs. Somewhere in the distance were the sounds of screams; it seemed the movement of the undead herd had passed this spot.

'Not looking for a shooter, eh?' Trev said as he walked past the dismembered corpse of the foreman. '"Smart way's to round 'em up and bring 'em into town",' he mimicked, poking the dead man's head with his boot. 'Not too flamin' smart, are you?'

'Trev!' Swanny whispered. 'We need to get a car or something. Stop messing about!'

Momentarily stunned by Swanny's rare display of backbone, Trev complied. They both had guns now, though Swanny didn't realise the rifle from the hostel wasn't loaded. It made him feel better at any rate.

There was a noise behind them, and the pair of petty thugs turned, only to see a morbidly obese police officer. Trev swore.

'Behind you,' the man said calmly, raising his pistol. The pair turned, firing at the camel that lurched drunkenly towards them. Swanny panicked and threw his useless rifle at the undead beast, which the stranger dropped with a well-placed shot to the eyes.

'You there,' the cop said. 'Forgot to do your bag up.' Swanny looked down, saw the *kroners* sticking out of the open duffel bag. The man had a pistol levelled at Trev, and gestured for Swanny to drop the bag.

'Over my dead body,' Trev said, lifting the shotgun. He was so focussed on the fat man that he didn't hear the camel until it pounced on him, all peg teeth and grinding punishment. Swanny squeaked with dismay, and was frozen with fear. Several camels were running towards them, honking and slavering, broad feet kicking up the dust as they charged. The policeman grabbed him by the collar, jerked him into a different direction. Swanny was too terrified to object.

'I've a score to settle with you,' the fat man said, 'but you and I have bigger problems. I know you can shoot, you shot my brother-in-law.' He handed Swanny a revolver, which the young man took with disbelief.

'We need to get fuel, and we need to leave. Help me and I promise not to leave you for the camels.'

It was a no-brainer, even for Swanny. They almost made it too.

At long last, the dead man staggered into Alice Springs. How long he'd travelled was beyond his limited understanding, but he'd finally made it as far north as he'd ever been in his previous life. It was glorious, a dream come true, and he took in the vista with a moaning wordless amazement.

Hordes of the undead staggered around in the streets, half-eaten and moving. Even more of a surprise, the great spitting beasts of the desert were there. In a few instances, the camels were quite happy to let the more damaged undead ride around on them.

Shuffling forward, the zombie was greeted with moans of recognition and acceptance from the newly raised dead. Let the fresh ones fight over the other places. The dead would always have this town.

AFTERWORD

'Undead Camels Ate Their Flesh' was written as my week-four story at the Clarion South workshop, when Gardner Dozois was our tutor. I'd intended to write a serious Big Idea piece to impress him, and all I could come up with was this piece. In response, Gardner led the class in a rousing rendition of 'Undead Camels Ate My Flesh', sung to the tune of 'Camptown Ladies Sing This Song'. The man is a legend!

This story is everything I would love to see in a movie . . . some sort of messed up Mad Max/George Romero disaster with a healthy dash of black humour. And camels.

—*Jason Fischer*

CECILY SCUTT is a Perth writer and storyteller in love with the crossover between the local and the fantastic. Her short fiction has appeared in the literary journals *Southerly, Westerly, Hecate,* and in *Eidolon.* Her story 'Descent', which appeared in *Dreaming Down-Under,* was an ABC Radio National Short Story in 2003 and 2005.

An award-winning performance storyteller, she is always booked for Children's Book Week in Western Australia, where she tells her original stories of fridge ghosts, clockwork whales, bathyspheres, the boy who took the Bag of Winds to school, and refugees abducted by the Moon. Her performance stories for adults have reached conferences, national festivals, literary readings, cafés and libraries. A series of these tales was featured on the Faster Than Light radio show in 2001.

Cecily is currently working on the second draft of a first novel, and the first draft of a second.

Her story 'Europa' is a lyrical and poetic meditation on home, memory, myth; and a personal voyage on Homer's wine-dark sea, which is due north and west of Fremantle, Australia . . .

EUROPA

CECILY SCUTT

The old jetty is crowded, but I can't see Yanni, even from the yacht's high prow. I lean on the hot railing and scan the milling groups. Perhaps he won't turn up. Behind me Mick stoops around the sail, and the boat knocks against the jetty's stumps, mast arrogantly scratching at the sky. My newly ex-boyfriend, in immaculate ironed whites. 'Where's the old codger then?'

'He has to catch a bus, doesn't he. He'll be here.'

But perhaps he won't. I imagine him hunched over the table of his tiny flat, trapped by fear. He would have the blinds pulled down.

The boy leans at the side of the ship . . .

Yanni's white head threads through the crowd at shoulder height, bobbing like a lost fishing float. He is the only person here without sunglasses. A kind of shabby red blanket bulges in one arm. Finally he sees my wave.

I look away from Mick's classic 'Meeting my Elders' act; the slightly raised voice, the use of 'Sir'. Yanni merely scowls, standing four-square on the jetty's edge. 'We are not aristocrats here. My name is Yanni.' He glances at the gleaming hull and continues more formally, 'I say thank you now for letting me come on your boat.'

I expect him to be nervous on the water, clumsily gripping the rail, but he jumps in smoothly and helps with the canvas. I sit out of the way, next to his faded bundle, and wonder if it is only deep water, then, that is the problem.

The yacht shudders from its mooring and angles out across Fremantle harbour. The sun beats off the sail. When Yanni moves to the bows Mick leans forward.

'Ginny, I'm sorry about Friday, hey ...' I think of Mick, slurring through seven vodkas, declaiming to an entire party that my dress, which he'd persuaded me to buy, was too short, and my laugh, apparently, too loud. Then he'd cried all over the same dress, out on the back veranda.

'Whatever, Mick.' If I hadn't promised Yanni, I wouldn't be here. But Yanni has no phone to ring. And I said I'd help him go back to his country. Old as he is, this could be a last request.

He is crouched at the front now, eyes on the western horizon. Something in the tense muscles of his neck makes my own knuckles tighten on my knees.

The boy leans at the side of the ship and imagines . . .

I met Yanni feeding the ducks. A tiny man in a checkered shirt, crooning at the water's edge. The back of his head pink where every fortnight the barber runs his shaver up through white bristles.

'This one,' he tells me, 'was some people's pet. One day they go on holiday, just dump her here. She was too frightened to eat.' He says it *frroiten*. Every day he brings her special breadcrumbs. She knows his whistle.

He tells me young people are too *frroiten* too. No one joins the union, fights for the workers. Before he retired, he was in The Party. 'I am always in the front line,' he says.

I see him often after that. Soon he is dropping by my house, bringing me Greek newspapers, 'to see the pictures', and grimacing over my coffee. In Greece, he says, they take their politics seriously; when the Communists march, even the Chancellors of the universities parade in their robes behind the red flag. 'I wish I could go there,' he says, squinting at the smudgy text. 'I could meet my cousins, too, before I die.'

'Why don't you?'

'I'm too poor. It's too far.' He sloshes cold coffee around his mug and fumbles with the newspaper. 'Also,' he says, 'I don't like the sea.'

'You could fly.' *I could help you*, I am about to say.

'Even so —' He frowns at the window. '— you must cross it.'

Nudging through the Suez Canal, the ship rides high above the ground, ramparted like a castle. The boy runs from side to side, shabby boots clumping on the salty deck. To the right, the smog of the great stack wallows back across pallid Egyptian desert; to the left rise the red hills of the Sinai, grinding suddenly out of the land.

Red beyond red beyond red. Like the cliffs of Hell. Like his own home mountain captured through the stained glass of their village church. When he was smaller he thought the tinted slopes were burning. Breathless, he runs from the deck to fetch his mother.

'Red, red, will Australia be red?' he chants, as he drags her to the port rail. In the westering light he can see their shadows drifting on the banks beyond, fluid and elongated.

'I don't know. Wait and see.' Her scarf is slipping back and scarlet gleams in the dark hair at her temples. Seeing his eyes there she tugs the black cloth away. 'In Australia all the women walk bareheaded in the street. They wear hats only to keep off the strong sun.' She shakes her head and her hair slips in tendrils round her shoulders. She is beautiful.

Still he looks doubtfully at the sailors grinning and staring in the stern. He holds her hand. 'Will we be happy there?'

'Yes.' The red hills parade slowly past.

Out of Aden the ocean opens green and empty. The ship steams across the sea like a snail across a mudflat, slow and solitary. The boy watches the water for dolphins.

His *mitera* has discarded her black scarf, and smiles at the other passengers. The Greeks on board will not talk to her — a widow or worse, travelling alone, why is she not with her family? — so she speaks with the English, practising for the new country. Each night she washes his linen shirt in the basin, and brushes her glossy hair with oil.

One English couple give the boy a set of marbles. On the sunny deck the Tom Bowler streaks like a bee towards the yawning side. Too slow, he watches a canvas shoe descend, the glass circle lifting in calloused fingers. The sailor smiles slowly, holding it out to the woman in black, while across the deck his crewmates watch.

The child slides past his mother's waist to take the marble from the man's hand. His voice is like the English lady's finch, lonely and precise: 'Thank you sir. Mama we need to go down now.'

The sailor's gaze slides down her dress. He doesn't move as the boy tugs his mother away. Her hand is cold. Behind them the sailors' voices rise.

From the dark bunk he watches her stand by the tiny porthole. Orange light from the deck above flares beyond the spray-flecked glass. She lifts her hand to wipe away the room's steam, and over the engine's grumble he hears her breathing change.

'Mama! Is there something there?'

As she turns from the glass her eyes are strange. Her loose hair slides on her shoulders. 'Yanni, just a dream. Go back to sleep.'

Outside, the night sea shifts and surges.

The boy leans at the side of the ship and imagines the drop . . .

'What about women, you know, after the revolution?'

'Everyone will be equal. All the people. All the workers together.' He is standing at the edge of the pond, peering into the tea-dark water, ducks squabbling around his feet.

'But it seems to me ...' I squeeze the last of the bread between my fingers, 'doesn't it seem to you it's not just about money?'

He stares at the scummy surface as if searching for something. 'I say to you before, it is power, it is who makes the things.'

I am thinking about the men on the building site just opposite, who shout at me. The man outside the cinema who makes strange smacking noises with his lips. Mick's friends Steve and Gaz, who despise girls if they're ugly, and hate them if they're not. 'Why didn't you ever get married, Yanni?'

He is quiet for a minute. 'When I come here, there were not many Greek girls — not to marry an orphan with no family. And my English is not so good. Also ... it is a hard life for women. My mother had a hard life in Greece, before she left. She ran away, I found out later.' He looks at me across the muddy bank. 'Not like you, Geenee. Here the women are very free.'

I fold up the paper bread bag. It makes a forlorn crumpling noise. 'I suppose.'

'If I had met you when I was young, Geenee, I would have married you,' he says, and gives me his sad, generous smile.

... imagines the drop down the wall of the hull ...

The swell grows as Fremantle recedes. Rottnest Island slips past to the left, and the spray increases. A line of clouds blurs the northwest horizon, but here the sun still flattens itself on the white stretch of sail.

Yanni is motionless in the bows. Mick slouches long-legged in the stern, singing the same three lines of a song over and over. Every now and then he gives me his sad-puppy look. I am thinking of his swagger, which mars his beautiful legs, smudges the gold of their outline in the sun. What scared me at the party was how many of them nodded, looked at him with sympathy as he sputtered out accusations. I wish again I hadn't come.

At noon the wind drops suddenly. Land is a purple blur behind us to the east as Mick rises to secure the limply flapping sail. 'What now?' he asks me.

'The anchor,' says Yanni, not turning his head. The back of his neck looks sunburned. Mick scowls and shuffles to let the sea anchor out.

Yanni rises stiffly and moves over to where I'm sitting. His face is burned and tense. As he unfolds his crimson bundle I almost start to laugh. It is an old cape, braided at the shoulders — like something from my childhood dressing-up box. Only his stiff breathing stops me.

Casting it over one arm, he makes his way back round the sail to the bow. He turns to the darkening northwest, shakes the red cloth in the sun, and calls out. I think his words are Spanish, not Greek. They sound dim and muffled in the still air.

Mick is incredulous. He grabs my elbow and whispers loudly in my ear. 'What the hell is he doing?'

'Shhh. I don't know! It's a symbol or something. He's afraid of the sea.'

'Crazy old coot.'

Yanni calls out again. His spine is straight. This time the words clang against the metal of the water — weird and archaic. I can't move my eyes from his slight figure, tense against the shifting of the boat. I feel how small he is, how small we are, a tiny stick-and-bone bundle on the swaying desert of the sea.

Yanni is breathing in to call again when Mick's shout breaks across it: 'What the FUCK is THAT?'

Past Colombo the men in uniform search the ship. They toss about the child's bedding. They jostle in the doorway and speak only to each other. One holds up a worn and embroidered petticoat, and shakes it in the dim cabin. The sun from the porthole softens it with light. His mother holds his shoulders hard. She is gazing out the round window.

'You have more trunks?' the leader says in English. The woman stares at the sun-filled glass, and her son shakes his head. 'Where is your husband?' asks another man, too loudly.

This is what the child remembers: the long corridor of the lower deck, the taste of his own wrist in his mouth, the door closed behind him.

When they leave, they drop the petticoat in the corridor outside.

The boy leans at the side of the ship and imagines the drop down the wall of the hull; the sudden shock of cobalt, down, down through warmer currents to cold. Since the men came, his mother has locked her cabin door, and will not speak. When he talks of Australia she is silent.

In Australia he will build her a house. She can sit under the olive trees in the sunlight and stare at the moving leaves. If strange men come to the house he will send them away. He will buy her a floppy hat to cover her hair. They will be happy.

Later, in the new country, he will call it a dream, riven by the engine's changing roar. The child climbs the steep below-deck stairs. Ahead of him the woman's hair blows back, slowly, like seaweed: the soiled petticoat is trailing in her hand. She throws the scrap of cloth into the sullen orange of the wake, gleaming in the deck flares. She raises her arms. She is calling.

Huddled by the wall, her son watches the sea divide. Watches immensity roll across the dark towards her. Sees her turn back towards him, turn away again.

Wakes night after night in his Fremantle foster home, shaking and screaming at the harbour down below.

. . . the sudden shock of cobalt . . .

The clouds on the horizon are boiling suddenly, flattening into massive anvil shapes. I can see wind whipping across the sea, rushing towards us. And a wave, a cloud, a shoulder, heaves up from the water, impossibly high.

Yanni cries out and flaps the cape high. The wave-mountain turns, and a last gleam of sun catches on green glass near its head: horns.

The Bull slouches across the water towards the boat. It moves with a horrifying smoothness, and leaves no wake. Now only its knees are covered by the ocean below. It is huger than a dream.

The red cloth flutters in the wind. Mick is clutching the tiller, mouth stretched wide. The monster lowers its head and charges. In the dark muscles of its shoulder I see fish, moving, but its eyes are hot and ancient. The yacht heels over as the wind of its passing flings the boom around.

'Hai!' cries Yanni, staggering against the mast, and he whirls the red banner again. In a world turned to grey and violent green it glows like a beacon. Behind us, the Bull turns ponderously and falls through the air towards it. I push liquid from my face to see the glass scimitar slicing for Yanni's head.

'No!' I scream hopelessly at the shadow massed above us. 'Get *away*!' My shoulder shoves Yanni to his knees, and the tip of the horn snatches the red cape from his arm. But the Bull has already pulled its head up. It stands in the water beside the wallowing boat, swollen as a cloud, and sways its head slowly back and forth. 'Get *away*!' Hysteria shudders my breath. 'Get *off*!'

The great mass heaves a step backwards. The wind is dropping. In the sudden silence I can hear Mick choking and retching in the stern.

Yanni climbs slowly to his feet. He looks defeated. The cape spreads out in the water below us, sodden and sinking. He cranes his neck back up at the Bull and says something. This time I am sure it is Greek.

After a long moment, the molten shoulder turns, and the immensity of back roils with movement. At the green joints of the knees seaweed swirls. The Bull lurches away, thrusting through the waves with enormous, muscular strides. Near the horizon it merges with the surface, and the returning sun glints green on the last gleam of horn.

. . . down, down . . .

After a while of silence, Mick moves to find the anchor. Yanni lifts his head from his knees.

'Well I know now, Geenee,' he says heavily. 'I can go back to my country now. So I say thank you for this. And also to your friend.' He rubs his prickly scalp, looking diminished and bitter.

'But . . . Yanni . . .'

'I see now. You must call him up. And even then, you can tell him to go.'

Coughing the last of the salt from my lungs, I almost miss the rest.

'And so she didn't, my *mitera.* She didn't tell him to go.'

. . . through warmer currents to cold.

Halfway back to shore the sea is a glinting plain again. A fresh westerly skips us across the surface like flying fish. Mick is concentrating on sail and tiller, and won't speak to me — I wonder what he saw, and who he will blame. My own thoughts are circling through immensity, dark translucence, muscle.

'Yanni?'

He looks up from the last of the bailing.

'Can you teach me the words?'

'They're Greek. In this country better you learn Vietnamese.' His forehead furrows. He strips off his overshirt and passes it to me. 'You should wear more clothes, Geenee.'

His eyes are nowhere near my sodden T-shirt, but my skin flinches, pulling my arms across my chest. 'I meant, those particular words.'

In the afternoon light his eyes become curiously flat, rejecting. My grandmother had that look — the effect of cataracts on brown eyes, that's all. We are both silent, listening to the cold sound of the wind in the cables.

I trail my hand in the glassy water. The waves have edges like blades. I slide my gaze down their green sides, searching, hungry for the gleam of horns.

Cecily Scutt

AFTERWORD

What's the name for the thing that comes before a bigger thing? An outlier, a scout before the army, a harbinger, a herald . . .

'Europa' is a harbinger story for me — it heralded a novel project. Not that anyone in this story appears in the novel, but here are Greek myths, migrant ships, the Western Australian coastline. But in the novel, it is the maze's prisoner — the bull-headed Asterion — who is bundled into the hold with a sack over his head, bellowing desolation through the hull, then lost beneath our hard, bright, windy streets . . .

'Europa' is for my friend George Stathopoulous.

— *Cecily Scutt*

ROSALEEN LOVE is an Aurealis Award winner and one of Australia's best short story writers. Her deliciously wry, funny, and ironic stories have gained her international attention. She writes about science in a variety of ways, from the academic study of the history and philosophy of science and future studies, to science fiction. Rosaleen has worked as a university lecturer in both the history and philosophy of science and professional writing and is currently a Senior Academic Associate in the Faculty of Arts at Monash University, Clayton, Australia.

Her writing career began in 1983 when she won the Fellowship of Australian Writers, State of Victoria Short Story Award. Since then, she has published three brilliant short story collections: *The Total Devotion Machine and Other Stories, Evolution Annie*, and *The Traveling Tide*. Her stories have been included in mainstream as well as science fiction anthologies and magazines in Australia, Great Britain, and the United States. Her most recent nonfiction book is *Reefscape: Reflections on the Great Barrier Reef.* She is currently working on a collection of essays.

The wild confection of a story that follows could have only been written if Rosaleen were channelling Isaac Asimov, R.A. Lafferty, Richard Feynman, George O. Smith, Agatha Christie, and Gertrude Stein.

You'll see . . .

RIDING ON THE Q-BALL

ROSALEEN LOVE

Mikey rang Lula whenever Earth was pointing in the right direction in the torsion field. 'I'll be quick. I've not much time before the field drive flips me over to the other side. I have to tell you something.'

That was why, when Lula was a child and the phone rang, she rushed to be the first to pick up. Sometimes the calls were for her.

With everyone else, Lula chattered away on the phone, but with Mikey she learned the value of listening. From call to call, Mikey taught Lula the principles of zero point energy, and what the view was like from the other side of the Milky Way.

Lula grew up knowing all about dark energy, except nobody else had ever heard of it, and it was hard to tell people about Mikey's calls from the other side of the galaxy. Lula absorbed the lessons of the torsion field, not knowing where and when they might come in handy.

It is not surprising that Lula grew up to be a futurist, her mind open to the realities of life on other worlds, firm in her conviction that one day she would meet Mikey somewhere out there, if not in the flesh, then in an alternate mode of existence that might, conceivably, be better.

One day Lula was summoned to the office of Creighton Trucking and Aerospace, her biggest client. She advised as a consultant, juggling the strategic plans, doing the vision stuff. Bread and butter work. Creighton was her favourite client. They were into transport, but wanted to be in aerospace. 'That's what I call visioning,' said Lula whenever she dealt with them.

Lula dropped by at the office of Lucille and Gaynor, assistants to the boss.

'We called you in, Lula, because we didn't know where else to go.' Lucille dressed butch but girly with it, her name embroidered in pink roses on the pocket of her khaki coveralls.

'We called you in, Lula, because we knew you wouldn't laugh.' Gaynor dressed girly but butch with it, her trucker's T-shirt teamed with a layered purple skirt.

'We think the company may be in some kind of trouble, but we don't know what.' Lucille prodded the numbers on the fax machine.

Models of spacecraft, rockets, and landing modules hung from the ceiling of Creighton Trucking and Aerospace. A huge mural covered one wall, showing trucking, heading out from Earth towards the moon, Mars and beyond. The truckers wore spacesuits. The astronauts drove trucks. Rays from a benevolent smiling sun beamed down from above. A rainbow arced from one wall across the ceiling to the opposite side of the room.

As Lucille poked the fax machine, it suddenly sprang into action. A sheet of paper chattered its way from one side to the other.

Lucille froze. Gaynor jumped.

'That fax,' said Gaynor, 'That's part of the problem. Oh, Lula, it's Hitcher! He's disappeared. Here one minute, gone the next.'

'Hitcher, he said this, "I've come to warn you . . ." and then, when I turned round to ask him what he was on about, he wasn't there.' Lucille sobbed. 'He was standing right here, by the fax.'

Gaynor said, 'I suppose, it's only part of the problem to say he's disappeared, but then, he wasn't meant to be here in the first place. So you could say the problem isn't that he disappeared, it was that he was here at all.'

'It's like he came in one day, materialised, I think now, looking back on it, I think that must be what he did. You see, I'd been asking Gaynor for an assistant, when she went off on holidays, and Gaynor went off, and Hitcher appeared. So I thought she'd arranged it.'

'But I hadn't,' said Gaynor.

'He was standing beside the photocopier when I came in, looking a bit shaky and I saw him, thought, well, he's the temp, he's been sent to help me through this busy patch.'

'No way,' said Gaynor, 'I haven't a clue who he is, where he's come from.'

Lucille said: 'There were times . . . he was a bit sparky, you know, like he'd get near pieces of electrical equipment and sparks would fly? I did wonder about that, what he was wearing. He looked like he wasn't really comfortable in his clothes. As if he wasn't comfortable in his skin. But what he was wearing, you know, it was just like me. These coveralls, and his name, Hitcher, in roses just like mine, and I've never had any problem with static.'

'I want to get this straight,' said Lula. 'There's this guy, who's gone now, who was a bit sparky and who didn't fit his clothes, his skin, whatever . . .'

'The first time I thought something was odd. I asked him to photocopy and he went across and did this thing he does, all sparky, and he gave me the photocopies, but then I realised I hadn't given him the code to type in. But perhaps I'd left my number keyed in, it wasn't cancelled, my number? And he was here all day, being helpful, you know, a whiz at filing and he checked out the computer and it works so much better now.'

'Now, here's the really weird bit . . .' said Gaynor.

'Then after about a week, Gaynor rang in, and I said it was great having help, I was getting the backlog all sorted out? And she said, I never sent anyone? And I said to Hitcher, where are you from, who are you, and that's when he said, I've come to warn you, and I turned away because the fax machine went berserk, and all the phones rang at once, and there were sparks flying everywhere, and when I turned back, Hitcher was gone and there was an odd smell of burning nylon in the air.'

Lula listened with mounting excitement. It was something she'd been waiting for all her life, without knowing quite what it would be. Hitcher was her kind of man. Materialising. Spontaneously combustible. Here one minute, gone the next.

'And we're like, an aerospace company. Was he some kind of spy from, I don't know, some of the big guys, like, Lockheed? Boeing?' Lucille sat down.

Gaynor stood up. 'Except, you know, Lula, we're not really yet into aerospace. It's just we want to be, when it happens. We're really just truckers, but we want to truck to space.'

'I know,' said Lula, 'Most forward thinking of you.'

'Should I tell the boss? What can I tell the boss? Hitcher got through security somehow. He got through the usual checks, and then he said I've come to warn you. And he looked so sad, just before he left.' Lucille stood up.

Gaynor sat down. 'It's not like we're big time, like NASA. It's the boss's baby, this rocket. He wants to send it to the moon. It's a new kind of propulsion he's into, but it's not like it's going to run Boeing out of business. Or Lockheed. It's just a prototype, a model just two metres long. I don't know anything more about it. It's the guys in R&D who do that stuff.'

'He came to warn us, Lula,' said Lucille, 'as if something is about to happen. We've got some consultancy money left over, enough for a day. Take it. Spend the rest of the day looking round. See what you can find.'

'Do something, Lula, we need your help. So we can go to the boss and not look so stupid,' Lucille pleaded.

Lula took the job, not knowing what it was, and feeling way in over her head in either industrial espionage, or fraud, whatever. All she knew, she wanted to find out as much as she could, and fast. She wanted to meet Hitcher. If it wasn't already too late.

'We do have a photo. There's a camera in the corridor, and we got Charlie from Security to print one off for us.'

Hitcher was dark, serious, unsmiling, as if the weight of the universe lay on his hazy shoulders.

Lula took the photo and asked around. She soon found everyone knew Hitcher. To Ross in the law department, he was Mitch, the consultant sent to sort out intellectual property issues. To Bill in trucking, he was Pitcher, an IT whiz with the rosters. To Fletcher in finance, he was Pushka, the tax expert invited to tidy the year's returns. At the factory site, he was Hutch, the spot welder.

Ross, when pressed for more information, got a bit huffy. 'What do you want to know about Mitch for? That stuff's commercial-in-confidence. I'll tell you one thing though. Loved his suit. Armani three-button pinstripe flat-front . . . to die for.'

It was with the engineers that Lula found her first lead. George said, 'I want to use the rules and get the right answer. I want this rocket to stay in the air, go where I want it, and come back.'

'It's this guy, you know him?'

'Hutchkin? He was great. He's this physicist sent from head office. Hutchkin said, when I showed him what the problem was, "It won't work, that way, not like that it won't." All that torsion field stuff was like way above my head.'

'Torsion field?' Lula made a note.

'Yup. Never heard of it till then, but now I do. It wasn't rocket science, it was quantum physics. The wave function of the universe? Never heard of it. But the way he explained things, it made sense. He gave me rules to follow.'

'What rules?'

'The law of conservation of energy, for starters. I mean, I know all that, but the way Hutchkin put it, it's the law of conservation of dark energy that you've got to take into account, and when I did that, and I tell you, we're the only rocket company in the world working on dark energy as rocket propellant, then a few things clicked into place, and the next rocket we launched was a right zippy little sparkler.'

'Did you happen to notice what he was wearing?'

'Blundstones. Plaid shirt. Jeans.'

'Like you?'

'Just like me. He's an engineer.'

At the end of the day, Lula reported back to Lucille and Gaynor. 'Multi-skilled. He's been all over. Hitch, he turns up when and where he's needed, as if he knows he's needed. Then he leaves, but people aren't too puzzled, because he was only a temp, or a consultant.'

'He knows all about the business?' Lucille asked. 'We've got to tell the boss. Big Charlie won't like it.'

Hitcher, Pushka, Mitch, whatever, came when he was needed and fixed things up. He went where he wanted, no passes, no keys, no passwords. He appeared. He disappeared. Lula felt a prickle on the back of her hands, the thrill of the chase. Hitcher was her kind of man. If indeed he was a man. Could be, he was more like a collection of molecules brought together by the torsion field, so that now you see him, now you don't, as he dissolved and vanished into the ethereal wind.

I've come to warn you, said Hitcher — and then he was gone. What he meant to say, in the moments following the moment he wasn't there any more, was this: I've come to warn you, it's not a good idea doing what you're doing in R&D, creating a bubble universe in a jet propulsion stream while that fax machine in Lucille's office is sparking with sleptrons and neutralinos because of this trapped ø-type Q-ball I'm trying my best to free. Only minutes from now the gravity lens will be in full refractory mode, and all hell will break loose. Furthermore, Lucille, as a friend, I have to say with that fax machine of yours, the reason why half the faxes you send never arrive is because in its inner workings six laws of your universe (though not of mine) are being violated with every pulse of the ink jet feed.

And if he'd managed to say all that, Lucille would never have taken it all in, except for the bit about the fax machine, which, intuitively, she would recognise as true.

* * *

Hitcher's story: What Lucille can't yet know, is, I'm inside the fax machine, looking out. It's what I came here to fix — this Q-ball that's been the problem with the fax machine. Q-balls — they've been roving round the universe since the Big Bang, and mostly, they're no problem. They just zip though materials like these machines and out the other side, and straight through the centre of the Earth, and off to the edge of the universe, much the same now as when they were first created. This Q-ball though, it's been warped a bit, got its ø-field in a Möbius knot and it's stuck here. Playing up.

When I say I'm looking out from the edge of the Q-ball, it's only in a manner of speaking. I'm more tweaking the space-time continuum, twisting the geodesic warp drive, and throwing a gravity wave round a corner and behind. All to keep this Q-ball stable. For as long as I can.

Time to send a fax.

Fax: For Lula

From: Hitcher

I have come to warn you . . .

The fax machine burst into flames. A piece of paper, singed at the corners, flew out of the machine and clear across the room, scattering sparks as it went.

Lucille tugged the electricity cord from the socket.

Gaynor poured coffee on the flames.

Lucille picked up the fax by an unburned edge. 'Hey, it's from Hitcher! For you, Lula.'

'How's he know about me?' asked Lula.

'I've come to warn you,' said Lucille. 'It's what he said to me.'

'That fax machine's a write-off,' said Gaynor.

'Forever,' said Lucille.

As the instant coffee with its dose of artificial sweetener hit the flames, the dark energy from the rogue Q-ball made a break for it. The entity known as Hitcher was ready. Taking advantage of the instability in the space-time sub-axis, Hitcher thinned his consciousness one slepton thick and spread it round the inside surface of the Q-ball. He went with the flow, then sucked himself back, one squark at a time. Then Gaynor picked up the fire extinguisher and threw foam on the caffeine-slepton mix. That was it. That did it. The bulge redoubled its efforts, the dark matter inside the Q-ball not quite meeting the matter outside. The ø-field tightened the Möbius knot and caught a ride on the gravity wave.

The Q-ball sphere expanded to embrace first the coffee, then the foam, and then Lula, Lucille, and Gaynor.

'Aarrkkk,' said Gaynor, as the room fell away and expanded outwards in a sphere of light. 'Uh Uh Uh.'

'That fax machine, it always was big trouble,' said Lucille, as she slipped into a new state of being.

'So this is what it's *for*, dark energy and such.' Lula opened her mind to the bright new world.

The sphere expanded rapidly. Squarks co-exist with quarks, sleptons with leptons, each occupying their own space in the universe of spaces; dark matter occupying, as it does, the interstices within un-dark matter. Q-balls are the stuff of dark matter. It's not like matter and anti-matter, where the two meet, but in explosion, Boom! A new black hole. More, matter and dark matter actually co-exist within the framework of the universal laws of nature, violating only those laws that were meant to be broken. Faster than light travel becomes possible, though technically not so. Conversion of matter to dark energy, and (possibly) back again may happen, depending on the proportionate implosion of cosmic anarchy.

Hitcher did his best to stop the inside getting to the outside and the outside getting to the inside. On the outer surface of the Q-ball the conscious entities that were Gaynor, Lucille and Lula found instantaneous transformation. They are the creatures of quarks and leptons. Hitcher is the stuff of squarks and sleptons. Matter encounters dark matter, and the universe is forever changed.

— Welcome. We are Hitcher-Mitch-Pitcher-Pushka-Hutch-Hutchkin. Hitcher.

— We are Lula-Lucille-Gaynor.

— Gurgle. Glug. Waark.

— Not Gaynor. Not talking yet. What's happened? What have you done?

— It wasn't me. This ø-type Q-ball, it's bad news. I'm trying to get rid of it.

— Hitcher, Lucille here. You weren't truthful. You said you were a temp.

— I never said I was.

— You let me think you were.

But you would never have believed me, if I told the truth.

The entity that was Hitcher strained at the seams, doing its best to keep a tight grip on the edges.

Lula looked out on the office where she has just a few minutes before been standing, upright, possessed of her usual two arms, two legs, body and head, then a normal regular human woman, now, what was she? Now it was as if she was looking at the world from the perspective of a consciousness smeared atoms thin over the surface of a rapidly growing sphere. She couldn't see her arms or legs, or Lucille or Gaynor, though she sensed them close to her, and Hitcher, if that was really Hitcher, the voice coming from within her head — her brain, no her mind, whatever it was. Hitcher appeared as an extra sense, something that gave her access to a consciousness above and beyond her own, incorporating those close by, Lucille and Gaynor, in the one expanded entity. She sensed the office ceiling looming closer, its spacecraft models swaying in the ethereal wind, until she whooshed up through them, through the roof and into the sky. The building of Creighton Trucking and Aerospace was left behind, and — It's true, thought Lula, the future truly is a river bearing us away. But this is just not possible.

— In your world, yes, but certainly not in mine. It's happening.

— Where are we? What are we? Why are we, where we are, what we are? Lula sensed herself leaving the world behind. She saw mountains, rivers and oceans in rapid retreat below.

Oblivious to the panorama, Hitcher continued. — There's this point now, and from this point, a whole heap of things are possible, might happen, but only some do — only some *seem* to happen. But what if they all happen, but we don't know, because we're caught on this time line here, and not that one over there?

— Like the future is a quiver full of arrows?

— We're at this point from which the possibilities diverge, but we'll know only one future that will come of it. But there are others.

Lula watched the Earth shrink in size to a sphere as seen from space.

— I did try my best to fix things before they got to this stage, said Hitcher. — But if you will use dark matter as rocket propulsion at the same time you've got a ø-type Q-ball stuck in the fax machine, while Ross is trying to patent the intellectual property on stuff he can't begin to understand, forcing George from R&D to confine the bubble universe in the jet propulsion stream; and as for the income tax complications, you are aware that making mistakes there can make the space-time axis throw a wobbly and — there's more. Later. Let's fix this mess first.

— How could we know?

— About Creighton? That it's a centre for the flux of synergistic energies, on the cusp between the universes of matter and dark matter? You know now.

— Uh Uh Uh.

— It is? But what's this? Hitcher, is that our Earth down there? And the moon, so tiny?

— You've got it.

— Why are we here? Where are we going?

— Got to go. Can't stay. The Sun will go neutronic.

— Is that the solar system, Mercury, Venus, Mars?

— Got to get going. We're heading for a small hole, over near the edge, the containment facility for rogue and errant Q-balls. We've got a choice, see? The future here's like a forked path. The choice is — do nothing, and the Earth explodes. Do something, we get to save it. Some choice. Don't want the Sun to be a neutron star, no way. Slurps up the sleptons like you wouldn't believe. No, we're taking this ø-type Q-ball to the cosmic dustbin.

— There's something you're forgetting. Us. We didn't ask for this. It's like you asked us to step into a cab, and when we do, the driver is wearing a blindfold, and can't see a thing, and it's out of control and nobody knows where we're going. The next thing we do is we all crash together.

Then Lula realised that it's like she's always been told: the moment of transition, of transformation, no one ever sees it coming. Change is sudden, sharp and discontinuous. The old gives way to the new. Everything seems clear until the moment when nothing is clear, when the people that once were people, the entity that once was Hitcher, the fax machine that was once a fax machine, become entangled in a mutually transformative experience.

Hitcher says, and he's the boss of this world, this conjunction of worlds, he knows more about it than they, the collective consciousness of Lula, Lucille and — well not Gaynor, she's lost her voice in the Ughs and the Erks and the experience has been a bit outside her comfort zone and she's not coping as well as . . .

— Yuk yerk yikes.

Leave her out of it, then, the merging. Lula-Lucille has come to feel it's perfectly natural somehow to be riding a transparent Q-ball at faster-than-light-speed, on the way to save the planet from destruction.

As a futurist, Lula always followed Dator's dictum — any useful idea about the future can often appear ridiculous, at least when it is first suggested, before it takes flight. Doors that open all by themselves? Crazy. Rockets that fly to the moon? Impossible. Lula, Lucille and Gaynor riding a Q-ball, on a mission to save the universe from destruction? Totally ridiculous.

Except it was happening.

— I'm a futurist, said Lula of Lula-Lucille, introducing herself properly to Hitcher. — I don't believe we met, not as the old me, the old you.

— Lula, it's Lucille here, tell Hitcher we want to go home. Gaynor's not feeling so good.

The Q-ball grows as it bounces through the universe. Inside the ball two universes co-exist. One is the creation of dark matter. The other, both within and without, is the everyday world of un-dark matter, where on the edge Lula-Lucille and Gaynor exist in a higher state of excitation. Plop, plop, plop, the bubbles of dark matter rise up from under.

— Lula again. Hitcher, we seem to have picked up one of the rings of Saturn.

— Whoops. Give it a wriggle and a shake. Can't go taking one of the rings of Saturn with us, not where we're going.

— There it goes. Now about this future, this straight line stuff, past-present-future, even past-present-multiple futures, isn't that a bit too simple? Aren't things more intertwined, more like the future already exists in the present, bubbling up from underneath like mud baths in Rotorua or Yellowstone, plop, plop, plop. Ripples spread out and they bump into each other and become all interconnectedy.

— Hitcher here. Interconnectedy? There's this time here, and the lines go off and diverge and there's no going back. But what if you can go sideways? Get interconnectedy that way? That's the Oort cloud down there, by the way.

— We're starting to get a tail, like a comet.

— Lovely, isn't it? They're proto-comets. They can tag along.

— I'd be enjoying this a lot more if I knew where it was going to end.

— Simple enough. Here we have divergent futures and we are jumping between them. Just because it sounds impossible doesn't mean it is.

— True, said Lula, that's Dator's Dictum, to which I adhere, as a principle of my profession.

— It's not impossible. It is in agreement with the law of the conservation of mutually inconsistent futures.

— Of course, said Lula. I was forgetting what Mikey told me.

— That's why Mikey thought of you, Lula, because you'd understand.

— It is my kind of thing, said Lula.

In the state of cosmic anarchy, exotic matter rules. The solid stuff of hands, faces, legs, arms, eyes, ears is left behind, mere appearances cloaking a deeper quantum reality. Inside the Q-Ball, the ø-type energy surges, seething with plopping goo, on a mission to draw the non-Q universe into itself.

— Where are we going? What's this hole?

— Just a small one.

Inside the Q-ball, Hitcher mobilises his squarks and sleptons. Outside the starry skies whiz past, blurred like in spherical time lapse. Lula-Lucille gets her act together. — This hole, it'll be the end of the journey?

— As always. But I always think the journey matters more than the end.

— Hitcher, we don't want to just end. Pfutt. Pfoot. Phut. We didn't want to come on this trip. You dragged us along. Once you get sucked into a cosmic containment facility, that's it? End of journey? End of life? We want to go home.

— Hang on here. I have to renormalise the group flow to a fixed point for the emergence from the Galilean substratum.

— Hurk Hark Hirk.

— You mean, to the point where Ohm's quantum potential acts instantly?

— How'd you know?

— Mikey told me.

— Mikey sent me to you.

— I had this friend, when I was little, Mikey, and he used to send me messages from space, but I never told anyone about him, or I tried to, and nobody believed me.

— Arwwkk Orrkk Warrkkk, Gaynor cries to the void.

Lucille joins in. — Uh Uh Uh Urk.

— We're talking about the same Mikey, I take it: the multitudinous integrated K-type energy ying thing?

— To me, he was just a friend called Mikey, someone who rang me up from far away, whenever Earth was pointing the right direction in the torsion field. He taught me the principles of dark energy, and that's why I'm not as surprised as I might be at being here, now. What about you? You know Mikey too?

— We are all aspects of Mikey in the eyes of the universal observer without whom the quantum universe would not continue in existence. That is how I see it. And Mikey sent me to find you. As if he knew you'd help.

The Q-ball is a dark nutshell universe on its way through the larger-scale universe that is the universe of ordinary matter. Q-balls have existed from the beginning of the universe, their dark gravity distorting the paths of visible stars and galaxies. But a rogue and errant Q-ball, just one can hit a neutron star and blow it to pieces.

— Not that your sun is a neutron star, yet, but this Q-ball, this one from your fax machine, why, it only takes one like this to turn rogue on you and guzzle up all the protons and neutrons in the vicinity of Earth. Then before you know it, it spurts out streams of pions and muons, and the resulting Cerenkov radiation will dazzle you all to death. So, got to get to that hole before the end of your universe.

— Do we have to go all the way with you? Can't we just wait till the torsion field flips us over to the other side. You go visit the hole by yourself.

— We're getting close.

— We want to go home! Lula now speaks for Lucille and Gaynor, both, for the moment, totally out of it.

— There is another future, you know, in which you never left Creighton Aerospace. You want it back? Time lines diverge, there are many possibilities for many futures. We're the creatures of an eternally existing self-reproducing multiverse, and this is not the only way for possibilities to be realised.

— We want that part of the multiverse we used to call home.

Lula knew what to do. She had to let Hitcher go. Such a pity, when she'd only just met him, and he seemed a nice enough guy, for a cosmic entity. He was cute, but dead serious, and not a whole bunch of fun, but then, you wouldn't be, if you had an entire universe to save. But not for nothing had she learned the lessons of the torsion field. All it took was a tweak of the space-time sub-axis, and a twist of the ying co-ordinates thing, and . . .

In the office of Creighton Aerospace, Lula reported back to Lucille and Gaynor. 'This is what I've found out about Hitcher. Seems he really was sent here to help you. He knows a bit about everything — Renaissance Man. Mate of Big Charlie. Seems Hitcher met the boss on a plane when they sat next to each other in First Class. They got talking and one thing led to another. Hitcher turned up. Did his various jobs. Now he's gone.'

'He was a bit of a philosopher, for a temp,' said Lucille. 'He was different. I liked him, even if his clothes didn't fit, and when he spoke he crackled a bit. It's so hard to find good help, and he was good.'

'Didn't something just happen to that fax machine? Some kind of fire?'

Lula's career went from strength to strength. Her mind was truly open. How well she knows the secrets of the universe, that out there in the cosmic void there are dark matter earths and dark matter suns. There are dark matter people and plants and animals and bacteria and viruses. She and her Earth-kind are the stuff of quarks and leptons. Others beyond are the stuff of squarks and sleptons.

So it was that Lula could ask just the right questions at planning meetings to get people sparking off each other. Afterwards, they might wonder what it had been about, as they reached a consensus that was often too whacky to be reported back to the boss. The group statement that came from the meeting would be a pale shadow of the cosmic breakthrough they achieved, together with Lula, where the solution to where the company would be in the future was totally wild and far out of this world. The journey was what they remembered, not the end point, lost in some cosmic generality that was, at the time, both deeply felt and known to be a glimpse of the eternal truths, the essence of which they could never quite remember but which they knew to be the most important thing that had ever happened to them in their lives.

AFTERWORD

I've long been brooding about the prospect of writing a short story sequence about a futurist detective. I love the feng shui detective short stories of Nury Vittachi, whose detective, C.F. Wong, solves crimes through the logical application of the allegedly scientific principles of feng shui. I wanted to create a character who solves problems using the principles of Futures Studies. For a few years, I moved in futurist circles, and found them a diverse, whacky and congenial group of people. I wanted to write about futurists at work, just as Vittachi fleshed out the work of the geomancer. I've made a number of attempts at creating a story sequence, but, as I write, I find it's either my futurist detective, or, in this case, her sidekick, who speeds towards the far edges of the galaxy on a one-way trip. Perhaps I could try a prequel.

— *Rosaleen Love*

LEE BATTERSBY was born in Nottingham, United Kingdom, in 1970, and moved to Australia when he was five. He is the author of over seventy stories, which have been published in the United States, Europe, and Australia. His work has appeared in markets as diverse as *Aurealis, All-Star Zeppelin Adventure Stories, Year's Best Fantasy & Horror*, and *Australian Woman's Day*. A collection of his work, entitled *Through Soft Air*, was published in 2006. Since winning the international Writers of the Future competition in 2001, he has collected a number of awards, including the Aurealis, Ditmar, and Australian Shadows, as well as twice winning Australia's only ongoing science fiction competition, the Katharine Susannah Prichard SF/F contest.

He was a tutor at the Clarion South writers' workshop in 2007, and has run workshops and tutorials for the Katharine Susannah Prichard Writers' Centre, the Fellowship of Australian Writers, and the Queensland Writers' Centre. He lives in Perth, Western Australia, with his wife, writer Lyn Battersby, and their three children.

Here he writes a story of family, love, necessity, and survival in the icy wastes of the future . . .

IN FROM THE SNOW

LEE BATTERSBY

It is snowing outside the house. Snow is dangerous. You leave tracks, and tracks can be used to follow you. I am to stay inside. Father will not permit me outside, not until I am fully trained. The Darrington boy went out last winter and brought the weight of the gallows down upon his whole family. There are few families left. Snow is too great a risk.

Last Snow, the family acquired a cookbook. We have had a year to practise pickling, preserving, bottling. We are not so reliant upon fresh food as we were. It takes time to build up reserves, and we have always been cautious gatherers. Travellers are rare this season. Snow makes things difficult for everybody. Still, Father is out amidst the white world. Travellers are rare, but our need is great. Our need is always great, and Mother is pregnant again. I have been left to guard the house. I am the eldest male, and in the last two years I have grown large and strong. Large enough and strong enough to defend Mother and the children. Even Father eyes me warily. All I need is experience. In the meantime, I sit in the front room and watch snow forming patterns through the windows.

I pick out flakes and stalk them as they skitter across my field of vision. They make for good tracking practice, jumping and diving like rabbits across a field. I am so caught up in my pursuit that I am taken by surprise when a shape looms out of the darkness, grey against black. Snow dies against its borders. I leap back from the window.

'Mother! Get the children.' I race for the door at the side of the house. Only a fool rushes toward the enemy. 'Into the kitchen.'

The kitchen is a stone vault at the centre of the building. Everyone in the family knows how to use a knife, a pot, a kettle of boiling water. Within its confines, even babies become attackers. As I hit the door I hear Mother shouting at the children. I cast them from my thoughts, push through the door and into the cold.

The door swings shut behind me, locking into place. No entrance into the house can be opened from the outside. Either I will signal my return with the correct knock, or I will not return at all. No member of the family gives themselves up, not even our dwelling. I hit the ground and roll away at an angle, diving across a snow bank and behind the oak where it looms across the entrance. As I rise I slip the hunting knife from the sheath at my thigh. No cause to use my throwing knives: miss, and they are lost until the Thaw, and we cannot afford to lose precious edged weapons. The swirling snow gives me cover. I will get close enough to strike. Not experienced, but I do know my trade. To move quickly without being seen is at the heart of all we do.

It takes me less than a minute to gain the front of the house. The figure stands ten feet from the door, swaying as the wind buffets it. He is smaller than I first thought, and lighter in frame. He topples and falls headlong into the snow. I crouch, knife hand tucked into the angle of my hip and thigh. I have used this ruse to capture prey: fall as if weakened, then spring upon the unwary Samaritan who comes to help.

The ground is too cold to hold the ruse for long. Sooner or later, a movement will betray the supine figure. Breath stings my nostrils. I tilt my head, directing the streams of warm air towards my chest. No puff of moisture shall reveal my location. The figure on the ground does not move. Unless he moves now, the intruder will freeze to death. I wait a minute more, then sneak around the far side of the mound of whiteness building up over his body. So long without movement, there is no risk that he will be able to overcome me. Even so, I will not hurry my attack.

I approach until I am no more than two feet away, close enough to strike but out of reach of a sudden lunge from the ground. The coating of snow does not move. I tense my thigh muscles, crouch, and launch myself. The prey does not react. My knees strike the middle of his back. My knife sweeps down, and stops an inch from where the throat lies beneath the snow. Something is wrong. This is no attacker. An attacker would have moved. I lean back, use my empty hand to expose the body. It lies face down, unmoving, barely breathing. This is no man, set on usurping my home, my family. She is a woman, pale face against paler snow, dark hair shaken loose from the hood of her cloak by the fall. Her lips are turning blue. She is the first woman I have ever seen outside the family group. I waste seconds staring at the unfamiliar lines of her face, the exotic cast of her cheeks, her closed eyes, her neck. I scoop her up with a single movement, run to the door and bang out today's knock against the wood. I wait, stamping my feet until the entrance inches open, then barge past Mother and into the kitchen.

'Blankets,' I order. 'And boil the kettle.' Mother favours me with a black expression, and I growl at her. 'Move.'

She scurries to obey. I use the woman's body to clear the table of obstructions, then lay her down. Some of the smaller children press close to look. I snarl at them until they back away. Mother returns, her arms full of bedding. I tear blankets from her grasp and throw them across the limp body. The kettle arrives and I pour water over a towel, fold it in quarters, and wipe her face and limbs. She groans and twists from the contact. I persist, and her protestations grow more insistent.

In less than a minute, she sits up and stares at her surroundings. The children, brave attackers all, squeak and dart behind nearby hiding spots, including Mother's legs. I would punish them, but I cannot take my eyes from the woman. She sees me watching her, and opens her mouth to scream. I shoot a hand forward and clamp it over her mouth.

'Don't.'

She stares at me with wide eyes. I look away for a moment, determined not to notice how blue they are. Mother tutches. The woman's nostrils flare as she drags in air. I push harder, mashing her lips back against her teeth. She winces. Were my hand not over her mouth her scream would be from pain. I lean close, so that my eyes fill her vision.

'Don't scream,' I hiss. 'They'll kill you.' Now that the children have grown used to the strange visitor they have returned from their hiding. Ragged-haired and smiling, they would frighten anybody. The woman inhales once, twice. I give her head a short shake, just enough to bring her attention back to me.

'When I let go, you sit still. Otherwise …' I nod towards the children, then slowly remove my hand from her mouth. She watches me, fear brightening her eyes. Only when my hand is back against my chest does she relax, though her eyes dart here and there. I straighten, allowing her a small measure of room. Mother nods in the corner of my vision, a small sign of respect.

'Good,' I say, and fold my arms. 'What is your name?'

I get no response. Either she is too frightened, or I have been warning a mute. Mother speaks.

'She's shivering.'

'Hmm.' I point to little Belis. 'Some wine.' She runs to do my bidding. I am fond of Belis. She is obedient and sharp. Within a minute she returns and hands a mug to the woman.

'Drink.'

She does so, eyes fixed upon me over the edge of the mug. She chokes after the second swallow. A gout of wine spills over her shirt. I watch it trickle across her chest. Mother hisses, and I shake my head.

'Your name.'

'Marell,' she says, averting her eyes. I study the incline of her face, the softness of her skin. She is younger than I had at first thought, perhaps no more than sixteen or seventeen. My own age. The skin of my throat begins to itch. I take back the mug and hand it to Belis. Marell uses her sleeve to dab at the corners of her mouth.

'Thank you.'

'You're welcome. Now,' I perch on the table next to her. 'What were you doing out during the Snow? This is no place for a solitary traveller. You're not from a family.'

'Family? What do you mean?'

Mother and I exchange glances. Some of the younger children gasp. Mother silences them with a stare. Such looseness will be punished later. I keep emotion from my face.

'You're alone?'

She pauses before answering, and I become aware of how heavily we are leaning towards her answer. I click my fingers, and the children disperse. Within seconds the sound of fake play reaches us from the surrounding rooms. I am not fooled. There are ways to listen without seeming to do so, and our children are well trained. Marell seems not to notice the falseness. She relaxes, and her voice gains some strength.

'My caravan … we were travelling south, to Ealdwic. My father and mother, myself, and three retainers. A man, he jumped out of the snow . . .' She stops, looking past me at events too fresh to be ignored. 'He killed Mother with his teeth … Father …'

Mother and I glance at each other over the top of her head. Father hunts wild, on occasion, when the odds are in his favour, or he forgets himself.

'What happened?'

'He killed them. Everyone. Even after Vine shot him he just kept going. There was so much blood. So much …' She raises her hands to cover her eyes. 'I just ran, ran out into the storm, just to get away. Had to get away … Mother …' Tears overcome her and she bends into herself, voice swept away by the fear and grief. I place an arm around her shoulder and make comforting noises. Mother signals Anna.

'A warm bed for her, and a shot of the sleeping broth. Set one of the little ones to watch. Get me when she wakes.'

Anna half-carries the weeping Marell away. The sound of her crying disappears up the stairs before Mother speaks.

'Shot.'

I nod, eyes fixed upon the door. 'A caravan of six.'

'You know what we have to do?'

I nod again, and stand. 'I don't want her harmed.'

'What?' Mother turns her head, sharp as a bird. 'And what do we — ?'

'If Father is dead.' I step over to her, and realise just how much bigger than her I have become, how much taller. I can look over her without lowering my chin, and she shrinks the tiniest fraction at my closeness. 'If he is dead, then I am — '

'If,' she says, voice hard with the challenge. 'If not . . .'

I shrug. 'If not, he'll return.' I turn from her and make my way to my room. I am the oldest child. I have the greatest share of responsibilities. My room is the largest in the house, besides the kitchen and Mother and Father's bedroom. What little I own fits comfortably within: my weapons and pack; what few clothes I do not already wear; a small wooden ball on a string, the only childhood toy that has not been passed on to a younger one. A single bed. It is enough. And yet, standing in the doorway, I am struck by a flash of dissatisfaction. I see Marell with me, inside the room, and realise just how small it is, how there is nothing in here for anybody, not even me. The moment passes. I grab my cloak and knife, and shrug my pack over one shoulder. I do not bother to close the door when I leave. There is nothing to take.

In the kitchen, I fill the pack with a skin of wine and enough meat to last. Mother catches up to me as I tuck the last strands inside.

'That's the last of it.' She nods at the pack.

'I don't want her harmed.'

'Father wouldn't hesitate.'

'Father isn't here.' I draw my cloak around me and pull it tight. We walk to the door, and she pats me down, fussing. She is Mother, after all.

'Be careful.'

'A caravan of six.' I open the door. A blast of arctic hate strikes me in the face. 'Whichever one of us returns, we'll get through the winter.'

'Kester . . .' Mother raises her hand to my face, holding it there for a moment before letting it fall. 'He'll be injured, if he's not dead. Are you sure — ?'

'It had to come.' I smile, hoping it is not the final smile I give her. 'This is how we go on. The strongest will lead.'

I turn from her, and step out into the storm. I do not even hear the door close.

I am no more than a dozen feet from the house when the wind grabs the edges of my coat and hurls me to the ground. Father would kill me for coming out in this weather. At the least, he would give me a beating that would leave me unable to hunt for weeks. A body lost to the Snow is a waste of hunting equipment, and hunting is all we have to sustain us. A family can breed, but knives are hard to come by.

It takes me half an hour to reach the gate at the far end of the property, and another hour to cross the frozen river into the World. Father is too experienced to be caught in the open. Either Marell is right, and he lies dead amongst the wreckage of her caravan, or he has found shelter. If that is so, then I will die. I am under no illusions. I am young and strong, but Father has led our family for many years. There is no better hunter on the cliffs. Even injured, he will recognise my challenge and kill me.

Marell claims she was on the way to Ealdwic. Her driver would have skirted the cliffs and headed for the inland roads. I turn to the east, straight into the teeth of the wind, and take one step, then another. This journey will be a matter of single steps. I will not count them, simply look for the next snow bank, the next tree, anything I can hide behind to catch my breath and wipe the frozen snot from my lips.

It is more than three hours before I reach the nearest pack road, a distance I would run in less than half an hour at the beginning of a normal hunt. Our family does not stalk this road: too close to home, too high the chance of discovery. Other families have used it, but then, nobody in this region has a hunter like Father amongst them. He is the reason we are so strong, and why we go hungry on so few nights. Without him, we are a lesser pack. Without his presence standing guard, others may see a chance to take our home. Not everybody has firm walls around them, cooking equipment, cushioned furniture. The wind blisters my skin. I pull the furs up closer to my eyes, bend my head, and push forward, one step after another.

I cross the pack road in a crouch. There are no other families about, not in this weather. But Father has raised me well. I do not take unnecessary risks. I laugh at the thought. This whole expedition is a risk of the highest order. Still, training is for life. I duck and run, slide into a hollow on the other side of the road, unsheath my knife and strain my ears against the wind. No sound comes, no sign to show that my progress has been spied. We families do not attack each other, generally, but anybody abroad in this weather might be hungry enough.

I stay this way for long minutes, senses searching the surrounding wastes. It is a fine balance: stay still too long and I will freeze, and be lost to the family. Move with undue haste, and I might be caught by a stalker, killed, and still be lost. Once I am sure I am alone I straighten, sheath my knife, and expend precious energy upon a few jumps to circulate my slowing blood. Then I am off, running as best I can through the mounting drifts towards where I hope the Ealdwic road is still recognisable.

It verges on dark when I reach the caravan. It rushes out of the gloom, not on the Ealdwic road as Marell had said, but closer, on the lane between the abandoned trading outpost of the older tribes from across the straits. I crest the rise that separates the lane from the surrounding meadows, and stare down at the ruined caravan with a frown, nestling my back against the partial shelter of a fallen tree.

Something is wrong. I scan the remains of the battle. The lane runs between two rises that afford some shelter from the elements. Even so, snow covers the area in a thin layer, obscuring much I would like to see before I venture down to pick at the corpses. The caravan has overturned, its wheel smashed against a marker stone that has been half-pulled from the ground by the impact. This was not the camp Marell had mentioned. Someone attempted escape, and it resulted in their ruination. At least one body lies amidst the wreckage. Snowbound lumps litter the laneway. I tentatively identify half a dozen as human, and mark out another dozen or so as worthy of examination. Father was hunting, and if he is dead, I need to complete the task. That means gathering tools, anything that might be of use to the family. It also means making sure no survivors crawled away to bring the world down upon our heads. If no food is to be found in skins or bottles, I will have to carve the best meat from the bodies of the travellers.

But these tasks can wait. I have realised what is wrong. I cannot see Father, nor any trace of him. That means only one thing. He is still alive. Dead men leave more trails than a live man who takes care to cover his presence.

I crouch against the tree long enough for the breath to sting as it leaves my nostrils, scanning for signs of Father. I do not expect to find any. I can hide from even the most determined pursuer, and what I know, Father taught me. I suffer a moment's depression at the thought. Then it occurs to me: this training is my best chance of locating him. I may not know everything Father does, but I only have to pick up the scent of his trail, the signs that only one trained as I am could locate. My imagination will supply the rest.

I shift my gaze back to the beginning of my search pattern, and, despite the pain of the cold, slowly scan across the ground again. This time, I do not search for Father. I look at the progress of the fight, playing it out in my mind, placing figures against the white backdrop. When my mental battle ends, I replace Father's image with my own and look once more at the surrounding cover. Where would *I* go? Where would *I* hide? What would *I* do to conceal myself from discovery?

There: a slight disturbance in the rise of a nearby hillock, unnoticeable to the gaze of a pursuer, but affording anyone behind it an uninterrupted view of the landscape below. Once I have it in my sights I discern other signs of Father's progress: tiny depressions that speak of paused footsteps; a hollow where a body may have rested, or fallen; a branch that bears more snow than those around it. I visualise my progress up that slope. In doing so, I know where Father lies. One question remains. Does he lie so still by choice? I will not find out from my present position. There is no way to delay what must come. I wince as frozen muscles propel me to a standing position, and take care to stretch as I leave my cover and stride down into the centre of the clearing, exposing myself to his view. I turn towards his hiding place, and raise my face.

'Father,' I say, my voice clear and empty of fear. 'I am here.'

No response. I did not expect one. He occupies the high ground. He won't come down to me, even in voice. I walk up the rise, my hands visible at all times, making no attempt to hide the signs of my approach. I crest the rise. A shallow depression lies between hillocks, a hollow scoured out of the ground by wind and rain, deep enough for an overhang of vegetation to conceal the figure propped up by the edge of the hole. A casual observer would take him for dead.

'Father.' I kneel before him, tilt my head to show my open throat. He gives no indication that he is other than the corpse he resembles. I keep my position, eyes lowered. Slowly, an inch at a time, he raises his hand and runs a finger along the line of my throat, from ear to shoulder blade, then lets his hand drop. I exhale and sink backwards into a sitting position.

'How bad is it?' My eyes race across him, looking for injury. He opens his arms and lets his jacket fall open. A rash of red stains the side of his shirt.

'Not my worst,' he says. I hear the pain he tries to hide. I lean forward, and peel the shirt away from his skin, exposing the bullet wound to view. He does not flinch or inhale too sharply. He has washed the wound with snow: I do it again, and then he does wince and hiss between his teeth.

'The ball is still in there.'

'Not too far.'

I sit back on my haunches.

'Can you walk?'

'Well enough.'

'Then why . . .?' I gesture at his hideaway, and the world outside.

'It was worse when it happened.' He matches my gaze, hunter's eyes steady. 'Why did you come?'

'Mother was worried. You've been gone too long.'

He waits for a long time before replying. He knows my lie. We both recognise it. Finally, he nods, and his grip changes upon his knife.

'Help me up.'

'Yes, Father.' I lean forward, using the movement to disguise my hand as I draw my knife from its sheath. Even so, he is ahead of me. His thrust causes me to drop my shoulder sideways and barge into him. His knife whistles past my ribs. Father grunts and falls back against the cave wall. I follow him, slamming my body into his. He groans and pushes me away, heaving himself off the rough surface. We fall out of the hollow in an untidy bundle. He reaches for my shoulder blade with his free hand. Fingers tuck underneath it and pull. I scream and thrust my head forward against the bridge of his nose. It crushes under the blow. He reels back, the small respite giving us both time to find our feet and crouch into a fighting stance, balanced upon the balls of our feet, bodies turned to present the smallest possible target for the other's blade.

Neither of us speaks. Neither offers explanation or question. We both know the why of it, and what awaits us. We circle the tiny depression, backing up the slight rise of each hillock in an attempt to find an angle of attack. For the first time I look at Father not as hunter, or imposing head of our family, but as opponent. He is smaller than I, and holds his injured side as far away as possible, favouring his off hand, his less-used grip. But he is still faster of movement, hard, unforgiving, like a biting snake. And Father always kills without thought or mercy. I am no longer his son. He will not hesitate. He lunges, and I swivel away from the strike, bringing my unarmed fist down towards his wrist. I miss, and he twists his fingers across the knife's hilt, slicing sideways in a movement I could not replicate without hours of practice. The blade misses my flesh, but his fingers, hard as wood, crack against my forearm, deadening my grip. I leap backwards and risk shaking my arm to drive the blood back along it.

Father smiles, a sharp, humourless sign of satisfaction. He presses forward, his blade nipping at my desperate ripostes. I back up the incline, feet sliding on the snow. He follows slowly, not rushing, using the speed of his arm to keep me on the defensive. I reach the top of the hillock. My foot slips over the sudden decline of the far side, and I slide to one knee. Father steps forward to strike. I continue my movement, letting my chest thud against the ground, splaying my arms out as I hit. My right arm sweeps around, and I feel the drag as my knife bites the flesh of Father's calf. He yowls and falls backwards, sliding down the hillock on his back. I dive after him, letting the full weight of my body strike him before he has a chance to find his feet. Something cracks. He flings me off in a burst of strength. I land on my hands and feet, and swing round to face him, limbs tense for another rush.

Father kneels before me, head hung low as he gasps in great lungfuls of air. The wound at his side has opened further during his fall. Blood seeps below the hem of his shirt. His knife arm hangs at an awkward angle, and his hand is empty. I wait, but he does not move. I see the handle of my knife under his left leg. He can not draw it out: his shoulder is broken, and any movement to recover the blade will drag the broken ends of bone across each other. I draw myself to my feet and circle him at a safe distance, just outside a body's length. He makes no move to track my progress. I crouch behind him and place my forehead against his back.

'Father . . .'

He raises his working hand to his shoulder. I raise my own, and we lock fingers. He squeezes, and the pressure of his fingers passes on his love, and pride, and his plea to look after the family. We hold the contact for a dozen breaths, before his grip loosens and his hand falls back to his lap.

I break his neck, swift and clean, and close my eyes as he slumps to the ground.

I kneel in the snow until cramps in my legs cause me to cry out as I stand. When I can ignore the task no longer, I turn Father's body over so he lies on his back, open eyes gazing at a point somewhere beyond my toes. I retrieve my knife from its resting place between his legs. Beginning at his head, I run fingers over Father's body, removing his clothes and folding them into the satchel I find tucked into the back of his hollow. His knife sheath lies empty against his thigh. I untie it and sling it over my shoulder while I work. A small bracelet of hair and stones circles his wrist. I cut it free and place it amongst the clothes, then quickly move across his skin, checking for any other implements that may benefit the family. I find nothing. His knife lies a few paces away. I pick it up. It is longer and heavier then mine, the most obvious mark of his position as head of the family. I heft it a moment, testing its balance against my grip. Then, looking down at his sightless eyes, I tie his sheath around my other thigh, and slide the knife inside. After assuring myself that nothing else lies inside the hollow, I hang the satchel over my shoulder and drag Father's corpse over the rise and down to the ruined wagon at its base. I sit him against the wagon, so that his dead eyes watch me as I circle the battle scene, building a pile of resources in the middle of the space: utensils, clothing, skins of food and wine in quantities too big for a single man to carry. The lumps under the snow resolve themselves into men, faces and throats slashed by a single knife, arms caked in frozen blood where they were thrown up in a futile act of protection. Several firearms appear beneath my searching fingers. I examine each in turn, then replace them. Knives are silent, and only need sharpening. Once I have completed looting I turn my attention to the wagon, lying like a broken beast at the outer limit of the clearing.

It sits on its side, the far wheel buckled and broken where a place marker has shattered the rim and caused it to topple against the old rocks that litter the edge of the rise. Personal effects lie scattered beyond, boxes thrown clear to smash open upon impact. I spend a minute or so sorting through them, picking out a hand mirror and some hair combs and a straight razor. The rest I return to their boxes, dusting them with handfuls of snow until only the most dedicated search would reveal any interference. By the time the Ealdwic authorities realise the wagon is not going to arrive, it will be the middle of the Snow, and the wolves will play havoc with the wreckage before searchers ride out in the Thaw. Even so, that is the future, and it does not do to discard habits of care and caution. I make the site safe, then move on to the wagon itself.

I find the woman at the back of the wreck, under a tangle of boxes and farming implements. She lays face up, arms outflung as if some great blow has struck her chest, hurling her upon the ground like a dead calf. Her throat is a ruined hole, and I do not need to see the teeth marks to know who tore it out, or how. Frozen blood coats her fingernails. The fresh scars I spied upon Father's back as I undressed him were proof enough. This woman is more than just another corpse to be stripped and ransacked. I finish wiping the snow from her face.

Even through the blood and the carnage of Father's feeding, I recognise her. I have seen these eyes before, the bridge of this nose, the cheekbones, now bitten by frost and slashed by an errant stroke of

Father's knife. I have seen this face alive. Younger, fresher, but most definitely *this* face. I inhale with the sudden shock, turn my gaze away and blink my eyes back into focus.

'I will tell your daughter that you fought,' I say, and lower her eyelids with my hand. A thin band of silver circles the base of her throat, preserved amongst the damage. I lift her head, reach round the back, and unclasp it. Placing the chain on my thigh, I sever a lock of her hair with my knife, then wind it and the chain together until they form a wristlet, twisted tightly together and held in place with a quick knot. Later, once I have reached safety, I will melt a small measure of wax over the knot to seal it. For now, I slip it around the handle of my knife and sheath it, pinning the memento between leather and flesh.

'I will make sure she knows,' I say, and take care to cover her body with reverence. I return to the centre of the clearing and the pile of materials I have salvaged.

I am large, and strong, and on a day of perfect weather I can carry almost double my body weight into the loping run we use when hunting. But I am tired and injured. No amount of wishing will let me bear the plunder I have accumulated. I work quickly, separating those things which will benefit the family from those that will merely prolong my comfort. I discard everything not useful to more than one member of the family. In the end, I take a skein of wine to sustain my journey homeward, and load myself with clothing, utensils, and two snares of solid metal from the back of the wagon. Several empty jars constitute a rare prize, and I spend several minutes considering ways to carry them. Preserving what vegetables we grow will help immeasurably next Snow. I choose a dozen, and thread the fastenings of Father's jerkin through their clasps, hanging them from my shoulders like a tinker's wares. The rest of the salvage I return to their original spots, as best I remember, save a haunch of dried meat and several packets of seeds which will be a blessing, come the Thaw. For long moments I contemplate taking my knife to one of the corpses. Fresh meat is unheard of at this time of year, and my knife marks would soon be covered by the teeth of hungry wolves. In the end I decide against it. I have neither the strength nor room to carry a worthwhile burden of meat, and should I fall and die, and be discovered in the Thaw, what I have will mark me as a solitary looter, dissuading any rescue party from searching further afield. If I stop to satiate my hunger now, I may never find enough strength in my legs to leave. A tightening belly is the greatest spur.

As many ways as there are to protect the family, there are an equal number of ways to betray them. Father would make no mistake, and now neither can I. Thought of the dead traveller's flesh reminds me of another need. I return to the wagon, and praying my apologies to the dead woman's spirit, slice several thin strips from Marell's mother's inner thigh. Her petticoats hide my cuts. Scavengers will do the rest.

The meat is moist, and tender, and I slip it inside the cuff of my jacket, except for the strip I place under my tongue. I will draw upon the dead woman's wisdom as I travel, suck her courage and love from the meat. When I return to Marell, we will already be family.

I have only one thing left to do, and then my journey homeward can begin. I reach into the wagon and pull out a long, oiled skin, opening it to reveal the rifle that lies inside. Father showed me, once, how to work such a weapon, when I had hunted with him on enough occasions to prove I was worthy of further teaching. Anything can be a weapon, he told me, and all weapons must be understood.

I load the ball and powder from the packets within the skin, tamp them down, and heft the weight of the rifle as I turn to face Father's corpse. The searchers in the Thaw must see an enemy, a cause for the carnage around them. And the trail needs to end here, with that enemy defeated and dead. I aim down the barrel, at the spot just above his right eye. I want to say something, to make some sort of apology. But that is not our way. What we do is always for survival. I press the trigger. The flint catches. A single boom echoes across the open space.

Father's head snaps back, and forward, and the ruined eye socket that stares at me bears nothing of his likeness. I turn away, repack the rifle, and begin to clean the site of my presence.

When I am finished, I climb the rise over which I first arrived, and view my work, nodding in satisfaction. The site lies as I discovered it, and the snow will soon muddy even the few tiny marks I made in leaving. The journey home will be hard, and dangerous, but I can undertake it in the knowledge that the hunt was successful, and the family will remain safe from pursuit. And I am alive.

I shoulder my burden, lean into the wind, and begin the journey home.

It takes two days to reach the house, two days of trudging through thickening snow banks, slipping across puddles of ice, and tucking my face further and further down into my coat to deflect the shards of pain that shatter against my skin with every gust of wind. By the time the house shimmers through the storm, and I slump against the doorway with just enough strength left to drop my fist against the wood in the right series of knocks, my eyes are all but sealed shut, and I no longer feel anything except the icicles in my lungs. I scarcely register the arms that drag me inside, or the bodies that crowd around me in front of the kitchen fire, lending their warmth and welcome to the heat creeping into my bones. By the time I open my mouth and accept a few swallows of mulled cider, I am *too* warm, and shrug children from my chest and shoulders. Soon, I struggle out of my over-garments and stand alone, swaying, in my shirtsleeves, gesturing to whoever is nearest for another shot of the revitalising cider. My mug is refilled. I swallow it in one long draught, cough, and spit into the fire as the dram hits my throat and spreads its magic out along my limbs. I turn away from the flames. The family has gathered around the far edge of the table, Mother at their head.

'Kester,' she says, as much warning as greeting. I give her a small, acknowledging smile.

'Mother.'

I retrieve the pile of treasure from where it was stripped from me, and heft it onto the table. Youngsters are despatched to store the haunch of meat, and snares, and take the seeds down to the cellar. Mother takes possession of the jars, and places them high upon a shelf, out of the reach of little fingers. When everyone has returned, I pull my satchel from the pile.

'Gather everyone here.'

'Kester — ' Mother steps forward, arm half-raised.

'Now.'

She stops, and turns to the children.

'Quickly.'

We wait, not looking at each other, until the whole family arrives. Marell is amongst them. She is dressed in family clothes, her hair tied back in the way Mother prefers. She stands between two older boys, towards the back of the group. When the entire family is assembled, I open the satchel. I remove Father's clothing, and spread it out on the table so everyone can see. I hear shock, and some of the children strangle back cries. Mother stands with a hand over her mouth. Her eyes are fixed upon me. She knew, the moment I arrived at the doorway. Now she can not pretend otherwise. I untie Father's knife from my thigh, then step around the table and present it to her. She takes it without word, and I turn my back.

Mother is quick and fierce. I barely hear the knife as it slips from the sheath. I twist just as she lunges, catching her arm under my own and continuing the movement so she strikes the table with the front of her stomach. I lift her up so she lies face down amongst Father's clothes. I pin her there with one hand and rake her skirt up with the other, exposing her hindquarters to view. I step over her leg, part her thighs with mine, and unbutton myself. I enter her in a sharp, violent thrust. She lies silent as I take her, letting me come in no more than a dozen short strokes. But it is enough. When I am finished I stand back, draw my trousers up and refasten them. She stays still for perhaps half a minute, then slides from the table and turns to face me. We meet gazes. She bends her head, and presents me the knife. I take it, recover the sheath from where it has dropped, and slide in the blade. Mother drops to her knee, and ties it to my thigh. I hold my hand out to her. She takes it, rises, and stands at my side.

'Take her.' I point to Marell, stiff with shock by the doorway. 'Take her to her room, and educate her. Make sure she understands.' The wristlet lies amongst the pile of treasures still to be distributed as gifts. I will give it to her, when she is ready. For now, there is much to be done. I must make my family safe for the Snow, and ensure that the infants are weaned, so their mothers will be ready to bear children when I visit them in the Thaw. And Marell must be taught her role, like Mother was taught before her, and she must understand her place in the family, as Mother understands hers.

Mother turns to me, and in front of the family, kisses me.

'Yes, Father,' she says.

AFTERWORD

Stories come to me from all sorts of places, but often a number of current obsessions will intersect in such a way that I'll see them in a new light and be able to write about the resulting view. In this case, I fused a lifelong fascination with Sawney Bean with an illustration I recalled fronting an old Kate Wilhelm story, filtered through a documentary I watched about a pride of lions, and this is what came out.

Much of my work often springs from a sense of loss, and my characters often fulfil the actions of the plot despite the isolation and monstrous requirements it forces upon them. That probably says something deeply profound about my state of mind, but, in truth, no story is worth telling unless it imposes sacrifice upon the protagonist, and emotional and/or psychological sacrifice is, for me, the most telling. A friend once accused me of being genetically incapable of writing a happy ending — they were wrong, but I don't manage it very *often*. That same friend also said I'd grow up to be Warren Zevon, so at least their view of me is entertaining!

In early 2007 I suffered a catastrophic hard-drive crash, in which I lost all my work. (Yeah, I know. I make backups regularly *now.*) 'In From the Snow' only survived because I was line-editing a hard copy at the time. It's nice to see it in print: like Kester, it's a survivor.

— *Lee Battersby*

Aurealis and Ditmar winner TRUDI CANAVAN is the author of the bestselling Black Magician Trilogy, which includes *The Magicians' Guild, The Novice,* and *The High Lord.* All three books entered Australian top ten SF bestseller lists and went on to sell internationally. Neilsen BookScan rated the trilogy as the most successful debut fantasy series of the last ten years, and in 2006 it had sold over 500,000 copies.

Her second trilogy, Age of the Five, also received bestseller success. *Priestess of the White* reached number three in the *Sunday Times* hardback fiction bestseller list, staying in the top ten for six weeks. In 2006 she was offered a seven-figure advance for a four-book contract to write the prequel and sequel to the Black Magician Trilogy.

In the story that follows, Canavan conjures up a dusty, magical room in Melbourne's Flinders Street Station so that we may see for ourselves the Draconian nature of consequence . . .

THE LOST PROPERTY ROOM

TRUDI CANAVAN

In the park, people were dancing in the rain, laughing and cavorting. Trinity rolled her eyes skyward. This pathetic drizzle was not worth getting soaked over. Already, patches of blue were visible as wind hurried the clouds onward. It would take much more than this to break the drought.

The rain might relieve her of the chore of watering her garden. She was heartily tired of bucketing grey water from the washing machine, shower and kitchen onto her plants. Restrictions only allowed her to use fresh water twice a week, and her small fernery needed a lot more than that.

As she reached the shelter of Flinders Street Station, she paused to shake and then fold up her umbrella before joining the queue of people filing through the turnstiles. The ticket machine sucked in her ticket then spat it out, the clunk within excessively loud and heavy for the processing of such a light bit of card. Once on the train she opened her bag and took out the cover of her umbrella, carefully placing it underneath her wet umbrella on the seat beside her. Then she took out her knitting.

Pausing to admire her handiwork so far, she smoothed the neat stitches of a striped sock, then set to work. Suburbs, bridges and stations flashed by unnoticed as she knitted through the tricky patterning of the heel. Counting stitches and rows. Slip, knit, slip, knit, turn, purl back across. As always, the absorbing rhythm soothed her. Eventually she recognised the familiar sound of the boom gates a suburb from her station. She was just two rows from the end of the heel. One station to go before she must pack it away. She hunched over her work. Her needles and fingers flew. As the train pulled into the station she finished the last stitch, stuffed her work into her bag and hurried out of the train.

The air was full of glitter. Sunshine lit thousands of tiny droplets as they drifted toward the ground. A sunshower. Pretty.

As the train pulled away from the station the droplets abruptly gained weight and size. She groped for her umbrella and froze, her stomach sinking as she realised it was still lying on its cover, on the seat beside the one she had just vacated. On the train.

The rain hammered down on her head in mockery. She ran to her car.

Reciting directions under her breath, Trinity made her way down the corridor, not completely sure coming here had been a good idea. Her shoes clacked on the hard grey linoleum floor, the sound echoing loudly no matter how lightly she tried to walk. At the end of the corridor a window framed a square of perfect blue. The rain of the afternoon before might as well have been a dream, for all the good it had done. None of the gardens or parks she had glimpsed out of the train window looked any less brown and withered. The dams and reservoirs were still between twenty and thirty per cent full, according to the morning news.

The directions she had been given stated that the room she sought was at the end of the corridor. She thought back to the call she had made that morning.

'Hello? Is this "lost property"?'

'Yes. How can we help you?' The voice had been sexless, but had the dryness of old age.

'I left my umbrella on the train last night. The girl I just spoke to said that if anyone has handed it in it would have come to you. Did you receive any umbrellas since then?'

'Oh, we get lots of those. Sometimes dozens of them, if it's been raining a bit. Was this last night, did you say?'

'Yesterday afternoon, about five.'

'Well, it might not have come through to us yet. Why don't you come in this afternoon?'

'Can't you ... can I leave my phone number? Could you call me if one comes in like mine. It's black and —'

'It's better you come in, dear.'

Trinity hadn't argued. Old man or woman, like all mature aged workers in this day of privatisation and downsizing, he or she was probably understaffed. She doubted there was anybody free to hunt for her umbrella among all the others that came in on rainy days. It was surprising, really, that a service like a lost property room still existed.

So she had asked for their opening hours, scribbled down directions, and left work early to retrieve her umbrella on the way home.

Now, reaching the end of the corridor, she wondered for the hundredth time since making that call if one umbrella was worth losing an hour's flexitime and getting lost in the bowels of Flinders Street Station.

Then she felt a now-familiar pang of loss. The umbrella held memories. Good memories of a holiday, a spontaneous purchase and friendship made and treasured. She didn't want to let go of that umbrella any more than she wanted to let that long-distance friendship to end. Perhaps that was silly.

Anyway, she was here now. The door she faced wore a small metal sign that read: 'The Lost Property Room'. She sighed and knocked. A moment later the door opened and an extraordinarily tall old man beamed down at her.

'Come in,' he said, his high voice recognisable from the phone call the day before. She found herself in a small room. Opposite the entrance was another door, but of carved and polished wood — surprisingly ornate in this place of utilitarian practicality. The old man slipped behind a thoroughly modern desk of glass and metal and checked a notebook.

'Trinity Hunder,' he said. 'Lost an umbrella, right?'

'Yes,' she said, reaching for her purse and identity cards.

He waved at the carved door. 'Go on in.'

No security checks, then. Not just old fashioned décor, but old fashioned trust. She shrugged and moved to the door. As she reached out to the handle he made a small noise.

'One word of warning,' he said. She turned to look at him. His expression was solemn. 'Only take what is yours.'

'Of course,' she replied. Not so trusting after all, she mused.

The wooden door opened easily. Beyond it was a corridor, shelving on both sides, lit by strips of weak fluorescent lights. She had almost expected oil lamps or candles, to match the door. The room extended a long way, the far wall indistinguishable in the dim, dusty light. She stepped inside and turned as she sensed the room was broader than just this long corridor ... and caught her breath in wonder and dismay. So many rows of shelves extended into the distance, she could not see the end of them.

The Lost Property Room was enormous.

'How am I going to find the umbrellas?' she asked aloud. A moment later she noticed the shiny bronze letters at the end of each wall of shelving. 'Cr-Da' shone proudly at the end of the shelf to her right. Smiling, she started walking.

She still hadn't spotted the far wall when she came to the 'Uk-Us' sign. Walking between the shelves, she chuckled as she saw the row of small guitar-like instruments painted with hibiscus flowers and hula girls. They must get a lot of stringed instruments, if they had an entire shelf just for the ukulele.

A mysterious array of bones, some freshly white, others dark with age, puzzled her until she saw the label 'ulna' on the front of the shelf. Perhaps mislaid by a medical student? A disturbing alternative occurred to her. But surely any skeletons found on trains were handed over to the police.

Conscious that time was running short before her usual train home, she quickened her pace, passing purple light globes in several different shapes, jars of a dark brown powder, strange discoloured metal disks — some with Celtic knot patterns worked into their surface, a small glass-topped box containing a collection of pretty butterflies and a biology specimen jar with a strange cord-like object floating within.

At the end of the shelf she found the umbrellas. Just as she expected, there were a lot of them.

Paper parasols were piled alongside frothy lace and fur-trimmed fancies. Brightly coloured and patterned cloth and plastic contrasted with the more common black and navy. Sizes ranged from huge beach umbrellas in cream or rainbow colours, to tiny children's umbrellas, and even some that must be for dolls. Of the usual, city worker's umbrella, far more of the straight, metal-tipped kind were here than the collapsible kind she preferred. Yet both kinds were endlessly varied, some bearing monograms of famous designers or menswear manufacturers, company logos or the team colours of several different sports, cartoon characters or artwork. Some were plain, some sported carved wooden handles, some were cheap plastic, some wore slip covers and others were naked.

Of the one she had lost, there was no sign. She went through the shelf once, then again more carefully, running her hands over them, picking them up and putting them down again. All in vain. Her umbrella wasn't there. Either it hadn't reached the Lost Property Room yet, or someone had picked it up on the train and decided to keep it.

Disappointed, she stepped back and regarded the collection before her. All these umbrellas. And she was umbrella-less. Then she looked closer. Some of the less modern ones were dusty. Fingerprints marked where she had touched them. Clearly they had been lost long ago.

Their owners hadn't come back to claim them, and probably never would. What harm would there be in taking one in place of her own? She remembered the old man's warning, but shook her head. It wasn't like she was stealing, since they no longer belonged to anybody.

Still, it might upset him. Examining the dustier umbrellas more closely, she thought back and asked herself if she'd given him any particular details of her lost umbrella. She could remember saying it was black. She might have described it as collapsible.

Of the dusty, collapsible umbrellas, one had a wooden handle carved into a simple but delightful representation of a duck's head. Smiling, she picked it up, took out a tissue from her bag and carefully wiped the dust away.

It would do. She felt a pang of guilt as she strode toward the exit, but pushed it aside. The umbrella was going to waste here in the dusty, hidden rooms of the station. She was giving it a new home. A good home.

To her surprise, when she stepped outside the building, it was raining. With a smile of happy satisfaction, she opened the umbrella and let the last of the dust wash away.

On the television screen, images came and went as relentlessly as the rain outside. Trinity sighed. Why was drought always followed by flood? Why did too much have to come on the heels of too little?

It had been raining so long now it seemed that it had always been raining. But she knew that wasn't true. Thinking back, she sought her last memory of the sun shining, then laughed at the irony. It had been the day she'd replaced her umbrella.

Trinity looked out at her garden and frowned. Where it had once been dry and withering, now her rejuvenated plants sagged in soft, unsupportive soil and the grass had turned to mud. She hadn't had to carry buckets of water out from the house for weeks. Instead, she'd had to pot up a few of her more fragile plants and place them in sheltered positions.

Unfortunately the rain was not filling the dams or reservoirs. It was strangely local, falling mainly on her side of the city. The only time it had fallen elsewhere had been the day she had visited her mother. Of course, it had rained not just on that day, and not just at her mother's house, but all the way to her mother's house, making the drive unpleasant and a little hair-raising. Her mother had accused Trinity of bringing the rain with her.

A map now appeared on the television as the weather report continued. She sighed again as she saw the single patch of blue over her suburb.

'These are freak weather conditions,' the charming young weatherman said. 'The cloud cover remained in place all night, despite a change of wind direction. In the last few days it moved toward the city during the day, then back to the east. All this time it has been growing smaller, but conditions within the rain storm are increasing in strength rather than weakening. The Bureau of Meteorology has never recorded a phenomenon like this before. They have issued a warning of a possible mini-tornado and advise residents to secure all loose items and to remain inside . . .'

A chill ran down Trinity's spine. Into the city and back again. Like it was following her. *'You've brought the rain with you.'*

Shaking her head, she turned the television off and picked up her car keys. She pictured herself trying to explain to her boss why she hadn't come to work. *'The Bureau of Meteorology said I should stay home and secure all loose items.'* At least it was better than *'There's a freak storm following me around.'* She took a step toward the door then, hearing a squelching noise, looked down.

A slowly growing dark patch was spreading over the carpet.

'No!' she gasped. The flood of water was coming in under the front door. Rushing to the entrance, she opened the door and stared down at a large pool of water lapping at her front step. It spread from her door out to cover half her front garden and driveway. As more water spilled into the house she snapped out of her shock.

She needed something to block it. Sandbags. They always use sandbags during floods. Grabbing a coat from her hat rack, and some plastic garbage bags, she hurried out the back door to the gardening shed, soaking her shoes and stockings as she discovered more puddles. The sands she used for potting mixes would have to do. She filled the bases of the bags, rushed back to the house and patted them into place around the door.

It was hard to tell if it was working. And the sodden patch of carpet had grown much larger. Not large enough, she decided, to justify calling the State Emergency Service. They were, no doubt, occupied with fallen trees and power lines — much more important hazards than a little wet carpet. Sighing, she picked up the phone book and found the number for her insurance company.

After twenty minutes on hold, she took out her mobile phone and called the office to warn them she was going to be late. Then she returned to listening to the recorded message of the insurance company's line, slowly grinding her teeth in frustration.

'HellohowcanIhelpyou?' a voice finally said.

'My house is flooding,' she began. 'The rain won't stop and —'

'Oooh! Do you live in that street where the freak storm is?'

Trinity opened her mouth to answer, but no sound came out. Her whole body was suddenly cold. Her heart raced with a superstitious fear. To her horror and surprise, she realised she was about to burst into tears.

'Hello?'

She hung up. Taking deep, calming breaths, she looked around. Somehow rain was pounding against the windows on *both* sides of the house, despite the shelter of the eaves. The woman's words '*... that street where the freak storm is?*' repeated in her mind. *That* street. *Her* street. Was the storm that small and concentrated now? Why was it concentrated on her house?

Suddenly she badly wanted to get out of the house. She fought back panic and made herself look at the patch of wet carpet realistically. It didn't appear to be growing. *And it wouldn't, if she left the house and the storm followed.* She needed to call the insurance company back, but she could do that from work or from her mobile phone.

Let's test this theory that the storm is following me.

As she stepped outside, the rain began to pound with fresh intensity. Opening her umbrella, she splashed to the car, unlocked it as quickly as she could and ducked inside. The umbrella did her little good. The rain seemed to be falling sideways. Looking down at the bloated splodges of water on her good jacket, she groaned. Once she got to work she would have to delay starting on her duties even longer drying her clothes under the hand-dryer in the women's toilet.

Starting her car, she turned on the wipers. Rain pounded the windscreen so hard, there was only a blink of time in which to see the world beyond. Carefully, she backed out into the street.

She turned onto the main road. Between the snap of the wipers she was relieved to see the road was empty of cars. The gutters were overflowing, so she stuck to the centre lane. Ahead she sensed as much as saw the curve of the rail bridge.

Then her car abruptly slowed, suddenly straining as if something grabbed at the wheels. She yelped as water sprayed up around both sides of her car and surged over the bonnet. Then she cursed as she remembered that the road dipped as it went under the bridge. A puddle always formed when it rained. Between sweeps of the wiper blades she could see that the puddle was more the size of a large pond.

The car began to bob like a boat as it half-floated in the water. Cold enveloped her toes. She looked down and cursed again as she saw that water was pooling around her feet. As it deepened she felt the car sink, its tyres scraping the bottom of the pond. Peering through the side window, her heart skipped a beat. The surface of the pond lapped at the car just below the windows.

This puddle was also a lot *deeper* than the usual one.

As the water inside the car rose toward her knees she grabbed the door handle, then paused. Opening the door would only let in water faster. The level outside was still below the window. She took hold of the winder and began to turn it. When it would no longer wind any further, she grasped the edges of the window and pushed herself up and out.

It was not easy, and at the last moment she lost her grip and tumbled out into the pond. Yet as water closed over her head she felt panic subsiding. She was not afraid of drowning, only of being trapped in her car. Getting her feet under herself, she stood up.

The pond came to her waist. She was soaked from head to toe. But, looking around, she saw that nobody was nearby to see.

The water in her car was brimming over the seats. She reached inside and grabbed her belongings. Wading out of the water, she turned to look back at her car. Rain stung her face. She turned away, but it continued to drive into her eyes.

Slowly she turned around. Felt her stomach turn over. The rain was driving toward her from every direction.

She was in the centre of the storm.

She *was* the centre of the storm.

The world seemed to shift. Suddenly it was a place where the impossible — the ridiculous — could happen.

But if it's true, and the storm is following me . . . what caused it to? When did this start.

She looked down at the umbrella in her hand.

'No,' she heard herself say. 'It can't be. That's crazy!'

A white flash dazzled her eyes, then a second later the air, water and ground vibrated with the deafening boom of thunder.

Abandoning her car, Trinity ran for the train station.

Her shoes left wet footprints on the grey linoleum floor of the corridor. The soles squeaked as she walked, the noise humiliating, but not as much as she imagined the next few minutes would be.

The Lost Property Room door opened at her knock. The tall old man looked her up and down, taking in her still-dripping clothes and matted hair, then smiled.

'Come in.'

She followed him to the desk. Placed the umbrella on a clear section of the glass top.

'I'm giving this back,' she told him. 'It isn't mine.'

His smile disappeared, but it appeared to take an effort. 'No?'

'No. I ... ignored your warning. Mine wasn't here and this was all dusty. It ... well ... it seemed like it, er, needed a new home.'

The old man nodded. 'And it proved to be an ungrateful house guest.'

She stared at him, reluctant to give voice to the crazy conclusion she had come to. But nobody else was ever going to believe her. Nobody except, perhaps, this old man. She was never going to mention it to anyone ... but it was a secret that might just drive her crazy if nobody else ever acknowledged it.

'Am I mad?' she asked, 'or did this create the storm that seemed to ... that followed me around for the last few weeks?'

He smiled. 'You're not crazy.'

She looked down at the umbrella, drew in a deep breath, and sighed. 'Rain. We needed the rain. But not where it fell.'

'Would you be willing to take it where it would do some good?'

She looked up at him. Fear warred with something else. Something that tugged at her, promising glory and satisfaction. Could she end the drought?

Thunder boomed outside. The glass in the windows rattled. A warning.

Slowly she shook her head. 'Yes, but I think it's gone too far for that. I don't think I'd make it to anywhere the rain would do good.' Picking up the umbrella, she turned away and walked to the wooden door. The old man said nothing as she twisted the handle, opened the door and stepped into the room beyond.

It was pitch black inside. She groped her way forward, wondering how she would tell when she had reached the aisle the umbrellas were stored in. After passing several shelves, she paused to reach up and feel for the letters.

The room flickered into existence around her. Looking back, she saw the old man standing by the door, one hand over a light switch. He smiled crookedly, then disappeared back into his office.

Striding down the room, Trinity found the right shelves and moved to where the umbrellas were stacked. Taking out a few tissues, she wiped the duck-handled umbrella dry, buttoned it closed and placed it among the other collapsible models.

Turning away, she made her way back to the door

Back on the train, she took out her knitting and began work on the cuff of a sock.

If only she'd grasped the magical qualities of the umbrella sooner, she could have taken a trip out to a dam or two, or toured the places where crops were failing and livestock starving.

But then it wouldn't have been a punishment for her theft. And then she realised something else: her ruined carpet and car were not the penalty. Knowing she'd missed such a great opportunity was.

As the carriage turned to cross a bridge she looked out of the window. A bank of clouds stretched over the city, spreading as far as she could see. Sheets of rain fell like lazy grey curtains. Despite herself, she felt her heart lift with hope.

'Now that,' she whispered to herself, 'is more like it.'

AFTERWORD

'The Lost Property Room' was inspired by the experience of a friend, years ago, who lost an umbrella on a train and discovered there was a lost property room at Flinders Street Station, full of an amazing range of mislaid items. She didn't find her umbrella, but the person in charge said she could just take any umbrella she wanted, so she took one with a carved handle in the shape of a duck's head. I loved the idea of this room, full of lost treasures, and of people seeking something they'd lost but coming away with something different. I wonder if it still exists.

— *Trudi Canavan*

Bestselling author JOHN BIRMINGHAM is extremely versatile, as adept at writing speculative fiction, fantasy, and bestselling thrillers as he is at writing mainstream history, sport, crime, gonzo journalism, and humour. His first book — *He Died with a Felafel in His Hand*, which he calls 'the Chernobyl of share house literature' — became a comedy bestseller and a youth cult classic, and was later turned into a play (the longest running stage play in Australian history), a film, and a graphic novel. He won the National Award for Nonfiction in 2002 for *Leviathan*, his biography of Sydney. His other books include *The Tasmanian Babes Fiasco* (the bestseller sequel to *He Died with a Felafel in His Hand*), *A Felafel Guide to Sex* and *The Felafel Guide to Getting Wasted, How to be a Man, Dopeland: Taking the High Road Through Australia's Marijuana Culture,* and *Off One's Tits: Ill-considered Rants and Raves from a Graceless Oaf Named John Birmingham.* He is also the author of the crime novel *The Search for Savage Henry* and the Axis of Time trilogy, which includes the novels *Weapons of Choice, Designated Targets,* and *Final Impact.*

Birmingham writes that he was distracted by the first incarnation of *Dreaming Down-Under*, inhaling it in one big gulp when he should have been earning his keep elsewhere. That distraction was a left-handed gift, though, encouraging him to switch genres to alternative history/technothriller with *Weapons of Choice.*

He says that his story in this collection, 'Heere Be Monsters', pays off that karmic debt.

HEERE BE MONSTERS

JOHN BIRMINGHAM

(Extracted from the address of Lieutenant-General Sir Watkin Tench to members of the Royal Society, in London, on 25 January 1808, to mark the twentieth anniversary of the discovery of the Scourge.)

You will forgive me, gentlemen, if I do not dwell on the preliminaries of the matter which has these recent years inflamed the fearful wondering of every soul extant upon God's earth, be they monarch, basest commoner, republican or Bantu savage. My colleagues Surgeon White and Admiral Hunter have both enjoyed considerable success with their journals of the voyage from the Mother Bank to the forbidden seas. The publication of our late Governor's notes as an addendum to their work provides an immoderate weight of material preceding the events at Port Jackson for those inclined to so immerse themselves.

If I might begin with the ordinary, as a solid footing for the extraordinary which quickly follows it, we had famously anchored for a number of days at Botany Bay and found it unacceptable as home for the new colony. The waters were very open and greatly exposed to the fury of the southeast winds, which when they blew, caused a heavy and dangerous swell. At a distance of a league from the mouth of the bay was a bar, on which at low water not more than fifteen feet were to be found. Within this bar, and proceeding for many miles along the southwest arm of the bay, was a haven in which any number of ships of the line might permanently shelter, were it not for lack of fresh water, a thirst unrelieved by any source within the bay as we first found it.

I emphasise that point. As we *first* found it.

The Governor, having despatched a small party north to examine the inlet noted by Mr Cook, and having had reports of a commodious and well-watered anchorage, resolved to remove the camp from its original situation to one more calculated to inspire confidence in our survival. A grim irony, that, you'll warrant now.

Our passage took up a mere few hours, but in that time we did not simply move from the rather exposed and unsuitable anchorage at Botany Bay into the deeper harbour of Port Jackson. We rather travelled from a position of pleasant anticipation and general relief at the termination of our long voyage, into a hell of unimaginable contour and unfathomable depth.

As best all who lived can tell, it was the white squall which marked the crossing of the line from an ordered world, where God's design is apparent to all who look, into the darker Inexplicable where we now dwell. The Fleet was proceeding in fair order, as we had done for nigh on two hundred and fifty days. HMS *Supply* had the vanguard, and in her sailed Governor Phillip. The fastest of the convict transports —

Scarborough, *Friendship* and *Alexander* — were not embarrassed in their efforts to keep station, a claim my own tub, the *Charlotte*, could not dare make without gross outrage to truth and modesty. We wallowed some distance behind the leaders, penned in on all sides by the remaining hulks and store ships, shepherded on our way by brave little *Sirius*.

There was no warning of the tempest. You will have heard seafarers make claim of wild storms blown up without caution, when what they truly mean is that whatever warnings they did enjoy were rather short and the transition from tranquillity to the devil's own maelstrom was effected without delay, a matter of some minutes, perhaps.

As an officer of His Majesty's Royal Marines, I too have had my fill of storms at sea and would not confute any mariner a small measure of exaggeration in such things. They have earned the right. In doing so, however, such tales rob my own of the immediacy and hazard I must now impress upon you.

At one heartbeat I stood on deck, adjacent to the barricado, our final defence against any uprising from below. The waters were gentle, and slipped by our flanks with a slight hiss and the occasional plop of wavelet against wood. The moon's reflection was a silver sword upon the deep and I was chatting pleasantly with my friend Surgeon White, enjoying the hard brilliance of the increasingly familiar southern stars in the night sky, as we recalled our damnable luck in the affairs and intrigues of *l'amour* with the ladies of St Sebastian. We had both arrived in that port aflame with the reports of Dr Solander, who had written of Portuguese beauties throwing nosegays at strangers for the purpose of bringing on an assignation. White and myself, not an entirely unhandsome pair I'm sure you'll agree, were so deplorably unfortunate as to walk every evening before their windows and balconies without once being honoured by a single bouquet, even though nymphs and flowers were in equal and great abundance.

These memories did we rake over like spent coals, enjoying the warm, still night, when at the next heartbeat we were all about beset by a storm of such insensate violence I would not be aghast to discover it had blown straight from the mouth of hell. It is possible the good surgeon cried out. I am certain I did, but so enormous was the shrieking of wind and hammering of rain, that I could hear nothing beyond their savage caterwauling din. Smashed to the deck as if by a great invisible fist I was attempting in extreme distress to settle accounts with my maker, for annihilation must surely be the only outcome of such a development.

And then another heartbeat, gentlemen, just like the thudding within your own breast pockets at this precise moment, and we were clear of it, or rather it of us, for of the storm there was no sign, beyond a strange contrary fog which had settled like a cloak upon the fleet. Besides the mist there was not a puff of breeze, nor drop of rain beyond that remnant moisture which now dripped from our sails and rigging. The silence was enormous in its own way. As deafening as the roar that had proceeded it.

I heard the raw curses of the *Charlotte's* crew, and the beginnings of a panic below decks amongst our human freight, when there came a great crash and the awful splintering of timber which bespoke a collision between two ships. It was impossible to tell, what with darkness and fog — and one must admit of it, *fear* and confusion — but a naval lieutenant soon hurried past with news of a mishap involving the *Borrowdale* and *Golden Grove*.

I am sure you will agree that it is to the credit of the British race, and our maritime tradition, that no lives or ships were lost in the next hours (although, perhaps for some it were best t'was otherwise). Great cliffs stood to our portside and we had been driven a good way towards them, but the masters of the Fleet and their fine men quickly shook off all consideration but that of returning order and a settled command to our affairs. When Governor Phillip was satisfied that no great damage had been done to his host, that *Borrowdale* and the *Grove* were still seaworthy, and that we might proceed, he signalled from *Supply* to heave to, and, as innocent and unknowing as babes, we did just that.

Would that our intelligence of the great changes afoot was not smothered by the fog that had remained after that unholy tempest? Might we have stood off and sent much smaller armed parties to investigate? Might we have withdrawn and quarantined the Scourge for all time? I see some of you nodding vigorously, but of course, to have done so would have betrayed the nature of dauntless inquiry and adventure by which Empires such as ours are built. And without the Scourge, of course, there could be no knowledge of the wonders which attended it. We might be gathered here by candlelight, rather than electronical glass. These notes before me would consist of stained scrawls, inked by quill, rather than neatly composed by mechanical typewriter. And the cornucopia of marvels recovered from that benighted place would have been prey to Spanish brigand or French privateer, rather than devoted to the betterment of man's finer instincts and designs, as manifest in the achievements of the British Empire.

Could the American colonies have been won back without the repeating gun? Could all those children now alive and growing to strengthen the sinews of the Empire have done so without the miracle patents and potions and pure knowledge of the Hippocratic arts we snatched from the jaws of hell and brought safe home? Would the blockade of the forbidden seas by the Royal Navy have any real chance of sustained accomplishment without the steam engine, ironcladding and the radiola? As much as horror has come into the world, so has a countervailing magic with which to combat it. I hope you will indulge me these digressions, for, as I age, they are much upon my conscience.

At that point however, some twenty years ago tonight, my deliberations were centred squarely on immediate concerns. I had greater than one hundred convicts in my charge, twenty of them women, and forty-one marines with which to guard them — although I must confess some of my men took to their husbandry duties with questionable vigour, and I cannot today recall a single female transportee who had not found herself a connection amongst the men of the regiment by the time we reached Port Jackson. I have at times pondered the virtue of such vice, asking myself if we might not have survived in the numbers we did aboard the *Charlotte* were it not for the bonds of family which had been struck below decks on the voyage out.

I had ordered the chains struck off my prisoners almost as soon as we had departed home waters, an indulgence which I am proud and happy to relate was not abused by the wretches, or not so much as greatly matters. Disinclined to return them to their fetters I was nonetheless concerned lest riot should ensue upon our making landfall. It had been much discussed amongst the officers, and Chaplain Johnson, always greatly exercised by questions of morality, had predicted a bacchanalian outbreak of sin as soon as the prisoners were free to have at each other. I must admit I was more concerned for the safety of our precious stores than for the ethical temper of my pick-pockets and whores.

Lest high spirits should lead to a general debauch, in which months of provisions might be utterly destroyed, I loudly ordered all of my men to stand to with muskets, sabre, bayonet, spare ball and powder. I am convinced I stand here before you today in possession of my life and immortal soul because of that precaution. I might add that thirty seamen sailed on the *Charlotte*, and although the majority of them were given to the busy task of navigating an uncharted, fog-bound harbour at ebb tide, their master Mr Gilbert, ensured that his men too were alive to the possibility of mayhem.

We proceeded up the passage, the cries of the pilots and fathom sounders flat and alien, smothered by the mist no doubt. Of the shores there was little to be seen at this juncture. It was still dark and the fog shrouded all. Those few times we strayed close enough to make out anything, the slopes seemed steep, and luxuriantly wooded. Points of light burned here and there, a sight we had grown used to as we hauled up the coast. Natives, we presumed, gathered around their campfires, some of them considerable infernos as best we could judge.

The first intimation of disaster was not long in coming. Positioned as we were towards the rear of the Fleet we discerned the cries and alarums from ahead, without understanding what encouraged them. As I was later to discover, the *Supply* had struck a buoy.

A floating buoy in a harbour never transited by civilised man.

In short order, more shouts and sirens reached us in the rearguard as those in the van encountered evidence of the cursed miracle into which we had blundered, or been cast. As the sun rose and quickly burned away the fog we found ourselves, not resident of some empty cove at world's end, but inexplicably surrounded by a city, not of the new world, but of another world entirely. A sharply strengthening breeze from the south cleared out the remaining fog within minutes, presenting to us the spectacle of a metropolis to call London dwarf, of blues and whites and light, bathed in sun to blind the eyes. I stood there a pilgrim to this New Jerusalem. It was only as we drew closer I found no hammering of industry, no cacophony of voices, or the clip clop of horse traffic. There was a low, constant and most unsettling *moan* which drifted over us, but I ascribed this to the passage of the sirocco through our rigging.

Many, if not all of you will have seen the photographic imagery of the dead city known as Sydney. A city of monoliths, of magnificent colour and textures and angles and omnipotent scale as to overwhelm the senses. I need not recall to you the familiar sights of metal and glass towers, some of them awash in flames and spewing clouds of roiling black smoke into the sky. As dawn brightened, the harbour itself was revealed as an inky pool choked with debris and dominated by the broken hull of a gargantuan iron vessel, unlike any ship of His Majesty's Navy, at least in those days. I could see now a veritable flotilla of smaller craft, their lines sleek and almost painful to the eye. Abandoned all of them, or so we thought.

As the temperature rose, the southerly wind carried over us the first of many terrible revelations. The foul, cloying air emerging from the broken teeth of those soaring towers was as rank as a charnel house on a summer's day. The miasma of putrescence and burning flesh threatened to overwhelm me, and I, you will recall, had ample experience of life below decks and not far removed from the bilge water of the good ship *Charlotte*.

Surgeon White appeared at my side, a looking glass in hand.

'It is an impossible vision,' he croaked. 'A thing that might be dreamed of by a Wren in the grip of opium.'

My uncomprehending eyes followed his shaking hand and I perceived it too, a vast claw, raking the sky. It seemed the cunning work of giants, fled from the lands of men and returned here at the ends of the earth. It was terror and it was madness and it was glory, and it made one feel like an ant beneath the boots of God himself.

'What holds it up?' I whispered.

'The Will of God, sir,' said Surgeon White. 'It can be nothing else.'

Behind the impossible erection, which we know these days to be a haunted opera house, a massive stone and metal arch spanned the waters of the inlet. It glittered in the morning sun. A dream of iron and wire and stone, its arch almost a mile in length and suspended at over five chains above the harbour. On both banks I presently espied great stately homes. Some of them afire. But of people we saw little. A shambling figure here and there. One or two others darting hither and yon across rooftops in the distance. Some waving, possibly crying out to us. Of their fate I know nothing, but suspect the worst.

We advanced towards the magnificent bridge, a creeping sense of wickedness and malignity growing stronger as we delved. I have seen much battle at the closest of quarters in service to His Majesty, but I lie not now when I tell you that never has fear threatened to unman me as completely as it did on that bright morn'. Surgeon White must have perceived my unease, for he gripped me on the arm and pressed a tot of rum upon me.

'Some medicinal advice, if you will have it, Captain Tench?' he muttered.

'Yes,' I choked back in reply.

'One tot immediately for every fighting man, and any man who will fight to save himself and his fellows.'

'Why ...' I began, meaning to inquire further, but the gentlemen's grip only tightened. 'Do you not feel it, Watkin? Inside of you? We are in the presence of evil and I fear it means to strike. The men will look to you for strong leadership. You must provide it, or we will die here. I feel it in my meat.'

The gooseflesh crawling up my arms and the ice water in my bowels knew the truth of it. I took the rum in a swallow and ordered Mr Baker, my sergeant at arms, to break out two days grog ration and distribute it with all haste amongst the private soldiers. Then to see to a further distribution amongst Master Gilbert's men, and every convict who was willing to bear arms.

Yes, I see some of you shake your heads at that. I understand your perplexity, that we had gone in such a brief interval from guarding these miserable vagabonds at bayonet point, to placing in their gnarled hands the very weapons with which they might undo us. You must take it as testimony to the malevolent nature of our surroundings that such a drastic course seemed entirely appropriate. Sergeant Baker, a thirty-year man, did not so much as bat an eyelid. With sallow face and haunted eyes he merely nodded and hurried off to do my bidding, his fingers stroking the ammunition pouch at his waist as he went.

We all felt it, the oppressive presence of evil and grave madness.

It was at that moment that I perceived a vision so reassuring in its familiarity that it seemed placed within this fantastic tableau as a mockery to the rational mind, a jape to reinforce the loss of balance we all felt when reeling back from the apparition of the damned city. It was a stone fortress, a Martello Tower as they are called of late, which would not have caused surprise had it been spied in any port where the King's law is writ. A mere glimpse, I had, before the *Borrowdale* and *Sirius* passed in front of her, but in that interlude, I knew I had seen men at the ramparts. Armed men. It was a revelation to add to a book of revelations, but before I could order my thoughts around this new development it ceded precedence to another.

The first appearance of the Scourge.

Satan's handiwork did not present as such of course. T'was Surgeon White, with benefit of a long looking glass to his eye, who saw them on the promenade of the opera house. A woman and boy came first, running as though the hounds of hell snapped at their heels. They emerged from the far side of that soaring bleached structure of giant seashells, and behind them came a shambling mob of hundreds. The low moaning of the wind, I belatedly recognised as issuing from human throats. Hundreds of them.

'Look,' he said, a redundant instruction, as I had been alerted to the excitement on shore by the sudden tacking of *Supply* towards water's edge. Our sister ships manoeuvred about in the semicircular quay, with *Sirius* pulling up next to the stonework fort, where a furious communication ensued between the occupants and the commander of the Marine detachment aboard. Too distant to hear any of it, I noted the precautions of the *Sirius*, the guns trained upon the stronghold, and could not help but admire the courage of the master and crew. In any duel of cannon the wooden ship must surely have fallen to a redoubt of solid rock. Would that we had known what armaments lay within of course! Captain Hunter might not have been so quick to follow Nelson's dictum that no captain can do very wrong if he places his ship alongside that of the enemy.

The greater drama, to my eye, lay on shore, where the mob had surrounded woman and child in a tightening half-circle. She, a red-headed lady, was most remarkable for being dressed in her underthings, a rather thin blouse of some kind and what appeared to be unconscionably brief white pantaloons. She looked frantic for escape, but saw as I did, that there was nowhere to go but into the deep. Her son, who seemed to be about seven or eight years of age and dressed in mud-coloured shorts and a blue sleeveless jerkin, was pulling at her hand, obviously urging her in the direction of the water.

'Sergeant Baker!' I yelled. 'Your best marksmen into the rigging now! Covering fire for the woman and child on my order.'

'Yes sir,' he replied and set to snarling and snapping in his reassuring way, sending half a dozen musket men aloft with loaders and a spare gun each. He knew his work, did Baker. Master Gilbert too needed no telling his duty, and we began to move towards the scene as he brought the helm about.

I had the looking glass from Surgeon White and, training it upon the fugitives, both leapt into view with faces strained by a mortal terror such as I had never seen etched upon human features, no matter the extremity of peril. The boy at that point stared at me, I am certain of it. He yanked at his mother's arm again and pointed in our direction. She turned from the closing mob, and saw the reassuring bulk of the *Charlotte* and *Supply* closing in. The brave woman wasted no time, but grabbed the lad by his right hand and dragged him into the water.

'Ready the gig!' roared Captain Gilbert from just behind my ear, causing me to leap near out of breeches and boots. 'A fighting party, if you please, Mr Hood. That boy and his mother will drown otherwise . . .'

But, for a wonder, both could swim! And they struck out directly for us. At this very moment the loudest voice I have ever heard bellowed forth from the ramparts of Fort Denison. Had it issued from the same proximity as Gilbert's roar, behind my ear, I am certain it would have blown out my brains, such as they are, from their resting place within my skull.

All turned as one, by which I mean no exaggeration. Every single soul upon the deck and in the rigging of the Fleet's vessels twisted towards the source of that shout.

'Get out of the —— way! Move aside and give us a clear field of fire,' boomed the voice. I saw a man with a red trumpet to his mouth and assumed the amplified roar could only have issued from that instrument, although it still seemed too loud to me.

At any rate, whatever intercourse had been pursued between Hunter and the defenders of the fort, the *Sirius* promptly made way and then came the specific instant that I, as a military man, knew the world had forever changed. Three score men *and* women did I spy mount the ramparts of Fort Denison, all of them armed with miniature muskets. They took aim and opened fire.

The immediate concatenation was deafening in a fashion that any one of us might recognise, but there came no respite for reloading. No second or third line stepped up to provide volley fire. The same thirty or more shootists simply squeezed their triggers again and again and again, until the uproar of gunfire was so constant and so huge that it overwhelmed all else and pained the ear as greatly as any long naval engagement with artillery.

Beside me Surgeon White swore, as small geysers erupted in the water around the woman and child, and for all the world I would have wagered that these savages had demanded we move aside so they be allowed to shoot down their own kind. The command to return fire was in my throat but *Supply* ran up signal flags ordering us to stand fast. I could scarcely credit it, and my head swirled with the outrage of the thing, but presently I saw the reason of it.

The fugitives were being pursued in the water by fiends which appeared to rise from the harbour floor, and their comrades were providing covering fire of an accuracy I would not credit had I not witnessed the affair myself. Examining the scene anew, I discerned a division of responsibility among the firing party, with a portion given to protecting their mates, while others engaged the mob.

White muttered curses and shook his head as he passed the glass back to me.

'What make ye of yon slaughter?' he asked.

The vast mob had piled up at a stone barrier, waist high, which impeded all forward motion. Not a one of them attempted to mount it, as modest an obstruction as it was. Instead they stood rocking back and forth in a rhythmic motion, moaning as one while they were methodically felled by scarifying gunfire. The thing of it was this. Every single shot seemed aimed at their faces. Only once or twice did I witness a round strike home below the neckline, and then with the most salutary effect — which is to say *none at all.* From a short observation it became apparent that these monsters were immune to all but the most serious of wounds, a lead ball sent directly into their brains.

And monsters they were. Less than one hundred yards now separated us from the nearest of them and such propinquity allowed of an uncomfortably intimate inspection.

'They should be dead,' avowed the good Surgeon White. 'Look at them, Tench. Just look at them.'

He did not need to reiterate the suggestion. I could not look away. I stood transfixed by that phantasmagorical sight. The recently imbibed grog lay unsteady in my vitals, threatening to rise as the stench of them assaulted us. One does not like to speak ill of the dead, gentlemen, but here I must. No member of that horrific rabble was whole of body. Their exposed flesh was a rich palate of advanced decay and gangrenous mortification, shining in sickly hues of mottled greens and grays. All manner of atrocity and flagellation had been visited upon their flesh. I witnessed those with limbs hanging by the merest thread of skin, with guts opened and viscera spilling, throats torn and faces flapping, jaw and skull bones shining whitely in the dawning morn'.

And the stench! The smell of the Scourge, the high, putrid, stomach-churning reek that accompanies them, is not easily conceived unless experienced by prior ill fortune. The lowest bilge or the ripest midden is as nothing to the miasma that emanated from that dreadful horde. There is something about the infection that seems to magnify the natural aromas of decay and effluvium the human body produces post mortem, such that even from our removed vantage, I was struck quite physically by the rankness that reached out to us. I heard several of the crew retching beside me, and felt my own gorge rise, yet with an effort I regained control and turned back to Surgeon White.

'What hell is this, sir?' I asked in shaking timbre. 'Some malady of the soul *and* the flesh? A disorder of the mind? Some voodoo curse? I have seen Zombees of the Carib, Doctor, but naught of them do I see here. Here I see but monsters.'

'Aye,' said White, his voice a whisper, a drift of ash. 'Monsters. Captain Tench,' he continued, reaching a moment of decision. His speech accelerated like a fast steam ship with boilers roaring. 'I cannot vouch for my speculations but on the evidence I must avow to a suspicion that some malady *is* at work here. Some sort of rabid infection, perhaps transferred in the saliva, or in the blood itself. I must advise you, sir, to order your men that under no circumstances are they to *come to grips* with these fiends, even if it means surrendering honour to expedience and retreating in the face of them. Destroy the head, sir. They must *destroy the head* by whatever means available, but not by hand to hand combat. A club, a sword, a bayonet thrust directly into the brain pan. Anything to stay beyond arm's length. Ball and powder, of course, would be best.'

He grew wistful at that, squinting at the distant rifle company of Fort Denison. I knew that he, just like I, was wishing to Our Lord for weapons such as those as yet unknown allies did enjoy.

I called up Sergeant Baker and bade him in the strongest terms to pass on the physician's warning. The first of the convicts appeared from below, blinking in the light, and dealing with a thousand confusions, not the least of which were occasioned by the armaments pressed on them. Baker and his men pushed them forward to the gunwale, with furious and lurid imprecations to do their duty as Christians and Englishmen, no matter how poorly they had once measured up as subjects of the crown.

Now musket shot began to pour upon the mob from the decks of our own vessels, our meagre volleys adding drips and drops to the flood of fire still raging from the fort. Only a broadside from the *Sirius*, unexpected and terrifying, drowned out the staccato uproar, and then but briefly. The withering cannonade of grapeshot from half of one dozen six pounders and three of her eighteen pound pieces swept over the foul assemblage onshore like an evil wind, disarticulating rotten arms and legs, bifurcating trunks like hollow tree stumps, turning whole bodies to a rancid mist and yet . . . and yet . . . still some lived! If living it could be called. With a hand now preternaturally steady I raised glass to eye again and surveyed the carnage only to reel inwardly at the vision of some demonic wretches, inadequately fragmented by the broadside, dragging what remained of their leavings back towards the water's edge. An intact cranium attached to a half or more of torso appeared to be vessel enough to contain whatever motive force drove them on. Only a discrete blow to the brain itself provided an assured *coup de grace*.

As orders to this effect rang out across the fleet, including from myself to *all* the fighting men aboard good *Charlotte*, I watched as her gig, almost forgotten in the wider horror, reached the woman and child. Both flung themselves into the reaching arms and hands of our gallant tars as though attempting to jump from a boiling pot. One of the poor, brave men, however, not swift enough to escape a reaching, rotted claw, suddenly screamed and toppled over into the water, which began to boil around his thrashing form. The foam turned red and he soon disappeared below. No order to heave to was needed. The small boat crew leaned into their oars with vigour inflamed by mortal terror as they raced back towards their mother ship.

As escapees and rescuers scrambled up the nets of the *Charlotte*, dripping nightmares followed them and I was thankfully spared leisured contemplation of the morning's wickedness by the demands of our defence. The nets I had cut away with all despatch, and those few devils who made it to the top before the severance were held off with gaffing hooks while a single shot to the head was organised and administered by Sergeant Baker.

The poor woman was delirious with fear and her boy shaking as though possessed by a fit of St Vitus. 'Sweet mother of Christ,' White called out over his shoulder as he hurried to their aid. 'Look upon fresh hell, Captain Tench.'

I followed where he pointed and felt my gorge rise as I too comprehended the new and awful exigencies of this battle. Four of our transports packed with convicts, stores and livestock had withdrawn to a safe distance from the fray, or so it had seemed. But these most exemplary precautions had taken them beneath the span of that great steel bridge and whilst all had been distracted by the terrible spectre of the walking dead to our port, on starboard an horrendous *mise-en-scène* unfolded. Hundreds of ghouls dropped through the air like fat, blackened fruits. Descent and the prospect of destruction upon impact seemed not to bother them at all and quickly I was given to comprehend the reason of it.

Even as their bodies struck spars and mast, parting in an obscene spray of chunk and offal, the ruined vestiges smashed into wooden decks and, presuming no damage to the cranium ensued, they recommenced their assault. Many simply speared into the deep, and many were indeed destroyed by the crushing or severing of skulls. But enough made it down there, gentlemen. Enough.

I shudder now to think of it, even though my own sight of the holocaust was oft impeded by distance and the intervening bulk of our other ships. Through the glass I saw all that I needed. A score or more of the plague carriers made the *Borrowdale* while I looked on, all but helpless. Some of the fiends survived by mere dint of crashing down atop some unfortunate crewman or marine and, horror upon horror, commenced without delay to feast upon them. The screams which reached across the water and over the uproar of gunfire will follow me to the very gates of heaven, where I can only hope I might finally receive blessed surcease. Just one incident of this satanic cannibalism did I allow myself to witness, and that because I could not avert my eyes in time. I confess myself paralysed by the horror. Half a devil fell upon one of the few free woman travelling with the Fleet, the wife of a comrade indeed, and well known to me from the advantage of fond memories. I recognised her at a distance from her gay bonnet and parasol, which I well remember from pleasant walks with that poor family about the common of their village back in Dorset.

The thing which struck her — for although science tells me it had once been a man or woman, I could not now privilege it with any appellation beyond that of a foul and soulless *object* — the thing, trailing gizzards and great ropey lengths of corruption, crashed into her shoulder and drove her to the deck. Would that the force of the blow had killed poor ——. Alas she was but momentarily stunned, and quickly revived by the painful stimulus of first one, then two, then three of these creatures making a meal of her. Brave woman that she was she cried out her defiance and had at them with the only weapon to hand, her broken parasol. I saw it rise and fall repeatedly, but to no effect, and the resistance soon ended as all life ran from her wounds. As horrific as this was, worse followed as my colleague's only love soon rose from the heap of her tormentors, and now suffering the most appalling disfigurements, joined in the assault on her former friends and shipmates. I saw her bite the neck of a corporal of marines whose only fault was to attempt to spirit her to safety and as he fell with great jets of his lifeblood painting the ambulatory corpse of ——, I turned away.

As any professional military man will attest, however, there is much succour to be had in attachment to duty and necessity. Of that I had an elegant sufficiency, as we now found ourselves ordered by the Flagship to sail into the diseased heart of that horrendous encounter beneath the bridge, there to take on any survivors who might yet escape.

Pride is a deadly sin, gentlemen, but I am proud that not a man amongst us on that day resiled from certain death, and what was more, from equally certain damnation. Even the prisoners, now armed with the means to revolt if they so wished, proved themselves not entirely beyond redemption as each gripped whatever weapon they now held and, spitting either prayers or curses at their fate, made ready at the end to die as free men. For none of us saw any way in which we might possibly achieve the stated aim of our orders. We were surely headed to our doom.

Our passage there was not without incident, as you might imagine. We were increasingly besieged by those water-logged corpses drawn to us by the flight of the woman and child. A veritable raft of them did form o'er the next minutes, a floating carpet of moaning reaching phantoms that surrounded every ship on all sides, necessitating much cooperation between the firing parties of each vessel, and our new chums in the fort.

My own makeshift force however, I ordered to hold fire, knowing that we would presently require every advantage accruing to us through the possession of a well stocked armoury. Master Gilbert brought the helm around for a rendezvous with the *Lady Penhryn*, the nearest vessel, upon which a furious but sadly hopeless struggle was enjoined. It was vexing. Of all of the ships of the Fleet, the *Lady*, with the majority of women transportees, had but two lieutenants and three privates of His Majesty's Marine Forces. A small, valiant party still held out on the quarterdeck, where these three marines and the same number of tars blocked all attempts by the shambling hordes to have at a dozen or more screaming women and children clustered at the stern.

Below them lay many corpses of the dead, in pieces. They stabbed, slashed and hacked at a solid writhing mass of reanimated flesh as it all but *poured* up the steps towards them. The deadly winnowing education of combat had taught these few defenders the efficacy of striking only at the heads of their attackers, among whom, I am sorry to say, were numbered many former comrades and shipmates, including the afore mentioned regimental officers, both friends of mine while the light of God had flickered within their breasts.

Sergeant Baker had a firing line of our marines drawn up in short order and I instructed them with all despatch.

'Aim for their heads, lads,' I called out. 'The heads and . . . fire!'

Ten flints struck as one, followed by a single roar. The gun smoke lifted to reveal a small clearing, felled in the midst of that evil mass.

The second line stood forward and unleashed their volley in the same fashion to even greater effect and the rousing cheers of the *Charlotte's* complement. Sadly I saw one of *Lady*'s marines slip and slide into the flailing mob, screaming proud defiance to the end. His partner smashing his skull as he fell, before returning to the dreadful repetitive work of cracking monster heads with a pair of iron bars.

I saw, a dozen chains away, a similar battle raging on the decks of the *Sirius* which had drawn up beside the *Golden Grove* and I could but wish them Godspeed.

Our own trial began at this point as we had drifted within the shadow of the giant bridge and exposed ourselves to invasion from above.

'Look to the skies,' I called out as Sergeant Baker began to roar at his reserve of armed prisoners, goading them from their fearful reverie as the very first crash of a demon slamming into the boards of our own deck resounded. A terrible, dull, crunching thud it was, an impact which speared the beast headfirst into solid oak, thus ending the immediate threat, but only for a moment.

They soon came upon us as a biblical rain of toads. Dark, heavy and pounding down like the fists of Satan himself. What a job of work it was, maintaining an orderly supporting fire upon the vile horde of inhumanity that had infested the for'ard decks of the *Lady Penrhyn*, whilst all the time being mindful that something worse than death was probably plummeting towards one from the heavens.

But Baker, a soldier's soldier, had done my job for me, as the very best of non-commissioned men will always do. A corporal and five privates all armed with Ferguson pistols and axes were duly detailed to the single task of spotting imminent and unwanted arrivals on board the *Charlotte* and warning any who stood in danger of being thus felled to move themselves with extreme haste. Such of those vile creatures which did make it down *relatively* intact and hungry for fresh meat, were consigned to oblivion by this party, all save for one.

A scrape and the metallic clink of chains upon the deck sounded behind me. I turned and was confronted by a woman. One of ours gone over to the darkness. Her white, dead eyes and a slack jaw identified her as being contaminated. Shocked, I saw the child at her breast still suckling but it too had been cursed. She looked at me and uttered one, guttural word ... '*B r a i n s*' ... as she reached out to me with a clawed hand. I had become immotile, this woman had given life to her child on our perilous voyage and I had promised to bear witness to her wedding with William Bryant and now ...

A sick-making crunch cut off her rasping call for my grey matter and she toppled like a rotten tree given out at the roots. An iron axe head protruded from her cleaved open skull and behind her stood the near naked woman we had rescued from the fore court of the Opera House.

'I am most grateful, madam ...' I began, but lost my words as she stepped forward and despatched the zombie child with a shot from what I took to be a pistol, although its design was in kin with the sharp angles and prepossessing bulk of so much machinery in this benighted hellhole.

'Sweet as,' she said tightly and somewhat incongruously before striding to the gunwale, taking a spot in the firing line as though a woman might do such a thing without a second thought, and unloading a second helping of death, this time permanent, upon the hellish multitude there swarming. Like her fellows on the stone fort, she handled a firearm with preternatural ability, placing her ball seemingly wherever she chose.

Good *Charlotte* crunched into the flanks of her dying sister ship, and lines to the embattled party were made fast as every muzzle available to us was trained upon the remaining ghouls. Now sitting directly under the bridge, we were spared the airborne hazard for the moment and could concentrate our best efforts upon effecting the escape of our comrades.

Many, if not all of you, will have read Surgeon White's account of the rescue, which I must tell you fails miserably in one respect, by neglecting to credit the surgeon with his own most fearless role. A wide plank did he have laid between our vessels and with two pistols in hand he proceeded over, heedless of the fatal seas alive with the undead just beneath his feet. One unfortunate pitch or toss and he would have joined them down there.

More tars and marines followed him, setting up an impenetrable barrier past which none without a soul might pass. In this way, with safety lines secured to the few surviving passengers of the *Lady Penrhyn*, did we evacuate that poor accursed wrack.

Others, I am afraid, were not as fortunate. Whether by ill luck or lack of fair preparation, the *Sirius* did not return from her mission. She was overrun, and with her the other store ships and transports. Our commanders signalled us to withdraw from any further contretemps beneath the bridge, and, barring a short interlude where once again we received the enemy from above, we repaired from the battle without much further incident.

I deduce by the strained faces before me tonight that I have done enough to present to you some intimation of our vile circumstances, but, gentlemen, believe me when I say that whatever repulsion you may feel, was felt one thousand fold in our gullets on that day. Indeed, it would not be much of an exaggeration to admit to you that a shadow of repugnance has followed me through my days ever since.

And yet, I stand here, before my friends and colleagues, ready to bear witness and to avow my preparedness to do whatever necessary to preserve this realm from the terror of the Scourge, which every day threatens to spread beyond the Forbidden Seas to infect virgin lands and souls.

It cannot pass, gentlemen. And it shall not. Not while the British Empire stands vigilant and immeasurably strengthened by the scientific wonders salvaged from that dead city inexplicably cast down amongst us from the god-forsaken wastes of the twenty-second century.

John Birmingham

AFTERWORD

I was deep into researching my big fat history of Sydney when I saw version one of *Dreaming Down-Under*. I shouldn't have picked it up. I should have kept on at my research into the sand dunes of Surry Hills, but I am a bad, naughty, easily distracted author, and such a hefty tome, promising hours of enjoyable time-suckage, was too much for me. I think I read it in about two days, during which time nothing else got done.

It set me to thinking about writing my own bit of spec fic, which I soon started, as an alternative to playing computer games to wind down at the end of the day. Long story short, that brief, unintended experimentation eventually saw publication world wide as the Axis of Time series. Since that day, I've always felt I owed a debt to *Dreaming* and the authors who worked so hard to drag me away from my paying gig as a serious, nonfiction guy.

And so here I am, paying that off. The setting for the story, you'll see when you read it, was directly influenced by my research for *Leviathan*.

The other thing that was a bit spesh about this story for me was that I wrote it in close collaboration with some of my readers, specifically with the 'Burgers', the regular inhabitants of the toxic swamp that is my personal blog, Cheeseburger Gothic (birmo.journalspace.com). I've always been comfortable having a lot of contact with my readers and the Burger operates as a sort of friendly tavern where anyone can pop in for a brew and a chat.

Over the years I've gained a lot from having those scurvy dogs at my back. I've run a lot of ideas for my books and even my journalism past them and have been blown away by how generous and useful have been their suggestions and offerings and tip-offs about raids by the Feds.

I'd wanted some way of paying them back as well, and *Heere Be Monsters* is it. I cannot claim sole authorship of the story, which is a ripping little zombie yarn by the way, because at every turn the Burgers were there with their own helpful thoughts and contributions. They can all claim to be coauthors, and as such we've decided to donate *our* story fee to research into sexually transmitted disease amongst koalas. They're randy little buggers and they just can't help themselves. So are the koalas.

Some time after this book is published I'll post up the various drafts of *Monsters*, and anyone who cares to check them out can do so. You might even find the evolution as fascinating as I did.

—*John Birmingham*

ROWENA CORY DANIELLS writes for both children and adults and has been involved with speculative fiction as a fan, bookshop owner, small press assistant, graphic artist, and writer for over thirty years. With her writing group, ROR, she has sold a children's series to ABC Books. Rowena's book *The Evil Overlord* is the third of The Lost Shimmaron series. Her Last T'En fantasy trilogy appeared in Australia, the United States, and Germany. Over the years Rowena has served on both state and national bodies to promote writing and the speculative fiction genre. In her spare time she married, had six children, and spent five years studying each of these martial arts: Tae Kwon Do, Aikido and Iaido, the art of the Samurai sword.

Here Daniells investigates a killer virus that could cure us all by Christmas . . .

PURGATORY

ROWENA CORY DANIELLS

I loved long weekends. Not because I took time off, but because it meant the rest of my team left me alone to work without interruption. Not this long weekend. This time I was going to put my future on the line to prove our antiviral worked and I was going to break the Code of Research Ethics by administering it to my partner, Nathan.

I'd come in early Saturday morning to combine the antiviral with a primitive head-cold virus that I'd synthesised, modifying it to create the perfect carrying agent for my antiviral. The head-cold was designed to strike rapidly and be highly contagious. Dating from last century, I doubted anyone would have immunity.

And I was going to infect Nathan against his will.

I felt only a twinge of guilt. After all, we'd created the antiviral to destroy a virus that had caused the deaths of millions. Infecting Nathan without his informed consent was morally and ethically wrong but if I didn't do something I'd lose him. And I couldn't bear to lose Nathan after losing Ebony.

A river of grief travelled its familiar path through my body, swamping all other emotion. I accepted it willingly. They'd offered me therapy to lessen the loss of my infant daughter but I'd refused because I believed this dishonoured her memory.

I would have tested the antiviral on myself if it had been possible but I was one of the ten percent who were naturally immune. In the computer simulations the antiviral worked in approximately two hours but we couldn't test it on lab animals because the virus interfered with brain function in a very specific way, so specific that only human testing would reveal if it had been destroyed. So it had to be Nathan.

After adding the antiviral and its carrier agent to my favourite perfume oil, I slipped it into my satchel. This one dose was enough to start a chain reaction. Once Nathan inhaled it and became contagious, the head-cold carrier would pass through the population like the proverbial winter flu. The majority of the infected population would be cured by Christmas.

Christmas!

My laughter echoed off the tiled walls. The hysterical note frightened me and I broke off mid peal, standing there in the sudden silence fighting a sense of dislocation.

The antiviral should have been tested on foreign prisoners. After all, they'd forfeited their rights by infiltrating our society to disrupt it, unconcerned by the loss of human life. Since they were motivated by religious mania, testing the antiviral on them would be satisfyingly ironic. But getting permission to use foreign prisoners would mean approaching the Council of Social Engineers and, because of the ramifications, they would debate it and by the time they made their decision, Nathan would be irrevocably lost to me. His aberrant behaviour was killing my love for him by degrees. He'd become so detached, there were times when he was a stranger. I'd told myself his actions were prompted by the virus but logic and emotion are distant cousins.

This had to be done.

I locked up, using my thumbprint to enforce the security code. Already, I was anticipating how I would approach Nathan. First I'd tell him we'd made a breakthrough and then I'd lie to him. I hated the thought, but I had no choice.

As I approached the last checkpoint of Facility Security I told myself no one could possibly guess what I meant to do, but I felt sick. I'd make a terrible spy.

Jarden straightened at his post. One of the many human back-ups to the Security System, he must have been annoyed to learn he was rostered on over the long weekend. Not clever enough to reach Careerist status, he had to be satisfied with a Sinecure, a make-work job. The credit he earned at his Sinecure provided the extras of life. In a society where housing, food and medical care were the right of every citizen, it was the extras that gave people status.

'Going home early, Lilli, that's not like you,' Jarden teased. 'I thought you were a workaholic.'

'I've seen the light.'

'What, converting to Catholic Romanticism?'

'God forbid!'

We both laughed and I headed for the monorail. Like me, Jarden was one of the natural immunes. It was odd but intelligence didn't protect one from the virus's effects. Nathan was brilliant but because he was infected he would argue that he didn't need to be cured, trapped in the virus's delusional loop. Only when he was back to normal and completely rational would he thank me. And then he would be his old self. I'd missed him terribly these last five years.

When Nathan first started exhibiting symptoms, I didn't understand what was happening. His attack had blossomed into a full blown infection in a matter of days, prompting me to pursue this area of research. The discovery that religious mania was a communicable disease had made headlines across the world and caused a great deal of anger, hence the Facility Security.

The tricky thing about viruses was that we could produce a vaccine but it was only useful if people were not infected and it turned out everyone was, even the immunes were carriers. In the vulnerable ninety percent, the virus was latent until triggered and the trigger was stress. Who lived a stress free life?

Yes, I was breaking my professional code of ethics by curing Nathan without his consent. But conviction filled me. This antiviral would save so much unnecessary suffering and death. It was the goal of every citizen to contribute to our country and I was no exception.

The monorail travelled along the ridge, down to where our pole-house stood on a steep spur overlooking Greater Brisbane. It was midday and the city's solar panels turned their faces to the sun like obedient sunflowers. Since Nathan and I were both Careerist we could afford to pay for these inspiring views. Nathan was an Installation Artist. Anyone with the brains could study and become a Careerist in their chosen field, but only those with real talent could become Artistic Careerists. They were valued because they held up a mirror, helping society see itself warts and all. Nowadays Artistic Careerists had the acclaim that sportsmen and women had once experienced. I knew, because history had been one of my obligatory humanities subjects. Back then it had struck me as bizarre how a whole society could share a mass delusion over the outcome of a football match. We'd come a long way, so it came as a shock when religious mania reared its ugly head; that it could affect Nathan made it personal for me.

When I first met him he'd already attained Careerist Celebrity Status and I had only just achieved my official Careerist accreditation. The discovery of the true source of religious mania had made everyone at the Facility Research Celebrities. I'd shunned the attention. My goal was results.

When I jumped off the monorail the heat hit me. Inside, with our smart-architecture, it would be pleasantly cool. I approached my front gate where bougainvillea trailed defiant red arcs across the driveway. With no private vehicles, this cement drive was an anachronism from before the Decline, before the Council of Engineers saved us from ourselves.

I dodged the bougainvillea thinking I must give the bush a trim. We'd put it in when we first came here, just before Ebony was born. The plant had thrived in these six years, unlike our poor little girl.

We'd felt betrayed when we discovered there were some things the marvels of modern medicine could not prevent.

Breathless, I ran down the drive and across the front veranda to the door. 'I'm home early, Aunty Flo. Where's Nate?'

'Nathan is in the studio,' the smart-house replied, sounding just like a maiden aunt from an Agatha Christie novel. Nathan had chosen its persona. It had amused him back when he'd had a sense of humour, and I hadn't the heart to change it.

'Begin recording Aunty Flo. This is to be sent to my work colleagues at the Facility.' I wanted Tri and Yasmin to have a copy of what happened this afternoon so we could review it together on Tuesday. 'Hi Guys. I can't wait any longer so I'm giving Nathan the antiviral. The time is noon, Saturday. Wish me luck. Oh, and for the record, this was done without Yasmin's authority. I take all responsibility.'

'Do you wish to send this recording now?'

'No, keep recording. Send it Tuesday morning.' They were simple creatures, smart-houses. We'd had to edit Aunty Flo's safety margins to avoid misunderstandings in Nathan's studio.

The door opened and I stepped inside, kicking off my outdoor shoes and dumping my satchel on the antique hall stand. Glancing to the stand's mirror I caught sight of myself. I was windswept from my run down the street, hair coming loose from the ponytail and brushing my shoulders, eyes alert with excitement like a kid on Christmas morning.

Christmas again. We hadn't given up our holidays when we discarded religion.

According to the Social Engineers, religion was a primitive people's insurance policy. Where once people had implored the gods to keep their crops safe from pestilence, we genetically modified our food to be pest resistant. We should have been beyond superstition, yet we suffered from a resurgence of religious bigotry. The Social Engineers had been tolerant at first, but this last year they had begun to crack down on extremism.

Well, now I had the cure. I put a dab of perfume behind my ears and between my breasts. It was vanilla, my favourite. Nathan would not suspect a thing. Again, I felt that pang of betrayal.

Ready to do battle, I headed for the studio.

Peer Gynt's *In the Halls of the Mountain King* thundered through the house. Nathan always played dramatic classical music when he was working. I used to find it endearing. Now it annoyed me.

The first two months after Ebony died he didn't work at all and I'd feared something in him had died with her. Then he discovered the Catholic Romanticists and began his CR Period. His pieces had sold really well at first because of the novelty value and the power of his creativity. This very power had helped trigger converts in a society grown desperate for meaning. But, as the burgeoning religious movement gained momentum, costing people their Sinecures, Careers and lovers, resentment built and the Social Engineers had *suggested* that Nathan refrain from exhibiting or selling his work. He resented this fiercely.

Since his infection had become full blown five years ago I'd bided my time, hoping he would work his way through it. I missed the old Nathan, desperately.

My stomach churned with excitement. If this worked, apart from Tri and Yasmin, no one needed to know that I'd compromised my professional ethics. Nathan could announce that he'd had a change of heart and we'd move on, sadder and wiser, but together again.

I relished the cool of the polished boards on my bare feet as I went down the long hall. The studio stretched across the back of the house. With huge windows along three sides it looked through the bush canopy to the city. It was like living in a tree house. When I'd originally seen this room I'd thought it was the perfect place to raise a child. Ebony had been a month short of her first birthday when she died, just old enough to appreciate the brilliant lorikeets that came down to feed in the native trees.

Once again, I experienced that terrible sense of loss. And yet again, I savoured it. After six months the Counsellor had advised us to have another child. As we were both Careerists we had a licence for two, but by then Nathan had discovered Catholic Romanticism and didn't want to bring a child into a godless world. That had really annoyed me but I'd been close to making my first breakthrough about the true nature of religious fervour and was willing to give him more time. Now five years had passed and I was needy for another child.

Brilliant, tree-dappled light streamed into the studio, blinding me after the darkness of the hall. I blinked. Where was he?

There on the floor. Was he hurt? My heart lurched as I tried to make sense of what I saw. My partner lay stretched out, arms flung to each side, legs crossed at the ankle, naked on a life-size canvas. About fifteen centimetres deep, it was an impressionable-canvas, an innovative piece of technology he had designed, and he had already begun to sink into it. Later he would sculpt the form and set it with hard-light.

'Are you all right?' I had to shout to be heard over the music's crescendo.

He jerked and turned his head to look up at me. For a heartbeat he didn't recognise me, then he frowned impatiently. I'd disturbed his work. Even wilfully ignorant as I was of Catholic Romanticist Lore, I recognised his subject. A powerful spasm of primitive anger flashed through me.

'Music off, Aunty Flo,' I ordered. Sudden silence resounded in my ears. After a couple of heartbeats, I heard the birds singing in the treetops through the wide open windows. 'I came home to share my good news with you, Nate.'

'I have good news, too,' he said, making a visible effort to be sociable. We'd been going through the motions, hoping we could regain that old love for a long time now. It was painful. He managed a smile. 'The CRs have contacts in the Alliance of First World Nations. They're going to smuggle my new exhibition out so it will be seen. The Voice of our Times cannot be Silenced.' He'd started talking in capitals when he'd converted to Catholic Romanticism. I hated it.

'We've made a breakthrough on the antiviral,' I blurted.

'Oh?' He'd grown cautious after learning that we'd pinned down the viral sequence that induced religious mania. Naturally, because he was infected, he refused to believe it was a physical illness. The virus must have lain dormant until his immune system wavered under the onslaught of Ebony's sudden decline and death. In the first extreme phase he'd insisted she visited him as an angel. His withdrawal from reality had left me to mourn her passing alone and, when I realised what had happened to him, I mourned the loss of what we'd once shared.

I licked my lips and crouched so that we were about an arm's length apart, him lying naked on the impressionable-canvas, me kneeling like a penitent on the floor. I picked my words with care. 'Nathan, I want you to know that I love you dearly, even after everything we've been through since Ebony died. And that is why I'd like to kiss and make up.'

Liar. Trickster. Firmly, I silenced the inner voice.

He sat up, pulling his back and arms free from the canvas with an audible sucking noise. His interest in my offer was obvious. We both glanced to his groin and smiled.

I leant forward. Let him kiss me, let him nuzzle my neck and breasts, let him inhale the antiviral. I was certain the virus would be eradicated but I didn't know how this would affect him while it was happening, or how he would rationalise the sudden change. What ever happened, I would be by his side.

Our lips touched. Savouring the sensation, I prayed that I would soon have my old lover back. I cradled his head, feeling the Nodals on his temples. He'd had them implanted before I met him, back when this new technology had been used only by Psychological Resonance Interfacers. Back then, I'd admired him for his innovation. The Nodals allowed him to download emotion and impression directly into his impressionable-canvases. Now, even people on basic Sinecures had Nodals implanted to heighten their appreciation of all forms of art. I'd refused. My mind was private.

He climbed out of the impressionable-canvas and it slowly resumed its original shape. I came to my feet. Unsealing my top, I let it hang open then offered my hand. His fingers were hot and dry in mine. I led him to the cushion-laden divan where I had modelled for him so often. As I sank into its familiar depths I pulled him down after me and a kick of desire made my heart race for I meant to seduce him. Call me old fashioned but I'd have to edit the recording. I didn't want to share this intimacy with my work colleagues.

Nathan nuzzled my breasts, reclaiming my attention. I delighted in the soft brush of his hair on my skin. He lifted his head and turned away from me to sneeze, covering his face with his hand.

A wry grin tugged at his lips. 'Sorry. Must be coming down with something.'

'Don't worry.' I wanted to laugh with joy. The primitive head-cold was the perfect carrier. Every breath Nathan expelled would propel the infection into the air. Everything he touched would hold a trace of the virus which could survive up to forty-eight hours outside the human body. 'I love you, Nate.'

He reached for the catch on my pants and I lifted my hips so he could peel them off, stripping my lower half bare. His knee sank into the divan between mine. He lowered his head and inhaled my scent appreciatively, then sneezed again.

'Sorry, Lill.'

I shook my head. He'd forgive me tomorrow. I pulled him down to me. 'You'll see. It'll be like it was between us.'

I reached for him. He was so hot and ready, he groaned.

'Like it was . . .' he whispered. Then his eyes widened as the glaze of desire was replaced with comprehension then growing fury. He pulled upright. 'You've created the antiviral? That was your good news.'

I nodded. I couldn't lie. I held my arms out to him. 'Be pleased for me, Nate.'

He brushed my hands aside. 'You've infected me with it, haven't you?' His voice rose dangerously. 'That's why you think it will be like it was.'

I sat up, trying to put some distance between us, frightened by his intensity.

'They warned me, told me to leave you. They said you were the tool of Satanus.' His feverishly bright eyes fixed on me, all hint of the Nathan I loved banished by religious mania. Face flushed, he lifted large hands. 'Truly, you were aptly named, Lillith.'

'Oh, for god's sake, Nate!' I couldn't keep the scorn from my voice. 'Can you hear yourself?'

He lunged for me. I scooted off the end of the divan. He was fast. He tore the shirt off my back as I got away. I'd gone six steps when I glanced over my shoulder and tripped over the lip of the impressionable-canvas. I fell full length into it. Before I could pull myself from its sticky embrace he landed on me.

Betrayal burned in Nathan as he forced the heretic's face into the impressionable-canvas. Outrage fired him and the defiler's struggles only incensed him.

When the struggles ceased he dragged himself from the impressionable-canvas to stare uncomprehendingly at the body, stretched face down.

It did not move.

The heretic was dead.

Sad, but necessary, even inevitable. The heretic had refused when he'd suggested she give up her research. She'd turned her face away from the Mother, Father and Son towards Satanus.

He stood trembling, the heat of fever raging in him. Loss curled through his belly, painful and intimate. He'd intended this canvas to be a tribute to Mary's Son, sacrificed to save human kind, now he had made the ultimate sacrifice for his faith.

If this was what Catholic Romanticism demanded of him, so be it.

Leaf-dappled sunlight played across the rise of her buttocks. The artist in him appreciated the effect. She'd always had the perfect female body, sweet curves and slender ankles. Her body had inspired him so many times . . .

In that instant he saw the perfect composition. Taking her limp form he rearranged it so that she became the archetypal female half-trapped, rising from the impressionable-canvas, all sinuous curves. Adding more mixture to support and encase the form, he used hard-light to set each layer.

The shafts of leafy sunlight moved across the floor from midday to midafternoon. As golden light filled the studio, Nathan lifted his latest piece, standing it upright. It was a bas relief.

A Soul in Purgatory. Lillith, the temptress, caught in mid-struggle, trying to pull free of her own sin. The pale veined faux-marble finish was perfect, sensual yet cool.

Immersing himself in the image and what it meant to him, he plugged the impressionable-canvas's input leads into his Nodals to create the imprint. Intensity churned through him. He let it run its course. It was cathartic, as always.

Pleased, he withdrew the Nodal leads and checked that the impressionable-canvas had made the recording. Now his audience would be able to plug in and immerse themselves in his Art.

To be sure, he had to test it. Steeling himself, he inserted the output leads into his Nodals and waited receptive, as he took in the beauty of *A Soul in Purgatory*. A wave of tortured emotion hit him, forming a sensory loop with the sculpture.

When he could take no more he staggered and unplugged. This piece was his best yet. No wonder his work had won so many converts to Catholic Romanticism.

And his new exhibition would do the same, taking his unique vision to the world. He glanced at the time. Nearly 2 pm. They'd be here soon.

Now that he wasn't working he felt terrible, thick headed and feverish, so hot that everything wavered. A shower would help him freshen up. But first he lined up all his pieces for the exhibition and tested each one for nuance of feeling, arranging them in the order that they should be experienced. When he was done, he was certain that no one would be able to walk out of his exhibition without being moved. By this time he was feeling a little numb.

Still naked, he stumbled off to the bathroom and ran the shower ... fresh water from the tank, solar heated. He felt no guilt letting it pour over his back and neck. In a kind of mental stupor he stayed under for ages until Aunty Flo warned him that he was seriously depleting their water store.

Bleary, he stepped out, dried off and dressed, running a comb through his hair. Why had he let it get so ragged? And he needed a shave. Why had he let himself go like this? No wonder Lillith had been dropping hints.

Lill ... a cold sensation made his stomach lurch. They'd had a fight, another one, only this time he couldn't remember what it was about or why. He'd been angry and that's all he remembered.

At a run, he burst into the studio. It was alive with late-afternoon light that shifted constantly as the treetops writhed in the breeze. He paced the length of the exhibition where Lillith's form was reproduced over and over in exquisite detail. Where was she?

He came back to the newest sculpture. *A Soul in Purgatory*.

Even though the artist in him could appreciate the sculpture's lines, for some reason sick dread filled him the longer he looked at it.

He lifted the leads and slid them into his Nodals as he stared at the tortured figure trapped in the glistening faux-marble. A wave of vile emotion swept him and with it came the memory of the physical sensation as he thrust her face into the mix despite her futile, desperate struggles. His sick but loving, painstaking arrangement of her body as he encased her in the faux-marble came back to him.

With an inarticulate howl he pulled the links from his Nodals and staggered a few steps to stare at his new exhibition. Over and over the variations of that same perverse emotion appeared in his work. How could he have lost touch with reality? The horror of it filled him with revulsion. Only god could absolve him of this crime. But the thought did not resonate, uplifting him, instead it was completely hollow.

Devastated, he took several steps back, then ran for the nearest open window, leaping out into the treetops, crashing down through the branches to the bush floor four storeys below.

'I'll fast forward this bit,' Yasmin said. She hit the button and caught Tri's eye. Both of them were nervous, presenting the smart-house evidence to the Council of Social Engineers. The Director of their Facility had made it clear he'd washed his hands of them. Yasmin had to clear her throat before she could speak over the silent antics on screen. 'Their smart-house closed the window when the wind rose. And it let the CR Activists in when they arrived. You can see them here, searching for Nathan. When they couldn't find him they tried out the exhibition.'

On screen the ordinary looking activists plugged their Nodals into the artworks and reacted with fast-forward abandon that was almost comic.

'Remember,' Tri said, 'the cold virus remains contagious for up to forty-eight hours and Nathan touched all of those artworks while he was infectious.'

The Social Engineers exchanged looks that Yasmin didn't attempt to interpret. She just wanted to come out of this with her Careerist status intact.

She swallowed. 'By the time the Activists loaded the artwork onto their truck they were all suffering from the first signs of a head-cold.' She switched off the recording, turning to face the long table. 'From there some of them went to the airport. The rest went to their homes —'

'To infect their significant others,' Tri said, unnecessarily didactic, she felt.

'And the exhibition?' the most senior Social Engineer asked.

Tri left it up to Yasmin.

'It was a long weekend here. We didn't get the recording until we came in this morning. The Exhibition was flown overseas, set up and given a gala opening, celebrities, media ... the works. Since then, thousands have plugged in to experience the "Catholic Romanticists Revival".'

'Those thousands will have infected tens of thousands. The antiviral is loose,' Tri said, a shade defiantly. 'You can't stop it.'

Yasmin held her breath.

The senior Social Engineer glanced to her colleagues.

'What will you do?' Yasmin asked, mouth dry.

'Nothing.' The Social Engineer stood, signalling the meeting was over. 'You'll sign a Confidentiality Agreement and continue your work. Agreed?'

'Oh, yes.' Tri laughed.

Yasmin agreed, but she didn't stop shaking until she was back at her desk. Then she switched on the religious media channel and waited.

AFTERWORD

'Purgatory' is one of a series of stories set in near-future Australia run by Social Engineers. The subject of religious mania, its effect on societies and individuals, has always fascinated me. Darwin waited twenty years to publish his theory on evolution because he knew it would change the way we saw the world. If we could inoculate people against religious fanaticism, would we hesitate?

— *Rowena Cory Daniells*

RUSSELL BLACKFORD is a Melbourne-based writer, critic, and philosopher who teaches part-time in the School of Philosophy and Bioethics, Monash University. He is Editor-in-Chief of *The Journal of Evolution and Technology* and a Fellow of the US-based Institute for Ethics and Emerging Technologies. His publications include three novels for the *Terminator* franchise, collectively entitled *The New John Connor Chronicles.* His most recent book is *Kong Reborn* (2005), a sequel to the original *King Kong* movie.

Blackford is an internationally prominent critic and scholar of the science fiction and fantasy genres. With Van Ikin and Sean McMullen, he co-authored *Strange Constellations: A History of Australian Science Fiction.* He is one of the main contributors to *The Greenwood Encyclopedia of Science Fiction and Fantasy* and also wrote the entry on science fiction for a major on-line reference work, *The Literary Encyclopedia.* His philosophical and related work frequently deals with issues involving the relationships between science and society, and with humanity's future prospects. This work has appeared in a wide range of journals and magazines, including *Meanjin, Quadrant, Australian Law Journal, Journal of Medical Ethics,* and *American Journal of Bioethics.*

Blackford's work in the field of science fiction and fantasy has won him a swag of awards, including the William Atheling Jr Award for Criticism or Review on three occasions, and both the Ditmar Award and the Aurealis Award for his 1996 short story, 'The Sword of God'.

In 'Manannan's Children', Blackford the philosopher examines the idea of immortality, while Blackford the storyteller sweeps us headlong into the living breathing palpable world of distant Irish myth and legend . . .

MANANNAN'S CHILDREN

RUSSELL BLACKFORD

They'd chased a deer, which had bolted in terror from the forest, then run to a round grassy hill and vanished over the top. At the top of the hill, Finn and Oisin pulled back on their horses' reins and wrapped their heavy cloaks more tightly against the bitter cold wind from the sea. Down on the shore was a lady, also on horseback, with the lapping waves and the sinking red sun behind her.

Oisin's breath caught and his heart seemed to melt like heated gold within his ribs. She was incomparable!

The lady rode a majestic, shimmering stallion, as black as adamant. She called out to the heroes, father and son, and they rode down to meet her, white-bearded Finn going ahead. Oisin couldn't take his eyes from her.

Her horse had a jewelled bridle of fine leather, but she rode without a saddle. She wore a long white gown, embroidered in crimson, which she'd gathered around her thighs, leaving her legs bare and free. Sea water dripped from her pale feet. Her hair was long and yellow, woven with gaudy flowers, crimson, gold and purple. Her eyes were blue as mountain ice, her lips full and red. On a golden chain slung round her neck, she wore a silver horn, scarcely longer than a man's hand.

She seemed to gaze into Oisin's heart as she spoke. 'You are sad, heroes.'

'Do you know who we are?' Finn said impatiently.

'You are Finn and Oisin, rulers in this land of Erin. Yet, your hearts are sorrowful.'

'We were hunting to forget our cares.'

'So,' she said, 'does a victor of battles have cares?'

Finn seemed to swell up even larger in his saddle. 'Our cares are those of men who fought on the field of Gabhra, where Fenian betrayed Fenian. They're the cares of men who went into the hell of battle and returned, leaving behind kinsmen who'd become the food of ravens.'

'Then perhaps you should rest from them,' she said in a voice of infinite kindness.

For a long moment, Finn was silent. Then he said bluntly, 'Who are you, lady? *What* are you?'

'I am Niamh. I come from a country far away.'

Surely, Oisin thought, this creature was one of the Immortals — reckless Manannan's children. She showed no fear of the heroes who confronted her — tall, strong-armed Oisin and his mighty father. Nothing mortal could have stood for long against the pair of them. Finn looked like a huge dolmen stone with an iron helmet planted on top of it.

'My father rules there,' Niamh said, 'as you do in the shores and towns and forests of this kingdom. His name is Aengus.'

'Then what brings you *here?*' Oisin said, finally discovering words to speak, as if a spell had broken.

Her chin lifted slightly at that. 'I have chosen a man. King of the Fenians.' Her breast heaved beneath her gown, but she spoke to Finn in an unwavering voice. 'Oisin will be mine.'

Within his own breast, Oisin's heart pounded like a madman's drum. Manannan's children were creatures beyond mortal notions of life and time and death. This one had chosen him! That might be a blessing or a curse, but what did it matter? He had only to look at her, at the beauty shining out of her.

'Why choose my son?' Finn said gruffly.

'That's for him to know, milord, if I lead him to make sense of it. But it's not something I'm going to shout about all over the wide world of mortals.'

'Is my son not mortal, then?'

'If he dwells in my country,' Niamh said, 'he will live no life such as mortals understand.' She spoke to Oisin directly. 'Speak now, prince of the Fenians, will you give yourself to me gladly, with your whole heart?'

Years seemed to pass as Oisin dismounted from his horse, stepped quietly to her, then knelt at her feet. He drew his long iron sword from its leather scabbard and held it out before him, point downward, resting it in the sand. His giant hands knotted on its hilt. 'I am yours,' he said. 'Lady, I am yours only.'

'Then ride in my arms.'

One last time, Oisin glanced at his father. Standing, he sheathed the sword and leapt onto the back of the black stallion, sitting in front of the wondrous lady. Niamh leant into him from behind, her soft breasts pressing into him through his cloak. He was a hero of many famous battles, but his body trembled.

Finn made no gesture or speech to dissuade him, perhaps as enchanted as his son; the old, unconquered king, who had fought relentlessly against monstrous creatures and beaten the assembled might of the Fir Bolgs, was powerless to oppose Niamh's will.

'We go now,' Niamh said. 'We have very far to travel. Farther than you can imagine.'

To Oisin's uncomprehending senses, they appeared to ride across the sea itself, the green waves reaching up to their feet. 'You are one of us,' Niamh said.

'I am yours now, Niamh, I belong to your father's kingdom.'

Her arms wrapped around his chest; her breath was close to his ear. 'No,' she said. 'That's not what I told you just now, hero of the Fenians. Listen to me carefully, Oisin. *You are one of us*. One of Manannan's children. You always were. Think about that.'

'My love, I hear you, but I don't understand.'

'Then let me give you understanding. For all his mighty strength, your father is old and white-whiskered —but he sired you in the lust of his youth. How long ago was that, then? You have lain with many women and made warrior sons of your own. By now, your face should be wrinkled and your hair as silvery as a herring.'

'You say I appear young for my age? That's not so uncommon.'

'But it is seldom so marked. Trust me on this, my lover. When it is seen, it leads to comment, to questions. The mortal folk are starting to notice. A few more years, and there would have been talk, foolish talk, then foolish action. You would have needed to take the blood of more Fenians with your sword and heavy arm — except that I came to you in time to put a stop to it.'

He thought of the battle of Gabhra, where Fenians had turned upon Fenians and almost destroyed each other. His eldest son, Osgar, had died in that battle.

'Forget it for now,' Niamh said — then she sang to him, songs of unending youth and joy. For days, they rode over the sea-swell, the sun rising and setting many times in a cloudless sky. One day, he heard the sound of a different music on the wind. The stallion's ears pricked, and he galloped towards the sound. Grotesque trees with smooth bark and roots like stilts grew out of the water, first in ones and twos, then peculiar groves of them, then a whole forest marching out from the shoreline into the sea.

Brightly coloured birds and strange large insects flew around. One blue butterfly was as big as Oisin's hand.

They rode to the shore and up the beach beyond the highest mark of the tide on the yellow sand. The air itself smelled sweet. Niamh released him from her embrace, then swung from the horse in an elegant motion, fluid as a sea wave. Oisin followed her, feeling clumsy beside her movements.

She tethered the horse to a tree, then faced her new lover, frankly looking him up and down in admiration. 'As I told you,' she said, 'the blood of Manannan's children must flow in your veins. Surely, it has dominated your mortal blood. Like me, you do not age. I claim you as one of our own.'

She took the flowers from her yellow hair, then gathered her hair in one hand as she raised the golden chain over her head. Gently, she laid it down at her bare feet, careful to get no sand inside the little silver horn. Then she smiled shyly, showing perfect white teeth. She crossed her arms: right hand on left shoulder, left on right. In another elegant motion, she peeled the gown down her body, then stepped out of it, her skin like alabaster. 'I am yours, Oisin, and you are mine.' She walked to him and began to undress him, starting with the cloak, which now seemed so out of place. Still it was like a dream. Then she added a single word, 'Forever.'

They lay together in the sand, loving and sleeping and loving. Finally, the sky drew black, with the firefly lights of an ocean of stars overhead. Oisin slept dreamlessly, then awoke to a new day with the yellow sun already high above them. Niamh was running to him from the waves, but this was a *different* Niamh.

Her body was strangely altered — her skin had turned a golden brown. She was shorter and rounder, narrower across the chest, and her breasts were as flat as a young girl's. Her neck had grown longer, and her arms and shoulders looked powerful. As she approached, she changed once more, becoming slimmer and taller, her chest-wall arching out and her breasts growing larger. She lay by his side — now restored to the form he already knew so well — laughing and wriggling against him.

A *shapeshifter*. So, what was she, really? Which was her *true* form? The Niamh who'd run to him from the sea just now was not an ugly creature, far from it, but that had not been *his* Niamh. She was truly inhuman. How could he make love to *that*?

But his body betrayed him. She took him deep into her, straddling him as she moved like the rolling waves. 'Forever, my love,' she said. '*Forever.*'

Oisin gazed out at the sea. There was nothing but the clear blue water and the strange trees, the forest of them growing thinner toward the horizon. 'Where is this place?' he said.

Niamh cast a pink seashell into the small, lapping waves. 'You will not find it on the maps of mortals,' she said. She hugged him, pressing her naked body close to his. 'Our country is called Tir na n-Og. We live on the islands of the sea — or under the water itself!'

'Under the sea?'

'So I said, my love.'

'But how can you live under the sea and breathe the sea's waters? It's not possible.' But even as he said the words, he felt their foolishness. What did *possible* and *impossible* mean when it came to the deeds of this strange, beautiful creature? He had already seen the impossible many times. What was one more impossibility, that it should trouble his waking thoughts?

'We have certain powers,' Niamh said. 'I shall teach them to you. We can shape our own bodies as you have seen me do, but that is not all. We can also shape the world around us, at least as it appears to others.'

'Illusions? *Glamour?*'

'You can call it by such words, if you wish. One day, such things will seem like foolish tricks. They will seem like nothing at all to you.'

She stretched out beside him, head resting on her palm, her fine body balanced on elbow and hip. Even as he admired her beauty, she changed again, becoming the version of Niamh who had run to him from the waves the previous day: darker, more rounded, yet more muscled in the places where she needed strength for swimming.

'Our control of our bodies is not entire,' she said, 'not total. There comes a certain point, if we seem to change, when it is what you call *glamour*. There are parts of us too fine to change — fine-*grained*, I mean, like timber. Flesh and hair and bone are made of very tiny stuff. The tiniest parts we can merely shift about.'

'Shift about?' he said, feeling stupid.

'Yes, my love — like building blocks smaller than grains of sand.'

She returned to her long-limbed, more human form, taking only seconds to shift shape, then stood and shrugged into her gown. As Oisin tugged on his sturdy breeches, Niahm wandered down to the waves, lifting her hem and skipping in the shallows.

'One day we will understand more,' she said, as he followed her to the edge of the water. 'Perhaps we can leave the wide Earth itself and let mortals squabble over it. Meanwhile, many of us find life under the sea freer and richer than on dry land. My father has a great underwater city, hidden from mortal eyes. This island is a different part of our kingdom. It is the Island of Dancing.'

She walked back to the little horn, where she'd left it on the sand. She stooped to pick it up, then raised it to her red lips, blowing one long note.

From the woods above the sand, there came a note in answer.

Moments later, a band of young men and women filed out of the woods, two by two and hand-in-hand. They wore simple cloaks and gowns of a pale sea green, with crimson embroidery like Niamh's. The leading couple stepped up to her and bowed. They led the way through the woods to a large clearing with huts, a well, and a sandy square. Here, a young man greeted them, almost a male version of Niamh, with the same red lips and blue eyes. 'Joy fills the stars!' he said.

Niamh kissed him on the cheek then stepped back, taking Oisin's hand. 'Joy fills our hearts,' she replied calmly.

Some of these children of Manannan had silver instruments: horns, harps, and many bizarre devices that Oisin did not recognise. They played and danced, mocking the power of death and time, their dance winding through the woods to the yellow sands, down to the sea, then back once more. All day long they danced, then feasted in the evening on fruits and fish, talking and laughing and sometimes glancing upward at the clear sky and the glittering stars.

That night, Niamh led Oisin back to the beach, where they lay together in the warm sand. In the morning, they ran to shore, Niamh changing form and Oisin finding he could do the same when she commanded it. They plunged into water as warm as blood, letting it flow into their bodies through their open mouths — then out of them through fishy gills they had grown on their long necks. Soon, they swam out to deeper waters, past the stilt-like trees. They explored shelves of bright coral, and made love under water.

Afterwards, they walked on the shore in their human forms, not bothering to dress, and Niamh told him more stories of the land of Tir na n-Og.

They danced with Manannan's children. Late that night, Oisin asked her about something that disturbed him. 'You and all the dancers appear young, but all about the *same* age — between the years of twenty and thirty, I would think.'

'And you appear the same,' she said, 'though you have seen fifty winters. We reach the time of our perfection, then age no more. Sometimes we go secretly in the lands of mortals, looking for those who belong to us.'

'But where are your own children?' Oisin said. 'With all this merriment and lovemaking, why are there no children here on the Island of Dancing? Don't you miss their pranks and laughter?'

Niamh sighed. 'In Tir na n-Og, we choose not to have them,' she said. 'You know that we have power over our bodies. To conceive or not, at our own will, is easily within our powers.'

'Then you are not barren?'

She laughed at that. 'Is that what you thought, my love? Of course not!'

'In my land,' Oisin said slowly, choosing his words with care, 'they say that the Immortals can have children only if their men lie with mortal women.'

'That is a silly story invented out of jealousy,' Niamh said. 'We *choose* not to have children — but it was not always so. Centuries past, when the first of us were discovering each other, before Tir na n-Og was founded, things were different. We made love and gave birth to children just as mortals did. But when Manannan's children lay with each other, sometimes they birthed a mortal child — imagine that, if you will, in a country where the parents live forever.' For a fleeting moment, infinite sadness crossed her face. 'We can't prevent it happening. There is some … some *mechanism*' — she said the word distastefully, as if she despised it but could find no better one — 'of our bodies, too fine-grained for us to understand and control. It is something deep within how we are. Until we have mastered that, our women choose never to have children at all.'

She was silent, and he realised that he pitied her. 'I'm sorry,' he said, feeling the inadequacy of words.

'No, my love,' she said, 'don't misunderstand me. We have many, *many* consolations.'

'But how can you find out more if you devote your lives to revelry?'

She gave an almost secret smile. 'There's so much to tell you. I brought you to the Island of Dancing because it is a paradise. Not every part of Tir na n-Og is like this. But stay with me here. I love you.'

One hundred years passed on the Island of Dancing. Oisin swam in the sea, revelling in his new powers, fishing with bare hands among the coral. In the nights and mornings, he made love with his Niamh. They danced through the day, then feasted in the warm, sweet evenings, returning to the beach to sleep together in the starry night.

Then it changed. One day, they ran down to the water's edge, shifting their bones and muscles as they changed to their watery forms. But something washed up on the beach at their feet. Oisin looked more closely and saw that it was a broken wooden lance. He held it up in the bright daylight. How far had it drifted? Across what seas? The shaft was ingrained with dirt from some warrior's hands. The iron point was rusted, but dried blood remained on the shaft.

And he remembered.

He remembered battles, fighting side by side with Finn and Bran, and other great Fenian heroes. He recalled how the dead lay heaped on one another in that last mutual slaughter between Fenian and Fenian on the field at Gabhra, how the horses had seemed to wade in blood, how it had dripped from their legs and bellies at the end of the terrible battle. An emptiness stole into Oisin's heart like winter, and suddenly he found himself weeping, weeping openly for Osgar and all the other Fenians who had died, or been hacked and mutilated — the ones who'd wished they were dead, who'd thought the dead were the lucky ones.

Niamh held him as he wept and sobbed on her shoulder, grief-stricken beyond any consolation.

When their bodies parted, he realised that they could not stay on the Island of Dancing. They dressed in silence — Oisin's heavy winter clothes lay untouched and unharmed on the beach, as if mere days had passed, and not a century — then found the black stallion where they'd left him that first day on the island. Like them, the horse was no older, and it was no worse for being tethered for all that time. Strange that Oisin had never seen him since they'd come ashore — but now, when they needed him, there he was. Silently, the two Immortals mounted the black stallion, then sped across the waves.

'Don't be sad, my love,' Niamh said. 'We shall never die till the day Manannan reaches out from the sea of stars, and the sun grows old and huge like your father, Finn, and consumes the Earth forever. Perhaps we can cheat that fate as well. Perhaps we need never die.'

'But to what purpose?' Oisin said. 'We create no life, we accomplish nothing. We just go on like this forever.'

'We will learn to understand life,' she said as they rode along. 'Mortal sages have tried to understand it, but we will outshine all their learning.'

'*Who* has tried to understand it?'

'The Hellenes and Romans — peoples you do not know — have teachings about life and the seeds of life. They tell how life begins in the woman's womb, how it grows and changes, how the child resembles both father and mother, sometimes leaning to one, sometimes the other way. Have you never wondered at that? We strive to improve the teachings of mortals. If life can be understood at all, then the children of Manannan will find out how. Nothing is more important to us. And, after all, we have eternity.'

'These Hellenes and Romans —' Oisin said.

'Yes?'

'What do they say about life? What have they learned about it?'

'That does not matter so much, my love. Our own philosophers have disproved their teachings.'

'What?'

She told him how a philosopher of the Immortals had once asked Aengus to remove a dozen does from the bucks during the rutting season on an island of Tir na n-Og. 'Our woodsmen secluded a dozen of the does after they all had mated,' she said.

Later on, half the does had been killed and cut open. Strangely, no trace of male seed had been found within them. Later still, the does that had been kept alive were all found to be carrying fauns.

'Do you see, my love?' Niamh said. 'All the slain does must have conceived as well, but where was the male seed?'

Oisin pondered it. He could neither dispute her reasoning nor see where it should lead him.

'Among the Romans,' she said, 'they who rule the greater part of the mortal world, some say that a child grows from a mix of male and female fluids in the womb. Others say that the male seed shapes the female blood. But we have never observed such things. So much for the fancies of mortals about life and birth. They are entirely disproved.'

'At least for *deer*,' Oisin said, trying hard to understand.

'If for deer, my love, why not for other such beasts? Why not for mortal humans? Why not for Manannan's children as well?'

'So, what does it *mean*?'

'It all means nothing, I suppose.' Her tone had a sour trace. 'It shows how little is known, even by the wisest of the mortals, and even by Immortals like us. Yet — somehow — life must form from the mingling of male and female together. We believe that the male seed quickly leaks out, or is absorbed in the womb, but a small amount remains, so tiny that our eyes could never see it, however much we try to improve them with our shape shifting. We take our characters from living particles so fine that even we can scarcely imagine them. That is why we cannot control them. And so the women of my country choose not to bear children.'

She spoke no more as they crossed the sea, which grew cold and misty. Instead, she sang to him — heroic songs of old battles and heroes.

Oisin could not see in the mist to know how often the sun rose and fell, but many days must have passed as they journeyed. At last, they heard the sound of breakers crashing on rocks. Soon, all round them, the water was smashed into white foam, and a black tower rose abruptly from it, looming sheer from a base of dark, twisted rocks. The tower's sides approached each other at an angle, as if it might be, in reality, a prodigiously stretched pyramid rising to a point far above. But its top was obscured from sight in the sea mist. For all Oisin could tell, the tower might have risen forever into the sky and the ocean of stars.

The black stallion strode over the breakers and spray, then onto the rocks. 'Where are we now?' Oisin said.

'Hush, my love. You'll see.'

They reached a huge, battered wooden door. It looked like great siege engines had pounded it, but never broken through. The stallion shivered, and Oisin could see no way forward — but then the door opened inwards like an invitation to the land of the dead. They entered the dark tower, and the door clanged shut behind.

Niamh dismounted, her bare feet silent on the hard floor. Oisin followed quickly. They were in a huge hall full of statues carved from the twisted rock, and he loosely tethered the horse to one of them. There were no windows or torches in here, but the hall was lit with a green phosphorescence that was everywhere and nowhere.

More huge doors led out of the hall in every direction, and they approached one on the right-hand side. It opened before them, then shut behind. They entered further halls, Oisin trying to memorise the pattern of doors that had opened for them, for when they needed to find their way back.

In the fifth hall, a dark-haired woman in a pale green gown was chained by her outstretched arms between another two statues. One of these was a laughing giant, the other a great dragon with teeth longer than daggers. It strode on two legs, like a bird of prey, with huge, scaly wings. The woman's head was bowed, but she looked up as they approached. She was weeping softly, her face set in a sad smile even, as tears welled out of her ice-blue eyes and rolled down her pretty cheeks.

Niamh spoke quietly. 'We will free you.'

Oisin drew his sword. 'Who has chained you like this? Who must I slay?'

The woman shook her head. 'Flee while you can.'

He swung the heavy sword and cleaved one of the chains where it fastened to a ring of iron set into the dragon statue. Now the woman could move, though she was surely sore and stiff. There was still an iron band on her wrist, dangling its length of rusted links. With a second powerful stroke, Oisin cleaved the other chain, and the woman was free. He sheathed his sword and looked carefully at the bands on both the woman's wrists. The bands were not perfect, fused circles, but thick strips of metal bent round until their ends almost touched. Oisin gestured for her to be still, and he pulled at one of those metal strips with all the force in his immensely strong arms.

Slowly, he unbent the metal, then threw it clanking on the stone floor. He rested to get his breath, then opened up the other strip of iron — grunting with the effort — and slid the narrowest part of the woman's wrist through the gap he'd made.

'You're doomed,' the woman said. 'You should have run.'

'We'll see about that,' Oisin said. 'Come with us if you wish.'

They approached the door to yet another hall. It opened before them, and they entered. This hall was the largest yet. Like the others, it was full of statues of dragon creatures and other ancient monstrosities.

'Take *that* door,' Niamh said, pointing.

Oisin went alone this time, drawing out his sword once more, and pointing its naked blade ahead of him. The door swung open, and he found himself in the open air, on a grassy plain overlooking a cliff. He could hear the sound of waves crashing below. The sun was rising in a misty sky. Oisin scanned the plain, finding nothing but more statues: dragons, three-headed giants, grotesque creatures of every sort. Then there was a sound from somewhere nearby. It was almost like a dog's barking, but somehow different, not like any dog Oisin had heard in mortal lands. Then it came again — louder this time. The evil sound put a shiver up his back. He turned slowly, waving his sword from side to side. One of the statues was coming to life.

It was a scaly creature, larger than any man, even the greatest heroes of the Fenians — larger than Finn himself, larger, indeed, than mighty Bran, who was too big to sit on a horse. The creature was obscenely naked and unarmoured, but it carried a sword in one hand and a battle-axe in the other. Its upper body moved and it made that barking sound once more. Its lower quarters were still immobile, but it gradually moved more and more of its parts, testing itself for life, as if it grew out of the stone. It uttered a different sound this time, a plaintive wolf howl, as if frustrated at the slowness of the change from statue to living thing.

Suddenly, it could twitch its legs. Its next sound was a bark of triumph. The creature gathered into itself, opening its slavering, toothy mouth. Its eyes — the same black as the rest of its body — turned white, then red. They fixed on Oisin, and the nameless creature barked sharply. It lifted its powerful arms with their bladed weapons, then jumped towards Oisin with the hopping motion of a gigantic sparrow.

As the sun made its long climb through the sky, Oisin exchanged blows with the creature. Sword rang on sword and battle-axe. Like Manannan's children, the creature was a shapeshifter and a master of illusions. One moment, its body was a hideous writhing like a mass of eels, the sharp blades of sword and battle-axe whirling from the midst of it. Then it leant into Oisin in the form of a drowned sailor, water dripping from its body, swinging its blades at the last moment when Oisin hesitated. It appeared as a giant fir tree with bladed branches — this was a feat beyond any mere shape shifting. It became a clawed dragon, then took the graceful form of Niamh herself. Oisin ignored all these changes. As the red sun sank into night, he prevailed.

With a sudden lunge, he broke through the creature's wall of ribs and his sword blade found its heart. The creature screamed and barked and fell. Oisin *swung* his sword this time, chopping the creature's head from its body. With a backbreaking effort, he lifted his enemy's huge body, which was even weightier than it looked. He carried it to the edge of the cliff, then hurled it into the sea-surge below.

Holding the severed head as a trophy of victory, he returned to Niamh and the other woman. They searched his body for wounds, rubbing them with lotions. The three of them feasted on stewed meat and roots from a black iron cauldron that the woman found in one dark corner, and drank red wine from a stone jar.

In the morning, the dark-haired woman was gone, taking up the freedom she'd been granted, whatever it meant to her. Niamh and Oisin found a rug of otter skins. There they made love with a joy enriched by victory. She wrapped her soft limbs around him, and shuddered and cried out as they joined together.

For three more days, they feasted, slept and loved. The cauldron and the jug never emptied. On the fourth morning, they walked together on the plain of statues and heard that barking sound. A shiver went up Oisin's spine, and he turned to face the scaly creature. It was moving slowly, but then more quickly, its eyes turning to white, then red. With a grim joy in his heart, Oisin drew out his sword. Blade beat on blades once more, until the end of the day, when the Fenian prevailed and cast his enemy into the sea below.

For one hundred years, Oisin feasted and battled and loved his beautiful Niamh, his taste for victories never quenched. But then, as he cast his enemy into the sea one more time, he saw how the breakers tossed up a green beech bough on the rocks below.

And he remembered.

He remembered a time with Finn, his father, sheltering under a beech at Almhuin — and then memory grew from memory in a flood that overwhelmed him and brought him weeping to his knees. Niamh appeared and ran to him, cradling him in her white arms and comforting him, kissing his eyes and cheeks. But nothing could make the tears stop.

She left him, then returned with the black stallion. They mounted in silence, and the magical horse leapt over the edge of the cliff, then ran like a long-legged fly on the surface of the water.

For days they rode. 'We go to the Island of Forgetfulness,' Niamh said, 'for your memories defeat our happiness.'

Oisin shook his head. 'I was happy for one hundred years, then for another hundred.'

'But our lives go on forever,' she said behind him. 'One hundred years, or two hundred, is nothing to us. We have the great Forever to fill up.'

'To dance or love or fight forever is vanity. There must be something more.'

'Though we live for ten thousand years, or ten thousand times ten thousand, we can never see or know all that there is,' she said, 'for the universe can never be bounded.'

'Not even by the gods?'

'If Manannan truly exists, he is the god of a greater ocean than mortals imagine. I mean the ocean of infinite space, of the never-ending islands of stars. But that is as it should be, for a greater universe means a greater god. A god who made the confined little universe that mortals believe in would not be worthy of our worship.'

'Then we should stride out into Manannan's universe. We have magical powers. Is it so difficult?'

'No, my love, we cannot do that, at least not yet. We have certain powers, all of them natural to us, none of them magical. The stars must be infinite in number, and the universe an endless ocean of them, but they are not for us. *Not now.* We know of no way to travel on that vaster sea.' She pressed more tightly into his back, as if she feared losing him. 'We are bound to this Earth, and I fear we've already drunk its pleasures.'

'But not the knowledge of it, Niamh.'

'No,' she said thoughtfully, 'not the great knowledge it contains. As I told you, the very small eludes our attempts to understand it — as much as the infinitely great.' She let him go, leaning away, just touching him lightly with her delicate hands. 'Perhaps you would find the search for knowledge and wisdom less vain than years of dancing or victories.'

'I am a warrior,' he replied sadly. 'That quest is not for me. Take me to the Island of Forgetfulness.'

Niamh wept for a time, but then she sang — sad songs of loss and old memories.

Again, they journeyed for days, through a mist that became thicker and colder as the time passed. At last, they found themselves wading through white foam along the edge of a desolate stony shore. Where a stream flowed into the ocean water, the black stallion began to walk up the shoreline and into a forest of immense, wrinkled trees, each of them wider than a house. Hanging from the boughs of these trees was a long, gourd-shaped fruit that smelled as sweet as honey. For hours, the stallion walked on dark tracks that became steeper the longer the journey went. Then he stopped, as they left the forest and found themselves at the top of a hill looking down on a valley floor — on a wide, grassy plain.

The horse whinnied and picked his way down.

Here were a thousand men and women, not unlike the folk of the Island of Dancing, but sleeping silently on the ground. Now and again, one moaned and woke for a moment, made some gesture or dumb action, then fell back into a slumber. On the ground beside the men were weapons of all kinds: swords and spears, arrows, battle-axes, war hammers and maces, shields and armour, battle conches and horns. Scattered across the valley, rising from the lush, tall grasses, were more of the gigantic honey trees, and the honey-sweet smell was all around, heavy as the taste of mead.

As the sky darkened and the stars came out, birds and animals moved fearlessly among the sleeping Immortals. One of the sleepers was vast in size, larger than any mortal — as large, perhaps, as the nameless creature that Oisin had slain so many times on the Island of Victories. This enormous sleeper was covered with gold jewellery. Niamh and Oisin stopped by his side and dismounted from the black horse. Niamh blew a single note on her horn, and the sleeper woke. He raised his hand as if in blessing, and Oisin felt all his memories of battles, victories, betrayals rise within him in a riot. With them came the memory of endless vain revels on the Island of Dancing, endless futile combat on the Island of Victories. All of it seemed to flash before him at once, then dissolve like a summer cloud. He felt purified.

'Forget,' the sleepy giant said. 'Forget it all.' He lay back in the grasses, returning to his slumbers.

Niamh and Oisin let the stallion go free to do as he would. They breathed the honeyed air and lay down in the grass, too sleepy even to make love. In his dreams, Oisin forgot everything of heroism, war, merriment, and sexual joy. His dreams were as peaceful as a blanket of snow or the slow-growing ivy on a wall.

At times, the brightness of the noon sun brought him awake, or the presence of some animal — then he breathed the sweet air and smiled on his Immortal lover, sleeping by his side. But after a hundred years, he and Niamh chanced to wake at the same time, disturbed by a raven eating a ripe honey fruit where it had fallen. The bird scuffled about busily, showing no sign of drowsiness. Then there was another such bird, and yet another. No more — only the three. But that was enough.

Oisin *remembered.*

The ravens were like those that had feasted on the endless dead when kinfolk fought with kin on the field of Gabhra. Oisin's eyes met Niamh's. 'I can never forget,' he said.

She nodded sadly, or so it appeared. But then she said, 'It is just as well. I am glad of it. Come.' The black stallion ran towards them, unchanged in another hundred years, and they mounted on its back.

'Where do we go now?' Oisin said.

'You are ready to return to the land of mortals.'

'No. I have forsaken it for you.'

'There is something I must show you.'

Yet again, they rode for days, speaking earnestly of their future. This time, Niamh did not sing, but only talked and listened. But she gave him a warning. 'Touch nothing, my love. If once you give way, then you will never return to the Islands of Dancing and Victories. Your soul will be weighed down with time.'

They rode on waves the size of mountains, past innumerable islands, past sights stranger than mortals' eyes had ever seen: many-limbed kraken, each of these monsters larger than a mortal village; even vaster leviathans that chewed on the kraken like crusts of bread.

One day, there was the sound of horses and geese. Niamh and Oisin had reached the lands of mortals. They crossed the country of Erin from west to east. All was changed as they rode through the countryside. The battle camps of the Fenians were gone. The great fortress of Dun Ailleann was a mound of broken stone. Villages paid worship to a strange god of death and rebirth, while hard-handed folk tilled the soil, skilled with ploughs, not shield and sword and spear. For all their toil, they were puny, considered beside the least of the heroes of old.

'Three hundred years have passed,' Niamh said, 'and the Nazarene god has triumphed.'

Oisin shook his head, disconcerted. 'What god is this? I know of no Nazarene god.'

These farmer folk with their insipid deity worked and loved and hoped; they were not entirely contemptible. For all that, Oisin wept. Three hundred years all gone ... The land was no longer fit for heroes.

In a field at Glenasmole, two men carried a heavy rock, staggering and sweating with its weight, trying to load it onto a wagon. Oisin did not hesitate, though he never knew whether he acted out of pity or contempt — or simply out of pride that a use could still be found for his heroic strength. Leaning from the horse, he seized the rock from them and flung it easily on to the wagon. Then he remembered Niamh's warning.

He fell from the horse's back and it flew westward across the mortal land, heading for Tir na n-Og, bearing Niamh with it.

Heavy with the weight of three hundred years of memories, Oisin seemed to fall down a steep-sided abyss, as deep as the tower on the Island of Victories was tall — its bottom lost from sight. Down, down, into oblivion.

He swooned, then awoke, then swooned again. Yet once more he awoke, but was somehow less than himself, some of his faculties missing, though how could he tell such a thing if it were the case? Some power outside himself seemed to be assessing him and making its report.

Oisin gave in and slept.

The next time he woke, he was alone on a grassy hillside in cold mist. Gradually the mist parted, and a figure came toward him. It was Niamh.

'I thought I'd never see you again,' he said.

'I never said that, my only love. I said your soul would be weighed down with time. Did I not speak truly?'

'Where are we?'

'In my father's kingdom. Come with me.' She stretched out her hand, and he took it, standing with her help, then finding he needed no help at all. He shook her hand away; he was assessing himself. He felt strong and light. All his powers seemed to be back. *All* of them? Could he still shift shape, as he'd learned on the Island of Dancing? He held out his right hand as an experiment, inspected its back, reacquainting himself with each nail, every freckle and hair, stretching out his fingers like a spider. Concentrating as he'd been taught, he made the fingers grow longer, joint by knuckled joint, then shaped his nails into retractile claws like a cat's. Niamh watched patiently as he returned the hand to human shape.

'How did we get here?' Oisin said.

'We rode for three hundred days over land and sea, using roads and bridges and ships. I assure you, my horse cannot fly over the waves as I made it seem, but what I told you is true. This kingdom is very far from the land of Erin. It is everything I said — a kingdom of islands and ocean.'

As the mist vanished, the day grew warmer and clearer. Supernaturally clear — he had never seen with such clarity, not in his days as a hero among mortals, not on the three enchanted islands.

At times since he'd met Niamh, he'd felt as though living in a dream. This was the opposite. Everything *before* this moment now seemed dreamlike.

'I don't understand,' he said, thinking back through his adventures. 'You're leaving out the Island of Dancing, the Islands of Victories and Forgetfulness. It's three hundred years or more since I first met you in my own land. You showed me what it has become.'

'It has not changed,' she said. 'Not yet.'

'But I saw it.' Yet that, too, seemed like a dream.

Niamh shook her head and smiled sweetly. 'I am sorry to have deceived you. I merely showed you its future.'

'You can see the future?' he said, incredulous.

'Its *possible* future.' Once more, she took his hand. He neither returned her reassuring grip nor broke away, letting his hand become a dead thing in her grasp while he thought about what she was saying. 'We believe,' Niamh said, 'that the cult of the Nazarene god will triumph through all the great empire of the Romans. Then it will find its way to the Fenians' land. I showed you what your home may look like in three hundred years. Mortals prefer such faiths to the wild gods of heroes. Eventually, one god will be universal, at least among the Romans and their neighbours.'

'What about your god, Manannan?'

'We are not so attached to our god, or to the idea of a god. We worship the endless sea of stars. If Manannan made them, well and good: in that case, he is a greater god than any other. But we don't know the origin of the stars. We don't even know our own origin, for all that we call ourselves Manannan's children.' She released his hand and walked away slowly, as if hoping he would follow.

But a bitterness entered his heart. So much vanity! Even the icy clarity of his senses might be some new kind of illusion.

Niamh stopped and turned back to him. Her breast rose and fell beneath the embroidered gown. 'There is so much that we don't know,' she said. We are scarcely more advanced in our philosophy than the mortals. I told you how little we understand of conception, the inheritance of our natures, the growth and development of life.'

Her words were meaningless, like lumps of stone dropped in an icy lake. 'The last three hundred years that I seemed to live were some kind of trick, weren't they?' he said. 'That's what you're telling me. More of your *glamour*. None of it ever happened.'

'It happened,' Niamh said. 'It was no dream. But little was exactly as it seemed to you. I told you on the beach of the Island of Dancing. Certain powers are natural to us and one of them is the ability to confuse the minds of mortals.'

'But I am not a mortal, or so you told me.'

'I spoke the truth. But you are untrained, my love. Besides, you were only partly confused. As I hoped, you broke the *glamour* on every occasion, smuggling in your spears and beech boughs and ravens. Oisin, will you come with me or not?'

'To where, lady? Where would I go with you after all this?' Words of the embittered heart.

'To my father's city,' she said.

'What if I don't?'

'You will live forever, all the same — but time will weigh even heavier on your shoulders. What is it that you want in life that can keep you occupied *forever*? Dancing? Battles? Perhaps forgetfulness? You have experienced them, or their semblance, and you know now that they alone cannot sustain an immortal life. So what then? Do you want a life among the mortals, changing your name and your home each decade to avoid suspicion? You can have any of those things, if you seek them out, but I've taught you that they're not what you really want — they're not enough. Am I wrong about that, my love?'

'By now, I'm too confused to answer.'

'If I'm wrong, they're all yours for the finding and taking — but they're not for me. Not them alone.'

She stepped toward him, but he gestured her away angrily. Now they were both like fish floating deep in an icy pool, each waiting for the other to come to life. 'How do I know this is not another trick?' he said. 'Another illusion? More *glamour*? How can I be certain of anything from now on?'

'You can't, Oisin, you can never be sure of things, though I tell you truly that none of our conversations were tricks and you're not currently moved by *glamour*. But you'll have to find a life for yourself in a universe where such things can be. Is that too much to ask of a hero?'

'Then what was it all about?' Everything was so clear, at one level of his thoughts. Yet Oisin understood none of it. It tortured him.

'You have been gifted with three hundred years of feeling and experience,' Niamh said, 'in preparation for eternity — all packed into just as many days. All of us are put through that preparation when first we're called to Tir na n-Og. It helps us to find out what we really want in an immortal life. My love, you're stronger than ordinary men. You can shift your shape and become even stronger, more versatile, more beautiful.' She shrugged. 'You need never die. But, if you choose to prey on the mortal world with all your strength and your powers, you'll have to say farewell to me.'

'You think *that's* what I want?'

'It's not for me to know, but understand that I could not go with you in the mortal lands, for I know what I want and it's not what the great world is offering. Stay with me in Tir na n-Og.'

'Must I decide now? *Just like that?*'

'No. You can walk with me a while. Or walk behind me, I don't mind. I'm going to see my father, Aengus.'

'What happens then?'

She walked, and he followed, several steps behind. Over her shoulder, she said, 'The world, the universe, is an infinite ocean of stars. I told you that before.'

'So you did, lady.'

They walked for an hour. Silently. Then she turned and said, 'I haven't told you *this*, my love. The stars themselves are stranger than you think.'

A shudder went through him as he realised she must be right, that she spoke truthfully. He listened to her with care. Over the past hour, the anger had all gone out of him. Now he was merely numb. He needed to find some new feeling in himself.

And as she spoke, each new word seemed to find a place pre-set for it in his thoughts. Yes, it had to be like that, once you reckoned beyond the everyday appearances of things. 'Oisin,' she said, 'there is a star that the Romans call *Jupiter*. On one of my father's islands we have built an observatory — a place where we convene to study the sky.' She walked backwards now, as she spoke to him, happier than he'd seen her since . . . when? Those first days on the Island of Dancing. 'Do you know what, Oisin? There are starlets circling Jupiter, as the moon circles this Earth!'

He started to speak, but she gestured him to silence.

'There's even more. We can sharpen our own eyes, and add still more to their powers with lenses made of glass. When we observe the star called Saturn, it appears to have a moon flanking it, stationary, on either side as it faces us, though no one knows how that could be. One of our philosophers says that such starlets must always travel in circles. She says that there is a vast ring of innumerable tiny starlets all the way around Saturn. That might create the same kind of appearance. We see no motion, because there is no gap between starlet and starlet.'

Oisin caught up with her and took her arm, less gently than he might have, but not so roughly as he'd have done an hour before. 'I told you I am a fighting man,' he said. 'Do you expect me to spend eternity gazing at the sky trying to understand the universe? It would be worse than the Island of Dancing.'

She winced in his grip, and he relaxed it, then let go entirely.

Niamh's close-lipped smile was infinitely calm, infinitely joyous, infinitely sad. You could find anything and everything in her smile. 'There is always something *new*, my love,' she said. 'Don't you yet understand? Sometimes new stars appear in the sky. I have sharpened my own sight with shape shifting and glass instruments, and I've looked closely at the Earth's moon. I've studied its surface like you'd survey a plain spread out below you from a hill.'

'And seen what?'

'I've seen great mountains and huge, round craters like strange dry seas! Perhaps the moon is a world like our own, one that died. No one knows among the Immortals. But we think that the Earth is itself a starlet dancing about the sun, which is only a star in the infinite ocean of stars that I told you of.' Infinitely joyous, infinitely sad, her smile said, *Come with me, Oisin. There's so much to learn in a universe like this.*

'But I'm a warrior,' he said. 'I've been a warrior for all my years, since they trained me as a child. I can't change now.'

She looked upward into his eyes, gesturing wildly, shaking her head. 'Fifty years is nothing,' she said. 'It's *less* than nothing.' She grew taller — just slightly, the merest use of her powers. Then they were equally tall. 'You can change and grow many times. You can lead many kinds of life, each more fascinating and intricate than you can think of. Would it really be so bad?'

He felt like his skin was hardening and cracking. *Like a snake's.* Then he laughed. Another illusion. But it was painful to think about change.

'The universe is large enough for heroes and for lovers to bloom in,' Niamh said. 'It's mysterious enough that no hundred years need ever resemble the one before. And *you* need not be the *self* of a hundred years before.' She laughed. 'You can't be a warrior all your life, my love, not with the length of life ahead of *you*. Eventually, you'll have to grow up ... or else put an end to your immortal life. It's not so bad to grow up. *And to grow up is not to be any one thing.* Not just a dancer and a lover, not just a warrior. Do you understand? One faraway day your wiser self will look at your present-day self like you now look back at your childhood. And later still — another day — that wiser self will seem like a child in its turn.'

He couldn't accept her words, not *just like that*. It was all too strange, and there were three hundred years of illusions behind him. Besides, there would always be uses for a warrior — *surely!* Uses more varied, less futile, than on the Island of Victories. But he had never seen so clearly as he was beginning to today.

Niamh's hair, her eyes and lips, were beautiful — so he kissed her. She was warm and lovely and strong. They broke apart again, but he gave her his hand.

Together they walked to the sea, shedding their clothes and weapons. Everything would be safe here in Tir na n-Og. The sun was high overhead when they changed their shapes. Absurdly, he realised that, in all his time on the Island of Dancing, a hundred years of experience, he'd never learned to *talk* beneath the waves. They'd communicated with gestures and actions. Now they'd need to speak, as well, or something similar. He'd learn. There were so many things to learn. But he'd already mastered the breathing. The skills she'd taught him were real enough. No, it had not been wholly a dream — whatever else it had been. A preparation, she'd said. A time of testing and learning.

They swam, deeper and deeper, their bodies changing, and changing yet again. They touched each other's strange, webbed hands.

They swam to her father's city.

AFTERWORD

'Manannan's Children' is based on the story of Oisin and Niamh from Irish mythology, perhaps best known via W.B. Yeats, who retold it in the magnificent verses of his great narrative poem, 'The Wanderings of Oisin'. Much as I love Yeats, I've given the story an extra twist. I've taken its meditation on mortal and immortal lives, and re-examined its questions. For me, the poem asks, 'What would make immortality bearable?' or even, 'What might make it good?' At any rate, those questions haunt my characters; they're a sub-text to all Oisin's adventures with radiant, immortal Niamh. But I see no reason to give the usual rationalisations of death.

Can life go on forever? No, not forever, not even with the best science we could ever have ... but is it really so bad (as we're often told) to wish that it could? We live in a wonderful universe, and it would take many lifetimes to tire of it all. In fact, the wonder need never end.

— *Russell Blackford*

MARGO LANAGAN has published poetry, novels and speculative fiction short stories for adult, young adult, and junior readers. Her collection, *Black Juice*, won two World Fantasy Awards, a Victorian Premier's Award, two Ditmars and two Aurealis Awards, and was shortlisted for the *Los Angeles Times* Book Prize and made an honour book in the American Library Association's Michael L. Printz Award. The story 'Wooden Bride' was shortlisted for the James Tiptree Jr Award, and 'Singing My Sister Down' was nominated for many other awards. Her third collection, *Red Spikes*, published in Australia in October 2006, was shortlisted for the Commonwealth Writers' Prize and longlisted for the Frank O'Connor International Short Story Award, was nominated for a World Fantasy Award for Best Collection and is the Children's Book Council of Australia Book of the Year for Older Readers. Margo lives in Sydney and has just completed a fantasy novel, *Tender Morsels*, which will be published in late 2008.

The dark and edgy story that follows is a disturbing and unforgettable dystopian vision of prejudice, alienness, sexuality, and the environment . . .

THE FIFTH STAR IN THE SOUTHERN CROSS

MARGO LANAGAN

I had bought half an hour with Malka and I was making the most of it. Lots of Off girls, there's not much goes on, but these Polar City ones, especially if they're fresh off the migration station, they seem to, almost, enjoy it? I don't know if they really do. They don't pitch and moan and fake it up or anything, but they seem to be *there* under you. They're *with* you, you know? They pay attention. It almost doesn't matter about their skin — the feel of it, a bit dry and crinkly, and the colour. They have the Coolights on all the time to cut that colour back, just like butchers put those purply lights over the meat in their shop, to bring up the red.

Anyway, I would say we were about two-thirds the way there — I was starting to let go of everything and be the me I was meant to be. I knew stuff; I meant something; I didn't *givva* what anyone thought of me.

But then she says, 'Stop, Mister Cleeyom. Stop a minute.'

'What?' I thought for a second she had got too caught up in it, was having too good a time, needed to slow things down a bit. I suppose that shows how far along *I* was.

'Something is coming,' she said.

I tensed up, listening for sounds in the hall.

'Coming down.'

Which was when I felt it, pushing against the end of me.

I pulled out. I made a face. 'What is it? Have I got you up the wrong hole?'

'No, Mister Cl'om. Just a minute. Will not take long.'

Too late — I was already withering.

She got up into a squat with one leg out wide. The Coolight at the bedhead showed everything from behind: a glop of something, and then strings of drool. Just right out onto the bedclothes she did it; she didn't scrabble for a towel or a tissue or anything. She wasn't embarrassed. A little noise came up her throat from some clench in her chest, and that clench pushed the thing out below, the main business.

'It's a puppy?' I said, but I thought, *It's a turd?* But the smell wasn't turd; it was live insides, insides that weren't to do with digestion. And turds don't turn over and split their skin, and try to work it off themselves.

'It's just a baby,' Malka apologised, with that smile she has that makes you feel sorry for her — she's trying so hard — and angry at her at the same time. She scooped it up, with its glop. She stepped off the bed and laid it on top of some crumpled crush-velour under the lamp. A white-ish tail dangled between her legs; she turned away from me and gathered that up, and whatever wet thing fell out attached to it.

This was not what I'd had in mind. This was not the treat I'd promised myself as I tweezered HotChips into artificial tulip stalks out at Parramatta Mannafactory all week.

The 'baby' lay there working its shoulders in horrible shruggings, almost as if it knew what it was doing. They're not really babies, of course, just as Polar 'girls' aren't really girls, although that's something you pay to be made to forget.

Malka laughed at how my faced looked. 'You ha'n't seen this before, Mister Sir?'

'Never,' I said. 'It's disgusting.'

'It's a regular,' she said. 'How you ever going to get yourself new girls for putcha-putcha, if you don't have baby?'

'We shouldn't have to see *that*, to get them.'

'You ask special for Malka. You sign the — the thing, say you don't mind to see. I can show you.' She waved at the billing unit by the door.

'Well, I didn't know what that meant. Someone should have explained it to me exactly, *all* the details.' But I remembered signing. I remembered the hurry I'd been in at the time. It takes you over, you know, a bone. It feels so good just by itself, so warm, silky somehow and shifting, making you shift to give it room, but at the very same time and this is the crazy-making thing, it nags at you, *Get rid of me! Gawd*, do *something*! And I wouldn't be satisfied with one of those others: Korra is Polar too but she has been here longer and she acts just like an Earth girl, like you're rubbish. And that other one, the yellow-haired one — well, I have had her a couple of times thinking she might come good, but seriously she is on something. A man might as well do it with a Vibro-Missy, or use his own hand. It's not worth the money if she's not going to be real.

The thing on the velour turned over again in an irritated way, or uncomfortable. It spread one of its hands and the Coolight shone among the wrong-shaped fingers, going from little to big, five of them and no thumb. A shiver ran up my neck like a breeze lifting up a dog's fur.

Malka chuckled and touched my chin. 'I will make you a drink and then we will get sexy again, hey?'

I tucked myself in and zipped up my pants. 'Can't you put it away somewhere? Like, does it have to be there right under the light?'

She put her face between me and it and kissed me. They don't kiss well, any of these Offs. It's not something that comes natural to them. They don't take the time; they don't soften their lips properly. It's like a moth banging into your mouth. 'Haff to keep it in sight. It is regulation. For its well-being.' Her teeth gleamed in another attempt at smiling. 'I turn you on a movie. Something to look away at.'

'Can't you give the thing to someone else to take care of?' But she was doing the walk; I was meant to be all sucked in again by the sight of that swinging bottom. They do have pretty good bottoms, Polars, pretty convincing.

'I paid for the full half-hour,' I said. 'Am I gunna get back that time you spent . . . Do I get extra time at the end?'

But I didn't want extra time. I wanted my money back, and to start again some other time, when I'd forgotten this. But there was no way I was going to get that. The wall bloomed out into palm-trees and floaty music and some rock-hard muscle star and his girlfriend arguing on the beach.

'Turn the sound off!'

Malka did, like a shot, and checked me over her shoulder. I read it in her face clear as anything: *Am I going to get trouble from this one?* Not fear, not a drop of it, just, *Should I call in the big boys?* The workaday look on her face, her eyes smart, her lips a little bit open, underneath the sunlit giant faces mouthing on the wall — there was nothing designed to give Mister Client a bigger downer.

Darlinghurst Road was the same old wreck, and I was one loser among many walking along it. It used to be Sexy Town here, all nightclubs, back in history, but now it's full of refugees. Down the hill and along the point is where all the fudgepackers had their apartments, before the anti-gay riots. We learned 'em; we told 'em where to stick their bloody feathers and froo-froos. That's all gone now, every pillow burned and every pot of Vaseline smashed — you can't even buy it to grease up handyman tools any more, not around here. Those were good times when I was a bit younger, straightening out the world.

It didn't look pretty when we'd finished, but at least there were no 'packers. Now people like me live here, who'd rather hide in this mess than jump through the hoops you need for a 'factory condominium. And odd Owsians, off-shoots of the ones that are eating up the States from the inside, there are so many there. And a lot of Earth-garbage: Indians and Englanders and Central Europeans. And the odd glamorous Abbo, all gold knuckles and tailoring. It's *colourful*, they tell us; it's got *a polyglot identity that's all its own and very special.* Tourists come here — well, they walk along Darlo Road; they don't explore much either side, where it gets *real* polyglot.

I zigzagged through the lanes towards my place. I was still steaming about my lost money and my wasted bone, steaming at *myself* for having signed that screen and done myself out of what I'd promised myself. There was nothing I could do except go home and take care of myself so I could get some sleep. Then wake up and catch the bike-bus out to Parramatta, pedalling the sun up out of the drowned suburbs behind me.

That EurOwsian beggar girl was on my step again, a bundle like someone's dumped house-rubbish. She crinkled and rustled as I came up. When she saw my face she'd know not to bother me, I hoped.

But it wasn't her voice at all that said, 'Jonah? Yes, it *is* you!'

I backed up against the opposite wall of the entry, my insides gone all slithery. Only bosses called me Jonah, and way-back people who were dead now, from my family, in the days when people had families. Grandparent-type people.

Out of what I had thought was the beggar girl stood this other one that I didn't know at all, shaven-headed and scabby-lipped. 'Fen,' those lips said. 'Fenella. Last year at the Holidaze.'

'Oh!' I almost shouted with the relief of making the connection, although she still didn't click to look at. She put her face more clearly in the way of the gaslight so that I could examine her. 'Fen. Oh, yeah.' I still couldn't see it, but I knew who she was talking about. 'What are you doing in here? I thought you lived up the mountains.'

'I know. I'm sorry. But, really, I've got to tell you something.'

'What's that?'

She looked around at the empty entryway, the empty lane. 'It's kind of private.'

'Oh. You better come up, then.' I hoped she wasn't thinking to get in my bed or anything; I could never put myself close to a mouth in that condition.

She followed me up. She wasn't healthy; two flights and she was breathing hard. All the time I'm, like, *Fen? But Fen had* hair. *She was very nearly* good-looking. *I remember thinking as we snuck off from the party: Oh, my ship's really come in this time — a normal girl and no payment necessary.*

She didn't go mad and attack me for drug money when I lit the lamp and stood back to hold the door for her. She stepped in and took in the sight of my crap out of some kind of habit. She was a girl with background; she would probably normally say something nice to the host. But she was too distracted, here, by the stuff in her own head. I couldn't even begin to dread what that might be.

'Sit?' In front of the black window my only chair looked like, if you sat there, someone would tie you to it, and scald you with Ersatz, or burn you with beedy-ends.

She shook her head. 'It's not as if there's much we can do,' she said, 'but you had to know, I told myself. I thought, Maybe he can get himself tested and they'll give him some involvement, you never know. Or at least send you the bulletins too.'

I tipped my head at her like, *You hear what's coming out your mouth, don't you?* I'd just about had it with women for the night, this one on top of Malka and of Malka's boss with the cream-painted face and the curly smile, all soothing, all understanding, all not-giving-a-centimetre, not giving a cent.

Fen was walking around checking my place out. No, there was nowhere good for us to settle; when I was here on my own I sat in my chair or I lay on my bed, and no one ever visited me. She came and stood facing across me and brought out an envelope that looked just about worn out from her clutching it. She opened it and fingered through the pages folded in there one behind the other. 'Here, this one.' She took it out and unfolded it, but not so I could see. She looked it up and down, up and down. 'Yes. I guess. May as well start at the beginning.' She handed it to me. 'It's not very clear,' she apologised. 'I wouldn't keep still for them. They'd arrested me and I was *pissed off.*' She laughed nervously.

It was a bad copy of a bad printout of a bad colour scan, but even so, even I could work it out. Two arms. Two legs. A full, round head. For a second there I felt as if my own brain had come unstuck and slopped into the bottom of my skull.

'It's . . . It's just like the one on the sign,' I said, with hardly a voice. I meant the billboard up on Taylor Square — well, they were everywhere, really, but I only biked past the others. People picnicked under the Taylor Square one; people held markets and organised other kinds of deals; I sometimes just went up and sat under it and watched them, for something to do. Protect Our Future, it said; it was a government sign, Department of Genetic Protection, I think: a pink-orange baby floating there in its bag like some sleeping water creature, or some being that people might worship — which people kind of did, I guess, with all the fuss about the babies. This was what we were all supposed to be working towards, eh — four proper limbs and a proper-shaped head like every baby's used to be.

Fen looked gleeful as a drugger finding an Ambrosie stash. One of her scabs had split and a bead of blood sat on her lip there.

I went to the chair; it exclaimed in pain and surprise under me. 'What else?' I looked at the envelope in her skeleton hands.

She crossed the room and crouched beside me. She showed me three bulletins, because it was two months old. Each had two images, a face and a full-body. The first one gave me another brain-spasm; it was a girl-baby. *The hope of the line*, said the suits in their speeches on the news screen down the Quay; their faces were always working to stop themselves crying by then; they were going for the full drama. *Man's hope is Woman*, they would blubber. *We have done them so wrong, for so long*.

In every picture the baby girl was perfect — no webbing, no cavities, no frills or stumps, and nothing outside that ought to be in. Fen showed me the part where the name was Joannah. She read me the stats and explained them to me. These things, you could tell from the way she said them, they'd been swimming round and around in her head a long time. They came out in a relief, all rushed and robotic like the datadump you get when you ring up about your Billpay account.

When she finished she checked my reaction. My face felt stiff and cold — I had no blood to spare to work it, it was all busy boiling through my brain. 'It's something, isn't it?' she said.

'You and me under the cup-maker. It only took a few minutes.'

'I know.' She beamed and licked away another drop of blood. 'Who would've thought?'

I was certainly thinking now. I sat heavily back and tried to see my thoughts against the wall, which was a mass of tags from before they'd secured this building. I needed Fen to go away now — I couldn't make sense of this while she was here watching me, trying to work out what I thought, what I felt. But I couldn't send her away, either; this sort of thing takes a certain amount of time and no less, and there was no point being rude. It takes two to tango; no one knew that better than me.

After a while I said, 'I used to walk home behind that Full-Term place.'

'Argh,' she said, and swayed back into a crouch. 'You've got one of those skip stories!'

I nodded. 'Mostly it was closed, and I never lifted the lid myself.'

'But.' She glowered at me.

'If someone had propped it open, with a brick or, once, there was a chair holding it quite wide? Well, then I would go and have a look in. Never to touch anything or anything.'

'Errr-her-her-herrr.' She sat on my scungy carpet square and rocked her face in her hands, and laughed into them.

'One time —'

'No, no, no!' She was still laughing, but with pain in it.

'One time someone had opened it right the way up —'

'No!' she squeaked, and put her hands over her ears and laughed up at me, then took them off again and waited wide-eyed.

'And taken a whole bunch out — it must've been Ukrainians. They will eat anything,' I added, just to make her curl up. 'And they'd chucked them all over the place.'

'No-no!' She hugged her shins and laughed into her knees. This woman had done it, this scrawny body that I couldn't imagine having ever wanted or wanting again, had brought a perfect baby to nine months. In the old days she would have been the woman who *bore my child*, or even *bore me a child*, *bore me a daughter*, and while I had to be glad she wasn't, I . . .

Well, to tell you the truth, I didn't know what to think about her, or about myself, or about those loose sheets of paper around her feet, and the face that was Fen's, that was mine, two in the one. Joannah's — my name cobbled together with a girl's. I didn't have a clue.

'It's true,' I said. 'All these —' I waved at the memory of their disgustingness against the cobbles and the concrete, across the stormwater grille.

'Tell me,' she whispered. 'It's mostly the heads, isn't it?'

'It was mostly the heads.' I nodded. 'Like people had hit them, you know, with baseball bats, big . . . hollows out of them, every which side, sometimes the face, sometimes the back. But it was . . . I don't know, it was every kind of . . . Sometimes no legs, sometimes too many. It was, what do you call those meals, like at the Holidaze, where it's all spread out and you get to put whatever you want of it on your plate?'

'A smorgasbord?'

'That's it.'

'A smorgasbord of deformities, you reckon?'

'Yeah.' *Deformities*, of course — that was what nice people called them. Not *piggies* or *wingies* or *bowlheads*. Not *blobs* for the ones with no heads at all.

'And don't tell me,' said Fen, 'some of them were still alive.'

'Nah, they were dead, all right.'

'Some people say, you know? They see them moving?'

I shook my head. My story was over, and hadn't been as interesting as *some people's*, clearly.

'Well,' she said, and bent to the papers again, and put them in a pile in order.

'Let me see again.' She gave them to me and I looked through them. It was no more believable the second time. 'Can I have these?'

'Oh no,' she said. 'You'll have to go and get tested and take the strips to the Department. Then they'll set you up in the system to get your own copies of everything sent out.'

'That'll cost,' I said glumly. 'The test, and then getting there — that's way up, like, Armidale or somewhere, isn't it? I'd have to get leave.'

'Yes, but you'll get it all back, jizzing into their beakers. Get it all back and more, I'd say. It's good for blokes; you have your little factory that only your own body can run. They have to keep paying you. Us girls they can just chop it all out and ripen the eggs in solution. We only get money the once.'

'They have to plant it back in you, don't they?'

'They have to plant it back in *someone*, but they've got their own childbearers, that passed all the screenings. I don't look so good beside those; where I come from used to be all dioxins. My sister births nothing but duds, and she's got some . . . mental health issues they don't like the sound of.'

'But you brought this one out okay, didn't you, this . . . Joannah?'

'Yeah, but who knows that wasn't a fluke? Besides, I don't want that, for a life. They offered me a trial place there, but I told them they could stick it. I met some of those incubator girls. The bitchery that went on at that place, you wouldn't believe. Good thing they don't do the actual mothering.'

She took the papers from me and we both looked at the top one with its stamp and crest and the baby looking out. Poor little bugger. What did it have to look forward to? Nothing, just growing up to be a girl, and then a woman. Mostly I think that women were put here to make our lives miserable, to tease us and lure us and then not choose us. Or to choose us and then go cold, or toss us aside for the fun of watching us suffer. But you can't think that way about a daughter, can you? How are you *supposed* to think about a daughter?

'Well, good on you, I say.' I tried to sound okay with it, but a fair bit of sourness came through. 'Good on both of us, eh,' I added to cover that up. 'It makes us both look good, eh.'

She folded the papers. 'I guess.' She put them away in the envelope. She gave a little laugh. 'I hardly know you, you know? There was just that one time, and, you know, it wasn't like we had any kind of *relationship*. I didn't know how you were going to take this. But anyway.' She got up, so I did too. She was no taller than me — that was one of the reasons I'd had a chance with her. 'Now you know everything, and . . . I don't know what I thought was going to happen after that! But it's done.' She spread her hands and turned towards the door.

I believe it used not to be like this, people being parents. Olden days, there would have been that whole business of living together and lies and pressures, the *relationship*, which from what I've heard the women always wanted and the men kind-of gave them for the sake of regular sex. Not now, though; it was all genes and printouts now. Everyone was on their own.

I closed the door after Fen, and went and sat with my new knowledge, with my new status. It was some kind of compensation for the rest of my evening, for not getting Malka properly to myself. What's more, I might end up quite tidily-off from this, be able to drop assembly work completely, just sell body fluids. I should feel good; I should feel excited, free and stuff. I should be able to shake off being so annoyed from my poor old withered bone. Some people had simple feelings like that, that could cancel each other out neatly like that.

What I hadn't told Fen, what I wouldn't — her of all people, but I wouldn't tell anyone — was that I used to go home behind the Full-Term place because there was always a chance there'd be someone in labour down the back wards there. And the noises they made, for a bloke who didn't have money then, who was saving up his pennies for a Polar girl, the noises were exactly what I wanted to hear out of a woman. No matter I couldn't see or touch them; it was dark, and I could imagine. I could hang onto the bar fence like the rungs of some big brass bedhead and she would be groaning and gasping, panting her little lump of monster out, or — even better — yowling or bellowing with pain; they all did it different. And some nurse or someone, some nun or whatever they had in there, would be telling her what to do. *Oh, what a racket!* she'd say. *You'd think you were birthing an elephant! Now push with this one, Laurie*. And I'd be outside thinking, *Yeah, push, push!*, and somewhere in the next yowl or roar I would spoof off through the fence and be done. There was nothing like the night air on your man-parts and the darkness hiding you, and a woman's voice urging you on.

There's always the buttoning, though, isn't there? There's always rearranging your clothes around your damp self and shaky knees, zipping, buttoning, belting. There's always turning from the bed and the girl, or the fence and the yowling and the skip there, and being only you in the lane or hallway, with no one missing you or needing you, having paid your fee. You're tingling all around your edges, and the tingle's fading fast, and that old pretend-you floats back out of wherever it went, like sheets of newspaper, blows and sticks to you, so that then it's always there, scraping and dirty and uncomfortable.

I turned out the lamp and crawled into bed. Now stars filled the window. In the old days of full power and streetlights, Sydneysiders saw bugger-all of those, just the moon and a few of the bigger stars. They say you couldn't see the fifth star of the Cross, even. Now the whole damn constellation throbs there in its blanket of galaxy-swirl. People were lucky, then, not knowing what was out there, worse than a few gays poncing about the place, worse than power cuts and restrictions and all these 'dire warnings' and 'desperate pleas', worse than the Environment sitting over us like some giant troll or something, whingeing about how we've treated her. Earth must have been cosy then. Who was it, I wonder, decided we wanted to go emitting all over the frickin universe, saying, *Over here, over here! Nice clean planet! Come here and help us fuck her right up*. That was the bloke we should have smashed the place of. The gays, they weren't harming anyone but themselves.

I jerked awake a couple of times on the way down to sleep. *My life is changed! I am a new man! They'll show me proper respect now, when they see that DNA readout*. To get to sleep, I tried to fool myself I'd dreamed Fen visiting. Passing those billboards every day, and Malka's baby this evening — everything had mishmashed together in my unconscious. I would wake up normal tomorrow, with everything the same as usual. Fen's scabby lips, the proper kisses, full and soft, we'd had behind the cup-maker — thinking about those wouldn't do any good. Push them into some squishy, dark corner of forgetting, and let sleep take me.

AFTERWORD

The image of Malka's 'baby' being born and the fog around that image of Jonah's disgust and scorn for Malka were the first things that arrived when I wrote this story. I had quite a lot of the first scene in a notebook but hadn't thought out the ending when Jack suggested I contribute to *Dreaming Again*. I think it was pretty much the only story I had going that was set in Australia, so I took it up and searched around that scene for the context. Oh dear, oh dear, not a nice context. I did have fun drowning the eastern suburbs, though.

— *Margo Lanagan*

RJURIK DAVIDSON is a freelance writer and editor who travels widely and has lived in Perth and Paris. He has written short stories, essays, screenplays, and reviews and has been short-listed for the Ditmar Award for Best Short Story three times, the Aurealis Award once; and he won the Ditmar Award for Best New Talent in 2005 and Best Short Story in 2007. His stories have appeared in *Year's Best Australian Science Fiction and Fantasy*, volumes one and two; *Australian Dark Fantasy and Horror 2006*; *Fables & Reflections*; *SciFi.com*; *Aurealis*; *Borderlands* and elsewhere. He is the Reviews Editor at *Overland* magazine and currently resides in Melbourne.

In the next story, Davidson takes us to a land redolent with rich scents, a place of strange, surreal, decaying beauty that takes its place in the mind and memory just as J. G. Ballard's evocative *Vermillion Sands* stories did for a previous generation.

Here is a story of possession . . . and abnegation.

TWILIGHT IN CAELI-AMUR

RJURIK DAVIDSON

The front of the house is overgrown with weeds, allowed to grow wild and free as they do on the hills behind Caeli-Amur. It's a grand old façade: pillars to the side of the double doors, which stand open; windows high on the second floor overlooking the tree-lined street. In this part of Caeli-Amur, furnace trees line the sides of the road, their round bulbs overhead like lanterns in the night, collecting the heat in summer, emitting it in soft warm glows during winter. Now the sun's light has softened so the cobblestoned streets, the other grand houses with their balconies and domed roofs, the horse and carriage that I've just left by the side of the road, seem faded.

With trepidation, one foot after the other, stopping and then again advancing, I enter Director Didion's house.

'Madame Didion, Madame Didion?' My voice echoes strangely around the entry hall with its two staircases that rise along each wall and join on the overlooking balcony above. Half-dead vines crawl from immense pots along the staircase rails, their brown leaves drooping, once-yellow candle-flowers trying desperately to pierce the gloom. They would have been magnificent once, fitting of Director Didion's house, but now their withered trunks, knobbly and dry, remind me of dead bodies found high in the mountains. Candle-flowers are not one of the plants that Didion created, but grow wild in certain marshes south of Caeli-Amur where at night, if you can bear the swarms of airborne insects and avoid falling into one of the treacherous bogs, the flowers light the air like a thousand magical flames scattered by some romantic god. The plants Didion designed always had a more dangerous beauty.

Open doorways gape to either side of the entrance hall, and shadowy forms seem to move there in the darkness accompanied by scuttling noises. At any moment I expect creatures to burst through those doorways, but it is surely just my feverish imagination. Nevertheless, rumours come to mind that I have not thought of for fifteen years, since I was a student following in Didion's dark shadow at House Arbor. There, jealous inferiors had concocted all kinds of spiteful stories: of his hidden secrets and sexual depredations, of how he had taken other thaumaturgists' works and pretended they were his own, of how he favoured those students loyal to him, and excluded the brightest and the best.

I sneeze. Dust. Dust everywhere, a thin layer coating the floors, a powdery sea.

'Madame Didion?' *Where is she?*

Advancing beneath the staircases, I pass into a corridor on the opposite side of the room. Along the walls stand statues of bizarre creatures or gods, trunks sprouting from their faces, strange implements in hand. There are doors between each statue, and everywhere dead plants: once writhing silk-vines frozen and stiff, baby furnace trees in alcoves, their bulbs collapsed like empty bladders, or desolate sticks emerging from dry pots. I try not to sneeze. Already my nose is becoming blocked.

'Madame Didion?'

I look through the door to my left, and there she is, seated on an intricately patterned couch. A table has been pushed up against the wall and fruit sits in a bowl, small orange and grey balls merging with each other. The smell of something rotting hovers in the air. A fat, black cat scuttles beneath my feet and bolts down the hallway.

'Oh,' says Madame Didion, looking up towards me, her eyes tiny in her cadaverous face. 'Oh, I didn't hear you come in.'

'The door was open.'

'Oh, I know,' she says. 'I leave it open. I don't care.'

'But people might come in.' Images of thieves flash into my mind, with old Madame Didion helpless and frail on the couch.

'They don't,' she says.

'I suppose it's not the area for it.'

There's an uncomfortable silence for a moment and I shift my weight from one foot to another.

'Well sit down,' she says irritably, in the tone that she would use with a servant.

She has an extraordinary face, so old that it resembles a skull. The terribly thin skin has shrunk around the bones beneath. Red splotches dot her face and her hat casts a faint shadow, as if she's hiding herself from view.

I sit in a chair opposite hers and neither of us speaks. She rubs one bony hand with the thumb of the other, purple veins running beneath the white skin. She doesn't look at me, but stares away at an angle towards the middle of the room. Another cat, this one with patches of white and black and ginger, pokes its head around the corner of the doorway, examines the scene for a moment and disappears.

I want to ask her about the notebooks, to have her collect them so I can get out of the house, but it is too soon and it would be rude. I shift in my seat unable to find a comfortable position. I have been warned: she does not want to give up the notebooks.

'Have you seen the house?' she asks eventually.

'No.'

'Of course not. I keep thinking you were one of his colleagues. But I suppose you're much too young.' She speaks as if he were here, as if he were still alive.

'I'm thirty-six,' I say in my defence.

'Yes,' she says, 'too young. He's been gone a long time you know.'

I search for something to say but only remember the reports of his affairs and his domineering temper; of how he struck his students with a knotted rope as he paced behind their chairs, leaving them stammering and red-faced and all the more likely to forget his formulae; and how, as if to make up for these cruelties, he lavished them with opulent gifts of rare spices and pieces of ancient or lost technology.

'But even so,' she says in an unusually reserved manner, each word measured to reduce its effect, 'I remember him like it was yesterday. He was considered quite handsome in those days. A dashing figure, really.'

'I've heard only the best things about him,' I say, 'stories of his brilliance.'

'Everyone liked him,' she says.

'Well, his achievements were enormous. We've all studied his theorems. His *Formulae for the Merging of Plant Species* is still the basic text in the House. And the new species — well, *Toxicodendron Didion* still protects the outer walls of House Arbor's palace.'

She sits up straighter as I speak and the edges of a satisfied smile play on her face. She must have basked in his triumphs for all those years and I thank the gods I'm not a woman. I couldn't bear to be excluded from House Arbor's laboratories, or from intrigues between the Houses. But then I'm a thaumaturgist and a man. One day I may even become Director.

'Come,' she says. 'Let me show you the house.' She stands and she seems smaller than I had first thought.

The house has vast expanses, great empty sitting rooms filled with coffee tables surrounded by delightfully embroidered chairs, now colourless beneath the dust, and some visibly mouse-eaten. Despite these holes the chairs are still arranged just so.

'He liked *order*,' she says definitely. 'He liked things to be in their place.'

The dust overwhelms me again and I sneeze.

'You're sick,' she says.

'Oh, it's nothing.'

We pass through a ballroom, the walls lost in the gloom. Outside, the sun must be descending fast. 'We danced here. You should have seen the dances!' She leads me along grey corridors. 'We had many servants, you know. How the house was abuzz!' Kitchens lay off to the side. Somehow we end up in a wild and overgrown garden.

We follow a path that runs up along the middle of the garden which lies silently in the twilight. To both sides the weeds and grasses and bushes are so thick as to be impenetrable, their colour taking on an extra shade of blue-grey, an intimation of the approaching night. Some lean over the path, green turning to brown as the year moves on, leaves dropping and mounding up on the side of the path.

We come out into a central patio, two long lines of tear-flowers, fully five feet tall with heads like bloodied plates, running parallel to each other on the sides. Around them there are no weeds and the earth looks freshly turned and fertilised.

'Here are my flowers,' she says. As we approach, the flowers lean towards us and emit that faint wailing, like the cries of faraway children, and nectar slowly runs from their heads and down their petals. They recognise my thaumaturgical power — that is what they are designed to do. I stop and Madame Didion walks on. I note, with some surprise, that the flowers turn away from me and follow her, as she passes. Perhaps they have grown accustomed to her.

She reaches in, touches one and it shivers in delight, its petals undulating, calling her closer. I want to reach in and pull her away from its deadly calls but they are her flowers, and she has no doubt been here a thousand times. The only danger is to me.

As she walks along the rows, the tear-flowers, wailing and weeping, lean in further towards her, their heads following her down the path. A few notice me and turn indecisively before they lean back towards her.

A greenhouse stands on the other side of the courtyard, creeper vines covering it and enclosing it, passing through the broken panes inside.

She passes along the other side of the patio and reaches out as the flowers on that side join the crying and weeping. 'They have a wonderful sound, don't they? Almost melodic, like an aria,' she says.

'They do,' I say, even as I resist the pull of that mesmerising call. One does not lie down in a row of tear-flowers. No — *they like their blood and bone*.

'How long have you had them?' I ask.

'The same length of time they've had me,' she says beaming. Her face is alive here — the flesh around her cheekbones suddenly rising, the eyes wider and sparkling. Suddenly she doesn't look so old.

'So how many notebooks are there?' I ask.

'Notebooks?' she raises both hands, palms upwards as if the notebooks don't matter and shrugs. 'Oh, three or four.'

'Oh,' I say, 'I thought there were six.'

She suddenly stops and turns towards the flowers, her back to me. 'Oh, yes,' she says almost inaudibly, 'six.' She steps closer to the flowers and, by instinct, I step towards her. The flowers lean in and nestle around her, caressing her face with their petals. Their nectar drips onto her shoulder. I should pull her away, but she is fine. And I don't wish to get too close to them. Already I feel like walking among them, listening to their mournful music, lying down beneath their flowing tears and closing my eyes, sleeping. There I would never wake, but would dwell in strange reverie, semi-conscious, sucked through their roots and up along their stems so that, even as I lay half-alive at their base, we would become one living creature — the flowers and I.

She steps backwards. 'Let me show you the rest of the house.'

'But the notebooks . . .'

'Ah yes,' she says. 'Come on then.'

Retracing our steps, we reach a vast dining room, the table set for a banquet. There are no notebooks to be seen.

'There he is!' she says. 'Magnificent, isn't he?'

The portrait shows a stern man, powerful. He has grey hair, and an angular, harsh face. His eyes stare out with fire and passion. It is painted in the style of the forties, so there's something unreal about it: the power and the sternness of the portrait reside simply in the form. House Arbor has always used that style, still does to this day. I try to reconstruct what he would have looked like, to distil the reality of the man from the pomp and façade of the painting.

'Yes,' I say, 'magnificent.'

'He was a good man. He served House Arbor all his life. He was loyal, to all of us, and look, he built us this house and he gave us three wonderful children. And they gave us grandchildren. What more can you ask for?'

'Your children, they work for the House?'

'No, they are up north, in Varenis.'

'So you never see your grandchildren?'

'Oh no. Anyway, I wouldn't want them to come here. I'd scare them.'

'Well, you are quite . . . powerful,' I say.

'I think they'd be scared by how old I am,' she says.

'So these notebooks . . . are they all about thaumaturgical anabolism and hybridisation?' I ask.

She looks up at the portrait and then away again as she speaks: 'He practically invented it, you know. He would retreat into the library, all kinds of philosophy and theory spread out on the desk. You should have seen him. And the delight of discovery! When he first recognised how to augment the speed of plant growth by the connection of previously unrelated thaumaturgical formulae. The way, suddenly, a whole new world opened up in his mind and everything seemed wondrous and strange.' I'm taken aback by the way she stares off into the distance as she speaks.

'And then later,' she says, 'he found he could use some of the same equations not just to speed up the growth of plants, but animals too. And why not humans?'

'But it was never done,' I say.

'Who knows what the House did? He was a theoretician; he did all the formulation of the initial foundations of that branch of thaumaturgy. He was an innovator. He created new plants, but they were mainly for theoretical research. What Arbor did with that knowledge, it kept to itself. Perhaps you know — you're a thaumaturgist for the House.'

'I don't know,' I say, and she smiles, knowing that I could not say even if I wanted to. She nods and looks back up at the portrait.

'Talented . . .' she says slowly.

She turns suddenly towards me, and leans in, an innocent look on her face, pleading and beckoning, almost siren-like. 'Does the House really need them? I mean, after all these years?'

I bet she used that look to seduce many a man when she was young. It's an unfair thought, but it comes to me just the same.

'Perhaps you could make copies . . .' I say, but the absurdity of it strikes me and in any case, House Arbor would never allow it. Control, order, system — these are the House's watchwords.

She curls her lip, and again I feel like a servant. 'Does a painter make do with duplicates of a painting? A writer, copies of his first manuscript? An original is an original. Anyway, these are in his handwriting, a piece of him. You think a copy can reproduce *him*?'

Foolishly I stand at attention, like a chastened child, but her voice softens again. 'I mean . . . they're the last thing I have to remember him by.' Behind those words I hear the entire edifice she has created, the entire world of her life and her place in it, defined by her relationship to him, the innovator, the originator.

I look around the room and back to the painting. He seems to be challenging me, daring me to betray his memory. I look at Madame Didion and she shrinks backwards, turns away and says, 'They're in the library.'

She stands still for a moment and then, in a broken voice says, 'Excuse me for a moment.' She shuffles quickly back into the corridor where she sobs, high and uncontrolled. I remain still, before the portrait of her dead husband as she weeps on the other side of the wall, emitting low and uncontrolled gutteral sounds and great heaving breaths. We stay there, on opposite sides of the wall, like mirror images of each other, as the house descends into yet a darker shade of gloom. Finally the sobbing stops and shortly afterwards she comes back into the room.

'I'm looking forward to showing you the library,' she says, 'I'm sure you'll like it.'

It's a whole wing, the library, with stairs rising to antechambers, little grottos filled with ramshackle shelves, some entirely covered with grassy mould or lichen, as if thin green blankets have been thrown over them. But no! I think. Not the books! What wonders could be lost in there?

I follow her into a splendid circular domed study, with a massive desk made of oak resplendent under the glass ceiling, the sky now a darkest shade of blue. The dust has taken this place too but Madame Didion is oblivious to it.

Everything has a ramshackle feel, disorganised and cluttered. Piles of yet more books stand beneath the shelves, towers threatening to fall onto each other. Scrolls in a great sea to one side of the desk, which is cluttered with tiny statues and fountain pens and ink wells and mechanical watches and incense burners and other assorted knick-knacks. It is so *disorderly*.

'Are the notebooks here?'

She looks away breathing rapidly, her small chest rising and falling. I put my hand to my face. She looks like she might cry again and I shift my weight from one foot to the other. I hope she doesn't cry again.

Madame Didion looks back at me for a moment. Her gaze holds mine and we wait, as if to see whether the other will break. I cannot ask her again for the notebooks.

'Here they are,' she says finally, and reaches up to a book-filled shelf. She pulls down two large books. Didion's famous notebooks. I look at them, with their thick leather binding. Dust makes the brown leather appear grey.

She holds them in her hands, and rubs her bony little thumbs over the soft leather and the fine engravings, once silver but now only residues remain. She rubs the books the same way she rubbed her hands earlier.

'You'd better take them,' she says, but instead of giving them to me, she places them on the desk, away from me, and steps backwards. A parchment sits on the desk; my eyes strain in the darkness to make out a spidery handwriting laying out formulae, equations, paragraphs of reasoning. Beside the parchment lie the pages of a manuscript. Neither is dust-covered.

'Six?'

'Oh yes, the others are up there on the shelf. You'd better get them.'

We stand there, in some sort of counterpoint. Perhaps I could only take four, then at least she'd have two left. But I know it's impossible. The items will be taken to the House Arbor Palace, itemised, shelved, studied by the House Thaumaturgists. Dissertations and critiques will be written, lectures and debates organised. Careers will be made. I must take them all or questions will be asked.

'It was you, wasn't it?' I ask.

'I don't know what you're talking about, dear.'

'You were the one, not him. You. I saw the way the flowers leaned in towards you. *Your* flowers. And these: *your* notebooks.'

'Oh, don't be ridiculous.' She turns away, looks for no reason towards a shelf on the wall. 'Don't be silly,' she says again, quietly.

But even now I can see the sheen of thaumaturgy around her. I've studied Carel's *Ontology of the Thaumaturgical Universe* and Taslin's *Structure and Augury*. I can read the powers in the air; I can put together formulae and equations, one after the other, connecting and intertwining them just so. I can see her aura now that I'm looking for it, wavy and old in the darkness that encloses us. Her pride will keep her secret until death, and I will not betray it.

'Take the books and I'll show you out,' she says.

She leads me through that massive and empty mansion, the dust billowing about us. It is almost completely dark now, and dead plants emerge from the gloom like ghostly relics of some ancient desert and the doors gape like even blacker holes in the night. When we come to the entrance hall the candle-flowers on the vine try desperately to emit a tiny yellow light.

'Aren't they beautiful,' she says, standing next to the grand staircase.

I try not to sneeze as I make my way to the grand entrance doors. I pass through them and look back. She stands there, beside the half-dead vine, like a ghost herself.

'Shall I shut the doors?'

'Don't bother,' she says. 'I don't care.'

'People might come in.'

'They don't.'

I nod (though I doubt she sees it in the darkness) and turn away.

'Why don't you come again?' she says. 'We've had such a lovely time.'

I turn back. 'Yes. Perhaps I will.' I feel guilty saying it and, as if it will make a difference, add: 'I think I might.'

And then I turn and head out of Director Didion's house and up to the street. Stars twinkle between quickly moving clouds. The horse and carriage stands silent and waiting on the street: the horse's head down and unmoving, the driver waiting patiently as is proper when transporting a thaumaturgist of House Arbor. The bulbs on the furnace trees have begun to glow, and even now, as autumn is upon us, I can feel the faint warmth emanating from them, like little fires hanging in the night. It will not be long now until winter.

AFTERWORD

The most interesting characters are often those torn by a number of contending forces. And those sorts of characters are ones who stand on the borders — of race, class, gender, sexuality, politics. What interested me especially was the ways in which Madame Didion sees herself and her place in the world. I've always been interested in the ways in which we deceive ourselves because we gain some kind of benefit, even if that benefit is outweighed by the cost. The union bureaucrat, the government environmentalist, the career feminist — all of these are lodged in a contradictory position, and all have to generate an idea of themselves, an identity which can make sense of these contradictions and, at the same time, justify them. In order to do so, a lot must be left unspoken. In any case, there are two parts to *all* of us. There's our public face: the part of us we deem fit to show the world, the mask we put on in the morning. Then there's the internal life that we hide away: thoughts and dreams that we don't tell anyone. Because of this, what we say is not quite what we think. Part of getting to know someone is to penetrate through the mask to this hidden identity. This story is about that process. It's about those times when the secrets are unable to be kept hidden.

— *Rjurik Davidson*

JANEEN WEBB is a multiple award winning author, editor, and critic who has written or edited ten books and over a hundred stories and essays. She is a recipient of the World Fantasy Award, the Australian Aurealis Award, and a three-time winner of the Ditmar Award. Her current novel series for young readers, The Sinbad Chronicles, has been called a 'seamless interweaving of the stories of Sinbad and Ulysses' and 'a great combination of mermaids, genies, pirates, leviathans, witches, magic carpets, windsurfing, and lip-gloss.' The series includes *Sailing to Atlantis* and *The Silken Road to Samarkand*. She is internationally recognised for her critical work in speculative fiction and has contributed to most of the standard reference texts in the field. She holds a PhD in literature from the University of Newcastle. Janeen was co-editor of *Australian Science Fiction Review*, and also co-editor, with Jack Dann, of the original *Dreaming Down-Under*. She divides her time between Melbourne and a small farm overlooking the sea near Wilson's Promontory.

Due to circumstances beyond her control, Janeen has not been writing lately. Sometimes it really pays for the editor to be the writer's spouse because I knew where she had hidden her last unpublished story. The result of some expert cajoling on the part of your editor is the publication of the wry, witty, turn-the-world-upside-down tale that follows. Here is a quintessential Adam and Eve story, the first dinosaur story … of sorts, a poetic homage to Milton, and a show-don't-tell killer response to all those creative creationists espousing the logics of intelligent design …

PARADISE DESIGN'D

JANEEN WEBB

'No one must speak of this, ever.'

'He'll know,' Michael said glumly.

'Obviously,' said Raphael. 'What Gabriel means is that we don't need the news to get out elsewhere.'

'And as long as we tidy up here, there's no reason it should,' Uriel added. 'He's very protective of His little experiment. Hardly anyone's allowed to come here.'

The four archangels looked down again at the untidy pile of bloodied feathers that was all that remained of their brother, Floriel. Beside him lay the corpse of the guilty T. Rex, still smoking from the fiery sword thrust that had dispatched it.

Michael shuddered. 'It's still got feathers in its teeth,' he said, 'and shreds of Floriel.'

Gabriel winced, and readjusted his own shining wings. 'We're only here because He sent us to guard His pets,' he said. 'So what was Floriel doing here anyway?'

'Designing flowers, he said.' Raphael shrugged. 'I warned him about these monsters.' He gestured at the corpse. 'Just look at the teeth on that thing.'

'So how do those two' — Uriel gestured briefly to where Adam and Eve crouched behind a huge cycad, watching wide-eyed and unafraid, — 'manage to go about completely unscathed?'

'He forbade it. All the carnivores are blocked from attacking His pets in His Garden,' Raphael replied. 'It would be a different story outside the Gates.'

'I guess He just forgot to include angels in the ban,' Michael said. 'He's not infallible.'

'Don't let Him hear you say that,' Gabriel said urgently. 'He's a bit touchy on the subject, ever since you-know-who rebelled.'

'Let's not even think about that, just in case.' Uriel looked around nervously. 'And what exactly are we going to do about the monster?'

Gabriel smiled his dazzling smile, and raised his flaming sword in salute. 'I think a little landscaping is in order,' he said.

The others smiled back.

'Molten rock? Landslide? Raging torrent?' said Raphael.

'I thought something simpler — something small enough to do the job without attracting attention.'

'Well?'

'I propose that we should just slide this little bit of land and vegetation into that little hollow down there, and then apply some heat and pressure. That way we can bury the evidence and, after the flames die down, the pit will look like a natural pool.'

'Clever,' said Uriel. 'I like it.'

'Then let's do it,' said Michael. 'These things are best done quickly.'

All four archangels raised their swords then brought the fiery tips down in the one place. Rock collapsed, lush jungle toppled into the hole, and the remains of the Tyrannosaurus Rex slipped down after it. After a few moments, all that remained was compacted earth and a deep tar pit, black and sticky, although tell-tale red flames still licked the surface and noxious vapours swirled about the valley.

'It'll soon be still,' Gabriel said. 'I think it looks fine.'

'But won't other animals fall in and be trapped?' Michael said, looking meaningfully to where a curious stegosaurus had already wandered perilously close to the brink.

Raphael shrugged. 'He didn't forbid collateral damage,' he said. 'There's no shortage of wildlife here. There were lots of small things living in that bit of jungle. Maybe a few fossils will add to the charm of the Garden.'

'Too late to worry about it now,' Uriel said.

The stegosaur had already toppled in. Suspicious-looking bubbles were rising to the surface.

'We'd better warn the pets,' Gabriel said.

'How do we warn creatures that have no knowledge of sin or death?' said Michael. 'They witnessed the whole thing, and they don't even look worried.'

'They're trained to obedience. We just tell them,' Raphael said. 'I'll do it, if you like.'

'You can try,' said Michael. 'Maybe they can understand.'

Raphael walked slowly towards the humans. 'Do not be alarmed,' he said. 'I bring you tidings.'

Adam stood to meet the angel. 'Hail, thou wondrous celestial messenger,' he said solemnly.

Raphael ignored the sniggering of his brother angels behind him. 'I bring you warning,' he said. 'For your own safety, you must not go near the new pool. It is dangerous.'

'Can we not drink from it?' asked Adam.

'No,' said Raphael. 'It is unfit for you.'

Adam looked around him, hesitating until Eve came forward and took his hand. They both looked up adoringly at the angel.

Raphael tried again. 'It is important that you do not go near the new pool,' he said. 'Can you both remember that?'

'That's three things, ethereal one,' Adam said.

'What?'

'Three things we must not eat or drink: fruit from that tree, fruit from the other tree, and now water from the new pool.'

Raphael nodded. 'That's right,' he said. 'Those three things are not fit for such as you.'

'We will remember, shining one,' said Adam.

'We will remember,' Eve echoed.

'Then all is well,' said Raphael, fervently hoping it would be.

Michael snickered. 'That was convincing,' he said.

'Not to worry,' said Gabriel, wrinkling his perfect nose. 'The smell should keep them off.'

Raphael shrugged. 'I tried.' He glanced around hurriedly. 'Any sign of trouble?'

'Nothing so far,' said Uriel.

'Probably too busy laughing,' said Michael.

'Wonderful!' Satan's laughter resounded from the iron Gates of Hell, echoing through the cavernous depths.

Beside him, sitting at their ease, Sin and Death were laughing with him.

'Do you still want to be bothered corrupting the pets?' Death asked.

'Oh yes,' Satan replied. 'The sport's too good to miss.'

'Then I suggest you wait till nightfall,' Sin said, still laughing. 'Those angels will be tired of guarding the Gates of Paradise by then. They've had a busy day.'

'Quite so,' said Satan. 'But they don't sleep. Any suggestions about how I should break in?'

'Mist is always good,' said Death. 'Anything can happen in a dense mist.'

'Good idea,' said Sin. 'Fog and mist are such useful things.'

'I'll think about it,' said Satan.

*   *   *

'Everything seems quiet enough now,' Raphael said. He was leaning against the Gate, lit only by the glow of his sword.

'True,' Uriel replied from the opposite gatepost. 'But the fog still seems very thick around the tar pit. We've lost a triceratops now, and a few smaller creatures besides.'

'Stop worrying about the dinosaurs,' said Raphael. 'There's nothing we can do to stop them going too near the pool. And anyway, the vapours will probably dissipate with the sunrise.'

'I suppose so.'

Both angels watched carelessly as a thick, long tendril of mist snaked silently towards a herd of drowsing brontosaurus.

'Our labours await, my dear,' said Adam, yawning and stretching in the first rays of morning sunlight. Pterodactyls soared overhead in a perfectly blue sky, their harsh cawing echoing across the lush landscape of Eden. The air still smelled faintly noxious.

Eve looked up, all innocence. 'I thought I might work alone this morning,' she said. 'We could achieve more if we divide the tasks between us.'

'But darling Eve, we must stay together. Hast thou forgotten that an angel warned me against a malicious Enemy who envies our happiness and seeks to destroy us? Together, each can offer aid to the other and the Enemy cannot circumvent us, but each of us alone is more vulnerable. I think it best that I should guard thee.'

Eve drew herself up. 'All Earth's lord,' she said, 'dost thou doubt my firmness to God or to thee? Dost thou fear I am so weak that my love and faith can be so easily shaken? Dost thou truly think so little of me?'

'Of course not, darling Eve, daughter of light,' Adam replied. 'I do not doubt thee. I sought only to avoid the attempt — if the Enemy sees that we are together, he will not assault us. If we are apart, he may try, and I would not have thee in harm's way through my own neglect.'

'And are we then to dwell in fear, constrained by an unseen foe? Are we to be always together because we doubt our integrity to resist the Enemy?'

'But Eve, daughter of heaven, the Enemy may be too subtle for us. I was told he has seduced angels.'

'That does not mean he will seduce us,' Eve said firmly. 'And besides,' she smiled, 'what is faith, love or virtue if it is never tested?'

Adam sighed. 'As God has given us free will, I will not constrain thee. But Eve, I beg thee, seek not temptation.'

'I am forewarned, my lord and husband,' Eve replied, already leaving.

Eve was deep in the Garden, humming to herself as she twisted tender new tendrils onto their supporting trees, when the brontosaurus spoke.

'Hail, Queen of Eden,' it said.

Eve looked around, but could see no one. 'Who speaks?' she said.

'I, sovereign mistress,' said the tempter through the brontosaurus that carried him. 'Do not be alarmed. I have long admired and adored thee, and now I have the means to tell thee.' The elongated, snaky neck bent low before her as the giant creature bowed.

'But how can this be?' said Eve. 'The tongues of brutes cannot pronounce the language of man.'

'Empress of Eden,' the creature replied, 'I shall explain all, if you command.'

Eve nodded her assent.

'There is a tree,' the tempter said, 'whereon hangs wondrous fruit of red and gold, the fruit so high above the ground that you could not reach it, nor can other creatures. But I, with my long neck, am able to pluck the fruit and eat my fill. And so I did. And, beauteous mistress, from that very moment there was a strange alteration in me — both reason and speech, so long desired, were mine, and knowledge too, though my shape changed not.'

'There are many trees that grow in Paradise, so various that many are yet unknown to us,' said Eve. 'Can you say where grows this tree, and how far?'

'It will be my greatest pleasure, lady of Paradise, to conduct thee there. The way is not long.'

'Then lead on,' said Eve.

The tempter turned the dinosaur, and Eve followed in its swaying wake, musing on the ungainliness of the beast, until it stopped at last before one of the trees of prohibition.

'Strange creature, I fear we might have spared ourselves this journey,' Eve said. 'The fruit of this tree is wondrous indeed if it has caused such effects in thee, but God has commanded that of this tree we may not taste or touch. So it must be fruitless to me, though there is fruit in excess.'

'How strange,' the tempter replied, 'that God has made you lords of all in earth or air, yet forbids you to eat certain fruit.'

'We are forbidden,' Eve said simply, 'lest we die.'

'How can you believe that,' said the brontosaurus, 'when I who have eaten of the fruit stand alive before you? I who have now risen above my lot by eating of the fruit tell you that it brings knowledge, not death.'

Eve hesitated.

The tempter pressed on. 'Would a loving God deny you knowledge that will so enhance your care of this Garden? Would He not rather applaud your enterprise? Is He not a fond parent, waiting for the day that you put off childish ignorance and, knowing good and evil, become as He is. For, celestial lady, if a brute such as I am raised to your human level through eating of the fruit, would not you, in proportion, be raised to godlike status? You are already a goddess in beauty — should you not seek to match that beauty with understanding?'

'I don't know,' said Eve.

'Wherein lies the offence that you should seek to know what can be known?' said the tempter. 'How could your knowledge hurt God?'

'I don't know,' said Eve.

'Then look more closely at the fruit,' said the tempter. The brontosaurus reached out, delicately plucked a ripe fruit and dropped it at Eve's feet. 'How can it do any harm?'

'I don't know,' Eve said a third time.

She stooped and picked up the rosy fruit, surprised by the smooth texture of its sun-warmed skin. She caressed it, held it to her face, and then found herself inhaling its fragrance. Her mouth watered at the divine smell of it, and before she had thought further she was nuzzling it, licking it, nipping it with her white teeth. The tiniest spot of juice broke the skin, just enough for her to taste.

The world changed.

Eve bit then in earnest, burying her face in the fruit. Rich juice ran down her naked skin and fell dripping from her perfect breasts as, heedless of the watching brontosaurus, she engorged greedily and without restraint, hungrily eating death in her ecstasy.

The tempter had to look away.

When Eve was finally satiated, she wiped her hands on her naked thighs, leaving sticky trails there as she turned back, flushed, to the tempter. 'I need another fruit,' she said. 'As I am your sovereign lady, I bid you fetch it for me.'

'Certainly, my lady,' the tempter replied. 'But is it wise to eat more of the fruit before you truly learn its effects?'

'I need it for my husband,' she said. 'If you are right, and God is not angered, then all is well. But if He has seen, and decrees my death, then I shall be no more and Adam will be wedded to another Eve. I cannot bear that thought, and so I am resolved that he will share with me, for well or woe.'

'Your wish is my command, empress,' said the tempter. The brontosaurus obligingly stretched up and brought down another fruit.

Adam looked up in surprise as his wife came to him, carrying a new-picked fruit that exuded ambrosial aromas.

'I am making a garland for thee, beloved,' he said, offering her the armful of flowers he had been gathering against her return.

'Thank you, my lord,' she said. 'But I have a more important thing for thee.' She held out the fruit.

Adam stared at it, wondering why she blushed so deeply to look upon it.

'I met a strange creature,' she said breathlessly, 'who proved to me that the tree forbidden is not a tree of danger, as we were told, but a tree of divine effect to make as gods those who taste. The brontosaurus had eaten of the fruit and was not dead, but newly endowed with human sense and speech and reason. So I also have eaten, and in growing to godhead have now understood that my future bliss will be tedious if not shared with thee.' She looked at him with pleading eyes. 'Fate will not now permit me to renounce Deity for thee, my lord, and so you too must eat of the fruit, that we may be again equal in love and joy.'

'My wife, my darling, thou fairest of creation,' Adam stammered. 'What hast thou done?'

'Nothing that is not for thy benefit, my lord.'

'Nothing? Thou art lost — defaced, deflowered, and now to death devoted. Did'st thou not suspect that the creature may have been the Enemy of whom we were warned?'

Eve hesitated.

Before she could frame an answer, Adam went on, talking to himself, trying to reason out his dilemma. 'But how should I lose thee,' he said, 'and live again alone in this wilderness? How should I be parted from thee, thou who art flesh of my flesh, bone of my bone, how should I live without thee?'

'That need not be, my lord,' Eve said, moving closer to him, her movements sinuous, beguiling.

Adam reached out to her, embraced her, inhaling the perfume of forbidden fruit from her hair, her skin. He breathed deeply, feeling the stirrings of lust. He nuzzled her neck, licking the residue of death's juices, and was lost.

'Give me the fruit,' he said.

Taking her by the sticky hand, he raised the fruit to his mouth and bit down upon it as he led her, smiling, into the depths of their green bower.

'That was close,' said Gabriel. 'I've never seen Him so angry.'

'Lucky for us He agreed that we could not have prevented the Enemy from entering the Garden as mist,' Raphael said. 'We could have been sharing the fate of the hapless brontosaurus.' He shivered in sympathy.

'That is unfortunate,' Michael said. 'But He has a point.'

'But the poor creature was innocent,' said Uriel. 'It was terribly confused when the Enemy stopped inhabiting it.'

'But it still wanted to eat the fruit,' said Michael. 'And what one brontosaurus eats, so do the rest. You'd have to agree that a herd of suddenly sentient dinosaurs would create problems for Him.'

'True,' said Uriel. 'But I still think that taking away their bodies and leaving their necks and heads to become serpents was extreme. The tallest of creatures are now the lowest, condemned forever to crawl on their stomachs and eat bitter dust.'

'They'll survive better outside Eden that way,' said Raphael. 'They are banished too, don't forget.'

'Well, He couldn't leave them here, could He?' said Gabriel. 'The temptation would always be there, and serpents could still coil themselves up the Tree.'

'Too late to worry about it now,' said Raphael. 'He has spoken.'

'And the pets are condemned to make their own way in the world outside the Garden,' said Uriel.

'I feel bad about that,' said Michael. 'We didn't protect them very well, did we?'

'We tried,' said Raphael. 'But we can't help them now.'

'Why not?' said Gabriel.

'And disobey Him?' Michael said incredulously.

'Of course not,' Gabriel replied. 'But I'm thinking that we can at least atone for our part in this whole miserable episode.'

'How?' Raphael asked.

'Well,' said Gabriel, 'He has decreed who should go from the Garden, but He hasn't said anything about who should stay.'

'Good thinking,' said Uriel. 'Maybe we can help them survive a little longer.'

'Let's do it,' said Michael.

Adam and Eve walked miserably towards the Gates, downcast and uncomfortable in their awkward clothing of leaves tied on with lengths of vine.

'It's the best I could do,' Eve whined.

'Obviously,' said Adam. 'It's your "best" that got us into this mess.'

The archangels stepped forward as the humans drew level with the Gates.

'Stop bickering and listen up,' said Raphael, hefting the fiery sword for emphasis.

'Greetings, thou celestial messenger,' Adam began.

'Forget all that,' Michael said sharply. 'Are you ready to leave?'

Adam nodded dejectedly.

'Then get going,' Raphael said, opening the Gates just wide enough for the two humans to pass.

'We're giving you a head start,' Gabriel added in a theatrical whisper. 'Make the best of it.'

Puzzled, Adam and Eve stepped beyond the lush portal that had opened in the tropical wall of rainforest, and through into a harsher land. Hard at their heels a horde of serpents slithered and slipped through rising dust in a frantic rush for cover. The air was thinner, the sun hotter, the vegetation sparser. Everything was different. Eve tried to take Adam's hand, but he shrugged her away, radiating bad temper. She walked on, feeling the first prickles of sweat and sunburn. The palm-frond skirt felt scratchy, the ground was rough beneath her bare feet. The child in her belly kicked — the first murderer was restless too.

The howl of a hunting T. Rex pierced the air. Eve looked back, and felt for the first time the thrill of physical fear.

Behind the fiery swords that barred the way, velociraptors clamoured at the Gates of Eden.

AFTERWORD

The Genesis for 'Paradise Design'd' was a television interview in which I saw apologists for 'intelligent design' insisting that there had been dinosaurs in the Garden of Eden. I then recalled that Milton had neglected to include dinosaurs when explaining the ways of God to man in *Paradise Lost*, and concluded that a further story was needed to remedy that lack. The dinosaurs, alas, were behaving badly.

— *Janeen Webb*

TRENT JAMIESON lives in Brisbane. He has had more than sixty short stories published over the last decade, including 'Slow & Ache,' which won the 2006 Aurealis Award for best science fiction short story. His work has been published in *Future Orbits, Agog, Andromeda Spaceways Inflight Magazine, Daikaiju!, Encounters, The Devil in Brisbane, Nemonymous 4, Nowa Fantastyka, Aurealis, Eidolon* and *Altair.* His short story collection *Reserved for Traveling Shows* was published in 2006, and his first children's novel, *The City and the Stony Stars,* is part of the Lost Shimmaron series published by ABC Books.

'The New Deal' is a wild storm of a story, dark as the twisted alleys of a ruined, deserted city. Revelations come in blinding flashes in this hard-boiled surrealistic detective tale about sex, death and undeath, and deals with those dangerous and devious powerbrokers on high . . .

THE NEW DEAL

TRENT JAMIESON

'You hear about the new Deal?' Jacobi asked, crouching down by the nearest body on the flat corrugated iron roof.

Ulmer shrugged. 'Just rumours, nothing definite. Last one wasn't so good. These two aren't going to benefit.'

He took a step back from the bodies, careful to stay on the line of nails marking the beam beneath. The roof was rusty; it creaked with his movement.

Jacobi grinned and brushed flies from his cracked lips. 'These blokes been dead a while.'

'No shit.' Ulmer squinted down at the dead blokes, then at Smoketown beyond the roof, the city swinging like a curse of concrete and steel up Beacon Hill; dark steeples, and flat roofed towers. A storm, days in brewing, rose above it all, bleak sky and detonations stretching up and up, almost to the snake god Nehebekau's overarching gut. No rain though. Not yet.

On the western edge of town, John Shabtee's doll factory belched black smoke that mingled with the cloud. Nearer, no more than a block distant, cows were being slaughtered in the abattoir. Ulmer's ears rang with the thuk, thuk, thuk of the air gun and the bovine shrieks. The blokes on the roof had stopped shrieking days ago.

Jacobi passed him a wallet. No ID, just forty dollars in twenties. There was also a photo, family shot; wife and kids. That sort of shit hit Ulmer every time, just ate him up. The photo was old, Pre-Deal, peeling up at the corners, smudged with hope and yearning. He slipped the wallet in a zip-lock bag, tucked the photo in his pocket. Ulmer grimaced; he knew the dark places that stuff took you to in this Post-Deal world, but he kept the photo, and if Jacobi noticed he didn't say anything.

Ulmer split the money with Jacobi. Standard practice; not worth the paperwork.

The other corpse had nothing but a pair of glasses, too scratched to be worth anything, and a rabbit's foot, hollowed and weighted with a small lump of lead. Ulmer slipped the rabbit's foot in his pocket too.

'Sacrifice, certainly not theft, always somebody trying to make their own deal.' Ulmer motioned at the dark over Smoketown, a thick black smudge like a sketch of depression. 'Maybe call up the storm.'

'Sacrifices aren't this subtle. This is old school haruspication.' Jacobi pointed to the neat incisions in the corpse's torsos, the care with which the livers of each victim had been placed on their chest. The bloke on the left's wire-rimmed glasses weren't even spattered with blood. Jacobi glanced towards the dark horizon. 'And that storm's been brewing longer than these bastards have been dead. Can't tell you what the querents were trying to divine from these guts, but I can tell you what they're saying.' Jacobi grinned. 'Storm's coming.'

Ulmer took a lazy swing at him.

'Too slow, mate.'

Ulmer grunted. He wiped the sweat from his brow. 'Let's get to work.'

* * *

Storm broke as they turned away from the corpses. Jacobi sprinted to the edge of the roof. Ulmer followed fast as he dared because this was no mild precipitation, but rage. They couldn't do anything about the bodies; they were too short-staffed, although Ulmer was certain Jacobi would soon be making a call to Mr Shabtee. The doll maker would find a use for them.

All that iron and lightning tensed Ulmer up as they clambered off the roof. Jacobi seemed unperturbed, still he jumped when the storm snatched half the roof free, and he crossed himself when the bodies, laughing, lifted and tumble-flew through the air, west *against* the wind. Ulmer could hear their cackling clear above the rain and thunder.

'Now that shit I don't like.' Jacobi had dropped to the ground, almost to his knees. He rose unsteadily from the crouch.

Ulmer was already dashing for the car, even if he wasn't designated driver. Mud that had been dust a minute before sucked at his boots. He watched the dead blokes' stumbling shrieking flight. 'Seen worse.'

Jacobi stank up the car with his sweat and his music. Bobby Darin, *Mack the Knife* or *Beyond the Sea*, Ulmer didn't know; his brain shut out the lyrics once he recognised the voice.

'Hate that shit.' Ulmer wiped the rain from his face; he could feel the soot there, in his skin.

Jacobi turned up the volume. 'You drive, you pick the tunes.'

That shut Ulmer up. He couldn't drive, that part of him hadn't come over, P*ost-Deal*. But you couldn't dwell on what you lost, because it wasn't just memories or skills. The dealmakers had bartered more than half the population out of existence. You couldn't dwell on the things and people you'd lost. When it came to the Deal, you had to remember that things had been bad, real bad. Start thinking and you'd start sinking, spiralling down, into those dark and reaching days, into the various calamities.

Ulmer considered winding down the window, to let out the stink and the music rattling around in his head, but the rain still pounded from the bleak clouds. So he drowned in music and stench, and the car crashed into Smoketown. Piece of shit car. Piece of shit tunes.

He bummed a cigarette off Jacobi. His partner scowled. 'You owe me a few of those now.'

'I'm good for them,' Ulmer said. Jacobi turned up the volume some more; the speakers rattled.

The wipers tick-tocked on their fastest setting, Smoketown swam behind their swinging beat. They passed the brothels, the dolls out; their smooth wooden limbs and breasts slick with rain. Jacobi leered, even though he had a doll waiting at home. Ulmer watched them, suspicious of their predatory movements, their calculated desire. He could feel them from his balls up. Smoketown was a city of longing, pent up, like that storm. But with no release.

Storm didn't last long, mostly spent by the time they reached the stationhouse.

Dorian sat at the front desk, flicking through a dog-eared porno magazine. He lowered it without shame, took their guns and counted out the bullets with sweaty fingers, his fingertips smearing the desk.

'Bullets all there. Or we'd be telling you they weren't.' Jacobi snarled.

Dorian flashed his black teeth. 'Your time of the month, eh, Jacobi?'

'You shut up.'

'Bean in?' Ulmer asked.

Dorian laughed. Bean was always in. Chained to his desk, literally; a silver chain, links an inch thick. Part of the Deal. Some things hadn't come over. Other things had, and one of those was Bean. Bean was always in; down below, in the basement, filing, running through the paperwork, following leads, and listening, always listening.

'Bean doesn't need to see this,' Jacobi said, and Ulmer could tell he was thinking of his desk and his notes and all that paperwork. Job was mostly paperwork.

'You don't need to come,' Ulmer said, heading out to buy his offering.

Jacobi didn't look back. 'Suit yourself.'

'Bought with a dead man's cash. You're all class.' Bean sniffed at the burger, fries, and Coke that Ulmer had dropped on his desk.

Ulmer ignored the slur. 'To your taste?' He inquired, about as formal as he got.

Bean wiped at the sweat beneath the neat part in his hair. 'Always hungry, Ulmer. Crack your knuckly bones and suck the marrow out, if it weren't for this chain.' Bean leant over the desk. His dead breath washed against Ulmer's face.

'Thank Christ.'

'No. Not Christ. Something darker, something crueller. Like they say, you don't make deals with gods, though people never learn. Isn't it enough that there's a god in the sky, and that I'm down here. Don't you people know when to stop?'

'If people stopped making deals, I'd be out of a job,' Ulmer said.

Bean swallowed the food down in a couple of gulps. The soft drink he took a little longer on, his big black eyes never leaving Ulmer.

'What do you want?' Bean asked.

'Two dead blokes,' Ulmer said, and gave him the details, sketched the knife marks, the position of the bodies in relation to the major celestial points.

He pulled out the heavy rabbit's foot. Bean's eyes widened a little at that, with theatrics, or genuine surprise, Ulmer wasn't sure. Ulmer put the rabbit's foot on the desk. Bean leant down and sniffed it. He popped it in his mouth. He spat it out, his face twisting in a grimace. 'This isn't a rabbit's foot. It's an arrow pointing somewhere, like the haruspication. It's a message.'

'What's it say?'

Bean finished his soft drink. Dropped the bottle in the bin, wiped the water mark from the desk with a paper towel; dropped that in the bin too.

'It says, you don't want to pursue this.' Bean slid the foot back to him, Ulmer noted he was careful to touch it with just the dark squares of his nails. Ulmer picked it up. Bean had lost interest, his eyes already straying to the papers piled up in his in-tray. 'Do your paperwork and leave it on someone else's desk. You're too thorough.'

'Inside job?'

'Shit yeah. You leave it alone, or you'll regret it.'

Ulmer thanked him and got out of there, and home, not sure what to do. The photo of the dead bloke and his family in his pocket.

* * *

Ulmer woke just as irresolute, went and bought some cigarettes, and coffee, and caught up with Jacobi at the stationhouse.

'I don't understand you.' Jacobi picked the cigarettes Ulmer owed him out of his pack, careful in every selection. 'You make a good wage, better than me. And you piss it all away, always hanging out for the next pay check. One day you won't make such a good wage, what you going to do then?'

Ulmer snatched the packet from his partner. 'Piss a lot less.'

'Seriously, you could live in a nice place, up on Beacon Hill. You could save. You could get yourself a doll.'

'I'm not buying a doll.'

Jacobi laughed. 'Explains the calluses.'

'We've got work to do.' Ulmer pulled the rabbit's foot from his pocket. 'Bean tried to warn me off this.'

'And we're still hunting?' Jacobi raised his hands in exasperation. 'Ulmer, we're not here to solve crimes. We're here to make sure that it all runs smoothly, that people don't start making any more deals. Get what comfort you can from the small amount of suffering you might reduce, but realise it's just a small amount of suffering, and that people are always making deals.'

'That's where you're wrong,' Ulmer said. 'At least this time. You don't get warned off unless it's something big. Maybe something to do with this new Deal.'

Jacobi shrugged. 'All right, but if it is, not much we can do. Not exactly our purview.'

'But we can find out.'

'Maybe, but not today. We've got other things to attend to. Doll Factory today.'

Mr Shabtee waited for them, at the gates to the Factory. He passed them both fat envelopes. Ulmer slid his into a jacket pocket; he looked up and down the street. 'Let's get this done,' he said.

Mr Shabtee's eyes narrowed. 'Why? You got something better to do?'

Mr Shabtee waited a while. Ulmer said nothing. 'Yeah, you got nothing better to do.'

They passed through the gates. Factory wasn't the right name for this place. The Dolls weren't made here, just repaired; they came from the desert, unearthed by the winds. Shabtee's men dragged them back here and cleaned them.

Jacobi whistled. 'Shit, that's a lot of wood.'

And there were; hundreds of dolls, twitching and hanging from their wires. Mr Shabtee nodded. 'Winds have been blowing strong in the desert. Lots of dolls. Lots of nightmares too, our boys have been picking spiders from their flesh.'

Ulmer and Jacobi looked over the bodies, checking they were kosher, that no human flesh was used. Not checking too close. Ulmer had heard that you had to have something human in the doll, something to activate them; an organ, a piece of brain. One of them bled from its painted nose.

Mr Shabtee clucked and delicately wiped the blood away with a handkerchief. 'Messy,' he murmured.

'Make sure it doesn't happen again,' Jacobi mock admonished.

They signed his clearances.

'Thank you, lads,' he said, folding the paper away in a pocket, whistling for his workers to get back to work. 'See you next month. Oh, one more thing.'

Ulmer raised an eyebrow.

Mr Shabtee coughed, looked a little embarrassed, like it wasn't his job to ask for favours. 'My lads say they saw a dead bloke on the edge of the desert road.'

'And they didn't bring him in?'

'We don't send you to get the dolls do we? He was out there, dead and not dead, if you know what I mean; all haruspicated.'

Ulmer pulled out the photo. 'This the guy?'

Mr Shabtee squinted. 'No.' He grinned conspiratorially. 'Buy that photo off you though. Know a lot of collectors who are into that shit.'

Ulmer slipped the photo back into his jacket pocket.

'Wouldn't have taken you for one of them,' Mr Shabtee said. 'Nostalgia's poison.' Ulmer ignored him.

'He isn't,' Jacobi said, though he gave Ulmer an odd look.

Ulmer brought out the rabbit's foot. 'You know what this is?'

Mr Shabtee gave a dry cough. 'You get rid of that.'

'Don't make deals with Old Gods, eh?'

Mr Shabtee blinked. 'You've got better stuff to do, believe me.'

'What kind of world do we live in?' Ulmer asked, counting out his bribe, leaning against the bonnet of the car. It was all there. 'Dead and not dead. All this shit.'

Jacobi flicked a cigarette stub at a passing truck — cattle from down south for the slaughter yards. 'You know what kind of world we live in.' In one sweeping gesture he encompassed the snake-bound sky, the dusty road, the city. 'It's one we can live in. Before the Deal things were bad, not just what happened at the Poles. Darkness was coming, and it would have drowned all of us. When that thing happened in Perth, shit my best mate lived there. I saw the screaming earth, the Swan River nothing but a slick of blood. None of us could have lived with that. It was never going to be a good deal.'

'I remember waking that first day,' Ulmer said. 'In a bed that was mine, but wasn't, and I walked out, and there it was, the sky not blue, but ruddy with the belly of the snake. Ah, and that was the least of it.'

Another truck rumbled by, lifting up dirt red as the sky.

'Shit you're maudlin today,' Jacobi said. 'You got that rabbit's foot?'

'Yeah.' Ulmer handed it to him. Jacobi threw the rabbit foot after the cattle truck.

'What you do that for?'

'Shabtee wasn't bullshitting. Christ, Ulmer, even Bean told you to drop it. I'm looking out for you.'

'Bullshit, you're scared.'

'Not denying it.'

'Well, it's going to get scarier. I'm driving out to the Cold Desert. See if I can find that dead bloke.'

'You can't drive.'

Ulmer looked Jacobi square in the eyes.

The air smelt like cattle, and the shit of cattle, and dust. The air smelt old and sere and used up. But their lungs still took it, still sucked up each breath.

'I don't like you much right now,' Jacobi said.

More Bobby Darin. Ulmer supposed he deserved it, but it didn't stop him grinding his teeth all the way to the edge of town. The road petered out a few minutes walk from the ridge that bordered the desert. There was a good path up the ridge, but it was steep, and both were panting by the time they reached the top. They paused and stared back over at Smoketown and the bleak black sea that washed against its eastern shore.

'I hate that place,' Jacobi said. 'Hate the sea.'

'Why?' Ulmer put his back to the city and the sea. 'You didn't lose as much.'

'Fuck you!' Ulmer was surprised at the anger in Jacobi's voice. 'So I wasn't married. Yeah I didn't have kids, for them old bastards to deal away, but I lost my ma, I lost my sisters. I got on.' Jacobi sighed. 'You ever think that, maybe the Deal wasn't to save us, but to save them?'

'Sometimes,' Ulmer said. He let it drop, neither of them believed it.

The air clear enough that Ulmer could see Nehebekau's belly occluding the sky, dark where it neared the horizon. People didn't like to talk about the snake god, just like they didn't like to talk about the sea. Sometimes a meteor or some other such thing might punch its way through Nehebekau's flesh and a brief and bloody rain would ensue.

The other side of the ridge faced the desert. One of the dead blokes, the one with glasses, sat there on the desert's edge. It turned when they approached, then stood up; Ulmer could see the hole the haruspication had left, bones gleamed.

'You don't want me. I've not the teeth for it.' The dead bloke's voice came slow and soft.

Ulmer frowned. He glanced over at Jacobi. His partner shrugged; neither one of them wanted to get much closer. Sometimes things hunted in the sand; dolls that had got a bit of life in them, and a lot of hunger.

'Come over here.' Ulmer took a deep breath, sidled up close, near enough to grab the dead bloke, if he was quick.

The dead bloke opened his mouth, and Ulmer could see the cracks and stubs, barely had teeth at all.

It stepped onto the sand.

'No you don't.' Ulmer reached for him. Something beneath the sand got to the dead bloke first. The dead bloke went under. Ulmer caught a glimpse of a rolling doll's eye and long smooth wooden limbs. Ulmer lost his balance, fell back on his arse, then scrambled back away from the sand.

'Shit.' Ulmer got to his feet. A hundred metres away, a doll's head jutted from the sand, driftwood pale, a wooden hand poked out not too far west of it. Wooden fingers flexed then stilled.

'You want to risk it?' Jacobi's voice had an edge, a tension Ulmer wasn't used to hearing. Maybe Jacobi was starting to enjoy it a little.

Ulmer laughed. 'Not a chance. Let's get back to the car.'

Ulmer's room possessed the aching tension of a thousand perfunctory wanks. It smelled of sweat and smoke and cheap wine. He got out the photo.

Dad, arm around his wife, her dark hair luminous in the reflected light of the flash. The kids smiling. It wasn't even a good photo, not very well framed, eyes all red. And yet he yearned for this moment captured. He thought of his own wife and kids. And that spiral of thought led only one way.

Where were they?

Smoketown was what you get when dry old men make deals. And they had given up the women and children. Ulmer was prepared to entertain the idea that it had been unintentional. Gods liked their irony, they liked complications. Desperation should not be something you bring to the table. But the world had been going to hell. He'd seen things in those days, before the Deal. Things that could make a man believe in demons and gods, and how they might just tear everything apart.

Tears streamed down his face, but they gave no relief. He cried. He cried. He folded the photo away.

He showered, but the water offered no comfort; hard and frustratingly unctuous, it didn't lather but lingered. He went to bed, the sheets gritty as his skin, gritty with the leavings of his skin.

He dreamt his wife called him across the dark. There was a rage there, an accusation of love unfulfilled. Deep down he knew he had let this happen. They all had. He'd never understood the Deal. But who really understood half of what was going on, what they agreed to? Still, he ran through all that night, ran towards the voice. Because there had to be a way he could turn it all back.

Bean's appearance was sudden, the dream shifting, like the Deal had shifted their world. 'Enough there, chief. You're making it personal and if we all did that we'd have a right mess on our hands.' He lifted the chain with one hand. Ulmer could see where the metal fused with his flesh. 'You want to be personal, you think about this chain. You think about what's happening to Jacobi. Those things are intimate enough, those things hurt. He's screaming, Ulmer. Do you think your wife screamed, do you think your kids howled out their pain?'

Ulmer woke, eyes snapped open. The dead bloke's face was in his window. The one with the teeth. The bastard grinned. Ulmer snatched his gun, but the bloke had gone. He got up, dressed, and called Jacobi.

There was no answer. The phone rang out twice. He checked the time, two o'clock in the morning.

Two blocks away, just two blocks to Jacobi's apartment. He ran all the way.

Ulmer's shoulder hurt from battering down the door, slowed him down as he fumbled for his gun.

The doll had wrapped itself around Jacobi; its hands buried to the wrists in his bowels, haruspicating something, lifting up organs for closer scrutiny. Its head snapped around towards him, big, unblinking eyes, bloody lips twisted in a smile.

'Let him come first,' the doll said in its wind-up voice. 'There are worse ways to die.' It rose to its feet, and bits of Jacobi, tangles of bowel and gut, rose with it, and then fell away.

Ulmer fired. His first shot smashed the mirror behind the doll's head, and made it a crown of doll reflections.

'Worse ways to die.' It sounded almost remorseful, as it rushed towards him.

Ulmer fired again. The bullet took off its head. He fired again, through the belly. The doll stumbled and fell, its bloody hands swinging, catching his legs. Ulmer kicked at its arms, then crushed its delicate joints beneath his boots. The wood was fleshy and hollow. It bled dark fluids. Ulmer kicked the doll away from him. He crouched over his partner and closed Jacobi's eyes. In the cavity of his partner's belly, Ulmer saw the rabbit's foot. Jacobi had thrown it away yesterday. Ulmer fished it out.

He could hear the sirens drawing near. He suddenly felt suffocated in that room, the air too hot. He loosened his tie, and got out.

'I thought I would see you,' Bean said.

Ulmer slid the paper bag holding the burger and fries across the desk. Bean unfolded the bag, he plucked out a fry. His nose wrinkled, but he ate the fry anyway, gobbled it down, and the next, and the next.

'I heard about Jacobi,' Bean said between mouthfuls, the fries not crunching but cracking, and far louder than they ought in his mouth, little bony detonations. 'I told you to leave this alone.'

'I know you did.' He pulled the rabbit's foot from his pocket. 'Jacobi threw this away, and it came back.'

'Not so lucky for him, was it?'

'So what do I do?'

'Leave it alone.'

'And if I can't?'

Bean unwrapped the burger, slid the whole thing in his mouth and swallowed. He wiped at his lips with a napkin. 'When did you last go to the beach? Find me one of those dead blokes. If you can't leave it alone. Find me one of them, and bring it back here. You do that and you'll have your answer.'

Ulmer lit a smoke. His hands shook.

The black dunes of the beach steamed, the dark water crashed in. He sat just out of the water's reach. Few came here, few cared to scrutinise the things that washed ashore, the implications of these fragments of past; invitations written on soft paper, ink bleeding from submersion; children's toys; nappies and video cassettes that wouldn't play, but had notes like 'Wedding', 'Sharon's first Birthday' written on them. They were all, as Ulmer's dream had been, accusatory.

Ulmer came here precisely for that reason. He sought the pain.

There was a storm building, and he stood, with his back to it, facing the water, the restless dark.

Alone. Not quite. A figure stood, watching him, down the beach.

'I know you,' Ulmer said and walked over to him, touching his gun, periodically, for a modicum of comfort.

The dead bloke smiled.

'Where's your mate?' Ulmer asked. 'Still in the desert?'

The dead bloke shrugged.

'I've got something for you.' Ulmer passed him the photo. The dead bloke shook his head and passed it back. Ulmer folded the photo and put it in his jacket pocket.

Ulmer considered cuffing him, then changed his mind, he didn't want it attached to him. 'You coming with me?'

The dead bloke nodded.

When they reached town, Ulmer bought a burger and fries, and a soft drink.

'You can't take him down there,' Dorian said, looking up from the front desk.

'I think I can.'

Ulmer tapped his pistol. The desk sergeant was quick, but Ulmer was faster. He pumped two shots into Dorian's chest. The big man grunted. Doing you a favour, Ulmer thought, as Dorian fell dead on his porn. He reached over and pulled the keys from Dorian's pocket.

There was a bell ringing somewhere. He didn't have much time.

He could feel Bean down there, waiting, like lungs waiting for the next breath, like a heart between beats. The dead bloke grinned. Like he was waiting to see how this played out.

Ulmer could hear people running; someone shouted out his name. He fired a shot down the hallway.

Ulmer took the dead bloke down to the basement, locking the doors behind him as he went.

* * *

Ulmer put his offering on the desk. A few storeys above, someone kicked at a door, wood splintered.

'You know what I am?' Bean asked, his eyes weren't on the food, but trained on the dead bloke at Ulmer's side.

Ulmer shook his head.

'Nehebekau and me, we made a deal. I stay down here, and he stays up there.'

'Sounds like a good deal.'

Bean laughed. 'You know that's shit, Ulmer. The thing is you humans start making deals, and they diminish you. Bit by bit. Sure you wanted a better world, a safer world from that coming dark. You think this is a better world?

'And that's the way it's always been. People are always making deals, Ulmer. A new deal's been made, from above, and, like always, you little people you just play them out. Truth is you're living in our world now, Old Deal, New Deal, it was only ever going to get worse. If you had been looking you might have seen it in those dead blokes' guts, or Jacobi's, you might have realised you were jumping hoops. It ain't fair and I pity you, as much as I can with all this hunger.'

Another door crashed from its hinges. People shouted.

The dead bloke walked over to Bean. Ulmer shot the dead bloke in the leg. Slowed him, didn't stop him. The dead bloke lifted the silver chain to his mouth. He opened his jaw, bit down. The silver links shattered.

Bean filled the basement, all that released presence, though he still sat behind the desk. He smiled, and that grin widened, and widened and widened. He hadn't touched the burger this time. He pushed it carefully, distastefully to one side.

Ulmer fired at Bean's head, once, and then again. The bullets just passed through him; Bean didn't even blink.

'I'm going to make you a deal,' Bean said. And he didn't move his lips. The words just slithered in Ulmer's skull, like they were a garrulous parasite or an infection. 'You're not going to like it. But it's the best you're going to get. There's no one batting for you now. I'm going to give you a few minutes to run. Hey, you might even get longer on account of what's approaching.'

The last door broke.

The cops were coming for Bean, coming to contain the beast. But he knew they couldn't any more. He knew that Bean was right, a new Deal had been struck, Bean'd suck their bones dry before he was done; and then he would be coming for him.

Outside old Nehebekau would be gone. Gods liked their complications. No sheath of snake, just cold void, cruel and endless. And Bean.

'I said run.' Bean's voice filled his head.

Ulmer ran. His fellow coppers, a half-dozen men, moved out of his way. He cursed them for it. That they should let him pass so unchallenged. That they should go to their deaths so easily.

But he didn't stop, didn't look back. He ran up the stairs, his breath and his pounding heart roaring in his head, filling the space Bean's voice had made.

Behind him, in screams, and gunshots, and wet, horrible noises, the New Deal unfolded.

AFTERWORD

'The New Deal' came about as a confluence of my desire to write something Noirish, a visiting exhibition of Egyptian relics, including shabtis, at the Queensland Museum, the Kevin Spacey/Bobby Darin biopic *Beyond the Sea*; and the introduction of new Australian Workplace Agreements. Proving, I suppose, you never know where a story's going to come from.

— *Trent Jamieson*

DIRK STRASSER has had over thirty adult and children's books published. He won the Ditmar for Best Professional Achievement in 2002 (with Stephen Higgins) and has been short-listed for the Aurealis and Ditmar Awards a number of times. His *Ascension* series of fantasy novels have been published in Australia and Germany, and he is the author of *Graffiti*, a children's horror/fantasy novel.

He has had SF/fantasy/horror short stories published in magazines and anthologies in Australia, the UK, the USA, and Germany, with several stories appearing in 'Best of' anthologies and lists in Australia and the United States. Some of these stories can be found in magazines and anthologies such as *Universe Two, Borderlands 4, Metaworlds,* and *Alien Shores.* He co-edited *Aurealis* magazine from 1990 to 2001 and founded the Aurealis Awards.

Born in Germany in 1959, Strasser has lived most of his life in Australia. He is currently employed as a Senior Publisher for Pearson Education Australia, and is living in Melbourne with his wife and two children.

In the rich and elegant voyage of greed, discovery, and betrayal that follows, we travel to the New World with the the Spanish conquistadors only to discover yet another new world . . .

CONQUIST

DIRK STRASSER

'You see, my men suffer from a disease of the heart which can only be assuaged by gold.'

— *Hernán Cortés*

'Even if the snows of the Andes turned to gold, still they would not be satisfied.'

— *Manco Inca*

The following is the first English translation of four fragments from an obviously much larger account that came to light in an archive in the Museo Nacional de Arqueología, Antropología e Historia del Perú in Lima. Cristóbal de Varga is a verifiable historical figure, a distant cousin of both Hernán Cortés and Francisco Pizarro who, unlike Pizarro and many of the other conquistadors of his time, was highly literate. This very facility with words has lent credence to those that claim these fragments and the greater work from which they have been derived are merely the fevered imaginings of a man frustrated by his own lack of success in an age where others were making their fortunes.

Translator's note

On the eve of the Holy Trinity in the year of Our Lord 1542, I, Cristóbal de Varga, humble servant of His Imperial Majesty Charles V, King of Spain and Holy Roman Emperor, led my four hundred conquistadors through an *entrada* into a new world. I have decided to write of the wonders of this world that lie beyond the wonders of New Spain in the hope that others who may also discover the *entrada* in the mountains of Peru will contemplate entering only with the full knowledge that I bring. Only thus will those who follow be able to complete what we have begun for the glory of Our Lord and for the Empire on whose horizon the sun never descends.

Let me speak firstly of the moment of passing through to this new and beautiful world whose strangeness far surpasses even that of New Spain. We knew at once that the very air had conspired to change as we urged our horses and dogs through the shimmering curtain that hung in vertical folds like thin veils of snow across the narrow pass. We all reported a sensation which infused the familiar deep Andean cold with an alien bitterness that sliced for a moment into the marrow of our bones. Then, in an instant, it seemed we had entered a landscape over which a new sun shone, for the sky had turned a strikingly deep crimson. And while the same mountains towered around us as they had done, the snows had receded from the peaks, as if we had suddenly lost a season, and smoke and bright sparks issued forth from the summits and hidden crevices.

As, single file, my cavalry, foot soldiers and crossbowmen emerged from the *entrada*, it appeared from where we stood on the earth of the strange world that these men were being miraculously conjured from nothing. We could see no white veiled curtain once we had passed through, and one disembodied horse head after the other seemed to float momentarily before it was conjoined with its body. And it was for good reason, on that day, that we named this curtain an '*entrada*', for once we had crossed that veiled bridge, we could not return. When the last of my soldiers and horses had emerged, I sought to reconnoitre momentarily to the Andes of New Spain, wanting to explore the nature of what I perceived as a gate, only to discover that it was not in truth a gate, but only an entrance in the one direction.

Those who hear my story may believe that a deep fear entered the hearts of these humble servants of the Empire at this moment. And yet I, Cristóbal de Varga, must tell you that those who would believe this do not know the true heart of a conquistador. We have hearts that feel fear, only a fool would deny this most human of emotions, but the heart of a conquistador will hone this fear into action. It was the conquistador heart that led my countryman Hernán Cortés to scupper his own fleet and overcome the evil sacrifices of the Aztecs Motecuhozuma and Guatemoc, and it was the conquistador heart which gave Francisco Pizarro the courage to conquer the Empire of Atahuallpa and Manco Inca with a smaller company than I commanded. And it was the conquistador heart that now drove us, for the glory of God, to embrace the unknown and wondrous rather than seek to escape it.

Under my directions, my most loyal captain, Luis Velásquez, staked the Cross of Burgundy standard into the harsh ground and I declared this land, in the name of the Emperor, as a Viceroyalty of New Spain, and claimed for His Majesty Charles V a fifth of the gold that my expedition would find. My carpenters fashioned a large cross and we placed it on the site where the *entrada* had led us to this new world. Our padre, Bartolomé Núñez, blessed the site, though he feared it could be the work of the devil, and we began our trek into the unknown and to forge deep into this strange land.

On the third day we were set upon by a large party of high-helmeted *enanos*, thickset dwarven men with wild beards and dark eyes. They thrust at us with three-pronged *horcas*, lances of dark shining steel that could pierce our armour, and were it not for their obvious fear of our horses and the sting of our muskets, our tale could have ended at that first encounter. We fought against this new assailant, who was so unlike any of the Indians of New Spain, with fury and skill, and managed to capture one before those that remained alive fled into the smoking mountain crevices from which they had erupted.

The captive *enano* would not speak at first, offering us only stares and silences from behind his beard, and Padre Núñez expressed his fear that he and his people were demons. I implored, in the name of Our Lord, that we only sought peace and proffered this dwarven man maize cakes, salt pork and beads as a sign of our good will towards him. After he finally chose to eat, he began to speak in a tone like a growling dog. The Inca translators that travelled with our company said the language was neither Quechua nor Aymara, nor anything related to these two Incan tongues. We knew then that we were truly in a new world beyond the New World.

I examined the dwarf's plumed helmet and to my joy saw it inlaid with what appeared to be the highest quality gold. I held it up to him, saying, '*Oro, oro*,' hoping that he would understand the Spanish word for gold. He appeared to comprehend me almost immediately, but then turned away from me, refusing to meet my eyes. I took this to mean that he knew what we sought, and he knew its value. It was from that moment that I was certain that we had found a source of gold that would exceed the wealth found by Pizarro in the Incan capital of Cuzco.

We took this *enano*, who we later learned was called Halín, with us as we continued our expedition. Although he was swift to learn Spanish, he never lost his fear of horses and dogs, and would never march near them. We treated him well, hoping to gain his trust so he would be able to aid us in our quest, but though we spoke freely at times, he remained surly and would never speak on the subject of gold.

I was most intent on discovering who ruled in this land, which we simply called *Nueva Tierra*, and whether it contained any great cities and powerful kings. Halín spoke of kings as if they only existed in the past, and was wary when I spoke of His Majesty. The dwarf told us of the two peoples of *Nueva Tierra*, using Spanish words to denote them for he held the pagan superstition that true names should never be divulged. The *enanos*, those dwarven like himself, built their homes into mountainsides in hidden valleys and deep under the ground. The other peoples, the *duendes*, were taller than Spaniards and were, in Halín's words, 'of light and wing'. The two races seemed in an unrelenting state of conflict with no resolution, although in recent times they had lapsed into an ill-defined truce.

In my discussions with Halín I tried to uncover the source of the conflict between the *enanos* and *duendes*, for I knew we would be able to use this to our advantage. I had learnt the lessons of Cortés and Pizarro, and attempted daily to extract information I could use, but Halín spoke as if words were coins and he did not wish to pay more than he had to. Padre Bartolomé Núñez spoke to Halín of the need to surrender to God's will, accept the mercy of Christ our Lord, and cast down any idols that he worshipped. Though Halín showed interest in the padre's words, he did not accept them as the truth, and claimed he did not worship any idols.

On the twentieth day under the crimson sky of *Nueva Tierra*, we entered a steep-sided valley and, as night started to fall, we discovered we were suddenly encircled on both slopes by the flames of ten thousand torches. Through the fearful silence that fell upon us, we heard the booming of a single drum. While the courage of my men was beyond question, we all began to tremble at the sound of that forlorn drumbeat in a valley far from New Spain. Our horses reared, their breath clouding in the bitter dusk, and our dogs cowered and whimpered like pups.

We drew our swords and loaded our muskets and crossbows. I gave the order for our cannons to be primed with powder as the drums sounded through the sinistering sky. I commanded Halín to shout words of peace at what we could now see in the gleaming torchlight was an army of his people, fully armoured and brandishing their gleaming trident *horcas*. His voice echoed through the valley, but while he had rapidly learnt Spanish, none of us knew enough of the *enano* tongue to be certain of what his message was.

'They wish you to return to your lands,' reported Halín once a response had been shouted to us from the darkness.

My reply was that we bring greetings from our king and that we wished only to pay our respects to their leaders and trade for gold. I offered gifts and honour to a delegation of *enanos* to discuss our presence in their lands.

As the night drew further into blackness, the drumbeat finally ceased and several of the lights on the eastern slope began to move towards us. The *enano* delegation insisted on meeting us far from our horses and dogs. The leader, Tagón, whose face was almost entirely enveloped by a coarse beard, wore a peaked helmet that towered above the others, and he carried a three-pronged *horca* that reached almost twice his height.

After both of us claimed, through the interpreter Halín, to be people of honour, I spoke again of friendship from a powerful distant king and of our desire to trade for gold. Tagón said there was little his people valued more than gold, and that there could be only conflict if the strangers sought it in their lands. I understood then, watching this dwarf's wild eyes as he spoke, that were we to satisfy our mission, there was no choice for us here but to take the gold of this world by force, prising from the grasping hands of each *enano*. This conclusion gave me no pleasure, other than the pleasure of certainty, for I am no uncivilised savage and my sole motivations were the glory of Spain and Our Lord.

Padre Núñez then came to Tagón, holding a crucifix in one hand and a bible in the other, saying the *enanos* must submit to the truth of the Word of God in this Book and denounce their gods. The interpreter Halín said that he would attempt to impart the meaning of the padre's words to Tagón, but that the words *God* and *gods* could not be translated accurately into their language. Padre Núñez placed the Holy Script into Tagón's hands, demanding that he repent his sins and declare his love for Our Lord. Tagón opened the bible and squinted in the torchlight at several pages. He declared that these words said nothing to him and held out the book for the padre to take. When Padre Núñez refused to accept its return, staring instead into the eyes of the *enano*, the two remained locked as if in mortal, unmoving, combat, until Tagón finally released his hold on the bible and let it fall to the ground.

Padre Núñez pronounced the *enanos* to be demons, as he had suspected, and beyond salvation. I had no choice but to order the immediate capture of the delegation. It was fortunate that the *enanos* did not expect us to break the agreement of our meeting, for their slow reaction to our attack enabled us to avoid any bloodshed.

In an effort to avert a pitched battle, I commanded that my most loyal captain, Luis Velásquez, shoot a cannonball into a bare hillock at the entrance to the valley as a show of our power. A thunderous roar echoed through the valley and the acrid smell of gunpowder permeated the air. Through Halín, I offered peace and called on the *enanos* to submit to our king.

Let there be no doubt that we feared annihilation since for every one noble conquistador, there stood a hundred *enanos*, tridents in hand on the eastern and western slopes that towered above us. I myself trembled like a child and could barely hold my crossbow. Yet our strength lay in the certainty of Our Lord and the unshakable conviction that we were performing His Will.

And when the solitary drum recommenced its mournful, sonorous beat, we knew that our lives were now held in God's hands. We said our prayers to the Almighty as the lights of the *enanos* began to crowd down the slopes towards us, and their raw battle cries tore at our hearts like jagged blades.

Our crossbowmen hit countless marks, but it was our muskets that gave us an advantage during the initial attack. The *enanos* clearly had no understanding of how to defend themselves against guns, and these weapons destroyed their front ranks, making it difficult for those pressing behind them to break through. Our cannons wreaked a thunderous havoc on the dense clusters of *enanos*, although the advantage of our artillery diminished the closer the *enanos* drew.

Once the first of the dwarfs reached us, our advantages were significantly diminished. They fought with the fury and strength of the demons we now believed them to be, wielding their sharp-bladed *horcas* with powerful arms and brutal determination. Their armour was at least the strength of ours, and we resorted to thrusting our swords at the exposed portions of their helmeted faces and attempting to wound their legs. If it were not for the dogs and horses, we would not have withstood the first pitch of blade-on-blade battle. The *enanos* who appeared so fearless against us, quaked at the sight of our war-hounds. And our steeds allowed our cavalry to charge and retreat countless times in a tactic that destroyed any battle rhythm the *enanos* could muster.

Although we, thanks be to God, defended ourselves with skill and bravery in the face of that initial onslaught, we were so grossly outnumbered that we could launch no counter thrust, lest our defences be left weakened and we were forced to parry from our exposed position in the middle of the valley. As the deaths of our attackers mounted, we realised we had their measure and grew bolder in our blade work. Though these dwarven men were as courageous as any soldiers I had encountered, they clearly could not change their tactics mid-battle, and we beat off the attack before dawn, but were too exhausted to chase those *enanos* who retreated carrying their dead from the valley.

We buried our own dead and staunched our wounds and those of our horses with the fat of the fallen *enanos* who had not been taken, for our dressing supplies were limited and we feared that the campaign could be a long one. We had lost twenty-four good men and two hounds during the attack, but could only guess at the casualties of the dwarfs. After Padre Núñez had performed the blessings for our fallen comrades and we had erected a cross, we prayed for the strength to continue. With Luis Velásquez and my other captains, I spoke to the captured leader Tagón who assured us through Halín that his kinsmen would not make peace if we marched further into their lands, and that they would learn from their losses and strike again. I took this, at first, to be merely the pride of a captured leader speaking, but Halín confirmed that his were a stubborn people who would continue on a course of action even when that course appeared the most horrific folly.

Three of my captains counselled that we should be seeking a return to New Spain, but agreed in the face of my arguments that we did not yet know anything of the other people of this land, the *duendes*, and that an alliance with them was the path forward. I then questioned Tagón on these tall people who Halín had described as 'of light and wing'. He informed me that they lived in the regions beyond these mountains and that, unlike his people, their minds shifted constantly and they could not be trusted. I asked him if they possessed carved objects of gold, and he said that they had many such objects and that they were valued for their spiritual power rather than for the gold itself.

I spoke to him of the greatness of Our Lord and God, but the only word he could find in his language for a god was closer to the Spanish word *mago* or wizard.

We moved from the valley the next day because we feared another encirclement on the eastern and western slopes. The more I spoke with Tagón, who was eager to learn of our people and our God, the more I felt in him a kindred spirit. I sensed that all I had to do was explain fully our beliefs and he would consent to a baptism in the name of Our Lord. Padre Núñez remained suspicious, claiming the *enanos* as demons had no capacity for accepting Christ as their Saviour, and that Tagón was only seeking to discover our weaknesses through his questioning of our customs and beliefs.

On the forty-third day under the smoking peaks and blood-red skies, we were traversing a high narrow pass when the *enanos* struck again, as Tagón had said they would. We had been eating and sleeping with our weapons at the ready, never removing our armour in anticipation of another attack, yet nothing could have readied us for the numbers and fury we encountered. They had, as we had been warned, learned from our first encounter, and had chosen a battleground where we were most vulnerable and our horses were of limited advantage. The mountain winds whipped at us as the *enanos* swarmed up the slopes towards us in full battle cry with shining armour, brandishing their *horcas*. This time they were stubbornly intent on bringing down our horses, and they attacked them with fury, mortally wounding several of them before we pulled our cavalry deep into our formation for protection. Having lost this advantage, although our dogs continued to defend us ferociously, the battle became a grim blade-on-blade combat, where we were not only outnumbered by greater degrees than in the previous attack, but had less space to manoeuvre.

We were exposed without a path of retreat, and no conquistador in the history of New Spain fought with such courage and skill against such overwhelming adversaries. I can only thank Our Lord for his gift of wisdom as it appeared we would all die a noble death in that strange and far-flung land, when I sensed that the *enano* battle plan was to destroy our horses and that nothing that would happen in the heat of the conflict would sway them from this course. I ordered our horses to be presented as momentary prizes for the dwarfs, only for us to quickly encircle the *enanos* who blindly followed their strategy to their doom. When we were finally able to turn the cannons down-slope and shoot at the waves of dwarfs still swarming towards us, we dared to hope that we could once again be granted a victory by God.

It was at the very moment when the outcome of the battle was in its most perfect balance that the sky seemed to lighten like a bright dawn springing to life at midday and a frosted wailing filled the air. Despite the danger that lay upon us, we all looked up, as if entranced, to see a gleaming army of winged men-like creatures, armed with silvered bows and gilded arrows, descending from the heavens. The *enanos*, too, ceased their battle fury and stared skyward, and both our peoples were thrown from our entrancement only as the first flurry of arrows rained down. As we lifted our shields to protect us from this new onslaught, I sensed that the arrows were meant for the *enanos*, and not my soldiers. I sought out Tagón, who remained chained at the heart of our formation, and he confirmed these were the *duendes* of which he had spoken.

Padre Núñez shouted his thanks to the heavens that the angels had come to our aid, and the dwarfs, now caught between two armies, were slaughtered like no army in history. So few *enanos* remained at the end of the battle that most of their dead could not be carried away. In the silence of our victory, Padre Núñez spoke some words in glory of Our Lord, and we erected a cross before we marched across to the valley beyond the high pass on which we had been exposed.

There the silver-winged leader of the *duendes*, who gave his name as Ithilium, alighted before us with his captains, his face shimmering like sunlight on water, and spoke to us in a tongue so strange it sounded to our ears as the wind passing across mountain peaks. Tagón refused to face this foe, but Halín spoke their strange language and interpreted for us, although he reported the *duende's* words with anger and contempt. Ithilium offered flattery and praise, promising to share with us the treasures and spoils of the final *enano* defeat, and his only demand was that all the remaining *enano* prisoners in our custody be killed at sunrise.

During the night I sought counsel with my captains on the course we should take at dawn. Padre Núñez exhorted us to kill the remaining *enanos*, as we had been requested to do, and join the angels in the final battle to destroy what remained of the demons. While most of the captains agreed with this counsel, Luis Velásquez, whose mind and heart I have always placed the highest faith in, spoke of both the *enanos* and *duendes*, despite their appearances, as men like us, not the demons and angels of the Holy Writ. Would not any peoples, he appealed, attack those who entered their lands in battle armour and carrying weapons? Were not the most warlike and barbaric nations of New Spain, even those who tore out the hearts of their enemies and ate their flesh, capable of accepting the Lord? Were silver-winged creatures who shone like the sun and spoke like the wind to be trusted merely because, as they flew down from the heavens, they appeared as we imagined angels to appear?

After much discussion, I announced to my captains that I would retreat for some hours to ponder our fate and the choices it had thrust upon me. I spoke again to Tagón and Halín, whose steadfast nature I had grown to like and trust since his capture. Tagón showed no surprise when I confided to him what Ithilium had demanded of me. He spoke, as he had in the past, of what he called the 'words of the wind' that the *duende's* spoke, referring not simply to the sound of their tongue, but the very changeability of the meaning of what they say.

Well before sunrise I had made my decision and informed my captains that we would seek the *duende's* friendship, but not surrender to their demands to put our *enano* prisoners to death. Padre Núñez protested with vehemence and the captains other than Luis Velásquez now stood against me, their weapons raised. There was no will among those captains to battle what they believed to be angels in defence of demons, and Padre Núñez convinced them I had been infected by a strange fever. Velásquez, sensing events had conspired against both of us, then too turned on me, brandishing his sword in support of the others as I was placed in chains.

I can only give thanks for my humble life to the quick-wittedness of my most loyal captain Luis Velásquez in convincing the other captains who were once under my command that he was at one with their mutinous plans. In the depths of the night, he and a dozen of his most trusted soldiers came to me and freed me from my chains, informing me of their true convictions. There, under cover of a darkness filled with the memory of countless corpses, we made our fateful decision. After we had released the *enano* prisoners, we rode away furiously, led by Tagón who rode behind me on my horse despite his fear, and we entered a hidden valley before the sky of *Nueva Tierra* began to turn the now familiar crimson of dawn.

So ends the largest of the four fragments of Cristóbal de Varga's account. I have used the original Spanish words where the meaning of the English equivalent would be misleading or inadequate. The word enano *simply means 'dwarf', and perhaps the English term may have sufficed, which is why I have used it at times, but the Spanish word* duende *translates as 'elf' or 'goblin', and we have sufficient description to be certain that this nomenclature would be totally inaccurate. The last three fragments provide further insight into the nature of the* entrada *which translates as an 'entrance' or 'portal'. It is impossible to be certain exactly how much time has elapsed between the first and second fragments, but estimates have placed the following events somewhere between three months and one year after Cristóbal de Varga's escape.*

Translator's note

Still, I could not fully trust Tagón's people, who remain by nature a secretive race, despite the hospitality they have shown me and those few men who remained loyal to me. Although Tagón and those *enano* leaders who survived the slaughter have assiduously learned our tongue while we still struggle with theirs, my efforts to bring the Word of Our Lord to them remained thwarted and it seemed to me they listened to what I have to say only out of an awkward politeness. Whether they worshipped no god, idol or being of any kind, as they maintained, I could not say, for this claim could merely be a symptom of their secretiveness. I was now firmly convinced, however, of the existence of their souls, and I persisted in preaching God's mercy to them.

Though the *enanos* steadfastly refused to take us to their towns and cities (and we can only assume they must have these), and would not even divulge their general location, Tagón eventually decided he would show his gratitude for our actions against the *duendes*. He announced that, together with a small company of his soldiers, he would lead us on an expedition to the smoke-shrouded mountain that he claimed contained the *Boca D'oro*, the Mouth of Gold, the source of the exquisite high grade gold that adorned their helmets.

While Luis Velásquez counselled that the *enano's* purpose in bringing us to this place could be entrapment, my counter was that I had seen no duplicity in the motives of these dwarven men and that they had sworn to share with us equally the gold of the expedition once the royal fifth had been taken for Emperor Charles.

By mid-morning of the second day of our journey to the *Boca D'oro*, we had no choice but to leave our mounts behind, as the incline and loose stones made the path treacherous for our horses. After a further three days climbing, our armour weighing heavily on our back and the air growing strangely hotter as we ascended, we entered the smoke plumes that clouded the summit. Soon the *enanos* lifted their shields, and Tagón warned us to do the same, as we drew closer to the fiery peak that thundered like a storm above us. Despite the smoke, I could see the gilded arrows shoot from what seemed a flaming lake of molten gold cradled by the mountain top. With their free hands, the *enanos* held out urns they had brought to capture the glowing rain, showing great skill in anticipating the flight and not allowing the fiery gold to sear their skin. To our joy, on inspection of the contents of a filled vessel, we could see the most pure gold cooling to an exquisite shine before our eyes. Tagón gave us each an urn and counselled us on the techniques of catching the golden arrows.

I can only describe the feeling as joyous, as Luis Velásquez and those twelve conquistadors who had remained loyal to me scoured in all directions in the heat of that brilliant sun-lake, capturing the rain of gold in our vessels until they were filled to the brim. And the wonders of that moment at the jaws of the *Boca D'oro* were soon to be intensified to even greater heights when a chance gust of wind cleared the smoke momentarily. To our astonishment, hovering above the centre of the lake of molten gold, was revealed a scene so achingly beautiful to us that we could only stand transfixed and hold our breaths within us. There, as if a window had been opened in the air, were the snow-capped mountains and blue sky of New Spain as we had known them.

Although the smoke soon obscured the vision, we knew at once that we had found an *entrada* back to our world. Our joy soon turned to ash, however, as we concluded that there was no boat or other means that could be used to traverse the heat of the flaming lake. Tagón told us that he had seen 'the vision of the blue heavens', as he referred to it, on his other expeditions to the *Boca D'oro*, but that he had not thought that the place it showed was real. I questioned Tagón on whether he had seen such a vision elsewhere, but he said it was unique to the lake.

The passage of time between the second and third fragments of Cristóbal de Varga's account is even less certain. It could be a substantial period. While there have been some studies that have pointed to subtle stylistic variations in the third and fourth fragments compared to the first two, these will necessarily be less evident in the English translation.

Translator's note

Betrayal can numb your soul like the coldest of frosts. I do not accept its bitterness lightly and I pray fervently to always have the will to battle the illusive rapture that it promises. Yet I also recognise that the affirmation of one must sometimes necessarily mean the betrayal of another, and I could only place my faith in the Lord that I have chosen wisely.

So it was that I turned my back on the *enanos* and led those few men that had remained loyal to me to the high lofts of the *duendes*. There, where the winds keened in wild rhythms against our armour, we were captured and brought in chains before Ithilium by whose side stood Padre Núñez. It was in the face of this tall bright-winged angel in a palace of marble and electrum that I revealed my betrayal. As the *duende* leader had now learned our tongue, I offered him directly the means to destroy their enemy, promising to reveal the secret paths to the hidden cities of the *enanos*. For Padre Núñez and the captains and soldiers who had formerly been under my command, my offer was of limitless gold and the means to return with it to New Spain.

Such was my bargain that both Ithilium and Padre Núñez immediately embraced me, barely hesitating to hear what I required in return. When those soldiers from whom I had parted heard of my promises, they, to a man, returned with great joy to my command and we were all once again united in spirit and intent. Padre Núñez spoke of how he had brought the *duendes* to Our Lord and how all the winged ones had allowed themselves to be baptised in His Name. My confession that I had made no progress with the *enanos* only confirmed to Padre Núñez what he had always believed: that these demons had no soul and could not be saved even through our most pious efforts. In returning to New Spain laden with gold for the glory of His Imperial Majesty and the Empire, we knew we would accomplish all that we had set out to do, and our tale would be spoken of whenever the feats of Hernán Cortés and Francisco Pizarro were lauded.

I can barely speak of the exquisite rapture we felt on the day that soon followed as the *duendes* each lifted a conquistador into the sky and carried us, as if we were a host of angels, across the crimson heavens of *Nueva Tierra* to the *Boca D'oro*. There, those of my men who saw the fiery lake for the first time rejoiced in its splendour and filled vessels I had encouraged them to bring with the flaming rain of gold that flew from its molten surface. And their joy grew to still greater heights when, as had occurred on my last expedition to this mountain peak, the smoke dissipated for a moment, and floating above the surface of the lake in the distance appeared a window to the blue skies and familiar snow-capped peaks of the Andes.

There could no longer be any doubts that my plan would be successful. The *duendes* each grasped a soldier firmly and, spreading their glorious silver wings, began their flight across the lake, taking care not to be scorched by the gilded flames that shot skywards. Thus it was that my men, laden with vessels of the captured golden rain, were carried towards the *entrada* to New Spain.

I must say, *my men*, for Ithilium gave no order for me to be lifted skyward and instead approached me in a manner that brought me great displeasure. The *duende* leader had me immediately disarmed and spoke to me sternly in his clear but breathful-accented Spanish of his disappointment that I had not given him the true secrets of the *enano* cities. I protested that I had told him no falsehoods, but my words fell on deaf ears. When the smoke of the *Boca D'oro* suddenly cleared again, my eyes turned to the lake and I saw the *entrada* appear once more, with my men held by the *duendes* almost upon it.

Then it was that something occurred which no man should ever have the misfortune to behold. I have witnessed many battles and countless deaths as a conquistador, but the scene before me on that day is a scene that only the devil himself could conceive. With a wind-blown order from Ithilium, one by one, the duendes released their grips on my men and allowed them to fall from the sky into the molten gold of the lake. The screams and struggles of those who could see what was about to happen to them were something beyond bearing. There was no defence against this most hideous of crimes for we had placed complete trust in the *duendes* and my men had no opportunity to reach for their swords, and had this been possible, it would still not have saved them from their fate.

It was with a strangled heart that I saw my most loyal captain, Luis Velásquez, fall into the lake, momentarily rising to the surface like a golden statue of a screaming man, only to sink again, never to emerge. With the *entrada* still visible above the *Boca D'oro*, I shuddered with the thought that the last thing my dearest friend Luis Velásquez would see was the blue skies of New Spain within reach before him.

I turned my fury on Ithilium, but he now had me constrained by chains and my invectives had merely the effect of the ravings of a madman from whom all control had been taken. Ithilium's calmness was as if his betrayal was as natural as the wind over which none of us had any power. In his almost voiceless Spanish, with words that chilled my soul, he spoke of the joy of baptism that his people had now exchanged with mine.

That this text was indeed written by the conquistador Cristóbal de Varga is generally accepted. Stylistically the material has been shown to correlate strongly with his other known writings. The other Spaniards mentioned in the fragments have been confirmed as members of his expedition into the eastern Andes in 1542. The only other historically verifiable fact in the account is that no member of de Varga's expedition of discovery and conquest was recorded as returning to Lima. The final fragment is the shortest of all.

Despite its brevity, it presents us with information from which we can glean the circumstances under which Cristóbal de Varga wrote this account.

Translator's note

As a young man I had always believed it is the outcomes of battles that determine a soldier's life. I cannot say that I still hold this to be true. Perhaps the decision not to enter a battle is of greater importance. I have learned many things among the *enanos*. In truth I am in far greater debt to these steadfast dwarven men than to His Imperial Majesty, and had they not rescued me from my imprisonment by the *duendes*, I have no doubt I would have suffered, if not the same fate of my men, something far more grave.

The inevitable conclusion that I will never return to New Spain, let alone to Spain itself, has seared my soul, but after so many years, I have finally become resigned to it. I take some solace in my nightly solitude that I have never, in truth, betrayed my most faithful friends, the *enanos*. And yet, I wonder endlessly at the twistings and turnings of my own mind, for, in reality, I had nothing to offer the *duendes* when I proffered my fateful bargain so long ago. It was a bargain based on a falsehood, as I had not been entrusted then with the knowledge of the *enano's* hidden cities. Perhaps these people with no god and no idol are far wiser than I am. Perhaps they were aware that I would have betrayed them if I had known their secrets, rather than merely feigning that knowledge to the *duendes* in order to trick them into aiding our return to New Spain. It pains me to admit I do not know what path I would have chosen had I, in fact, been in possession of those truths that the *enanos* had not yet entrusted to me.

So it is that a man makes his decisions and lives by them, and then ultimately dies by them. Nothing will return my soldiers to any world that I have ever visited, nothing will right the deaths I have caused through my actions, and nothing will truly ease the pains in my heart. I can only tell my story, as I have done in these, my last days, in the hope that someone may one day read it and take something from its pages.

Tomorrow I will, with the aid of my most loyal friends Tagón and Halín, climb the slopes to the *Boca D'oro* a final time. There I will attach this account I have so painstakingly written to an arrow, and when the smoke clears over the golden lake and the *entrada* appears, I will aim my crossbow at the vision. And, God willing, if my aim is true, my tale will arc unscathed over the gilded fires as they rain their seering treasures upon its pages and reach the blue skies of New Spain.

This translation was made directly from the original fragments archived in the Museo Nacional de Arqueología, Antropología e Historia del Perú in Lima. I can confirm the other studies of the originals which have stated that many of the pages are flecked with droplets of gold.

Translator's note

AFTERWORD

I've often wondered what sort of damage the Spanish conquistadors would have done if they had found their way into a new world beyond the New World. 'Conquist' started as a quest for hidden dwarf treasure by a people with a ruthless lust for gold and an unquestioning sense of piety and duty. Somehow the story ended up more than this.

— *Dirk Strasser*

PETER M. BALL grew up on Australia's Gold Coast, which gave him a chance to see the allure of the unreal in vivid neon colours. He did a creative writing degree with the goal of becoming a poet, but realised he'd much rather be writing speculative fiction. He attended Clarion South in 2007, continues to work on a PhD in Gothic Speculative Fiction, and works as a writing tutor at Griffith University.

Here is a heart-stopping story of coming-of-age, of perversion, enslavement, and the pale and beautiful twice-born dead who can transform you forever...

THE LAST GREAT HOUSE OF ISLA TORTUGA

PETER M. BALL

She enters my name as Tobias Truman. I watch her ink the delicate curve of the capitals, the ostrich-feather quill dancing as she writes. My name is entered below Mr Drummond's, his below the Captain; two of the three marked with the swooping X that denotes status as paying guest, a true patron of the house rather than tag-along visitor.

The Madam ends with a final flourish that leaves the quill poised above a well of ink. Her needle-sharp eyes study me, peering through the thick veil of her lashes. I fidget beneath her gaze until she smiles and turns towards the Captain with a raised eyebrow.

'And the boy?'

The Captain spins on his unsteady legs, stares at me through the haze of rum and ruin that accompanies him whenever we put ashore. He considers the question for a few moments, mocking finger to his pursed lips, the barest hint of a smile visible through the tangled mane of his beard.

'The boy? What do you say, Benjamin? Should we give the boy his first tumble?'

Mr Drummond scowls. He is a bookish man, despite his first-mate's bluster. Short and straight as a ramrod, still every bit a schoolmaster despite his years at sea. He gives the Captain a short nod, neat and efficient.

'Aye,' he says. 'Let the lad sample the wares, if he's fool enough to agree.'

I am. Fool enough to agree, fool enough to seek this out, fool enough to abandon my London name and London comforts for the *Black Swallow* and a cabin boy's berth. Fool enough to risk my secrets, just to see the last of the Old Houses in action.

I'm fool enough, and I tell them so.

'Please, Captain.'

There is a pause then, an empty lull that I've learned to recognise as the first sign of a coming storm. I can feel a thrill of fear run down my back, the hair on my neck standing to attention. The Captain's smile grows slowly, like the shoals of a hidden reef coming into view too late.

Mr Drummond's face a grim mask, concealing the clumsy knot of desire and loathing. Taciturn, is Mr Drummond, and a pederast at the best of times. He has sought to take my innocence for the last year, despite the Captain's orders to the contrary.

The Madam waits patiently, the nib of her pen paused above the ledger. A bead of ink swells on the tip. I may not have the Madam's experience, but I have always been a quick study. I understand my place in this struggle, my role as a sharp knife used to tease the flesh of Ben Drummond's throat.

The Mate has thought our struggle beneath the Captain's notice. Ben Drummond has rarely needed to practise such subtlety; the buggery of cabin boys is common enough, even aboard respectable vessels. Had I set sail on another ship, under the command of any other captain, the question of my first tumble would have been decided long since and its tragic consequences already played out, for better or for worse.

I have been lucky with the *Black Swallow*, with her crew and her captain. Luckier than I deserve, fool that I am, so far from home in my thirteenth year. I force myself to affect excitement, an eagerness to see what lies beyond the velvet curtains. My stomach churns, a queasy roil worse than the sickness that plagued my first day on open water.

The Captain shifts his gaze between Mr Drummond and me, leering as he fishes coins from their hiding place beneath his shirt.

'For the boy,' he says, dropping a tarnished gold disk onto the Madam's creaking table. The Madam palms the coin, adds a flourishing X beside my name. Mr Drummond's eyes draw deep into his skull.

'Yes,' he says. 'For the boy. May the whores treat him gentle on this special night.'

There is laughter then, laughter from both men; Mr Drummond's heaving cackle joining with the Captain's booming roar. A cold chill settles into my gut as the tension between them eases, the same chill I get when the *Swallow* is becalmed and laying fallow in the water.

There are times when it's better to weather the storm and see where it takes you, but I have heard the stories about the Old Houses and I know them better than any man aboard the *Swallow*. I have connived my way here, using Mr Drummond's hunger as best I can, but I find myself suddenly afraid of what lies beyond.

The Captain claps my shoulder, pushing me towards the tattered velvet curtain. I draw a deep breath and step across the threshold, into the House of Pale Flowers, last of the great, Old Houses of Isla Tortuga, ready to find the twice-born whore who will transform Toby Truman forever.

The Madam leads us along the cobwebbed hall, along the floorboards that have been worn smooth with the rolling gait of a hundred thousand sailors, past the walls lined with the yellowed skulls of the dead. The Captain walks beside her, exaggerating his drunken stumble. Occasionally he reaches out, rubbing the cranium of an old friend, staining his fingers with bitter oil and dust. Mr Drummond walks by my side, a quick march with a stiff back, eyes focused on the door at the far end, gazing down the impossible length of the hallway.

It's the noise that surprises me as we walk, the raucous roar of a drunken crowd dancing and singing to the quick beat of a rolling shanty. Something about the noise seems strangely inappropriate, given the stories that surround the Old Houses; every tale tells of the silent ladies, unable to utter a single word on pain of death, quiet as the graves they were rescued from, even in the throes of passion. It seems sacrilege to engage in such revels in their presence, an insult to their sacrifices, even if their customers have never put much faith in God or the church.

It was different once, if you believe the stories. They say the Old Houses were sacred places, the home of lost secrets and forbidden loves, everything a pirate needed to warm his waterlogged heart.

'You've picked a good night,' the Madam says, pausing before the oak door that ends the hallway. 'There is only a small crowd; if you'll amuse yourselves in the parlour for a time, our girls will be with you shortly.'

Then she pushes the door open and the roar of the parlour is doubled; it hits us like a cannon's retort, impossibly loud and stung with a sudden flash of heat. The parlour stinks of pipe smoke and hot blood, the broken voices of seafaring men singing along with an off-key piano.

I once heard a crewman call this place the last great house of ill-repute, his voice full of quiet reverence, but I see little to revere in the human flotsam that litters this room. They litter the overstuffed divans and driftwood tables, with grey-fleshed girls limping on twisted legs or serving drinks with an arm that has been broken and poorly set before healing.

A dead girl emerges from the throng, ready to lead us to the table. Her left eye is missing; the flesh around the empty cavity an angry and puckered scar. She holds forward three fingers, then waves her hand to indicate we should follow.

As she turns, I can see the clumsy stitching that has repaired a wound to the back of her skull. It looks deep; like the aftermath of an axe-blow or the crushing weight of an iron belaying pin. The stitches hold the black flesh closed, barely concealing the rot at the seam.

Mr Drummond strides past me, following her as she cuts through the crowd of flesh. I hesitate for a moment, hands on my ears, trying not to breath in the scent of unwashed sailors and death. The weight of the Captain's arm settles across my shoulders, his thin lips drawing close to my ears.

'Relax,' he says. 'They use the broken girls as waitresses; the pretty ones are kept for the back rooms.'

I nod. The Captain offers me a wide grin, his first genuine smile of the evening.

'Come,' he says, hot breath tickling my ears. 'First we'll drink, then we'll make merry. You'll forget that they're dead soon enough.'

He guides me into the throng with a steady hand. We move carefully through the press of bodies, pausing so the captain can greet old friends he finds among the crowd. Mr Drummond has ordered by the time we reach the table, the waitress depositing three copper mugs filled with the Captain's favoured concoction of rum and gunpowder.

'To your health,' the Captain says. He throws his head back and takes a long draught.

Mr Drummond doesn't drink at first, simply sits with his back to the wall, eyes darting as he sweeps the crowd for familiar faces. He is a cautious man, hiding his nerves behind a scowl, always searching for those that would do him harm.

The Captain deposits me in a seat by the wall, the seat closest to Ben Drummond and his eyes of cold flint. Deposits me here with a quick wink and a leer of pure joy, a leer that assures me I have little choice in my position. His game continues, until he says otherwise. It's closer to Mr Drummond than I've been in a year, closer than I'd want to be under normal circumstances.

I stoop in my seat, a clammy sense of fear in the pit of my stomach.

Mr Drummond leans his skinny weight onto the scarred driftwood of the tabletop. He steeples his fingers, holding them before his mouth, a lingering gesture from his days as a man of learning.

'Relax,' he says, soft enough that the Captain can barely hear. 'You've got nothing to fear from me, not here.'

I nod, once, but it does little to quell the nerves. There have been incidences aplenty aboard the *Swallow*, despite the Captain's close watch, too many close calls for me to take Mr Drummond at his word. He makes a rough gurgle in the depths of his throat, a sound that's almost a sigh, and he turns his cold eyes towards me.

'Relax, Toby Truman,' he says. 'There are darker pleasures in this world than you can offer, and plenty here to satiate even my appetites.

The Old Houses are dangerous enough without worrying about me. Save your trembling for something that deserves it.'

There are stories aplenty about Ben Drummond, tales as dark and unfriendly as any you've heard over a midsummer campfire. They say he tutored a governor's child once, before his appetites forced him to take to the sea. They say he's been banished from ship after ship, cast off for deeds that even a buccaneer crew could not sanction. They say a great deal, these stories I've heard, and they imply much that is worse.

But the stories of the Old Houses are darker still, and the stories about the Pale Flower are often darkest of them all, so I choose to believe him, just this once. I let myself relax, let myself lean back into the rickety comfort of my chair and sip my drink while the Captain's order fills the table with rum and brandy and pipes filled with opium and fine tobacco.

The Captain breathes a white plume into the air, exhaling smoke like a contented dragon as we watch the crowd thin and disappear into the back rooms of the bordello. He has his boot propped on the driftwood table, a wooden cup dangling lazily from his fingers.

I take my time and study the crowd, watching even the bravest sailor flinch when he's forced to address one of the silent waitresses. They are mangled creatures, the victims of violent deaths, brought back with hurried stitching and missing parts. Mournful, misshapen creatures; women who have been destroyed by their deal with the black spirits that sponsor the Old Houses.

There are few men who are truly comfortable here, though the Old Houses have been pirate dens since the first buccaneer set foot upon the shore. They flinch and they look away, unwilling to deal with the walking dead regardless of their anxious glances towards the curtains and the whores' boudoirs. They are men who are plagued by fear, drinking and dancing only to escape the inevitable. It isn't long before I wonder why they've come.

Only the Captain seems truly at home. He revels in the promise of debauchery, in the willing violation of the natural order that the Pale Flower represents.

Mr Drummond does not revel, though he hides it well. His face is old leather, stretched across the skull, perfect for hiding the minutia of expression. He drinks cautiously, refusing the Captain's offer to share a pipe, stays alert to the impending possibilities of the evening. His drinks are pushed to my corner of the table, pushed across with quiet gestures he believes the Captain does not notice.

'Drink,' Mr Drummond tells me. 'It will help with your nerves.'

I drink a little, choking on the angry tang of rum. I keep my eyes on the serving girls, on their horrific wounds and scars, on the heavy curtains that occasionally part and allow one of the throng access to the back rooms and the ladies who dwell there. On the grimace of fear and confusion that flashes across each patron's face, as though unsure exactly why they're taking the next step.

'Captain,' I say. 'They look afraid.'

The Captain is drunk now, truly drunk rather than some feigned act. He roars with laughter.

'Of course they're afraid,' the Captain says, his roar cutting through the crowd like a shark's fin. 'They don't know the secret. There is an art to loving an Old House harlot. Don't you agree, Mr Drummond?'

Mr Drummond gives a short, crowing laugh.

'He doesn't believe me,' the Captain says.

'It would appear not, Captain.'

The Captain's lip curls into a sly smile, his eyes shining through the smoke haze.

'That's Ben's choice,' he says. 'His to make, despite the danger.'

'Danger, Captain?' Mr Drummond says.

'Danger,' the Captain says. 'Though not the type you'd think. True, there is always danger when sleeping with a woman, no matter who she may be. But the ladies of the Old Houses are different, they get beneath your skin. The memory of them gnaws at you during the lonely nights at sea, nibbling away your soul until there's nothing left. Therein lies the art; learning to love them while the opportunity presents itself, then letting the memory go before it destroys you.'

Mr Drummond scowls, thick brows meeting above his hooked nose.

'Love, Captain?' he says. 'Love is the stuff of poetry and children's tales, not the base currency of the Old Houses. Where does one find love here, among the dead?'

The Captain smiles, touches a finger to the side of his nose.

'Love is inescapable, Mr Drummond, even in the Old Houses. For we are creatures married to the sea, unfit for loving ordinary women. The ladies are dead and reborn, unfit for loving an ordinary man. We are all outcasts in the eyes of god, so we love each other as best we can. It may not be the love of your poems and fairy tales, I'll grant you that, but what they offer us is true enough for my purposes.'

'You're a romantic.'

'Who isn't, these days? We all bear the mark of romance, though we hide it like the first signs of plague.' The Captain peers at us from beneath the brim of his hat. 'Take note, young Toby, Mr Drummond may doubt me, but he hasn't yet said that I'm wrong.'

Mr Drummond snorts, taking a long draught from his cup. He places it, empty, on the table.

'Misguided,' he says. 'But not wrong. It was different, once, before the Frenchman and his army of street-whores.'

He stands and inclines his head, calling our attention to the curtain leading into the rear rooms. The Madam is waiting there. I can make out a cluster of girls behind her, pale and regal, resplendent in shimmering gowns and their necklaces of silver and gold. Overdressed for harlots, but the Old Houses have always known that women and wealth go hand in hand when it comes to raising a pirate's ardour.

'It's time,' Mr Drummond says. For the first time I can hear a slight current of fear below the croak of his voice. His left hand, his whipping hand, flexes and curls in anticipation of what's to come. 'My advice, boy, should you want to take it: get what you need, leave everything else behind. Remember that you sleep with the dead tonight, and there's precious little you can do to change that. Any feeling you see in them is just a hopeful figment, wished into being by your own desires, as ethereal and intangible as mist on the sea.'

It is the Captain who selects my partner, a dark-haired girl named Beatrice with skin as pale and clear as the china dolls I played with as a child. She leads me into a boudoir that smells of clove incense and stale sweat; a heavy fugue that hangs in the smoky air, so thick I can barely see the rafters above us.

Beatrice holds my hand between her cold fingers, leads me into the heart of the smoke where a lounge and bed lays waiting. Her cold hands guide me, seating me on the plump lounge whose leather is ripped and rent.

'Sit,' she says, and I am so shocked that I do so with mouth agape, like a wounded fish sucking for air upon the deck.

'Would you care for a drink? Something to smoke? We have some fine opium, if you'd prefer it?'

Her voice is unnaturally dark and rich, a sombre funeral dirge chafing to break into a lively waltz once the audience's back is turned. I shake my head, mute, and she arranges herself with languorous grace upon the threadbare cushions of the bed.

'You can talk,' I tell her, and I'm sure there's a quaver in my voice as I do so. She nods, smiling at me, her lips drawing into a winsome curve that belies her idle authority in this exchange. I feel a sharp heat rising into my cheeks.

'The ladies of the Old Houses do not talk,' I tell her. 'They are silent as the graves they were rescued from, and nearly as trustworthy when it comes to keeping a man's secrets.'

She shrugs, a practised gesture that sees her bosom heave with fluid grace.

'We do not speak to men,' she says. 'A necessity of the contract, but one that's good for business.'

'Then why speak to me?'

She shrugs again. I wince, suddenly aware of how complacent I've been, so long at sea, so long undiscovered and surrounded by men. It is easy to hide among sailors, among men unfamiliar with women beyond a few trysts at shore, willing to see a boy simply because they cannot imagine anything but in my place.

The skin at the base of my neck itches, my face is scarlet. I am not yet ready to return home, to abandon the sea and take up the safe life my mother planned for me. The dead girl revels in my discomfort.

'There must be some mistake,' I tell her, doing my best to keep the nerves from my voice.

'There must,' Beatrice agrees. 'Though it is strange, is it not? That a lady of the Old Houses can talk to a man? Break the compact without the spectre of death coming to claim her?'

'Strange,' I agree. Beatrice shrugs a third time, letting the slit of her robe fall open a little wider. The flesh of her chest is smooth and pale as cream, marred only by the livid scar of a bullet hole next to her left breast. I find myself tempted to reach out, to stroke the vivid knot of poorly healed skin.

'Perhaps,' Beatrice says. 'Stranger things have happened, in a house such as this.'

She turns, drawing her robe closed, the legacy of her first death disappearing beneath layers of crimson silk.

I draw my feet up, hugging my knees close to my chest, feeling childish for the first time in months.

'So,' I say, quietly.

'So,' Beatrice agrees. Her voice is like liquor now, lush and harsh and heavy with promise.

'What happens next?'

'Traditionally, there is an exchange,' Beatrice says. 'We do what is necessary to sate your desires, or what we can do, to that end, in the time we have. Some men remain a work in progress.'

'And then?'

'And then we are done,' she says. 'Then you go on your way, sailing off on your ship, and the memory of our time together gnaws at you, just as your captain promised. It gnaws at your soul and nibbles at your dreams and swallows you whole in order to pay my tithe.'

'Just like that?'

She nods, gravely, her voice devoid of mockery.

'Just like that,' she says. 'It is something of a sacred duty.'

'And what happens if you fail?' I ask her. 'What happens if I come here desiring nothing?'

Beatrice smiles, leaning forward as though preparing to whisper a final secret. I lean in, close enough to taste the sea-salt and pickling wine that lingers beneath the heavy scent of her perfume.

'Everyone desires something,' she says. 'They don't come here if they don't.'

One pale hand curls around my hair, drawing me closer. She kisses me and her lips taste like gravestones, like sodden dirt mixed with warm copper, like the hunger of a starving man.

It is a good kiss, powerful, a lure to reel me into the unfamiliar territory of her bed. I know better than to follow, but it takes more strength than I have to resist.

I succumb, briefly. We do not make love, though I allow Beatrice to unravel the tattered strips of my disguise. We do not make love, but her cold hands caress my face, my ribs, the hollows of my knee. We do not make love, but her kiss is cold against my lips and filled with promises.

For a moment I allow myself to feel hopeless within her grasp, writhing and twisting like a fish on the line that knows it will be drawn up onto the deck. Then it is over, halted, nothing more than a momentary weakness. Beatrice lays my head on the pillow, gently wraps me in the cold shadow of her embrace.

We lie together, quietly, a narrow shiver running the length of my spine. She has discarded her robe, allowing me to see the puckered scar once more, a ghost-pale reminder of a pistol shot to the heart. This time I do reach out, tracing the knotted flesh with my finger. It's strangely warm, as though touched by some lingering spark of fire from the lead slug that ended her life.

'Did you know them?' I ask; it's an incautious question, one that takes her off-guard. Beatrice looks down, presses her finger against the old wound, rubbing it lightly with her cold hands.

'I knew them,' she says, finally, her voice little more than a whisper. 'Not well, perhaps, but well enough.'

'Do you remember?' I ask. 'I mean, you hear stories, girls sold to the Old Houses before their times; still living, even if they're told otherwise; their flesh left cold and clammy by magic, to give the illusion of the grave.'

Beatrice smiles gently. I notice, for the first time, the reddish tinge of old blood on her teeth.

'I remember enough,' she says. 'It isn't something you'd recall clearly, given the choice, but I remember enough to be sure. To know that they brought me back, called me home to uphold my side of our bargain, bound me with silence and duty in exchange for my life.'

A cold thumb presses itself against my forehead, resting in the space between my eyes.

'Where do you hear such stories, little pirate?'

It's my turn to shrug.

'And why are you interested? What do you care for the poor, dead girls of Isla Tortuga?'

Beatrice studies me. There are stories about eyes and windows, so I know enough to close my own, to lock away the memories of my mother and her pale flesh, of the nightmares she offered me as bedtime stories until I was old enough to run away. Some days I can still hear her echo, all the old warnings she offered me, explaining that the world was a cold place for women and a colder place for a courtesan's child.

With closed eyes I permit myself to remember my mother; her violet eyes, the soothing chill of her hands, the ghostly heartbeat that made a lie of her graveyard pallor.

She hated my love of the sea, my infatuation with pirates and sailors, my soul that would not be tamed by books and tutors and the fruits of her wealth.

But it was a cold hatred, the final ember of an extinguished fire, trapped beneath the eternal frost that chilled both her body and soul. I sometimes wonder if she wept when she discovered her child was a runaway. It seems unlikely.

Beatrice is staring when I open my eyes, still waiting for an answer. I look at her, catching a glimpse of ghostly memories hemmed in behind her grey pupils. I see pain and sorrow and not enough joy, the same echoes that lived in my mother's head, buried deep beneath the sultry languor of her eternal stare. Beatrice gives me a slow smile, disarming in its honesty. We have both given something away here, letting our secrets live a little closer to the surface than we'd like.

When she speaks, her voice is little more than a whisper: 'How long have you been at sea, Tobias Truman?'

And though it has only been a year and three months, it still feels like forever, the weight of the days bunching like a clenched fist deep in my chest. Beatrice touches a tear as it rolls down my face, holds it before me on the tip of her lily-white finger.

'This is not an answer, little pirate?'

'Maybe not,' I tell her. 'But everyone has their secrets, and the wise sell them as dearly as they can.'

I have been gathering tears for a year now, hoarding them up like my own private ocean. Beatrice takes me in her arms, cooing quietly as I scatter her bed with my gathered sorrow, a hundred tiny shards of salt-water that I dare not carry back to the sea when I leave.

Beatrice shows me to the hall when our time is done, closing her door behind me with a gentle smile and a farewell kiss. The Madam waits nearby, ready to lead me away. It's a long hall, lined with doors, each leading to another boudoir, another pirate, another dead girl playing at life. I listen carefully as the Madam leads me past them, straining my ears to pick up every heaving breath and grunting drive as client after client expends his seed. There are no women among the voices, no matter how I strain, just masculine moans and manly groans as the moment of climax is reached.

For a moment, barely longer than the space of three breaths, I could swear I hear Mr Drummond's hollow cackle. The sound is followed by the familiar snap of the lash, the wet sound of flesh flaying off bone. My steps falter, causing the Madam to pause. She looks down at me, her eyebrow raised.

'Any desire,' she says. 'It's the role of the Old Houses. We try to fulfil any desire, and we take what we need in return. He cannot hurt them.'

'He wants to,' I tell her. 'He wants to hear them scream.'

The Madam offers me an elegant shrug.

'The dead do not scream,' she says. 'They do not speak, they do not sigh, they are silent as the grave. This is immutable, even in the face of desire.'

'So I've been told,' I tell her. 'But they could speak, if they wanted to. They could give him what they wanted.'

The Madam regards me carefully, silent as the night. We stand there, amid the whisper of a dozen clients behind closed doors, the muted buzz of the lounge in the distance.

Eventually the Madam nods.

'They could,' she says, 'but they won't. It would be the end, the talking; no man would come here, once the secrets are revealed.'

She stares at me, her eyes ancient behind the thick layers of make-up.

'Do you understand, little pirate? Do you know what I'm saying?'

There is a flicker of breeze in the hallway, setting the candles dancing. I think of my mother, powdered and cold, living out her life under my father's thumb. She wore the mask of a lady as it suited her, but there were precious few disguises that concealed her true nature.

I look the Madam in the eyes and nod.

'Reputations must be maintained,' I tell her.

The Madam smiles.

'Yes,' she says. 'I suppose they must.'

Then she takes my arm and she walks, returning me to the velvet curtain and the lounge beyond.

The revel has been tempered by the passing of time, whittling away both noise and numbers until the room is near empty and the voices muted.

The Captain is waiting for me, feet on the table, broad smile clamped around an ancient pipe. I sit down at the table, taking a long swallow of the mug he pushes into my hands. It's warm and harsh, like drinking fish scales.

'So that's that,' he says. 'Was it everything you expected, after the stories you've heard?'

I shrug, unsettled, wondering if I've left some gap in my disguise.

'Nothing is ever what you expect of it,' I tell him. 'Why should this place be any different?'

The Captain nods, the feather on his hat weaving a solemn dance; he pulls his feet off the table with a single fluid gesture, climbing to his feet.

'Mr Drummond will not likely emerge before dawn,' the Captain says. 'It's probably best that we don't wait. We should return to the ship, let you get a good night's sleep while you can. We break port in two days, and he's always worse after a night in Tortuga.'

I nod, getting ready to follow him. The Captain lays an arm over my shoulder as I stand.

'Did you find what you were looking for, Tobias Truman?'

He gives me a wolfish smile, but his eyes are serious beneath the brim of his hat. I consider the question for a long moment, studying it as though he'd asked my opinion of a precious jewel. I savour his interest, his desire to treat me as part of his crew; I'm acutely aware that it cannot last forever.

'Perhaps, Captain,' I tell him. 'But at least we can be sure that I got what I wanted.'

This will all end soon enough. One day soon there will be clues that are impossible to hide, and there is no going back once they're out in the open. I know my future, and I am destined to be landlocked if I survive the moment of discovery. I do not have the stomach for a lady-pirate's life, fighting to hold my place among the crew.

'What about you, Captain, did you get what you wanted?'

The Captain smiles at me.

'Nothing more, nothing less,' he says. 'Just as they promise.'

And he leads me out of the room, into the streets of Isla Tortuga, back to the ship that I can call home a little longer.

AFTERWORD

Gothic literature is full of dangerous attractions, with characters destroyed by their desire for someone or something they shouldn't have fallen for. Popular culture is full of zombies that are little more than a genderless, sexless swarm that goes for brains rather than the body.

'The Last Great House of Isla Tortuga' was conceived at the point where those two thoughts met, with an attempt to create a zombie who possesses some of the dangerous gothic allure that's traditionally associated with vampires and ghosts.

— *Peter M. Ball*

Multiple award winner ISOBELLE CARMODY began her first novel, *Obernewtyn*, in high school and has been writing ever since. She completed a Bachelor of Arts and a journalism cadetship while she finished the novel. *Obernewtyn* was shortlisted for Children's Book Council Book of the Year Award; and its sequel, *The Farseekers*, was an honour book in the CBC awards. Her award-winning Obernewtyn Chronicles have established her at the forefront of fantasy writing for young people.

Her fourth book, *The Gathering*, was joint winner of Children's Book Council Book of the Year Award and was second in the Western Australia Young Readers Book Award. She has since then written more than twenty books. The title story of her short-story collection *Green Monkey Dreams* won the Aurealis Award for the best young adult short story; and her novel, *Darkfall*, the first book of the Legendsong series, was shortlisted for the Aurealis Award for Best Fantasy novel. She has also won the coveted Golden Aurealis for her young adult novel *Alyzon Whitestarr*. Her books have been translated into many languages; and she has just completed *The Stone Key*, which is the next to last volume in the Obernewtyn Chronicles. The National Library of Australia has recognised the importance of Isobelle's work by recording an interview with her as part of its oral-history program.

And you, gentle reader, are about to enter one of Isobelle's lucid dreams. A word of warning, though: you are entering a trap …

PERCHANCE TO DREAM

ISOBELLE CARMODY

For Marjorie

Anna woke knowing she had been dreaming, but as so often with dreams, to wake was to forget. Strange to remember vividly that she had dreamed, yet to have no recollection of the dream. On the rare occasion that she did remember, the minute she tried to describe it, the dream would dissolve. Pinning a dream down was like trying to catch hold of a skein of smoke.

Leaf claimed it was possible to train yourself to remember dreams by writing down anything you could recall, after which you could analyse them. It would be nice to believe that dreams had meaning but her feeling was that they were nothing more than a churning of the thoughts and events of the day. Dream analysis was all of a piece with tarot cards, the zodiac and ley lines. Wishful thinking. Not that she would dream of saying so to Leaf. Dear, overweight, dreamy, compassionate Leaf was one of those people whose longing for meaning was so strong and lovely a part of her nature that even their cynical friend Izabel could not bear to do more than poke occasional gentle fun at it.

Anna yawned and turned over to find that she was alone. For just the slightest moment, she felt uneasy. Then she laughed at herself for undoubtedly David had gone to town to get fresh chocolate croissants and papers. These and the coffee that he would brew when he returned were part of their Saturday ritual. He would carry the lot in on the enormous antique tray left to her by her grandmother, complete with a sprig of something from the garden. He had done this the very first Saturday they had awakened together, and he never forgot.

She smiled smugly at the ceiling and told herself as she had done once or twice every day of the three years that she had known him that she was incredibly lucky. It was not until three months after he had been introduced to her at Izabel's retrospective, and only days before they had married, that Anna discovered that he was almost six years younger than she was. She had been horrified and he had laughed at her, asking how knowing their ages changed anything. Amazingly he seemed not to care at all about the age difference, so they had married and suddenly all those long lonely dispiriting years broken by occasional lovers who did not wait to see her face in the morning light were over. She was now that incredible, dazzling thing: an object of love and desire.

'The gods will get you for gloating . . .' she warned herself, and though it was a joke, a little shiver of disquiet ran down her spine because at some level she did feel that this much luck had a price tag, and that sooner or later, she would have to have a leg amputated or get cancer to balance the books. 'Idiot,' she muttered, deciding that she had better get up and have a shower before she got any more morbid.

Pulling back the quilt to air the sheets, she found herself trying to remember what she had done the previous night. Maybe she had got drunk. She almost never drank, but it was possible she had tried one of the strange drinks David sometimes brought home from his trips abroad for her to try. But if she had got drunk, surely she would remember the early part of the evening, even if she had forgotten the rest.

'Early onset of senility,' she muttered, and drew open the curtains.

She gasped, for instead of the sunlit dew drenched garden with the sea shimmering behind it, there was a mist pressed up against the glass, obliterating everything but the cloudy shapes of the nearest bushes. Then something black flew out of the mist and smashed against the glass, shattering it and showering her with cutting fragments. She screamed.

Anna sat up, heart pounding, and felt her face with trembling fingers, but the skin was smooth.

'A nightmare,' she whispered and lay back to ponder the doubled oddness of dreaming you were waking, only to find you had woken into another dream. She looked at David's side of the bed and wondered if she had subconsciously registered his quiet departure and that had been the seed for the dream. She was too wide-awake now to go back to sleep, so she got up and pulled on her kimono. Then she crossed to the curtains and drew them open.

To her astonishment, the garden and the road and the sea were all hidden behind a thick mist, just as in her dream. She stepped back from the window, but nothing came hurtling out of the mist. She laughed shakily and turned to make the bed, reminding herself that mists were not so extraordinary on this part of the coast. In fact, they were common in summer, and sometimes she got into the car and drove only to find the sun shining two kilometres away. It was one of the things she liked about her little stretch of the coast, that weather here was often anomolous.

Showering, she thought how as a child she had loved walking through the mist to school, pretending that she would pass through some hidden magical gate into a world full of adventure and danger, where she would find friendship worth dying for and the truest of true love, not to mention meaning and purpose. But of course there was only one world and only one way to escape it. So she had remained in the world with her grief-sapped father, the ghost of her mother and her bitter, half-mad grandmother. When her father finally committed suicide, she had continued living with her grandmother, whose corrosive bitterness scoured anyone with whom she came in contact, and her granddaughter most of all. The old woman had died when she was twenty-four, leaving Anna a small amount of money and her furniture. The house had gone because of something to do with capital gains tax, and it was only when Anna decided to sell an enormous lounge setting that she had been keeping in Leaf's shed for lack of space in her minute bedsit, that she discovered it was an antique. As were many of the pieces of furniture crammed in her bedsit and Izabel's attic. Where her grandmother had acquired them, she had no idea. Perhaps someone had left them to her, or she had brought them as a job lot when she had left her philandering husband to set up on her own all those eons ago.

Their sale had brought in enough money for a new car, the cottage by the sea, and had enabled her to quit her job as an art teacher and paint. That she had then exhibited shyly and found unexpected success as an artist seemed to be part of that excess of luck that sometimes worried her.

'I don't know how you can see yourself as lucky,' Izabel had said when she had once voiced this apprehension. 'Your mother dies of cancer and your selfish father kills himself, leaving you in the clutches of your vicious, tightfisted cow of a grandmother. I'd say you paid in advance for your luck, if that's how it works. Mind you this much luck is totally wasted on you, Anna.'

'He wasn't selfish,' Leaf had reproached their vivid friend gently, for she had gone to school with Anna and had known her father. 'He was just so sad. Think of it, his mother left his father and never allowed them to see one another again, and then his wife gets cancer and dies. I think he stayed alive as long as he could for Anna's sake.'

'Oh bully for him,' Izabel sneered. 'He kills himself when she is thirteen, which everyone knows is the worst age to have anything like that happen.'

'All ages are the worst age to have that happen,' Anna had murmured, but neither of them heard her.

Had she been scarred by her parents' deaths or her grandmother's terrible bitterness, she now wondered as she towelled herself dry. She did not feel scarred but she supposed those things might be at the root of her excruciating shyness; especially with men. She had never been able to imagine that anyone could love her and Izabel maintained that was why no one did. According to her, men only wanted what they couldn't have. They were natural hunters and Anna's meekness and lack of confidence made her as exciting as a tortoise. Anna conceded her shyness, but maybe that was her nature as much as the circumstances of her childhood. And it was not as if she had ever been glamorous like Izabel, with her flaming red hair and gorgeous face and body. Nor did she have Leaf's irresistable charm to distinguish her. She was merely ordinary looking and awkward of manner, and it had seemed foolish and vain to try to change that with clothes or make-up, as Izabel always urged. That would be too much like donning a mask, and if someone were won by it, then she would be doomed to wear it forever. Better to remain herself and alone.

Then David had come into her life. She could still see Izabel in her peacock coloured coat, smiling as she introduced them, and David's serious eyes above his soft wondering smile. 'I might be a little out of my depth here,' he had confessed, voicing her shy discomfort.

Slowly she rubbed into her face some of the expensive cream she had brought at his insistence when they had flown back from Paris, but she did not wipe the clouds from the mirror. Better not to look at her pale, plain face with its mouse-coloured eyes and mouse-coloured hair. It was not so much her mousiness that bothered her as the lines about her eyes that betokened her age and the slight thickening of her body, which might be the beginning of a middle-aged spread. Revolting phrase. As if you got soft and runny and incapable of holding your form when you got older.

Pulling on her favourite primrose silk kimono, she went to the kitchen to look at the clock but was distracted by the sight of the mist through the kitchen window. It obscured not only the back garden but the enormous hill that rose greenly up behind the house. Beyond it lay the vast wilderness of the national park. When she first used to come here she had been able to walk from her back door across blackberry-choked fields and up to the top of the hill where she would gaze at the forest that spread as far as the eye could see. But the older couple that had brought the land behind Anna's encompassed the hill and they soon poisoned the blackberries, repaired the fences, and put in a bad-tempered bull to discourage anyone trying to climb them. They were possessive ex-city folk with a loathing for cats, and twice Anna had been forced to go to the council to rescue Electra after she had been lured into one of their traps. David disliked them intensely and had more than once suggested she simply make an offer of money for their land, which the pair would be unable to resist. But Anna had not wanted to do that. She did not like the neighbours any more than he did, but life was full of people with plans that elbowed you and stepped on your toes, and you could not buy out everyone. Life was about adapting and finding a way to live with other people.

Anna frowned, remembering a rare argument with David about the neighbours, in which he had accused her of being too passive. It had happened a month after the wedding, and a few days after David had first met Leaf. She had always wondered if her friend's support of her refusal to act against the neighbours had precipitated the quarrel. 'Don't you ever want anything passionately enough to fight for it?' David had demanded. 'Will you always simply take what life gives you and strive for nothing?'

All at once the mist shifted and thinned so that suddenly Anna could see the bottom of the neighbour's hill. Unexpectedly, there was a man in a long black cloak striding along its flank! Leaning on the sill and squinting, she decided that it was not either of her neighbours, who were both grey haired, for this man had shaggy black hair. Besides, the neighbours never walked anywhere. They used a noisy two-stroke tractor to traverse their property and even to collect the mail from the postbox at the front of the house. The man might be a visitor, in which case he would know about the bull. But what if he was a hiker and had come down the creek from the national forest?

Anna stood there indecisive, until the memory of David's accusation of passivity drove her out the back door, across the veranda and through the trees to the waist-high fence which was the real border of her land. 'Hey!' she called.

The man stopped abruptly and looked across at her. He stood so still that he reminded her of a deer or a fox caught in the headlights of a car. Belatedly it occurred to her that she was wearing nothing but a thin kimono and was all alone. When the man began to come towards her with swift, purposeful strides, she had to resist the impulse to back up, reminding herself that she had called out to him. His face was extraordinarily pale, and if not for his dark eyes and his black brows and hair, she would have thought he was albino. That his clothes were black, only accentuated his palour so much as to be an affectation, except that somehow, despite his queer clothes and dramatic good looks, this man did not strike her as the sort who desired attention.

'I just wondered if you realised this is private land,' Anna said when he finally stopped on the other side of the fence. 'There is a bull, you see. It's not mine,' she added and then she blushed at the foolishness of her words. Why was it that she was unable to utter a single sensible sentence when she met someone for the first time?

Still the man did not speak, and although his Slavic features showed little of what he was feeling, she had the strong feeling that he was astonished, though she could not imagine why. Surely she was not such an amazing sight wearing a kimono in her own back yard.

'My husband and I saw you from the kitchen window. We thought you might not have realised that you had got onto private land. There is the bull you see. The neighbours let it loose and it has a very bad temper ...' She stopped, abruptly realising she was babbling on like an idiot. The man might not even speak English. That could be the explanation for his sombre, old-fashioned clothes and his silence.

'I did not realise there was a place here. The mist,' the man finally spoke, pointing behind her. He had a slight but definite accent, which she thought might be Russian or maybe Hungarian.

'This is my land. Mine and my husbands,' Anna said, then she blushed for surely in mentioning David so often and pointedly she was making it all too obvious that he was *not* at home. Get a grip, she told herself in Izabel's sharp clear tone. She said calmly, 'The land you are on is not my land. But I am trying to warn you that there is a bull loose.'

'A bull?' The man turned hastily, lifting his hands as if to defend himself. She saw from the breadth of his shoulders under the cloak that he was strongly built. But after a moment, he relaxed and glanced back at her. 'The bull is not yours?'

'No. The bull and the land you are on belong to my neighbour,' Anna repeated, unease giving way to exasperation. 'You must go along the fence there to reach the road.'

'The borders of this place are strong,' the man said, his dark eyes now seeming to examine her closely. 'I could not enter without being invited.'

This was such a peculiar thing to say that Anna wondered if the man had understood anything she had said. She said firmly but kindly, 'Just go that way. Follow the fence down to the road.' She turned and headed back to the house.

'Wait,' the man called. 'Will you tell me your name?'

Anna turned only to find that the mist had thickened so that she could no longer see the man or the hill. But some impulse made her call, 'My name is Anna. Goodbye.' She ran lightly through the trees to the porch and was inside the house before it occurred to her that it was a long time since she had moved so swiftly and easily. Maybe Leaf was right in saying that ageing was all in your mind. Then Anna grinned, remembering that Izabel had responded sourly to this pronouncement by saying unfortunately it was all in your body.

Anna looked out the kitchen window again, but the mist was thicker than ever and she could see no sign of the man. She hoped he had understood and was making his way to the road. Maybe when David came, he would go and pick the man up and offer him a lift to town. He had seemed very persuaded when Leaf had given him her random acts of goodness to counterbalance a world full of random acts of violence lecture; funny how he had gone from calling her a feather-brained hippie to admiring her genuine kindness and compassion. Thinking of David reminded Anna that she had come into the kitchen to look at the clock. It showed three o'clock, which was impossible. She put her head against the clock, and sure enough, there was no ticking.

She shrugged. The real wonder was that the old clock had ticked on for so long, rather than that it had stopped. She grinned, thinking how often David had asked how she could endure something so ugly. The clock was in fact quite hideously ornate but Anna liked it anyway. Or maybe that was why she liked it. Ironically, it was the most valuable by far of the things her grandmother had left her, and David said she ought to sell it before it broke or was stolen. But she had refused, saying it was the only thing out of all her grandmother's furniture that she liked and they had more than enough for their modest needs and for quite a few wants as well. It would be a nest egg for their old age.

Anna went into the living room to look at the little clock on David's desk. Incredibly, it had stopped at three o'clock too. This was odd enough to give her pause because one clock ran on batteries and the other on an intricate antique system of tiny pulleys and pendulums. She was tempted to call Leaf, who was bound to have a vague but thrilling sounding theory that would cover the mist and the stopped clocks, but she resisted the impulse and returned to the kitchen. She reached out and touched the antique clock affectionately. She would take it up to the city, to the old watchmaker who had valued it, next time she went and get it repaired. In fact she might drive up with David on Monday. It would be fun to go with him for a change. Maybe she would book the Windsor for the night and they could stay and even see a show. Or go to a Jazz club. David would prefer that. The more she thought of the plan, the more it appealed and she went to find the hotel number, thinking that she could just pack a bag for them and slip it into the boot of the car and make the whole thing a surprise. She would wait to tell him until he said disconsolately that he supposed they had better head for the hills.

Finger poised to dial, it occurred to her that David had not said that for some time. In fact the last time they had gone to the city, he had only said cheerfully, 'Let's call in and see Leaf on the way home.' The contentment in his voice had been profound, and she had stared out the window of the car to stop him seeing how moved she had been to hear him call the cottage home. She shrugged and dialed, then she stopped. There was no dial tone. The phone was dead. She stared into the receiver in disbelief; first the clocks and now the phone.

Maybe it was just the third thing. Leaf always said everything came in threes.

Anna's stomach rumbled loudly and that decided her. Instead of waiting, she would drive into town. No doubt David had been waylaid and if he had tried to ring, she would not have got the call. Would he have got some sort of signal or message to let him know the phone was out, or would he simply think she had gone to the beach? It was possible that the mist had rolled in after he left, and only extended as far as Point Defiant. She had a mobile of course, but there was no reception unless you drove out to the point. She debated walking along the road to the neighbour on the other side to find out if their phone was out as well, but they might not be down for the weekend.

The phone began to ring. Anna stared at it incredulously then she dived on it, snatching up the receiver. 'David?'

No answer.

She was about to hang up, when she realised she could hear someone speaking, but it was as if they were very far away. She pressed the receiver hard against her ear and strained to catch the words. 'I'm sorry,' she heard. 'I never wanted this. I never meant you to be hurt . . .'

'Izabel?' Anna whispered. 'Is that you?'

But now there was only a faint humming sound. Anna set the receiver down slowly and deliberately, and lifted the receiver again to dial David's number. Then she realised there was no dial tone.

'This is impossible,' she said.

She went to the bedroom and threw off her kimono, pulled on jeans, canvas shoes and a frayed red T-shirt that had once belonged to her father and went to get the keys to her car. But they were not on their hook by the door. She stared at the bare nail incredulously. David had taken her keys along with his own once ages back but she had driven in another nail since then, so their keys had hung on different hooks. The only answer was that he must have absent-mindedly put his keys on her hook the previous night when he had got in. Normally it would not have mattered, but so many queer things had happened already that morning that their absence disturbed her. For some reason, she thought of the pills Izabel had given her when she had been so nervous before her first show that she had kept vomiting.

'Vomiting is not good PR,' Izabel had announced, and she had given Anna a pill to calm her nerves. After the show, she had presented Anna with the bottle, saying that it looked as if she was going to have to endure many more shows. She had been right, for Anna had been inundated by offers from galleries and agents after that first night. But she had never taken any more of the pills for shows. She hadn't liked the way they made her feel as if she was wrapped up in cotton wool, all her senses numbed down.

Suddenly there was a loud thud against the window. Anna started violently but there was no broken glass. She drew a long steadying breath and went outside to see if the bird was lying in the grass, stunned. She thought how uncanny it was to have this happen after she had dreamed of something smashing the window. Of course birds frequently flew into the oversized windows David had insisted they install in the cottage. It might even be that she had subconciously registered a bird hitting the glass when she slept, and had simply incorporated it into her dream. Certainly more birds hit the windows when the fog was in. But there was no bird lying under the window so it must have managed to flap away after all. Or else Electra had been even faster than usual.

As if her thoughts had summoned the siamese cat, Electra was by the door waiting to be let in, blue eyes guileless.

'Don't you think this is a very weird day, Electra?' she muttered as they came back into the kitchen.

'Not really,' Electra answered in exactly the sort of raspy smokers' voice Anna always imagined the cat would have if she talked. Then her mouth fell open at the realisation that *the cat had talked*! Electra yawned elaborately, showing a pink tongue and sharp white teeth. 'I hope you are not going to be boring and do the whole oh my god the cat is talking routine.'

'This has to be a dream,' Anna said faintly.

'What else?' asked Electra drily.

'I'm *dreaming*!' Anna repeated. Relief washed over her at the realisation that this was the answer to all the strangeness of the morning. The mist, the foreign man, her inability to remember the previous night, even the birds hitting the windows; they were all part of a dream. But that meant she had dreamed of waking two times in the course of a dream, without ever actually doing so. The thought made her feel dizzy. Then it struck her that she was not just dreaming. She was *lucid* dreaming; she was aware of dreaming while she was dreaming. According to Leaf, that meant she could direct her movements in the dream, and wake when she wanted just by voicing the wish aloud. But the experience was so amazing and novel that she had no desire to wake.

'I don't want to wake,' she said.

'Fortunate, under the circumstances,' Electra muttered obscurely, as she began to groom her tail.

'This really feels real,' Anna said.

'What is reality?' Asked Electra.

Anna looked down at her. 'I always imagined you would sound like this.'

'Which is why I sound like this,' Electra said. 'So are you going out?'

'I can't. David took my keys by accident,' Anna said. Then she remembered she was dreaming. The real David was probably lying right beside her sound asleep. In fact, Leaf claimed that when you dreamed about a person, it was only the bit of you that the person represented, so it was actually she who had taken her keys.

All at once Leaf herself was sitting at the kichen bench cupping a mug of green tea in both hands. Only instead of one of her voluminous tent dresses, she was wearing a close fitting emerald green silk dress with a long train that hugged her multitude of curves and trailed across the terracotta tiles, and rather than being cropped into a white blond dandelion, her hair hung well past her waist and was bound into a loose plait from which fetching wisps escaped. She looked wonderful.

'I'm dreaming you,' Anna said.

'Of course,' Leaf responded, beaming. She bent down and picked up Electra, who began at once to purr. Anna was startled to notice that the cat's eyes had turned the same shade of green as Leaf's own.

'What does it mean that I keep dreaming of waking?' Anna asked.

'You mustn't look for the obvious in dreams,' Leaf said in her gentle pedantic way. 'To understand the meaning of a dream, you have to regard it as a message from the parts of you that are intuitive and voiceless, rather than reasoning and rational. In a sense, a dream is a code and you have to find the key if you want to unravel its meaning. Sometimes it will be a recurring image or event, or it might be one of the people you dream about that is the key. I mean, whatever it is that they represent for you.'

Anna frowned. 'Let's see; I dreamed of David being missing, and of mist and of birds hitting the window. Of the clocks being stopped and the phone not working. And I dreamed of Electra talking and then you appeared.'

'Not me exactly,' Leaf corrected her. 'I probably represent an aspect of your personality, too. You must think of me as a symbol.'

'Of what?'

'I'm not sure. Dream symbolism is very subjective. But if you want an educated guess, I would say that I symbolise the spiritual, imaginative aspect of your persona, and you have conjured me because whatever it is that your subconscious is trying to tell you is to do with intuition rather than facts.'

'What about Electra? What does she symbolise?'

'Well of course not everything in a dream is a symbol. For instance, *you* are not a symbol and it might be that Electra is simply Electra, but the fact that she spoke is surprising. It suggests to me that she represents a part of you that does not usually voice itself. Given that she is an animal and a cat in particular, I would say she represents atavistic aspects of your nature. Jealousy or rage perhaps.'

'But I don't feel either of those things,' Anna protested.

'Electra could also simply represent animal awareness; Your primal sense which existed in humans before reason. But don't get hung up on a single aspect of the dream. Tell me about this dark man? Is he attractive.'

Anna shrugged. 'He was a foreigner wearing black old-fashioned looking clothes. He had the palest face, too. I was trying to warn him about the neighbour's bull and then he said something odd. I can't remember it exactly, but something about not being able to visit my place unless I invite him.'

'Sounds like a vampire,' Leaf said. 'I hope this is not going to be a nightmare.'

Anna laughed. 'He was just a hiker that got lost in the mist.'

'Your mist,' Leaf reminded her. 'Your hiker.'

'What about David taking the keys?'

'It suggests to me that part of you has been set aside or misplaced in your relationship with David.'

'That's ridiculous,' Anna protested. 'I knew you didn't like him. It's because he's younger isn't it?'

'If that's what I think, it's what you think,' Leaf said mildly. 'In fact I did have reservations about him to begin with. It was something of a shock to come back from a trip and find you married, and he was always so controlled that I felt he was playing a part. But you know all of this because I told you. Yet in the end, I came to see that under the coolness and sophistication, he is a man in pain.' She laughed, adding, 'No, I don't wonder any longer why you are with him. These days it's Izabel who says he's not right for you.'

'But she introduced us!' Anna protested, but she thought of the whispered voice on the phone; Izabel apologising. But that was a dream. *This* is a dream, Anna reminded herself.

'Tell me what aspect of the dream stands out most for you,' Leaf asked. 'Sometimes that is the best way to understand a dream.'

'I guess it's that I dreamed of waking but I was still dreaming, and then I woke again, but I'm still dreaming,' Anna answered.

'Sounds as if you are trying to wake,' Leaf said. 'Tell me about the clocks.'

'They stopped. That antique of Gran's and David's little electric travelling clock. One runs on battery and the other has a mechanism that works on a pendulum but they both stopped at the same moment. Three o'clock.'

Something smashed into the kitchen window and Anna jumped and swung round in time to see something dark fly up and out of sight. It looked a lot bigger than a bird but when she turned to ask what Leaf had seen, she found that her friend and her cat were gone.

There was a knock at the front door. Anna stood for a long minute, then she went through to the front door and opened it. The foreign man was standing on her doorstep. 'Anna,' he said.

'This is a dream,' Anna said.

'I know,' agreed the man, 'I was only able to penetrate this far because you gave me your name. The giving of a name is always an invitation. Have you been beyond the boundaries of your dream yet?'

'Beyond?'

He nodded his glossy head. 'If you wish, I can escort you. It can be daunting in the beginning to go beyond your dreams. But I have been exploring around your area lately and there is nothing too bad. No nightmares. I came because I saw the hill but I could not find the house because of the mist. Then you called me.'

'I don't understand a thing you are saying,' Anna said. 'Are you trying to tell me that you are not part of my dream?'

'I am a part of your dream in this moment, but I can leave it and retain solidity and form and identity as I travel though the larger dreamscape. As you can. It is one of the advantages of being a long dreamer.'

'What is a long dreamer?' Anna asked, beginning to feel uneasy.

'A person who has been asleep long enough for their dream to have become solid. This means you can leave your dream and return to it without it vanishing. And once you become a lucid dreamer, you can direct your course as I have done. Of course, there are short dreamers who lucid dream, but they cannot travel outside their own dreams because the dream will immediately dissolve, causing them to wake.'

'But am I ... I mean, why am I sleeping for a long time? What happened to me?'

He shrugged. 'Car accident, failed suicide, embolism, bomb explosion. Could be anything really.'

'You mean I'm in a coma,' Anna gasped. All at once she felt weak.

'Let me help you,' said the man, but he did not move. Then he said, 'You have to invite me. I can't breach the boundaries of your dream.'

'I'll come out,' Anna said.

'I'm not a vampire,' the man said. 'But you should try not to think about such beings else you will summon one and they are very difficult to deal with. We may not be able to be killed but we can feel fear and pain very vividly.'

'You read my mind!' she accused.

'Not really. You projected an image into my mind of me as a vampire. But listen, let me show you what I mean. We should have a very good view of the dreamscape from the top of your hill.' He held out his hand.

'What is your name?' Anna asked.

He smiled. 'I am Nicholas and knowing my name will allow you to summon or repel me from your place. But it is rude to summon a person physically. You must say my name and allow me to come to you. Remember, though, that if you speak the name of a short dreamer, it can sometimes make them lucid but more often it will cause them to wake.'

'You mean I can go into other people's dreams?'

'Have I not been saying so?' Nicholas asked. 'But remember, the dreams of short dreamers are unstable and like to vanish when you are in them. Then you will be drawn back to your own place. But you will pass through the void and that is a place of pure nightmare. Best to learn the signs that tell you a dreamer is about to wake, so that you can abandon a dream before it abandons you. Come.' He held out his hand again and, after a hesitation, Anna stepped outside telling herself this was a dream and ordinary rules could not possibly apply. She expected his flesh to be cold to match his pallour, but his hand was warm and strong as it closed about hers.

They went down the side of the house to the back yard, past her car. She was startled to see that it was not her new car in the driveway but the little green Volkswagen she had brought out of her first earnings at teachers' college. She touched it affectionately as she passed and was shocked when it purred.

'Things are often as you imagined them in dreams,' Nicholas said, reaching out to pat the car. At the back of the yard, he leapt over the fence and then he helped her over it, adding, 'Best not to think about the bull you mentioned the other day.'

Anna stared at him. 'The other day? I saw you less than an hour ago.'

His winged brows lifted. 'Time is subjective here.'

They climbed the hill, which was as steep as she remembered from years before. Anna grinned to think how it would irritate her neighbours to know that she had appropriated their hill as part of her dreamplace. But thinking of the neighbours made her think of David and her smile faded. 'Am I in a coma then?' She asked flatly.

He was a little ahead and he looked back at her. 'It would seem so.'

Anna suppressed a surge of claustrophobia. 'But I can wake, right? I mean, I can wake up eventually.'

'It is possible. But the longer you sleep, the less likely it is that you will wake.'

Anna wanted to ask how long he had slept, but there was a remoteness in his face that prevented her voicing the question. They toiled up the last steep sloping part of the hill, and then turned to look around them. The hill had bought them above the mist and they had a panoramic view in all directions. But what Anna now beheld was not what she had seen the last time she had been to the top of the hill, save for the part of the hill that ran down to her house, or what would be her house, if it was not hidden in mist. There was no sign of the beach or the sea. Beyond the mist, a vast city rose up, which was bordered by a desert on one side and on the other by factories and housing estate homes in a rigid grid of streets. Further away was a wood, and a lake and then what looked like a castle, but in between each, there was mist.

'Those are all dreams?' Anna asked.

'This is the dreamscape. The solid seeming parts are dreams and the mist is void. But those solid places will vanish as soon as their dreamers wake. That is what makes your hill so unique. It is a true fixed point and so it can be used to navigate by. The nearest solid place beyond it is a wood with flaming trees.'

'Is that the dream of another long dreamer?' Anna asked.

'It must be so, but I have never found them. It may be that the dreamer has taken the form of a tree rather than becoming lucid. True long dream travellers are rare.'

Anna felt dizzy at the alienness of what he was telling her. Nicholas said sharply, 'Don't! If you let go, you will go back into the void and drag me there with you.'

'Won't I just wake?' Anna asked.

'An ordinary dreamer would do so, but waking is no simple matter for long dreamers. The best way to describe it is to say that there is a gap between waking and dreaming, and that is the void. To get from one state to the other, the dreamer must pass over the void. But while ordinary dreamers have a bridge to cross, long dreamers do not.'

Anna nodded slowly. Then she drew in a breath of surprise, because over his shoulder she saw that the city was beginning to shimmer and lose definition. Nicholas followed her gaze, then he said, 'Someone you know is waking.'

'Someone I know?'

He nodded. 'The dreamscape is formed of dreams resting alongside one another. Of course it is in constant flux as dreamers wake and sleep, but usually, each dream is surrounded by the dreams of those who think of their dreamer most often.'

'So the desert and that housing estate and the city are the dreams of my friends?' Anna asked. 'What will happen if I go there? Could I speak to them?'

'You can enter their dreams easily enough because they are not solid enough to have barriers. But then you must find the dreamer. If you can do that and if they have taken a form that permits you to question them and allows them to answer, and if they do not wake, of course you can speak with them. But what would you ask?'

Before she could frame an answer, an enormous oversized raven swooped into life in the sky above them and dived on them. Anna screamed and threw herself to the ground, but Nicholas stood over her batting at the bird until it flew away. When its shrieks had faded, Anna rose on legs that shook. 'What is it with these birds?'

'There have been others?' Nicholas asked, looking worried.

Anna nodded. 'Two, I think. They crashed into the windows of the house. What are they?'

'Warnings from your undermind,' Nicholas said. 'It seems that some part of you does not want answers.' He held out his hand and Anna was horrified to see there was a gash on his arm from which blood dripped freely. He glanced around. 'Let's get down from here.'

'I want to visit one of the other dream places,' Anna said.

They went to the housing estate. They reached it by walking along the road that passed the front of Anna's cottage. Nicholas explained that roads and paths were archetypes, and because all dreams contained them, a lucid dreamer could move from one dream to another using them, so long as they could visualise their destination. 'That is what makes the wood of flame trees and your hill so important. Because this is a land of constant change, and yet they do not change. Fortunately, we also saw the dreams surrounding yours from the top of the hill.

'I don't know whose dream this could be,' Anna said doubtfully, and they made their way along streets lined with houses that were all exactly the same.

'Try one of the doors,' Nicholas suggested.

Anna went up the nearest path and knocked at the door. She heard the sound of movement and then the door opened to reveal a small, grubby child with dirty straw yellow hair. 'What do you want?' he demanded.

Anna stared at him, not knowing what to say. 'We wish to see your mother or father,' Nicholas said, smoothly.

'No one but me's home and I ent to talk to anyone,' said the child. He shut the door.

Nicholas looked at Anna expectantly. 'I don't know him,' she said.

'Don't be so sure,' he warned. 'People are not always as you would expect to see them in dreams. They can take on forms that express their inner selves, or some aspect of it.'

But Anna shook her head. 'The only man who is close to me is David and that child could not have been him. David grew up in England in a village. He told me that his father was a history professor at Oxford.'

'Let us try another house,' Nicholas said.

They did and to Anna's amazement, the same boy answered the door. 'We need to speak urgently with your parents,' Nicholas said firmly.

'They're out at work and I'm not supposed to let anyone in,' said the boy, but less aggressively than before.

'What does your father do?' Nicholas asked. 'Perhaps we could visit his place of work.'

The boy glared at him and suddenly there was a pit bull pressing at the security door. 'Go away or I'll let Ghengis Khan out.'

Anna gave a start and Nicholas gave her a swift, searching look. 'It *is* David,' she whispered. 'He told me once that when he was a child, he had a dog called Khan.'

'David?' Nicholas addressed the boy.

'That's my middle name,' the boy said suspiciously. 'How did you know? Did my dad send you?'

'David, do you know a woman called Anna?'

The boy recoiled and all at once he was not a boy but a middle-aged man with thinning blond hair and a paunch. Anna was shocked to see that it was David, but a much older and coarser David than she had known. 'Anna's dead or as near as makes no difference,' he said in a surly voice half-slurred with drinking. 'It warn't my fault. I couldn't help how things came out. I had a plan and then I fell in love. How could I have expected that? And a lot of good it did me. I ended up with nothing.' The man stepped back and slammed the door closed.

'I don't understand,' Anna said.

Nicholas only took her elbow and led her back to the street and along it. 'Let us find somewhere to sit and talk. Do you feel hungry? Hunger is an illusion of course, but eating is always pleasant, I find.' Anna let him lead her out of the housing estate and back along the road towards the mist that hid her cottage. Once within it, the smell of the sea was very strong, and Anna felt a powerful longing to wake and walk on the beach. Perhaps she had projected the thought, because instead of leading her up the path to the house, he guided her down the path through the bushes that edged the road, to the little beach that she had visited so often. Nicholas bade her close her eyes and imagine a picnic she had enjoyed.

Somewhat bemused, Anna obeyed, imagining the picnic her father had prepared for her twelfth birthday. It had been a month after her mother died, and she had been allowed to ask Leaf. Her father had got a restaurant to prepare the food and it had been delicious.

'Perfect,' said Nicholas and Anna opened her eyes to find exactly this picnic spread out on an eggshell blue cloth. It was still misty but the air was warm and sweetly scented by the little purple flowers that grew along the track leading from the road to the beach. Nicholas sat and drew her down beside him, lamenting the single wine glass.

'It was my father's. I was a child,' Anna said.

'We will share it,' Nicholas suggested, and he uncorked the bottle deftly, poured some of the ruby dark wine into the glass and offered it to her. She sipped a mouthful, looking at him over the rim of the glass. Then as she passed it to him, she asked him why he was helping her. He took a long drink and then he said gently, 'Long dreamers are always searching for other long dreamers.'

'Why?' Anna asked taking the peach he had given her and absently smoothing the down.

'In part, for the solidity of their dreamplaces. But also out of loneliness. It is impossible to form any sort of relationship with an ordinary dreamer. Even lucid dreamers can only communicate until they wake. So we search for others of our kind. Of course even a long dreamer can wake, or retreat into the void. Or . . .' He stopped abruptly.

'Or die?' Anna concluded softly.

He turned his face towards the invisible waves.

Anna was silent a while, then she said gently, 'I understand what you are saying, Nicholas, and I am sorry for your loneliness. But I have to tell you that I mean to wake as soon as I can figure out how. Don't *you* want to wake?'

He gave her a strange look. 'There are wonders here that you could not imagine in your wildest dreams, Anna. I have seen a mountain of glass that shines like a diamond in the sun, and there is a white sea so vast I think it must be God's dream. And you can change things. You can use the stuff of dreams to build anything. You can change yourself.' He looked at Anna and saw her expression. 'What is it?'

She shook her head. 'I don't know. I had the feeling that I had heard you say that before. Can you have déjà vu in a dream?'

'You can have anything in a dream,' Nicholas said.

'I can't have my life,' Anna told him.

'Life is only another kind of dream,' Nicholas said, but he spoke softly, as if to himself.

They finished their picnic meal in silence, and then Anna stood up and said resolutely that she wanted to try visiting the desert. 'I need to know what happened to me. I need to understand the things David said in his dream.'

'The words he said may not mean what they seem to mean,' Nicholas said, as he rose too.

'They mean something,' Anna said determinedly.

They went up the leafy path to the road, but instead of coming to the road and seeing the mist swathed cottage on the other side, they were standing on the rim of the desert they had seen from the top of the hill.

'Any idea of whose dream this might be?'

Anna shook her head. 'No one I know is like a desert.'

He shrugged and set off across the desert. 'Perhaps, then, this is an unknown face of someone you know.'

They had walked for several hours when Anna noticed trees rising above a bare dune in the distance. It was an oasis! She set off towards it, the sand slipping away under her feet. They ran for a long time tirelessly, but also without getting any closer to the oasis. Finally Nicholas stopped. 'It is a mirage.'

Anna said nothing, for now she had seen a woman dragging herself up the shifting face of a dune with painful slowness. Anna noticed with horror that the woman's hands were covered with blood. Nicholas laid a hand on her shoulder as she would have reached out to help the woman. 'Be careful. If you touch her and she is the dreamer, she will very likely wake. Try talking to her.'

Anna nodded. 'Can I help you?' she asked.

The woman turned to look at her and Anna was astounded to see that it was Izabel, but not the elegant, sophisticated Izabel of the real world. Her face had been burnt to a terrible blazing red, and her eyes looked out in staring madness. Her lips were cracked and bleeding as if she had chewed them, and her hair was so filthy it looked grey brown instead of red. But all at once the madness faded in the wild eyes.

'Anna?' Izabel rasped, and her face twisted in a ghastly mingling of despair and rage. 'I never meant you any harm. I swear it. It was all his idea. He said you were soft and that it would be easy to gull you. But then he changed. He said he had not meant to fall in love but that it changed everything. He told me that he would give me money, but it was never the money I wanted. I never meant you any harm. I just couldn't see straight I was so jealous. I lost control.'

The desert began to tremble and a great terror flowed through Anna. She tried to stand but the ground was shuddering violently. She turned and saw Nicholas reaching out to her. Instinctively, she threw out her own hand, but it was too late. The world dissolved into the squeal of tyres and the grinding shriek of metal. Then there was a bone-crunching impact and terrible, excruciating pain. Then silence.

Anna woke.

She was lying in her bed in a rumpled tangle of sheets. She thought with bewilderment of the vividness of the dreams within dreams she had experienced and thought it was no wonder the bed was a mess. 'At least I know that when you hit the ground in a falling dream, you do wake up,' she muttered. She turned to find David was not in bed. 'Déjà vu,' she said. 'Déjà vu squared.'

She sat up and rubbed her face, remembering the bird smashing into the glass, and the one that had swooped her on the hilltop. Warnings from her undermind, the dream man had named them. Anna's thoughts shifted to the dream Izabel in the desert. She had not named David, and yet it was David she had been referring to. Then there had been David before that, saying that he had a plan, and that he had not expected to fall in love.

All of it had been a dream, and yet Leaf always said dreams contained messages from the subconscious. And so, what was she being told? Anna thought of Izabel in her peacock coat, introducing David. How beautiful she had looked that day. Anna had taken it for the glow of pleasure at her exhibition, but in fact nothing had sold that night, nor in the weeks that followed. Normally that would have enraged Izabel, but in fact she had dismissed the failure of the show lightly, saying that the next one would have the proper gallery and pre-publicity. It had not occurred to Anna to wonder what she meant.

What had the plan been then? David was to marry Anna, and after a time, divorce her? Izabel had known her well enough to realise she would not contest a reasonable claim; especially if they had come to her and confessed to falling in love. She would have accepted it as the natural fate of a plain woman. Then Izabel and David would have money and one another. Except that according to Izabel, David had fallen in love with her.

Anna heard the sound of crockery in the kitchen, and wondered if she had the courage to go in and confront him. After all she had no evidence. But if David had fallen in love with her, perhaps it did not truly matter that he had begun by pretending love. Except that it did. In that moment, Anna understood that loving David had been more a matter of loving someone who could love her. Anna got up slowly and drew on her kimono. She was trembling and her whole body ached as if she really had fallen from a great height. Entering the kitchen, she said, 'I had the strangest dream last night . . .'

She stopped, for the man making coffee was not David but Nicholas. The room swayed and shimmered but Nicholas leapt across the room and took both of her hands in his. 'Look into my eyes, Anna. Look into them and stay. Don't retreat.'

Slowly the shimmering faded and the room lost its strange radiance. Anna looked down at Nicholas' hands, clasped so tightly about hers that his fingers were white. A sense of déjà vu washed over her. 'I'm sorry,' he said, loosening his grip. 'Are you all right?'

'How long has this been going on?' Anna whispered, looking up into his dark eyes.

His expression grew very still, his eyes watchful. Then he breathed out slowly. 'Countless times, but you have never got so far before. Last time you retreated after confronting Izabel.'

'Was it always the same? The other times?'

He shook his head. 'Last time it was a jungle for Izabel, and David was working in one of the factories with his father.'

'He married me because of the money. Izabel loved him and he wanted the money so they deceived me. Then he fell in love with me . . .' She sat down at the kitchen bench and Nicholas set a cup of coffee before her.

'I hope I have done it well enough. The implements here are unfamiliar to me.'

Anna took the coffee. Then something occurred to her. 'How did you come in here? I thought you couldn't unless I invited you.'

'You screamed my name as the desert dream broke,' Nicholas said. 'It allowed me to bind myself to you.'

'But what if I had retreated into the void? I could have, couldn't I?'

He nodded. 'You could but . . .' He shrugged.

Anna nodded, but she was thinking of the blood on Izabel's hands, and the screech of tyres and the sound of grinding metal. The broken glass when the bird had hit the window. 'I think there was an accident,' she said softly. 'I think I was in a car with Izabel and something went wrong. Maybe David had told her he would not leave me. She said she lost control.' She shivered and wondered if they were both in a hospital; Izabel in an ordinary room and she in a special ward for comatose patients. Maybe David was sitting beside her, holding her hand, longing for her to wake.

She rose and went to the window, noticing that day had turned suddenly to night. The mist had thinned to veils of gauze and beyond them, the sea shimmered and glittered in the light of a full moon. 'Does night come here, then?' she asked.

'Night and day; winter, summer, autumn and spring; full moon and high noon. But they might not come when you expect and they are more often reflections of a dreamer's mood than of the natural state of the world,' he answered.

'Thank you for helping me,' she murmured.

'Thank you for giving me purpose,' Nicholas said. 'It is more precious than you can know.' He lifted her hand and kissed it.

'I need to go to the city,' Anna said.

The city was no ordinary city. As they walked along the road towards it, Anna saw that the skyscrapers were actually ruins wound about with some sort of leafy creeper, and what she had taken for roads were actually long stretches of dark lawn broken here and there by moon-sheened ponds and shimmering silver streams. Night blooming lilies grew in great clumps, filling the air with a heavy languorous perfume, but even as they moved through the city towards what Anna sensed was its heart, the sky began to lighten towards dawn and birds began to sing.

'This is beautiful,' Anna said.

'We have not been here before but ... it is strangely coherent,' he said, answering her unvoiced question. 'Dreams are not usually so,' he added. As they moved deeper into the strange city, the sky turned pink and gradually the light increased until it was a rich beautiful dawn. Then Nicholas pointed down the street to a grassy intersection where there was an immense marble fountain. Sitting on the edge of it bathing her feet was an enormous green skinned woman with flowing yellow hair. Squirrels and birds were perched fearlessly on her shoulders. Then the giant woman turned her face and Anna saw it clearly.

'Leaf,' she said softly.

The giant woman's eyes widened as her mouth curved into a smile of delight. 'I am so happy to see you, Anna,' Leaf said. 'I always believed I would, one day.'

'You are a lucid dreamer?' Nicholas said.

The goddess Leaf nodded. 'I meditate before I sleep.' She seemed to look at him more closely before asking, 'What is your name?' He told her adding that, like Anna, he was a long sleeper.

'Tell me about David,' Anna said.

Leaf sighed, 'Poor David. One can't help pitying him for in the end he really lost everything. I have not seen him for a long time, but the last I heard, he was living in a unit somewhere on one of the new housing estates. Izabel begged him to come and see her, but he refused. I suppose it was shame.'

'You know about them?' Anna asked.

'Izabel told me the night of the accident. I truly believe it was an accident though she lied about you driving, of course. The police worked that out almost at once and then she had that terrible trial. The prosecutor was very savage with her. She would have gone to prison, I believe, if she had not had a breakdown. She never did recover completely, though she does have good periods, and the money you left between us enabled me to engage a nurse to take care of her. After I heard what Izabel had to say, I did not think you would wish me to produce the will you made leaving everything to David. I took Izabel some herbal medicines and offered to open her chakra a while back, but she was never very receptive to such things.' She looked at Anna, and her expression became very serious. 'I hope that you do not trouble yourself about David. He was never worthy of you, my dear. I knew it when he came to tell me that he was falling in love with me not a month after I met him.'

'You!' Anna stared at her, and then she began to laugh. 'Of course he loved you! Who wouldn't?'

Leaf laughed, too. 'Quite a lot of people, actually.' Her smile faded. 'I did pity him of course. One could not help it. But his aura was so yellow, my dear. That is always the colour of spiritual weakness.'

'His aura?'

Leaf nodded, blond curls tumbling. 'I see them, you see. I always have. Yours is a lovely shade of violet with streaks of gold and the tiniest bit of green. Much prettier than the muddy brown and mauve aura you had before.' She beamed at Anna.

'What about Nicholas?' Anna asked shyly.

Leaf looked at Nicholas, whose skin was so white against his black clothes and hair. 'You must tell her, young man. There can be nothing real without truth.'

Anna looked at them in bewilderment. 'Tell me what?'

Nicholas sighed and nodded, glancing out the window to where the last vestiges of the mist were vanishing. 'I swore that I would tell you, if ever you became fully lucid. I have waited long for this moment and now that it has come, I fear it. You asked who I was and I told you Nicholas. I gave myself that name because I have no memory of anyone giving me a name in the real world. I can only suppose from this that I fell into a coma soon after I was born. I do not know why my parents kept me alive, nor how long I lived, for as I told you, time flows unevenly. But I think they must have kept me a very long time, and that this is why I did not vanish here, when my body died. I knew it had happened because my dream place vanished and I fell to the void. I had been there before and I knew it was difficult for a long dreamer to get free of it, but now I learned that without flesh, it was virtually impossible. I do not know why I fought so hard and so long to escape, but at last after eons of nightmare, I found my way back here to the dreamscape. I vowed never to fall to the void again, for I knew that it was a miracle I had escaped, and I would not manage it a second time.'

'But you . . . you stayed with me when my dream broke,' Anna said.

He nodded. 'I hoped that this time, you would not retreat. And I was right.'

'You risked much for loneliness,' Anna said.

'You speak of loneliness who do not know it as I have known it. When first we met, I was lonely almost to madness. You endured my madness with compassion, though you do not remember, and you allowed me to share your quest for truth. And then you vanished into the void. I waited and kept watch and in time you came again but you did not know me. That was hard, but I grew accustomed to the forgetting, for countless times you retreated into the void and each time, I searched and found you. In the beginning, I sought you for companionship and sanity, and then as time passed, for friendship. The last time, I thought that you would finally come to the truth you sought, but you were not ready and again you vanished. This time, it was as if my soul went with you into the void. I waited and I watched, and then one day, I saw your hill. I could not find your house, which meant you were not yet lucid, but I continued to search, knowing that you had at least come from the void. Then one morning you called out to me. And when I saw you, I knew that I would rather go to the void forever, than to let go of you again.'

'You love me?' Anna asked, something inside her unfurling.

'It would seem so,' he said, then he added gravely, 'But I do not expect you to love me.'

'I . . . I'm afraid your expectations will be thwarted then . . .' Anna said shyly, and she held her hand out to Nicholas, who took it, his pale face lighting up with joy. Then he stiffened and looked about them.

'Quick,' he said urgently, and he leapt to his feet and pulled her to the door.

Leaf woke, smiling, to find the nurse shaking her gently.

'You fell asleep again, Miss Leaf,' she chided. 'You ought to have gone to bed. She doesn't know you are here. The monitors have shown no evidence of brain activity in all the decades she has laid here. Most people would have thought long ago about switching off the life support machines.'

'I am not most people,' Leaf said placidly. 'As to these clever machines, they may show no evidence of brain activity, but are they sensitive enough to measure the activity of a soul?' She reached forward to pat Anna's withered hand and said softly, 'For all we know she is dreaming. Imagine the sort of dreams that might come to one who never wakes.'

The nurse suppressed a shudder, thinking how ghoulish old people were. After all, what sort of dreams would someone that old have, even if there was anything left in her capable of dreaming?

AFTERWORD

I have been writing for a lot of years. More years than I, frankly, want to think about. I like thinking about all that writing, just not all those years. I'm an insomniac. I've never seen it as a curse. I'm the only person I know who was not tired with a baby waking her every two hours. Sometimes I was awake waiting for the baby to wake. My partner never had to get up at night. I didn't even want him to. My daughter is now showing strong signs of the same insomnia. One day recently, she said, 'What do people do who can't sleep when other people can?' I said smugly, 'Feel smug, because think of all that time they are wasting while we get to be awake and think and read and write and daydream. They waste years and years of sleeping, and we get to be awake instead.' On the other hand, my partner sleeps enough to make up for my daughter and me and possibly several other children. He also dreams vividly and often. I never dream, except the occasional nightmare involving vampires. Unfortunately, I'm never the vampire; only its prey. Maybe that is why I write so much about dreaming. I've been doing that for as long as I've been writing, too. 'Perchance to Dream' came to me when I started wondering what would happen if instead of never sleeping, you never woke; if life was truly a dream . . .

— *Isobelle Carmody*

ABOUT THE EDITOR

JACK DANN is a multiple award winning author who has written or edited over seventy books, including the groundbreaking novels *Junction*, *Starhiker*, *The Man Who Melted*, *The Memory Cathedral* — which is an international bestseller — the Civil War novel *The Silent*, and *Bad Medicine*, which has been compared to the works of Jack Kerouac and Hunter S. Thompson.

Dann's work has been compared to Jorge Luis Borges, Roald Dahl, Lewis Carroll, Carlos Castaneda, J. G. Ballard, Mark Twain, and Philip K. Dick. Dick, author of the stories from which the films *Blade Runner* and *Total Recall* were made, wrote that '*Junction* is where Ursula Le Guin's *Lathe of Heaven* and Tony Boucher's "The Quest for Saint Aquin" meet . . . and yet it's an entirely new novel . . . I may very well be basing some of my future work on *Junction*.' Bestselling author Marion Zimmer Bradley called *Starhiker* 'a superb book . . . it will not give up all its delights, all its perfections, on one reading.'

Library Journal has called Dann 'a true poet who can create pictures with a few perfect words.' Roger Zelazny thought he was a reality magician and *Best Sellers* has said that 'Jack Dann is a mind-warlock whose magicks will confound, disorient, shock, and delight.' *The Washington Post Book World* compared his novel *The Man Who Melted* with Ingmar Bergman's film *The Seventh Seal*.

His books have been translated into over thirteen languages, and his short stories have appeared in *Playboy*, *Omni*, *Penthouse*, *Asimov's*, 'Best Of' collections in Australia and the United States, and many other major magazines and anthologies. He is the editor of the anthology *Wandering Stars*, one of the most acclaimed American anthologies of the 1970s, and several other well-known anthologies such as *More Wandering Stars*. *Wandering Stars* and *More Wandering Stars* have just been reprinted in the United States. Dann also edits the multi-volume

Magic Tales series with Gardner Dozois and is a consulting editor for TOR Books.

He is a recipient of the Nebula Award, the Australian Aurealis Award (twice), the Ditmar Award (three times), the World Fantasy Award, the Peter McNamara Achievement Award, and the *Premios Gilgamés de Narrativa Fantastica* award. Dann has also been honoured by the Mark Twain Society (Esteemed Knight).

High Steel, a novel co-authored with Jack C. Haldeman II, was published in 1993. Critic John Clute called it 'a predator ... a cat with blazing eyes gorging on the good meat of genre. It is most highly recommended.' Dann is currently writing *Ghost Dance*, the sequel to *High Steel*, with Jack Haldeman's widow, author Barbara Delaplace.

Dann's major historical novel about Leonardo da Vinci — entitled *The Memory Cathedral* — was published to rave reviews. It has been published in over ten languages to date. It won the Australian Aurealis Award, was #1 on *The Age* bestseller list, and a story based on the novel was awarded the Nebula Award. *The Memory Cathedral* was also shortlisted for the Audio Book of the Year, which was part of the Braille & Talking Book Library Awards.

Morgan Llwelyn called *The Memory Cathedral* 'a book to cherish, a validation of the novelist's art and fully worthy of its extraordinary subject.' The *San Francisco Chronicle* called it 'A grand accomplishment', *Kirkus Reviews* thought it was 'An impressive accomplishment', and *True Review* said, 'Read this important novel, be challenged by it; you literally haven't seen anything like it.'

Dann's novel about the American Civil War, *The Silent*, was chosen as one of *Library Journal*'s 'Hot Picks'. *Library Journal* wrote: 'This is narrative storytelling at its best — so highly charged emotionally as to constitute a kind of poetry from hell. Most emphatically recommended.' Peter Straub said, 'This tale of America's greatest trauma is full of mystery, wonder, and the kind of narrative inventiveness that makes other novelists want to hide under the bed.' And *The Australian* called it 'an extraordinary achievement.'

His novel *Bad Medicine* (titled *Counting Coup* in the US), a contemporary road novel, has been described by *The Courier Mail* as 'perhaps the best road novel since the *Easy Rider* days.'

Dann is also the co-editor (with Janeen Webb) of the groundbreaking Australian anthology *Dreaming Down-Under*, which Peter Goldsworthy called 'the biggest, boldest, most controversial collection of original fiction ever published in Australia.' It won Australia's Ditmar Award and was the first Australian book ever to win the World Fantasy Award. His anthology *Gathering the Bones*, of which he is a co-editor, was included in *Library Journal*'s Best Genre Fiction of 2003 and was shortlisted for The World Fantasy Award. His latest anthology, *Wizards* (co-edited with Gardner Dozois and titled *Dark Alchemy* in the UK and Australia), made the Waldenbooks/Borders bestseller list.

Dann's stories have been collected in *Timetipping*, *Visitations*, and the retrospective short story collection *Jubilee: The Essential Jack Dann. The West Australian* said it was 'Sometimes frightening, sometimes funny, erudite, inventive, beautifully written and always intriguing. *Jubilee* is a celebration of the talent of a remarkable storyteller.' His collaborative stories can be found in the collection *The Fiction Factory*.

The West Australian called Dann's latest novel, *The Rebel: An Imagined Life of James Dean*, 'an amazingly evocative and utterly convincing picture of the era, down to details of the smells and sensations — and even more importantly, the way of thinking.' *Locus* wrote: '*The Rebel* is a significant and very gripping novel, a welcome addition to Jack Dann's growing oeuvre of speculative historical novels, sustaining further his long-standing contemplation of the modalities of myth and memory. This is alternate history with passion and difference.' A companion James Dean short story collection entitled *Promised Land* has just been published.

As part of its *Bibliographies of Modern Authors Series*, The Borgo Press has published an annotated bibliography and guide entitled *The Work of Jack Dann*. An updated second edition is in progress. Dann is also listed in *Contemporary Authors* and the *Contemporary Authors Autobiography Series*; *The International Authors and Writers Who's Who*; *Personalities of America*; *Men of Achievement*; *Who's Who in Writers, Editors, and Poets: United States and Canada*; *Dictionary of International Biography*; *Directory of Distinguished Americans*; *Outstanding Writers of the 20th Century*; and *Who's Who in the World*.

Dann lives in Australia on a farm overlooking the sea and 'commutes' back and forth to Los Angeles and New York.

His website is jackdann.com.